Praise for *Silver Wolf, Black Falcon* . . .

"McKiernan's fans—as well as those of Terry Brooks and Terry Goodkind—will enjoy his usual array of thin-skinned, power-mad evildoers, hearty, honorable good guys, and grand magical fireworks."   —*Publishers Weekly*

"In the tradition of Tolkien, the author blends lore and prophecy with vivid battle scenes and emotional drama."
                                                                —*Library Journal*

. . . and for Dennis L. McKiernan's bestselling Mithgar novels

"Once McKiernan's got you, he never lets go."
                                                —Jennifer Roberson

"Some of the finest imaginative action. . . . There are no lulls in McKiernan's story."   —*The Columbus Dispatch*

"McKiernan brews magic with an insightful blend of laughter, tears, and high courage."
                        —Janny Wurts, author of *Grand Conspiracy: Alliance of Light*

"McKiernan's narratives have heart and fire and drive. His images and characters bring the power of the archetypes to his exciting adventure stories."
                        —Katharine Kerr, author of *Days of Blood and Fire*

continued . . .

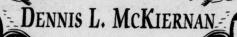

DENNIS L. MCKIERNAN

SILVER WOLF, BLACK FALCON

A ROC BOOK

ROC
Published by New American Library, a division of
Penguin Putnam Inc., 375 Hudson Street,
New York, New York 10014, U.S.A.
Penguin Books Ltd, 27 Wrights Lane,
London W8 5TZ, England
Penguin Books Australia Ltd, Ringwood,
Victoria, Australia
Penguin Books Canada Ltd, 10 Alcorn Avenue,
Toronto, Ontario, Canada M4V 3B2
Penguin Books (N.Z.) Ltd, 182–190 Wairau Road,
Auckland 10, New Zealand

Penguin Books Ltd, Registered Offices:
Harmondsworth, Middlesex, England

Published by Roc, an imprint of New American Library,
a division of Penguin Putnam Inc.

First Roc Hardcover Printing, June 2000
First Roc Paperback Printing, June 2001
10 9 8 7 6 5 4 3 2 1

ROC REGISTERED TRADEMARK—MARCA REGISTRADA

Printed in the United States of America

PUBLISHER'S NOTE

This is a work of fiction. Names, characters, places, and incidents either are the
products of the author's imagination or are used fictitiously, and any resemblance to
actual persons, living or dead, business establishments, or locales is entirely
coincidental.

BOOKS ARE AVAILABLE AT QUANTITY DISCOUNTS WHEN USED TO PROMOTE PRODUCTS OR
SERVICES. FOR INFORMATION PLEASE WRITE TO PREMIUM MARKETING DIVISION, PENGUIN
PUTNAM INC., 375 HUDSON STREET, NEW YORK, NEW YORK 10014.

To Martha Lee McKiernan
So it began and is

Acknowledgments

Appreciation and gratitude to Daniel Kian McKiernan, without whose help the transliterated ancient Greek used as the Black Mage magical language would never have been; to Partha Deb, Associate Professor of Economics, Indiana University and Purdue University at Indianapolis, for his transliterations of Hindi used as the language of the Mithgarian Kingdom of Bharaq; and to Martha Lee McKiernan for her enduring support, careful reading, patience, and love. Additionally, much appreciation and gratitude goes to the Tanque Wordies for their encouragement throughout the writing of *Silver Wolf, Black Falcon*. Lastly, I would say of all the languages used herein—some of my own devising, others of known nationalities—any errors in their usage are entirely mine.

Contents

Foreword   xiii

Author's Notes   xvii

Prologue: Flight   1
Winterday, 5E1009 [The Present]

1. Travail   3
Year's Long Day, 5E983 [Twenty-Six Years Past]

2. Joy   13
Spring–Autumn, 5E993 [Sixteen Years Past]

3. Auguries   21
Autumn, 5E993 [Sixteen Years Past]

4. Revelations   27
Autumn, 5E993 [Sixteen Years Past]

5. Draega   40
Autumn–Winter, 5E993 [Sixteen Years Past]

6. Departure   44
Winter, 5E993 [Sixteen Years Past]

7. Onset   49
Summer, 5E994 [Fifteen Years Past]

8. Vow   54
Autumn, 5E999 [Ten Years Past]

9. Promise   58
Winter, 5E999–1000 [Ten and Nine Years Past]

10. Foretellings   67
Summer, 5E1003 [Six Years Past]

11. Progression   73
Spring–Autumn, 5E1003 [Six Years Past]

12. Passages   89
October, 5E1003–January, 5E1004
[Six and Five Years Past]

13. Crossings   108
January, 5E1004 [Five Years Past]

14. Discovery   120
Summer, 5E1003–Summer, 5E1005
[Six to Four Years Past]

15. Tocsin   125
Summer, 5E1005 [Four Years Past]

16. Priming   127
October, 5E1004–September, 5E1005
[Five and Four Years Past]

17. Conquests   139
Summer, 5E1005–Autumn, 5E1007
[Four to Two Years Past]

18. Choices   143
October, 5E1008 [Fifteen Months Past]

19. Outset   158
Spring–Autumn, 5E1008
[Twenty-One to Fifteen Months Past]

20. Journey   162
October, 5E1008–January, 5E1009
[Fifteen to Eleven Months Past]

21. Erg   178
January, 5E1009 [Eleven Months Past]

22. Oracle   193
January–February, 5E1009
[Eleven to Ten Months Past]

23. Guile   208
February, 5E1009 [Ten Months Past]

24. Reflections   210
February, 5E1009 [Ten Months Past]

25. Khem   227
February, 5E1009 [Ten Months Past]

26. Tales   239
March–April, 5E1009
[Nine to Eight Months Past]

27. Hindrance   254
April, 5E1009 [Eight Months Past]

28. Jangdi   256
April, 5E1009 [Eight Months Past]

29. Engels   270
April, 5E1009 [Eight Months Past]

30. Interlude   277
May, 5E1009 [Seven Months Past]

31. Phael   284
May, 5E1009 [Seven Months Past]

32. Falcon   291
May–September, 5E1009
[Seven to Three Months Past]

33. Invasion   302
September–December, 5E1009
[*Three and a Half Months to Days Past*]

34. Pursuit   318
September–December, 5E1009
[*Three and a Half Months to Days Past*]

35. Neddra   326
December, 5E1009 [*Days Past*]

36. Muster   331
December, 5E1009 [*Days Past*]

37. Fortress   335
December, 5E1009
[*A Day and Three-Quarters to a Quarter-Day Past*]

38. Flight   346
Winterday, 5E1009 [*The Present*]

39. Vadaria   358
December, 5E1009 [*The Present*]

40. Recountings   370
December, 5E1009–January, 5E1010 [*The Present*]

41. Dendor   377
January, 5E1010 [*The Present*]

42. Grotto   382
January, 5E1010 [*The Present*]

43. Raudhrskal   384
January, 5E1010 [*The Present*]

44. Leave-taking   386
January, 5E1010 [*The Present*]

45. Prey   394
January, 5E1010 [The Present]

46. Adonar   401
January, 5E1010 [The Present]

47. Mithgar   410
January, 5E1010 [The Present]

48. Strife   424
January–February, 5E1010 [The Present]

49. Asea   431
January–February, 5E1010 [The Present]

50. Skirmishes   443
January–March, 5E1010 [The Present]

51. Rualla   446
February–March, 5E1010 [The Present]

52. Argon   453
March, 5E1010 [The Present]

53. Perilous Waters   458
March, 5E1010 [The Present]

54. Blood and Fire   461
March, 5E1010 [The Present]

55. Morass   469
March, 5E1010 [The Present]

56. Retreat   478
March, 5E1010 [The Present]

57. Trine   483
Springday, 5E1010 [The Present]

58. Homecoming　　　　505
March–June, 5E1010 [The Present]

AFTERMATH AND ECHOES　　　　517

59. Aftermath　　　　519
June, 5E1010–March, 6E1 [The Present]

Epilogue: Echoes　　　　523
Times Following [. . . And Beyond]

Afterword　　　　533

About the Author　　　　535

Foreword

This is perhaps—*perhaps*—my last Mithgarian novel.

Including this tale, I have written eight epics spread over twelve books, and one collection of Mithgarian stories . . . and there is one graphic novel based on the first story in that collection.

All of these tales fit in an overall story arc, an arc which "historically" begins with *The Dragonstone* and progresses (in order) through, *Voyage of the Fox Rider*, the *Hèl's Crucible* duology, *Dragondoom*, *Tales of Mithgar*, *The Iron Tower* trilogy, *The Silver Call* duology, *The Eye of the Hunter*, and ends with *Silver Wolf, Black Falcon*. Oh, I didn't write them in that order, but "historically," that's where they fit into the arc. Hence, *Silver Wolf, Black Falcon* is the last tale in the arc, the last tale in the overall theme, the tail of the tale so to speak. If you are wondering what that overall theme might be, I'll tell you.

But first, let me digress just a bit:

In each of the stories I try to take up some central issue, idea, or philosophical or metaphysical question; oh, I'm not talking about good versus evil, the forces of light versus the forces of darkness as a theme, although such can be read into my stories. Yet as a theme, good versus evil is a bit too general.

Instead I try to explore more specific issues that mankind has struggled with for millennia, issues such as: predestination versus free will; the nature of evil; the connections between events in terms of cause and effect, and whether or not all things are connected; the ability of the "common man" to rise to meet the challenge; the falsity of the romance of war; faith, reason, religion, and dogma; and man's effect on the environment: these are some of the issues involved in the Mithgarian mythos. I don't think I provide any concrete answers, but issues such as the above do provide much food for thought, things to ponder in idle moments (if nowhen else).

The reason I interject these questions and ideas and philosophical or metaphysical inquiries into the tales—issues which the characters take up while journeying across Mithgar or while sitting in a comfortable setting—is to give the tale some *substance*.

You see, a tale gets its *energy* from conflict and peril and challenge, but a story which is nothing but conflict—e.g., five hundred pages of continuous combat—although quite acceptable in some computer games, in stories gets old very fast.

And so, although peril and conflict and challenge give the tale its energy, it needs something else to give it substance . . . and, among other things, a tale gets its substance from the ideas embedded within. However, a tale with nothing but questions, philosophy, metaphysics, and issues quickly becomes a dry treatise, a dissertation, a thesis.

The trick is to find the right balance between energy and substance.

Oh, don't get me wrong, there's a lot more to a tale than conflict and peril and challenge . . . and ideas and issues and questions of a substantial nature: there's character, description, dialogue, special effects, a story to tell, and so on.

And of course, *all* of these things need to be balanced, and I hope I've done a credible job.

But I do believe that weaving issues into a story gives it an extra and worthwhile dimension, and perhaps you'll find the substance herein to your liking.

And with that I say—

—Oops! I almost forgot: I promised to tell you of the overall issue in the entire arc of the Mithgarian tales. Is it good versus evil? The forces of light versus the forces of darkness? All of the above? Perhaps. Perhaps you'll see it that way. But for me, I don't think it's quite as grand an issue as that; for me it's a straightforward theme, though still a complex one: the common thread in the entire arc is the struggle of those who believe in liberty and freedom, in free will, in freedom of choice—in the freedom to control one's own destiny—against those who would take those things away, a struggle which in more ways than one continues unto this very day.

—Dennis L. McKiernan
January 1999

Author's Notes

*S*ilver Wolf, Black Falcon tells the tale of the Impossible Child. It is a story that has roots stretching back into the far past, yet in this novel the tale begins on Winterday, 5E1009, but almost immediately jumps back twenty-six years to Summerday, 5E983. Fear not though, for the story indeed will catch up to its beginning and then pass it on the fly.

The story of the Impossible Child was reconstructed from several sources, not the least of which were the addenda to Faeril's Diary, fragments of which yet exist, and in the burnt part of a Jingarian scroll, which I managed to reconstruct due to advances in infrared scanners.

And speaking of that Jingarian scroll, a correction: when I wrote the epilogue to *The Dragonstone*, I made an assumption as to what was written in that area that was damaged by fire, and I incorrectly stated that the fisherman had taken his catch back to his village and there had made his discovery. Since the time I wrote that epilogue, by the good graces of advances in infrared scanning, I now have managed to descry the ideographs on that burnt part of the scroll, and in this telling of the Impossible Child's tale, I have written the fisherman's story as it was set down long ago on that long-lost scroll.

In addition, when writing a previous work—*Dragondoom*—the reference I used—*Commentaries on the Lays of Bard Estor*—had also been partially burned, assumptions I made about the Sundering have since proved erroneous: 1) At the time of writing *Dragondoom* I assumed that Mages came from Adonar when in fact they come from the Mageworld of Vadaria; and, 2) I also assumed that the Draega had been stranded on Mithgar because of the Sundering. In the telling of the Impossible Child—in particular, Dalavar Wolfmage's words—I have corrected these flaws . . . and should a revised version of *Dragondoom* be printed the faults will be corrected therein as well.

I apologize to my readers for the previous inaccuracies, and I shall take greater pains in the future to avoid such mistakes. Yet because my primary sources are so meager, in places in this tale (as in all others) I fill in the gaps with assumptions; in the main, however, the tale is true to its root material.

As occurs in other of my Mithgarian works, there are many instances where in the press of the moment, the Humans, Mages, Elves, and others spoke in their native tongues; yet to avoid burdensome translations, where necessary I have rendered their words in Pellarion, the Common Tongue of Mithgar. However, in several cases I have left the language unchanged, to demonstrate the fact that many tongues were found throughout Mithgar. Additionally, some words and phrases do not lend themselves to translation, and these I've either left unchanged or, in special cases, I have enclosed in angle brackets a substitute term that gives the "flavor" of the word (i.e., <see>, <fire>, and the like). Additionally, sundry words may look to be in error, but indeed are correct—e.g., DelfLord is but a single word though a capital *L* nestles among its letters.

The Elven language of Sylva is rather archaic and formal. To capture this flavor, I have properly used *thee* and *thou*, *hast*, *dost*, and the like; however, in the interest of readability, I have tried to do so in a minimal fashion, eliminating some of the more archaic terms.

For the curious, the w in *Rwn* takes on the sound of *uu* (*w is* after all a double-u), which in turn can be said to sound like *oo* (as in *spoon*). Hence, Rwn is *not* pronounced Renn, but instead *is* pronounced Roon, or Rune.

Finally, there are highlights of various historical events referred to in this story. For those interested in more detail, I refer you to the works listed in the front of this book.

Auguries are oft subtle . . . and dangerous—
thou mayest deem they mean one thing
when they mean something else altogether

PROLOGUE

Flight

Winterday, 5E1009

[The Present]

Deep snow cascading in its wake, up the mountain steeps
plunged the Silver Wolf, a yawling pack of Vulgs baying
after. A howling Ghûl on a gasping Hèlsteed surged up the slant
aft of the pack, and struggling alongside the corpse-foe and his
scaled steed, a yowling band of Rûcks and Hlôks clambered up
the cant as well. Black-shafted arrows flew upward, some aimed
at the Silver Wolf, others aimed at the dark falcon crying in rage
in the churning skies above, both arrows and falcon buffeted by
the shrieking winds aloft as the boiling wall of the oncoming
storm drew nigh, and a forerunning blast drove snow swirling up
from the ground.

The 'Wolf bore a burden concealed in a harness slung across
its back, and about the neck of the pony-sized creature dangled
a ring on a chain. Something as well glistened about the neck of
the falcon above—the bird itself black as night, the glisten as
from silver and glass.

Hunters and hunted, up the steeps they strove, the 'Wolf now
and again glancing at the ebony falcon above, yet pausing not in
its lunging run, while behind came the howling foe. Of a sudden the Hèlsteed squealed and pitched backward down the slant,
the scaled creature smashing atop the Ghûl, bones cracking under
the crushing weight of the beast. Yet snarling out commands,
with spear in hand the corpse-foe rose to his feet and took up
the chase afoot, though the Hèlsteed did not as it lay in the snow,

its head and neck twisted awry, its cloven hooves drumming a tattoo of death.

Now the black falcon called out a *skree!* and veered to the right, but the Silver Wolf did not change its course to follow. Again the falcon called out, but the 'Wolf plunged on upward, toward the stormy heights above. Calling out once more, the falcon stooped, folding its wings and plummeting toward the 'Wolf below. Just as it unfurled its pinions—*thuck!*—a crossbow bolt pierced it through, and with a wracking cry it tumbled down through the air to fall to the snowy slopes.

Even as the Rûcks shouted in glee, and in spite of the howling pursuit, the Silver Wolf veered rightward to come to the felled bird. And gently, in mouth and gently, the 'Wolf took up the wounded falcon, careful not to disturb the piercing quarrel, and then the argent animal plunged onward, up the steepening slopes, snow flying out behind.

And still the Vulgs came after, the huge black Wolflike creatures now gaining on the silver foe.

Up they ran and up, up through the screaming wind, while the black skies above seemed to darken yet further. At last the Silver Wolf topped the slant to come onto a circular flat, and ahead and curving 'round to the sides towered the hard face of a sheer stone bluff, trapping the small plateau in its looming embrace, trapping the 'Wolf and the falcon as well.

The 'Wolf—the Draega—moved forward and gently laid the black falcon to the soft snow, then with a low growl whirled 'round and padded back to the precipitous lip of the dead-ended, stone-held flat.

Downslope, the yawling rout of Vulgs and Rûcks and Hlôks and the Ghûl lunged upward, fangs bared, blades drawn, arrows and quarrels nocked, cruel barbed spear in hand, murder in their viperous eyes. In the distance beyond and barely glimpsed through the blowing white stood a massive black fortress, its ebon walls streaked with glazes of rime and long white runs of hoarfrost.

With another low growl the 'Wolf turned its back to the oncoming peril and stepped toward the wounded falcon, and in that moment the howling blizzard swept over all, hurtling stinging snow shrieking across the whole of the mountainside.

CHAPTER 1

Travail

Year's Long Day, 5E983

[Twenty-Six Years Past]

The first twinges of contraction began just after the *Ha-Ji* dawn came to the Steppes of Moko, and young Teiji, her belly swollen large, was escorted to the birthing tent, where the midwives awaited. They placed Teiji on a birthing stool, seated above a shallow pit lined with a mat made of woven straw. Along with the biting stick, the juice of the yellow poppy was prepared to ease the pain were it to become severe. Incense was set to smoldering, filling the yurt with a soothing scent. Water was boiled and swaddling cloths made ready, as well as cloths to clean up the blood and to deal with other needs. And they laid out precious scented oils and soaps for the cleansing after. Too, they discreetly brought in the brace of ceremonial blades: a bronze delivery knife to be used in the event the mother failed and her belly needed to be opened; an iron deliverance knife should the child be malformed, the throat to be cut, the curse quickly laid to keep it from tainting the tribe. But none expected either blade to be used, for after all, this was Ha-Ji, the longest day of the year, an auspicious time if ever there was one.

Chakun, who had just turned eleven and was attending her first ever birthing duty—she would be married in a year or so, and no doubt be with child quickly after, and so she needed to know these things—came running back from the high steppe stream, waterskin in hand. The chill water was for the cooling of Teiji's brow; it would be Chakun's task all day.

Throughout the rest of the camp, tea was brewed to be sipped by the women of the tribe, and they settled back to wait. As to the men of the tribe of Cholui Chang, they would not ride their sturdy ponies across the steppes that day but would instead dance 'round the central fire and drink strong *ammall palro ch'agi*—fermented mare's milk—for Teiji, the youngest wife of the *chuyohan*, was to give birth.

As dawn came to the village of Yugu, there on the shores of the Jingarian Sea, Wangu set out in his small craft, the battened sails angled to make the most of the early-morning offshore breeze, for surely on this the longest day of the year he would haul aboard a catch worthy of being taken to the grand market in the great port city of Janjong.

He was headed for the waters off the eastern shore of Shàbíng, the small rocky isle standing like a sentinel on the edge of the deep abyss. And as he sailed he readied his many-twined silk line; perhaps this new one was heavy enough to withstand the pull of even the greatest of fish, unlike the last one, which had broken under the strain of something large and unseen.

In the yurt, Teiji's labor became more intense, her groaning more pronounced—though her water had not broken—while outside the sun rode up in the sky, the long day growing hotter with each passing candlemark. Young Chakun was sent yet again to the cold stream to refill the waterskin and, as she had done before, she passed wide of the men drinking 'round the campfire, avoiding their sidelong glances and disturbing comments.

Wangu tied his new silk line to a short length of precious metal chain linked to his greatest hook, and baited the claw with the mesh bag filled with fish entrails. He said a brief prayer to the gods of the deeps and cast hook and chain overboard, paying out the heavy silken line, the impaled net of intestines disappearing into the depths beneath. Not far behind Wangu the tilted crag of Shàbíng jutted up out of the sea, the rock face stern and unyielding as it stared down into the abyss below.

*   *   *

It was just after midmorning when Teiji's water finally broke. Chakun, soothing Teiji's brow with a cool damp cloth, looked on in amazement as the liquid gushed out, a pinkish tinge to the flow. As the midwives got Teiji to her feet to walk her about in the tent yet again in order to bring on the child, Chakun was given the task of replacing the delivery mat in the pit and carrying the soiled one to the central fire and casting it in. When the wisp of a girl pitched the dampened delivery mat into the curling flames, the men gave a great loud cry of gladness, for it meant Teiji was nearer to bearing. The flames bloomed up to consume the straw, yet Chakun did not tarry to see it burn but instead hurried swiftly away, for some of the men were staring at her, their wide drunken grins unsettling. She got back to the birthing tent just as Old Tal took her hand from between Teiji's legs after measuring the amount of dilation, and then the elderly woman frowned and glanced up at the other midwives and shook her head: "Not even a little finger's width." Chakun felt a stab of fear in her breast, for this was ill news, or so she deemed. And even though Teiji had not heard these words above her own moaning agony, still her groans seemed to come all the louder.

Tzzzz . . . ! the line hissed out as something took the fish-gut–baited great hook and ran.

"Ai!" shouted Wangu in glee. "I have you now!" And he reached for the free-running silk and caught it up, only to cry out in pain and jerk away as the gossamer cable scored against his palms. Leaning over the stern board, he plunged his forearms into the brine of the Jingarian Sea, the salt stinging but soothing his rope-burned hands.

And yet leaning over, he watched as the line ran out and out, and then—*Tung!*—it twanged as it snapped taut, the knot around the aft cleat holding fast. But then whatever had taken the bait began hauling the boat backward through the sea, water churning madly and slopping over the board.

Wangu's eyes widened in fright. "What have I caught?" he shouted to the sea. "Or what is it that has caught me?"

The sun rose up through the skies, crossing the zenith at last to move into the west, as Longday slowly passed. And in the birthing tent of the tribe of Cholui Chang, Chakun covered her ears to shut out Teiji's screams, but still she could hear them, in spite of having her eyes shut as well.

And as two sturdy midwives more dragged than walked Teiji within the tent, the other midwives looked at one another with great concern, for the young wife was in dry labor, and still the signs of delivery had not changed: the baby would not come.

Once again they placed Teiji on the birthing stool, and Old Tal set her ear to the swollen belly and listened in spite of the shrieks. And she pressed her hands to the flesh and lightly squeezed and pushed here and there, and Teiji screamed all the louder.

The old woman then turned to the others. "The child is alive and in the proper position . . . not trying to come hindwards to the world."

And then Tal prepared another measure of the juice of the poppy to quench Teiji's hard pain, though the last yellow dose had seemed to have little if any effect.

Backward flew the boat, water churning over the stern. Wangu bailed frantically in a desperate attempt to stem the gushing tide. And just as he thought he would have to cut his precious new line to keep the boat from foundering . . . whatever had taken the bait stopped in its run.

Perhaps it is dead.

Still the fisherman bailed.

Do not be stupid, Wangu. It now but pauses in the drag of the boat. . . . Aiee! What if it plots dark evil?

Wangu madly bailed.

And then from underneath something struck the craft a great blow, pitching Wangu from his feet. He struggled up in time to look over the starboard wale, and glimpsed the great grey shape as it swam down and away.

"*Aie!*" groaned Wangu. "It is a *shâyú.*"

Once again the boat was hauled backward through the Jingarian Sea. And Wangu readied his knife. *Precious or not, if the monster I saw decides to dive down into the abyss and drag the boat under, I will cut the line.*

Even so, it galled him, for did not "Wangu" mean "stubborn"?

His father, Kwàile, had given him that name for being resolute, even as a child. And the great shark would bring much gold in Janjong, could he but land it, for its fins made the best of medicinal soups, while the heart and liver and other organs would bring much on the market as well, especially the eyes, which are said to be used by witches and such in their far-seeing spells. The brain, too, was treasured by witches, for they used it to know what evil men were thinking, or so it was said. The meat of the shark was certainly precious, for it would give strength to those who ate it. Precious also was the cartilage, for it was said to ward off the malignant disease that eats one from within. And the teeth would bring in a measure of gold, for warriors sought them as amulets—they bestowed ferocity in battle. Aye, if he could but land this shâyú, it would serve him well.

Wangu readied his boathook, the heavy iron barb on the spear-like spar, the nearest thing he had to a fighting weapon aboard.

And then he began bailing again as the boat was hauled backward through the sea.

Shrieking and shrieking, Teiji thrashed about on the ground, unable to sit or stand or walk. Midwives futilely tried to soothe her, and though Tal knew that too much of the juice of the yellow poppy was deadly dangerous in itself, still she tried to get Teiji to take some more, though it did not seem to help at all.

And Chakun bathed Teiji's forehead with cool water, the eleven-year-old now unable to cover her own ears to help shut out the shrieks. If this was what it meant to bear a child, Chakun vowed she would *never* get married but would join the priestesses of Moko instead, and await the prophesied Mage Warrior King to come.

Whump! Its slashing teeth bared in a gnashing jaw as it gnawed on the iron hook and chain, the shark slammed into the side of the leaking boat again, the great fish rolling so that its dead-black eye stared coldly up at screaming Wangu.

Dread coursing through the fisherman's veins, with all his might— "*Eyahh!*"—Wangu stabbed the iron prong of the boathook into the monster once more, the barb spearing again through the tough hide of the creature and deep into the flesh below.

Once more the shark wrenched about, Wangu nearly losing his pole as the monster wrested away through the shallows. Wangu and his boat were trapped up against a sheer rock wall on the west side of the stony crag of Shàbíng, where the shâyú had dragged the man in his craft, as if to pin him against stone and then wreak a crushing, slashing revenge. Again and again the shark had attacked, and again and again a wailing Wangu had stabbed the hook into the beast. And now the shâyú turned away once more to ready another charge.

As the shark surged away, Wangu managed to jerk the boathook out of the pierced hide at the last moment, and he clutched the pole tightly, for it and the battered boat were all that stood between him and death.

"I am named Stubborn," shouted Wangu above his own weeping moans of rage and fear. "I am named Stubborn . . . Stubborn of the family Sûn."

Out in the brine a heave in the water turned and sped back toward the boat: the shâyú was coming again.

Wailing in terror, with a two-handed grip Wangu readied the boathook once more.

As the sun lipped the horizon, Teiji gave one last scream, her voice so hoarse it was but a whisper . . . and her jaw clenched tightly, and she snapped the biting stick in two. And then Teiji fell limp, the life going out of her. Chakun's heart raced as Old Tal bent over and put her ear to Teiji's breast and listened. The elderly woman rose to her knees and barked out, "Bring the bronze delivery knife. Teiji is dead. Mayhap we can save the child."

Chakun turned her face away as Tal took the knife in hand and slashed a long cut through dead Teiji's belly, blood seeping out.

Standing in the shallows and laughing hysterically and using the boathook as a lever, Wangu managed to roll the dead shark into even shallower water. The monster was seventeen feet long and must have weighed a ton and a half or more. Still, the water gave it a bit of buoyancy, and so it was the bulk Wangu struggled against and not the creature's heft. Even so, the sun was sinking, and Wangu needed to harvest what he could ere night fell and other sharks came following the blood trail. With the shâyú now rolled three-quarters over and braced against the rocks, Wangu unsheathed his gutting knife and, grunting and cursing, managed to hack a long, deep cut through the great shark's underside. He then plunged elbow-deep into the gashed-open gut of the shâyú to gather in the precious organs, but his hands encountered—*What is this?*—something unexpected. Hard and smooth and spherical it seemed . . . or mayhap an ovoid. Slowly he lifted it out—*Waugh!* It was a crystal, or perhaps a jewel. No! It was jade! Or was it?

They drew the child forth from its dead mother's cloven belly, and squalling cries filled the tent. Chakun was given the task of cleaning the babe, a boy, while Old Tal searched in her bag for gut to tie the cord ere cutting it.

As Chakun cleansed the child of matter, she saw a dark mark twining 'round his neck and up the back of his head and over.

Cord in hand, Tal turned back from her bag to see the mark as well. "Bring the iron knife of deliverance," said the old woman, her voice cold, her features glacial. "This child is cursed."

"But it's just a baby," protested Chakun.

"Nevertheless," hissed Tal, holding out her hand for the knife, "born in pain and death and blood it killed its mother; it has a mark; it must be slain, its throat cut ere the curse can spread to the tribe."

Tears in her eyes, Chakun turned the squalling child onto its back . . . and gasped out in wonder, for there on its forehead the mark ended.

"Yong!" cried Chakun. "It is the mark of a Yong!"

Standing out starkly on the forehead of the child was the face of a Yong—a Dragon—its sinuous body snaking back over the head of the babe, its tail wrapping 'round the tot's neck.

All the midwives moaned and fell down in worship, for the *Masula Yongsa Wang*—the Mage Warrior King—had come at last.

Wangu's eyes widened in amazement, for he held an oblate spheroid of translucent, jadelike stone, flawless and pale green and lustrous—some six inches through from end to end, and four inches through across—and it seemed to glow faintly with an inner light. He held the orb up in the dying rays of the setting sun, the crimson luminance casting back scarlet gleams like glints of candescent blood.

Out into the camp the child was carried—Chakun afforded the honor, for wasn't she the first to see the sign on the child's face? She marched to the main fire, all the midwives in a respectful train after, Tal at their head. When Chakun reached the circle of men, she stepped boldly through and she called so that all could hear—*"He shall be known as Kutsen Yong"*—and she held up the child for all to see, the mark on his forehead standing out starkly, reflecting his name—Mighty Dragon. Moaning in obeisance, all the men fell down in worship, for the long-awaited Mage Warrior King had chosen *this* tribe to first set foot among.

Old Tal stepped forward and said, "Teiji is dead, and the child will need milk."

"The milk of a mare?" asked Cholui Chang, the chieftain, still on his knees.

The old woman looked down at him in outrage. "This is the long-prophesied Masula Yongsa Wang, the one before whom even the Dragons themselves will bow. Nothing less than the full of a woman's breasts will do."

An icy chill fell over the camp at these words. Cholui Chang rose up and looked about, and he strode to the gathering women of the tribe. And he snatched a wee babe from its mother's arms, and, as she screamed in horror, he slew it with a stroke of his knife.

Aiee! This fish was even more precious than I thought. Nevertheless, there is a harvest to do before the night hunters arrive.

Into his boat Wangu set the jade stone and then returned to the shark. Swiftly he reaped the heart and the liver, and then he took the eyes. As to the brain, he would harvest it on the morrow, if any of it was left, for Dame Fortune—Lady Yùnchi—had guided his boathook, and the iron point had crashed through the head and stabbed through that organ on the shâyú's final run, killing the great savage beast.

Wangu turned to the shark fins, managing to hack off the pectorals ere darkness fell. And in the dimness he clambered into his battered boat, the floorboards awash with brine, and ere falling into exhausted sleep, he bailed most of it out.

Sometime during the night, Wangu was awakened by a loud thrashing as scavengers came and took their toll. But by sunup they were gone.

The next morning it was decided: while weeping Kkot—her week-old son, now dead—would wet-nurse the child, Chakun would be the principal handmaiden and see to Kutsen Yong's every need. After all she was the first among them to recognize the Masula Yongsa Wang, and she was all of eleven, certainly old enough for the task.

And the Mage Warrior King must be served.

There was a great deal of meat left on the shark, but what had remained of its organs was gone, for the scavengers had torn large chunks from the sliced-open belly on inward. Even so, competing with crabs, Wangu salvaged much of the precious flesh; it would bring a good price in the nearby great port of Janjong.

Finally, Wangu turned to the mouth and, working carefully, pried teeth loose, for he knew the serrated triangular bones would bring gold from the imperial guard. As he reached in to take another, of a sudden the great jaws snapped shut, and screaming in horror, Wangu drew back but a stump where his left hand once had been.

Even in death, the shâyú extracted its revenge for the fisherman's dark deeds done.

Far to the south in the land of Jûng, a yellow-eyed being set out northward for Moko, for not only did the signs say the time had come, his subsequent raising of the dead girl had also revealed his relentless foe was near.

And even as the yellow-eyed one fared away, to the west a black-haired Elf came across the border and into the land of Jûng. He bore with him a crystal-bladed black-hafted spear, and about his neck he wore a small blue stone on a thong. Into the land of Jûng he rode, to finally come to the great central city where the warlord of warlords ruled. There the Elf inquired after a yellow-eyed man, and although a few of those he asked knew of this reclusive, sinister being, none who had seen him knew where he had gone, though they did know it was recent. One by one, the Elf followed each of the roads out from the city, riding for league upon league, inquiring at steads and inns along the way, asking after the yellow-eyed man, but it was as if he had vanished into thin air, for none had seen him pass by. Disappointed once again, the Elf finally turned his horse back to the west, and left behind the land of Jûng.

Under the remnants of a once-great volcano, where the land for leagues upon leagues juddered and jolted and trembled, in the rock far below lay a vast, fiery chamber, magma bubbling and surging and occasionally breaking free to erupt anew. Here it was millennia past Black Kalgalath had laired, the great Fire-drake sending his aethyric self into the molten inferno below. Still that was in a time now gone, the mountain itself long destroyed, and only ruin and devastation remained.

Deep in the stone and faring from points afar, a number of huge beings made their way toward this fiery Hèl, their broad hands splitting open the granite before them and sealing it after as they moved through solid rock. They were coming to draw the molten stone back into the earth, down and away from the surface, to quell this land of its incessant juddering, for the time was drawing nigh, and this was Dragonslair.

And in Dwarven-carved chambers hidden within a black mountain in far Xian, sleepers began to waken and stir and murmur of the verging Trine.

CHAPTER 2

Joy

Spring–Autumn, 5E993

[Sixteen Years Past]

Lightning flared and thunder hammered and the rain came drenching down. And as the four Warrows sat at supper—Faeril and her brother Dibby, and their sire and dam, Arlo and Lorra—above the brawl of the storm came the thud of galloping hooves and the flare of a horn cry.

"What the . . . ?" Dibby leapt to the fogged-over window, rubbing a hole in the wetness, peering out, Arlo at his side, but both Faeril and Lorra stepped to a bedroom.

Again came the horn cry, closer now.

Faeril hurried back into the room, her knife-filled bandoliers settled across her chest, the three-foot-one young damman girting a long-knife about her waist.

Lorra, too, was accoutred in throwing knives.

Dibby turned. "Lor," he breathed, seeing the weaponry, "d'you think there's like to be danger?"

"Mayhap, Dibs," answered Faeril, and Dibby rushed to catch up two knobbed staffs, one for himself, the other for his sire. Small they might be, these Warrows, yet resolute warriors at times.

Now a rider thudded up to the cote through the driving rain, trailing a remount behind, water and mud splattering.

" 'Tis a man on a horse, a remount too," muttered Arlo, peering through the rain-streaked pane, the vision dim, distorted by water.

But lightning flared as the rider dismounted and cast back his hood. "Nay," said Faeril, "not a man, but an Elf instead! . . . 'Tis Jandrel from Arden! Something is amiss!"

Faeril had met the Elf some eight years ago, when she and Gwylly—the last of the Lastborn Firstborns—had gone to Arden Vale to follow a prophecy entangled with the return of the Eye of the Hunter, a long-haired star that came streaking through the heavens but once every ten thousand years. And along with Dara Riatha and Alor Aravan—Elves of Arden Vale—Faeril and Gwylly had followed that doom when the harbinger had scored the winter night skies, its luminous tail streaming after. And miraculously they had recovered Urus alive, the Baeran finally freed from the glacier. But monstrous Stoke had been freed as well, an evil set loose on the world once again. They had pursued this vile being across half the world and finally had run him to earth. Yet in doing so they had paid a terrible price, they had lost Gwylly . . . Gwylly, Faeril's mate. . . .

Faeril rushed out into the downpour. "Jandrel! Jandrel! What is it? What is wrong?"

A great smile burst across Jandrel's wet face, and he caught up the golden-eyed damman, a silver lock streaking through her black hair, and whirled her about, water cascading down over both. "Wrong? Wrong? Why, my own sweet Faeril, what could possibly be wrong? I have come to fetch thee, back unto Arden to witness the miracle. The first Elven birth in Mithgar ever!

"Dara Riatha is with child!"

"You mean, she's had a baby?"

"Nay, she is pregnant! She carries Urus's child. Isn't it wonderful?"

"But, Jandrel, that is impossible! Elves cannot get pregnant on Mithgar. And even if they could, Humans and Elves between them do not bear children."

"Aye!" Jandrel grinned at the Waerling. "Did I not say it was a miracle?"

Jandrel set her down. "Riatha sent me. Canst thou leave on the morrow? She wishes thee at her side when the child comes."

Cold rain hammered upon the two. "Is it that quick? When is she due?"

Jandrel laughed, his face lighted with joy, and he spread out his hands, palms up. "Ah, wee one, no one knows. We have no experience with miracles at all. The last any Elf saw an Elven birth was more than five thousand years agone, on Adonar, ere the Sundering. And with Urus being the father, who can say when the child will come?"

Dibby and Arlo came splatting out in the rain, Dibby carrying Faeril's allweather cloak, casting it about the damman's shoulders. "Your horses are too big to fit in my pony stable," called Arlo through the downpour, "but they can take shelter in the byre yon." The Warrow looked up at the Elf. "And like your horses, you yourself are too big to walk through my door, but if you don't mind crawling in, we've got supper on the table, and there's plenty for you as well."

The very next morning—the tenth of April, 5E993—Faeril and Jandrel readied themselves to go.

Mid the tearful good-byes between Faeril and her family, Jandrel led the horses nigh, and with a final kiss for sire, dam, and brother, Faeril mounted up, the Elf lifting her to the saddle. And in the damp morning, running at a good clip they set out for Arden Vale, the Elf galloping in the lead, the damman mounted on the tethered horse coursing behind. And ere they raced beyond sight along the eastward trace, Jandrel lifted his horn to his lips, the Northwood ringing with his farewell call.

They changed horses in Stonehill and again in a stable in the Wilderland, as fifty or more miles a day they rode, seventeen to eighteen leagues, with Jandrel varying the pace of the run so that the steeds would last. They covered the nearly six hundred miles in but eleven days.

Riatha was radiant, and Urus beamed.

Faeril's intent gaze studied the golden-haired Dara, eyeing her tall, slender, five-foot-six frame. "They said you were with child, but I don't see . . ."

Riatha laughed, her eyes pale grey, all but silver. "As best as can be determined, the child is not due until autumn . . . October, mayhap."

Faeril mentally counted. *Five months, or six.* "How can this be, Riatha? I thought that Elves bore no young on Mithgar. And that there was no issue between Humans and Elves, ever."

" 'Tis remarkable, true. Yet Urus and I deem it is because of his nature. He is something besides Human."

"A Cursed One," rumbled Urus. "Or so I always thought, till now."

Faeril looked up at Urus, the Baeran huge at six-foot-eight and twenty-two stone. "And now . . . ?"

"Now I am a Blessed One," replied Urus, grinning, wrapping his arms about Riatha, the Dara all but lost in his massive embrace.

After consulting with Urus and Riatha, Alor Inarion, Warder of the Northern Regions of Rell and Lord of Arden Vale, sent representatives to the Great Greenhall to fetch a Baeran midwife, for the Elves had little or no experience in bringing forth a child—certainly not of late. And when she came, she was a strapping woman, some six-foot-one or -two. Yet her way was gentle, and her name was Yselle, and she and Riatha became fast friends.

Over the next weeks and months, marvelling Elves from throughout Mithgar came to be present at the birth.

And in the artisans' halls of Arden, workers of precious metals and gems and ivories—and other materials worthy—began fashioning gifts for the child, even though they knew not whether it would be male or female.

Among these workers was a wee damman, learning the art of fine chain crafting, for Faeril would prepare a birthing gift with her own hands. And she fashioned a crystal pendant on a platinum chain, the pellucid stone remarkable for the figure within, that of a bird, a falcon, wings unfurled as if poised on the verge of flight. The crystal had been given to her by Riatha as a gift from Inarion years past. Six-sided down its length, it was, each end blunt-pointed with six facets, some three-quarters of an inch across from flat to opposite flat, and four inches from tip to tip. At that time it had been perfectly clear, entirely without the bird. Yet upon her encounter with the Oracle Dodona deep in the desert Karoo, the crystal thereafter contained the falcon, though how inscribed completely within the limpid stone, none could say. And although Faeril treasured the stone, since the crystal had originally come to her from the Elves of Arden Vale, it seemed only fitting that it should be passed on to Riatha's child.

Why the damman chose platinum over gold or silver or even starsilver to make the chain, Faeril did not know, yet when she had touched the metal, she knew that this was meant to be. And all during the crafting, an elusive thought slid 'round the corners of her mind, always just beyond seeing, always glimpsed, but not recognized. Yet on the day she finished the crafting—chain glittering, crystal sparkling in the bright sunlight, a poised falcon within—suddenly there seemed to echo in her mind something Dodona had said to her in the crystal in the Kandrawood ring:

"You travel with one who is to bear the hope of the world, and she is worthy."

Faeril paused in her smithing and caught her breath as again Dodona's words echoed in her mind: *"You travel with one who is to bear the hope of the world, and she is worthy."*

Whelmed by the thought, Faeril sat down, staring at the crystal in her hand. *Could this be what Dodona had meant? That Riatha is to bear a child who will be the hope of the world?*

But she remembered as well something Aravan had said: *"Auguries are oft subtle ... and dangerous—thou mayest deem they mean one thing when they mean something else altogether."*

Faeril kept her thoughts to herself, wanting to ponder Dodona's words longer ere sharing her insight. And oft she gazed at the clear crystal, the one with the bird inside.

And as if a floodgate had been loosed, visions and phrases inundated her mind as she recalled her first dangerous journey down into the depths of that transparent stone, a journey that took place one warm spring evening some seven years past as she sat in the moonlight in Arden Vale and stared at the crystal in hand, and without warning found herself falling through glittering space:

Of a sudden she glimpsed an Elfess—Riatha?—she could not say, and standing behind was a huge man, mayhap a Baeron. Next came a rider—man or Elf?—on horse, a falcon on the rider's shoulder, something glittering in his hands.

And she shouted out words in Twyll, the ancient tongue of the Warrows, words that meant:

> *"Rider of Impossibility,*
> *And Child of the same,*
> *Seeker, searcher, he will be*
> *A Traveller of the Planes."*

And even after the chain was done and the crystal pendant affixed, as Faeril sat alone in her riverside cottage, her mind returned again and again to those visions, to those words, to those divinations:

> *Rider of Impossibility, Child of the same . . .*
> *Child of the same . . .*
> *Of the same . . .*
> *Rider of Impossibility . . .*
> *Child of Impossibility? . . .*

Riatha's child: the impossible child?
Faeril's heart hammered in her breast. *Is that it? Riatha's child, the impossible child? Seeker, searcher, he will be the Traveller of the Planes?*
If that is so, well then, oh my. . . .
Her mind awhirl, Faeril prepared a pot of tea, and then sat without drinking as it grew cold, lost in her thoughts, lost in possibilities.
Falcon on his shoulder, something glittering in his hands . . . ?
Faeril held up the pendant, the crystal she had borne across much of Mithgar, seeing the falcon inside. *Does this have aught to do with the falcon on his shoulder?*
And again Aravan's words echoed in her mind: *"Auguries are oft subtle . . . and dangerous—thou mayest deem they mean one thing when they mean something else altogether."*

On the ninth of October, 5E993, at the mid of day, in a hall crowded with watching Darai, in seemingly effortless labor, Riatha was delivered of a boy child. Faeril was at her side during the birthing, Midwife Yselle and two chosen Darai aiding in the delivery.

But after they had cut and tied the cord and had washed the newborn, it was Faeril given the honor of bearing the yawling infant out to Urus, the Baeran pacing as if caged. And when she handed him up, Urus took the tiny child in his great arms, gentle as a waft of air, and he lifted back the soft blanket covering the babe, and looked long at his son, the tiny face wrapped 'round howls. Turning to Inarion, he said, "Looks somewhat Elvish, somewhat mannish, but squalls like a newborn cub."

Together they stepped to the porch of the great hall, out where all had gathered, and Urus raised his child overhead, toward the new moon clasped in the arms of the old. And he called out unto the waiting assembly: "On this day is a miracle, for on this day Riatha has delivered a child. Our son is born."

And a mighty shout flew up to the sky.

The celebration went long into the night, wine flowing, shouts of joy, trills of laughter, wild dancing, feasting and drinking, bards singing and telling tales. . . .

That night, too, at the child's side someone left an exquisitely carved stone ring, set with a gem of jet, sized to fit a large man's hand. Whoever had left it had gotten in and out without notice. How? None knew. Yet on that very same night the celebrants heard foxes barking in the woods.

Aravan came the next day, the tall, slender, black-haired Elf riding in from the south, and he bore a gift for the child: a gold-encased glass-covered tiny arrow used to find true north.

On this day, too, in the glade of celebration there was an Elven naming ceremony, presided over by Inarion, the Elf Lord speaking in Sylva. And to this sacrament were gathered all the vale's occupants and visitors, for none had seen or heard the words of the rite in more than five thousand years.

And Inarion sprinkled the crystal water upon the newborn's forehead, intoning, "Water!" and touched the child's tiny hands and feet to clean earth held in a clay vessel—"Earth!"—and with a branch of laurel wafted the fragrant smoke of smoldering eldwood shavings over the babe—"Air!"—and illuminated the sleep-

ing newborn's face with the light of a burning branch of yew—
"Fire!"—and touched a lodestone to his wee hands and feet and
temples and heart—"Aethyr!"

At last Inarion turned to Riatha. "And what shall be his name?"

Riatha looked up at Urus, and then down at the child. "He
shall be called Bair."

"Bair," whispered Inarion in the babe's right ear and then in
the left, and then he turned to the gathering. "Darai and Alori assembled," announced Inarion, "from this day forward he shall be
called Bair!"

Alor Bair! rang out the response, thrice altogether.

The child yawned and nearly wakened, but did not. And on
this day, the day of his naming, Bair was one day old; yet no
matter his age, when compared to all of eternity, his life was just
beginning.

CHAPTER 3

Auguries

Autumn, 5E993

[Sixteen Years Past]

A week after the birth of Bair, Aravan came seeking Faeril. He found her sitting amid the last of a patch of summer wildflowers high along the banks of the Virfla—the Tumble River—the water plunging, swirling, eddy pools gurging as the braw stream furiously hurtled toward a distant sea. Aravan sat down in the sward at hand and laid aside his crystal-bladed black-hafted spear.

"Thou didst summon me?"

Faeril looked away from the rush and to the Elf and brushed back her stray silver lock. She pensively nodded but said not a word and stared down at the water again.

Aravan peered across the river and into the sky where a hawk soared back and forth above the tall grass. Finally, he said, "The Emir of Nizari is slain."

Faeril's eyes widened, but she said nought, and only the purl of the flow and the *skree* of the far-off hunter broke the silence between them, as the fading fragrance of the declining summer flowers drifted away on a pine-scented breeze. At last Aravan said, "Thou didst not ask me to join thee merely to sit without speaking a word. Something troubles thee."

Faeril sighed and pointed at the river below. "Just as the waters do whirl and plunge, so is my mind atumble."

"Atumble?"

"Aye. With visions I have seen and heard and been told about, with visions you know of as well."

"Visions."

Faeril nodded. "Visions, auguries, redes."

"More than one," mused Aravan, his soft words not a question.

"Yes, Aravan. More than one. It seems that several are coming together—three, four, mayhap more, others of which I know not—as if something momentous looms."

"Say on, Wee Faeril."

"I don't know where to begin," said the damman. But then she turned and looked at her cottage sitting some distance away. "I suppose it was when my very being fell into the crystal the first time, there in the moonlight yon. . . ."

Faeril sat on the stoop of the cote, emptying her mind of all distraction, trying to <see> as she peered into the depths of the crys—

—*She fell through glittering space, silvery glowing crystal panes tumbling past, or was she tumbling and the panes still? . . . she did not know. Mirrored reflections from angled, crystal surfaces sparkled about her, and the whole of creation was filled with the ring of scintillant wind chimes, tinkling, pinging, chinging, the sound surrounding all. Down she spun and down, into a shimmering sea of argent light, of luminance and glimmer and flash . . . and there came the peal of crystal bells ringing near and far. And as she tumbled past translucent planes, over and again she saw reflected a glow of a golden flame—at times multiple images, at other times but one—a steady and slender shaft of light; and suddenly she realized that it tumbled as did she, and knew it to be her own reflection, perhaps her very soul.*

Still she fell endlessly, down and down within, glittering hexagonal panes turning about her as crystalline chimes chinged and tinked in the nonexistent wind . . . in the blowing aethyr.

And even though falling, she felt no fright, her spirit steady, her soul filled with chimes and light and wonder.

In the glittering transparent surfaces where glowed her own reflection, past the golden light beyond the multiple windows of sparkling crystal, she could discern images, some vague and un-formed, as if unfocused, others sharp and strange. Images, vi-sions: they flashed by rapidly as she fell down among the scintillant panes—shadowy armies marching, a field of roses red, a murky black pool rippling, a great bear, enormous pillars loom-ing, stars glittering, water whirling, grey mist swirling, and more, much more—images vague and distant, others near and sharp, and all fleeting, all nought but glimmers and glances.

Of a sudden she glimpsed a Dara—Riatha? She could not say—and standing behind was a huge man, mayhap a Baeron. Next came a rider—man or Elf?—on horse, a falcon on the rider's shoulder, something glittering in his hands.

And Faeril felt words echoing from her mouth as she called out something. What? She did not know, even though the words were in Twyll, for she could not hear them, and she knew not what she said—the words were not her own.

> *Ritana fi Za'o*
> *De Kiler fi ca omos,*
> *Sekena, ircuma, va lin du*
> *En Vailena fi ca Lomos.*

And onward she fell, endlessly, down and down, the images of Dara and Baeron and rider and falcon left far behind, Faeril twisting and turning among a myriad of golden reflections of her soul as crystal panes tumbled past, shapes and forms and figures glimpsed beyond.

But then there came a voiceless cry, someone inaudibly weep-ing, and she listened knowing that somehow it was important, and somehow familiar, this mute voice calling noiselessly, this unheard grieving, this silent—

—Even as Faeril opened her eyes she could hear Gwylly weep-ing and whispering her name. And he was holding her hand and stroking her fingers. His visage swam into view and steadied. "Don't cry, beloved," she murmured. . . .

"Yes, I remember," said Aravan. "I was there. For three days thou didst lie unconscious, Gwylly ever at thy side, else we would never have known the rede thou didst say."

Faeril sighed, a vision of Gwylly shimmering in her suddenly brimming eyes. Brushing away the tears, she said, "Aravan, do you recall the words? —What they meant?"

Aravan nodded. "Rider of Impossibility, Child of the same—"

"You do remember," agreed Faeril.

Aravan cocked an eyebrow.

Faeril took a deep breath and then said, "Bair is the Impossible Child. He will be the Rider of the Planes."

"How dost thou know this?"

Faeril sighed. "The second time I was in the crystal it was with Dodona, and he told me this: 'You travel with one who is to bear the hope of the world, and she is worthy.' "

Aravan frowned in reflection. "I remember." Then he looked at Faeril.

"It was Riatha we travelled with, Aravan. And she has borne a child—an Impossible Child—one I believe who is destined to be the Hope of the World."

Aravan nodded slowly. "That is but two prophecies. Thou didst say there were more."

Faeril nodded. "A vision, Aravan, I saw in the crystal: it was of a rider, a man or an Elf, with a falcon on his shoulder and something glittering in his hands."

"Something glittering?"

"I couldn't tell what it was, Aravan. I was looking at the rider and falcon, and the image flashed by and was gone before I could see what the glitter was."

Aravan sighed, then said, "That makes three auguries which seem related, yet thou didst speak of four."

Faeril nodded. "The last is one I have but heard of: Rael's Rede, the one concerning a sword."

Aravan's eyes widened, and he said:

> *"Bright Silverlarks and Silver Sword,*
> *Borne hence upon the Dawn,*
> *Return to earth; Elves girt thyselves*
> *To struggle for the One.*

"Death's wind shall blow, and crushing Woe
Will hammer down the Land.
Not grief, not tears, not High Adon
Shall stay Great Evil's hand."

The knuckles of Faeril's interlaced fingers turned white at Aravan's words, and she said, "It is a terrible rede."

"Yet thou dost believe it pertains?"

With effort, Faeril relaxed her intertwined grip. "I do. They all seem to go together. Riatha has borne the Impossible Child who will be the Rider of the Planes and bear the Silver Sword to Mithgar when great evil brings woe to the world."

Again silence fell between them, and still the Virfla tumbled. Of the distant sweeping hawk there was no sign.

At last Faeril said, "I saw it in the myriad panes of the crystal—the future—or so I do believe. And who knows how many other auguries may be involved, visions I did not see, all coming together at once?"

Aravan frowned and pursed his lips.

"Yet there is this, Aravan," said Faeril, "you said it yourself: 'Auguries are oft subtle . . . and dangerous—thou mayest deem they mean one thing when they mean something else altogether.' "

Now it was Aravan who sighed, and he slowly shook his head. "Nevertheless, Faeril, I ween thou hast guessed the right of much. Mayhap Bair is indeed the Rider of the Planes, the Dawn Rider, the one who will bear the Silver Sword to the world. Yet who can say how that will come about . . . and when? Only the gods could know. And so, I cannot abandon my own quest for the finding of the Dawn Sword, nor for the yellow-eyed slayer of Galarun, for I am sworn."

Again silence fell between them, but at last Aravan said, "Hast thou told aught to Riatha, to Urus?"

Faeril shook her head, *No.*

"Then I bid thee to share what thou hast guessed, for keeping it unto thyself may have consequences dire."

"Just as may the sharing," responded Faeril. "What I say will surely color the way Bair is raised, for ill or good, who can foretell? . . . Not I, Aravan. Not I."

"Nor I, Faeril. Yet heed: in knowledge lies strength; in ignorance, weakness. 'Tis always better to know even part, than to know nothing at all."

Faeril slowly nodded, heeding his words.

They sat without speaking for a while, and still the river hurtled onward, and in the distance across the flow a hawk rose up from the grass, a partially consumed rabbit in its taloned grasp. As Aravan watched the raptor soar up into the sky, he said, "I leave on the morrow."

Faeril sighed. "Whence bound?"

"Easterly. . . ." After a moment he continued. "When Stoke nearly answered my question as to the whereabouts of Ydral, he vaguely gestured east."

"But, Aravan, there is a whole wide world to the east."

Aravan shrugged. "I have time, Faeril. I have time."

The next day Aravan was gone down Arden Vale, heading for the southern outlet, a passage secluded behind a plunging cataract, mist swirling up to hide all. And after they had waved him goodbye, Faeril turned to Riatha and Urus, the Baeran holding Bair in his arms. "Come," said the damman. "Let us sit awhile. I have something to tell you . . . something to unfold."

CHAPTER 4

Revelations

Autumn, 5E993

[Sixteen Years Past]

Six weeks after the birth of Bair, as a November snow drifted down, there came in the dawn the belling of bugles echoing up the vale, the relayed notes signalling that welcome visitors had come by the road under the falls and into the Hidden Stand. Yet the way under and in was nigh a day's journey south were they coming in haste, and even longer were they moving at a leisurely pace. Still it was not even noontide when the sentries standing ward on the southern approach to main holt glimpsed movement through the gentle falling as seven loping figures, seven Draega, seven Silver Wolves came running, all but unseen within the gliding white. And as they passed through a stand of ghostly birch, out came padding six Silver Wolves and a striding man, or was it an Elf? —Nay! 'Twas neither.

Dalavar Wolfmage had come.

Man height he was, six-foot or so, and as with all Magekind his eyes held the hint of a tilt and his ears were pointed, though less so than those of Elves. His hair was long and silvery-white, and it hung down beyond his shoulders, its sheen much the same as Silver Wolf fur, though somehow darker. In spite of his whitish hair, he looked to be no more than thirty, though in truth the measure of his years was counted in millennia. He was dressed in soft grey leathers, a silver-buckled black-leather belt at his waist. His feet were shod in black boots, supple and soft on the land. His eyes were as piercing as those of a falcon, their color pale grey. He bore no visible weapons and did not carry a staff.

Amid a great flurry of talk and speculation, Dalavar made his way unto the coron-hall, and there within he met with Alor Inarion, while the six Silver Wolves, large as ponies, settled outside to wait.

"I have come to see the child," said the Wolfmage, brushing aside the welcome, "and to speak with his sire and dam in private. The matter is urgent."

Since there was but one child in the Vale, Inarion did not ask who. But before the Alor could respond, the Wolfmage added: "Too, I would tell you to ward this vale well, for attempts will be made on his life."

Inarion's eyes widened, and he looked in startlement upon his guest. "Attempts on Bair's life?"

Dalavar nodded brusquely. "Aye."

"When?"

Dalavar turned up a hand. "While he is yet vulnerable. But as to the time and place . . . that I do not know."

"Why would anyone wish to slay a wee babe?"

Dalavar frowned and for a brief moment it seemed that he wouldn't speak. But then: "He has a destiny to fulfill, one that evil does fear. To say more would jeopardize all."

Inarion canted his head in acceptance, and a hard glint came to his eyes. "None has of yet invaded the Hidden Stand, for it is concealed and we do ward it well. Even so, we shall strengthen our measures to ensure none ever does."

Dalavar nodded and then said, "I would now see the child."

"Has he yet been imprinted?" asked Dalavar as he looked up from the babe to Urus.

Urus frowned. "Imprinted?"

"Patterned," replied Dalavar. "Impressed."

"Impressed with what?" asked Riatha, taking up the child and holding him in a protective embrace while stepping back from the Wolfmage.

"The essence of an animal," said Dalavar. "He—"

Riatha gasped. "Animal!" And she hugged Bair close.

"—is a shapeshifter, just as is his sire."

Riatha looked from the wee babe to Urus—Urus who some-times took on the form of a huge Bear—and Urus in turn looked at Dalavar, and his voice came soft and there was pain in his eyes. "My child is cursed?"

Dalavar cocked his head. "Cursed?"

"You said he is a shapeshifter, as am I," replied Urus, as if that explained all.

"Nay, Urus. As it is with folk everywhere, shapeshifters in-cluded, there are good and bad among all, Gyphon's Spawn the exception, of course. Hence, just as you are not cursed and I am not cursed, nor are others who change form, then neither is Bair cursed. Even so, he will shift shape, and we must choose with what essence he will be imbued, just as I chose for you."

Astonishment swept over Urus's features. "You chose . . . ?"

Dalavar looked about the cottage. "There is a long tale here for the telling. Will you prepare some tea and perhaps a modest meal, while I see to my friends outside? They need to hunt, for we have been long on the journey, and we did not pause to take game. When I return, we will speak of you and your parents, Urus, and of—"

"My parents!" blurted Urus. "But I don't know who they are, who they were. I was a foundling, raised in the Great Greenhall by Uran and Niki and Uncle Beorc, but as to—"

Urus's words jerked to silence as the Wolfmage pressed out a hand in a call for quiet. "I know," said Dalavar softly, "for I did approve it all." And with that he stepped outside.

Dalavar pushed back from the table, the shreds of a haunch of venison left lying on the platter, the meat eaten cold upon slabs of bread and washed down with cups of hot tea.

"I thought I was a trencherman," said Urus, pouring golden brandy from a crystal decanter into three pear-shaped goblets, "but clearly I have met my match."

Dalavar smiled as he took up his glass and warmed it in his hands. "As I said, we were long on the journey and did not pause to hunt."

Riatha took a small sip from her goblet and then said, "Now about Urus's parents . . ."

Dalavar nodded and set his glass to the table.

But even as Urus leaned forward, all attention, there came a knock at the door. Urus sighed and stood and stepped to the entry.

It was Faeril, a cloth-covered loaf of fresh-baked bread in hand.

She looked up at Urus holding the door wide and then to Dalavar. "Oh, I didn't know you had compan—"

"A Waerling!" exclaimed Dalavar. He looked across at Riatha. "Here in the Hidden Vale?"

Riatha nodded. "Aye. She is a most trusted friend."

"Here," said Faeril, holding out the loaf, "I'll just leave this and go."

"No, no," said Urus. "Stay. Our guest is about to tell me of my parents, and he has news of import about Bair."

"Your paren—? Bair?" Faeril's gaze flew to the small cradle, and she rushed to its side. "Is he all right?" And as she looked in she hugged the loaf of bread to her breast as if it were a child. Sighing in relief, she turned to the others and whispered, "He's asleep."

Then a frown came over her features and she marched to the table and confronted Dalavar. "Now what's all this about Urus's parents? And what is the news about Bair?"

Dalavar broke into a soft chuckle. "Just like a Waerling."

Faeril's jaw shot out. "Just like a Waerling, eh? And when have you ever met one?"

Smiling, Dalavar said, "Back in the Great War of the Ban. Beau Darby I met first, followed by Tipperton Thistledown. Spunky, they were, just like you."

Faeril's mouth formed a surprised *O*. "Beau Darby, Tipperton Thistledown: you met them?"

"Others, too."

"Oh my."

Riatha, grinning, said, "Faeril Twiggins Fenn, may I present Dalavar of the Wolfwood. Dalavar, this is—"

"Dalavar!" Faeril's eyes widened. "Why, I've heard of you: back when we were hunting Stoke, I asked Riatha if he might have gone into your forest."

"I would not abide such a monster to set a foot therein," said Dalavar.

Faeril nodded. "That's what Riatha said."

With a rumble, Urus cleared his throat. "Mayhap we can tell old tales to one another later, but for now I would hear what Dalavar has come to say." And he poured out a tot of brandy for Faeril and pulled up another chair.

And when all had settled, Urus turned to the Wolfmage. "Now, you were saying . . . ?"

"Long past, ere I was born, ere even the counting of Eras, when the ways between all Planes were yet whole, there occurred a terrible crime: the rape of a Mage. A Seer, she was, and though she could at times foretell events which would occur, she had no inkling of the fate that awaited her, there in her tower among the spires of the Grimwall south of the Quadran and west of what was to become the forest of Darda Galion.

"They came to her turret in the dead of night, a raiding party of Foul Folk. Looking for treasure, for plunder, for murder, and they were led by one she could only describe as a yellow-eyed Demon, and that but in her screams."

"Demon!" blurted Faeril, and she turned to Riatha and asked: "Like the one spoken of in the legends? Like in the tale of Arin and Egil One-Eye?"

Riatha in turn looked at Dalavar, and he said, "Nay, not like the one nigh the Temple of the Maze, for that was a true Demon, summoned by Ordrune to deal with Sir Ulry and all his subsequent seed.

"No true Demon was the raver who assaulted the Seer in her tower, but a profoundly vile creature of another sort, a *thing* of Neddra some might miscall 'Demon,' but one I would call a Fiend. I believe it was more likely the get of a true Demon upon a Spawn of Neddra—whether it mated with Rûck, Hlôk, Ghûl, or some other creature, that I cannot say—but no matter what, 'twas an evildoing of Gyphon, I ween."

Riatha gasped, as did Faeril, and a grim look came upon Urus.

"Such is the one Aravan pursues," said Riatha, "for he, too, is a yellow-eyed Fiend."

Dalavar shook his head. "The one Aravan pursues, I believe, is the offspring of another of the Fiend's ravagings, the foul creature spewing its seed into someone of Mithgar—Human, I would think—for from Eiron's recounting of Galarun's Death Rede, Aravan's foe looks to be more manlike than the Fiend I tracked down and slew."

"You slew it?" asked Faeril, her eyes wide.

Dalavar nodded. "Nigh the Stones of Jalan. In league with Modru it was, and through a surrogate Modru named it my bane and summoned it to slay me, but I was the victor instead, more by chance than design, for I killed it in blind rage . . . and slew the surrogate as well."

Silence fell upon them all as Dalavar took a long pull from his glass of brandy, but at last Urus said, "Be that as it may, you were speaking of the rape of a Seeress."

"Aye," replied Dalavar. "The Fiend took her brutally and left his seed in her womb, and then flew away."

"Flew?" asked Faeril.

"In what I could gather from her ravings, it changed into a Fell Beast and upon leathery wings took unto the air."

"Like Stoke," said Faeril. "A Fell Beast was one of his shapes."

Urus growled and turned to Dalavar, "And you say shapeshifters are not cursed?"

Dalavar turned up his hands.

"What of the Seeress?" asked Riatha.

Dalavar sighed. "She was left for dead by the Fiend, but instead did survive, and six months after this ravagement she bore twins: my sister Ayla and me."

"Oh my," breathed Faeril, and she looked with shock upon Urus and Riatha to find them as stunned as she.

Dalavar reached out and took the crystal decanter and refilled his goblet. "Her name was Seylyn—my mother—and screaming and raving and weeping, she was discovered by Elves who came to her mountainholt tower. They tended her dearly, but in spite of their comfort and aid, could not make her whole again.

"There was a Silver Wolf among the Elves—Greylight was his name—and when we were born he imprinted my sister and me."

"Again you use the word 'imprinted,' " said Riatha, concern in her features as she glanced toward sleeping Bair.

Dalavar sighed. "Seed from the loins of our demonic sire, both Ayla and I were shapeshifters, too, just as was he. 'Twas but good fortune that the first sentient animal we bonded with was a creature of Adonar, a Draega, a Silver Wolf."

Faeril gasped in astonishment. "You mean shapeshifters take on the form of the first animal they encounter?"

Dalavar held out a hand and shook his head. "Not the first they encounter but the first they are drawn to and those who are drawn to them. As I said, it is a bonding."

"And you say that Bair is to be imprinted?" rumbled Urus, uncertainty in his eyes.

Dalavar nodded. "Just as were you, Urus."

"Oh my," said Faeril. "Oh my."

"Thy tale is not finished," said Riatha in grim determination, unwilling as yet to concede to the imprinting of her son.

Dalavar canted his head in agreement. "Indeed it is not, Dara."

At that moment, Bair yawned and awakened, and Urus took him up, the child fussing to be changed and fed. After the babe was cleansed and diapered once more, Urus handed him to Riatha, and she bared one of her full breasts to the babe, which he took to eagerly. And as he suckled, Riatha said, "Say on, Dalavar."

The Wolfmage took another sip of his brandy and then continued his tale, pain lurking deep in his eyes:

"Our mother never recovered, and after lingering for a decade in madness, she died screaming, terror bursting her heart. Ayla and I were not quite ten.

"Eras came and went, and my sister and I each trod our separate ways. But a millennium or so past, Ayla sent me a message: she had found true love with a Baeran man; Brun was his name." Dalavar looked Urus in the eye. "They were your sire and dam, Urus . . . or should I name you nephew?"

Urus's mouth fell open, and Riatha jerked in surprise, Bair frowning up at her as he struggled to find the lost nipple. And Faeril said, "Oh my."

"Your sister was my mother?" breathed Urus.

Dalavar nodded, smiling gently.

"And Brun was my sire's name, a Baeran?"

Again Dalavar nodded, but his smile faded into sad eyes. "Shortly after, I came to their holt in the Grimwall—not far from here, I might add—to see them and their newborn child. But when I arrived, I found them slain: Ayla beheaded—by a silver-edged blade, I ween, for she was truly dead—and Brun impaled on a Ghûl's barbed spear. The place was ravaged, for Foul Folk had come and destroyed all. But in the nursery I found a Ghûl and several Rûcks torn asunder, their remains scattered about, as if some great beast had engaged in the battle as well; yet there was no beast among the slain, and no sign of a child, the cradle bare. Even as I set the wrack aflame in the early dawn—a fitting pyre to my sister and her mate—from a cradle blanket I saved, Greylight and the pack picked up a scent, and together we followed your trail. We finally found you in a hollowed-out bluff, in the care of a friend of Brun's: a great brown Bear, a sow, dried Rûpt blood on her claws. Wounded, she had borne you to safety by your swaddling clothes, and when I found you, you were nursing."

"Bear's milk?" said Riatha, a faint smile on her face, Bair now suckling on her other breast.

Dalavar's eyes softened, and he said, "Bear's milk, aye. From the look of things, she had of recent lost a cub of her own."

Urus sighed. "So my dam and sire were slain by Spawn."

Dalavar nodded. "I deem the Foul Folk were sent."

"Sent?"

"Aye. To murder your parents and you. But you were spirited away by the sow."

Faeril looked up at huge Urus. "But why would someone send the Foul Folk to kill Ayla and Brun and baby Urus? Was it out of maliciousness?"

Dalavar shook his head. "Nay. I believe whoever sent them had foreseen that Urus was but one step away from fulfilling a long-prophesied destiny."

"What long-prophesied destiny?" demanded Urus.

Dalavar gestured toward Bair. "The birth of the Dawn Rider."

"Bair?" asked Riatha, clutching the babe closer.

A look of distress fell upon Faeril's face. "Oh my, but I was right."

"Thou art certain?" asked Riatha.

Dalavar nodded. "He bears the blood of four worlds and four Races: Adonar, Vadaria, Mithgar, and Neddra; and the blood of Elvenkind, Magekind, and Mankind, as well as that of a Fiend."

Faeril gasped. "Will he be . . . normal?"

Dalavar nodded. "As normal as am I; as normal as is Urus; as normal as is Dara Riatha." Dalavar looked at Urus and said, "I deem it is the blood of the Fiend, Urus, which allows those like us to crossbreed with those of a different Race."

Silence fell among them, but then: "Oh my," said Faeril, looking at the child at Riatha's breast. "If Urus was in danger, then what about Bair?"

Dalavar sighed. "I fear he is in danger, too. Yet here in the Hidden Vale he is well protected."

Distress fell over Riatha's face, but she had a firm set to her jaw.

"Who would do such a thing?" gritted Urus. "—Send Foul Folk to slay my sire and dam, I mean—and threaten the life of our son."

"Thou, too, my love," said Riatha, softly. "Whoever did so send them, it was to slay thee as well."

Urus nodded and clenched a fist and repeated the question again: "Who would do such a thing?"

"Someone who has glimpsed the future," replied Dalavar, "and would not have it be."

"Like Arin Flameseer?" asked Faeril. "I mean, she saw a grim future of devastation wrought by the Dragonstone. But she found that token of ill and averted its fate."

Dalavar held up a hand of caution. "Perhaps. Yet tokens for good or ill have ways of fulfilling their own destinies."

Riatha frowned and said, "But Arin Flameseer was working to prevent a disaster, whereas if thou art right, Dalavar, then whosoever sent those to slay Ayla and Brun and baby Urus, and who may be a threat to my Bair, works to foster affliction."

"Aye," replied Dalavar, "yet list: my own dam, Seylyn, was a Seer, and at times I, too, have had <sight>. This I do know and will say: many things are coming together and Bair has a destiny to fulfill, but I cannot tell all I have <seen>, else it might change what is to come. And heed: Bair *must* be raised free of prophecy, else he will spend his waking life trying to fulfill the same."

Tears filled Riatha's eyes, but she nodded her agreement.

Faeril, too, canted her head in assent.

But Urus sprang to his feet and paced back and forth in rage, smacking a fist into palm. Finally, he stopped before Dalavar. "Is there nothing we can do to thwart this vile Seer?"

"One thing," replied Dalavar. "Protect Bair well within the Hidden Vale, yet allow him to walk with Aravan wherever Aravan goes. More I will not say."

"Aravan is like a *jarin*—a brother—to me," said Riatha.

Dalavar nodded. "So I have <seen>. Foster much of Bair's training to Aravan, yet you, Urus, must train him as well, especially in shifting shape. And you, Riatha, must teach him even as a child in the rite of the turning of the seasons."

Urus stopped his pacing and sat down, his fists clenched hard, his knuckles white.

Riatha gave over Bair to Faeril, the wee babe finished with his meal and asleep once again. And the Dara took Urus's hands and gently unclasped them and smoothed out his fingers.

"You did not finish your tale," said Faeril, stepping toward the cradle. "You and the Silver Wolves found Urus with a Bear. Was he, um, *imprinted* by her?"

"Not quite," said Dalavar, "for the sow had not been with him overlong. But by the time I found them, the sun had set and night had fallen, hence once again free of Adon's Ban the Foul Folk began searching anew; I could hear their horns calling. And then I heard an answering Vulg cry, and I knew that if the Vulgs joined the Foul Folk, they would scent the track as did we."

"What did you do?" asked Faeril as she eased the well-fed, sleeping babe down into his wee bed again.

"I could not put Urus at risk, and so we ran," said Dalavar. "And then we had a stroke of luck: we came across a band of Pyska."

"Pyska?"

"Hidden Ones," said Riatha. "Fox Riders."

"Oh. I know them by that name," said Faeril. And as she returned to the table and clambered back into her chair, Faeril remembered the time she first went to find Gwylly, when she and her pony passed through foreboding regions of the Weiunwood, great forested haunts where moving shadows seemed to flit at the corner of her eye. Gwylly had been astonished that she had ridden safely through places he named Forbidden. Later on she had heard of Fox Riders living in these banned places and how they could draw darkness unto themselves when they wished to remain concealed, though some said their gathered shadow could not fool Warrow eyes, especially up close.

Faeril shook her head to clear it of these vagaries and took a sip of brandy. Of a sudden, she frowned, trying to capture an elusive thought. And then she had it: "I say, there were foxes barking in the woods the night of the day Bair was born. Could Fox Riders have—?" Faeril turned to Riatha. "Hoy, now. Could they have delivered the ring? It was done in secret. No one saw anyone come and go, and if they enwrap themselves in shadow . . ."

Dalavar cocked his head. "Ring?"

Riatha stood and stepped to a bureau and pulled a drawer and took out a small wooden box, which she opened and placed on the table before Dalavar. Inside was the ring, made of stone and set with a gem of jet and sized to fit a large hand. Inside the box as well was the crystal pendant, the one embedded with the image of a poised falcon.

"Hmm. . ." mused the Mage, taking up the ring. Then he frowned in concentration and peered hard at the stone. "<Wild magic>," he muttered.

What? asked Urus and Faeril simultaneously.

Dalavar looked at them. "This is imbued with <power>, but not that of Magekind; some would call it <wild magic>. From its crafting I ween it came from the Hidden Ones, but as to whether from the Tomté, Vred Tres, Liv Vols, Pyska, or others . . ." Dalavar shrugged.

"A magic ring?" breathed Faeril, then sharply: "What does it do?"

Dalavar turned up a hand. "I can only say it holds <power>, but what it might do, I know not, for it is magic wild."

Faeril looked from Dalavar to Riatha and then back again. "Is it like Aravan's stone?"

Dalavar cocked an eyebrow. "Aravan's stone?"

Faeril nodded and said, "The one about his neck which grows cold when some kinds of peril are near. It came from the Hidden Ones, too—Fox Riders—just like this ring."

"If it came from the Hidden Ones, then I would say it holds <wild magic> as well."

Dalavar put the ring in the box and took out the crystal pendant, the chain dangling down. He touched the links, his eyes elsewhere, and murmured, "A *significant* metal." Then he gazed at the pellucid stone and turned it about, admiring the falcon within. And he looked hard at this gift as well, his eyes widening. "This once held <fire>."

Faeril glanced at Bair and then to the pendant. "It is not dangerous, is it?"

Dalavar placed the crystal and chain beside the ring and closed the lid of the box. "No more so than other crystals, reservoirs all, matrices for holding <fire>. Yet this one is now <attuned>."

"To what?"

"To the spirit of a falcon, I believe." He pushed the small box across the table to Riatha.

As Riatha opened the lid again and stared down at the ring and pendant inside, Urus cleared his throat. "So as you fled the Foul Folk, you ran across a band of Pysks."

Dalavar took up his brandy and nodded. "Aye. That was when I chose for you, Urus, for I knew if I left you this night with the Bear, that would be the shape you would take. Yet I turned the guarding of you—a wee babe—over to the Pyska, for their arrows are deadly and I believed you would be safe. I instructed them to take you to the Baeron in the Great Greenhall, and then Greylight and I and the rest of the pack went hunting Foul Folk and Vulgs." Dalavar took the last swig of brandy in his glass and waved off Urus's offer to renew.

"The Pyska rounded up four more Bears, boars to escort the child to safety. How they persuaded boars to travel together and the sow to allow them nigh, that I cannot say, yet travel in a band they did. Perhaps they sensed what you were, Urus, for Bears and Baeron seem to have a bonding, as do Baeron and Wolves. Regardless, off you went in a convoy of Pyska and Bears, the sow carrying you by your wrappings.

"But in the candlemarks sometime before dawn the Bears and Pyska ran into an ambush—Foul Folk who were ranging wide."

Urus nodded. "That's the morning when Uran and Uncle Beorc found me hidden under a stone overhang, dead Bears lying nigh, slain by Rûckish black arrows"—Urus frowned—"but Uncle Beorc told me they were all boars, not a sow among them."

"The sow was the first one slain and she lay just beyond the ridge," said Dalavar. "After the boars carried you to safety, they, too, were slain."

Urus growled, and the muscles in his jaw jumped as he gritted his teeth. But then he took a deep breath and let it out and said, "Well at least the Spawn got what they deserved, for my da and uncle said they found the arms and armor and ashes of Foul Folk, deadly Pysk arrows among the remains. They said it looked as if the Spawn had slain all the Bears, but had been slain by Fox Riders in turn, and then blown to ashes when the sunlight came and Adon's Ban struck even their corpses. As they carried me away that early morn, both of them said they saw Fox Riders high on the ridge above."

Dalavar nodded. "They did. The Pyska had been waiting for me to return, for they had no way to carry the babe—you—without the help of the someone larger: the Bears or Draega or me. They did take your soiled swaddling clothes and used them to lay a false trail, just in case the pack and I had not slain all the Vulgs. That was when your da and uncle came."

"Did you kill all the Vulgs?" asked Faeril.

"Aye," said Dalavar. "The Foul Folk as well."

"Good," said Faeril. "Now on with your tale."

Dalavar turned to Urus. "For five days altogether the Pysks and I followed your da and your uncle as they took you toward the Great Greenhall, both of them chewing up rations to feed you and squeezing berry juice into your mouth, along with giving you water, and I could see you were fussy but thriving under their gentle care.

"Finally, they reached a Baeron village in the Great Greenhall, a forest where Foul Folk fear to tread. And when I saw that Uran and Niki would keep you, I knew you would be fostered well."

Tears suddenly brimmed in Urus's eyes, and he grasped Riatha's hand. "I was indeed fostered well, my friend, and I thank you, Wolfmage Dalavar, for revealing my lost lineage to me."

As Dalavar held up a hand of negation, Faeril turned to Urus and said, "Shouldn't you call him Uncle Wolfmage? He is your kin, you know."

CHAPTER 5

Draega

Autumn–Winter, 5E993

[Sixteen Years Past]

Of a sudden, Faeril fixed Dalavar with a sharp gaze. "I say: and just where have you been, *Uncle Wolfmage*? Why have you taken so long to come and see Urus? To tell him this tale? Tell him of his parents? Do you just abandon nephews willy-nilly? He is your kith, you know."

Dalavar burst out in laughter and looked at Urus. "Did I not say 'Just like a Waerling'?"

Faeril grinned, but doggedly added, "Nevertheless . . ."

Dalavar held up his hands in surrender and said, "Throughout the years, I occasionally came to see Urus in the Great Greenhall, though not directly. Instead I observed him from afar, and at times I took on an Elven disguise and listened to what was said of him. He was loved and respected and faring well. Even so, he had a right to know of his lineage, and I decided I would tell him when he came of age—thirty, by my reckoning."

"Hmm," said Faeril. "Thirty is when Warrows come of age, too."

"Thirty was when I was chosen to be chieftain of my clan," said Urus.

Dalavar nodded. "As I was told. Yet when you turned thirty, I was elsewhere, dealing with events afar. Three winters after, I came to find you, but by then you were gone from the Great Greenhall."

"I was hunting Stoke," rumbled Urus, and his eye took on an echo of rage. "He had cruelly slain a warband of Baeron."

Again Dalavar nodded. "Aye. And over much of Mithgar did your hunt take you."

Faeril nodded and looked from Urus to Riatha and smiled. "That's when you two met." Then she turned to Dalavar and frowned. "But that doesn't explain why you didn't seek Urus out. I mean, that was a thousand years ago."

A faint smile crossed Dalavar's lips. "If you will recall, Lady Faeril, Urus was trapped in a glacier for that same thousand years, until you came and dug him out . . . a mere five years past."

Faeril's face turned red in embarrassment. "Oh, right," she mumbled but added, "Well then, you're excused."

The cottage rang with Dalavar's laughter, and he gasped, "I repeat: just like a Waerling."

In that moment there came a scratching at the door, and when Urus opened it, he found a slain stag lying on his doorstep, a pack of Silver Wolves lolling in the snow beyond.

Urus hauled on ropes looped over the limb and hefted the deer into the air by its hindquarters, the Baeran preparing to dress out the carcass. "We shall send some of this to the coron-hall," he said, tying off the line. "They will make good use of it there."

"Keep a haunch for yourself," said Dalavar, "to replace the one I ate."

"Oh, but I fully intend to," replied Urus, as he and the Wolf-mage watched the stag bleed out, nought but a gaping hole where its throat once had been, the snow turning scarlet below.

Then Urus took in a deep breath and let it out. "It would seem we have no choice in the matter. —About imprinting Bair, I mean."

Dalavar slowly shook his head, his silvery hair shimmering as would a waterfall. "Nay, for he *will* bond sooner or later. Even so, there is some choice in that you may select the shape he will shift to, does he bond to the creature chosen and does the creature bond to him."

Urus began cutting the musk glands from the buck's legs, taking great care so as to not taint the meat. As he cast a gland into a small basket to give over to the artisans of Arden Vale for the making of fragrant attar, he glanced back toward the cottage and said, "I will speak with Riatha."

Inside that small dwelling and standing at cradleside, Riatha turned to Faeril. "Although I would not have this foretold burden visited upon my Bair—my child the Rider of the Planes—it is prophecy, and little can be done. Too, in the matter of changing of shape, again it seems there is little choice."

Faeril sighed. "I suppose." But then her face brightened. "It didn't seem to hurt Urus, you know. In fact, being a shapeshifter saved his life more than once. Saved you and me and Aravan as well."

Riatha nodded morosely and stepped to a window and looked out across a wide span of snow to the tree where Urus was now skinning the buck.

Urus turned to Dalavar. "What would you suggest we choose for Bair's bonding? What animal, I mean."

Dalavar shrugged. "Something strong and swift and with endurance. Something clever and stealthy and savage at need, yet gentle otherwise."

Urus nodded. "Bears are strong and endure well, and are swift for short distances. As for savage . . . I have at times been quite brutal when there was a need. Gentle comes harder. As for clever and stealthy, I cannot claim such."

"How about a catamount?" asked Faeril, now rocking the cradle. "Or one of those great striped cats said to live in the east."

Riatha shook her head. "Though clever and stealthy and fierce, they are cats, and cats are quite feral, their loyalty doubtful. Whatever we choose for Bair, I want him to be steadfast to his friends, no matter what form he is in."

"As is Urus," said Faeril.

"As is Urus," Riatha agreed.

Urus carefully draped the deer hide over the waiting rack for stretching and scraping and curing later, and as he did so Greylight and the Draega pack came trotting out from the woods and toward the Wolfmage and the Baeran, the magnificent animals somewhat at play as they came forth from the trees, their faces grinning as they nipped at one another and dodged and darted and feinted, quick and agile in spite of their size. And both inside the cottage and without, Riatha nodded to Faeril even as Urus nodded to Dalavar.

In the eventide of Winterday, in a thicket of silver birch, a tiny Draega cub, walking on wobbly legs and pouncing on drifting-down snowflakes, played at the feet of Shimmer, the great Silver Wolf watching over her charge, a changeling whelp who once was a child named Bair.

CHAPTER 6

Departure

Winter, 5E993

[Sixteen Years Past]

On the fringe of the silver birch stand as darkness fell, Dalavar handed the pup to Riatha. "He is hungry. Call his name and give him your breast."

Riatha took the pup tentatively and held him to her bare bosom and softly said, "Bair."

Even as he sought the nipple, a dark shimmering came over the cub and swiftly it *changed*, and suddenly in the Dara's arms was a wee babe enwrapped in nought but a diaper.

"Oh my," said Faeril, as she gave over a small blanket to Riatha, "I have seen Urus, um, change, but with Bair it is somehow, I don't know . . . different? And I say, I have never thought of this before, but what happened to the nappy when he was a cub? Or for that matter"—she looked up at Urus—"what about Urus's clothes and such when he changes to a Bear? Where do they go? What happens?"

Urus looked at the damman and shrugged, and then turned to Dalavar.

Dalavar watched with satisfaction as Bair took sustenance, even as Riatha also looked at the Wolfmage, a question in her eyes. Dalavar smiled. "No one knows for certain, but some surmise that shapechangers have a special aura, something akin to <wild magic>. They speculate as well that shapechanging is much like the crossing of the in-between, where all things get enwrapped in the aura of the one crossing from one Plane to another and are simply borne along. But here is where it is different: in the case of a shapechanger, those things in the aura transform as well—clothing, weapons, gear—and when changing back, so are those things restored."

"Oh, I see," said Faeril, not seeing at all.

"Do all things transform?" asked Riatha, looking down at wee Bair. "That is, if I were to give Bair my sword Dúnamis, would it transform as well?"

Dalavar shook his head and touched a place at his throat where a starsilver nugget once rested. "Nay, Dara. Tokens of power do not transform at all, for they stand outside one's aura. Their <fire> is too strong. And Dúnamis is a token of power."

"Yet Dúnamis was borne across the Planes," said Riatha. "Just as were Black Galgor and Silverleaf's bow and other such."

"Aye," replied Dalavar. "All they need is to be conveyed by someone who has opened the way."

"Speaking of the Planes," said Faeril, "tell me again what it is that allows one to cross between. I mean, I thought the ways were sundered in the Great War of the Ban."

"They were," replied Dalavar, "all but the bloodways. This is the manner of it, Faeril: Had you the blood of the High Plane, such as do the Elves, then you could cross over to Adonar. Had you the blood of the Low Plane, such as do the Rûpt, then you could fare to Neddra. And had you the blood of the Middle Plane, you could cross the in-between from one of the other Planes to Mithgar. In spite of the Sundering, having the blood of a particular Plane allows one to cross from elsewhere to there . . . *if* the one faring the in-between performs the crossing rite."

Faeril nodded. "I see. And Bair will be able to cross to Adonar and back? To Neddra and back? To the Mageworld of Vadaria and back?"

Dalavar glanced at Urus and said, "Just as Urus could cross the in-between to Neddra—knew he the rite—and to Vadaria— if there were a way—and then return to Mithgar, so too can Bair cross to other Planes for he has the blood to do so; the bloodways are open to him."

Urus growled. "E'en did I know the crossing rite, still I would not travel to Neddra, except, perhaps, in pursuit of a monster such as Stoke."

Faeril vigorously nodded her agreement, but then she turned to the Wolfmage. "What about you, Dalavar: can you cross the in-between?"

Dalavar sighed. "I oft did before the Sundering, for although I was born on Mithgar, I did not think of it as home. Vadaria was more like my rightful place . . . and is where I spent much of my youth, learning Magekind ways. Yet with the destruction of Rwn, I can never go there again."

"Never?"

"Nay. Rwn held the only known crossing, and when it was gone, so too was gone the bridge between here and there."

"Oh my," said Faeril, "I am so sorry."

As if sensing something amiss, Shimmer stepped nigh Dalavar to settle at his feet, and Dalavar reached down and stroked her head.

"But you could go to Neddra, neh?" asked Faeril.

"I could, but like Urus, it is a place where I will not go, for then I could never return unto Mithgar; I have no blood of this Plane. And even were the way to Vadaria not destroyed, still I would not go, for a storm is coming to Mithgar, and much is yet to be done."

Faeril reached out and touched Dalavar's hand. "Here at least is where you have your 'Wolves."

Dalavar sighed. "They are not *my* 'Wolves, little one, but are my friends instead. Too, they are creatures of Adonar, and since the Sundering of the Ways, I cannot follow them there."

"Oh my. That's right. Although they could go home, they choose to remain at your side," said Faeril, stepping to Shimmer and hugging her about the neck. Shimmer took the embrace stoically. Faeril looked up at Riatha and said, "Loyal."

The Wolfmage glanced from Faeril to Riatha and back. "Loyal, indeed. I once told a warrior maiden that after the destruction of Rwn, I was stranded on Mithgar and the Draega stayed here as well, for they would not abandon me."

Faeril stepped back from Shimmer and frowned up at the Mage. "You did not tell her you could cross to Neddra?"

Dalavar ran a hand through his dark-silver hair. "Nay, I did not. At the time she and her companion were sworn enemies, and I could not let them know that I bore the blood of the Untargarda;

I could not let them think I was of Gyphon's Spawn, for much depended on their trust of me, much that is yet to occur. Their mission was vital beyond their own needs, and it was essential to convince them to go on, and for that I needed their confidence."

"Mission?"

"Aye. 'Twas Elyn and Thork—*One to hide; One to guide*—and they were after the Kammerling."

Faeril's eyes widened in surprise, and she said, "Goodness, but I have heard that tale, though not of your role in it. A sad story, that, and one of true love."

"Indeed," said Riatha, cradling Bair while reaching out to take Urus's hand.

But in that moment Faeril burst into tears.

"What is it?" said Urus, kneeling and embracing the damman.

"A story of true love," sobbed Faeril, clutching Urus. "Just as was Gwylly's and mine."

As they trudged in the darkness through the snow and toward the cottage, Dalavar said, "Say his name often to him, Riatha, Urus, for it is like a truename and will restore Bair to his rightful form. He must learn it well and know that it pertains to him, for without that knowledge he may take on the shape of a Draega, *become* a Draega, *remain* a Draega forever, never finding his way back. Should he change into a 'Wolf as a babe ere he learns his one true name, then give him your breast, Dara, and call to him, and just as he shifted from 'Wolf to babe this Wintereve, so shall he transform then."

Dalavar fell silent and glanced at Greylight's pack eagerly trotting alongside, and then said, "My mission here is done, and now I take my leave, yet heed: bear him to the Winterday rite of the changing of the seasons. Start him now, this very night, for it is vital that he learn, and even though he is but a wee babe, still the chant, the song, the cant, the paean will begin to impress. Sing it to him as well instead of lullabies, and pace the steps with him even though he cannot yet walk."

A puzzled expression on their faces, Faeril and Urus both looked at Dalavar, yet he said nought to enlighten them, though Riatha pensively nodded in understanding. "That I shall do, Dalavar."

Finally, they came to the back stoop of the cote, and Urus opened the door, and ruddy light of the fireplace seeped out to color the falling snow crimson. But Dalavar stopped short of the doorstone and cleared his throat. "Remember all I have said: train him well in shifting, Urus, and in the rite of the seasons, Riatha. Let him walk with Aravan. Be alert for those who would do him ill."

Dalavar looked to the east and then back at Bair. He raised his gaze from the child to the mother and said, "There is a terrible black storm coming, and your child is the Hope of the World."

And without another word, despite the bloodred glow cast through the doorway from the fireplace within, a gloom gathered about Dalavar, enveloping him, his shape changing, growing large, silvery-grey, with black claws and glistening fangs, the shifting form dropping to all fours, and where Dalavar had been now grinned a Draega, though one somehow darker than the others.

"Oh my!" exclaimed Faeril in wonder.

Yipping and yammering, the great Silver Wolves milled about, and of a sudden and almost as one they turned and raced away southerly through the drifting-down snow, to swiftly disappear in the nighttide darkness now clasping Arden Vale.

"Well then," said Faeril when she could see them no more, "I suppose that's that."

But standing in crimson light seeping outward to stain clustered shadows beyond, Riatha said, "Nay, Faeril, it is not done; instead it has just begun."

CHAPTER 7

Onset

Summer, 5E994

[Fifteen Years Past]

Chakun trembled in rage and fear. "*I* am the First Handmaiden of the Kutsen Yong, for *I* wear the conical hat, and so it is *I* who will decide."

Before her stood someone whose features took on the cast of an *akma*—the cast of a Demon—commingled with that of a man. Pale white he was, and Humanlike he seemed, but perhaps no mortal was he. Slender he was and tall, with straight black hair smoothed back and long fingers taloned and grasping . . . and wild, yellow eyes 'neath hairless brows. His face was long and narrow, his nose straight and thin, his white cheeks unbearded. He had come from the south the night of the birth of the Masula Yongsa Wang, the same night something had flown over the southern herd, something winged and hideous, the horses scattering in fear, the herd-warding tribesmen fleeing as well, fleeing to Cholui Chang to babble of the great flapping beast roaming the dark skies above. Cholui Chang blenched in dismay, yet declared it must be a Dragon come to worship at the child's feet. *Nay*, declared the herdsmen collectively, *no Dragon is this come to see his lord, but a Fell Beast of another sort.* Just what the creature might have been, none among the tribe could say, not even the elder priestess.

The herd warders alone had seen the creature silhouetted against the crystalline stars, but none doubted their word, for these were momentous times, what with the birth of the Mage Warrior King himself. Even so, Dragon or Fell Beast, no flapping creature of any sort came to pay homage to Kutsen Yong . . .

. . . although that same night a yellow-eyed man had come in among them, with his pointed teeth and long grasping fingers. All shuddered to see him, for mayhap he was a *Taeji Akma*—an Earth Demon—the most feared of all creatures, come to drag them down into the endless fires at the center of the world to scream in agony forever; all fell back as this yellow-eyed *thing* strode to the tent where Kkot wept for her own slain son even as she nursed the newborn lord.

And when Cholui Chang came running, the yellow-eyed man spoke: "*Jai* am Ydral, and Jai have come to tutor this lord in the way of the Wizard," he said in a hollow, whispery voice, a voice seeming somehow ancient beyond all years, belying his youthful frame. "Others can teach him the way of the warrior, but Jai will have him know of <powers>."

Cholui Chang thought to dispute him, yet when those yellow akma eyes fixed upon him, he nodded in meek compliance.

The news spread quickly to the other tribes—*The Mage Warrior King has come*—and all flocked to see this child of wonder, the prophesied Dragon mark standing forth on his brow. And they cried out in jubilation, for at last the time had come for them to follow this leader who would claim that which was rightfully theirs: the rule of all the world.

As the child grew, more and more tribes came to see him, more and more warriors gathered, and they sharpened their weapons of war and made ready to do battle, for it was their destiny to be the Masula Yongsa Wang's very own Golden Horde.

And all the while, the man, the akma, the one with the yellow eyes, had had the child—even as a babe—brought unto a black yurt, where he tutored him in the ways of Wizards, or so it was he did say.

On Longday of the child's fifth summer, his Golden Horde set out from Moko, crossing the border into Gaujiang, the northernmost province of Jinga. Long were the battles and bloody, yet the Overlord of Gaujiang could not stay the arms of the Golden Horde.

The next year they took the province of Kwailiang, and the following year another province; and another the year after.

And still in Ydral's black yurt he tutored the Masula Yongsa Wang in the dark arts, but as of yet the child had shown no capacity whatsoever in the ways of <power>. Nevertheless, Ydral continued the lessons; and though Kutsen Yong should have been but an innocent child, his nature turned ever more cruel, the fault of the yellow-eyed man, or so it was whispered at night.

With its numbers swelled by victories, after two years of rest, the Golden Horde turned east. They were striking across the province of Qilung, driving toward the great city of Janjong itself, there where the Emperor of Jinga ruled. And this time they faced the well-disciplined armies of the capital province.

But Cholui Chang was a canny warlord, and by feint and skill and hit-and-run tactics, the magnificent horse-borne warriors of Moko struck where least expected, and when pursued they drew the forces of the emperor into trap after trap. Yet when those forces weren't drawn after but took a stand instead, Cholui Chang would engage them in battle, the Golden Horde whelming down upon the emperor's overmatched troops. Nevertheless, it took three seasons of savage strife—from autumn through winter and spring—to finally come to the city of Janjong, its high walls made of stone.

But at last the city had fallen, the stone walls breached, the gates shattered, the defenders slaughtered—those that did not throw down their arms. With the city vanquished, the Golden Horde pillaged, plundered, raped—savage in their conquest. When Cholui Chang came to shout of this victory to his son Kutsen Yong, he found the youth in the company of Ydral; the warlord meekly spoke of the triumph, for although Cholui Chang was a fierce warrior, still he feared the akma with the yellow eyes.

And now Chakun, twenty-two years of age, stood trembling but glaring into those same yellow eyes, while in the near distance a great city burned, smoke twining into the sky. "I am First Handmaiden, and it is mine to see to his every need, and in this triumphal procession into Janjong *I* say where he will ride, and that is not in your dark wagon, nor at the head of his army upon a prancing horse like any common soldier; instead he will ride in his royal golden palanquin, surrounded by fierce Moko warriors and borne on the shoulders of the former overlords of Gaujiang, Kwailiang, Qizong, and Xinga, former kings who are now his slaves, for he is the Kutsen Yong."

Ydral smiled, his teeth but triangular fangs, like those of a shâyú. "Indeed he is the Mighty Dragon, the Emperor of All, yet he should be seen as a powerful warrior king and not as some pampered child."

"Fool!" hissed Chakun. "It is only the mighty who are borne upon the shoulders of kings."

Rage flashed in Ydral's eyes, swiftly quenched as he hooded his yellow gaze. With a slight bow he said, "As tji wish, First Handmaiden," and he turned on his heel and stalked away, his long, taloned fingers clutching and grasping in bridled fury.

And so Kutsen Yong was borne into Janjong on a golden palanquin, the shimmering silks of the aureate curtains swept back and tied so that all could see the Masula Yongsa Wang, robed in his bloodred raiment and sitting high in a gilded chair. And with poles on their shoulders and bearing the golden litter, four conquered kings trudged in chains, their spiritless servility plain. Surrounding the palanquin strode armed and armored warriors, swords in hand, their hawklike gazes sweeping everywhere. Trailing after the palanquin and walking barefoot came a thousand virgin maidens in diaphanous, pale yellow—brides of this child Emperor of All, brides gathered from across provinces conquered. And the citizenry of the capital city stood all along the processional route, the throngs herded there by the conquering warriors to line the way from the shattered east portal to the hurled-down gates of the palace. They cheered the Mighty Dragon as he passed, for to do otherwise would mean sudden death. And before the puissant Mage Warrior King, the impaled head of the former Emperor of All was borne high on a crimson pike.

Into the courtyard they strode, and up the one hundred steps, while the cheering behind rose in crescendo, prodded so by spears. At the top of the flight, the palanquin was turned about and set down on the landing, the virgins in their gossamer gowns halting on the wide steps below. The Mage Warrior King descended from his chair and stood where all could see, the First Handmaiden and the Royal Tutor a respectful distance behind, the four chained overlords brought to his side to kneel aflank and bow down in abject submission. And then with a gesture Kutsen Yong signalled to his father warlord, and four captains stepped forward and with single strokes of their swords took off the heads of the kneeling kings. And while blood flowed down the steps to wash the bare feet of virgins, the eleven-year-old child Emperor of All turned on his heel and strode into the unplundered palace, which now was rightfully his.

And inside the palace in a secret vault under the emperor's throne, an oblate sphereoid of a jadelike stone faintly glowed in the hidden dark.

And far to the west 'neath an arcane black mountain, well-rested Mages consulted their star charts and astrolabes and celestial guides to confirm that indeed the time of the Trine was coming.

While even farther westward and thousands of fathoms below the ruin of a blasted firemountain, great hands smoothed grinding faults to allow stone to slip past stone and relieve stress and strain far under. And slowly, ever slowly, the magma within the fiery vent leading to the vast chamber below was forced down and down.

CHAPTER 8

Vow

Autumn, 5E999

[Ten Years Past]

Trilling giggles, Bair, now nearly six, splashed barefoot in the water of the crystalline stream spilling down from the slopes above, while on the bank, Aravan, Riatha, and Urus sat watching.

"Is he always this happy?" asked Aravan.

Riatha nodded. "Aye, he is."

Aravan looked from Riatha to Urus. "And ye both do say he is in danger."

Riatha's silvery eyes glinted icily, her gaze sliding to the rise of the Grimwall Mountains looming in the distance, and Urus growled, "So Dalavar Wolfmage has said. Even so, we have seen no evidence of such these past six years."

Aravan's eyes widened. "Six years? Six autumns? Has it been that long since last I was here? It seems but yester that I was speaking to Faeril of Bair. And I—" Aravan's words jerked to a halt, and he pointed; where Bair had been a young Silver Wolf now lapped water.

"Bair!" called Urus.

The 'Wolf looked up from the stream to Urus, then resumed quenching its thirst, its tongue lapping rapidly.

"Bair," said Urus again, this time softly.

And a dark shimmering came upon the beast, and swiftly it *changed*—altering, losing bulk, gaining form—and suddenly there before them stood Bair grinning, his long shock of flaxen hair ruffling in the breeze.

Grinning as well, Aravan turned to Urus. "I see he has taken on some of thy shifty traits, though to Draega rather than Bear."

Urus sighed. " 'Twas the form we chose, with the help of Dalavar."

As Bair waded to midstream and peered into one of the pools, Aravan said, "Does he often take on 'Wolf shape?"

Urus smiled ruefully. "More than I would like. He seems not to heed my warnings: should he take on the shape of a Draega and forget his own true form, he could remain a Silver Wolf forever."

"A noble creature," said Aravan.

"A stubborn child," retorted Urus.

"Somewhat like his dam, neh?" replied Aravan, grinning.

"Pah," declared Riatha. "I deem 'tis the pot calling the kettle black."

Aravan raised an eyebrow. "Oh?"

Riatha nodded. "Thou hast pursued Galarun's killer for five millennia now."

Aravan's features turned grim. "I vowed to Coron Eiron I would find the one who slew his son and avenge him, a pledge I would not abandon."

Riatha reached out and touched Aravan's arm. "Oh, jarin mine, I but meant to show that thou art as resolute as I, if not more so."

"Resolute," snorted Urus, looking at Bair, the child once again in the shape of a Silver Wolf. "In the case of our son, *chier*, I call it willful instead."

The young 'Wolf ran splashing upstream, sparkles of droplets flying. Yet of a sudden it stopped . . . its form shifting once more into that of a child, and Bair now stood looking at the water, his head cocked at an angle, his pale grey eyes fixed on the burbling flow.

Aravan frowned and even though the amulet at his throat held no hint of cold, still he reached for the crystal-bladed spear lying on the grass at hand, and he called out. "What is it, *elar*? What dost thou see?"

Without turning, Bair called back, his voice piping, "The water, *kelan,* I am listening to the water-laughter; the brook is very happy here."

An eyebrow cocked, Aravan turned to Riatha and Urus.

"To Bair, all things live and feel and think," said Urus, gesturing about. "Be they plants, animals, rocks, soil, streams, the sky, storms, the mountains—it matters not the form—each thing has a spirit." Urus cast an arm about Riatha and smiled at her. "Or so says our child."

"Mayhap it is nought but the burble of the bourne he lists unto," said Riatha, returning Urus's embrace, "yet I ween there is more to it than that, for oft he speaks of the life he sees within each and every thing."

Aravan loosed his grip on the spear. "Given his heritage, mayhap Bair sees what the Mages name <fire>."

"<Astral fire>," murmured Riatha, nodding.

Urus sighed. "Perhaps so. Yet even though I bear much of the same blood as my child, I do not see such."

Riatha squeezed Urus's hand. "Mayhap it leapt over thee, chier, and landed upon our son."

Urus shrugged and did not reply.

In the weave of the chill autumn breeze twisting down from spires afar, they sat in silence for long moments, watching the child at play, noting that he often stopped to look intently at a thing, as if seeing or hearing something extraordinary, ere he wandered on.

He stopped at the edge of an upstream pool, where tall cattail rushes rattled in the swirling breeze, motes of soft floss spinning away from the fluffed heads. He laughed and called back, "The wind is teasing the reeds, kelan, and they do complain."

"They should instead be joyous, elar," replied Aravan, "for on the curl of the air floats the gossamer seeds, the get of the parents gyring off to far places to take root and carry on with living."

Again for long moments converse stilled while the child poked a long, thin twig into a hole in the bank. But finally Riatha turned to Aravan and asked, "Thy pursuit, jarin, found thee a trace?"

Slowly Aravan shook his head. "South of Jûng I went this time, south of the Straits of Alacca, for a yellow-eyed man was said to be living somewhere in the Ten Thousand Isles of Mordain. Yet three summers later I found him: an old man it was and not Galarun's killer . . . and his eyes were deep amber, not sallow."

Riatha reached out a hand to touch Aravan's cheek, yet she said nought.

Bair chortled and held up the long twig, a crayfish hanging on by one claw. Then carefully the child set the crayfish back into its hole and jiggled the stick loose.

"Jûng," rumbled Urus, "the realm, I know it not."

Aravan frowned. " 'Tis a dark league of warlords, loosely united under a mogul. Long past they did ally themselves with Modru and Gyphon; 'twas during the War of the Ban."

Urus growled. "Tell me: do they but adhere to Gyphon?"

Aravan nodded. "I deem so, yet it seems there may be another they seek to follow as well."

Riatha looked at Aravan, her eyes wide with an unspoken question.

Aravan shrugged one shoulder. "While I was in Jûng, I came across a caravan of people moving northward; they go to serve some child-king in Jinga—or mayhap in a land beyond—heeding a prophecy, they say."

Urus shook his head. "Another Human folly, no doubt."

Aravan frowned but did not reply.

Yet Riatha looked at Urus and said, "Speak not ill of prophecy, chier, for 'twas a prophecy we followed to raise thee from the dead."

Now it was Urus who frowned.

Bair came running up the bank and into his kelan's arms and squealed as Aravan caught him up and turned him upside down. As he righted the laughing child, Aravan said, "As Dalavar Wolfmage has bade ye, and as ye have asked, I will foster the training of this giggling whelp." But then the smile faded from Aravan's face, and his aspect turned deadly grim. "Yet should word come of a yellow-eyed man, then will I follow that glimmer, for my pledge to avenge Galarun takes precedence o'er nigh all."

CHAPTER 9

Promise

Winter, 5E999–1000

[Ten and Nine Years Past]

Oft did the Elves of Arden Vale see a huge Bear and a lithe Silver Wolf roaming the long woods of the high-walled gorge, the 'Wolf bounding ahead and running back to the Bear and then bounding ahead again, the Bear stolidly ambling along. And Darai and Alori alike would stop and smile, for all knew 'twas Urus training his son in the art of shapeshifting, a wondrous thing to see, yet a thing rife with danger:

"Da, tell me again about the man and the Bear and the boy and the 'Wolf."

Urus smiled down at six-year-old Bair, the lad hugging his knees and awaiting his favorite lesson. "Well, Son, there is the man named Urus, and there is the Bear. The Bear is a savage creature, where reason but barely prevails, for the Bear is driven by other urges, other needs from those of the man he once had been. The Bear is a thing of the wilds—not merely the man named Urus in the shape of a Bear, but truly a Bear, though one cunning beyond all others, a Bear who at times has strange un-Bearlike urges, urges and motives akin to those of Man, perhaps even akin to those of a particular man who just might be named Urus.

"Yet, the Bear who once was Urus only occasionally thinks along those paths; and although he might again *become* Urus, there is no guarantee he will. And *that* is a danger the Bear and Urus both live with: Urus might never again become the Bear;

the Bear might never again become Urus. The man Urus is aware of this danger; the Bear is not.

"It is the same with you, Son: there is a lad named Bair, and there is a Silver Wolf. And the 'Wolf is wholly a Draega, thinks like a Draega, acts like a Draega, though one cunning beyond all others; yet at times the 'Wolf who once was a boy will have un-Draegalike thoughts, thoughts akin to someone named Bair."

"But tell me, Da, the boy named Bair, won't he sometimes have Draegalike thoughts?"

Urus barked a laugh. "Indeed, I would think so, for Urus often has Bearlike thoughts, especially when engaged in battle."

"When will *I* have 'Wolflike thoughts, Da?"

"Perhaps in battle as well, though I believe it more likely you will think like a 'Wolf when you are hunting."

Bair nodded somberly, but then brightened and said, "Are we going hunting?"

Urus sighed. "Someday we will, though not today and not in the vale."

"Oh," said Bair, disappointed. "If not in the vale, then where?"

Urus looked westerly and said, "In Drearwood."

Bair's eyes widened. "*Ythir* and Kelan Aravan say that *Dhruousdarda* was once filled with Foul Folk and other dread things."

"It was, Bair. But now is not the time to talk of it. Instead tell me this: what so far is the lesson of shapeshifting?"

"That you are a man who at times thinks like a Bear and a Bear who at times thinks like a man. And I will be a 'Wolf who at times thinks like a boy and a boy who thinks like a 'Wolf."

Urus nodded. "Now heed me, Bair, for this is most important: it's when you are a 'Wolf who thinks like a boy named Bair that you can become that boy again. It is vital that you always remember that, that you always concentrate on your truename Bair when you are getting ready to shift from boyshape into 'Wolfshape, for only by the 'Wolf knowing your truename can you become a boy again."

"I already know that, Da. I think real hard about my boyname when I get ready to shift to 'Wolf *and* about my 'Wolfname when I get ready to shift back."

Urus looked at his son in surprise. "You have a 'Wolfname?"

Bair nodded.

"How did you get this name, Son?"

"When I was a puppy, Shimmer named me."

"Shimmer, the Draega?"

Bair nodded. "Her name is really, uh, Shimmer of Moonlight on the Water as the Gentle Breeze Brings Scents from Near and Far."

"A lengthy name, that."

Bair shrugged one shoulder. "As a boy named Bair, it took me a long time to know what Shimmer had said; but as a Draega it seems I always knew I had a 'Wolfname, Da."

They sat quietly for a while, but then Urus said, "And tell me, Bair, what *is* your 'Wolfname?"

"Hunter: the Seeker and Searcher Who Is One of Us but Not of Us." Bair frowned up at Urus. "She said one day I would know what it meant."

Urus sighed and nodded. "Perhaps one day you will."

Winterday came and with it the Elven ritual of the turning of the seasons, and all smiled to see six-year-old Bair among the males stepping out and chanting the rite, his piping voice canting, his wee legs gliding and pausing and turning, the lad in perfect synchronicity with that of the other Alori. Pacing among the Darai, Riatha smiled, yet her heart was filled with apprehension, for although Bair knew the steps and the chant perfectly, he knew not what they meant. It was not the ritual itself at the root of her worry, but rather what it portended for Bair, for its true meaning augured a destiny to come, a destiny rife with danger.

At the end of the rite, Faeril rushed to Bair and hugged him, the boy returning the damman's embrace. "That was splendid, Bair," she said, looking up at the lad, for now he was taller than she.

Bair grinned. "Let's eat, *Amicula* Faeril." And taking her by the hand, he tugged her away from the softly lit glade, with its colorful paper lanterns aglow, and toward the coron-hall, where the Winternight banquet awaited.

Winter snow was yet on the ground, though forerunning breezes heralded the oncoming of spring. And along the Crossland Road, a band of merchants slowly made their way toward

Crestan Pass afar; they would wait at the foot of the gap for the seasonal thaw to clear the way, for they would be the first ones over with their wares to sell in the lands beyond. But the pass lay a hundred miles hence, and where they now fared the dismal tangle of Drearwood loomed starkly to left and right, a place of dark dread in elden days, yet now said to be free of nearly all menace. Long past, the wood had been purged of Foul Folk in a summer-long bloody campaign, though some said that during the Winter War dark creatures had returned at the behest of vile Modru; whether or no it was true, the wood yet held an air of menace, as if the taint of evil endured. But riding in their wagons and with weapons at hand, the merchants felt reasonably safe ... as long as they stayed upon the way and did not stray beyond the bounds of the road and into that once-dreadful place. And so did the horses and wagons and men travel from west to east, the clop of hooves and the jingle of harness and the grind of wheels breaking the somber silence all 'round.

But then from within the tangle to the south there sounded the call of silver horns nearing, and the merchants halted, some to string bows and nock arrows, others to draw blades or take cudgels to hand.

Now they could hear the thud of hooves growing louder, and of a sudden a stag burst forth from the trees and fled across the road and into the forest again, and moments later a lithe pale 'Wolf the size of a pony dashed out from the wood in pursuit.

"By gar! A silver pelt!" shouted the lead merchant and raised his bow and took aim, only to have the bow knocked from his hands by a flung spear, even as riders upon fiery horses poured forth from the trees nigh.

As horns blew and the main of the mounted force thundered across the way and into the woods once more, two riders came unto the merchant train—one to ride to the spear and lean over and take it up again, the other to stop before the lead wagon, an arrow-nocked bow in hand.

"Who are you to nearly kill me," shouted the merchant, leaping down from the wagon to retrieve his weapon. "You could have broken my bow."

The merchant gasped as the rider with the spear rode nigh and cast back his hood. It was an Elf! "Had I wished to kill thee, thou wouldst now be lying dead in the road." The Lian couched the butt of his weapon into a stirrup cup. Then he called out so that all could hear: "I am Tillaron Ironstalker. And this is my companion, Ancinda Soletree."

His comrade cast back her hood as well. And with ice in her eyes and voice, she said to the one who attempted to bring down the 'Wolf, "Thou shalt not seek to slay aught in these woods but at desperate need."

Now Tillaron turned to the rest of the merchants, his eyes steely. "Do ye heed what the Dara said? None of ye shall slay aught herein except at last measure, and that but to save thy lives."

"Aye, my lady, my lord," said the merchant respectfully, the others mumbling deferential agreement.

In that moment a huge Bear padded across the road, as if following the Elven band.

The lead merchant made a slight hand motion toward an arrow in his quiver, but at a glare from Tillaron, he said, "Pardon, my lord, it is but habit."

"Were I thee," growled Tillaron " 'tis a habit I would break within the bounds of what we name *Dhruousdarda* and ye name Drearwood."

Ancinda's almond eyes narrowed. "Remember my words, merchant: thou shalt not slay aught herein but at desperate need."

The merchant unstrung his bow, and likewise all in the train did set their weaponry aside.

Ancinda then slipped her own bow into her saddle scabbard and the arrow into her quiver. She turned to Tillaron. "Yon went Urus, chier, and if he is nigh, the quarry is far."

Tillaron laughed and flourished his spear overhead and called out *"Hai!"* And he heeled his steed, Ancinda doing the same. As they galloped in among the trees, Ancinda raised a horn to her lips and a silver cry rang forth.

And then they were gone from sight.

While behind and exhaling a sigh of relief, the lead merchant wiped his suddenly perspiring brow. Clambering back into his wagon and taking up the reins, with a *chrk* of his dry tongue he urged the horses ahead, the train rumbling into motion after.

And far to the north the Silver Wolf now ran at the heels of the stag, both steering wide of the ancient dark temple deep in the heart of the wood.

As the stag roasted over the fire pit, with Flandrena and Tillaron spelling one another at turning the spit, Urus walked away from the blaze to make certain that the picket of Elven warders was well in place. Near the fire, Riatha sighed and turned to Elissan. "He is worried, is my chier, for 'tis the first time Bair has been beyond the bounds of Arden Vale."

"And I suppose thou art not worried?" said Elissan, her glossy dark hair asheen with ruddy glints from the flames.

Riatha smiled ruefully. "I am. Yet Dalavar Wolfmage told us that Bair should walk with Aravan, and 'twas Aravan who decided the boy needed to go on a hunt."

Elissan laughed. " 'Twas a boy who started on the hunt, but 'twas a Draega who finished it."

Riatha smiled, for in the very first moment the stag had been flushed and silver horns rang on the air, Bair had leapt from his steed, his sire shouting *"No!"* and racing afoot after. The child had not heeded his call, for even while running a darkness had come over Bair and from that hurtling shade had a Silver Wolf emerged to spring after the stag, and a Bear had thundered after the 'Wolf. But within the first furlong or so, the 'Wolf had left the Bear far behind.

Riatha shook her head. "Ever since Bair was but a wee babe, Urus has named him willful. I would have to agree, though today I deem him rash as well."

Elissan grinned, then sobered. "Fear not, for he is but a child and will grow beyond his rashness."

"Mayhap," replied Riatha, not seeming certain at all. "But he told his sire that when the stag sprang forth the boy named Bair simply thought like a 'Wolf."

"What did Urus say to that?"

"Urus growled and said that when the boy didn't stop, the thoughts of the man named Urus were akin to those of a winter-wakened Bear."

Elissan laughed, but then took Riatha's hand. "Look on the good, Riatha: Aravan was right, the boy did need go on a hunt, after all he has been working hard on his studies. He speaks three languages well—"

"Four," said Riatha.

"Four? What other than Sylva, Common, and Baeron?"

"Twyll, the Waerlinga Tongue."

"Ah. . . ." said Elissan, enlightened. "Four then. Regardless, he knows his numbers and is beginning to cipher. Too, he knows his letters. I plan on taking him to the archives to begin the study of scrolls and scribing."

Riatha glanced across at Bair, a pensive look on her face. "I do hope he takes to it as well as he has his other studies, for I deem he would rather be loosing arrows from his bow, or running the woods with a Bear, or climbing with Aravan . . . or going hunting, as today."

They sat without speaking for a while, but then Elissan said, "Dalavar Wolfmage had the right of it, for Aravan's hunt was successful and no harm came unto Bair."

Riatha sighed. "Aye, none did, yet Dalavar gave no guarantee of safety to that pairing."

"Still," replied Elissan, "the amulet Aravan wears at his throat will help ward Bair from harm, neh?"

Again Riatha glanced over to where Bair sat beside Aravan, the child casting small twigs into the blaze, the Alor staring into the curling flames without seeing aught of the fire, his mind elsewhere altogether, a sad look deep in his gaze. At his throat dangled a small blue stone on a leather thong.

"Aye, 'tis a wardstone," replied Riatha, "given to him by the Hidden Ones for saving two Pyska. It grows cold when things of vile menace are about, though it does not detect all such creatures."

"Still, it does detect evil," said Elissan.

Riatha shook her head. "Nay, Elissan, not evil, but mayhap peril instead . . . and that from only some of the foul creatures capable of causing harm."

Elissan frowned. "Such as . . . ?"

"Creatures from Neddra—Rucha, Loka, Trolls, Gargoni, and the like—those which fell at Hèl's Crucible. Too, it grows cold in the presence of Hèlarms—as well as some Dragons, though not all. Some creatures and folk seem to sense the stone, such as the Children of the Sea and other Hidden Ones, and they know him as a Friend; other creatures, perilous of nature, seem to shy away from coming nigh, wild dogs of the Karoo, for one. Yet even with all the amulet does, there are creatures of evil intent it does not descry, and that is why Urus set a ring of pickets and now does go on his rounds."

"What does it not detect?"

"It takes no note of Humans of ill purpose—pirates, thieves, brigands, and the like—these it does not warn of. Nor of other Mithgarian Races. Too, were a Dwarf to go mad, it would take no note. From Aravan's word and mine own experience with the amulet—gained while pursuing Baron Stoke—with but few exceptions, I ween it will detect nothing of Adon's or Elwydd's creations."

"Then that but leaves . . ."

Riatha nodded. "In the main it but leaves the creatures of Gyphon."

In that moment Bair glanced across at his mother, and then he turned to Aravan. "Tell me, kelan, who is the man with the yellow eyes?"

Pulled from his reverie, Aravan turned to the boy. "What didst thou ask, elar?"

"The man with the yellow eyes: what did he do?" asked Bair.

Frowning, Aravan took up a twig of his own and cast it into the fire. "When did you hear of him?"

"When you first came. You were talking to Ythir and Da."

"Ah, I remember. On the banks of the rill in which thou didst play."

Bair nodded but did not speak, his gaze fixed upon his mentor.

Aravan sighed. "He is an evil man, Bair, if man he is. Long past, during the Great War of the Ban, he killed a boon comrade of mine and stole a silver sword."

"What was your friend's name?"

"Galarun."

"And what is the name of the man who killed him, the man with the yellow eyes?"

"I think his name is Ydral. His son, a person named Stoke,

was an evil man, too, who also had yellow eyes, and there is an old saying: like sire, like son."

Bair shook his head. "My da has yellow eyes, but mine are grey, like Ythir's."

Aravan smiled. "Indeed, Bair, thine eyes are like unto thy dam's, though thou dost not quite cast as silver a gaze as does she. And I would not call Urus's eyes yellow, but would name them amber instead."

"Amber," said Bair, sounding out the new word and looking about for his father but not finding him.

They sat without speaking for long moments, and then Bair said, "What happened to the silver sword?"

Aravan turned up a hand. "It is yet missing. But if I find the man with the yellow eyes, then I believe I will also find the sword."

"I will help you."

With one arm, Aravan hugged Bair close to him. "Ah, little elar, unlike today's hunt, I would not ask thee on such a long chase, for I have been searching for thousands upon thousands of seasons, and—"

"I don't care how long it takes," said the child stubbornly. "I said I would help, and I will."

Just then Urus came striding back into the clearing, and Bair sprang up and ran toward him, calling out, "Da. Da. I am going to help Kelan Aravan find the man with the yellow eyes and get a silver sword."

A grim look came over Urus's face, and he glanced at Riatha, her own visage now drained of blood. Urus swung the child up in his arms and, forcing a smile, said, "Aren't you a bit young to take up such a quest?"

"No, Da. Besides, I promised."

CHAPTER 10

Foretellings

Summer, 5E1003

[Six Years Past]

With high clouds running down from the north before a blustery wind, Kutsen Yong, the divine emperor himself, did deign to come to the docks to see with his very own eyes what his warlords had wrought. Now a man of twenty, he rode in his silk-draped, golden palanquin, borne on the shoulders of the strongest of slaves, and all about strode his palace guard, swords and spears and bows in hand, their searching gazes alert. Behind on a lesser palanquin rode the First Handmaiden of the Masula Yongsa Wang, her conical hat now bejewelled. Next in line on a covered litter of his own rode a man with yellow eyes, his stare locked upon the palanquin of the priestess before him, his gaze filled with hatred. In the procession following came the lesser nobles and attendants, one of whom was a one-handed man, a man who had served the emperor of yore. All along the way, people trembled and fell to the ground in obeisance, their foreheads pressed against the cobblestones, their eyes hidden from sight, for none was worthy of seeing the Mighty Dragon in all his glory.

At last they reached the stone quays, and out in the harbor rode a vast armada at anchor, the ships filled with Kutsen Yong's warriors, ready to set sail for the shores of Ryodo, ancient enemy of Moko and Jinga alike.

The emperor was borne to the centermost quay, and there the palanquin was set down on its six legs and the golden steps unfolded, the emperor to tread down onto the red-and-gold carpet laid upon the stone, the twin figures of the Dragons of Fortune and Conquest woven within. The palanquins following were also set to stone, but no broadloom awaited the feet of either Chakun or Ydral. As soon as the First Handmaiden and the Royal Tutor had come to stand at the aft fringe of the rug, Kutsen Yong then glanced up to the thin clouds driving southward above and then down to the waves rolling in. At last he spoke to the kneeling priests of Jinga. "I would have an augury cast this day."

The oldest of the priests stood, the others following suit, and a delicate young girl verging on maidenhood brought forth a cage of white doves.

"*Mai* lord," hissed Ydral. "On this day *ahn* dove will not do, for *aun* minions set forth to conquer ahn mighty empire."

As the priests held in abeyance, Kutsen Yong canted his head in agreement. "What would you suggest, Lord Ydral? An eagle? A tiger? Something else?"

"Ahn maiden. Ahn virgin," replied Ydral.

Kutsen Yong nodded and pointed at the girl holding the cage of doves. "She will do."

Shocked, the priests made no move, but at a gesture from Ydral, four soldiers of the palace guard sprang forward. Striking the cage away from her hand to fall on the carpet and roll—doves calling out in alarm—the men hurled the girl to the stone of the quay and, ripping her clothes away, they grasped her by her thin arms and legs and held her down, her eyes wide in terror.

Kutsen Yong gestured to the leader of the cowering priests. "On with your work, old man, for I desire an augury."

The girl's shrieks filled the air as the priests eviscerated her with a hooked blade, some retching as they did so. And all during the gutting, Ydral's face bore a look of ecstasy.

At last the girl fell silent, and only the splash of waves and the sigh of wind and the cooing of doves filled the air.

With fearful glances at the emperor, the priests studied the entrails, and after a moment of consultation, "Great victories lie ahead" they all agreed.

As they cast the dead girl into the waters of the Jingarian Sea—waters stained yellow by the nearby outflow of the great

River Kang; waters taking on a crimson tinge as waves and undertow pulled the girl under to sink from sight, her innocent unseeing eyes staring up at the now-placid faces of the priestly butchers above—the signal was given unto the mighty fleet. Like petals of flowers unfolding, curved triangular sails filled with battens were raised, and with a northerly wind abeam and on a rough ebbing tide they set out upon the waters and toward the soon-to-be-conquered land of Ryodo, for victory was now assured.

Yet back among the attendants, a one-handed man who had formerly been a fisherman shook his head in disagreement; even so, he spoke not, since he didn't wish to have his pate join his missing hand, for surely this emperor was worse than any shâyú could ever be.

Weeks before, on the isle of Ryodo, the Golden Dragons and the Red Tigers temporarily set aside their differences, for word had come that a great fleet was assembling in the harbor of Janjong and that throngs of warriors and horses were waiting to be laded aboard. What else could be afoot but that this upstart emperor, nought but a boy, was preparing to invade the realm?

In a fury of activity in the days that followed, they fletched arrows and sharpened blades and polished armor and groomed horses and made ready to throw these uncouth invaders back into the brine of the sea, and they gathered unto the western shores and thereupon they waited.

Within five days of arriving, in the rising wind and through the driving rain they espied the first of the sails.

Shi! cried the Golden Dragons in one roaring voice.

Hakai! shouted the Red Tigers in thunderous return.

And upon the high dunes they stood ready, ready to swiftly move to wherever it was the ships of Jinga were bound.

And then more sails hove into view. *Shi! Hakai!* they thundered, raising their weapons on high.

And then more sails and more broached the horizon, until the entire sweep of the stormy sea was filled with Jingarian ships.

No Red Tiger, no Golden Dragon, no single warrior did now bellow of the death and destruction to be hurled upon the foe, for every voice was stilled by the awesome sight. Yet though they shouted not, they all grimly gripped their weapons, ready to fight to the last, though they knew they could not win.

With their lips clamped shut in grim silence, neither Golden Dragons nor Red Tigers uttered a word, but in their stead as if in challenge the wind rose up in fury and shrieked a wordless howl and drove a torrent down from the sky and lifted up great wild waves. And the fleet disappeared within a grey wall of rage.

As Kutsen Yong sat on his throne before his retinue, a messenger came striding into the great hall. Dropping to his knees and placing his head unto the marble floor, he waited for permission to speak. And when it was given, he said, "My lord, I bring ill news from our spies abroad: the fleet has been destroyed by a mighty typhoon. None whatsoever survived, including your sire, the Warlord Cholui Chang."

A shocked silence fell over the court, but for a whisper afar—"I knew it"—a whisper borne to the emperor's ears by walls cunningly arced to bring even the slightest of sounds unto the seat of the throne.

Kutsen Yong stood in rage. "Who said that?"

In the back of the chamber, all eyes turned to a one-handed man, and someone said, "It was Wangu."

Trembling, the one-handed man hesitantly stepped forward.

"Bring him to me," commanded Kutsen Yong.

Two men of the palace guard roughly took the one-handed man under the arms and rushed him forward to fling him down at the foot of the steps leading up to the throne. Cowering, the man placed his head to the marble floor.

"You knew it?" demanded Kutsen Yong.

"My lord, I but knew a terrible storm was coming."

"And yet you said nothing."

"My lord, who am I to gainsay the priests? I am but a lowly fisherman."

"Lowly fisherman?" demanded Chakun, the First Handmaiden stepping forward to the edge of the dais. "Then why are you here in the palace posing as an attendant?"

"Oh, my lady, it was the emperor who made me an attendant after he took from me my jewel."

"You gave me no jewel," hissed Kutsen Yong, and he raised a hand to signal a guard who stood with a sword in his grip.

The one-handed man fell forward prostrate and cried out, "It was the old emperor who took the jewel, and he raised me up to be master of the koi ponds."

"Bah!" sneered Kutsen Yong.

"Mai lord, wait," whispered Ydral.

Kutsen Yong turned to his mentor. "Why should I not have this fool's head? He is responsible for the destruction of my fleet."

"And the death of your father," said Chakun.

"Yes, yes. That, too, Chakun," said Kutsen Yong impatiently, waving a dismissive hand. "Well, Ydral?"

Ydral pressed out a palm in a gesture of delay. Then he turned to the one-handed man. "This jewel, describe it."

The man scrambled to a kneeling position, and with his eyes downcast he said, "It is this big"—he held his good hand out from the stump of his wrist to indicate its size—"like a melon, or one of those great eggs of the large birds who cannot fly which live in my lord's private garden alongside the pools of the koi. But no melon or egg is this gem; instead I would call it a rounded stone, a stone like that of pale jade, and yet this jade stone is more than it seems, for it glows with a faint inner light."

Ydral's eyes widened in shock.

"Where did tji get this stone?"

"I cut it from the belly of a shâyú, who took my hand in return."

Ydral sucked air between his teeth and he turned to Kutsen Yong. "Mai lord, no such treasure was found in the vaults of this palace, and so it must have been spirited away"—Ydral's eyes narrowed in speculation—"or still be here but hidden. Regardless, it must be found, for if it is what Jai believe, and can Jai discover its secret, then it will bring m— tji great power."

Gritting his teeth and clenching his fists, Kutsen Yong looked from the Royal Tutor to the First Handmaiden and then to the one-handed man. "Perhaps I will let you live, fisherman, until the jewel is found." Gesturing to the guards, he said, "Lock him away for now, and see he suffers no harm." He looked about the chamber at the other attendants, and added, "Instead, bring the priests who betrayed me, and bring their hooked knife as well, for they shall die the slow death of gradual evisceration for casting me false auguries."

Far to the west and within a black mountain, Wizards began gathering the many things needed to fend off disasters unknown. Just what would occur, none there could foretell, not even the most powerful of Seers. All that they knew was the Trine was coming, and a terrible calamity would fall on the Plains of Valon. And so they prepared for they knew not what; and so they prepared for all . . .

. . . or so they did believe.

Some five hundred leagues farther west and all 'round the ruin of a blasted firemountain, the juddering land began to still, the shuddering earth to quell. And deeply far under, the obsidian vent to the churning magma was finally sealed across with vast blocks of obdurate, black-granite stone. And then great hands began opening a channel to the waters of the snows lying high. And when the chill flow finally rushed down and 'round, roaring plumes of steam burst through the ground and raged at the sky aloft as the lava remaining above the barrier slowly began to cool. And great gemstone eyes looked on in approval, for the time of all times drew nigh.

CHAPTER 11

Progression

Spring–Autumn, 5E1003

[Six Years Past]

In the spring of the year, when Bair was nine and a half, out from Arden Vale fared five travellers: Riatha was mounted on a fine grey gelding, and Urus rode a great horse of the Baeron—the bay animal fully eighteen hands high, having white, feathered hair on its fetlocks; Aravan bestrode a spirited black stallion, while Faeril rode a dark brown pony, stolid in its ways; and midst them all rode Bair on a buckskin palfrey, small and swift and sure. They drew four pack animals after, for the journey before them was long: they were taking Bair unto the Baeron for training in the love of the land, in its ways, and in its nurturing. Even so, it was Faeril who remarked that little could be taught to Bair concerning the care of the land for, in addition to his Elven upbringing, his ability to see <life> in all things had given him deep knowledge of the ways of nature few if any could match.

In his other studies Bair had applied himself commendably, spending much of his days ciphering and reading and writing—in four languages, no less—and he burned many candlemarks poring over scrolls among the stacks of the archive, reading of Elven history, and of the ways of the worlds, reading, too, of many arcane and puzzling things he occasionally and randomly unearthed: the riddles and enigmas of redes and prophecies, of crystal seeing, of the Planes and of achieving the state for crossing the in-between, of <wild magic>, of tokens of power, and other such mysterious writings, most of which he did not then understand but believed he would when he was older, and so he set these scrolls aside, vowing one day to revisit them. And thus it was that Bair took to his studies, eager in the learning.

Yet as summer approached, Urus deemed it would be good for the lad to enjoy the full season outdoors. Besides, Urus would have Bair attend the schooling that he himself had endured.

And so, away from Arden Vale they went and to the Crossland Road, five travellers well armed: Urus with his great black-iron morning star; Riatha with her jade-handled sword Dúnamis, forged of dark silveron; Faeril with crisscrossed bandoliers holding her ten throwing knives, two of which were silver, the rest of which were fine steel; Aravan with his crystal-bladed spear Krystallopŷr; and Bair with sling and bow. If trouble did come upon them, they went forth well prepared.

East they fared some days and upward, up into the Crestan Pass high in the mighty Grimwall and over the apex, there where the Crossland became the Landover Road. Then down again, where they paid the toll to the Baeron warders at the foot of the eastern reach, and thence across the wide wold, aiming toward a forest afar: a weald called by some the Great Greenhall and loved, for it gave them shelter and sustenance; named Blackwood by others and feared, for therein was said to live creatures dire; but known to the Elves as Darda Erynian, the forest with halls of green. They crossed the mighty Argon River, riding the shallows at Landover Road Ford and thence into Darda Erynian beyond.

Southeasterly they turned within this forest, wherein they would ride for many more days, yet this darda held not their prime goal, for that lay a hundred or so leagues away: it was the Greatwood whence they were bound, to a village where many Baeron dwelled, south and east, beyond the River Rissanin, and they would be on the trail altogether a fortnight or more to cover the three hundred miles. And so southeasterly they fared, and now they were escorted by shadows in the woods, flitting thither and yon.

As sundown came and they set camp, Bair looked intently through the high-vaulted green galleries about. "These shadows which glance among the trees, kelan, they have light and life within."

" 'Tis the Fey, the Hidden Ones," said Aravan, clearing the

ground and setting a stone ring for a small and well-contained fire.

"Hidden Ones?"

"Pyska, for the most—Fox Riders—though now and again thou mayest see a Vred Tres or Liv Vol or Tomté or other such."

Faeril frowned. "Are these like Nimué? Was she a Hidden One?"

"Nimué?" asked Bair.

"A being who lived in a tree in a hidden grot in the Talâk Mountains," replied Faeril. "It was her knowledge saved Gwylly and me from dying of poison." Again Faeril turned to Aravan. "Was she a Hidden One?"

"Aye," replied Aravan.

Faeril nodded, and then frowned. "And what about these other ones: Vred Tres, Liv Vols, Tomté? I have never heard of such, at least not by those names."

Aravan smiled. "Mayhap thou dost know a Vred Tres as a Woodwer, or as an Angry Tree, though they do not resemble any tree I know; 'tis a being best described as a tangle of tendrils and vines which walks and wards this land; without their permission think not to hew any live wood, else thou shalt see their anger. A Liv Vol is a Living Mound; each some eight or ten feet high and twice as wide at the base, each hillock covered with a strawlike yellowish grass, or what seems to be grass; they, too, move about to protect this darda when urged by the small Hidden Ones they shelter, those named Tomté, who are much like Fox Riders in stature but even more shy."

"Ah," said Faeril, enlightened. "These shadows are mentioned but not named in Petal's diary, and Gwylly talked about such things, too, and he named them as did you: Fox Riders, Living Mounds, Angry Trees, and more . . . Groaning Stones, and other such. He told me tales of strange beings within some forests—the Weiunwood, mainly—tales of forbidding and forbidden places, shadowy figures half-seen, some gigantic, others small and quick. Some were said to be shining figures of light, while others were of the dark. Some were made of the very earth, while other beings were seemingly akin to stone, or to trees and plants and greenery."

"In those things, thy Gwylly was right," said Riatha, casting down an armload of deadwood. "Did he tell thee they do not abide strangers?"

"He did, saying that he'd heard of those who had challenged the woods, challenged the forbidden places, swearing that they weren't afraid and would prove it by walking through . . . would slay anything that threatened them. Gwylly said these would-be-heroes disappeared—entered but never emerged—were never seen or heard from again. But he also told of aid given to those in need. He was shocked to hear that once I had ridden through such a place there in the Weiunwood . . . asked me to go around next time. I didn't tell him that the Weiunwood was where the Warrows had settled in the last days of the *Wanderjahre*, long before they took up residence in the Boskydells." Faeril sighed, but then said, "Some Warrows yet dwell in those shaggy woods, mainly in the western part nigh Stonehill, and so I am not afraid to ride through—forbidden places, closed places, or not."

"Huah," said Urus, dropping his saddle to the ground, and then turning back to unlade the pack animals. " 'Tis good you are a gentle being, Faeril, and did not provoke the dwellers therein."

Aravan nodded and gestured all 'round. "This forest, Darda Erynian, is known by some as Blackwood of Old, a name to frighten many a person, for herein the Hidden Ones dwell, and they do not take kindly to unsavory beings."

Bair looked about, his grey eyes seeking, and he asked, "Pysks, Liv Vols, Vred Tres, Tomté: is that the sum of Hidden Ones?"

Aravan laughed. "Oh nay, elar, for there are many, here and elsewhere, spread across the world—forests, mountains, deserts, rivers, the sea—some remote, others not, some covert, others not. Many of these places thou wilt know the moment thou dost enter their domain, for they have a wondrous air about them. Other places thou wilt feel a deep foreboding upon stepping therein, and 'tis best to seek permission before proceeding. And as to the Hidden Ones, they are of many different kinds: Fox Riders, Living Mounds, Groaning Stones, Woodwers, Sprygt, Tomté, Ände, Children of the Sea, Phael . . . Fey and Peri of all kind, some I have no name for, some I've yet to meet."

"And they are named Hidden Ones because . . . ?"

Riatha growled, her silver eyes afire. "Because they've been hounded by Humans and have gone to ground."

Through forest and vale they wended with their flitting escort of shadows, fording clear streams as well as sparkling rivers, passing through Bircehyll, stronghold of the Dylvana—the green-clad woodland Elves of Darda Erynian. There they were welcomed and they tarried awhile, and feasted and exchanged tidings and sang in the moon-dappled nights.

But the time came for them to press on, and saying good-bye to many friends of yore, onward they fared.

And as they forded the River Rissanin to come into the Great-wood, the nature of their escort changed: Wolves it seemed or mayhap Bears or even huge men moved among the boles of the trees, there at the edge of vision.

"Some of these are not true Wolves," said Bair, "nor genuine are all of the Bears; they are more than they seem."

Urus looked at his son in surprise. "How . . . ?"

"Their <life>, Father. It carries a different light."

Urus sighed. "Would that I could see as do you, my son."

Bair shrugged and rode awhile without speaking. But then: "Da, are there shapeshifters among your folk, my folk?—I mean other than you and me?"

Urus nodded. "Ever is it told at the Baeron hearths that there are those among our folk who at times take on the shape of Wolves or Bears."

"I have seen it myself," said Aravan, Riatha nodding in agreement.

Urus frowned. "You have?"

"Aye," replied Aravan. "At the Battle of Hèl's Crucible. In the heat of combat, several great Bears appeared among the Baeron and fought against Modru's might."

Urus looked at Bair and grinned. "Did I not say that in battle sometimes I think like a Bear. It seems that others, perhaps in my lineage and yours, think so as well."

Bair laughed, and onward they rode, and now and again they would catch a fleeting glimpse of their elusive escort, primarily espied and pointed out by Bair, for their <life> carried a different light that only he could see.

* * *

"These once were alive but now they are dead," said Bair. "Only that tall one yet lives, and its \<life\> is low."

They had come across a vine-covered dell filled with huge broken stones—shattered, cracked, toppled and burst asunder—none was whole but one, and this a tall monolith, standing at the foot of the steep valeside. . . .

" 'Tis an aggregate of *Eio Wa Suk*—Those Who Groan," said Aravan.

Riatha nodded, her eyes glistering. "So many slain. What has befallen here?"

Bair strode to the last of the monoliths standing and placed a hand against the stone and laid his cheek alongside, as if listening. Some moments later his eyes filled with anguish and he looked at Riatha and said, "Its thoughts are slow and ponderous, not like those of ordinary rocks, which seem fixed, never to change. Yet this I can tell, Ythir: this tall stone, it mourns."

Faeril's eyes flew wide in astonishment. "Rocks have thoughts . . . ?"

Riatha, too, looked on in wonder. "Thou canst list to its bereavement, Bair?"

"I don't know what it is saying, yet had it a heart, it would be broken." Bair stroked the great stone and then stepped back, and the ground rumbled faintly.

Aravan cocked an eyebrow. "I thought that only the Pyska could converse with a Stone, yet it seems Bair can as well."

"I don't know what it said," replied Bair, trudging back up the valeside, "but it is so very sad."

With tears in her eyes, Riatha looked upon her child. " 'Tis enough that it knew you cared, and it wanted you to know."

Bair sighed and turned and looked back at the vine-laden vale with its uncounted shattered stones, and then he said, "Let us leave this place."

And they mounted up and rode on.

When they camped that night, Faeril said, "I did not know rocks have thoughts."

Aravan smiled at her. "Some believe the power of the Great Creator is in all."

Faeril frowned. "The Great Creator? You do mean Adon, right?"

Aravan shook his head. "Nay, 'tis one who is above all, or so those who believe in Him do say. Others say He does not exist, but rather 'tis pressing events and shaping forces in nature that determine that which comes about."

Faeril shook her head. "Well, Adon or no, Great Creator or no, nature or no, what I want to know is do rocks really think? I did not believe they were alive."

Aravan turned up his hands. "That I cannot say, yet this I do know: Bair sees some essence in all things which the rest of us see not."

Faeril turned to Riatha. "Is this what Bair sees in all things: the power of the Great Creator?"

Riatha shrugged. "All I know, Faeril, is that Bair says there is <life> in all."

"But in rocks?"

Riatha grinned and nodded. "He says they are alive in a strange way, their entire being fixed on only solidity. He told me the essence of streams is swift and ephemeral, and the basis of trees is stateliness; the core of zephyrs is playfulness; the marrow of great storms, raging. Whether or no he actually senses thoughts in these things, or rather some force within, that I cannot say. Yet he does have a <sight> we do not, and as thou didst see today, he did seem to sense the heart of a Groaning Stone . . . as the Stone itself sensed him: didst thou not hear the ground rumble? 'Twas the Stone acknowledging my Bair."

Aravan grunted in agreement, and then said, "Though I am a mentor of Bair in many skills and much lore, it is he who has oft led me in teachings of the <power> and the <life> that lies within all things."

Faeril raised her hands in surrender, and then looked about and took up a rock and held it to her ear.

Aravan was yet laughing when Urus and Bair came back into camp, their arms filled with wood for the fire.

Accompanied by their escort as they travelled southeasterly, of Wolves and Bears and men, and now and again perhaps a thing of tendrils and vines as well, down through the forest they fared.

Known as Darda Stor by Elves, the Greatwood was a vast timberland, some seven hundred miles long and two hundred and fifty wide. Yet guided by Urus, they rode straightly onward, and at last, together, they came unto a woodland village hidden among foliage green at the edge of a great treeless space in the midst of the forest, a village at the edge of the gigantic glade known simply as The Clearing, so broad that the woods beyond could not be seen, some thirty miles distant.

And this was where they were bound.

They gave over Bair to Brur, a huge redheaded Baeron, nearly seven foot tall, the one who would see to the lad's training, along with the three ten-year-olds who were already there—black-haired, black-eyed, small and compact Diego of Vancha; and blond, blue-eyed, slender Äldan of Valon; and finally, brown-haired, brown-eyed, Ryon of Pellar—royal sons sent there by their sires to learn to revere and keep the land as the sires themselves had learned. And though Bair was but nine and some, still he stood taller than any among them, though Äldan came within half a head of Bair. Prince Ryon, the son of High King Garon and Queen Thayla, stood nearly as tall as Äldan, in spite of his sire and dam's modest statures.

"I remember your parents," said Faeril to Ryon. "We met some years back, in a time before you were born. We had tea on occasion, your mother and I, and long did we talk. I liked her. But, oh my, you such a tall lad, my prince, and she just under five foot altogether, though not quite as short as I."

Faeril laughed and Ryon grinned as he looked down at her, the first Warrow he had ever seen, though that would change considerably in the years to come.

Riatha and Urus and Faeril stayed for a week in all, but then prepared to leave, for as Urus explained, the Baeron would teach the lads without the distraction of parents about.

Even so, Riatha was reluctant to go, but Urus said, "I would have him dwell here awhile, for he has not until now been in the company of others his age, just his elders in Arden Vale—his very much elders, I add. And with no children about in Arden,

I think him too old for his years. We must give him this summer. Let him cope with his peers, and enjoy the company of youth."

Riatha sighed and said, "Still, chier, there is always Dalavar Wolfmage's warning of peril he might yet face."

And though Faeril fretted, nevertheless she said, "Urus is right. He should have children about. Besides, didn't Dalavar Wolfmage say he should walk with Aravan, and since Aravan is staying with him . . ." She looked up at the Alor.

Aravan grinned down at the damman and then turned to Riatha and said, "Rest easy, *jaian*, for I will watch over him. Moreover, with the Greatwood guarded by those like unto the ones who escorted us on the way here, who of ill intent would dare cross into this forest? Hence, I say go and see Darda Galion and Bellon Falls and the Cauldron and Caer Lindor and other such. Come again at the end of the summer, when Bair's training is done."

And so Urus and Riatha and Faeril rode away that day, off to see Bellon Falls and the ruins of Caer Lindor and to visit Darda Galion, despite its being abandoned of all Lian, though not abandoned by Elves, for Dylvana warriors from Darda Erynian had come to guard it, turning away those who would loot from it, those who would steal precious eldwood.

For the whole of the summer, Bair and the three sons of kings roamed the woods with their guides. And they became fast friends and pledged to one another and roughhoused and teased and sang and learned to nurture the world. And in all that time Bair shifted shape but once, and that when a stag bounded by; the lad ran after, a cloud of darkness surrounding him, Aravan shouting "Bair!", while out from the hurtling shade sprang a Silver Wolf in full pursuit. Aravan glanced at Brur and shrugged, while Brur sighed in return. Yet the Draega ran no more than a furlong or so ere it shifted its shape back into that of Bair, and with a hangdog look he returned to the lads, whose eyes were by then quite wide, quite round. They drew back a bit in awe, but then Ryon stepped forward and slapped Bair on the shoulder and said, "Oh my, but that was splendid!" And then Diego and Äldan grinned and asked how did he do it and could he teach them as well? When Bair said one had to be born into it, they groaned in disappointment but accepted the fact, though Diego wished he himself could become a great cat of the mountains, while Äldan would be a swift steed. As to Ryon, he said he would become a golden griffin, had he a choice. It was only afterward that Bair realized that each had chosen the animal upon his crest of arms, and he knew if he ever had a crest of his own it would show a great Silver Wolf.

Brur let them chatter on for a while, but at last he urged them toward the next lesson: the preservation of great old trees and the selection of lesser ones to be harvested, as well as the planting of seedlings to replace those taken down.

Within but moments the wonder of Bair's transformation was forgotten, or so it did seem, though occasionally one prince or another would cast Bair a look in something akin to hero worship.

At the end of the summer, on Autumnday, when Riatha and Urus and Faeril rode back into the village, Brur came unto them and said, "Your son Bair and the keeping of the land, I deem he was my teacher instead."

Faeril cast Urus an I-told-you-so glance, but he turned to Brur and said, "Nevertheless I am glad he did dwell here awhile."

On that day as well, cavalcades rode with their charges out across the wide clearing, escorting the young princes away: Diego to Castilla in Vancha, Äldan to Vanar in Valon, and Ryon to Caer Pendwyr in Pellar, the seats of the various thrones.

But before they went, Diego and Äldan and Ryon came to Bair to bid him a farewell, and they all exchanged vows to aid at need should events warrant, little knowing how soon the time ere those vows would be redeemed.

That evening under the stars, with the crescent moon sliding down the sky chasing after the now-set sun, Riatha and Faeril and Urus and Aravan and Bair celebrated the changing of the seasons, stepping the rite and canting the chant beneath the sweeping skies.

Enveloped by moonlight and starlight and melody and harmony and descant and counterpoint and feet soft on the forest loam, they trod solemnly, gravely; yet their hearts were full of joy.

Step ... pause ... shift ... pause ... turn ... pause ... step.

Slowly, slowly, move and pause. Voices rising. Voices falling. Liquid notes from the dawn of time. Harmony. Euphony. Step ... pause ... step. Riatha turning. Urus turning, Bair at his side. Faeril passing. Aravan pausing. Counterpoint. Descant. Step ... pause ... step. ...

Singing, chanting, gliding, halting, all were lost in the ritual ... step ... pause ... step.

When the rite at last came to an end—voices dwindling, song diminishing, movement slowing, till all was silent and still—they once again stood in their beginning places: Riatha and Faeril facing north, Aravan and Urus and Bair facing south. The motif of the pattern they had paced had not been random but had had a specific design, had had a specific purpose, and the same was true of the song; yet as to the overall meaning, as to the hidden intent, all but Bair now knew ... a purpose he soon would discover completely upon his own.

As the stars wheeled through the sky, they took their Autumnday meal in the crisp fall air before a small campblaze, and they were exhilarated. And after cleaning their utensils in a nearby running brook and returning to the fire, Faeril turned to Bair and said, "You are nearly ten, my adopted *arran*, will be in but a fortnight and some, and I think you now old enough to keep this safely by. Here, you big tall thing, lean over."

As Bair leaned down, Faeril slipped over his head the platinum chain holding the falcon crystal she had fashioned into a pendant just over a decade past.

In wonder, Bair held up the stone in the starlight and marvelled at the incised raptor within and said, "My, but this is splendid." But then he frowned and added, "It holds a strange light, and yet whether or no it lives I cannot say." And then he hugged Faeril and said, "Thank you, amicula."

Faeril grinned and said, "I just wanted to give you a gift in celebration, for on this day you completed the Baeron school ... and taught them a thing or two, I might add. And there is this: I think I am not telling secrets out of turn, but there are two more gifts awaiting the day you reach ten."

Bair looked at the others, his eyes alight. "More gifts?"

"Aye," rumbled Urus, "but not until you turn ten, though there will be a boon ere then: while we were away, we did arrange with Balor, DelfLord of Kraggen-cor, a special birthday gift, though it will be weeks in the giving."

Bair frowned. "Balor? Kraggen-cor? Birthday gift?"

Riatha smiled. "Balor is a Drimm, Bair, a Dwarf, leader of the Drimmenholt they name Kraggen-cor, dubbed by the Humans the Black Hole, called Drimmen-deeve by Elvenkind."

"Oh, but I have heard of Drimmen-deeve," said Bair. "A wondrous place, or so I have been told."

Aravan nodded. "The mightiest of all Drimmenholts. I will take pleasure in seeing it again."

"You've been there?" asked Faeril.

Aravan nodded in remembrance. "When I crafted the *Eroean*, I went there to ask for starsilver to powder and mix in the paint for the whole of the hull from her waterline down. DelfLord Tolak of the Red Hills nearly burst a blood vessel when he heard what I was to do with it, for his were the Drimma crafters I engaged to build her. And he shouted in astonishment when I said it would take but a pound. '*A pound! A whole pound?*' he cried. 'Aye,' said I. 'I have a formula from Dwynfor the swordmaker.' He seemed to settle upon hearing Dwynfor's name, yet he asked me where I intended to get the starsilver. 'From Drimmen-deeve,' said I. When I did go there, DelfLord Durek was kind enough to yield up that amount, though he, too, thought it mad.

"And so it was then I walked the halls of Drimmen-deeve."

His eyes dancing with curiosity, Bair looked from Aravan to Riatha to Urus. "Um, about these gifts I am to g—"

"Bair," growled Urus, "the gifts will wait until your birthday comes."

"Yes, Da," said Bair, chapfallen. But then he immediately smiled and looked at the crystal pendant again, and hugged Faeril once more.

Bidding farewell to Brur, northwesterly through the Greatwood they fared, a half-seen escort wending alongside through the autumnal forest, the leaves shifting hue from green to yellow and scarlet and russet and gold. Small animals scurried along limbs and among leaves on the ground, rushing to store away provender for the winter to come, while high aloft flocks of redbreasts and chirpers and blackwings swooped and turned and swirled, gathering for the migrations ahead, while solitary crows sat high in the trees and jeered at those who would flee.

Faeril looked up at the blue sky above, then said, "I think I'll ride out to see Orith and Nelda when we are done in Drimmendeeve."

Urus grunted, but Bair said, "Orith and Nelda?"

Faeril glanced across at Bair. "Gwylly's foster parents. Humans. They live along the eastern eaves of the Weiunwood."

Bair looked at Faeril. "They are Humans?"

"Oh yes. They found Gwylly in a wrecked wain, his parents killed. By Rûcks and such. They raised him as their own son."

Now Bair turned to Urus. "May I go, Da? I've heard of the Weiunwood, a shaggy forest, and would see it for myself."

Urus glanced at Riatha. "Why not? I would see it for myself as well."

And so it was decided.

They fared over the Rissanin at the ruins of Caer Lindor, the remains of that ancient island fortress sitting midstream, a fortress overthrown by betrayal and destroyed in the time of the Great War of the Ban, nought but stone rubble now, its walls hammered down by Trolls. Yet here was a principal crossing over the waterway. Maintained by the Baeron, a pontoon bridge spanned from the southeasterly shore to the island ruins, and another pontoon bridge on the opposite side of the isle reached from there on across.

As they rode through the stone rubble remaining, rubble now covered in ivy and moss and lichen, Aravan sighed. "Here it was Silverleaf nearly lost his life, and many others perished"—he glanced at Faeril—"Warrows not the least of those slain."

"You were here?" asked Faeril.

Aravan shook his head. "On the day of betrayal, I was away on a mission Silverleaf had given over to me. My warband and I had gone west to see to the truth of those who sought sanctuary, to Olorin Isle in the Great River Argon and to Darda Galion beyond. When we returned, the fortress was nought but ruins."

"Who did this?" asked Bair.

"Foul Folk. A Horde."

Bair frowned. "And what happened to them?"

"Some were slain in the battle at the fortress. Many others perished at the hands of the Hidden Ones as the Rûpt fled these woods. Fully half of the Horde did not escape."

"Good," grunted Urus. "Nothing better than five thousand dead Spawn, except perhaps the death of the full ten thousand."

And on they rode.

They crossed the mighty Argon River on the ferries at Olorin Isle—ferries now manned by trustworthy men, and not by the perfidious Rivermen of old. They landed on the western shores of that great waterway at the far northern fringes of Darda Galion, the forest known by many as the Larkenwald, though it had been some five thousand years since any silverlarks had flitted therein.

Northwesterly they rode onward, now across the open wold and toward the foothills warding the approaches unto the Grimwall Mountains beyond, and to the Quadran therein.

On October the eighth, one day shy of the date of Bair's birth, they rode up a long, sharply rising valley hemmed by mountains about, an acclivity named Falanith by Elves, called the Pitch by men and others, and named Baralan by the Dwarves.

Up this vale they rode and into the arms of the Quadran: four great mountains of granite under which Kraggen-cor was delved: Loftcrag, lying to the immediate right, its dark stone faintly tinged blue; pale Greytower to their immediate left, its color to go with its name; ebon Grimspire lay leftward and ahead; and ruddy Stormhelm, to the right of Grimspire. It was to red Stormhelm they were bound, the tallest of the four, for there they would find the gate into Drimmen-deeve. They rode along the Quadrill, a crystalline stream flowing down from the Quadmere, a lakelet nigh the head of the vale fed by streams from the mountains above.

Past this broad pool they soon rode, and by a broken pillar on its western shore, a realmstone marking the bounds of Kraggen-cor.

Somewhere off to the right they could hear a distant rumble, as of a thunder of water. " 'Tis the Vorvor," said Aravan, riding alongside Bair. "A whirlpool entwined in the legends of the Dwarves."

"A whirlpool?" asked Bair. "Here in the mountains?"

Aravan pointed easterly. "Yon is a fold in the mountain stone, and therein a river bursts forth from beneath the mountain we name Chagor, also known as Loftcrag in the common tongue, but called Ghatan by the Drimma. The river tumbles into a great stone basin, to whirl 'round and then be sucked down into a hole in the bottom of the basin to disappear altogether.

"It is said that the first Durek was flung into the spinning maw of that whirling gurge by jeering Spaunen. Thus began the never-ending war between Drimma and Rûpt."

"But what happened to Durek?" asked Bair. "How did he escape the Vorvor?"

"He didn't," replied Aravan. "It sucked him down into the dark underearth and stranded him on the bank of a great underground river, yet he endured. And in the weeks after, he discovered vast tunnels and chambers under the stone of the mountains, tunnels and chambers which were to become Drimmen-deeve. How he survived during this time is not told, but it is said that the Utruni—the Stone Giants—aided Durek to freedom. Legend has it that the Dawn Gate, the gate where we are headed, stands at the very place Durek emerged into the light of day."

"Kelan, how did you come to have all this knowledge?"

"Ah, elar, I did sail the *Eroean* for millennia in the company of Drimma warbands. Voyages are long, and much time is spent telling of life and living."

Now they came upon a pave, a road leading unto the massive iron gates of the holt embedded in dark red granite. There they were hailed by Dwarven sentries, standing ward at the door. And a Dwarven captain was called, and when he stepped through the wide-open gates he said, "Welcome again, Lady Faeril, Lady Riatha, Lord Urus. And welcome to you, Lord Aravan. And this must be Master Bair, the one we are to train. Welcome, lad. I am Gatecaptain Dorn, and DelfLord Balor expects you all."

Even as the captain spoke the greeting, Bair's gaze swept across them all, for these were the first Dwarves he had seen. Squat they were, and broad, each standing some four to four and a half feet tall, but half again as wide at their powerful shoulders as was Aravan. Bearded they were, whiskers brown and black and ginger and red, a shade or so darker than that on their heads. Armed and armored they were, bearing warhammers and battle-axes. Black-iron mail over silken underpadding covered their chests and arms, and black-iron greaves clasped 'round their boots safeguarded the leg from knee to ankle. Leather pants they wore, and leather gloves as well, the fingers warded by black-iron platelets sewn on. And on their heads were black-iron helms, some with iron wings flaring, others with studs or spikes.

As the travellers dismounted to lead their steeds in, Bair looked at his father. "Train?"

"Aye, Bair," replied Urus. " 'Tis our special gift to you."

"Train in what?"

"In climbing."

Bair frowned. "But Kelan Aravan has already taught me to climb, Da, and I am rather good at it."

Aravan laughed. "Ah, elar, not half as good as thou wilt be when the Châkka—the Drimma—are finished with thee, for they are the best climbers in all of Mithgar."

Bair cocked his head to one side. "How can that be? They live underground, inside the stone of mountains."

Captain Dorn snorted. "Ah, boy, you have much to learn, for the insides of a Mountain need more climbing than the outside ever will."

Bair looked at Urus. "Da . . . ?"

Even as Dorn spun on his heel and headed for the gate, Urus turned up his hands and said, "So it is they do say."

And leading their animals and following the captain, into Drimmen-deeve, into Kraggen-cor, into the Black Hole they strode.

CHAPTER 12

Passages

October, 5E1003–January, 5E1004

[Six and Five Years Past]

With the hooves of the animals aclatter upon rock, through the portal known as the Dawn Gate and into an entry hall they went, past the great iron doors, Captain Dorn leading, Urus trailing, the others in between. Smelling of stone and delved out of the red granite of Stormhelm, the chamber before them was huge: perhaps two hundred yards in length and nearly as wide, the ceiling above some thirty feet high and covered with machicolations, murder holes from which would rain death—burning oil and melted lead and crossbow bolts and darts and other such—should an invader breach the outer gates. And along the walls were slots in the stone, arrow slits, through which more bolts would fly.

Past these formidable defenses they strode and toward a single outlet at the far end, an outlet which led into a broad corridor and down, down into the interior of Kraggen-cor, the shod hooves of the horses an echoing clatter from the nearby stone walls. And as they passed into this roadway, at Aravan's gesture Bair looked overhead where stood a wide slot above, in which he could see the edge of something made of black-iron, and deep grooves ran down the walls to mate with another slot across the floor.

"What is it?" asked Bair above the clack of hooves.

Aravan replied, "A gate above, a thick slab of iron, a great iron plate, set to drop down the grooves and into the channel below and seal the way."

Bair frowned. "Could not someone simply lift it?"

Aravan shook his head. "Even had someone the strength to do so, I ween when in place 'tis locked above."

"Ah," said Bair, enlightened. "And how do they pull it back up?"

"By a geared winch, I should think," said Aravan.

Down the wide corridor they went, the hallway lit with phosphorescent Châkka lanterns, the blue-green light casting a ghastly aspect over all. Down through this spectral glow they trod, along a gentle slope descending, murder holes overhead, a faint odor of oil drifting down, and after perhaps a furlong or so, the corridor came to an end. As he drew nigh the exit Bair saw another floor channel and more wall grooves, and ensconced in a slot overhead another thick iron slab awaited. They issued out onto a broad landing at the top of a short flight of wide stairs and paused, and Bair gasped in astonished surprise.

The steps led down to a broad shelf of stone, which in turn came to an abrupt end, the rock scissured by a wide rift. Black and yawning, a deep abyss barred the way: the ebon gape split out of a vast crack in the high rock wall on one side to jag across the expansive stone floor and disappear into another great crack on the opposite wall. It was a mighty barrier, some fifty feet across at the narrowest point, a hundred or more at the widest. Over the immense chasm spanned a broad wooden drawbridge, and a shielded winch on the far side stood ready to hale the counterweighted bascule up and away and lock it in place at need. Dwarven warriors warded the hoist and the bridge.

Beyond the mighty fissure the wide stone floor continued, and by the light of Dwarven lanterns affixed in wall sconces Bair could see the whole of a vast chamber: its extent was a mile or more, its width mayhap a half mile, its high-vaulted ceiling some hundred feet up, the roof of the chamber supported by four rows of giant pillars marching away to the end.

Gesturing outward, his voice sounding hollow in the vastness of all, Captain Dorn said, "Yon is the War Hall, the Mustering Chamber, should war ever again come to call."

"Then war has come here before?" asked Bair.

"Aye. Several times have Grg armies tried to conquer this place. But none has ever won across the Great Dêop against the assembled Châkka."

Urus looked surprised. "I was told an army of Spawn once occupied Drimmen-deeve."

"Aye, it is true. But they were conquered by Seventh Durek in the War of Kraggen-cor."

Urus looked at Riatha and then back at Dorn. "If no Foul Folk army has ever won across the Great Deep, then how was it they occupied this holt?"

Dorn's lips clamped shut, and it seemed he wouldn't answer, but at last he said in a low, grating voice, "They came swarming in after the Ghath drove us out."

Bair frowned. "Ghath?"

"A Draedan, a Gargon," said Aravan. "A terrible Fearcaster. None can withstand its—"

"We tarry," said Dorn, brusquely, as if to cut off all converse concerning one of Dwarfdom's darkest days, ashamed that the Châkka had fled, "and DelfLord Balor awaits."

Leftward he led them and down a ramp, and just as they came to the landing, to the left a stone door opened, one that was not there a moment before, so well concealed it was. A Dwarven warrior stepped out.

At Bair's quizzical look, Aravan said, "I deem it leads unto the defenses in the first hall: the arrow slits, the murder holes, the great iron gates set to block the corridor."

"Ah," said Bair. "Had it not opened, I would have never known it was there."

Dorn glanced back at the lad. "Secret Châkka doors are difficult to find, even when you know where they are."

To the right they turned and thence to the drawbridge, and as they passed over, Bair looked down. The walls of the abyss were smooth and sheer and dropped straight for as far as the eye could see and vanished into unguessable depths below. "How deep is this?"

Dorn shrugged.

Now they came onto the floor of the great War Hall, and there they paused to doff their cold-weather gear, for as Dorn said, "Kraggen-cor is warmer than winter and cooler than summer, nei-

ther hot nor chill but ever steady, made so by the rock all 'round."
Dorn called for several of the Dwarven warders to take the horses
and pony in hand and lead them to the stables; he bade them as
well to deliver the possessions of the visitors unto the guest quarters. Then rightward he turned to escort the travellers across the
hall, toward one of the many exits leading off into passages
carved through the stone.

As they passed one of the giant red-granite pillars, Bair saw
that the figure of a Dragon was carved twining up and around
the great fluted shaft.

"That's one of the new ones," grunted Dorn, seeing the lad's
interest.

"New ones?"

"Aye. Some Dragon-pillars were toppled during the Battle of
Kraggen-cor."

"When was this?"

"Um"—Dorn stroked his beard—"seven hundred seventy-two
years past." Dorn looked at the runes encircling the base of the
great fluted shaft. "This pillar itself was emplaced twenty years
later—"

"And so it is seven hundred fifty-two years old," interjected
Bair.

Dorn nodded.

"And you call it 'new'?"

Again Dorn nodded. "Aye. Compared to the others, it is but
an infant."

Into the passageway they stepped, and up a flight of stairs
and then another and another, the group turning left and right
and left and . . . until Bair lost count of the steps and the twisting way, for he was more interested in peering down the corridors they passed to left and right, some lit, others dark.

At the top of yet another flight of stairs, they came into a
long, narrow chamber, a rune-covered archway spanning the width
athwart the midpoint. "This is the Hall of the Gravenarch," said
Dorn. "It, too, is now restored."

Bair looked askance at the captain.

"It was collapsed," said Dorn, "as was the Mustering Chamber."

Bair stared at the stone overhead. "Even though the mountain above whispers of its strength, perhaps Kraggen-cor is not a safe place to be."

Dorn looked puzzled. "Whispers?"

Bair shrugged. "Whispers is not quite the right word, but the stone is <alive> with strength."

Dorn cocked an eyebrow. "It *is* the living stone."

Bair nodded but said, "Still you did not answer my question: with pillars falling and chambers collapsing, is Kraggen-cor a safe place to be?"

Dorn drew himself up to his full four-foot-six and gruffly said, "No safer place lies in all of Mitheor than here in Kraggen-cor. As to this chamber, it did not fall down on its own: instead it was wrecked by those you name the Deevewalkers, done so to cut off pursuit."

Frowning, Bair looked at Riatha, and the Dara said, "There is a written record of the Deevewalkers, Bair, containing the story within, recounted by Tuckerby Underbank and penned by his daughter Raven, for whom the book is named. It tells the full tale of the Winter War, at least from his point of view. In the scroll archives is a copy of *The Ravenbook*, one which thou shouldst read upon our return to the Vale, for it will tell thee much of the truth of war."

"Tuckerby was a Warrow," said Faeril, her voice tinged with pride.

"And Brega Bekki's Son, a Châk," replied Dorn, not to be outdone. "He, too, was a Deevewalker."

Out from the Hall of the Gravenarch they passed, turning leftward along a corridor. "Here we are on the Sixth Rise," said Dorn. "The Great Hall lies just ahead."

"Sixth Rise?" asked Bair.

"Aye, lad. All levels in Kraggen-cor, or in any Châkkaholt, for that matter, are taken with respect to the main gate. All levels upward from the Gate Level are called Rises; all levels downward are called Neaths. The War Hall lies at First Neath. Here we are at the Sixth Rise."

Bair frowned and then smiled. "Then from the War Hall we must have climbed, what? Seven sets of stairs?"

Dorn nodded and turned to Riatha and noted, "The lad ciphers well."

Now they came into a huge, dimly lighted chamber, fully a half mile from end to end and half of that across. And in the center and surrounded by glowing, phosphorescent lanterns sitting on pedestals of stone, mid the clangorous clamor of battle, Dwarves whirled in melee.

Uncertainty in his eye, Bair looked at Urus. "Da?"

Ere Urus could answer, Dorn said, "Rest easy, lad. They but do train."

"Trust the rope, boy. Trust the jam, the ring, the nail, the harness, and the rope."

Bair looked across at DelfLord Balor, the dark-bearded Dwarf clinging to the stone alongside him.

"I watched you set it well, the jam," growled Balor, his voice like gravel, his dark eyes aglitter. "The snap-ring is strong and will not break, and the rope is among the finest in all Mitheor, Châkka-crafted to soften the jolt. The rock-nails below are driven deep. Your harness will hold a dozen like you. So cast yourself loose and fall."

Clinging to the cool rock surface, Bair looked down at the stone floor some hundred feet below.

"Before I do so, DelfLord, I would know when such a maneuver is warranted."

Balor snorted, but said, "When arrows are flying, it is sometimes wise to keep the foe from discovering the range. Too, there are other perils you may wish to escape—a winged menace, a creature on a ledge, something dire in a hole or a crevice—dangers which can be avoided only with a fall."

Bair nodded, and then, taking a deep breath and gritting his teeth, he cast back and away . . . and fell.

Below, Riatha spasmodically clutched Urus's hand, her nails drawing blood from his palm as down through the air plunged Bair.

Thnn . . . ! The rope snapped taut but yielded, its elasticity absorbing much of the shock; even so Bair *Whuff!*ed with the jolt of it, and braced himself for the impact as he now swung inward toward the hard granite wall. He took up the shock in his legs as his feet landed squarely on stone.

Above, Balor turned to the Elf on the wall beside him. "You

taught him well, Lord Aravan. I expected him to be uncontrolled at the bottom, yet he landed feet true."

Aravan grinned. "He seems to take to it naturally."

Balor nodded and then looked down. "Talent he has, Lord Aravan, yet there is much left for him to master—to trust the rope among other things—yet that is enough for today."

That eve, the ninth day of October, Aravan gave Bair the golden-cased needle that pointed out the north, though Aravan did warn, " 'Tis a lodestone, Bair, and though it will nigh always find north, 'ware where thou dost attempt it, for it is also drawn to iron and to steel and to other lodestones nearby."

Bair looked at it. "Other lodestones? Then like draws like, would you say?"

"Or sometimes pushes it away," replied Aravan.

As those two were speaking of the mysterious power of lodestones, Riatha turned to Urus and handed him the ring that had been mysteriously delivered on the night of Bair's birth . . . by whom or what none could say. Stone it was, and exquisitely carved, and set with a gem of jet. "I know not why, *chieran,* but that thou art the one who should give this over to him seems fitting."

Puzzled, Urus looked at her. "Why so, chieran?"

Riatha shrugged. "It is sized for a large hand, more like unto thine than mine."

But Urus handed it back. "Somehow I think it more yours to give."

Now it was Riatha who asked, "Why so?"

"There is something about it which brings to mind the changing of the seasons," answered Urus, "the dance, the chant, the entire rite, and that is an Elven thing and not a thing of the Baeron."

Riatha shook her head. "But Baeron and others celebrate as well: Drimma, Hidden Ones, Waerlinga—"

"Oh, piffle." said Faeril. "Stop this chitter-chatter of who should give him the ring. Just give it." The damman then reached into her pocket and drew out a length of platinum links, much the same as the chain she had made for the crystal pendant. "I knew this day would come, and after I saw the size of the ring,

I made this; the ring is too large for Bair's hand now, yet he will grow into it, or so Yselle did say nearly ten years back. Riatha, you give him the ring. And when he sees it's too big to fit, Urus, you fasten it about his neck with this chain."

And so they did.

When Bair looked at the ring he said, "Stone it is, yet it has a <fire> within." He turned to Riatha. "Who carved it, and what does it do, Ythir?"

"I know not, arran, and neither did Dalavar Wolfmage."

Seeking an answer, Bair looked at Urus and then Aravan, and they both did shrug. But when he turned to Faeril, she said, "Perhaps it is a mystery you will solve someday."

Frowning, Bair again slipped it onto one finger and then another and another, yet even with a chain running through, it was too big for any, thumb included.

Nevertheless he turned and grinned and hugged and kissed them all. And just then the dinner gong rang, and so they did retire unto the Warrior Mess, where whatever was served that eve would be his birthday meal. . . .

. . . It was plain biscuits and gruel.

Long was the training and hard, and a month passed and then another, and Bair persevered through all, the lad's fingers at times bleeding from prolonged contact with stone. And every day Aravan climbed beside him, the Alor improving his skills as well. And Aravan insisted, and Balor agreed, that they should always climb with weaponry, for who knew what they might meet on the way? Of the two weapons ten-year-old Bair was skilled in, he chose to carry his sling. Aravan climbed with his spear slung across his back, and a long-knife at his thigh.

As they rested on a ledge during one ascent, Balor glanced over at Aravan and said, "Climbing with a spear would seem awkward at best, Lord Aravan."

"At times, DelfLord, it is," replied Aravan. "Yet Krystallopŷr is a *special* weapon and Truenamed. It is perilous in the extreme, and I would not have it more than a reach from my grasp, for should it fall into the hands of someone vile who came to know just how to invoke it, the damage it would do is beyond reckoning."

Balor grunted and eyed the smoky crystal blade warily, then nodded and turned to Bair. "Well, lad, it is time to resume. You take the lead on this pitch."

And on up the vertical rise they continued, climbing inside the black stone of Grimspire.

Only seldom did Balor take them outside to climb the flanks of the mountains, the DelfLord repeating what Captain Dorn had said: "The insides of a Mountain need more climbing than the outside ever will." And so they free-climbed and rappelled, and drove rock-nails into narrow crevices and lodged jams into wider ones, hooking snap-rings through and threading ropes and belaying one another, or climbing all alone. Up chimneys they edged, feet planted on one side, bracing back and shoulders against the other. And they swung free or ran across vertical surfaces, Balor ever calling out for the lad to "trust the rope," which meant much more than Bair merely trusting the rope, but trusting all equipment instead, once the boy had inspected the gear as well as inspected the setting of each jam and nail and ring, verifying the soundness of all. This and more did they do, each climb different, each difficult, each a harder test, whether it be climbing with scaling gear or climbing with none at all. For two months they struggled up and down and across rock faces—hands gloved and not, fingers chalked and not, feet booted and not, packs and other equipment borne or dangling from ropes or not, wearing armor and not, bearing weapons and not, and other such manners of equipage and hardship and trial—and at last Balor declared Bair fit to scale stone with any, though his skills fell short of the best.

It was now early December, and the DelfLord invited his visitors to stay for the celebration of Cheol, of Winterfest, for the time was drawing nigh. And when they accepted, Bair expected a spree, instead he found the hardships of such a Dwarven celebration, for on the ninth of the month, the Dwarves began a solemn twelve-day fast, and so did their guests do likewise.

"I swear, my stomach is eating itself," rumbled Urus.

"Me, too, Da," said Bair. "Twelve days on nought but a bit of bread and a mighty amount of water. Why do the Dwarves put themselves through such an ordeal?"

"The Drimma are a hard race," said Riatha. "Hard as the stone they delve." She grinned and added, "And starving themselves for twelve days somehow seems altogether fitting."

Aravan smiled. "E'en so, smell the air; the cooking has resumed, for 'tis Winterday now, and tonight begins the twelve-day feast."

"Smell the air, indeed," said Faeril, brushing her silver lock of hair from her eyes, as savory aromas drifted along the corridors and halls of the Dwarvenholt. "I think I'm going to drown in my own watering mouth."

Riatha laughed. "Wise are these Dwarves, my dear Waerling, for after twelve days of denial, no matter the edibles they serve— be it the coarsest of bread, the stringiest of meat, the most tasteless of tubers, the blandest of beans, the flattest of any food whatsoever—'twill be a meal fit for the gods."

Faeril grinned. "And I will eat it with zeal."

"Me, too," said Bair, then groaned, a chapfallen look on his face as he added, "even if it's biscuits and gruel."

They sat silent for moments, and then Aravan said, "When I fared on the *Eroean*, I had a Drimma warband—forty Drimma in all—as part of my crew. It was from them I learned the Drimm Tongue—Châkur, they name it. I also learned that on this night, Winternight, the Drimma consecrate themselves unto Elwydd, for they believe She created them. All of their crafting, all of their arts, all of their dedication to honor, they do so in Her name. This night, Year's Long Night, is the one they set aside for a renewal of their spirits, of their devotion to Her, and the twelve days fasting is part of that renewal. It is—"

A gong sounded.

Bair leapt to his feet. "Do we eat now?"

"Not yet, Bair," said Aravan, smiling. "It is but the sound to assemble."

Even as the Alor spoke, a tawny-bearded Dwarf came to the door of their chamber and announced, "I am Kelk. Mid of night draws nigh, and all are summoned."

Down they went from the guest chambers on the Seventh Rise and to the great War Hall below. And there among the red Dragon-pillars they found a great assembly of Châkka, even as others continued to arrive. And for the first time they saw gathered, slender figures covered from head to foot in diaphanous veils.

"Who are they, Ythir?" asked Bair.

Riatha put an arm about Bair and whispered, "I believe we now look upon those they call Châkia, the females of the Drimma."

Bair shook his head. "They are not Drimma, Ythir."

Her eyes wide, Riatha looked at her son. "Not—?"

"—Drimma," completed Bair. "At least I don't think so."

"Why would you say such?"

"Their <light> is not the same as Drimma, Ythir."

Riatha pursed her lips, then said, "Perhaps it is because they are female."

Again Bair shook his head. "I don't think so, Ythir. Male and female Lian have the same sort of <light> as one another. Male and female Baeron are alike as well, though different from Lian. The Humans we saw on Olorin Isle, the <light> around them is the same for the men and women alike, though different from Baeron and Lian." Bair gestured at the veil-covered Châkia. "But these females, their <light> is not like that of the males, and so I believe they are of a different Kind altogether."

"What of the young ones, Bair?" asked Riatha, gesturing at a solemn group of children standing nigh the Châkia.

Bair looked. "Oh, they're Drimma all right, Ythir, just like their sires. But did you notice one thing . . . ?"

Riatha looked, frowning. Then she shook her head. "What, Bair? What should I notice?"

Bair took a deep breath and then said, "There are no girls. Just boys. I wonder where are the girls? Do you think there are none at all?"

Before Riatha could answer, another gong sounded, and some Dwarves began crossing the bridge through the passageway toward the first chamber, where stood the Dawn Gate. Tawny-haired Kelk came to them. "We will go with the middle group of three to look at Elwydd's stars and praise Her."

"Ye go in three separate groups?" asked Aravan.

Kelk nodded. "Ever since Blackstone, only a third at a time go to praise her works. That way the holt is never undefended, never abandoned."

Bair looked at Riatha, an unspoken question in the lad's eyes, and the Dara said, "It has to do with Sleeth the Orm, Bair. I will tell it to thee later."

Riatha then turned to Kelk. "We need go with the last group"— here Bair groaned, but Riatha ignored him—"for afterward there is our own ceremony we step out this night."

Bair sighed, but made no other protest.

Kelk looked on in surprise. "You would be late to the start of the feast?"

"How long does it last?" asked Bair, forlornly.

Kelk smiled. "Twelve days, twelve nights."

"Oh my, but that's good news," said Faeril, turning to Bair. "Perhaps, my poor, nought-but-bones boy, you won't starve after all." And then she burst into giggles.

When the last third of the Châkka had gathered—Bair, Riatha, Urus, Faeril, and Aravan among them—Balor yet stood in a high, carved slot upon the ruddy flank of Stormhelm, and all eyes focused upon him, but for those of the Dwarven sentries ringed 'round, who watched with hard eyes the land and the skies instead, seeking any threat which might fall upon them from the snow-laden expanse of the Pitch and the slopes of the embracing mountains, and even from the spangled vault above.

And for the third time that night, the DelfLord lifted his face and arms to the star-studded heavens and raised his voice unto the sky, speaking the great litany, the unified response of the gathered Châkka alternating with his, cantor and chorale, the echoes of their invocation resounding among the stone of the Grimwall Mountains:

[Elwydd—
    —Lol an Adon]

. . . began the supplication, and in a low voice did Aravan translate as Balor and the assembly alternated:

Elwydd—
    —Daughter of Adon
We thank Thee—
    —For Thy gentle hand
That gave to us—
    —The breath of life

May this be—
>*—The golden year*
The Châkka—
>*—Touch the stars.*

Balor lowered his arms, and long after the belling echoes had ceased to ring, reverent silence reigned. And all that could be heard was the soft susurration of water running beneath the ice in the Quadrill below and the distant gurge of the Vorvor.

At last the DelfLord cleared his throat, and all faces but those of the sentries turned expectantly toward his. He gazed once more at the stars above, the spangle wheeling silently overhead. The waxing crescent moon had long set, but in the east were two of the wanderers: the Red Warrior rode high in the sky, while Slow Foot had just risen. Another moment passed and then another, and finally Balor cried out, "Here now at Kraggen-cor it is mid of night. Let the Winterfest of Cheol begin!"

A glad shout rose up into the sky, and Dwarves turned from the chill winter night toward the phosphorescent light of the Dwarvenholt beyond the massive open portals.

Yet five did not troop inward with the others, but remained behind under the starry skies to step out the Elven rite of the changing of the seasons as the silent Red Warrior glared down.

Year's Start Day was the last of the twelve days of feasting, and the very next morning the five visitors bade farewell to DelfLord Balor and to others who had become friends. And Balor assigned Kelk to guide them through the length of Kraggen-cor and to the Dusken Door some forty-four miles hence, for winter now hard-gripped the land, and all ways over the Grimwall Mountains were now impassable, blocked with unnumbered tons of snow. But the way under the Grimwall from east to west and west to east ever eluded dire winter's hand.

And so they gathered their horses and Faeril's pony, and the animals seemed eager to go, for although they had been ridden outside every day to keep them in fine fettle, still the weight of the mountain above appeared to press down upon them, or so Faeril surmised.

But as they said their good-byes, DelfLord Balor came unto them and gifted each with a small, hooded Dwarven lantern: brass and glass and needing no fuel as long as now and then they set it in sunlight for a while to restore the luminance therein. And one by one he solemnly spoke his farewells to each, yet when he came to Bair he embraced the lad and whispered three words: "Trust the rope."

"I will trust the rope," replied Bair, "as well as the jams and rings and nails and harness."

"I taught you well, Lord Bair," said Balor, smiling, and then gruffly adding: "Make certain you remember it all."

As the DelfLord stepped back, Kelk said, "Let us start, else it will be summer ere we arrive."

Mounting their steeds and following Kelk on his pony, westward into a dark passageway and away from the War Hall they rode.

Twisting through carven corridors and natural tunnels they went, their Dwarven lanterns lighting the path, down slopes here and up slopes there, Kelk leading them by ways along which there were no stairs for the steeds to manage. "I would not have them break a leg or become lame," said the Dwarf. "The path we follow is one which was delved for ponies and horse-drawn wains to travel: it spans from gate to gate."

Now and again they passed along crevasses left and right, and here Kelk cautioned them to tightly control the steeds, for some of the pits were without bottoms, or so Kelk did claim. Bottomless or no, for an animal to stumble into one would mark the end of the beast, to say nothing of the rider thereon.

At times riding, at other times walking and leading their steeds, and still at other times stopping at way stations to rest and water the animals and to relieve themselves, onward they went, while halls and corridors crossed and recrossed and joined and forked away from the passage they followed; millennia had gone into their delving, and had the five not been escorted, they would soon have been lost within the maze.

Occasionally, Bair peered at his gold-encased north-finder, and though it seemed to point steadily as more or less westerly they went, still Bair was turned about. Finally, in exasperation he put the lodestone needle away and did not look at it again that day. And as they took yet another rest, and the animals drank from a watering pool fed by underground streams, Bair asked, "How do you remember it all, Kelk? I mean, I'm entirely twisted around."

Kelk looked at the boy for a while, and it seemed he wouldn't answer. But at last he said, "I have been to the Dusken Door several times by this way, and we Châkka cannot lose our feet."

"Cannot lose your feet?"

This time Kelk didn't answer. And as the silence stretched out, at last Aravan said, *"Det nad ta a Châkka na, Sol Kelk."*

Kelk looked at Aravan in amazement. *"Da tak Châkur?"*

Aravan nodded and said, *"Ti."* And then he glanced at the others and then back to Kelk and said in Common, "I was taught by those in the Dwarven warbands who sailed with me on the *Eroean*."

Kelk nodded and then looked at Bair and said, "Lord Aravan is right; it is no Châkka secret, though it is not widely known: we Châkka cannot lose our footsteps, for wherever we travel by land, the path stays with us forever."

"What do you mean: stays with you forever?"

"I mean, we can retrace any path once trod, even were we blindfolded. And not only paths trod, but paths we travel by wagon or steed or by any other land-borne means. Only if we are unconscious or gravely ill when we go where we have not gone before, do we lose the way."

"Oh my, but what a precious gift," said Faeril. She turned to Aravan. "Does it work at sea?"

"No," said Aravan, even as Kelk said, *"Na."*

"What if you flew through the air like a bird?" asked Bair, fingering the crystal pendant at his neck.

The tawny-haired Dwarf laughed and shrugged his shoulders, but then said, "I know of no Châk who has flown like a bird, but I would think the answer is no; only on land and when of sound mind do we not lose our feet." Then he stood, saying, "The steeds have had water, and we must press on."

Onward they fared, stopping at what Aravan and Riatha both agreed was the time of the noontide, and no one questioned their call, for it was the gift of all Elvenkind to know at all times where stood the sun, stars, and moon, a gift Bair did not have. And as they rested they fed the animals a bit of grain, and they themselves took a meal: bread baked that day in Dwarven ovens, and some cold slices of roast left over from the twelve-day feast. Munching on apples and feeding the cores to the beasts, afoot they took up the trek again.

That night they rested in a chamber some halfway toward their goal. And there the stone through which they strode turned from red to black.

"Ahead lies Aggarath; behind is Rávenor," said Kelk, "the ones you name Grimspire and Stormhelm."

"In Sylva we call them Aevor and Coron," said Bair.

Kelk smiled. "The four Mountains of the Quadran are known by many names, those among them. But did you know another name given to Rávenor, to Stormhelm, to Coron, is The Hammer?"

Bair shook his head, *No*.

"It is because of the lightning which hammers his peak when storms abound."

Bair's eyes grew wide with the imagining of it, and he said, "Perhaps one day I will see such a storm."

A grim look came into Kelk's own eyes, and he studied the child's face and finally said, "Perhaps someday you will."

The next day they pressed onward, now travelling through granite of black, and still corridors and passages and tunnels joined and diverged and ran into darkness as generally southwestward they went, or so Bair's lodestone needle seemed to indicate. Up long slopes and down again did they fare, and as before they stopped at way stations along the route Kelk led them. And nowhere along the path they followed had they seen any other Dwarves, neither overtaking from behind, nor approaching from the fore.

"It is the winter," said Kelk, when asked, "and trade is light. Even so, we relax not our vigilance: the Dusken Door is well warded."

"But wait," said Faeril, looking at the way behind, "the whole of the Dwarvenholt just celebrated Winterfest; did the guard at the Dusk Door miss the feast? And if not, shouldn't some be heading back to stand ward there again?"

Kelk shook his head. "As with sentries everywhere, whether or no they miss a feast has nought to do with the duty; even so, the warders at the Dusken Door did not miss the Winterfest feast; they have their own well-stocked kitchens."

"Good," said Urus. "I could do with a hot meal."

"Me too, Da," said Bair. "Me too."

It was verging on sundown, or so Aravan said, when they came in among the chambers nigh the western portal. And they stabled the animals and watered and fed them and curried out the knots where halters and straps rubbed and where saddles and pack frames rode, and then they turned to take comfort of their own, beginning with a hot meal in the mess of the Dusken-Door Dwarves.

The next morning, following Kelk and dressed again in their cold-weather gear, the five led their horses and pony into the great West Hall and toward a massive iron gate standing shut against the far wall, where a Dwarven warband awaited.

"The gate glows with <light>, Ythir," whispered Bair.

Riatha smiled at her son. "Then it is a <light> thine eyes alone can see."

As they stopped before the portal, Kelk looked above, up past a loop of heavy iron chain dangling down from a geared mechanism overhead, up to a ledge where a sentry stood. The sentry peered through several small apertures and then called down, *"Droga wolna."*

"All clear," translated Aravan.

Kelk grunted and stepped to the barrier and placed his hand against one of the massive hinges. *"Gaard!"* he commanded, and slowly, silently, the great gate split in twain, an expanding vertical line of pale light showing where huge panels met. The Dwarves stood ready, weapons in hand, as outward the wide leaves swung into the dim winter morning, and a wintry wind swirled inward and 'round, bearing with it the sound of a nearby cascade.

The warband stepped through the open portal and into the chill beyond, into the dark mountain shadow, for the early-morning sun lay on the opposite side of the range.

Ere following the warband, Bair paused and looked at the great iron hinges. "The gate opens by word alone?"

"Only if a Châk bids it so," replied Kelk. "Else the chain needs be haled, the gears above to then engage and open or close the way. It is said the Dusken Door was crafted by Valki and enchanted by the Wizard Grevan, and Châk hand alone can open it with but a touch and a word."

Bair said, "I saw the <light> change, get brighter, when you said that word."

Kelk looked at Bair. "<Light>?"

"<Light> his eyes can see, but thine and mine cannot," said Riatha.

"Huah," grunted Kelk, then gestured toward the open way.

Leading their mounts and the four packhorses, out through the gate they went, out from the constant temperature of Kraggencor and into icy winter air, to find themselves under a great portico, itself on a broad semicircular plateau of rock, its sides falling sheer down into a wide moat arcing all 'round some thirty feet below. The moat itself was perhaps a hundred feet across, massive stonework making up its far edge. In spite of the portico roof, they could see the whole of that part of the outer mountain was a great hemidome of stone arching up and outward, the front edge a full quarter mile away, and it spanned more than a mile altogether from left to right. To their right along the back wall of the dome stood a great wooden drawbridge, its bascule now up, though the accompanying Dwarven warband had stepped to the winch to lower the way. The bridge spanned the moat and, just to the right of the bridge and below, a broad stream tumbled out from under the black granite of Grimspire to flow into the moat and fill it, and then spill over a formed lip in the stonework and plunge into the basin beyond, there to run in a stream and away toward a wide notch in the bowl-shaped land. Massive black-iron bars covered the crevice through which the stream tumbled out from the ebon mountain. Thin crusts of ice clung to the stone at the edges of the moat, but for the most part the rush of the flow and the shelter of the hemidome and the mass of the mountain kept the water of the moat from freezing.

Cranking the winch, the Dwarven warband lowered the wooden bascule to span the wide barrier. And as the deck lowered, the five led their steeds down a ramp from the portico to the plateau and toward the bridge, stopping just at the near end while the span sank toward the stone.

"Well then, my friend," said Aravan, as the bascule came to rest, "it is time we were on our way. *Châkka shok, Châkka cor,* Kelk."

"Shok Châkka amonu," replied the Dwarf.

And the five mounted up and rode across the bridge and followed a roadway along the back wall of the hemidome, until it curved down into the basin and then back up and out again. To their left they could see a tall spire, a carved stairway winding up and about, and atop it stood two Dwarven sentries, with a view of a cloven vale leading westward away from the mountain, the vale the only clear approach to the Dusken Door.

Now the road they followed came out from under the hemidome and descended a long switchback down the face of a high bluff to the floor of the valley below. And to the left the overflow water from the Dusk-Door moat streamed through the wide notch to cascade over a high linn and down, to tumble on stones at the base of the fall and then run in a streambed eastward. The road followed atop the north shore of the rill and along this way they went.

But Bair stopped long enough to turn and look back at Black Aggarath, and so did they all pause. Above the hemidome a great sheer massif of Grimspire rose vertically a goodly distance up toward the sky o'erhead.

And Aravan said, "They call that part of Aevor the Loom, and now I do see why."

Bair nodded and waved at the sentries on the spire and received a salute in return, then reined his palfrey west and *chrk*ed his tongue and rode onward, Urus faring alongside. Faeril took a deep breath and let it out and then turned to follow, with Riatha and Aravan coming after.

And they left Drimmen-deeve behind.

CHAPTER 13

Crossings

January, 5E1004

[Five Years Past]

Just ere the noontide, out from Ragad Vale they rode, did the five, out from the Valley of the Dusk Door to come to the Old Way, a trade route running from the western approaches to Crestan Pass in the north to the eastern side of the ford across the River Isleborne at the burned city of Luren in the south, the road running the full length of the land of Rell, a realm known as Lianion by the Elves. They turned northerly along this route, Riatha and Urus taking the lead, with Bair and Faeril coming next, and Aravan trailing all. The full of the afternoon they rode parallel to the great black flanks of Aggarath, the mountain seemingly right at hand, though the base of that dark loom was a goodly ten miles to the east. And when they made camp that eve, Aggarath yet towered over all.

The next day they passed Mount Redguard, where Vanadurin warriors—men of Valon—had sat watch upon Quadran Pass during the time of the War of Kraggen-cor, the Harlingar keeping ward on the gap to give warning should Foul Folk come marching down to fall upon the backs of the invading Dwarves, allies of the Vanadurin. This story did Riatha tell to Bair as they rode past the mount and came to where the Quadran Road split off the Old Way and led eastward up over the pass, a pass now blocked by snow. At this juncture the Old Way swung north-westerly, veering outward from the Quadran, though the travellers would ride for many miles ere they would escape the morning shadow of mighty Stormhelm.

On they rode and on, twenty or so miles a day, taking care to preserve their steeds for the long journey ahead. And in the early afternoon of the fourth day of travel, in a heavy snowfall, they came to the Red Ox, a small inn sitting in a gap in a spur of mounts and foothills reaching out from the Grimwalls to stand across the way.

They spent two days in the Red Ox, trading news, eating hot meals, and relaxing before the warm fire. They were the only guests at this time, for winter was not the best season for travel. And during their stay, at the lad's request and after much consideration, Aravan began teaching Bair Châkur, a difficult language to master at best, for it was a harsh and unforgiving tongue.

But the next day the storm had passed and, riding well-rested animals, onward they went, Bair and Aravan deep in locution. Northerly they fared across open land, the Old Way having swung northeasterly in a direction they were not bound, for the travellers were aiming for the Wilderland, lying west of north instead. The sun shone down and a warm wind came sweeping up from the south, and the relief it brought made it easier for the animals, especially Faeril's pony, the melt diminishing the snow.

Late on the following day they came to Rhone Ford, where they set camp.

The next morning they crossed over the frozen Tumble River and entered the land of Rhone. And now they turned northwesterly, aiming to cross the River Caire, were it frozen enough to bear the weight of their steeds; if not, they would follow along its banks all the way north to the Stone-arches Bridge and cross over there.

Within three days they came to the banks of the Caire, and across the frozen water they led pony and horses, the ice knelling under the hooves.

Now along the River Wilder, a tributary of the Caire, they went, and after six days of travel through the Wilderland they reached the Crossland Road nigh the mount known as Beacontor, the southernmost crest of the widely spaced tors of the Signal Mountains, which ran in an arc from Challerain Keep in the north to the Dellin Downs in the south. The only thing of note they encountered along the length of Wilder occurred the day before some twenty or so miles south of the Crossland Road, when on the eastern banks of the river they had come across a huge set of buhrstones all but buried in the land.

"A mill once sat here," had said Aravan.

"A mill?" asked Faeril.

Aravan pointed. "There lie the stones that ground the grain."

"I wonder what happened to it? —The mill, I mean," said Bair. "And who might it have belonged to?"

Aravan looked from Riatha to Urus and then to Faeril, each of them shrugging in turn.

"Some unknown miller," had replied Aravan, and onward they had ridden, setting camp a mile or so upstream as a light snow began to fall.

From Beacontor they rode westerly cross-country toward the distant eaves of the Weiunwood, and there along its marge they came to Orith and Nelda's small farm.

As they dismounted, a small brown dog came yapping, followed by a silver-haired man who stood in the doorway, peering through the twilight. And as Faeril rushed into his arms, the man called back into the house, "Nelda. Nelda. Hurry and see. Our Faeril has come to call."

"So this is the younker you went to see born," declared Nelda, holding Bair at arm length and looking upward into the lad's face. "And he is but ten?" She glanced at Urus and then back to Bair. "You must get it from your da, my boy, being so tall and all." She embraced Bair, but of a sudden her eyes flew wide and she stepped back and away. "Oh my, where are my manners?" She turned to Faeril. "Have you had aught to eat?" Nelda began rushing about the kitchen, poking up the fire. "I've a big pot of beans, and there's biscuits I could make. And tea. Oh yes, tea"— she set a kettle to boil—"and we've some root-cellar apples, and—"

"Mother Nelda," protested Faeril, "we don't—"

"Hush, child," said the woman, and she motioned at Bair. "This younker needs his vittles, growing as he is. Why, he looks to be half-starved. Orith, fetch more firewood." Then Nelda turned to Aravan and Urus. "Well, don't just stand there like a couple of shiftless idlers. Take care of your horses and the pony. We've a byre out back for their housing. I'll call you when supper's ready. You, too, boy: scat." As the males meekly shuffled out, Nelda paused, pondering. "We've only three beds, and there are five of you and . . ."

Leaving Faeril behind to visit with her Human "in-laws"—for they had raised Gwylly, though buccan he was, and Gwylly had been Faeril's mate—Riatha, Urus, Bair, and Aravan rode away westerly the next day as a snow began to fall. In spite of Orith's cautions—"There's *things* in there, things in the *closed places*, Hidden Ones better left alone"—they were going to explore for themselves the forest known as the Weiunwood.

As Orith's small brown dog ran in circles and yapped excitedly at the departing strangers, the animal pausing now and then to leap and snap at a drifting snowflake, Orith watched the four ride away, a worried frown on his lined face. "They know about the Hidden Ones, Dad Orith," Faeril said, "but fear not. They said they'd be back on the morrow." Then Faeril turned and caught up the excited dog, the damman laughing as she fended off a licking tongue. "I take it that you got this one when Black passed on, eh? What's his name?"

Distracted, watching the four ride away into who-knows-what-perils in the Weiunwood, "What?" asked Orith.

"This little brown dog, what is his name?"

"Brown," replied Orith sagely, looking to the west again.

Through the swirling snow the four rode under the eaves of the Weiunwood, that shaggy forest in the Wilderland north of Harth and south of Rian . . . Weiunwood, stark in its winter dress. Among the barren trees they rode, and still the snow eddied down. Picking their way through the woods, they came in among a stand of ancient oaks, and rode on through to pass into a wide glade and across and into another stand. And Riatha marvelled as they passed among the hoary trees of old Weiunwood, saying that it seemed nigh as aged as the Skög, a forest from the dawn of time. Onward they went, following a trail none could see, and yet now and again, shadows slipped among the trees wide along their flanks.

"Their <light>, their <life> is the same as those who followed us in Darda Erynian," said Bair, gesturing toward their elusive escort.

Aravan touched the blue stone on a thong about his neck. "I sense no peril, and this stone marks me as a Friend."

And onward they rode, stopping now and again to measure the girth of some of the massive oaks, the greatest they had ever seen.

"Come the season, I would think there'd be truffles here," said Aravan.

"E'en were this that season," rumbled Urus, "I think we'd best leave them for the denizens herein. —And don't give me that hungry look, Bair."

Riatha burst out laughing at the moue Bair made in return.

And onward they rode, the snow-covered loam soft to the horses' hooves as they made their way past yew and pine and maple and alder, past ash and cedar and wild cherry, past silver birch and dogwood and larch and laurel and tamarack and many others, some of which they could not name.

As evening drew nigh, they made camp in a small clearing near a broad stand of oak.

"Gather wood, lad," said Urus, "while I unlade the horses and your ythir and kelan set camp."

"Take only the deadwood, arran," cautioned Riatha.

Bair sighed and said, "I know," and set off into the oaks, taking up fallen branches along the way.

As the very onset of twilight began, in among the trees he went, gathering that which the wind had harvested and shaking it clear of snow. Soon he had an armful of branches. *Just one more billet, and then I'll turn back.* Onward he went.

But then . . .

. . . at his breast . . .

. . . a strange tingling began.

Dropping the wood aclatter to the white-laden ground, Bair placed a hand to his chest.

What is it?

Fumbling inside his down jacket his hand encountered—

The crystal? The ring?

Bair hauled out both the crystal and stone ring on their platinum chains about his neck.

The ring: its <light> has changed. Become brighter.

He gripped the stone and felt as if he were being drawn somewhere . . .

But where?

This way, something seemed to whisper.

Should I get my parents and Kelan Aravan? Or should I go just a bit farther first?

Following the tug of the ring, Bair went deeper in among the oaks.

Just a little farther.

And still Bair followed.

And he stepped into a small, snow-covered clearing, oak trees encircling all 'round, and there the stone ring on its platinum chain flared brightly and then began pulsing with a <fire> only Bair's eyes could see.

He peered at the jet stone on the ring and then up at the circle of oak—

What is this place? What is it for? What causes the ring to sing?

—and of a sudden in a rush of excitement he remembered the puzzling words of a scroll he had read one day in his studies, a scroll he had inadvertently come across in the archives almost a year agone now; a reference therein had made little sense then, but now in a burst of delayed illumination, he knew what it was he must try.

It did not occur to him that he should seek the counsel of his da, his ythir, his kelan, or even his absent amicula. No. He simply had to try. And even though it was not the turn of a season—not Springday, Summerday, Autumnday, nor Winterday—still, gripping the stone ring tightly in his left hand, he began the chant, the cant, and the step and glide and pause of the ancient Elven rite.

Bair's voice rose and fell, intoning the canto, the plainchant, the hymn, neither singing nor speaking, but something in between, his mind lost in the ritual, neither wholly conscious nor unconscious, but something in between. And moving in concert with the words, he stepped, glided, and paused, the gait arcane, neither dancing nor walking, but something in between.

And he moved about the tiny, oak-encircled glade, neither a field nor a forest, but something in between, stepping the steps in yielding snow, the footing neither solid nor fluid but something in between. And there in the twilight—a time which is neither day nor night, but something in between—Bair's voice became soft and then faint and then no more . . .

. . . for he was gone from Mithgar . . .

. . . for he was gone between.

Frowning, Riatha looked about and said, "Bair should have been back by now." She turned to Urus to see him step toward his goods lying on a tarpaulin in the snow, where he took up his black-iron morning star from its saddle cantle hook.

As Aravan glanced up from the new-set fire-ring of stones, Riatha began harnessing Dúnamis in its green scabbard across her back, the jade handle at her right shoulder. She drew the dark-silveron blade, even as Aravan stood, Krystallopŷr now in hand.

And weapons ready, in among the trees they swiftly went, following the lad's meandering tracks in the snow.

Soon they came to a scatter of deadwood. "Oh, Urus, the Rûpt," said Riatha, "do you think—?"

"There are no other tracks," growled the Baeron, scanning the snow, then looking into the branches above.

"And he is not running," said Aravan, somewhat ahead. "He walks instead, now in a straight line, or as straight as the trees permit."

"He is not shifted?" asked Riatha.

"No," replied Aravan, even as Urus began following the track.

Onward they urgently pressed, and within a hundred paces or so they came into a small glade, oak trees ringing 'round.

"Look. His tracks. They end," rumbled Urus, staring at the jumble of churned up snow. The Baeron's eyes swept back and forth. "He entered yet did not exit. —Unless . . . !" Urus gazed upward, scanning the skies, though little could be seen through the falling snow.

But Aravan, too, studied the trace of Bair's steps, and of a sudden his head jerked up and he turned about, gazing at the oaks. "Jaian, he stepped out the rite, and this is a crossing point."

Shock filled Riatha's face, and then dismay, and she slumped to the snow, her eyes filling with tears. Urus knelt beside her and took her in his embrace, but he looked at Aravan. "A crossing point to where?" Urus's voice fell to a whisper. "To Neddra?"

Aravan shook his head. "I think not, not to Neddra. Although I've not seen it before, I have heard of a crossing in the Weiun-wood, a crossing ringed about by oaks as is this. And if indeed this is that crossing, then it leads unto Adonar upon the High Plane."

Urus relaxed. "Good. Then he will soon cross back."

Her face stained by tears, Riatha gazed up at Urus. "Not immediately, chier, and mayhap not ever."

Now Urus's eyes widened in shock. "What do you—?"

Riatha stroked Urus's cheek. "There is an ancient benediction among Elves upon Mithgar: Go upon the twilight, return upon the dawn. Journeys unto Adonar can only be made at dusk, whereas travel to Mithgar must be made upon the dawn."

Urus looked about as the last shadowy glimmers of the wan daylight disappeared and the full of the nighttide swept over the land. "Then we will wait for dawn," he said, "for surely he will then come."

"Only if he knows when to do it," said Riatha, "and then only if Dalavar Wolfmage is right and he does indeed have the blood of this Plane to bring him back. Oh, chier, we should have told him. We should have told him of the rite and the crossings and the dangers therein, even though he is so young." Riatha burst into tears.

"Hush, my love," whispered Urus, holding her tightly, "and trust in the merit of our son."

Stepping and chanting, then pausing, then turning, of a sudden Bair saw that he was standing in a pristine field of undisturbed snow, the air clear, a few faint stars overhead, a crescent moon hanging low in the west, and lo! a smaller bright crescent was cupped in the arms of the larger, as if the moon had a daughter of its own. But Bair did not note this, as, still gripping the stone ring tightly, he fell silent, stopped his intricate gait, and looked about. He was in a small, circular, snow-laden glade with oaks ringing all 'round.

I was right.

Just as the scroll had said, the steps and chant of the Elven rite were key to going in-between.

But in-between where and where? Where am I now?

He looked about at the ring of oaks, fair matched unto the one on Mithgar, as the anchoring points for crossing the in-between needed to be, else no journey could be made. And the better the match, the easier the steps between. Yet with but rare exception, always would the chant be needed and the ritual steps be necessary, for perfect matches from Plane to Plane are uncommon and scattered, and for the most part unknown. And so, Bair's journey followed the traditional rite, the arcane chant and precise movements driving his set of mind to that deep state necessary to make the transition, to go between . . .

. . . or so had said the scroll.

And he had come unto a place he knew not.

Even though it was still dusk—the in-between time—had he desired to immediately return unto Mithgar from here, he could not have . . . or so did wisdom say.

But the problem of returning was not on his mind as he stood in the elsewhere twilight. Instead, he looked about at the winter-dressed oaks and the growing number of stars above, his eye spotting familiar constellations just beginning to appear, while here and there small animals slipped furtively athwart the snow-laden land.

Where have I gotten to? What is this place?

Bair walked across the small clearing and past the wooded ring of oaks. And out beyond that circle things were the same and yet not.

This is not the Weiunwood, but something alike.

He stood and drank in the air and light and silence and sights of the forest and of the sky above, finding all new yet familiar. And he was excited and apprehensive and filled with the elation of accomplishment, as well as the guilt for having done so without permission, perhaps a foolish risk he shouldn't have ventured.

What did the scroll say? Ah yes, I remember: Go forth upon the twilight, return upon the dawn.

He wondered if he should continue outward and truly explore, but decided against it. After all, he knew not where he was, and this could be Neddra on the Lower Plane, where Foul Folk dwelled.

No. I'll just wait here until the dawntime. Then I'll cross back over. And if there are Rûpt and such about . . .

He stepped back into the Ring of Oaks and walked to the center and concentrated upon his truename. A dark shimmering came over him, and a Silver Wolf, a stone ring and a crystal pendant on platinum chains about its neck, curled up in the snow to wait for the coming of light.

At the verge of the glade just outside the oak ring they waited; a track was worn in the snow where Riatha had paced the night. Aravan sat with his back to a tree, his spear in hand. Urus stood with his head bowed, yet whether he prayed to Adon, neither Riatha nor Aravan knew. It had stopped snowing just after mid of night, and the clouds had slowly migrated eastward, and now glimmering stars shone above. In the east the sky was washed with pale light: dawn was on its way.

And then just at the edge of hearing, a soft whisper drifted on the air. Riatha stopped her pacing. Urus's head snapped up. Aravan stood.

In the new-fallen snow in the center of the tiny glade a dim figure began to appear, moving in an arcane pattern, and the whisper became a murmur, a mumble, a mutter, a chant. Pacing, chanting, pausing, canting, turning, gliding—

—of a sudden, there stood Bair—

—in the glade, in the dawn, in the in-between time.

Tears running down her face, Riatha stood in the heart of the glade, Bair in her embrace, the Dara silent, just holding her arran tightly.

Tentatively, the lad returned her hug, and she pulled him against her all the more fiercely.

"What is it, Ythir?" asked Bair.

"Oh, Bair," she whispered, "we could have lost thee forever."

"Lost me?"

Riatha pushed back from her son, holding him at arm length. "There was no guarantee thou couldst return—"

"But Ythir, the scroll said—"

"Scroll? What scroll?"

"The one in the archives. The one about the rite of the turning of the seasons being used to cross the in-between."

"Oh, Bair, dost thou not realize the peril?"

"Peril?"

Riatha gestured about. "Thou didst not know where this crossing led. Thou couldst have stepped to Neddra."

"I don't know whether it was Neddra, Ythir."

"Bair, Neddra or elsewhere, it matters not. It could have been a place where peril silent or cunningly innocent or roaring in rage could fall upon thee in but moments, and thou didst spend a full night there."

"But I didn't, Ythir."

"Didn't what?"

"I didn't spend the night." At Riatha's frown, Bair added: "It was Hunter who spent the night, and peril could not come upon him unnoted, but would in fact yield him wide berth."

"Hunter?"

"Hunter: the Seeker and Searcher Who Is One of Us but Not of Us. The Draega, Ythir. The Silver Wolf I become. *He* is the one who spent the ni—"

"Bair!" snapped Riatha, and then more softly said, "Thy sire and I are sorely disappointed in thee . . . not for crossing the in-between, but because thou didst give so little thought to such a perilous undertaking as well as thy complete disregard as to what that crossing might mean."

Bair looked again to the dawn-shadowed brim of the glade, where his father had seemed to be weeping just moments before, his father who now stood with his great arms folded across his chest, the set of his stance one of ire. Behind Urus, Aravan looked at Bair and shook his head and then spun on his heel and strode away, his hard steps carrying him in the direction of their unused campsite of the eve before.

They rode in silence for most of the day, but at last Aravan asked, "How didst thou know 'twas an in-between crossing?"

Bair heaved a sigh of relief; *finally* someone had spoken to him. "I didn't, kelan. I just know the stone ring drew me there, and I guessed what it might mean."

Aravan looked at the ring on its platinum chain riding alongside the crystal pendant at Bair's chest. Then the Alor touched the blue stone at his own neck and murmured, "Wild magic."

Bair waited, but Aravan said no more, and onward they rode.

"Then it's true," said Faeril, peeling apples in Nelda's kitchen.

Riatha looked at her and cocked an eyebrow, the Dara kneading flour dough.

"That Bair truly is the Rider of the Planes," explained the damman. "I had been hoping Dalavar Wolfmage would prove to be wrong."

Tears formed in Riatha's silver eyes and broke free to run down her cheeks and fall glimmering into the dough. "So was I, Faeril. So was I. But it seems all along he was right."

CHAPTER 14

Discovery

Summer, 5E1003–Summer, 5E1005

[Six to Four Years Past]

Long did Ydral search for the jade-green, melon-sized, egglike stone the one-handed fisherman had spoken of, yet if it were still in the palace, its hiding place remained secure. Furious in his quest, the yellow-eyed man had had every nook and cranny, every cabinet and stand, every vault and chest and wall and floor in the palace thoroughly searched, thoroughly examined, and several secret panels and compartments were found, but none contained the stone.

Enraged, Ydral then had the palace grounds searched, the earth turned, diggers looking for a burial place; even the koi ponds were drained and excavated. And still nought was found but an ancient mummy enwrapped in golden silks, pearls and jewels bedecking the long-dead corpse, within a jade-covered sarcophagus the diggers had discovered buried in a garden grove. Ydral seethed at the find, for it held not the egglike stone he sought.

All of the former servants and slaves had been questioned, some to the death, with only incognizance forthcoming.

Failing to find the stone at the palace, every place the old emperor had ever visited was thoroughly searched as well, to no avail.

And Ydral in his tower had sacrificed many a slave, to his trembling ecstasy, yet his purpose wasn't merely pleasure, but instead to raise the dead, to raise the one just so murdered, for the dead could see many things in the world hidden from those alive.

And he asked them to speak of the whereabouts of the stone, yet that token of power not only proved to be unscryable to Wizards, but verily unto the dead as well, and they knew not of its place. And of the emperor who had hidden it: his beheaded corpse was unavailable to raise, for after the body had dangled from the walls of the palace for a year while the head rotted on a pike, the remains had finally been cast into the great River Kang to drift out and wander forever in the depths of the cold, dark sea.

Hence, from the dead nought whatsoever was learned of the glowing green stone, and with bludgeon and axe Ydral vented his wrath upon the corpses of those he had slain.

Yet as always, as he had done many times in the past, both before and after joining the Mokoans with their Dragon-marked boy, he did ask the dead if the Elf with the crystal-bladed spear drew nigh, and once again found he was far away.

In the dark of night, as Ydral sat on the emperor's throne in the dimly lit hall of state, contemplating in rage the fruitless search of the past year, a young female slave pushing a cart entered the hall, the girl approaching the dais, her eyes downcast. Ydral stood and stepped into the shadows of golden silk draping down from the canopy above and waited in darkness, eyeing the girl, considering just how he would proceed.

She wheeled her cart to the edge of the dais, and Ydral sank farther back into the dark, a long, thin-bladed knife now in hand, his yellow eyes glittering, his breathing a bit more rapid.

She took out a soft cloth from within the cart and began polishing the white-marble stone, carefully laying back the edge of the red and golden rug on which the gilded and bejewelled Dragonthrone sat along with its padded footrest. Ydral watched, anticipating his moves, anticipating her terror, anticipating fulfilling his need, as she shifted about on hands and knees. She stopped a moment and frowned, and the yellow-eyed man thought he might have been sensed prematurely. But no, instead she backed away from the throne long enough to fetch a tiny bristle-brush. And she began gently whisking at something on the marble stone. Ordinarily, Ydral would have paid the girl's ministrations little heed, yet something peculiar about her motion caught his eye, for she brushed in an undeviating course, as if following a narrow, straight line.

Ydral's yellow eyes widened and, knife in hand, he stepped forward from the darkness. The girl screamed in terror, and scrambled back and away and down from the dais, and cowed, her hands covering her face, her forehead against the floor.

But Ydral paid her no heed, and instead examined the stone she had brushed. A line so thin as to be nearly invisible ran straight along the flawless marble, and he stooped and touched it with his finger; it was a line of fine dust. But why would it run so straight? His eyes widening, Ydral dragged one of his clawlike talons across the line, and as the talon passed athwart the dust a nearly imperceptible *tkk* sounded, a *tkk* his talon felt: the dust lay in a hair-thin groove.

Excitedly, Ydral set his knife aside and moved about the throne, laying the rug back, following the almost invisible line. It went all the way about.

With the girl yet trembling in obeisance, Ydral stood and examined the chair of state, and after but a short moment, he found that with a twist of an armpost he could free the padded armrest. And when he swung the armrest up, from somewhere under the throne there came a soft *clk*. With effort, Ydral could then lay the chair back, a section of marble directly under the throne and attached thereto swiveling up as well.

From the inside of the discovered vault there came a soft green glow. And amid gems and jewels and golden coins lay an oblate spheroid of jadelike stone.

No one commented on the disappearance of a simple cleaning slave; after all, she was but a girl, and such things seemed to happen quite often in the new emperor's court.

And no one commented on the screams emanating from the court Wizard's tower, or the effluvium of death drifting down, for surely the realm was made stronger by his arcane divinations.

For nearly two years in secret did Ydral seek a way to unlock the mystery of the jadelike spheroid, for he knew it represented great power, and he would master the stone. Yet it defied him in all ways, no matter how many spells cast, no matter how many slaves slaughtered to increase his own power to bear against the stone. And he raged impotently, and cast impotent spells, and slaughtered nearly a thousand slaves seeking to gain command. For this was the stone the Dragons feared; this was the stone they bore to the Wizards of Black Mountain to guard, making an unthinkable pact in return; this was the stone which Durlok had destroyed an entire island to set free.

This was the Dragonstone.

Nearly two years passed in futility, until one moonless night . . .

"I was strolling by, Ydral, and I thought I would see my Wizard and discover why it is he has cost me so many slaves." Ignoring the scent of spilled blood, Kutsen Yong gazed about Ydral's sanctum, disinterest in his eyes, for in spite of his studies in years gone by it seemed the Mighty Dragon had had no talent whatsoever for things of a Wizardly bent. "Not that I mind, Ydral, for slaves are easily obtained. But still some think you are a"— Kutsen Yong shivered—"a *Taeji Akma*." Even though he was a man of twenty-two, still Kutsen Yong could not dispel the hideous tales of the Taeji Akma come to drag him down into the endless fires at the center of the world to scream in agony forever, tales hissed to him as a child in the night by Old Tal as a way to make him behave. In return, he'd had Old Tal strangled. But even so, the very thought of the Taeji Akma sent shudders up his spine. To cover his discomfiture, he took up an astrolabe and idly gazed at its markings while randomly sliding the pointer about.

Ydral cast Kutsen Yong a sidelong glance and stepped across the chamber to draw the man's gaze away from the hastily closed small casket holding the stone. "Mai lord, Jai am seeking divinations which will increase aun power, for Jai would make tji Ruler of All."

Setting the astrolabe down among scrolls, Kutsen Yong looked at Ydral and said, "But I *will* be the Ruler of All, for my destiny is plain for even the gods to see." He touched his forehead, his fingers tracing the Dragonmark over and back and down around his neck. "I am the *Yong Chuin*. Even now more warriors flock to my banner, and soon we will set forth to assail Ryodo again"—an enraged look swept over the emperor's face—"and this time we will conquer."

"Yes, mai lord," whispered Ydral.

"You will cast me an augury before we set sail, Ydral, and this time I would have no storms," spat Kutsen Yong.

Ydral bowed. "Indeed, mai lord."

Seemingly mollified, the young man idly turned a few pages of a tome, seeking illustrations, finding none, the arcane words in a tongue he did not know.

"I would also have from you a spell assuring my enemies suffer great pain."

"Indeed, mai lord."

Kutsen Yong turned to leave, but just as he reached the door, he stepped back to say, "Ydral, perhaps it is virgins you need." He casually laid a hand on the cloth-covered casket and slid aside the silk. "You told me yourself they increase the potency of spells."

Without purpose Kutsen Yong opened the lid—

—"Mai lord," said Ydral stepping forward—

—and looked within—

—"the stone was recently found"—

—and reached inside—

—"and Jai would see to aun safety"—

—and grasped the spheroid and took it up—

—As if awaiting the touch of this warrior king, this Kutsen Yong, this man of the Dragonmark, this Masula Yongsa Wang, intense light burst outward from the stone, engulfing the Wizard's sanctum, blasting through window slits to blare across the sky, fierce beams burning with a furious green brilliance like that of blazing witchfire.

And in that same moment, all across Mithgar, Dragons raised their heads in alarm.

CHAPTER 15

Tocsin

Summer, 5E1005

[Four Years Past]

An aethyric blast knelled through the world, and Mages within Black Mountain looked at one another in consternation, each wondering what had caused such a ripple in the aethyr. The Seers cast their spells to identify the source, but even the mightiest of the diviners failed. Only once before, millennia past, had they been so completely thwarted, and that was when trying to augur the whereabouts of the arcane Dragonstone, the Green Stone of Xian, a token of power gone missing, whether lost or stolen no one in Black Mountain knew, for the 'Stone itself defied scrying. Centuries upon centuries passed, yet at last the jadelike token had been recovered, though not by any of Magekind. Again it was given over to the Wizards for safekeeping, though not the ones under Black Mountain, but the ones on Rwn instead. And then Rwn was drowned deep under the sea, and with it the Dragonstone plunged down to the depths as well. Hence, even though Magekind could not identify the source of this present aethyric blast, surely the 'Stone could not be involved . . .

. . . or so the Mages did believe.

In isolated towers elsewhere across Mithgar likewise did Black Mages sense the pulse, and there were those among them who then began plotting the death of a prophesied youth.

*   *   *

And deep in the cooling lava below Dragonslair as the aethyric wave knelled, a silveron artifact flared once with a brightness, a stroke seen by gemstone eyes. And the great beings knew the time of the prophecy drew nigh.

CHAPTER 16

Priming

October, 5E1004–September, 5E1005

[Five and Four Years Past]

*T*ck-tak-clk-clat-clttr . . . Bair retreated before Riatha's running flèche, his wooden sword barely able to fend the quick striking of hers. But then she paused momentarily, inviting him to attempt the maneuver in return. And forward he rapidly sprang again and again, always driving off his rear foot, stomping and pressing her back and back. Yet of a sudden with nought but a flick of her wrist she disarmed him entirely.

Panting, he looked in amazement at his empty hand, and then at the sword yet spinning through the air, the weapon striking ground and gyring about on the edge of its guard before coming to a lazy, rolling rest.

"Thou didst let thy grip become too lax, arran," she said. "Recall what I said concerning the manner of clasping the sword—"

"Aye, Ythir, I do: grip the weapon as if it were a live bird: loose enough to keep from killing it; tight enough to prevent its escape."

"Aye, for looseness lends dexterity, tightness strength, a critical balance to be achieved. Thou didst try for too much nimbleness and thereby lost thy blade." She pointed at his sword with hers. "Thy little bird did fly away."

The eleven-year-old boy picked up his slender wooden weapon, nought but a long, slim rod, with a metal cup to guard the hand, a wire-wrapped hilt to grip, and a light pommel for balance. "I seem to do better with a heavier blade—a rapier, a saber, a falchion, and such—than I do with this weightless twig."

Riatha laughed. "Aye, those and a morning star like thy sire's to bludgeon with, my Bair, yet this is the best blade to teach finesse. Remember, arran, with many a blade, quickness beats strength every time."

"But, Ythir, you always told me cunning and guile will out."

"Only if thou hast had the time and wit to bring cunning and guile to bear, for at moments there is only an instant to react to an unforeseen threat, and then it is when thy weapon needs to be agile and strong, no matter what thou dost wield."

Bair pointed at the weapons rack. "From a morning star like my sire's to a sword like your Dúnamis."

Riatha nodded. "Everything in between as well as those beyond."

"Such as this twig," said Bair.

"That, too," agreed Riatha, and then without warning she attacked.

To add to Bair's bow and sling skills, they had begun his training in other weapons right after returning from the Wilderland. Riatha became his sword-mentor, to teach him a variety of styles matched to a variety of blades; Urus took up his training in axes and maces and flails and morning stars; Aravan took him in hand to add spear and lance and stave skills; and Faeril would teach him the skill of throwing knives. They did not expect him to become expert in all of this weaponry; rather they would have him not be at a loss should unexpected peril come upon him and should he have to fend with whatever might be at hand.

"The day will come when you will choose a particular weapon or two to bear at your side," said Urus, hefting his black-iron morning star, "but for now we will train you in several, such that when you do choose, you will do so from wide knowledge rather than ignorance raw."

Bair nodded, and then asked, "Da, can I become a master in each and every one?"

Urus cocked an eyebrow. "I have not lived long enough to answer that question. Speak to your mother. Mayhap she knows someone who has mastered all. Tillaron Ironstalker, Inarion, Flandrena, Aravan: all have splendid skill of arms, though they each do bear but a weapon or two."

"What about Ythir? Ancinda Soletree? Elissan? Other Darai? Do they not have such skills?"

Urus glanced at the morning star in his hand and smiled. "The Darai are indeed quite skilled in their weapons of choice—rapiers, bows, lances, and the like—for they have grace and finesse and quickness, all needed for such. But with a battle-axe, a mace, a morning star, a two-handed sword, any weapon needing strength for its heft and wielding, Darai are at a disadvantage."

"Ah, I see," said Bair.

Urus stood and looked down at his son. "Shield up, boy, 'tis time we began anew."

As they retrieved the throwing blades from the silhouette of one of the Foul Folk—a Hlôk-shaped, soft wooden target—Faeril said, "That was quite a throw, Bair. Did you mean to hit him in the knee?"

Bair laughed. "No, amicula, I was aiming for his heart."

"Well this one came a bit closer," replied the damman, pulling a blade from the left ear of the silhouette.

"Perhaps if I use my sling I could do better," said Bair.

"Perhaps," said Faeril, slipping the blade into its bandolier sheath. And then she paused, her gaze going soft in remembrance. "Ah, were Gwylly here, he could improve your sling skills. He was the best, you know."

"So I have heard," said Bair. "Ythir and Da and Kelan Aravan all say it was so."

As they walked back to the place of casting, Bair asked, "Do all Warrows use missile weapons? Bows, slings, things thrown?"

Faeril grinned up at the gangly boy. "Did you not read of the Deevewalkers?"

"Not yet," replied Bair. "But I will. I promise. Other things keep getting in the way."

Faeril shrugged. "Well, then, I'll tell you this: the Warrow Tuckerby Underbank used a sword in the Winter War, though his weapon of choice was the bow."

"Sword?" asked Bair. "It must have been specially made to fit one of your Kind."

Faeril grinned. "According to *The Ravenbook*, it was Bane, an Elven long-knife, given to him by Gildor . . . but a long-knife to an Elf is a sword to a Warrow." Faeril stopped at a line scratched in the dirt.

"Had he been trained in swordplay?" asked Bair.

Faeril shook her head. "No, Tuckerby wasn't trained, but when he did use the blade, he was most effective. On the other hand, Peregrin Fairhill and Cotton Buckleburr—Warrows in the Battle of Kraggen-cor—they were trained at swords, though I believe those two would have been better off with these"—Faeril touched her crossed bandoliers filled with knives—"or a sling or a bow. You see, even though we Warrows are quite quick, we are simply too small to go blade to blade against larger foes. Tuck and Cotton fought mostly Rûcks, an enemy nearer our size, though a hand or three taller still." Faeril drew a knife and flipped it in the air by its blade and caught it by blade again. "Missile weapons are our choice in the main—bows, slings, knives, and such, even rocks. Rarely do we select another, because we are of limited stature."

"Small in stature," said Bair, looking down at Faeril, "but large of heart."

Faeril grinned, then handed Bair the knife. "This time, my lad, try to hit something vulnerable."

Frowning, Bair hefted the blade and then took a step forward and planted and threw. The knife turned over and again, and struck the silhouette pommel-first in the groin. As Bair winced and sucked air in between his teeth, Faeril fell down to the ground laughing.

" 'Tis known as one of the great weapons," said Aravan, flourishing Krystallopŷr. "Thou canst stab with it—*hai!*—or use its blade as a cutting weapon—*uwah!*—nigh as well as a sword, though I must admit it has a long helve for such. Even so, the length of the haft extends thy reach—giving thee an advantage—yet if a foe gets inside"—he slapped the long-knife strapped to his thigh—" 'tis best to have one of these at hand. But stabbing and cutting are not the only ways to use the spear, for thou canst wield it in place of a quarterstaff—*an e dwa!*—or as a lance ahorse—*cha!* Lastly, thou canst cast it at a foe"—Aravan hurled the weapon and spitted a shock of hay—"yet I would not advise flinging any weapon away except if no other choice presents itself."

Bair frowned. "So, but for missile weapons—throwing axes, knives, sling bullets, and the like—it is best to not cast any weapon?"

"Only at desperate need, thus," replied Aravan. He whirled about and snatched up a sword from the weapons rack and, as he had done countless times on countless practice fields, he spun and hurled it at the rick, the weapon to slam blade-first to the hilt next to the embedded spear.

As Bair's mouth formed an *O* of surprise, Aravan said, "Someday I will teach thee that trick."

Nearly twelve, Bair sat on the ground facing Tillaron Ironstalker, the green-eyed, compact Lian one of his armsmasters of late. The Alor brushed back a stray lock of his honey-gold hair and said, "Tell me of the Rûpt."

Bair frowned, then said, "Which one?"

"Any and all."

"Well I only know what I've read in the archive."

"That will do."

Bair took a deep breath and, as if reciting schoolwork, said, "Um, the Rûck: taller than Warrows by three or four hands, night-dark he is, with skinny arms and bandy legs and batwing ears and the eyes of a viper: yellow and slitty. Wide-mouthed he is, with wide-gapped, pointed teeth."

Bair paused, and Tillaron asked, "Tell me of the Rucha's weapons skills."

"For the most they fight with cudgels and hammers—smashing weapons—though some use bows and black-shafted arrows, at times coated with poison. Yet their main strength is in their very numbers, for they swarm upon an opponent as do locusts swarm upon a field, or so say the scrolls."

"Well and good," said Tillaron. "Now let us speak of the Loka."

Bair nodded. "Hlôks: like Rûcks but taller and straighter of limb, man-sized in height. Their weapon skills are greater than those of the Rûck, and Hlôks usually bear scimitars and maces, though they are skilled in other weapons as well."

Tillaron nodded and gestured toward Ancinda Soletree, her hair honey-gold like that of her pledgemate, though a bit lighter of cast. The hue of her eyes stood somewhere between blue and violet, one a trace darker than the other. "She will play the part of the Ruch and the Lok when time comes to teach thee combat against those two Rûpt. I will play the part of a Ghûlk, and so tell me of that foe."

Bair smiled at Ancinda and received a like grin in return, and then the lad looked at Tillaron. "The Ghûl is deadly, known by some as the corpse-foe, for he takes dreadful wounds without hurt. Dead white he is, and man-size, and rides a mount known as a Hèlsteed, a steed like a horse but not. The Ghûls use cruelly barbed spears as lances, and saberlike tulwars should they need a sword."

Tillaron nodded. "How can they be slain?"

Bair took a deep breath. "Wood through the heart—a stake or spear or arrow or such. Beheading. Fire. Dismemberment. A silver sword. A special weapon, such as Ythir's Dúnamis or Kelan Aravan's spear." Bair glanced at Riatha and Urus and Aravan sitting nearby and listening to his recitation. Ancinda Soletree was gone.

"Is that all one needs to be concerned with when in combat with a Ghûlk?" asked Tillaron.

Bair shrugged. "I can think of nothing else."

Tillaron sighed. "Didst thou forget the Hèlsteed?"

Bair smacked himself in the forehead. "Oh, right. The Hèlsteed. Like a horse but not a horse. Cloven-hoofed. Scaled whip-like tails. Yellow eyes with slitted pupils. A terrible stench. Slower than horses but with greater endurance. The hooves can cut like hard-driven axes, and the tail is a deadly lash. The teeth are sharp, the bite foul, causing flesh-rot if not treated."

Tillaron nodded and said, "Many a good person has been felled for not being wary of the 'Steed, thinking it nought but a horse when it is anything but."

"Wary will I be, Ironstalker, should I meet up with such. —Oh, there is this about the Foul Folk as well: all of them use other weapons—whips, knives, strangling cords, scythes, flails, more—but the scrolls say they usually wield those I named first."

"Indeed, Bair. And forget not that just as the arrows might be poisoned, so might the other weapons bear venom as well."

Bair nodded and said, "The scrolls say that one can die days later from even the slightest of wounds from these."

"Just so," affirmed Tillaron. "Yet we are not here to speak of poisoned blades only, but to talk of the Rûpt, and there are other Spaunen thou hast not yet named, the Troll for one."

Again Bair took a deep breath and blew it out. "The Ogru is like a giant Rûck, twice as tall as a man. They have stonelike hides and enormous strength. They use great warbars, smashing aside whatever gets in their way. They have few weaknesses, but can be slain by a stab through the eye, groin, mouth, or"—Bair looked at Aravan—"or ear. Also, they have bones like stones and cannot swim at all; they sink like rocks and will drown in any water deep enough. Too, they can die from a high fall, or be killed by a large enough rock dropped upon them from a sufficient height. The soles of their feet are another weakness, caltrops are especially effective. Fire, too. —Oh, and this: *all* Foul Folk—Ogrus, Rûcks, Hlôks, Ghûls, Hèlsteeds, Vulgs—all will suffer the Withering Death if they step into Adon's light, the light of the sun. It turns them to ashes."

"I wondered if thou wouldst remember the Ban," said Tillaron. "Rather than face them directly, especially the Trolls and other Fell Beasts, *Draedani* and Cold-drakes among the latter, 'tis best to try to lure Foul Folk into the sunlight, or delay them from reaching sanctuary ere the night is done. Recall, lad, wit is ofttimes a better weapon than any cold iron or steel."

"Cunning and guile will out, eh?" asked Bair, glancing at his mother.

"Cunning and guile indeed," replied Tillaron. "Yet thou didst mention another foe: the Vulg."

Bair nodded. "Like a great dark Wolf, but not a Wolf. Ponysized. Has a virulent, poison bite. Usually runs in packs."

"And how wouldst thou combat such?" asked Tillaron.

"Simple," said Bair, and of a sudden in a bloom of vanishing darkness a Silver Wolf sat where the youth had been.

"Bair," snapped Urus.

With another gathering of vanishing shadow, Bair reappeared.

"But Da, that's how I would do it," protested Bair.

"One Draega take on an entire Vulg pack?" asked Tillaron quietly. "Is that cunning and guile?"

Bair frowned. "Well . . ." But then he fell silent. Yet after a moment he said, "It would depend on the number and place, I suppose, and whether I had time to plan."

"Good," said Tillaron. And then the Alor stood. "But now we need train thee in facing each of these foes."

"Who will play the part of the Ogru?" asked Bair, clambering to his feet as well. Then he glanced at sitting Urus and grinned. "You, Da? Are you big and ugly enough?"

Urus fell back on the ground, roaring with laughter, Riatha giggling, Ironstalker smiling.

Tillaron said, "Mayhap thine *athir* will indeed play the Troll, but we shall start thee with a Lok."

From behind Bair there sounded a shriek, and as the youth turned about, charging toward him with a scimitar raised to strike, there hurtled a man-sized, dusky, batwing-eared, leather-clad, yowling being, murder in its eye.

"*Waugh!*" shouted Bair, stumbling backwards, tripping over Tillaron's outstretched foot and crashing to the ground.

And then, standing above the youth, the dusky-skinned foe burst into silverlike laughter and reached out a hand to aid the lad to his feet, and Bair could see it was Ancinda Soletree, her face smeared with blackener, her batwing ears nought but a look-alike helm.

Tillaron scowled down at the youth and soberly said, "Take heed, my boy: in some instances there is no time for cunning and guile, and running away will do." And then he burst out laughing as well.

As twilight stole over the vale, Bair glanced from Urus to Aravan. "Tell me this: I named many Foul Folk today, and I know they come from Neddra, yet does anyone know of a place of crossing the in-between from here to there?"

They sat out before Faeril's cottage, the damman and Riatha inside preparing tea. Down at the foot of the slope of the land the Virfla tumbled and sang. Urus shrugged and looked at Aravan, and the Alor pitched a small stone out through the air to splash in the swirling stream. "During the Great War of the Ban, there was a company, a regiment I think, of Elves and men who crossed over to Neddra, there to harass the foe. The crossing they used was somewhere in or about the Gronfangs—just where, I cannot say, but somewhere nigh Modru's Iron Tower there on Claw Moor—a crossing they found by backtracking a contingent of Foul Folk who had just come to Mithgar from Neddra. The regiment needed great stealth to slip by Modru's fell bastion, for the Evil One's minions were nigh. At war's end, the Humans came home by the same route, emerging there nigh the Iron Tower, no Elves among them."

"No Elves?" asked Urus.

Aravan nodded.

"Why was this?" asked Bair.

Aravan sighed. "The Sundering had taken place, and only the bloodways lay open for Elves and men alike, and so each had to go their separate ways. The men reported that the Elven band had crossed over within sight of a black fortress, for an in-between unto Adonar lay nigh, the same in-between Gyphon used to invade the High Plane. And so it was the weary contingents did return from Neddra at the Great War's end."

"How did they know the war was over?" asked Urus. "With the Sundering dividing Plane from Plane, it is not as if messengers rode the in-between."

"From a fleeing Lok or Ruch, I believe, one who was escaping the Ban. They captured him and he babbled all, when they sorted out his words."

Bair's eyes widened. "There were those among the Allies who spoke the Foul Folk tongue?"

"Slûk it is named, Bair," said Aravan. "And yes, a few mastered that foul speech. And there are those among Elvenkind who yet retain skill in the tongue, in case there is a need."

Bair nodded and then said, "It seems a good language to know."

"Good language? Huah!" growled Urus. "I hope there never comes a time when you will need such, Bair."

They sat without speaking for moments, but then Bair said, "Crossings to Neddra, crossings to Adonar, stepping the in-be-

tween—yet I would have you tell me this: are there crossings to
the Mageworld of Vadaria?"

"There was one . . . once," said Aravan, his voice husky, laden
with sudden emotion. And he stood and walked downslope toward the Virfla. Bair started to gain his feet to follow, but Urus
laid a hand on the youth's arm and silently mouthed a *No.*

In that moment Faeril came to the doorstone. "Tea and sweet
biscuits are ready." And as Urus and Bair entered the cote, Faeril
looked about and asked, "Where is Aravan?"

"Down by the river, remembering," said Urus. "He will be up
by and by."

Awhile later, Aravan joined the others at tea, and the talk
turned to many things, Rwn not among them. Even so, Aravan
was yet in a morose mood and would not be drawn from it no
matter the subject, or so it seemed.

But finally, Faeril said, "You know, Aravan, I think you ought
to go and see Dodona, ask him where the yellow-eyed man is."

Aravan took a deep breath. "Mayhap I would . . . had he not
already answered the one question we were allowed."

"Who is Dodona?" asked Bair.

"Yes, he did give an answer to that question," replied Faeril,
"though wrapped in an image it was."

"Who is Dodona?" asked Bair again.

"Quite an image, too," said Riatha. "Wrapped about a riddle,
I would say."

Bair stood and stepped to the center of the room and then
sang in a high, clear voice:

"Tell me, my dear Ythir,
Tell me, Aravan,
Tell me, Da named Urus,
Or, amicula, if you can . . ."

As all eyes turned to him in amused surprise, of a sudden his
voice dropped to a growl. "Who is Dodona?"

"That was splendid, Bair," said Faeril.

Bair threw up his hands in frustration. "Splendid it may be,
amicula, but answer the question it does not. Would you please
just tell me who Dodona is?"

Faeril shrugged one shoulder. "Oh, him. He's an Oracle we found in the Karoo."

Bair frowned. "In the desert?"

Faeril nodded.

"An Oracle, you say?"

Again Faeril nodded, then she turned to Aravan. "He will know where Galarun's killer is—and the Silver Sword."

"He has already answered the one question we were allowed," repeated Aravan.

"But that was *my* question he answered," said Faeril. "Not yours. Perhaps he will give you the revelation you seek."

"To find the Silver Sword?" asked Bair.

Aravan slowly shook his head. "The time of the sword is long past, I ween. It was to be used against Gyphon in the Great War of the Ban, or so we did surmise. But Gyphon is banished to the Abyss beyond the Planes and so the sword now has no use. Nay, if I could get but one answer, it would be the whereabouts of the yellow-eyed man. Even so, there is this: I deem wherever Galarun's killer is found, there also will be found the Silver Sword though a purpose it no longer has."

"No matter," said Bair. " 'Tis the yellow-eyed man we seek, for I will go with you."

Urus looked at Bair and shook his head.

"But I am pledged, Da," protested Bair.

"You were but a child of six when you swore that oath," said Urus, "and you are yet too young."

"I am nigh twelve, Da."

"Aye, but still too young."

Thwarted, Bair jumped to his feet and stormed to the door and out into the September night.

Urus started to rise, but Riatha said, "Let him walk off his ire, chier. He will see reason on the morrow."

Skeptically, Urus looked at Riatha but said nought.

Again Faeril turned to Aravan. "Well, Bair's childish vow or no, what about Dodona?"

Aravan sighed. "I will think upon it"—he looked to Riatha and Urus—"but not ere my pledge to ye and hence to Dalavar Wolfmage is done. If I do go unto the Karoo, 'twill be after

Bair's initial weapons training is rendered . . . mayhap three years hence."

Sitting on the bench outside the open window, Bair nodded to himself. *Three years it is, and then we go.*

CHAPTER 17

Conquests

Summer, 5E1005–Autumn, 5E1007

[Four to Two Years Past]

Even as the aethyric wave knelled throughout Mithgar, in a witchfire-lit sanctum atop a tall tower on the palace grounds mid the city of Janjong in the eastern realm of Jinga, Kutsen Yong stared at the flaring 'Stone, brightness streaming outward . . .

. . . and he laughed in triumph.

And as he did so, the spectral blaze of the 'Stone began diminishing, though brilliant still.

Cowering and shielding his yellow eyes from the ghastly blare, as the light faded Ydral risked a glance at the twenty-two-year-old boy-emperor. The young man now held the glowing, jadelike 'Stone on high as he turned about and about and cried, "I command them all. I command them all."

Ydral sucked air in between his sharpened teeth, daring to believe. "Mai lord?"

Kutsen Yong stopped his spinning and thrust the 'Stone toward the yellow-eyed man, but then snatched it back from Ydral's reach and drew himself up and haughtily said, "I command them, Ydral."

"Indeed, mai lord, but who?"

"The Yong, Ydral. All the Yong of the world."

"Tji command the Dragons, mai lord?"

"Did I not just say so, Ydral?"

Ydral's cold heart leapt with glee, for with such a token the whole of Mithgar would fall. And if Mithgar fell, then Gyphon would be set free of the Abyss to cast Adon down and rule all, to set Ydral upon the throne of Mithgar as His regent, to give over this boy emperor unto Ydral to do with as he wished . . .

. . . but only if the 'Stone did in fact command the Dragons would this be true.

"How splendid, mai lord," whispered Ydral, sweeping a hand outward. "Let us put it to aun test."

At Ydral's gesture, Kutsen Yong clutched the waning 'Stone to his chest and hissed, "Think not to lay a finger upon this, for it is mine alone to wield."

Ydral bowed and backed away. "Yes, mai lord. Plainly it is meant to be, for who else bears the mark of the Mighty Dragon?"

Now the emperor stared at the glimmering 'Stone and then touched his own forehead, tracing the birthmark up and around and down. And then, as if coming to himself, he turned to Ydral and said, "This test: what have you in mind?"

"Ryodo, mai lord. Tji are truly the Masula Yongsa Wang— the Mage Warrior King—as prophesied of old. Command the Dragons to conquer Ryodo, and let aun minions follow after and gather up the wealth. And when the foe is beaten, set aun trusted advisor—say, Chakun, the First Handmaiden—upon the throne of that vanquished realm to be aun regent."

"A glorious plan, Ydral," said Kutsen Yong. And he turned his gaze upon the Dragonstone and once more it flared with light as an aethyric summons silently rang forth in irresistible command.

In the skies above Janjong, mighty Dragons, Fire-drakes all, bellowed in impotent fury, while the citizenry below cowed inside their hovels and huts and dwellings, terrified by the swirling Yong with their fire and their saberlike claws and their great, thrashing, leathery wings. And down in the royal gardens, Ebonskaith sat and seethed and roared and blasted flame into the air, yet the insignificant Human before him held the Dragonstone come to life, and the great Fire-drake could do nought but heed and obey, for the awakened essence within the 'Stone held dominion over all of Dragonkind.

Next to the Human stood a yellow-eyed mongrel of man and Spawn and Demon, or so Ebonskaith's raging gaze did see, for the eyes of Dragons not only behold the visible, but the invisible and hidden and unseen as well . . . all but for the Dragonstone, an abominable, god-wrought thing Drakedom could not detect with cast-forth senses; nor could they directly look upon it without risking being plunged into an eternal madness of everlasting grief beyond measure.

And as the petty Human issued his imperatives, and Ebonskaith roared in powerless fury, the yellow-eyed mongrel laughed at the Drake who was unable to do aught but comply.

Ryodo fell in less than a month, Dragonfire blasting away opposition, and following in the Dragons' wake came the Golden Horde—warriors of Moko and Jinga—raping, murdering, pillaging, taking whatever they found of worth, leaving devastation behind.

In spite of her protests, First Handmaiden Chakun was set upon the throne of Ryodo, for what could be worse to this particular conquered enemy nation than to be forced to bow to the rule of a woman? . . . or so Ydral did whisper into the ear of Kutsen Yong.

And when Chakun set sail across the Jingarian Sea, Ydral danced in glee, for his greatest opposition in the emperor's court was now gone. That night there came horrid screams from his tower as Ydral celebrated his ascendancy.

In the following year, Jûng fell, along with the Ten Thousand Isles of Mordain.

The year after was one of consolidation, the emperor setting his favored ones upon various thrones. Wealth was gathered and sent to the palace in Janjong, along with selected slaves.

In this year as well, from conquered Jûng an old religion swept across the lands: the worship of the *Jìdu Shàngdi*—the Jealous God—and among the courtiers only Ydral knew it was one of Gyphon's many names.

And the Golden Horde continued to grow as more and more warriors flocked to the Dragon banner.

And during all of this time, Ydral stood by Kutsen Yong's side as the faithful and chief advisor, ever whispering into the emperor's ear. And as the year elapsed, ever did Ydral urge Kutsen Yong to turn his attention to the West:

"Mai lord, far to the west there are many nations and much wealth."

"I will see to them in my own time," replied Kutsen Yong, stroking the Dragonstone.

"Indeed, mai lord. As it is written in the stars, tji will be Ruler of All. Even so . . ."

Kutsen Yong frowned and looked at Ydral. "Even so?"

As if reluctant to speak, Ydral hesitated but, at an impatient gesture from the emperor, said, "In the West there is ahn who names himself the High King of Mithgar and sets himself above all."

"Even above me?"

"Yes, mai lord," whispered Ydral.

Kutsen Yong's eyes blazed with rage. "Then I shall personally show him the error of his arrogance."

"Personally, mai lord?" Ydral could but barely hold his jubilation in check. "But what of aun safety?"

Kutsen Yong leapt to his feet, Dragonstone in hand. "I am the Mighty Dragon, and nothing shall bar my way. Call my commanders. Call my mandarins. We have a conquest to plan, for I shall destroy this upstart and rule all his kingdoms as well."

"Yes, mai lord," whispered Ydral, stepping away from the throne. And as he strode from the chamber, he exulted, for now all of Mithgar would fall, and Gyphon would evermore rule.

CHAPTER 18

Choices

October, 5E1008

[Fifteen Months Past]

On Bair's fifteenth birthday the long-limbed youth stood six-foot-four and weighed just a pound or two under fifteen stone. His flaxen hair had turned even lighter as the lad had grown, a thing Faeril found contrary to nature. Yet contrary or no, his shoulder-length mane now held a silvery cast, as did his pale grey eyes. And on this natal day he was dressed in grey leathers, Inarion's gift to the lad. A hooded allweather Elven cloak hung from his shoulders, an elusive grey-green on one side, an evasive grey-brown on the other, and which side would be worn out depended upon the nature of the terrain and whether or no the wearer wished to blend in. The cloak was clasped at his neck by a jade brooch; both cloak and clasp given unto him by his Amicula Faeril. An Elven long-knife was girted at his thigh, a gift from Kelan Aravan, and a flanged, Dwarven-forged, black-iron mace hung from his belt, bestowed by his sire and dam; these two weapons, along with the bow and sling, were Bair's arms of choice.

And now in the glade of celebration, illumined by paper lanterns and by the stars and a moon just barely past full, he stood before the assembled Lian—the lad towering above all but his sire, Urus a hand or so taller still. Alor Inarion stood facing the youth, and both were ringed 'round by a circle drawn in the soft, rich loam of the vale. And the Alor called out for all to hear: "Long has it been since we have seen such a ceremony as we observe this night." Then Inarion turned to Bair and spoke: "Kneel, Bair, son of Urus, son of Riatha. Kneel, but a child."

Bair dropped to one knee before the Alor and bowed his head.

Then Inarion called out, "Who of the five will vouch for this child?"

"I will," came the reply, and Faeril solemnly stepped forward bearing a shallow silver bowl filled with crystal-clear water, and she took a designated place on the circle, her somber mien briefly broken by a fleeting but gleeful smile.

Now Inarion called out again, "Who of the five will vouch for this child?"

"I will," came the staid answer, and Ancinda Soletree stepped forward, and she held a clay vessel filled with fertile earth. She, too, took a place on the circle.

Once more Inarion called, and Aravan responded gravely and took his place on the circle, a silver vessel filled with smoldering eldwood shavings, a laurel branch in hand.

At another call, "I will," said Tillaron Ironstalker, his manner solemn, and he held a burning branch of yew as he took his place on the circle.

"Who of the five will vouch for this child?" asked Inarion.

"I will," replied dark-haired Elissan, adding, "and I am the fifth and last." And she held a lodestone cupped in her hands as she took her place.

Now Inarion received the bowl from Faeril and with his fingers sprinkled the clear water onto Bair and intoned, "The first of the five: water."

He scattered earth from Ancinda's bowl about the youth and said, "The second of the five: earth."

From Aravan's smoldering shavings, with the laurel branch Inarion wafted smoke onto Bair and said, "The third of the five: wind."

Taking Tillaron's burning branch of yew, Inarion illuminated Bair's face and said, "The fourth of the five: fire."

And lastly, using Elissan's lodestone, Inarion touched Bair's hands and feet and temple and heart and called, "The fifth and last of the five: aethyr."

Then Inarion called out, "Who is the one who gives the name?"

"I am," replied Urus, stepping to a point on the circle face-to-face with his son, "and the name is Bair."

"Bair," whispered Inarion into each of the youth's ears.

"Who is the one who will deliver him?" next called Inarion.

"I will," responded Riatha, directly opposite Urus, and she stepped into the circle and took Bair by the left hand, the hand nearest the heart, the lad yet kneeling.

Now Inarion looked at the youth and called out so that all could hear. "As was thy birth seasons past, so is thy birth this night, for thou hast been vouched for by the five, and thou hast been named by the one, and thou hast the one who will deliver thee. Thou didst enter the circle as a child, yet thou art a child no more. Arise, Bair, son of Urus. Arise, Bair, son of Riatha. Arise, Bair, keeper of the wide world and take thy rightful place. Rise up a Guardian named Bair."

And with Riatha holding his heart hand, Bair gained his feet. Now Alor Inarion slowly turned and turned as he called out to the assembly, "On this day we have a new warrior among us, yet even more so on this day we have one who fosters and cares for the land . . . and he is a Guardian named Bair."

Thrice a mighty shout lifted up to the sky from the gathered Lian as they called out, *Alor Bair!*

They held a spree in the coron-hall, celebrating a rite of passage not seen in millennia, and Darai and Alori played lively music and danced and sang and ate and drank and laughed and told riveting and humorous and sad tales, and Bair was the center of all. And as another wild pipe-and-drum reel played, Aravan sat down next to Faeril and said, "I believe I will go see Dodona, now that Bair's initial training is done."

"We shall go with you," replied Faeril.

Aravan shook his head. "Nay, wee one, for if thou or Urus or Riatha rode at my side, then Bair would come as well."

"But then, Aravan, I alone could go and—and—"

Faeril stuttered to a halt as Aravan held out a h ˙d to forestall what further she would say. "Nay, 'tis better thou shouldst stay here and see to Bair."

Faeril sighed and looked at the lad now dancing a wild fling with laughing Elissan.

"Too, in the past I have made many journeys alone across Mithgar seeking Ydral, if indeed that is his name, the yellow-eyed man who slew Galarun. Surely I can journey alone again, though I have little hope that Dodona will answer my question."

"You don't have to go alone, for—" Faeril began, yet Aravan raised a finger and shook his head again, but Faeril would not be hushed, and she angrily snapped, "Then why did you tell me, if only to say to me nay?"

Aravan smiled. "I did forget how determined thou canst be, Faeril, yet I tell thee this for I have a task for thee: a fortnight after I leave, I would have thee tell the others where I have gone so that they will not worry."

"But we *will* worry, Aravan."

"Even so, I would not have them deem I have merely disappeared, or that something foul has inadvertently befallen me. Too, by delaying a fourteenday, I will be long gone ere Bair knows of it, and 'tis better he remain safe here in the vale. Besides, as I say, there is every chance that Dodona will say nought, and I will return ere the spring thaw . . . or by summer at most."

Faeril ran a hand along the silver lock running through her black hair, and she reluctantly nodded and said, "Oh, Aravan—"

"Amicula, would you dance with me?"

The damman looked up and there stood Bair, panting a bit and grinning widely. Faeril forced a smile and said, "You great gangly thing, you would dance with me?"

In answer, Bair took her by the hand and drew her out onto the open floor. And the six-foot-four youth and the three-foot-two damman began a fling of their own, drums alone hammering out the pace. Soon Faeril was caught up in the joyous revel, and all Lian stopped to watch this hugely mismatched pair, the onlookers applauding and laughing as the two pranced and whirled and coursed about the floor.

At the end of the dance, when the drums fell silent, breathless and laughing and amid much applause, Faeril and Bair stepped to the board where refreshments sat. As she quaffed a heady dark wine, Faeril looked across the goblet's silvered rim, her gaze seeking out Aravan, but the black-haired Alor was gone.

*   *   *

"No, he is not up in the high meadows bringing the sheep down for the winter. Instead he has gone to see Dodona."

"What?" blurted Bair, springing to his feet, his chair falling aclatter.

"When was this?" asked Riatha.

"A fortnight past," replied Faeril. "The night of the celebration."

"He went without me," protested Bair, uprighting the chair once again but not sitting down.

"He went without us all, arran," said Riatha, shaking her head and looking to Urus.

"It is his mission," rumbled the Baeran, "his to choose as he will, and in this he chose to go alone."

Riatha sighed and nodded, murmuring, "As he has done many times before."

"But he went without *me*," spat Bair and, flinging down his napkin, he stormed out, slamming the door behind.

"Bair, it was his to choose," called Faeril after, but only the shut wooden panel met her words.

Urus looked at the door, and Riatha said, "Let be, chier. He is disappointed. It will pass."

"Would that he were less violent in his manner of saying so," replied Urus.

Faeril snorted. "This from the Baeran who when ired slams an axe into cords of wood as if he were slaying Rûcks?"

Urus grinned and shook his head. "At least it keeps us warm in the winter."

As the three continued their meal, from behind the cottage, there came the sound of a heavy axe blade cleaving wood.

The following day: "What are you seeking, Bair?" asked Faeril, entering the Coron's war chamber.

Bair looked up from the map table, vellums and charts spread wide. "Oh, amicula, I was simply wondering where in the Karoo Kelan Aravan was bound."

Faeril dragged a stool to the table and then clambered up to see. After a moment, she stabbed a finger down to the map and said, "Here is the place, though it is not marked—south and slightly west of this port city, here."

"Hmm," murmured Bair. "But how will he cross the Avagon Sea?"

Faeril searched among the maps and drew out another chart. She touched a finger to the vellum. "Likely he'll find a ship here at Arbalin Isle; it's almost directly south from Arden Vale, though quite a long way: four hundred leagues or so." She traced a route down along the Grimwall and across Gûnar and Jugo and to the coast, and then across the channel to the isle. "It's the shortest path to the Avagon Sea from here, and thence to the Karoo. Yes, most likely he'll head for Arbalin Isle; they have splendid ships and mariners there. —Say, did I ever tell you about the time Petal and Tomlin sailed from Arbalin?"

Staring at the map, Bair did not respond, his mind elsewhere. "Bair?"

"Wha-what?" The youth looked across at the damman.

"Did I ever tell you about the time Petal and Tomlin sailed from Arbalin"—Faeril traced another route across the map at hand—"through this part of the Avagon to the port of Castilla in Vancha?"

"Ah, no. I don't believe you did, amicula. Please do."

Bair's gaze returned to the map and he frowned in concentration as Faeril continued the tale. "Well, it seems there were rumors of an evil at the end of the Grimwalls, somewhere near the walled village of Sagra—right here—and they thought it might be Baron Stoke, and so . . ."

Another day passed, and in midafternoon of the following day, Riatha walked out to where Urus stood at the curing rack. "Have you seen our arran, chier?"

As Urus unlaced the deer hide, "No," he said, tugging the last thong through. "Mayhap he is with Tillaron or Ancinda"—Urus grinned and looked at Riatha—"or with Elissan. He's taken a fancy to her, I think."

"Tcha." Riatha shook her head. "If so, 'tis one-sided, and Bair is like to be disappointed, for Elissan and Flandrena are nigh pledging to one another. Besides, at fifteen summers, Bair is yet too young."

Urus set the cured skin aside and reached an arm about Riatha's waist and drew her unto him. "Oh, I don't know about that, my love." He slid his other arm about her. "At fifteen I did not think I was too young; still, at that time I felt as if I were cursed and could not take a mate. Of course, that was before I met you."

Riatha raised her face and they shared a gentle kiss. Yet held in the circle of his arms, she pulled back and looked up at him and cocked an eyebrow and said, "I would guess hadst thou felt differently, 'twould have been with someone nearer thine own age though, than the gap which exists 'tween Elissan and Bair."

"Hah!" barked Urus. "A gap to which Elvenkind seems to pay no heed."

Riatha grinned, and then said, "Fear not. When Bair comes into his own, I deem there will be one, or mayhap many, who will find him as fascinating as I do find thee."

Again they kissed, and Urus released her and took up the deer hide and said, "This needs softening." Then, as if in afterthought, he added, "Fret not for our son, my lady, he should be along by and by."

Riatha nodded and returned to the cottage, and the day waned, and still there was no sign of Bair.

In the twilight, there came a tap on the door. And when Urus answered, Faeril entered. She looked about and then asked, "I say, is Bair all right?"

Riatha frowned. "Why dost thou ask?"

"Well, I just saw Ancinda, and she said that Bair had missed his session with Tillaron. He was to learn the finer points of fending off Ghûlen spears."

Riatha looked at Urus and frowned. "He has never missed a time at weapons."

Urus stepped to the door of the youth's bedchamber and hesitated momentarily, but then opened the panel and stepped in. After a moment he called: "His mace is gone, long-knife, too. His leathers and cloak are also gone. And here is a note." Urus reappeared, parchment in hand. "It reads: I must keep my vow. Love, Bair."

"Vow?" asked Faeril, looking at Riatha, but the Dara turned up her hands.

"Late last night a Draega passed this post, loping southward, Alor Urus," reported Alaria. She passed her fingers through her dark brown hair. " 'Twas thine arran, or so we thought, out for a mid-of-night run."

"Are you certain it was a Silver Wolf?" asked Faeril.

Alaria nodded. "Although the moon had long since set, by starlight alone we could see 'twas a Draega. And since there is but one Draega in this vale . . ." Alaria turned up a hand.

"Where has he gone?" asked Faeril, turning to Urus.

Urus growled and gazed in the direction the Draega had run. "Yon, after Aravan."

"But-but, Aravan left"—Faeril frowned—"sixteen, no, seventeen days past. He is at least three hundred fifty miles away by now, heading for Arbalin. Surely Bair wouldn't—" Of a sudden Faeril gasped and said, "His vow! The promise he made when he was but a child, ten— no, nine years past. And the maps! Oh, no. I told him where—" Her words chopped short, and she turned to Riatha. "Urus is right. Bair has gone after Aravan, and it's all my fault, for I was the one who told him the way."

"Come," said Riatha, starting for the cottage, Urus striding alongside, Faeril trotting to keep pace. "We'll need our weaponry," said Riatha, "and foodstuffs, and remounts, yes remounts swift and many."

Faeril frowned. "Remounts? But surely we can—"

"A Draega can cover thirty or more leagues a day," snapped Riatha.

"Thirty?" exclaimed Faeril. "Why, that's ninety miles. Ninety miles a day?"

"Or more," said Riatha. "Yet if Aravan indeed is bound for Arbalin Isle and takes the most direct route, mayhap we can catch them at the main port ere a ship sets sail across the Avagon Sea."

"Well then it's clear my pony will be too slow for this chase. I'll tag along behind on one of the remounts, just as I rode with Jandrel."

"Well and good," said Riatha, then turned to Urus. "We must needs leave thy great horse behind, chieran, for he, too, is not swift enough."

"I'll gather my weapons and goods and meet you at the stables," called Faeril as she veered off in the direction of her own cottage.

*   *   *

Four candlemarks after full night had fallen, Riatha, Urus, and Faeril rode out from the Elvenholt, Riatha on a fiery roan and trailing three remounts on long tethers behind, Faeril on one of them. Urus rode a large black, four remounts in his wake, two of which were lightly loaded as packhorses. Faeril along with the rest of the burdens would be rotated among all nine horses as Riatha and Urus switched from mount to mount and changed over the cargo, too.

Away they rode at a goodly clip, following the trail through the woods, unwilling to ride faster until day came upon the land. Yet they rode even though it was night for they were determined to reach Arbalin Isle ere a ship to the Karoo could set sail.

South they coursed and south, hooves thudding against loam, yet they had not gone more than seven miles when—"Hola," cried Riatha, reining up short, the animals behind stuttering to a halt as well, Urus riding onward a few strides ere reining his mount around, the four remounts trailing him juddering to an uncertain stop.

"What is it?" cried Faeril.

"List!" called Riatha, holding up a hand for silence under the glittering stars.

Above the blowing and stamping of steeds there came from behind the faint sounds of distant Elven bugles ringing silver through the night.

"Oh my," hissed Faeril. "What does it—?"

Her words jerked to a halt, for mingled among the clarion calls there sounded the blats of Rûptish horns.

"Ardenholt is under attack," gritted Riatha, haling her horse about. "We must fly!"

Back toward the Elvenholt they raced, riding at a gallop in spite of the dark.

A candlemark passed and then part of another as they thundered through the night, hammering back along the path, dark silhouettes of trees passing to either side. And now they could see the glimmer of fire through the woods ahead, and hear the *chang* and *blang* of steel on steel mingled with shouts and cries.

They charged into the Elvenholt, cottages burning, battle raging in the ways between, Rucha and Loka bashing and cleaving, savage Vulgs rending and tearing, Elves lying wounded, some slain, others battling in the light of raving fire.

Through the heart of the main body of foes Riatha charged, deadly Dúnamis hewing, and where the starlit blade clove, black blood flew wide and Rûpt fell dead in her wake.

In Riatha's wake as well came Faeril on a galloping tethered steed, steel flying from her hands, Rûcks and Hlôks stumbling back, throats and hearts pierced by hard-thrown knives.

And midst the Vulgs a great Bear raged, savage claws severing, bones breaking with each massive blow.

Deadly was the battle, great gashing wounds slaying Rucha and Loka, crushing cudgels and cleaving scimitars felling Elves. In spite of the savage Bear, the Elves were driven back and back, for Vulgs are a terrible foe, and there were many among the Rûpt.

All of Faeril's knives were gone, the ten blades buried in ten Foul Folk now dead, and she was afoot, for the horse that had borne her lay slain, its throat slashed open by scimitar. And now the damman scrambled away, unarmed and in flight. She darted among yawling Rûpt and shouting Elves and the skirl of steel on steel, while all around fire burned, flames raging from roofs and roaring out through windows, each building a furious inferno in which nought could survive.

She ran for the smithy for therein were racks of weapons, one of which held throwing knives—a set she had forged for Bair, and she prayed he had not taken them south. But as she ran there came a cry above others—" 'Ware, Faeril!"—and she looked back to see racing behind a foe she could not outrun: 'twas a Vulg.

Faeril scooped up a rock, pitifully small; "Come on, you cur of Gyphon," she shouted, and drew back her hand to throw. But a silver form flashed past her—a Draega, a Silver Wolf!

"Bair!" she cried as the Draega slammed into the oncoming Vulg, and even as she called, more silver hurtled past.

Five Draega, six, no seven altogether crashed into the foe. And the targets they chose every time were Vulgs.

Now the tide of the struggle shifted, yet savagely it raged still. And into the strife came a damman on a pony, bandoliered knives again crisscrossing her breast, the little steed dodging this way and that as Faeril threw steel, making every cast count, and she shrilly shouted, *"Blût vor blût!"* in the ancient Warrow tongue of Twyll.

Back and back were driven the Foul Folk, back and back and back. More Spawn fell, more Elves, too, as the battle raved on.

Down to the Virfla they were driven, the Rûpt, down to the churning flow, and Rûcks and Hlôks splashed into swift and deep water, some to drown, their armor pulling them down. But not a Vulg reached the river, for they were all lying slain. And not a Rûpt emerged on the far side of the swirling flux: some were taken in watery battle by sword, others were pierced by arrows and flung knives or smashed by hurled slingstones to fall dead and be swept tumbling downstream. And still others were hauled under by enraged Lian warriors and drowned by hand alone.

And thus did the battle end.

They spent the rest of that night and all the next day and into the night treating the wounded and quenching the fires and cleaning up after the battle. As to the dead Foul Folk there was little to do but to take up arms and empty armor, for the sun had shone down on the corpses, and even for the slain the Ban held sway: at the touch of daylight the bodies had withered to ashes in an instant, to blow away on the wind.

As to their own dead, great was the mourning among the Elves, for many a death rede had been passed from the slain to the living. Such redes were both a blessing and a bane among Elves: a blessing, for it was a final message, a vision dear, somehow cast forth from heart to heart, from spirit to spirit, from mind to mind at the moment of death; a bane, for it came without warning as a devastating blow, and it meant a loved one had died, and those who received such death redes were whelmed in heart and spirit and mind, were whelmed to the depths of their souls. But even more so, to all of Elvenkind it meant that an immortal life had been quenched, for no matter the age—be it ten years or ten thousand or more—it was a life just a step along an endless way, a life just begun. And among the slain were Alaria and Flandrena and Jandrel; Faeril was most distressed over this last, for she and Jandrel had become good friends. Yet as the great pyres were set and the spirits of the slain were sung up into the sky and surviving Elvenkind wept, the wee damman consoled Elissan, the Dara devastated by Flandrena's death, his rede bequeathed to her.

As mid of night drew nigh, the weary rested, all but the healers and helpers, and they continued to tend. And down on the banks above the Virfla—

"I came across the tracks and the scent on the far side of the Grimwalls," explained Dalavar Wolfmage, "and since they seemed to be headed this way we followed as swift as we could."

Of the six Silver Wolves, only one—Greylight—lay in the grass nearby. The other five were again aiding the wounded, caring for those who had been Vulg bitten, for the Elven healers had not enough precious gwynthyme to treat all afflicted by the dark venom. And so the healers had turned to the Silver Wolves for aid, for the saliva of Draega was a natural counter to that deadly poison.

"Thou and thy friends didst come in the nick of time, I ween," said Ancinda Soletree, "for thine arrival did turn the tide."

"What I would like to know is how they got past the sentries," said Tillaron, his left arm in a sling, Ancinda at his side. He looked to Dalavar for an answer.

"There lies in the foothills yon"—Dalavar pointed northerly—"a dead Black Mage, or rather his ashes. It was he who slipped this raiding party unseen past the pickets above ere he was slain."

"Slain?" asked Faeril. "How?"

"His throat was torn out," replied Dalavar. Faeril waited, but Dalavar said nothing more.

"The question is not how, but rather why," declared Riatha. Yet she visibly braced herself for the answer she thought might come.

"They came to slay Bair," said Dalavar.

At these confirming words, Riatha reached out to take Urus's hand. Urus enveloped her grip in his own, and said to the Wolfmage, "As fifteen years past you said they would."

"Oh my," said Faeril, "I remember." But then she turned to Dalavar. "But Bair is gone from here."

Dalavar nodded as if he had known it all along. " 'Tis good, for those who seek his death believe he is yet in the vale."

"Good you call it," growled Faeril, "yet he is alone, following after Aravan. And when Bair catches Aravan, he intends to accompany him into the Karoo. And the sad thing is, it's all my fault, for it was I who told Bair the way."

"Nay, Faeril, 'tis not thy fault," said Riatha. "The blame lies with Bair."

"A headstrong, foolish lad," growled Urus.

Dalavar shook his head. "You are all three wrong. Oh, headstrong he may be, but foolish he is not. It is his destiny he follows . . . that much I have <seen>."

"Destiny or no," rumbled Urus, "when we catch up to him I am of a mind to—"

"I do not think that would be wise," warned the Wolfmage.

At Dalavar's tone, Greylight gained his feet, hackles partly raised, the Draega looking to the Mage for direction. Yet Dalavar spoke a <word>, somewhat like a growl, and Greylight reluctantly settled, turning about and about before finally lying back down.

Ancinda glanced sidelong at Urus. "I would not interfere in the raising of thine arran, yet think on this, Urus BearLord: had Bair been in the vale tonight, he might now be lying slain. Mayhap it is his destiny to be gone from here, as Dalavar Wolfmage has said."

Urus sighed and nodded and said, "Nevertheless . . ." but then he fell silent and looked to Dalavar for advice.

The Wolfmage glanced up the vale and gritted, "Down from the north they came, did the Spawn, down from the Grimwalls, murder in their eyes, searching in vain for a now-runaway youth. And there will come more raids on this vale, and you must prepare.

"As to Bair, there are some things I have <seen>, others I can only guess. Even so, this I say: Bair and Aravan are on a path of destiny, and should you follow, they will most assuredly fail, for you will change the very thoughts they will have, and thereby change the outcome."

"And if we do not follow . . . ?" asked Urus.

"I cannot foresee all, for something or someone blocks my <sight>, but this I do know: their chances are slim regardless, and failure looms large. Even so, 'tis better to have a slender chance than none whatsoever."

"This <sight> you have," asked Faeril, "you can <see> an immutable future?"

Dalavar turned up a hand. "Not immutable, nay. Instead, 'tis vague and ever shifting, many paths leading away from any given critical instant. To choose that which will happen is difficult at best, for some decisions are balanced on a knife edge, and events can fall to either side on nought more than a whim or a passing bird or a gust of wind or a blowing leaf or on nought whatsoever at all."

"Then how dost thou know we should not follow?" asked Riatha.

"In truth, I do not know. Yet I do believe that those two together—Aravan alone with Bair—have a minuscule chance to succeed, but should anyone else accompany those two, I think they have none at all. But there is this I *do* know, and I say again: more attacks upon this vale will occur, for the ones who would slay your son, who is blood of my blood as well, believe the lad is yet here. Hence not only are you needed to defend these borders, but you are also needed to act as decoys, for should they see you three riding south, they may suspect Bair is absent from Arden, and then they will cast their nets wider and find where he has gone."

Faeril gasped and looked toward Riatha and Urus, to find them grim of face. "A pox on all Mages!" spat Faeril, but then glanced toward Dalavar and raised a hand in mute apology.

Dalavar gazed away toward the Grimwalls, his sight focused well beyond, and he said, "There is a dark wind blowing from the east, and I know not what it portends. Yet this I do know: the Trine is coming, and rivers of fire and blood will flow on the Plains of Valon."

"Trine?" asked Faeril, her heart suddenly racing for no reason she could fathom.

"Fire and blood in Valon?" asked Riatha.

Dalavar looked from Riatha to Faeril. "The Trine is when the three Planes converge, and the barriers between are at low ebb. Even the boundary to the Great Abyss is weakened."

"Weakened!" Ancinda gasped.

"Can Gyphon escape?" asked Tillaron.

"Not without unforeseen aid," replied Dalavar.

"Won't the Black Mages try?" asked Ancinda.

Dalavar nodded, but said, "They might, yet to bridge that gap it would take a powerful artifact, one of Gyphon's own making, and neither I nor the Mages of Black Mountain have sensed such."

Riatha sighed and then said, "What of this disaster in Valon?"

Dalavar shook his head. "Even the greatest of Seers are blocked, and only know that a dreadful slaughter will occur in Valon at the time of the Trine."

Faeril groaned and said, "The Trine again. When will it come?"

"Seventeen months hence," replied Dalavar.

"Is there no way to stop it?"

Dalavar shook his head and pointed to the nighttime sky and asked, "Can you stop the passage of the stars, or the moon in the course of its track?"

Faeril shook her head. "No, I cannot, but this I can do: defend this vale against further incursions, unless we ride after Bair, that is."

She looked toward Riatha and Urus, their visages grim in the light of the glittering stars. Her face twisted in an agony of decision, and with tears standing in her eyes, Riatha turned to Urus and said, "We must let him go on his own, for 'tis a destiny he follows, and we are needed in the vale."

Urus wrapped his arms about Riatha and clasped her tight, and he cleared his throat but spoke not a word as he looked at Dalavar and nodded but once.

With tears in her own eyes, Faeril raised her face to the nighttime sky, her vision blurred beyond seeing, and she fretted about her Bair.

And far to the south beneath glimmering stars wheeling above, a Silver Wolf loped through the dark of the night and across the shadowy wold.

CHAPTER 19

Outset

Spring–Autumn, 5E1008

[Twenty-One to Fifteen Months Past]

By the spring of that year the long conquest began, the vast Golden Horde trekking westward, led by unnumbered horses and men, among which Kutsen Yong himself rode midst the swords and spears and bows and arrows of his personal guard. And high in the air above this great army, mighty Dragons circled, bellowing in rage at their degrading subservience, unable to do otherwise. Following after came a great train: wagons and oxen, men and women afoot, Ydral in an enshrouded horse-drawn van. And near the head of this enormous procession there came a huge enclosed wagon haled by forty red oxen; panel-sided and gilded, its golden spires rising up in the sunlight and glinting, it was Kutsen Yong's grand wheeled palace, and it rolled in the wake of the Masula Yongsa Wang and his invincible throng.

Up and down and across the lands great elements of the Golden Horde fared, cities and provinces falling before the emperor's power, despots and warlords and civilized mayors surrendering their realms and bastions and citadels and cities and towns and insignificant villages to the Masula Yongsa Wang, for none could oppose the irresistible might of Dragons, to say nothing of the army below. Bastion by bastion, city by city, province by province, and realm by realm, Kutsen Yong installed new mayors and warlords and placed ranking members of his Golden Horde upon provincial and kingly thrones; under these handpicked lackeys, he put in place the bureaucracy of his mandarins to arrange for crushing tribute. And in public displays of his unopposable authority he beheaded or impaled those who had ruled before. And where there was even a hint of disquiet he loosed his soldiers to thunder across the land, their reaving swords slashing down, hacking off legs and arms and heads and gutting the innocent, spilling their intestines out on the ground, while great dark-winged shapes wheeled in the sky, flame roaring from their throats, turning the day dark as night with the smoke of burning cities. Forests were hewn and fields salted, and rivers ran red with blood, and none were too young or old to suffer these edicted ends, much to Ydral's everlasting delight.

And when the Golden Horde had moved on, gorcrows and vultures by the thousands came to feed upon the slain multitudes, slashing beaks plucking out eyes, rending flesh, gulping down gobbets of rotting meat.

And long after the crush of cruel iron and fire had swept past, those who had managed to escape immediate death at the hands of the horde and the flames of the Dragons still continued to die— for riding in the train of war came plague, pestilence, and famine, the condemned survivors nought but skin and bones with great pustulent black buboes bursting forth and spewing out yellow poison. And scuttling among the stricken to feed upon the new-fallen came rats and beetles and many-legged crawlers and other creeping vermin.

And so it was as westward the Golden Horde marched, wide wings sweeping north and south, conquering and consolidating as they went, burning and raping and murdering all at the slightest sign of resistance. And in that steady advance toward blood-red sunsets, all of the remaining provinces of Jinga fell, as did the mountain kingdoms of Hutar and Sataya on the northwest bounds of Jûng, as well as the wide realm of Hmei across the western border of Moko.

And wherever the Horde went, temples and mosques and ashrams were cast down, idols destroyed, priests and monks murdered, new ones set in their stead. Pagodas were raised to replace the former houses of devotion, and the worship of the Jìdu Shàngdi— the Jealous God—was imposed upon all as the only religion allowed. Ydral consecrated many of these new temples himself, sacrificing men and women and children on the blood altars, trembling in ecstasy as he did so, yet always remembering to ask the dead if the Elf with the spear were near.

Thus did conquest sweep across the lands as westward the Golden Horde marched.

Kutsen Yong gestured toward the flame-engulfed city. "Ydral, I would have you release your plague when my Dragons and soldiers are done."

"As tji will, mai lord."

Kutsen Yong sat on his golden throne in his great rolling palace, though at this moment it stood still. The softly glowing jade-green 'Stone rested on a blue-velvet pillow within reach of his long-nailed right hand. With its wide panels cast back and away, the front of his grand palace was entirely open, nothing blocking the view, and Kutsen Yong looked out past the forty red oxen standing still in their traces and watched as Ashak, the capital city of the realm of Bulahn, burned, Dragons flying above. He turned to his chief advisor and gloated. "Who else can command such power?"

"None, mai lord," hissed Ydral. "Even the Drakes bow down to tji."

Kutsen Yong nodded and proclaimed with royal certainty, "It is fitting that I be ruler of the world."

"Yes, mai lord."

"Chakun often said that the gods favor me."

Ydral suppressed a frown. "Yes, mai lord."

"One of my concubines—from Jûng, I believe; one I gave to you—told me I am the favorite of the Jìdu Shàngdi, and I do believe it is true."

As if struck by sudden revelation, the blood drained from Ydral's pallid face, making it even more ghastly. Yet Kutsen Yong saw it not, for he was intent upon watching the city burn. Ydral managed to choke out, "Indeed, mai lord, tji stand at the Jìdu Shàngdi's right hand."

Kutsen Yong reached out and stroked the Dragonstone. "Perhaps He will make me a god, if I am not one already."

"Tji are divine," hissed Ydral, while in the distance Dragons swooped and destroyed a city and all the men, women, and children within, a city that had had the temerity to have had its gates closed when Kutsen Yong had ridden within distant sight of its entirely insignificant walls.

Horrid were the shrieks that night as Ydral sacrificed many, seeking confirmation from Gyphon—the Jìdu Shàngdi, the Jealous God—that he, Ydral, would be master of this world rather than some upstart Dragonboy. For it was he, Ydral, who had set in motion the events that would free his master from the Abyss to cast down Adon and rule over the whole of creation. Surely Ydral's proper reward was the regency of all Mithgar. And so Ydral sought an answer, his flaying knife stripping, his victims screaming. Yet the yellow-eyed man was caught up in the rapture of killing, blood-ecstasy shaking his frame, and if Gyphon answered, Ydral heard it not, held as he was in joyous thrall.

CHAPTER 20

Journey

October, 5E1008–January, 5E1009

[Fifteen to Eleven Months Past]

As night drew down on the land, Aravan sensed he was being followed, and yet the blue stone on a thong about his neck had not grown chill, hence, if peril were near, it did not come from Neddra. Even so, the stone did not detect all danger— Human brigands and highwaymen were among those it failed to discern—and so Aravan remained wary as he rode onward, his packhorse following, the flanks of Gûnarring Gap looming to either side: far on the left; at hand on the right. He rode past a shoulder of mountain and saw a jumble of huge boulders ahead, and angled for this shelter, a defendable place should hazard come.

In moments he reached the protection of the rocks and, dismounting, he drew his horses within. He pulled his bow from its saddle scabbard and quickly strung the weapon. Then he took his quiver of arrows in hand as well as Krystallopŷr, and he clambered to the top of the north-facing stone and waited, an arrow nocked, his spear at hand.

Moments passed and moments more, and then 'round the shoulder of mountain stone came padding a lone Silver Wolf, and around its neck on platinum chains dangled a stone ring and a crystal pendant.

Aravan relaxed his draw and murmured, "Elar," and even though he had but breathed the name, the Draega's ears pricked as if it had heard, then a darkness shimmered 'round.

*   *   *

Across the small campfire, Aravan looked at the lad. "Bair, do thy sire and dam know thou hast come?"

Bair sighed. "I suspect they do now."

"Thou didst not get permission to journey with me?"

Bair shook his head without speaking.

"Then shouldst thou not go back?"

"Kelan, I once overheard Amicula Faeril and Ythir discussing the words of someone named Dalavar Wolfmage who said I should walk with you."

Aravan nodded. "So he did say."

"Ythir and my amicula seemed to both agree that it was the right thing to do."

"Even so, Bair—"

"Is it that you do not want me?"

"No, Bair, it's just that—"

"Did I not make a vow, kelan, to aid you on your quest?"

"Aye. Even so, thou wert but a child."

"Kelan, am I not a Guardian, a child no more?"

Now it was Aravan who sighed, and for long moments he did not answer. But at last he said, "Aye, Bair, thou art indeed a Guardian."

As if unto himself Bair nodded and glanced at the slopes of Gûnarring Gap and stood in silence for a moment, but finally said, "Then come the morrow let us be on our way."

"I paced myself to overtake you in Gûnar, but I forgot I would need to eat, and to do that I would have to forage. Still, there was much game on the way, and Hunter provided swiftly and well."

"Hunter?" asked Aravan, stoppering the waterskin and taking up another to replenish as well.

"The name of the Silver Wolf I become. It is not the full name, but one which will serve." Bair finished scrubbing the pan and set it aside.

Aravan nodded and corked the second waterskin. He then stood and looked about the campsite. "We can share out the load between the horses, though I do not have a spare saddle for thee."

Bair laughed. "Kelan, I did not expect to ride a horse when

I caught up with you. Though I will camp with you at night, in the day it is Hunter who will accompany you to the shores of the Avagon Sea."

Aravan grinned and turned up his hands and shrugged, saying only, " 'Tis seemly."

For four days down Pendwyr Road they fared ere coming to the vast gap between the Gûnarring in the northwest and the Red Hills in the southeast, and there they crossed into Jugo. Turning south by southwest, across the broad, rolling plains they went, crofters in their November fields stopping to watch the amazing sight of a great Silver Wolf padding alongside an Elf on horseback, or now and again looking on gape-jawed as a pronghorn or other game fled for its very life, a huge silverlike beast racing after, a rider with a packhorse in tow galloping in their wake.

In the nights, Bair and Aravan stayed in inns in town or in crofters' lofts, or camped on the open plains, or in the lee of hills, or at the edge of thickets or groves when one was nigh as eve drew on. And they feasted on coney and antelope and marmot meat, Hunter living up to his name.

By night it was Guardian and Guardian who slept and warded by turns in camp—one sleeping, the other resting in shallow meditation, his senses alert to the world—but by day it was a Draega and a horse-borne Elf who made their way south, bisecting the realm of Jugo, the Red Hills far to the east, the Brin Downs far to the west. And thus did kelan and elar cross the rolling land.

And twenty-eight days after Bair joined Aravan at the Gûnarring Gap, they came to the town of Merchants Crossing on the shores of the Avagon Sea, for there docked the ferry that would take them the thirty miles across the channel to the seaports of Arbalin Isle. Aravan rode to the home of a nearby crofter, a friend from times past, and arranged for the boarding of his horses, saying he might be gone for a while. The crofter would take no fee for the steeds, saying that the horses would yet be there whenever Aravan returned.

Five days later found Aravan and Bair in the sea-trader city of Port Arbalin, for here gathered the captains and crew of every merchant ship sailing the Avagon Sea. Here as well oft came the chartered ships of Realmsmen, agents of the High King. Too, at times ships of questionable repute or provenance anchored in the sheltered bay—smugglers and freebooters and raiders and other such—some with royal commissions, others not. And from merchant or Realmsmen or freebooter did Aravan plan to arrange for passage across the Avagon, he hoped to the city of Sabra on the edge of the wide Karoo, though any port on that southern shore would do.

As for Bair, he was all agawk, trying to see all things at one and the same time, for this was the first city he had ever been in, and his head turned this way and that as he and Aravan made their way from the landing into the heart of the port.

They took a room in the Red Slipper Inn, a bawdy house to be sure, yet the most popular place for mariners on the entire isle. There as well occasionally appeared one or more unsavory sorts—cutpurses and swindlers and spies and the like—drawn by the thought of quick profit at the expense of unwitting dupes, though when unmasked as thieves and cheats and unscrupulous agents, ships' crews made short shrift of them, usually meting out swift and harsh justice on their own rather than summoning the city ward.

And into that den of questionable virtue did Aravan take young Bair. They stowed their goods in their quarters above and descended into the noise and laughter and shouts filling the crowded common room. And the chamber smelled of pipeweed and sweat and sawdust and ale, of roast and stew and salt, of cheap perfume and the spiced scent of hot mulled wine, and there was an iron tang in the air, as of blood or of metal quenched. On a small stage a bard was playing a lute and singing, but it was questionable as to whether anyone could hear him above the raucous din. Gaudily dressed women seemed to be everywhere, some laughing and sitting on mariners' laps, while others pulled their charges by the hand and led them up the spiral stairs to the bedrooms above. Some sailors shouted and placed bets as a pair of burly men arm wrestled; other seafarers played cards, and some diced for drinks. A few lay on the floor, dead drunk and oblivious to the world. Into this roar came Aravan and Bair, their passage among the revelers causing a bit of a stir, for not often did Elvenkind come this way, nor was it common to see a flaxen-haired lad looming taller than nearly all. And Bair thought he heard several voices call out *It be Cap'n Aravan.*

They came to a table more or less occupied by a couple of passed-out sailors: one lying atop, half-on, half-off; the other sprawled 'neath. Aravan dragged both away and deposited them in a nearby corner. As he and Bair sat down, he waved away three approaching doxies and summoned instead a serving girl and called for a loaf and a joint of beef and a flagon each, as well as two plates of stew. As they ate, Bair looked about the roiling room, his gaze passing over the mariners and merchants— a pair of these latter were Dwarves—the lad's eyes seeking fairer sights. He turned to Aravan and raising his voice to be heard he said, "These ladies, kelan, they do seem friendly."

Aravan laughed. "Hadst thou any coin, elar, they would be friendlier still."

Redness crept up the back of Bair's neck until his face was flush. "I didn't, uh— That is—" he stammered, while Aravan's laughter swelled. And Bair burst forth, "Oh, kelan, you know what I mean."

"Mayhap I do, lad. Indeed, mayhap I do." Again Aravan broke out in guffaws, while Bair turned his full attention toward tearing off a chunk of bread which he studiously applied to the beef juice swimming in his wooden trencher.

When Bair next gazed across the common room, he determinedly avoided looking at the women, instead peering anywhere but. And he noted some sailors at a large table who, in spite of the din, seemed to be whispering among themselves and casting surreptitious glances toward him and Aravan, while a few in their group turned about to openly stare at the pair. Finally, they got up and started toward the door, but then one of the mariners, a huge man, stopped and after a brief word to his companions, squared his shoulders, and, as the others waited, he turned and came toward Aravan and Bair, his jaw jutting out belligerently. Casually, Bair slipped loose the keep-thong on the flanged black mace at his belt. And then the man arrived, towering.

"Be you th' Elf Aravan," he demanded, "blue eyes, black 'air, crystal spear 'n' all?"

Aravan set aside his spoon and looked up at the looming stranger, a Gelender from his accent and the cut of his clothes.

Bair tensed, getting ready.

"I am," replied Aravan, his voice soft, but even so he was heard.

The huge man whipped off his cap and clutched it with both hands, twisting and crushing it, turning it about as he shuffled from foot to foot and bobbed his head in greeting, his sandy hair falling down across pale blue eyes set in a face gone all eager-soft. "Oi be Long Tom of Arbor in Gelen, 'n' many 'r' th' tales 'anded down t' me o' you 'n' your ship, th' *Eroean*. Moi griate, griate, griate, um, Oi-don't-know-how-many-griates, um, granther sailed wi' you long apast, back at th' end o' th' First Era, um, lemme see, that'd be, unh . . . wellanaow, Oi can't roightly say, but it were quite long past. 'Is name were Finch—"

"A carpenter; one of the best," said Aravan, as Bair relaxed and casually slipped the keep-thong of his mace back on its belt hook.

Long Tom beamed. "Lor', but 'at's right. A carpenter 'e woz. But me naow, Oi be a mait. Regardless, moi granther told tales o' adventures in striange lands, all but th' last'n 'e sailed. Did-n't say nowt about that final voyage. Sworn t' secrecy, 'e claimed, or so 'tis they say, th' stories wot woz 'anded down, that is. Kept 'is mouth ashut till th' day 'e died.

"Oyo naow, look at me 'ere anatterin' on, 'n' me ship is leavin' 'n' all, bound for Port Thrako in Alban. But Oi did want t' meet you 'n' interduce meself, Oi did. 'N' if you need a mait or a rig-ger, Oi'm y'r man, 'n' Oi stands ready should y' call"—Long Tom began backing away—" 'n' Oi'll be agoin' naow."

"No, wait," bade Aravan, gesturing Long Tom to a seat. "Wouldst thou have a flagon with us? A jack of ale? A jot of rum?"

"Hoo, naow, indeed a cup o' grog'd be roight t' moi taist, 'n' thank y', Cap'n. But as Oi says, m' ship be leavin' on th' out-flowin' tide 'n' all. . . ." Seemingly at a loss for further words in the presence of a legend, Tom's eyes lighted on Bair, and as if finding his voice once again—"Oi be Long Tom, lad, 'n' you be . . . ?"

"Bair."

As they shook hands, Tom's eyes widened in surprise at the size of Bair's hand, nearly as large as Tom's own.

"Oy, Tom," came a call across the common room, "th' tide'll be flowin' soon."

With a final bob to Aravan, the big Gelender backed off a few steps and then slapped his grip-twisted and -crushed cap onto his head and hurried away, Aravan calling after, "Fair winds, Long Tom. Fair winds."

Bair watched as the big man and his shipmates headed out, Long Tom animatedly talking, his companions casting looks back toward Aravan even as they passed through the door. Bair then glanced at Aravan. "This ship of yours—the *Eroean*—it must have been quite a craft to have been remembered all this time. I mean, tales handed down from the end of the First Era, that would have been nearly eight millennia past. And a secret mission at that."

A look of profound sadness swept into Aravan's eyes, and he did not reply, but instead peered into his jack of ale, finally taking a swig.

At that moment a loud argument broke out at a nearby table, followed by shoving and name-calling and then the crunch of knuckles on flesh, and soon the entire common room was filled with struggling, cursing men, chairs flying, cudgels bashing, the gaudily dressed women fleeing to the spiral stairwell, where they took station on the risers and shrilled obscenities and shouted encouragement, their voices lost in the furor. And in the churning midst of all, two broad-shouldered Dwarves were laying about with their fists while singing Dwarven dirges, an accumulation of dazed mariners sprawled in a pile at their feet.

Dodging a hard-flung chair, Aravan stood and, weaving like a dancer, led Bair through the swirling melee and toward the door. A time or two a brawler turned to attack one or the other of them, but backed off at seeing Bair's six-foot-four frame, to say nought of the black-iron mace in his hand. As for Aravan, Krystallopŷr was enough to deter even the most rabid assailant.

When they emerged, Aravan swept his arms wide and said, "Wellanow, lad, what dost thou think of the big city?"

But Bair was looking back at the free-for-all within the confines of the Red Slipper. "I say, Aravan, are you certain this is the best place to stay?"

Aravan laughed. " 'Tis quite lively, neh?"

Bair shook his head and followed the Elf as Aravan headed for the station of the harbormaster.

"Let me see, Captain Aravan," replied the keeper of the log, flipping through pages of the current port journal. "Ah, here we are: hmm . . . there's a Chabbain trader sailing in two days for Aban, there on the border with Sarain . . . but that's too far from the Karoo." He looked up from his records. "Besides, Captain, I wouldn't want you to have to sail on one of those Chabbain scows anyway." He turned another page. "Oh, here's a bark whose next port of call is Kalísh in Hyree; she'll head out within the week . . . now what would a Vanchan captain want in that port, I should wonder. Regardless, that's near the Karoo, a bit west, I believe." The man thumbed through several more pages, running his fingers down lists of the ships currently in harbor. "Ah, here's one: down in slip eighty-seven, there be a Gjeenian dhow lading cargo even as we speak. She'll be sailing on the morning tide. Heading for Sabra, just as you asked, or so it says here"—he looked up at Aravan—"right on the edge of the Karoo." The log keeper scanned through the rest of his list and finally closed the journal and said, "Except for those three, I don't see any others in the near term bound for the southern shore, though with the traffic lately, one or a hundred could come any day now, Captain."

Aravan canted his head. "I thank thee for thy aid." He held out a silver coin to the man, but the Arbalinian refused to take it, saying, "Captain Aravan, it was reward enough just meeting you."

Aravan smiled briefly and pocketed the coin. Then he and Bair walked away, Bair saying, "You have quite a reputation in this town, even though eight thousand years have elapsed."

Aravan waved a dismissive hand. "The tales grow in the telling."

Bair cocked an eyebrow, but said nought in return. Yet after a moment he frowned. "This doesn't seem to be the way to the slips. Where are we going?"

Aravan gestured toward the center of town. "First we shall outfit ourselves in appropriate attire, such that the Gjeenians will accept us, and then arrange for passage."

"What's wrong with the garb we are wearing?"

"Though Gjeenian shipmasters will trade with foreigners, they seldom take any aboard. Hence we must needs make ourselves presentable . . . less like the outlanders we are. Too, our garb, though fit for northern climes, will not serve well in the Karoo, where the sun is fierce and water is scarce and the nights are all too chill. The clothes we wear must protect us from the sun and help us use less water and keep us warm at night. There is a merchant not far from here who will provide us with all we need."

"In Kabla, the language of the desert, the headdress is called a *kaffiyeh* or a *ghutrah*," explained Khasan as he outfitted Bair, the merchant small and dark. Khasan had come to Port Arbalin twenty years past from a village in Khem on the western edge of the Karoo. He had brought with him many bolts of cloth woven from the finest Khemish cotton, and had set up a tailor shop, his specialty the making of clothes for the sundry travellers who would journey to the lands south of the Avagon Sea. And now he fussed about Aravan and Bair, at present outfitting the large youth. "It is held in place by a headband called an *agāl*. The cloak is named *jellaba*, or *abaya*. The shirt is a *brussa*. The pantaloons are called *tombon*."

"We shall want many blue tassels fastened here and there," said Aravan, turning about before a mirror and inspecting his own desert garb.

"Aiee, but yes, the holiest of colors, the color of the *Mlâyiki*," replied Khasan.

Bair frowned. "Mlâyiki?"

Khasan searched for a word in Common, but failed, and he appealed to Aravan.

"The Fjordlanders call them *Engels*—winged beings who live beyond the sky," explained Aravan.

Khasan stood on a step stool to drape a cloak about the shoulders of Bair, telling the lad, "You must enwrap this close around in the Karoo, *tawîl wahîd*, for it is most important to be well covered; not only will your robe and clothing protect you from the sun, they will also lower your need for water, for the sun and wind on bare skin will rob your body of moisture, causing you to drink more often, and water is most precious in the Erg. Do you understand?"

"Indeed, sir, I do," replied Bair.

"A most clever boy," crowed Khasan, leaping down from the stool, and then muttering to himself, "Blue tassels. Blue tassels," as he rummaged through several drawers.

By midafternoon, Aravan and Bair, dressed in their desert finery and bearing a bundle or two, strode down the docks toward the Gjeenian seagoing dhow tied up at slip eighty-seven. Two-masted she was and with triangular lateen sails, the ship some eighty feet long and forty feet at the beam. Pointed was her prow and it bore no fo'c'sle, and rounded her aft, a green-and-black flag flying from her sterncastle. Serpentine writing writhed across her fantail: *"Hawa Melîh,"* pronounced Aravan, reading the name. "We would call her the *Good Wind.*"

"Perhaps it's an omen," said Bair.

Aravan shrugged, "Mayhap," and he stepped to one of the Gjeenian crewmen lading cargo aboard and spoke to him in Kabla.

The dark-brown man looked up from what he was doing, and gasped and backed away, then turned and bolted for the aft cabins, shouting, *"Raiyis! Raiyis! Sheyâtîn! Sheyâtîn!"* And the other crewmen looked at Aravan and Bair in alarm.

"Adon, kelan, what did you say to him?" asked Bair.

Aravan shrugged. "I but asked to see the captain."

"Well, then, what was he screaming?"

Aravan sighed. "He called out, 'Captain! Captain! Devils! Devils!' "

Bair frowned. "Devils?"

Aravan nodded. "My eyes and ears. Your size. They think we are of Demonkind."

"Huah!" grunted Bair. "I'd rather be mistaken for an Engel." He then canted his head toward the aft cabins as a burly Gjeenian came forth, the crewman cowering behind.

Yet within but a candlemark or so, Aravan had arranged for passage to Sabra.

At first Captain Malaka had seemed reluctant to take on the pair, for with his tilted eyes and pointed ears, Aravan did exceedingly resemble a *Djinn*, a Djinn with a terrible spear, and with his great size Bair could be an *Afrit*, an Afrit bearing a dreadful black mace. Yet at the same time these strangers did wear blue, and no Demon could do such. Besides, the captain had sailed to Arbalin many times, and he had seen Elves before, and he had thought those might have been Djinni, though other sea captains said not . . . yet they were not from the desert lands, hence what could they know of Demonkind?

Regardless, the shipmaster of the seagoing dhow took on these two passengers, wearing blue as they were, for the one who might be an Elf spoke fluent Kabla, and the large one spoke Common quite well, and everyone knew that the forked tongues of Demons caused them to hiss and lisp.

Moreover, they offered gold.

Aravan and Bair returned to the Red Slipper to retrieve their goods, and as was its wont the tumultuous hostel was filled with a raucous din—laughter and gambling and contests of strength and wild whooping and drunks passing out, doxies plying their trade—and of the brawl that had taken place earlier there wasn't a sign, as if nothing untoward had occurred at all. Up the stairs went the pair, and along the hall to their quarters, Bair blushing to hear the gasping and sighs and moans and giggles coming from various rooms along the way.

Just ere dawn on the morning tide of the thirteenth of December, the *Hawa Melîh* rode out on the ebb, Bair and Aravan standing in the bow, a waning half-moon glimmering down into the dark sea below.

"It speaks of eternity, does the sea," said Bair, holding to the forward railing, "its deep <fire> breathing with the waves." Bair inhaled deeply. "It smells of salt, a clean scent, unlike some of the odors nigh the docks—day-old fish and the like."

"Aye, a welcome relief, elar," said Aravan, leaning on the railing and peering down into the water, the prow churning the brine to faint luminescence, "one we'll enjoy for many a day."

"How many days? I mean, just how far is it to the port of Sabra?"

"Some seven hundred fifty or sixty leagues as the gull flies, but given a headwind we'll add many more leagues in the tacking." Aravan turned and gazed at the set of the lateen sails and the stream of the guide pennons flying from the masts above. "Though should the wind remain abaft or abeam, as it does now blow, we could sail a straight course all the way."

"And how long will we be at sea?"

Aravan frowned. "The winter winds on the Avagon are blustery, Bair, and generally come from the northeast, as they do blow now, yet they are at times fickle, and may come from any quarter. Even so, seldom do they die altogether." He looked over the side to gauge the speed, and then said, "This dhow makes about six knots, I deem, hence, given the tacking we mayhap will do, and given that we don't become becalmed and dwell overlong in irons, I ween we'll be in Sabra some twenty-five or thirty days from now."

"Huah," grunted Bair. "And if we were sailing in the *Eroean*, then how long would it be?"

Aravan sighed but said, "Half or a third of that: eight to twelve days."

"Eight days to go, what, two thousand two hundred miles?"

Aravan nodded. "That's as the gull flies, elar. Yet were the wind to blow dead against, the *Eroean* herself would tack some three thousand miles altogether."

Bair gaped. "Three thousand miles in but eight days?"

Aravan nodded, then added, "Down at the bottom of the world where the polar air does roar, the *Eroean* has run before it at a speed nigh thirty knots, and we sailed over seven hundred miles in but a single day, hurled as we were by that wind."

"Adon," breathed Bair, "seven hundred miles a day?"

"Aye," replied Aravan, "but then we nearly lost the ship flying too much silk in that blast: two of the three masts gave way, shattering down adeck, and the seas were towering, the waves over a hundred feet from crest to trough—greybeards all—and in the dark of a blizzard we nearly crashed the ship 'gainst a mountain of polar ice."

"Lor', kelan, why were you in such straits to begin with?"

Aravan smiled. "Indeed we were in straits: the Silver Straits, to be exact, the rocky narrows round the horn of the Silver Cape, and in the cold dead of icy summer at that, when the South Polar Sea is arage. As to why? We pursued a Black Mage, and lost him there in the storm. Nearly lost the *Eroean* as well, but she held up and we made it to safety, driving snow, howling winds, broken masts, greybeards, mountains of ice, and rocks notwithstanding."

"It sounds grim," said Bair.

They watched as the water churned past the prow of the *Hawa Melîh*. Finally, Bair asked, "This, um, Black Mage—"

"Durlok," gritted Aravan.

"This Durlok: did you ever catch him?"

"Months later, elar. He no longer lives. It was the final voyage of the *Eroean*, or so I thought then. Yet I did sail her again during the Winter War, but no more, no more."

Aravan turned and walked away, and Bair simply watched him go, knowing that for some reason his kelan needed to be alone.

Southerly across indigo waters did the *Hawa Melîh* sail, Aravan and Bair living adeck night and day, in fair weather and foul alike, in a simple tentlike lean-to, for Captain Malaka would not have them sleep below with the crew nor in the aft cabins with himself and his officers; he still held suspicions concerning this Demonlike pair . . . though he supposed it was possible they could be blessed Seraphim instead.

The crew of the dhow remained cautious as well, flinching back whenever the two came nigh, in spite of the fact that they *did* wear blue. And the suspicions of the crew seemed borne out, for in the dark of Longnight these two did cast a spell, or so the mariners did believe as they watched the pair stepping through some arcane rite and chanting or singing or canting strange words, no doubt appealing to higher powers for aid or abeyance or some such. After all, what else could it be?

The wind remained more or less abeam for two weeks, and then died altogether, and Gjeenian sailors looked askance at their passengers, perhaps blaming them for the loss of air, or mayhap appealing to them to conjure up a breeze or to ask Rualla, Mistress of the Winds, to do so: perhaps they would step through a rite and chant and bring the blowing wind back. But the Djinn and Afrit, or the Seraphim, stood still and mute, and the sails hung slack, and no sailor dared to ask, and so Captain Malaka ordered a crew overboard in dinghies to tow the ship out of irons.

As the sun shone down on the deep blue Avagon Sea and men rowed through the glassy waters to the steady call of *Shadd!* ... *Shadd!* ... *Shadd!* ... Bair turned to Aravan. "Tell me of the *Eroean,* kelan."

Aravan looked up from the map he studied, then rolled up the thin vellum and slid it back into the case with the others. "What wouldst thou know, elar?"

"Everything: how she was built, where she was sailed, and where she now lies. She's not gone down, has she?"

Aravan shook his head. "Nay, elar, she is yet seaworthy."

Bair looked about and saw that no one stood near and quietly asked, "Well then, where is she now?"

In a like voice, Aravan said, "Tethered in a secret grot in Thell Cove."

Bair waited, but Aravan said no more.

Shadd! ... *Shadd!* ... The men rowed on.

Remembering the conversation of two weeks back, finally Bair said, "And she had three masts?"

Aravan nodded.

"What was her length?"

"Two hundred twelve feet from stem to stern, her beam a slim thirty-six feet at the widest, and she drew but thirty feet of water fully laded." Aravan turned to Bair. "From my time aboard Fjord-lander Dragonships I had learned much about how speed is related to the measures of hull length to width to draw, and so I designed her to be long and slim and shallow of draft and flying a cloud of sails."

Shadd! ... *Shadd!* ...

"Back when we went to Drimmen-deeve to sharpen my climbing skills, you said the Dwarves built her."

"Aye, 'twas a crew of Drimma from the Red Hills holt, along with a handful of men."

"Why Dwarves?"

Aravan said, "They are the best crafters of all, and I did want the best, for I designed her to be fashioned from the woods of many lands, and her metal fittings to be Drimmen-made, fittings that neither tarnish nor rust. Her silken sails, though, and rigging and ropes came from the looms of Darda Galion, spun from Jingarian thread."

Shadd! . . . Shadd! . . .

"How many in her crew?"

"Forty men and forty Drimma . . . and an occasional Waerling or two for, with their stealth and size, few can rival the Wee Folk as scouts."

"I remember on that same trip to Drimmen-deeve you spoke of Dwarves on the ship—warbands, I believe you said—but I didn't know they sailed."

"In the main, they don't, but indeed I took them on as a warband, for they are mighty fighters, and where I intended to go, danger would oft be nigh."

"Where did you go? What did you do?"

"We sailed over all the seas of the world, carrying cargoes at times, but chiefly looking for adventure: searching for treasure, exploring legends of lost cities and hidden tombs and abandoned hoards of gems and jewels and gold and silver, seeking to find the truth of those and other such fabulous myths. Over and again did the legends prove to be nought but fanciful tales, yet oft did we find they were not, and there were occasions when we found adventure and treasure and battle all in the same place, many times needing to fight our way clear."

Bair's eyes lighted up. "Oh, splendid ventures indeed. How long did you sail her on these quests?"

Aravan frowned. "As man measures time, some three thousand years or so."

Bair's jaw fell agape. "Three thou— Oh, kelan, why did you stop?"

A look of anguish fell over Aravan's face, and Bair thought he would not answer.

Shadd! . . . Shadd! . . . Shadd! . . .

Finally Aravan said, "Too many memories."

Bair frowned. "Too many memories of adventure?"

"Nay, elar. Too many memories of a love."

As Aravan fell silent once more, a puff of air swirled across the deck and set the slack sails to rippling.

Captain Malaka began shouting orders, and the dinghy crews cast loose the towing lines and rowed back to the dhow, and soon the *Hawa Melîh* was under way again, a light breeze on the larboard stern quarter fitfully filling her triangular sails.

*   *   *

Under a waning half-moon and on the inflowing tide of the evening of the twelfth day of January, some thirty-one days after setting out from Arbalin, the dhow *Hawa Melîh* sailed into the port of Sabra, a city trapped 'tween the rim of the sea and the edge of the great Karoo.

CHAPTER 21

Erg

January, 5E1009

[Eleven Months Past]

As Aravan and Bair made their way toward the Blue Crescent Inn, word ran rampant along the streets and byways before them, for thrice in the last twenty years or so had one of these two come through the city. And now he was back with his crystal-bladed spear along with a huge companion, mayhap the same one who had accompanied him once before, mayhap not; regardless it was a blue-eyed Djinn and a tall and terrible greyeyed Afrit who strode through the city that night . . . or so some did say. But then there were those who noted they both wore blue, the holy color, hence perhaps they were not Demons at all but blessed Seraphim instead. . . .

The pair spent the next two days haggling over the purchase of camels and waterskins and grain and other such, and it became clear they were going into the Erg, no doubt to their deep stone caverns where everlasting fires do roar and lost souls burn forever, shrieking in endless pain. Either there or to their concealed mystic castles on lush hidden lands where figs and pomegranates ever do grow and water does flow most freely.

It all depended upon whether they were Demons dire or Seraphim most holy.

Of course there were some who claimed that they were neither, but people holding these views had no doubt stood unprotected in the sun too long.

*   *   *

They spent the third night in Sabra at a caravansary just outside the central gate of the southern wall, where their supplies had been delivered, along with their camels and tack, for by edict of the emir, camels were not permitted within the city except to pick up or deliver cargo, and by sundown all of the ill-tempered, foul-smelling beasts had to be beyond the walls.

In the candlemarks just before dawn, they equipped and laded their waiting *hajînain* and *jamâl*: two dromedaries for riding; four pack camels for bearing the bulk of their food and supplies and goatskins of water. Mounting up and towing two camels each, in the predawn light they headed southward into the Karoo, the great curve of endless sand lying before them, a relieved populace remaining behind.

Underneath fading stars, south and away from the city walls they rode, the grumbling hajînain swaying beneath them in an ungainly gait, rocking from side to side with each forward step.

"Lor'," said Bair, "but they roll as did wallow the *Hawa Melîh* on the waves of the Avagon Sea."

Aravan laughed. "Ah, Bair, that is why they are called 'ships of the desert,' weltering as they do. Fear not, thou shalt become used to it ere we reach the dunes."

On through the fading night they rode, paling skies in the east, and just as dawn gave way to daylight, Aravan and Bair came to the brim of the Karoo, where long graceful curves of majestic sand dunes stretched away to the limit of the eye, the world an illuminated sea of golden beige and shadowed bronze in the glancing radiance of morn. Kelan and elar paused a moment before plunging on, taking in the commanding scene. To their left the sun rose upward, just breaking free of the eastern horizon. To their right the slow bend of the Erg carried it westerly, gradually veering northward to follow the arc of the land. In the near distance behind them lay the city of Sabra with the Avagon Sea just beyond. And before them stood the dunes of the vast Karoo.

"Lor', kelan, whence came all this sand?" asked Bair, his right leg hooked around the wide, padded crook of the camel saddle, the beast standing still but looking back at the city aft, as if to bolt away to a better place than that which lay ahead.

"I know not, elar. Mayhap the gods made it so."

"How far do we have to go through such?"

"By the route we take, from Sabra behind to our goal ahead 'tis a hundred fifty leagues, less three."

"Four hundred forty-one miles? On nought but sand?"

"Oh no, lad, as thou wilt behold, there is much more than just sand."

"Such as?"

"Thou shalt see," said Aravan.

"Hmm . . . not talking, eh? Just tell me this: will we come across any green or find water along the way?"

"Aye, at the Oasis of Falídii as well as the Kandrawood—water and greenery both."

Bair nodded. "I look forward to seeing this forest in the desert—the Kandrawood—our final destination."

Aravan shook his head. "Should Dodona answer my question, then final it is not for me. I shall be going onward from there."

"With me, kelan."

"Bair, it is to peril I go."

Bair canted his head in assent. "Indeed. And I am sworn to go with you."

"Bair, I would not apurpose subject thee to hazard."

Bair turned up a hand. "And I would not apurpose allow you to step into danger alone."

Aravan sighed. "We shall discuss this anon, elar."

"What is there to discuss?"

"Greater things lie before thee, Bair, than the slaying of a yellow-eyed man."

Bair cocked an eyebrow. "Such as . . . ?"

Aravan did not respond.

They sat mute for long moments, but finally Bair burst out, "All my life I have felt as if secrets and mysteries were being kept from me, as if you and Ythir and Da and even Amicula Faeril are under some vow of silence, secrets it seems you dreaded, for oft have I seen the disquiet in your faces, especially when we speak of the in-between crossings, and Planes, and even the Silver Sword. Mayhap in the Kandrawood, when or if you find your answer and we argue about whether or no I go with you, perhaps you will say what 'greater things' lie ahead for me, what hidden mission I might have." Bair gestured at the wide

Karoo. "Until then, kelan, the sooner started, the sooner done, or so I have heard many times."

Conflict in his eyes, Aravan looked upon the lad, but then he plied his camel stick and called out *"Hut, hut, hut!"* Bair doing likewise, and the two set forth, drawing the pack animals behind, all the camels *hronk*ing and *rrrunk*ing in rancorous protest at having to move again. Into the endless sand they went, Aravan in the lead, Bair trailing after, and soon the city of Sabra was lost in the distance arear, the tall minarets the last to disappear.

As the noontide drew nigh, Aravan stopped, and when Bair came alongside, the Alor said, "Though 'tis winter, still 'tis best we rest over the heat of the heart of the day and some beyond. We shall take pause here." And so, with calls of *"Raka! Raka!"* they bade the camels to kneel, the beasts awkwardly lowering into the sand, the riders then dismounting.

As Aravan erected a shade cloth, Bair retrieved food and a goatskin of water from their goods, while the camels, grumbling and sneering, instinctively hitched about to be in alignment with the sun, turning toward it so as to expose as little of themselves to its direct rays as they could. As Bair stepped back toward Aravan, he said, "What about the camels, kelan: what will they eat and drink out here in this forge of Hèl?"

Aravan roped the last corner of the shade cloth to a stake and said, "Fear not, elar, all is not barren dune, and tonight we will reach a pasturage, where they will forage."

"Pasturage in this?"

"Aye. Thorny bushes and desert grasses, growing in sheltered places. And now that it is winter, much dew will collect, and that is all the water they will need."

After the sun passed through the zenith and slid partway down the sky, Aravan and Bair struck their shade and took up the food bag and waterskin to bundle all back on the pack camels, the ill-tempered beasts growling and unsuccessfully attempting to bite their tormentors. Then kelan and elar mounted the yet-kneeling hajînain and—shouting *"Kam! Kam!"*—they got all the camels to their feet, each animal levering up hind legs first and then one front leg and finally the other, an ungainly maneuver at best, all camels *hronk*ing and *rrrunk*ing in vile protest even as they obeyed.

It was chill dark when they stopped that eve nearly forty miles south of the city, where they hobbled the camels in a pasturage of thorny bushes and sparse grass. They set their own camp and made a small fire in a modest brass brazier—burning charcoal they had brought along—and they brewed tea to take with their austere meal of sweet dried dates and hardtack. Preparing to settle for the night, from a fired-clay flask Aravan poured a thin ring of liquid about each bed site. " 'Tis *hruja* oil," he replied when Bair asked, "pungent of odor and taste, and scorpions will not cross a line thus laid."

Bair held up a hand in the breeze blowing. "The air is quite crisp, kelan, and I would think it too cold for scorpions to be moving about."

"It will get colder still, elar, and then shall the scorpions den in, but for the nonce the ground is yet warm enough for one or two to come calling."

"I'll take the first watch, then," said Bair, smiling.

Aravan laughed. "Leaving me to lie down with the pests, eh?"

In the starlight, Bair turned innocent eyes toward Aravan and asked, "Would I do such a thing, kelan?"

Aravan laughed all the harder, and he was yet chuckling when he took to his bedroll and said, "Wake me at mid of night, sly Bair."

It was the depths of the nighttide when Bair awakened Aravan. A coldness gripped the land, and their breath blew white in chill air, for it was winter and the skies were clear, no clouds above to trap the day's heat and keep the desert warm. The Elf took station on a nearby rock, yet Bair did not lie down immediately, but instead sat in the glimmering starlight and gazed at the spangle above. "Kelan, I have spent my part of the night wondering about something you said on the voyage across the Avagon."

"What was that, elar. I will answer if I can."

"You said you could not bear to sail the *Eroean*, for it bore too many memories of a love, and so you hid it away at the end of the First Era, putting to sea but briefly during the Winter War, after which you hid it away again. Yet the First Era ended more than seven thousand years past, and the Winter War is past as well, a thousand years gone, and . . . and . . ."—Bair turned to Aravan—"Oh, kelan, it was so long ago."

Aravan shook his head. "Nay, elar, to me it was but yesterday."

"Which? The end of the Winter War, or the end of the First Era?"

"When the First Era fell to cataclysm."

"Seven thousand years past," murmured Bair. "And this memory of a love . . . ?"

"My soul mate, my heartmate," replied Aravan, his voice nought but a whisper.

"Oh, kelan, I do not mean to dredge up ill memories."

"My memories of her are not ill, elar."

They sat awhile without speaking, nought breaking the vast desert silence but the grazing of camels. Finally, Bair said, "How did you meet her?"

His gaze upon the stars, Aravan took a deep breath and slowly let it out, a stream of whiteness curling in the air and vanishing. "We were in the Straits of Kistan and came upon a gig adrift flying a flag of distress, yet it was anything but, for this mariner had sailed the small ship out to channel center to await the coming of the *Eroean*. We wore around the wind and luffed up alongside the gig and took the sailor aboard . . . and when she clambered over the rail, my heart was lost in that moment. Reed-slender she was, and dressed in brown leathers. Her light brown hair was cropped at the shoulders and seemed shot through with auburn glints in the bright sunlight of that day. Her complexion was fair and clear, but for a sprinkle of freckles high on her cheeks, and her eyes were green and flecked with gold. And she was tall, the top of her head level with my startled gaze, for until that moment I had not considered that this sailor adrift was anything but male. Yet female she was, and I was lost in her eyes."

"What was her name, kelan?"

"Aylis. And my heart sang with the sound of it."

"And you say she was waiting for the *Eroean*?"

Aravan nodded. "She knew the ship and crew and all aboard

were in great danger, and she came to warn her sire, who was with us at the time; 'twas Alamar the Mage."

"A Mage?"

"Aye."

"Then she was of Magekind, too?"

Aravan nodded. "A Seer."

"Where is she now?"

Aravan did not immediately answer, and long moments fled into the past as the starry skies silently wheeled above, but finally he took a deep, shuddering breath and said, "She is dead, slain, she and her sire and all else who were on Rwn when Durlok cast his terrible spell. On that day my heart was reft from my soul." Unable to say more, Aravan stood and walked a short distance out into the desert, needing to be alone.

Tears in his eyes, Bair whispered, "Oh, kelan, I am so sorry."

In the chill winter air of dawn, the desert vegetation was wet with dew, droplets clinging to the thorny bushes and to the stiff blades of sparse grass. After kelan and elar broke their own fast, while Bair rolled bedrolls and gathered their goods, Aravan offered the camels a drink, but sneering in disdain they did refuse, having gotten all the water they needed from grazing upon the dew-wet plants. And he proffered them grain, which the camels eagerly ate; their appetites for such were insatiable. And then Aravan and Bair laded their goods on the pack camels and saddled the dromedaries, all beasts grumbling and growling, knowing that soon they would have to submit once more to the indignities of bearing these fools across the desert.

For four more days did they travel on a southerly course, camping in the eve, setting nightwatch, rising at dawn, resting in light meditation in the heat of the day. And Aravan, who had been this way thrice before—twice going and once returning—seemed always to locate pasturage for the camels to graze on at night, and the winter dew was such that they needed no water at all.

The land they crossed was desolate beyond redemption, filled with sand and rock and sparse vegetation. Yet there was an elusive beauty in its gaunt reach: hills of red rock reaching up from rust-red sand, fantastic whorls and striations exposed to the sun;

isolated towering rocks soaring hundreds of feet into the sky, as if here and there entire mountains had been carved down to their very cores by wind-driven sand, leaving behind great monoliths visible for tens of leagues; extended reaches of tussocky hummocks, where they let the camels graze; vast arrays of timeworn hoodoos, twisted stone pillars shaped by the wind, standing like unremembered fields of ancient obelisks dedicated to kings long forgotten; valleys of gravelly stone, rounded as if from water, though 'twas the wind and sand instead; dry *oueds* wrenching across barren land, silent testimony that water once flowed within their banks and might once again; towering flanges of upright stone running for hundreds of yards, holed through here and there, huge windows for viewing beyond; immense shallow circular pits, with walls and floors covered in crustal salt as if the whole of a forgotten sea had evaporated therein; wide stretches of flat rock reaching for a mile or more, called "beds of the giants" by the K'affeyah, the nomads of the desert.

But always they came back into dunes, the sands of the great Karoo, the face of the mighty Erg.

And though it seemed nigh lifeless, to Bair's eyes it all held <fire>.

Late in the morning of the fifth day of travel and some sixty leagues south of Sabra, they rode up a long dune, and Aravan paused when he came to the top of the rise. Coming up after and stopping beside him, Bair could see in the near distance ahead a sweeping arc of low stony mountains; cupped within its embrace was an extensive palm grove.

"There is the green I promised," said Aravan, grinning at Bair.

"What is it, kelan?"

"The Oasis of Falídii," replied Aravan. "A *djado* place."

"Djado?"

"Cursed," answered Aravan, "or so the stone obelisk does say."

"Cursed with what?"

Aravan shrugged. "I know not, elar. Thrice have I spent the night here, and nought of consequence occurred"—he touched the blue amulet at his throat—"though my stone did grow faintly chill on one of the eves. —Regardless, let us go down; a swim awaits us yon."

"A swim?"

But Aravan did not answer, instead calling out, *"Hut, hut, hut!"* his hajîn and jamâls surging ahead, sand cascading down the long slope in their wake.

Not to be left behind, Bair did likewise, and when he caught up, he asked, "Thrice? You were here three times?"

"Aye: once with thy sire and dam and Faeril and Gwylly and two Realmsmen—Halíd and Reigo—in pursuit of Stoke; and then twice more when travelling to and from the city of Nizari concerning a matter of justice long due."

"And you didn't discover why the place is cursed?"

Aravan shook his head. "Nay, I did not. And neither did Vanidar Silverleaf and Tuon and Halíd when they stayed here on the way to and from the Well of Uâjii."

Bair frowned. "Perhaps the curse has expired."

Aravan shook his head. "I think not, for if it had, this oasis would have dwellers within, for it is a rich jewel in the desert: it has water and shelter and fine pasturage and a broad date grove. Nay, Bair, if ever it were cursed, then so it is still."

"Hmm," mused Bair as they rode down the slope, the normally reluctant camels eagerly moving forward, "I wonder what it could be?"

"Halíd, a Gjeenian, once said that a place of djado is a place where Lord Death himself comes on a black camel, and if any are found at his *guelta*—at his water hole—they will forever ride with him through the endless dark."

"Huah!" Bair snorted. "I have little respect for the tales of the Gjeenians. You saw how groundless were their fears of us aboard the *Hawa Melîh*. As Amicula Faeril would say, 'Twaddle. It's all superstitious twaddle.' "

Aravan looked askance at the lad. "Be not certain of that, Bair, for oft are legends rooted in truth, or so my crew and I did find on many a journey of the *Eroean*. Nevertheless, we will spend the rest of the day here and the full of the night as well, for the journey is long and we can do with a bit of respite, djado or no. Even so we will keep a keen watch."

Past a small toppled obelisk they rode and into the oasis beyond, and Bair could see the remains of mud-brick buildings—their roofs caved in, some walls collapsed, other walls yet standing—all clutched tightly against the steep sides of a broad, boulder-laden knoll.

"So at one time this oasis *was* occupied," said Bair.

"Aye, but not now," replied Aravan.

Onward they rode, to come at last to a solid rock hillside, an overhanging stone bluff along its northern flank. Aravan called his camel to a halt, Bair stopping beside him. "Here we will camp," said Aravan, "for here is a great guelta, water aplenty."

"Lord Death's guelta?" asked Bair, grinning. "Should I keep an eye out for a black camel?"

"Tchaa!" chided Aravan, but he returned the grin.

They unladed the grumbling beasts and hobbled them, and set them free to graze, and though it was not the season, grunting, the camels eagerly surged into the nearby palm grove to search for fallen dates.

"Follow me, Bair," said Aravan. "We are in sore need of a bath." And he led the lad toward the stone bluff, where, under an overhang of sheltering ledge and fed by an underground spring, a great crystal-clear pool of sweet water lay. Without removing his garments or boots, Bair joyfully plunged in.

They pitched camp and washed clothes and hung them up to dry, and after the noon meal, Bair said, "I see what you mean about the richness of this place." The lad looked about. "Something dire must have happened here for it to be abandoned."

Testing the clothes for dryness, Aravan nodded in agreement, saying, "Not only dire, but long past as well."

"Kelan, I would see the obelisk which names this place cursed."

Aravan tossed a shirt and a pair of pantaloons to Bair, saying, "You will have to go unshod, for your boots are yet foolishly wet."

They made their way out to the fallen and half-buried obelisk, the modest stele some two paces long by Bair's measure, the width of each face six hands. On the upfacing plane some third of the way from its blunt-angled tip toward the flat of its up-rooted square base, Aravan brushed off the accumulated sand and then cast a light handful back across, carefully brushing away the excess to reveal a barely discernible cartouche. "Bair, here is the warning of 'Djado.' "

"Hmm," mused Bair, peering. "What is the language?"

"An old form of Khemish," replied Aravan.

"Here in the Karoo? Isn't Khem quite far to the east?"

"Aye," said Aravan. "Nevertheless, Khemish it is."

"Well then," said Bair, "perhaps someone dragged this big rock from there to here, and if so then perhaps the djado—the curse—lies back in the depths of that land."

Aravan turned up a hand. "Mayhap, elar, yet that does not explain why the oasis is abandoned."

Bair frowned. "No it does not." Still frowning, he brushed away more of the sand lying atop. "I say, what's this?" Revealed was a dark stone disk set in the obelisk a few hands below the first cartouche. "It looks like it's made of the black granite of Grimspire."

Aravan examined the embedded stone, testing with the point of his dagger along the thin line of join. "Whoever set this into the stele meant to have it stay." He slid the blade back into its scabbard.

"What does it represent, kelan?"

Aravan frowned in concentration and finally shrugged. "That I cannot say. It is no cartouche I have ever seen. Mayhap 'tis from the eldest of times of Khem, much earlier than the times of the form I learned. Yet the other symbol does say 'Djado,' a cartouche I do know."

"And the black disk may come from an earlier time?"

Aravan nodded. "Aye, elar: in Khem there are cartouches which mayhap none alive can read. Not only in Khem, but elsewhere as well: lying in the sands on the way to Nizari there is a toppled obelisk inscribed in that manner. Mayhap this dark cartouche is from that time, for I know it not . . . yet I ween it speaks of something most dark."

"How about an eclipse of the sun or the moon?"

Aravan shrugged. "Mayhap. Yet it could just as well symbolize the dark plague, or black poison, or any number of ill things, up to and including death, though the cartouche for death I do know, and this is not it . . . unless this cartouche is from that earlier time, in which case it well might be."

"Oh," said Bair, disappointed, but then he brightened. "Perhaps there are other markings on the stone, something to reveal its dark secret." He began brushing away the remaining sand atop, but nothing else was revealed. And then he dug into the sand along the flanks to discover the warning and dark circle on each of those surfaces, too. As to the side lying facedown, whatever might be there would remain hidden, for though it was modest, still the stone was too massive to roll.

Returning from the obelisk, they explored the ruins of the dwellings but found nought of import, and nothing to explain the abandonment of the oasis, though Aravan did say that when Gwylly was here, near one of the crumbling walls he had unearthed a Vanchan vambrace and a length of forearm bone.

Finally, the two went back to the campsite and rested in the shade, and the sun swung across and down in the west, as evening drew nigh.

When twilight finally came—their clothes completely dry, Bair's boots as well—Aravan and Bair donned their garb, making ready for the chill winter night. Aravan took up his blue stone by its thong and held it out to Bair. "In this oasis I would have thee wear this on first ward, elar, for tonight is the dark of the moon, and the amulet may give warning—grow chill—ere thou dost see peril draw nigh."

A puzzled look came over Bair's face the moment he grasped the small stone. "Kelan, it seems chill now."

Aravan pulled the amulet back and gripped the stone direct . . . and frowned. "Distant peril, or peril agrowing."

Holding the amulet, Aravan walked in a great circle to see if the coldness would wax and wane. "It seems faintly cooler in the southeast quadrant."

He looped the thong back over his head and took up his spear and gestured for Bair to arm himself. Then south and east they fared, with Aravan clutching the blue amulet and veering widely side to side, trying to isolate the direction of the danger.

And the dusk darkened as the nighttide swept on.

"It seems to be coming from that stone bluff ahead," said Aravan after several of these broad sweeps.

The brightest stars began to appear, the twilight failing rapidly in the equatorial latitudes.

"Look, Bair, see? Something. Pillars carved in the cliffside."
More stars shone overhead.

"The amulet grows colder still."

"Kelan, there's a door between the pillars."

Aravan nodded. "I see it."

Onward they strode, weapons at the ready, and then Bair said,
"Kelan, on the door is that same cartouche and black symbol."

Aravan did not reply as they stepped the last few paces to the
shallow recess carved in the stone of the bluff, where loomed a
somber, dark door, the panel some eight feet high and four feet
wide. A great iron ring dangled down from a ring-post—a handle to open the door. A stone plaque in the center of the portal
held the djado cartouche along with the black-disk symbol. A
broad stone step led to the door between the stone-cut pillars.
Some twenty feet or so to the left of the panel stood a tall, broad
slab on which many cartouches were carved.

Aravan glanced from the door to the stone slab and back.
Softly he said, "Some Khemish tombs are made like this, hewn
in stone bluffs, pillars carved from the stone of the rise aflank
of the entryway, a cartouche slab standing nearby telling who is
interred therein." Yet gripping the frigid amulet—"Keep ready
thy mace, Bair, for peril is nigh"—Aravan stepped away to the
left to study the broad, carved slab. Squatting before it and frowning in concentration, Aravan hesitantly read aloud, "Um . . . Beware . . . hmm . . . what's this? Ah. Beware the dark of the
moon . . ." Pausing, Aravan looked across at Bair, the lad standing with his flanged mace at the ready and glaring at the door.
"That's what the dark circle represents, Bair: the dark of the
moon."

"Tonight," growled Bair, "is the dark of the moon. And I do
not like waiting."

And as the last of the twilight vanished and full night came
on, Aravan again looked at the carved stone slab. "Beware the
dark of the moon, for, um, then comes the shade of . . . hmm . . .
the Lamia to—"

There sounded the squeal of iron on iron and Aravan looked
up—

—"Bair, don't!"—

—to see Bair twisting the iron ring and pulling the door wide—

—"Bair!"—

—and stepping back as—

—a shadow, a blackness, a *thing* of dark and deadly <fire> rushed forth and enveloped the boy, and Bair's scream pierced the night—

—and he was held in the thrall of pain—

—and struggle as he might, he could not break free—

—and his very essence was being drained from him.

Even as Aravan came running, *"Krystallopŷr,"* he whispered, Truenaming his crystal-bladed spear.

And still Bair's shrill screams cleft the dark, the force of them swiftly dwindling.

And then Aravan plunged Krystallopŷr into the blackness, praying to Adon that he didn't strike Bair.

"Eeeeeeee . . . !" a high-pitched wail keened through the night, and the darkness whipped away, vanishing into the tomb.

Bair collapsed to the stone step.

With his spear at the ready against the return of the *thing*, Aravan knelt beside the boy and touched a finger to the lad's neck.

Bair's pulse was thready, and his breath nought but shallow gasps.

"Endure, elar," gritted Aravan, and he stood and stepped into the doorway beyond, into antiquity, into the smell of ancient dust.

The faintest of starlight seeped into the dimness, and Aravan could see gloom and shadow and murk, and mayhap the shape of a sarcophagus on a raised stone block mid all. Aravan stepped inward . . . and then the *thing* of blackness was upon him. Yet Aravan slashed Truenamed Krystallopŷr through the darkness, and again there came a whining wail. And the *thing*, the shade, the black on black, shrank back. But now Aravan could discern it within the gloom, and he stepped forward and stabbed Krystallopŷr into the heart of the dark, and it shrilled and shrilled and tried to flee, but Aravan was now quicker and kept it impaled on the crystal blade. And then he slammed it down to the floor as its scream rose to a thin shriek, its shape dwindling, dwindling, the darkness mewling and jerking, trying to break free, trying to wrench away, but Aravan held it fast to the stone, and it could not escape. Its movements grew feeble, and its shrilling fell to a whine, a whimper, a whisper, and finally to silence. But with grim death in his eyes, Aravan did not let up on Krystallopŷr and kept the shade pinned, the Truenamed weapon draining the monster just as the Lamia had drained so many victims, the shadow shriveling, dwindling, to finally vanish altogether . . .

. . . to leave only the point of Krystallopŷr's deadly blade grounded against the crypt floor.

And the blue stone amulet about Aravan's neck no longer held any chill.

"Krystalloýp," whispered Aravan, again Truenaming his spear, stilling its lethal power.

And then he turned and stepped forth from the tomb to where Bair lay slack on unyielding stone in the dark of a moonless night.

CHAPTER 22

Oracle

January–February, 5E1009

[Eleven and Ten Months Past]

When Bair groaned awake in the firelight, Aravan swiftly stepped to his side and knelt and held out a cup of liquid. But Bair's eyes flew wide and he struggled upward. "The *thing*, kelan, the *thing* of dark burning <fire>!"

Aravan thrust forth a staying hand. " 'Tis slain, Bair. Rest easy."

Bair collapsed back to his bedroll.

"Canst thou sit up and drink this? It is a gwynthyme tisane."

Grunting, Bair managed to hitch up on one elbow, and as he reached for the cup, he moaned, "Lor', kelan, but I feel as if a camel dropped out of the sky and fell upon me."

"Thou hast been unconscious for two days."

"Two days!"

"Aye. All today and yester thou didst lay oblivious—"

"But two days? That is hard to—" Bair's words chopped short, and his eyes widened in discovery. "It was the dark of the moon when we came upon the tomb. But now—" He took a deep breath and let it out and pointed westward, where a thin silver crescent of a waxing young moon was sinking into the dark horizon. "Adon, it *has* been two days," breathed Bair.

"Aye," affirmed Aravan. "Now drink thy tea."

As he sipped the bracing tisane, Bair looked about in the night. "How did I get back to our camp?"

"I carried thee, Bair, and thou art no light load."

Bair drained the cup and set it aside, then, struggling—"I need to relieve myself, kelan"—he got to his feet with Aravan's help.

Waving off any further aid, Bair tottered to a nearby palm tree, and as he emptied his bladder he called back, "What *was* that thing, kelan?"

"A Lamia, Bair."

"Lamia? What's a Lamia. I mean, I saw it, felt it—the worse for me—but what *is* it?"

"A stealer of life, rooted deep in the legends of many a folk, the desert dwellers among them. Some say a Lamia is a serpent with the head and breasts of a female, while others claim just the opposite—a female with a snakelike head and neck. Still others say a Lamia can take on many shapes: that of a bat, a Wolf, a mist, a thousand running rats, a seductive female, all of them draining blood or draining the flame of life."

Finished, Bair returned to his bedroll, and Aravan helped him back down. "It was draining my <fire>, kelan."

"Aye, and it nearly slew thee in but mere moments."

"It felt like years. And the pain was, was . . . —Oh, kelan, I pray to Adon that I never experience such again. And I am so weak, so very weak."

Aravan nodded in agreement. "Thou dost need to rest and drink and eat, elar, to restore thee unto thy vigor. Here, I have prepared thee some barley broth." Aravan crumbled a bit of hardtack within the soup to give it more body, and then handed a cupful to Bair.

Slowly, Bair sipped the broth and nibbled on a biscuit of crue—a nutritious but rather tasteless waybread. He said nought as he did so, his thoughts turned inward instead. Finally, as he finished his meal and set the cup aside he said, "What I did— opening that door, unthinking, not waiting—it was the act of a fool."

"Brash thou wert, hasty thou wert, and indeed a fool thou wert. 'Tis the folly of youth."

"But surely, kelan—" In spite of his own words of selfcondemnation, Bair began to protest Aravan's affirmation, but Aravan thrust out a hand of negation.

"Nay, Bair. Thou hast named thyself a fool and a fool thou

wert. There are times in the press of the moment when bold-ness and dash will serve and serve well, but this was not one of them. There are many things of dire peril in this world, things that will slay thee in but a heartbeat, and rash acts only serve to hasten already hasty ends. The seasoned warrior knows this truth; the brash beginner does not."

"But kelan, how do I get this seasoning if not by facing dire peril?"

"Step by step, lad. Gradual ascent. It does not come all at once."

"Is that how you learned?"

A memory washed over Aravan, a memory from the Elven days of madness—a madness that lasted for aeons rather than mere days—a memory of the bloody morning when he was thrust into savage conflict as a youth no older than Bair.

"Is that the way you learned?" repeated Bair.

"Nay it was not."

"Well then—"

"This is different, Bair."

"How so?"

"Unlike when I first went into battle, in thy case we have a choice."

Bair growled and shook his head, but did not otherwise dis-agree, and they sat without speaking for a while, the crescent moon now gone from sight. But finally Aravan sighed and said, "This, Bair, is why I shall not take thee with me in pursuit of Ydral, but shall return thee to Arden Vale instead."

"But kelan—" protested Bair.

"Nay, Bair. Speak not. I have decided."

A chill silence fell between them as remote stars wheeled in the cold night above and, despite his exhaustion, sleep was a long time coming to Bair.

They remained for two more days at the oasis, Bair recov-ering his strength, the lad and his mentor barely speaking, a coldness between them even in the heat of the day. But in the dawn-time of the third morn, they made ready to leave, Aravan filling up all the *guerbas*—goatskins for carrying water—saying, " 'Tis good the camels foraged well on these lush pastures, for the days ahead will be hard on them."

Bair grunted noncommittally, and continued to break camp.

They rounded up the animals and saddled the dromedaries and laded most goods on the pack camels—all but a cautionary waterskin apiece and a few days' rations of food, which, as they had done in days past, they slung onto the riding hajînain—all the beasts growling and spitting at these vile two-legged beings who would forever enslave them. And when all was ready they mounted the dromedaries and—*Kam! Kam!*—commanded the animals to their feet. Westward they rode to the bound of the oasis, where they then turned south-southeast. As they passed by the fallen obelisk, Bair said, "Should we remove the Djado cartouche? After all, the Lamia is slain."

Aravan glanced at the stele and said, "We shall do so when we come back this way on our return to Arden Vale."

At these words the chill deepened between the two.

Far across the Erg they went, endless dunes of sand, the world filled with a warm sun by day and a frigid cold by night, the 'scape ever changing, never changing, as across dune after dune they trekked. Pasturage was nonexistent, and the only water to be had was held in their goatskin guerbas. They fed the camels grain, yet there was not enough to wholly sustain the grumbling, complaining beasts, and the animals began to draw on the fat stored in their humps, Aravan assuring Bair that the camels could bear up under such conditions for many days. And onward they went across the sands, each day riding till late morning and resting and dozing till midafternoon, then riding again until the eventide. They camped on bare sand and spoke little, though the chill between them had begun to thaw. And throughout the nights the warder on watch wore Aravan's blue stone amulet; although occasionally it seemed to grow cool, it never became icy cold.

Five days they fared, crossing endless dunes, seeing nought but frozen waves of sand, but on the morning of the sixth day, the camels surged eagerly forward. " 'Tis the water ahead," said Aravan, letting his dromedary set its own pace, Bair following suit. Onward trotted the camels, and within a mile they came to vast, shallow depression, scrub growing in the wide hollow, and in the distant center grew a handful of ragged palms, the fronds desiccated, yellowish and sickly. On the brim of the depression Aravan halted his camel, the beast complaining loudly.

"Do we camp here?" asked Bair, stopping alongside and glancing at the still-rising sun. "It's yet early in the day."

"Nay, not camp, but we shall let the camels forage the day, and then we move on at night."

"Why so?"

Aravan pointed, and among the palms Bair could see a mortared stone ring. "So . . . ?"

"It is the Well of Uâjii," said Aravan, "a place where evil once dwelled, an evil slain by Vanidar Silverleaf and Tuon and Halíd, though it nearly cost them their lives."

"Ah, Amicula Faeril told me that tale."

"Did she also tell thee that this is the place where she gained the silver lock that runs through her hair?"

Bair shook his head.

" 'Twas thine ythir's blade Dúnamis which did so, for when invoked it draws energy from those nearby to power the wielder's arm, and if the need is great the sword will draw life itself."

"And here the need was great?"

"Aye, and it took years from Faeril's life and left her with a silver lock. I am afraid she will not live the full span of a Waerling."

Tears sprang into Bair's eyes. "And you say my ythir did this to her?"

"To her and Gwylly and Halíd, mortals all. Riatha had no choice but to Truename Dúnamis, Bair; otherwise, all would have died."

"But surely . . ." Bair looked about as if seeking an answer to complete his unfinished thought.

"Come, Bair. The camels must forage and I would not spend the night in this djado place, this cursed place, for not only are the memories ill, but other such creatures may yet dwell herein. We will not draw from the well itself, but continue to use our guerbas, for we have enough water to last us all the way to the Kandrawood."

Down into the basin they rode.

*   *   *

In late afternoon ere the sun had set they fared away from the Well of Uâjii, and Aravan said as they rode from the basin, "There are but twenty leagues left ere we come to the Kandra-wood, a ride of no more than two days."

"The Kandrawood—does that name have meaning?"

"It is where a stand of kandra trees grow, a timber nearly as precious as that of eldwood. Kandra lumber is a rich golden hue with a fine, dense grain and a delicate and pleasing scent; the wood itself has a natural sheen, as if it contained an oil, though it does not burn like such, and it is resistant to aging and rotting and warping. I used some kandra in the construction of the *Eroean*, though I harvested it in the realm of Thyra rather than from the place we now go."

"Ah," said Bair, and then he fell silent as onward the two rode, their goal but some two days hence.

They travelled nigh six leagues from the Well of Uâjii, much of it in full night. They stopped among high dunes, and spoke little as they set camp, the relations between kelan and elar yet strained.

And now that they were less than two days from their destination, for perhaps the thousandth time Bair once again reviewed all of the reasons why Aravan *must* take him along, should the Oracle Dodona point the way. But each and every argument he mentally mustered was negated by his boneheaded act at the Lamia's tomb. All that was left was the leniency of his kelan, the chance that he would change his mind, but Aravan had made abundantly clear that in this he was unyielding. Bair slammed the last of the cargo racks to the sand and stalked off to stand atop the nearest dune and glare at the gibbous moon.

Aravan watched the lad go, and he knew the turmoil within Bair's heart, yet the brash boy was not ready in spite of his training, or so Aravan did believe.

They spent the cold night in chill silence, not speaking at the change of watch.

They came up a long stony slope to the wide rim of a deep, plumb-walled canyon in early morning, the rising sun yet low in the east. "Here we are, our destination," said Aravan, "or nearly so." They stood on the east brim of the gorge, near its northern end, and Bair could see the chasm held the shape of a crescent moon, running southerly and curving away to the west. Leftward and spread out across the distant floor was greenery—a stand of trees. And there came to Bair's ears a faint purl, and he turned his head side to side, trying to capture the elusive sound, and then he realized it was the sonant of a distant fall of water coming from somewhere below.

"A forest and waterfall in the heart of the desert?"

Aravan nodded. "The water comes from that which Halíd named *Ilnahr Taht*—the River Under. It flows out from the stone of the west wall and wends its way southerly a league or so to the east wall, where it plunges under stone again."

"Three miles, eh? But the gorge itself looks quite a bit longer than that."

"Seven miles it spans from tip to tip along its arc, and three-quarters of a mile at its widest, the walls a thousand feet high."

"That stand of trees I see: that's the Kandrawood?"

"Aye, Bair, it is. It fills the canyon side to side, along where the river flows, but the last two miles at each end of the gorge is barren of all but scrub—thorny bushes and sparse grass—forage for the camels."

"How do we get down and in? Rappel?"

"Nay, elar. Dost thou see the narrow slot cleaving full down through the western face? 'Tis our way into the rift. Come, the camels need fare."

North and west they rode and around the northernmost end, and then Aravan struck a course due south, away from the brink and back down the stony bordering slope. Some distance west of the brim of the gorge they came to a downsloping crevice in the land. Following this fissure, they tracked west away from the chasm until they came to the place where the fissure started.

"It is strait, but the camels can squeeze through," said Aravan, and with that he turned back easterly and rode into the twisting rent in the land, the camels growling at the close-by walls, dismayed at the idiot rider for leading them down between such. Bair followed, the way so narrow he could span its width with outstretched arms, and the farther he went, the deeper became the slot. Daylight faded as they descended, the unyielding walls rising about them, the air in the cramped notch quite chill, as if the warmth of day never seeped into this cragged and stony way. Down they went and down, faring along a rugged, rock-strewn floor, among boulders and fallen slabs, with rough, shadowed stone looming high overhead, a thin jagged line of blue marking the sky far above.

Deeper they went and deeper, twisting this way and that, the camels objecting loudly. But as they rounded a tight corner, Bair at last saw jagging up the stone before him a great vertical cleft filled with bright daylight; they had come to the end at last.

Squinting, he rode on outward and down a long slope of scree, and Aravan awaited him at the bottom, his camels a deal less noisy now they were free of the slot. Even so, they grumbled and fidgeted and cast rolling-eyed glares, for winter pasturage awaited them here if these dolts would only let them be.

But Aravan turned and rode southerly, his camels *hronk*ing angrily, as did Bair's when he followed.

"*Hut, hut, hut!*" Bair urged his hajîn forward to come alongside Aravan. "Where will we find Dodona?"

"In a ring of kandra trees," replied Aravan. "If find him we can."

Bair frowned. "How so?"

"He has a warding about the ring, and it turns seekers away. When we sought him before, we nearly did not succeed. The last two times I was here—going to and from Nizari—I did not e'en attempt to find Dodona or the ring."

Bair cocked an eyebrow. "Though I saw nothing untoward when we were up on the eastern lip above, now that we are in the canyon mayhap I can <see> this warding, this charm, given it has <fire>."

Aravan nodded in approval. "Mayhap indeed, Bair, thou *wilt* see. I had not thought of the gift of thy <sight>."

They rode onward, the vegetation slowly changing, becoming more lush, more succulent, the closer they came to the stand. At last they rode in among the kandra, and though these trees dwelled in the desert, palms they were not, but something else altogether. Large they were, their great limbs spread out like oaks, yet their leaves were small and bladelike, shaped as rounded stone arrow points—green on the topside and yellow on the bottom, and they quaked in the slight breeze as would aspen leaves tremble. And in their shade grew green grass, a thing Bair had not seen in the desert until now.

"This place is filled with <life>, kelan," breathed Bair.

Aravan looked at the lad and then at the surround, and finally he said, "Would that I could share thy <sight>, elar."

"I would that you could as well," replied Bair, as onward they rode.

Aravan turned rightward toward the sound of falling water, and soon they came to a wide, clear stream running in the shade of the overhanging branches of the kandra trees. Upstream a furlong or so, they came to where the pellucid flow poured out of a wide crevice in the face of the western gorge wall, to fall ten feet into a crystalline pool, a spray of rainbows dancing in a swirl of mist in the bright morning sun.

"Here we make camp," said Aravan.

Aravan and Bair unladed their goods and unsaddled the camels, and then they let the beasts drink their fill from the stream. When they were finished, Aravan and Bair led them just beyond the edge of the Kandrawood and hobbled them and set them loose to graze on the succulent fare.

As they walked back to the campsite, Bair asked, "When do we go to Dodona?"

Aravan glanced at Bair and said, "First we shall make ourselves presentable. Then we shall seek the ring of trees and speak with him, can we defeat the charm, and given that he comes at our call."

They bathed in the clear pool below the waterfall, using the cascade itself to rinse away the days of sweat and odor and grit and grime, and the clinging smell of camels. After washing their travelling clothes, they unpacked their spare garb from among their baggage and dressed.

"Ah, but it feels good to be clean again," said Bair as he wiped his boots with a damp cloth to clear away the dust of many days.

"Indeed," said Aravan. "Art thou ready?"

Bair slipped into his boots. "Ready, kelan. Now let us see if we can find this charmed ring of yours."

"Not mine, Bair, but Dodona's. And it may be the most difficult task we will have done so far on this journey, including defeating the Lamia."

Bair's mouth fell open.

Seeing the lad's dumbfounded look, Aravan added, "I tell thee, elar, finding Dodona is nigh impossible."

Bair turned up his hands. "Where do we begin?"

Aravan pointed vaguely. "When last I saw the ring of trees, it was here nigh the waterfall."

They stepped in the direction indicated, and within a pace or two they found themselves in a circle of trees, where stood what seemed to be an old man, with long white hair and a flowing white beard and dressed in white robes. His face was crinkled with age lines, and pale blue eyes looked out at them from beneath shaggy white brows. "Ah, here you are at last," said the man. "I have been waiting for you."

As Aravan's eyes widened in surprise at finding the Kandra-wood ring so quickly, "You are not what you seem," blurted Bair, "but are silver <light> instead."

"Is anyone ever what he or she seems?" asked the man.

"Nay," replied Bair. "I have always found them to be more."

At Bair's response a look of regard came into the eyes of the man, and he nodded in silent approval.

"Art thou Dodona?" asked Aravan.

The man turned toward the Elf. "It is a name some call me."

"But if you are Dodona," asked Bair, looking about at the perfect circle of evenly spaced kandra trees, their branches interlaced overhead, "what of the charm that wards this place? I was told it is difficult to find."

"Did you not hear me, boy? I said I was waiting for you."

"For me?"

Dodona nodded, then added, "For you and Aravan."

"Then thou wilt answer my question?" asked Aravan. "I have come to find the whereabouts of—"

"I know why you have come," interrupted Dodona, "and I will not answer, for though you again pursue a monster, more important outcomes are at stake. Besides, did not wee Faeril tell you that I am loath to aid anyone on a mission of death?"

"Aye, she did, but Ydral deserves death, mayhap e'en more so than Stoke."

"Mayhap indeed," replied Dodona, "yet that is neither here nor there."

Even as Aravan's face clouded, Bair said dejectedly, "Then our mission is wasted."

"Again, lad, did you not listen. What I said is that more important outcomes are at stake than the slaying of a single being. The Trine is coming, and you both must be ready."

"Trine?" asked Bair. But Dodona did not answer, and Aravan shrugged, for he knew not what Dodona meant.

"These outcomes," said Aravan, "I would know what they are."

"Heed me now," said Dodona, fixing Bair with his gaze. And then he looked at Aravan. "A great woe is coming from the East, the West is all unknowing, the South readies for war, and in the North lies buried the hammer." Of a sudden Dodona's hand snaked out viper swift and seized the crystal pendant on its platinum chain fastened about Bair's neck, and Dodona held it up and looked straight at Aravan. "And you, Aravan, you must learn to use this; the future of all creation depends upon it." Dodona let the pendant fall back to Bair's chest.

"Aravan use my crystal? Bu-but how?" sputtered Bair, looking down at the pendant and then to Aravan and finally back to the old man.

Dodona held up a single finger of caution. "This I will say: go to the Temple of the Sky, for there you can master the crystal."

Again Bair looked at the pendant. "But what will my crystal do?"

Dodona sighed. "I once told your amicula that all things are possible therein, but no more, no more, for it is impressed, and of that I will say no more."

Bair groaned in frustration but said, "If you'll not speak of what it will do, tell me this: after Aravan learns to use the crystal, then what?"

"A path will be chosen at the Temple of the Sky."

Bair waited for more to be said, yet Dodona revealed nought else. "That's all you are going to say? A path will be chosen at the temple?"

Dodona nodded.

As Bair growled in frustration, Aravan said, "And where is this temple?"

"In the Mountains of Jangdi," replied Dodona.

"That is quite far from here," said Aravan.

Dodona nodded his agreement, and added, "And there is perhaps not enough time to do all that must be done."

"Which is?"

"That I will not say, for to do so would likely change the outcome, or so I do believe."

Bair's eyes flew wide at Dodona's pronouncement. "But you are an Oracle. Can you not see all things?"

"I only see the myriad branching choices to be made, and the most likely path among all," replied Dodona. "Should any interfere with these choices through intervention of any sort—such as answering all questions, or laying out the exact course to take—then the future itself will shift to one which I have not seen. Along the way aid may come unbidden and assist you toward an end, yet I will only point out a beginning and not tell you where it might lead."

As Bair snorted in exasperation, Aravan looked at Dodona and asked, "And this is a necessary thing thou wouldst have me do? Go to the Temple of the Sky?"

Once more Dodona nodded.

Aravan pondered but a moment, silence falling over all but for the gentle rustle of leaves, and Bair realized that he could not hear the waterfall, though it was a mere few paces away. The preternatural hush was broken when Aravan said, "As thou hast asked so shall I do, but first I must return the lad to Arden Vale."

"No!" cried Bair in protest.

"No," said Dodona, quietly.

No? asked Aravan and Bair in unison.

"No," affirmed Dodona. He turned to Aravan, "Even though the boy did a foolish thing, a rash thing, a near fatal thing, at the tomb of the Lamia—"

"You know about that?" gasped Bair.

"—still he must go at your side, for I deem if you go without him, or he without you, and the hammer goes awry, then creation will fall, brought about by *a man born of a corpse.*"

What? blurted Aravan and Bair, again in unison.

"I cannot say more," replied Dodona.

Aravan frowned and said, "What if the hammer does *not* go awry."

"Then creation will stand," replied Dodona. "Yet heed: there will come a time of choice, and likely the wrong path will be chosen, in which event you and Bair are the last hope of the world, but also perhaps its doom."

Bair's eyes widened in startlement. "Hope and doom both?"

Dodona nodded, but before Bair could ask, the Oracle pressed out a staying hand and said, "I will not explain."

Bair groaned in exasperation.

Aravan shook his head. "Dodona, Bair is yet a brash youth, and I like this not if it puts him in jeopardy—"

"And I like not your liking it not," said Bair. "Jeopardy I will deal with—*we* will deal with—as it comes. And as for my *boldness*, I deem I learned my lesson at the djado tomb; even so, mayhap now and again, boldness will serve where cunning and guile will not. Besides, you heard Dodona, and he's an Oracle. And anyway it's *my* crystal pendant, and where it goes, so go I."

Dodona sighed. "Stop squabbling, you two, and listen: it is necessary for Bair to go, Aravan, for he is the Rider of the Planes—"

Bair frowned, trying to remember something he read in the archives, but it remained elusive, beyond his grasp, but Aravan's eyes widened with understanding.

"—hence, he *must* go with you, and you must go with him, and in the end you must go together and alone," concluded Dodona.

"Is there no other way?" asked Aravan.

Dodona shook his head and said, "None."

Aravan glanced at Bair and sighed, then reluctantly nodded his agreement.

Bair's face lighted up with joy.

"Beam not, boy," growled Dodona, "for a terrible trial lies ahead."

"A trial?"

"I have said all I may, save to warn you time is pressing."

He fixed Aravan with a sharp glare. "Go and go now, else the coming storm will leave you in its wake."

And without preamble or warning, Dodona vanished, leaving Aravan and Bair startled and alone in the hush of the ring of kandra trees.

"But wait!" cried Bair. "I have more to ask."

Dodona did not reappear.

"He has answered all he will," said Aravan softly.

Bair sighed in disappointment, and Aravan said, "Come, let us sit by the River Under and discuss what we have just heard." And they stepped from the circle, and once again the sound of the waterfall came to their ears. Yet, lo! though they had entered the Kandrawood ring ere the noontide, twilight was now on the land; it was as if time ran at a far different pace when in the presence of Dodona.

Bair frowned, pondering, and then stepped back toward the Kandrawood ring, only to find— "Kelan! It's gone! The circle of trees is gone!"

As if confirming a suspicion, Aravan nodded unto himself. Wide-eyed and shaking his head, Bair stepped from among the trees, and together they walked through the gathering dusk and into their campsite, each reflecting in silence upon the arcane ways of Dodona.

Later, as they prepared a meal, Aravan said, "Though this is a precious place of rest, we shall leave early on the morrow, Bair, for Jangdi is far to the east and Dodona has said time is pressing."

"What is a pressing time to an Oracle?" asked Bair.

Aravan shrugged. "I know not. It could be a day, a year, ten years, or a thousand or more."

"We should have asked," said Bair, "even though he might not have answered."

"All we know concerning urgency is what he said: there is perhaps not enough time to do all that must be done; too, he said the Trine is coming. Could we discover the meaning of that, then might we reason how long or short is the time, though I ween 'tis more likely to be short than long."

Of a sudden Bair clapped his hands and laughed. "The best

thing he said, kelan, was when he said it was necessary for me to go at your side and bade you to take me along."

"Grin not, Bair, for I shall keep a stern eye on thee, and I say now, rashness I will not abide. Hear this as well: were it not for Dodona, then truly would I have returned thee to Arden Vale, a place where thou wouldst be most safe."

CHAPTER 23

Guile

"Fall back! Fall back!" cried Elissan on a black horse thundering by, and silver horns rang out *Withdraw, withdraw!* while bugles blatted *Charge!*

Faeril let fly her last steel dagger to take a Hlôk in the throat, and then she reined her nimble pony 'round and fled before the foe, Foul Folk howling in glee as the Elven force broke and ran, and down the gorge of Arden Vale raced away the fleeing Lian, savage yawling Rûpt in hot pursuit, scrambling through the cold snow after.

Far beneath a bright gibbous moon sailing the clear night toward fullness, on the heights of the gorge an Elven archer waited in moonshadow for what was to come. And she watched as warriors galloped past and Spaunen came running behind, and not a single arrow was nocked nor a hard-driven shaft sent winging. *Not yet, not yet,* came the whispered command, as pursued and pursuers fled down the vale, eventually to be lost unto her clear Elven sight.

And the silvery moon serenely sailed on.

Away they fled and away, down the narrow vale, thundering horses and one lone pony fleeing before the storm, the Foul Folk afoot running after. Two leagues they fled and two leagues more, and the Spaunen began to lag, but lo! so did the Elven force begin to slow as well, coming nigh within the harsh Rûptish clutch. Seeing their foe now starting to flag, the Spawn howled in glee, renewed vigor coursing their veins, and they took up the race once more.

And there came another clash and clangor of weapons and the shouting of battle cries as the Rûptish forerunners overtook the waning foe; Rûcks fell dead in the milling melee, and Hlôks were slain as well; Elves were unhorsed, their steeds falling down, yet quickly the animals gained their hooves, and the Elves mounted up again or leapt up behind a comrade to ride double; but then the bulk of the Foul Folk were nigh upon them; yet once again the Elves broke free and fled just ahead of the main Spaunen force.

And the platinum moon continued to slide across the starry night above.

A league more did the pursuit run and another league after, and the Elves, the Elves, the damned Elves stayed just beyond the victor's grasp. It was almost as if they were trying to—

—gasping in startlement, the Foul Folk *cham* looked up at the moon now gliding down in the west; *"Gadak!"* he shrieked to his bugler, and turned and fled the opposite way as Rûptish blats blared through the cold night and signalled that daylight was coming.

Squealing in terror, the Foul Folk fled back along the way they had come, and on the heights above—*Now!*—came the command, and arrows sleeted down, dropping running Rûpt into churned-up snow, their blood leaking blackly away.

And all of the horses and the single pony of the fleeing Elven force turned and came riding after, the pursued no longer a lure, but a force now of vengeance dire.

Gasping and wheezing, back ran the Rûpt, fleeing toward distant refuge, slowed by a rain of death from above and cut down by galloping doom from behind.

They did not make it out of the gorge before deadly daylight came, and they failed to kill the single lad they had come to slaughter that night. Only ashes blowing in the wind marked what they had done, and soon even these were gone.

And in the clear light of early morn, Dara Riatha offered up thanks to High Adon that Bair was gone from perilous Arden Vale.

CHAPTER 24

Reflections

February, 5E1009

[Ten Months Past]

On the north bank of the Ilnahr Taht, Bair and Aravan sat and pondered as they ate their evening meal, winnowing through the cryptic words of the Oracle Dodona, glitter-bright stars wheeling above.

As Aravan took a bite of crue, "Something most dire is afoot," said Bair, setting his tea aside, his heart hammering with excitement, "something for us to quell. Did you hear what he said? The hope of the world, and perhaps its doom—that's what we are, though I'd much rather be a hope than a doom. Why do you think he said that? And what's all this talk of a buried hammer? And why did he call me the Rider of the Planes? And the crystal, what do you think he meant when he said—?"

"Elar, cease!" said Aravan, his free hand thrust out palm forward to stay the lad's rattle of words.

Bair's jaw snapped shut with an audible click. He took a deep breath and slowly let it out, then reached for his cup and took a sip.

Aravan finished chewing and swallowed and then said, "Let us take up what we saw and heard as it occurred, for at times the order reveals answers. Thereafter, we shall decide our course."

"All right," said Bair, breaking off a piece of crue and looking at it in disdain. "Even though I believe our course is set— we go to the Temple of the Sky in Jangdi—still there many things I'd like to know." He popped the crue into his mouth and 'round it said, "Where shall we begin?"

"At the beginning," replied Aravan.

"And that would be . . . ?"

"We found him immediately," said Aravan.

"We did at that," said Bair, then frowned. "You said he had a charm to make finding him difficult. But I say it was more than a simple charm, for, when I went back, the circle was not even there! And— Ah, I see: he *wanted* to be found."

"Aye, Bair, he did. Hence, as an Oracle he has seen something dire. How did he put it? A great woe is coming from the East . . . yet what that might be—war, famine, pestilence, scourge, or something else altogether—I cannot say."

"What's in the East?"

"Many nations: Ryodo, Jinga, Moko, Jûng, Lazan, the Ten Thousand Isles of Mordain, more. Of these, only Jûng has in the past been a threat to the West."

Aravan fell silent, and Bair said, "Dodona's next words were, 'the West is all unknowing.' What is the West, kelan? And unknowing of what?"

"The West, Bair, are the lands under the protection of the High King."

To Bair's mind's eye sprang a vision of Prince Ryon, son of High King Garon and Queen Thayla; and along with Ryon came images of Prince Äldan of Valon and Prince Diego of Vancha— the three he had trained with in the Greatwood.

Will they be in peril?

Not knowing the answer to his own question, Bair sighed and said, "All right. And the West is all unknowing of what? —The woe from the East?"

"Aye, or so I would judge," replied Aravan.

"Then why does Dodona have us haring off to Jangdi instead of sending us to Caer Pendwyr to warn the High King, to warn Prince Ryon?"

"I know not, elar, yet this I can guess: there is not enough time for us to do both, to warn King Garon and also to go to Jangdi and do whatever it is we must do."

Bair nodded in reluctant agreement, then wolfed down the last of his crue and swallowed the last of his tea. "And given that Dodona next said 'the South prepares for war,' it means war is coming, and the woe from the East could be invading armies and—"

"Bair, recall, as I said, it could just as well be some other ill," interjected Aravan, "pestilence, plague—"

"But kelan, war breeds war. And since the South prepares . . . Still, as you say, it might be something else. If so, I would very much like to know what." Bair stood and stepped to the flowing stream and rinsed his cup, and then drank of its pure water.

Aravan joined him at streamside and knelt to rinse his hands. "Much is cryptic and unknown to us, Bair, as is an Oracle's wont, and so we can only ponder until reason or events make things clear."

"Are we all unknowing, then?"

Aravan stood. "Not quite, Bair, yet when it comes to Oracles, 'tis an arcane maze we face, and we can only take it a step at a time, though now and again there may come a leap."

Bair took a deep breath and let it out. "Then let us take that next step through the maze: I repeat, he said, 'the South readies for war.' Tell me of the South."

They took seat on the bank again, and Aravan said, "The South is made up of several kingdoms on this side of the Avagon Sea, specifically Hyree, Kistan, Chabba, and Sarain, the ancient foe of the West, joined by others now and then—by Khem and Thyra and faraway Jûng. Indeed, some eighteen years past, when thine ythir and athir and amicula and I came back through Hyree, we did see warlike preparations being made and reported such to the High King, for we thought Hyree and mayhap others were once again preparing to invade across the Avagon Sea as they have done in the past. The King then did send Realmsmen forth into those lands and others to keep watch, and they are watching still. Hence, through the Realmsmen, the High King knows that preparations for war have been in the making for many a year. We could not then say whether or no an onslaught would be forthcoming, but we suspected it was so, for, worshipping Gyphon as the Southerlings do, eventual warfare seemed a certainty, though whether or no it would come soon, none could say."

"I would think there'd be no question of it," said Bair. "Does not preparation for war lead to war?"

Aravan smiled. "Ah, Bair, thou hast asked a question which has occupied many a sage throughout the aeons. For should no nation whatsoever prepare for war—no weapons of conquest, no soldiers, no power seekers—then war might never come. But given the world as it is, elar, war is oft prevented by a nation being well prepared, for then the cost to an aggressor would be entirely too great to bear, and so they do not invade. Yet there is another reason potentates and others in high seats prepare a nation for war, even though they have no intention whatsoever to fight; they do so as a means of maintaining power, pointing in alarm at those they name great enemies; they gather armies in the face of this false threat, and they foster the conviction that only they can lead the nation forth from the darkness to come."

Bair frowned. "But kelan, do we not also name those of the South great enemies, too? Do we not also prepare for war with no intention to fight, except, of course, at need? Do we not believe no matter what, we will be victorious? If so, how are we different from them?"

"Ah, Bair, we *do* name them enemies, yet not to sustain our leaders in power, but to maintain a readiness for war in the hope that such preparation will cause the foe to quail and remain within his bounds. And we believe in our inevitable victory, for not only are we well prepared, but we fight against oppression, and in the end freedom will out, though it take millennia. In these and in many other ways we are different from the South, for unlike them we do not worship Gyphon, who would have a world in which the strong dominate the weak, rather than aid them to better themselves, or at least not stand in the way."

"Does Adon aid the weak?"

Aravan shook his head. "I think not, Bair, except, perhaps, through His tokens of power. Instead He does not stand in the way, letting each person, each creature, each being, decide for himself the course of his life."

"That seems rather aloof of Him," said Bair.

"Aye, it is, yet we are free to choose and are not ruled in our daily living by a being we cannot oppose. —But we stray from

Dodona's words, and given what he said, then along with woe from the East, mayhap war *is* coming soon; if so, 'tis likely a war in which the Southerlings will be embroiled. We will have to hope that the Realmsmen's reports to the High King will be warning enough."

Bair sighed in resignation. "I suppose so, yet I can't help but feel that somehow Dodona's words would lend an urgency to the High King's preparations that might otherwise be missing. —Regardless, Dodona next said, 'in the North lies buried the hammer.' What might that mean? Do you know?"

His brow furrowed, Aravan took a deep breath and let it out and said, "The Kammerling."

"The Kammerling? What's that?"

"Thou didst not read of this in the archive? No? Ah, Bair, thou shouldst have taken to thy lessons in the history of Mithgar more assiduously—"

"But, kelan, I was more interested in languages, and with all the work in arms and armor and in climbing and other such, well . . . —Besides, Ythir said that endless days stood ahead, and that I would always have time to—"

Aravan threw up a hand of surrender. "Enough, Bair. Thy point is well made. I will chide thee no more."

"Then tell me of the Kammerling."

"Any who has read or heard the Legend of Elyn and Thork knows that the Kammerling—Adon's Hammer, the Rage Hammer—was lost in the ruins of Dragonslair."

"And this lies in the North?"

"Aye," replied Aravan. "And 'tis a hammer buried."

"What is this hammer, and how does it concern us?"

"As to how it bears on our mission, that I cannot say," replied Aravan. "However, there is this: Dodona said should the hammer go astray—the Kammerling, I deem—then we are the hope of the world."

Bair frowned. "But he also said we might be its doom."

They sat in silence for a while, Dodona's words weighing heavily, but then Bair said, "Tell me as much as you know of the Kammerling and of Elyn and Thork as well."

Aravan looked at the stars above. "I will tell thee the short of their tale; the long of it thou canst read for thyself when we return to the vale. As to their story, this is the way it was:

"Elyn and Thork were foes during the War 'tween Jord and Kachar: she a Jordian warrior maiden, he a Drimm warrior. Humans and Drimma were not the only ones engaged in the struggle, for reining terror over both sides was Black Kalgalath, the mightiest Dragon of all.

"Independently, both Elyn and Thork bethought to gain the Kammerling, a mighty warhammer also named Adon's Hammer, for it was said to have been forged by the hand of Adon Himself, though others dispute that claim. Regardless as to its maker, it was, and mayhap still is, a great token of power, and its doom was to slay the greatest Dragon of all, yet whosoever wielded the hammer would suffer dreadful woe. The Drimma named this token the Rage Hammer, for woven in this doom was the legend that the Kammerling could only be empowered by great rage.

"In spite of the legend that to the wielder great woe would befall, separately, Elyn and Thork set out to gain the silveron hammer, thinking that after the Dragon was slain they could use it against their enemies—the Drimma against the Jordians; the Jordians against the Drimma—for both were driven by great rage through the loss of close kith.

"Neither Elyn nor Thork knew the other had fared forth on the same quest, yet by happenstance they were cast together and they found themselves facing a common foe, and even though they were bitter enemies, they formed a temporary alliance. Yet in a day-after-day running battle, the common foe attacked again and again, and so the temporary alliance held longer than either Elyn or Thork had wished. But after many trials and tribulations, they pledged to one another that together they would seek the destruction of Black Kalgalath and then find a way to bring peace between their nations.

"In the end, one of the two slew Black Kalgalath with the Rage Hammer, and it was plunged into the firemountain of Dragonslair by Black Kalgalath in his death throes, and the mountain was crashed into ruin, and the Kammerling was lost down in the deep molten stone below, or so say the Utruni."

"Utruni: Stone Giants, eh?"

"Aye: the Earthmasters dwelling deep within the Living Stone of Mithgar. —Regardless, Bair, that is the short of the tale."

"But there is so much you didn't say, kelan. Of how Elyn and Thork found the Rage Hammer, who wielded it, and—"

"It is a splendid saga to savor, Bair, and not a tale for spoiling, hence I shall let thee read of this venture for thyself when we return to Arden Vale."

"Just answer me this, kelan: did the wielder suffer great woe?"

"Indeed, that part of the foretelling was true, Bair."

Bair nodded. "And nought else of the tale of the Kammerling bears upon our venture?"

"Mayhap it does, Bair, yet here and now I cannot say how. All I know of the Kammerling is that it held an augury to slay the greatest Dragon of all . . . and is now lost in the ruin of Dragonslair."

Bair peered at the ground. "In the North lies buried the hammer." Then he looked up at Aravan. "Is the prophecy you cite written anywhere? It would seem there is more yet to come."

"Mayhap the Mages know the text, yet at its heart it is an Utruni rede, for it is given to them the keeping of both the prophecy and the Kammerling, and none I know has spoken to them since the time of Elyn and Thork."

"Who now is the greatest Dragon of all, kelan, given that Black Kalgalath is slain."

Aravan pondered a moment. "Ebonskaith, I ween, is now the mightiest Drake of all."

"Then mayhap the Kammerling is fated to slay Dragon after Dragon, whelming whichever Drake currently holds the claim of mightiest—in this case Ebonskaith."

Aravan's eyebrows raised, then he shook his head. "Ebonskaith is pledged by the Dragonstone to keep the peace. Yet if he were not thus pledged, still, even were thy premise true, how it bears on Dodona's words, that I cannot say."

"Pledged by the Dragonstone? What do you mean by that, kelan?"

Aravan pointed to the stars above. "Elar, we have an early start on the morrow, and I will tell thee the short of that tale on the way to Jangdi."

"But there's more I want to know: why did Dodona call me the Rider of the Planes? And—"

"Bair," interjected Aravan sharply, "there is much time to explore these and other issues, for the way to our next goal is long. And as to why he named thee Rider of the Planes, that I must ponder whether to answer at all, for another did pledge us to say nought."

"I knew it!" cried Bair. "Did I not say that all my life I have felt as if secrets and mysteries were being kept from me, as if you and Ythir and Da and even Amicula Faeril are under some vow of silence? I also said that mayhap in the Kandrawood, perhaps you will say what 'greater things' lie ahead for me, what hidden mission I might have. Well, kelan, now we *are* in the Kandrawood, and to keep me in ignorance would seem folly, especially in matters of weight. How can your silence do other than bode ill for events yet to come?"

Aravan sighed and looked at the sky and remained silent for a long while, as if considering, pondering. At last he turned to Bair and said, "Thou art right, Bair; to keep thee in darkness *is* folly, or so I do believe. Once did I tell thine Amicula Faeril that in knowledge lies strength; in ignorance, weakness; and 'tis always better to know even part than to know nothing at all. Those words I have always lived by, yet in the raising of thee I did stray, for I was pledged. Nevertheless, in spite of Dalavar Wolfmage's warning and the pledge to thine ythir and athir, on the morrow I will tell thee all I know. But for now, elar, we *must* rest, for the dawn will come quite soon. And so let us sleep."

"I shall take the first watch," said Bair, "for I have much on my mind."

Yet Aravan shook his head. "Nay, elar, we shall both take to our beds, for in this vale there is no need to set ward; it is protected by Dodona from harm."

Grumbling in youthful impatience, and feeling as though he would never rest with all these questions whirling and tumbling across his mind, Bair unrolled his bedding and lay down, and lo! he fell straightaway into peaceful slumber, Ilnahr Taht and the waterfall singing him to sleep.

*   *   *

The next morning, Aravan opened his map case and took out several charts, placing one before Bair. "Here we are, elar, at the Kandrawood." Then Aravan shuffled through the other charts, selecting two more to lay out to the east of the first. He pointed to a place on the third map, the one farthest from the Kandrawood. "And here is Jangdi, a small mountain kingdom, north of Bharaq."

Bair frowned, his gaze sliding across the three maps. "It looks far from here."

With the span of his hand, Aravan measured. "Some sixteen, seventeen hundred leagues were we birds to fly"—Aravan measured a different path across land and sea and then land again—"but two thousand two hundred by the route we will take."

"Six thousand six hundred miles?"

Aravan nodded. "Most of it by water." His finger traced a course. "East of here and a bit south is a caravan route which will take us into Khem, to the city of Dirra on the banks of the *Nahr Sharki*—the River Eastern—some three hundred leagues all told. There we will go by boat down to the *Ahmar Jûn*—the Red Bay. Then we sail the northern coastal waters of the Sindhu Sea until we come to the port city of Adras in Bharaq. Then it's overland some three hundred leagues to Jangdi. When we cross into that land, we will ask the way to the Temple of the Sky."

Bair studied the maps, then traced a different route, saying, "Why not this way, kelan? Back to Sabra and then by the Avagon Sea up the coast to, say, somewhere along here in Sarain, and then overland to Jangdi—it looks shorter to me."

Aravan made a negating gesture. "Shorter by leagues but longer by days."

Bair frowned. "How so?"

"Too much of it is by land and through mountains where the travel will be slow—three or four leagues a day at most. Whereas by the route I propose—"

"Ah, I see," interrupted Bair, grinning. "Your route is mostly by water, and boats never tire as long as the river flows or the wind blows."

Aravan grinned in return.

But then Bair sighed and gestured at the maps. "Lor', Aravan, but how long will this take?"

Aravan frowned. "Some thirty days across the desert to Dirra; another five days down the river to the Red Bay; from there, mayhap another forty days to Adras, given a fair ship and good winds; and then another forty days overland by horseback to the mountains of Jangdi. And more days after to reach the temple; just how many, I cannot say."

"One hundred ten days to Jangdi, then," said Bair. "Just under four months. We should be there mid-to-late May."

"If all goes well," said Aravan, rolling up the thin vellums and placing them back in their waterproof case.

"I wonder if that's enough time," said Bair.

Aravan shrugged. "It will have to be time enough, Bair, else Dodona has sent us on a mission in vain."

"Aye, Aravan, but recall, he as good as told us that our chances of succeeding were exceedingly slim at best. Besides, we don't even know what our mission is, other than for you to master this crystal."

Aravan stood. "Slim to none our chances may be, yet regardless, 'tis all we have, and a crystal I must learn. Even so, there are missions I have undertaken where the knowledge afforded was less; some of which failed, some not. Yet, heed me, elar: as soon as we are under way, I will break my vow of silence and tell thee of two redes, both of which concern thee . . . two redes which mayhap bear on this mission as well."

Bair's eyes lit up, and he leapt to his feet. "You break camp; I will fetch the camels."

Within three candlemarks, the two were on their way, the camels *rrrunk*ing and *hronk*ing at having to bear these fools through the narrow dark crevice again—uphill no less—and away from the gorge where succulent sweet forage grew. And as they emerged, around the rim of the northern horn of the crescent gorge they fared and struck out east-southeasterly across the Erg, aiming for the caravan track that would take them into Khem.

As they trekked into the dunes, Bair rode forward to come alongside Aravan.

"Well, kelan?"

Aravan sighed. "I hope to Adon that I am right in telling thee this, yet as I said, I have always believed even a small bit of knowledge is better than none at all."

They rode some moments more, Aravan collecting his thoughts, and just as Bair became certain he would burst apart with impatience, Aravan said, "Long past in Arden Vale there dwelled a Dara named Rael, though she and her consort, Talarin, are now gone, having ridden the twilight unto Adonar. They named her Crystal Seer, for at times she could foretell events which were yet to come, though always they were couched in redes most obscure."

Bair nodded. "Amicula Faeril spoke of her, said there is a tale in *The Ravenbook*, where she did speak a rede unto Tuckerby Underbank concerning the Red Quarrel, though none understood its import then, nor that it was meant for him."

Aravan turned up a hand. "That is the way of redes and prophecies, Bair: their meanings are uncertain at best." Aravan paused and then frowned. "Hast thou not read *The Ravenbook*, elar?"

Bair shook his head. "Nay, kelan. Not yet. Oh, the very day after Amicula Faeril told me of the Rede of the Red Quarrel I went to the archives to read the full story myself, but I couldn't find it. —*The Ravenbook*, that is."

Aravan frowned. "But it is easily—" His words jerked to a halt, and then he murmured, "She hid it."

"What? What did you say?"

"I deem Faeril hid *The Ravenbook* from thee, elar."

"Why would she do such a thing? I mean, on more than one occasion she urged me to read it."

"Because of Rael's Rede."

"The one about the Red Quarrel? I don't understa—"

"Nay, Bair. Not that rede, but another."

Bair frowned in puzzlement.

Aravan held up a staying hand. "List. Faeril made a promise unto Dalavar Wolfmage to keep secret from thee a prophecy, a secret we all did pledge to keep, for if thou didst hear of it, the fear was that thou wouldst spend thy days trying to fulfill it, and Destiny would not then be served. Aye, Faeril did urge thee to read *The Ravenbook*, yet once she spoke of the Rede of the Red Quarrel writ large in that book, then do I think she did remember that recorded therein was another rede, a rede detailing a secret she had sworn to Dalavar Wolfmage to keep veiled. And so she hid the book from thee so that thou wouldst not come upon what was written ere its time was due. Yet though I made the same promise, it is one I am about to break, for, given what Dodona has said, I ween the moment has come to reveal all I know. And I will start with Rael's Rede, spoken long past, a rede which concerns thee."

Bair's jaw fell agape. "Rael spoke a rede about me?"

Aravan said, "We do think it is so."

"Then say on, kelan."

Aravan nodded and then intoned:

> *"Bright Silverlarks and Silver Sword,*
> *Borne hence upon the Dawn,*
> *Return to Earth; Elves girt thyselves*
> *To struggle for the One.*

> *"Death's wind shall blow, and crushing Woe*
> *Will hammer down the Land.*
> *Not grief, not tears, not High Adon*
> *Shall stay Great Evil's hand."*

Bair fell into thought, his camel lagging a bit behind Aravan's. And then the lad slowly shook his head and urged his mount forward again to come alongside. "Given what you have told me of the Silver Sword, this seems to signal a final conflict between Gyphon and Adon, kelan, and I don't see how that applies to me."

Again Aravan held out a staying hand. "I am not yet done, Bair. Heed, for there is another rede, one spoken by Faeril when she used a crystal—your crystal—to seek an augury—"

"Amicula Faeril spoke a rede?" blurted Bair.

"Aye, though 'twas not her design to do so . . . but then again mayhap it was the design of Another."

"Another?"

Aravan shrugged. "Adon, Elwydd, mayhap Another altogether. I know not, for as I did say: redes, prophecies, their meanings are uncertain at best, and whence they come none knows but for perhaps those we name gods."

Bair frowned down at the pendant. "And she used this crystal to do so?"

Aravan nodded. "Aye. Faeril used it—as did Rael use a crystal of her own—to serve as a focus to see into the future."

"Ah," said Bair, his eyes lighting up, "perhaps that's what you are to master, Aravan: the use of this crystal to see into the future. Surely, a peek at what is imminent should improve our chances greatly at whatever is to come."

Aravan's eyes widened at Bair's canny observation, and he looked at the lad and said, "Mayhap indeed thou hast struck upon what I am to learn."

Bair grinned, then sobered. "What was her rede? —The one Amicula Faeril spoke that had to do with me."

Aravan took a deep breath and intoned:

> *"Rider of Impossibility,*
> *And Child of the same,*
> *Seeker, searcher, he will be*
> *A Traveller of the Planes."*

"Seeker, searcher? That's part of my 'Wolf truename."

"Aye, Bair, it is. And thou art the Child of Impossibility, and, as we have seen, a Traveller of the Planes."

"Wait a moment. I thought the rede said Rider of Impossibility, not Child."

"Rider of Impossibility, and Child of the same, Bair, hence, Child of Impossibility. Thou art the Impossible Child."

"How can I be an impossible child?"

"Thou wert conceived of a Baeron and an Elf upon Mithgar, where such cannot happen, and thou wert born of an Elf upon Mithgar, where such births cannot take place."

"Tchaa," said Bair, waving a hand of negation. "I am born, hence, living proof that such is not impossible. Perhaps a Baeron and an Elf simply never mated before."

Aravan laughed. "It is clear to see, youngling, that thou hast much to learn."

Bair's eyebrows raised. "There have been pairings between?"

Aravan nodded, and then added, "But no progeny. Yet thy sire's blood is not pure Baeron."

"Not pure—?"

"Aye. According to Dalavar Wolfmage, in Urus's veins flows the blood of the Middle and Lower Planes and of Vadaria—the Mageworld—as well. In thy veins, to that mix, we can add the High Plane, from thine ythir's side. Hence, with such coursing in thy veins, the bloodways are open to thee, and thou art truly a Traveller of the Planes."

Bair gritted through clenched teeth, "I bear the blood of the Lower Plane? Of Neddra? Of the Foul Folk?"

Aravan canted his head in assent.

"Aargh!" shouted Bair to the sky, and at this unexpected yell, the camels broke and tried to run, yet the reins and tethers through the nose rings held fast, and with cries of *Wakkif!* and *Amahl!* and *Mishi!* Aravan and Bair managed to slow the beasts to a walk.

With the camels growling and glaring at Bair accusingly, Aravan said, " 'Tis deeds, not blood, which determine the worth of a being, though in thy case, 'tis the blood which makes thee the Rider of the Planes."

Bair sighed. "At the circle of oak in the Weiunwood, Ythir told me I did not know where the crossing led, and she added that I could have stepped to Neddra. Little then did I know that I truly could have gone, and that her words were true, what with Rûptish blood in my veins." He raised his hand and looked at it, murmuring, "No wonder my <fire> is different from all others."

They rode onward in silence for a while, Aravan letting Bair accept the knowledge just given. Finally, Bair asked, "Aravan, what is my lineage?"

"This much I do know," said Aravan. "Thine ythir is born of Daor and Reín, Elvenkind pure. Thine athir was born of Brun, a Baeron pure, and of Ayla, her blood of Magekind and that of a Fiend, or so Dalavar Wolfmage says."

"Fiend?"

Aravan sighed. "Dalavar believes it is the offspring of a Demon and one of the Spaunen, though which of the Rûpt he cannot say."

"And this Fiend was . . . ?"

"Dalavar did not name it, yet the Fiend took Dalavar's ythir by force—Seylyn, she was named; she was a Mage, a Seer— and from this ravishment Dalavar and Ayla were born."

"Dalavar is my kith?"

"Aye. Dalavar was Ayla's jarin, she his *sinja*. They were *dwa*. From their ythir they were given Mageblood, and from Seylyn through Ayla to Urus to thee comes that same Mageblood as well."

"Yes, but also by that line—from Ayla on down—I gain Foul Folk blood, too."

Aravan held up a finger, saying, "And, if Dalavar is right, the blood of Demonkind."

Bair's eyes widened in realization, and he raised his hand and peered again at his <fire>. "Adon, Aravan, what kind of creature am I?"

"The best kind of creature, elar," said Aravan. "Gentle-hearted, good, and true . . . one whose deeds speak well of him. One who will prove most worthy. One who is even now a boon comrade to me."

Onward they rode easterly, Bair deep in reflection, absorbing what he had just learned, Aravan pondering what might lie in store ahead.

That night in camp as they drank hot tea in the chill air and took a meal of crue, Bair asked, "But how does Amicula Faeril's augury relate to Rael's Rede?"

Aravan chewed and swallowed and then said, "Faeril had a vision when she attempted to scry the future. 'Twas of a rider— Human or Elf? She did not know, for the rider seemed in between, as thou, Bair, art in between—on a horse, a falcon on the rider's shoulder, something glittering in his hands."

"Something glittering?"

"Faeril thinks it was a sword, the Silver Sword of Rael's Rede."

"And this is the Dawn Sword? The sword Galarun bore, taken when he was slain? The sword said to be able to slay the High Vûlk Himself?"

Aravan turned up a hand. "I do so believe, yet it is not certain."

" 'Silverlarks and Silver Sword borne hence upon the Dawn,' " quoted Bair. "Is that what I am, Aravan, the one fated to bring the Silver Sword back to Mithgar?"

"So Dalavar Wolfmage and Dodona have said. The Rider of the Planes thou art, or so we all do believe."

"Oh my, if Rael's Rede does signal a final conflict between Gyphon and Adon, then this is a weighty thing, this responsibility."

Aravan nodded but did not speak, and his eyes were filled with compassion.

Bair stood and looked out into the desert. After awhile he asked, "When will this be, Aravan?"

Now Aravan stood and placed a hand upon the youngster's shoulder. "As to when, I cannot say, for all we have to guide us are Rael's Rede and Dodona's words: Rael said it would be a time of 'crushing woe,' and Dodona said, 'A great woe is coming from the East.' Too, he told us the Trine is coming . . ."

". . . and that we both must be ready," added Bair.

Aravan nodded. "Yet I know not this Trine, nor when it is due."

As they looked out across the desert night, Bair's mind was atumble with speculations and dreams and dreads, for he was not at all certain that he could measure up to the task given to him to bear. And feeling as if the weight of the world rested upon his shoulders, he sighed and took to his bed, Dodona's words to Aravan echoing in his mind—*you and Bair are the last hope of the world, but also perhaps its doom . . . hope of the world . . . its doom . . . hope . . . doom . . . hope . . .*

He was a long time falling asleep.

In the late marks ere mid of night, Bair startled awake, the dregs of a dream yet clinging, a dream wherein he spoke with Dodona, yet all he could remember of the conversation was—*". . . by a man born of a corpse."*

How can someone be born of a corpse?

Bair rolled over to see the silhouette of Aravan sitting on a tall rock in the moonlight, the Elf's eyes glittering in the silver radiance. Aravan did not stir, yet Bair knew that although the Alor rested in shallow meditation, he was nevertheless on ward.

Somewhere nearby a camel growled, complaining to its brethren of the sparseness of forage.

Bair settled down again to capture what little sleep remained ere it was his turn at watch.

... by a man born of a corpse ...

... of a corpse ...

... a corpse ...

... corpse ...

CHAPTER 25

Khem

February, 5E1009

[Ten Months Past]

On they rode the next day, and as they moved east-southeast-erly, Aravan told Bair of the Pledge of the Dragonstone, and the story of Arin Flameseer and Egil One-Eye and the others who quested for the Green Stone of Xian. The sun moved up and across the sky as Aravan told the full of the tale, and in late afternoon, just as he finished the telling, they came upon the caravan track and turned southeasterly along its reach, aiming for Dirra in Khem, though they would yet spend a fiveday in the sands of the Karoo ere reaching the borders of that land.

As they set camp that eve, Bair asked, "Where did it come from, this Dragonstone?"

Aravan looked across at the lad. "Whence it came, none knew, or would say, yet it seems the Dragons did fear it mightily, and that's why for the guarding of it by Magekind the Drakes pledged as they did: to refrain from plundering and raiding and from interfering in the affairs of the world."

"Yet some did not pledge, you said."

"Aye, just as some Wizards did not pledge, Renegades all."

"Black Mages and Cold-drakes, those who suffer the Ban?"

Aravan nodded. "Those who sided with Gyphon during the Great War."

"And the Dragonstone is now lost?"

Aravan took a deep breath. "Aye, Bair. It was in the vaults below the College of Mages in Kairn, the City of Bells." The look of tragic memory crossed his face. "And when Rwn was destroyed, so too was the Dragonstone lost."

"Perhaps it yet lies locked in the vaults, there far under the sea."

"Mayhap so, Bair. Mayhap so."

The next day as they broke camp, Bair asked, "Where is Arin Flameseer now?"

"She has ridden the twilight back unto Adonar."

"Gone from Mithgar? Why so?"

Aravan sighed. "After Egil died, Arin mourned for many long years. Finally, she crossed the in-between, seeking the peace and solace of the High Plane."

Bair laded one of the camels. "And did you say Rael is gone to the High Plane as well?"

Aravan nodded. "Aye. She and Talarin and Gildor . . . and others. They also sought the solace of Adonar, for the memories of those lost in the Winter War bore heavily upon them, Vanidor, Gildor's dwa, among those souls."

"Oh my," said Bair, touching the crystal pendant. "Arin and Rael: they are both gone. And here I was hoping there would be someone of Elvenkind who would truly understand the burden of this and lend you solace when needed." Then he lifted the crystal over his head. "Here, Aravan, take it, for it seems it was meant for you."

But Aravan pushed out a hand in negation. "Not yet, Bair. It is thine to wear until we discover otherwise . . . mayhap at the Temple of the Sky."

Bair settled the platinum chain back about his neck and said, "Until then."

On they rode and on, and on the fourth day rain came to the Erg, the oueds across their way swiftly filled to overflowing with racing water and forced them to an early halt.

On the sixth day they could see in the distance ahead a low range of mountains standing athwart the horizon, and the following midafternoon they rode up into a pass to come upon a caravansary, where they stayed the night. The proprietor, though surprised to see an Elf in his inn, did not think him a Djinn. The same could not be said of the proprietor's wife and three daughters, who, even though both cajoled and threatened by the innkeeper, made warding signs and refused to serve the two.

The following day, down into Khem they rode and away from the sands of the Erg. The land they fared through was arid, yet greener than that which they had left behind. And the farther southeasterly they rode, the more verdant became the world.

Throughout the next days it rained and rained again, the fitful winter storms sweeping across the 'scape, the camels growling at getting wet, expressing their haughty displeasure.

Now the two travellers rode into more fertile vales, here where the rain did reach, and days later found them faring among fields of cotton, the finest in all the world, or so said Aravan. And they passed among villages and towns, most small, some modest, and there the Khemish merchants were more than willing to haggle over the price of goods, though they looked at the two travellers askance.

Yet as they fared down across the land, every day they saw columns of riders and companies of men afoot moving northward—

The South prepares for war.

—some in the distance, with only dust in the air marking their line of march, others met upon the roads Aravan and Bair followed. And when the first of these brigades came toward the two, "Cover thy face, Bair, and hide all in the shadow of thy hood," hissed Aravan, pulling the drape of his own ghutrah about his features to cover all but his eyes, then casting his hood over as well, moving into the land beside the road to let the column pass, Bair following, the camels readily complying, for forage grew there.

As the Khemish soldiers marched by, Bair noted that the banner they bore was a white fist upon a field of black, the symbol repeated upon the breast of each man.

A man on a horse rode past, eyeing the pair suspiciously, yet just as it seemed he would continue on, he reined to a halt and turned and called out, *"Shu shurl?"*

"San'a min Sabra, Mlâzim," replied Aravan, sketching a salaam.

"Lawain' râyih?"

Aravan gestured southeastward. *"La Dirra."*

Apparently satisfied, the man called out, *"Rakka ysallmak,"* and turned his horse and rode on northerly.

When the column was far enough away, Bair asked, "What did he want?"

"He asked what our business was, and I told him we were traders from Sabra. Then he asked where we were bound, and I said to Dirra. And then he said, 'Rakka be with you,' and rode on, to which I did not reply."

"Rakka?"

"Another name for Gyphon. Didst thou see the emblem?"

"Yes. Clenched fist, white on black."

"They are known as the Fists of Rakka, an old religion oft put down but revived again and again by ill-meaning men."

They rode a bit farther and then Bair said, "This language of theirs: I am going to have to learn it."

Aravan nodded and said, "I will teach thee what I know, yet until thou hast a good grasp of the tongue, thou shouldst act as if thou art deaf."

And on they rode, day after day, Aravan teaching Kabla to Bair, the lad with his natural facility in tongues learning quite rapidly. Even so, when they dealt with townsfolk and tillers of the soil, Bair acted as if deaf, acknowledging no sound whatsoever.

Some twenty-seven days after setting forth from the Kandra-wood, they came to the walls of Dirra, its red minarets standing tall in the slanting rays of the morning sun, white fists embedded in circular fields of black standing out starkly high upon their sides. Their faces covered and shadowed in hoods, Aravan and Bair passed through the warded gate and into the narrow streets, the guards but cursorily asking their business, their questions so simple even Bair could have answered.

Through the tight twisted streets of the city they fared, pressing past the crowds, and down to the docks along the banks of the Nahr Sharki, the river flowing easterly from a range of mountains far to the west and passing through Dirra on its journey to the distant sea.

Ere the sun set that evening, Aravan had traded the six camels for a small ship and supplies.

"This craft will bear us all the way to Bharaq, Bair," said Aravan, as he and the lad laded the goods aboard.

Bair hefted a water keg and eyed the open-hulled vessel with skepticism. "If you say so, kelan. But it seems rather tiny to me; why, it can't be more than seven of my paces long, and two at the beam at most."

" 'Tis a two-masted bovo, elar, and quite seaworthy. She bears a triangular main and two jibs from the mainmast, and a spanker from the mizzen; it is quite common in the eastern Avagon Sea, especially nigh the Islands of Stone, where cargoes are light and nimbleness is essential."

"What's it doing here?"

"The Khemish captain I bought it from said he sailed it across the Avagon Sea to the Weston Ocean and down to the Cape of Storms and around and into the Sindhu Sea, hugging the coast all the way. After that voyage he came upriver to Dirra, where he gave up the sea altogether, saying that he'd had enough sailing for a lifetime. He's a merchant now, dealing in cotton for shipment down to Port Khalin on the Red Bay. He was rather glad to get rid of her; it seems the Khemish prefer their familiar dhows to ships of this sort, and so he had no buyer until we came along. It made the bargaining go swiftly and greatly to our favor."

Bair lifted the last water keg and set it down into the open hull. "What will we do if it rains?"

"Bail," replied Aravan.

Bair groaned. "Bail?"

Aravan laughed. "Oh, we've a storm canvas to cover from wale to wale, but it will leak regardless." As he rolled the barrel to its place by the others, Aravan glanced toward the lantern-lit city, for twilight was now on the land. "Here, now, let us lash all down tight, and then get under way. I've an ill feeling about Dirra and the Fists of Rakka herein. Too, the sooner started—"

"—the sooner finished," concluded Bair.

Swiftly they made ready, lashing down the goods and setting cargo within lockers affixed to the deck nigh the bow and stern. And just as full darkness fell, Bair cast loose from the dock and shoved off and leapt aboard, while Aravan raised the main. Sailing on a single canvas, Aravan maneuvered out from the piers and among craft riding at anchor, their bows pointed into the river current, their tethers holding them fast. Quickly the little ship was free of obstacles, and Aravan sailed into the swift heart of the river flow, and then he and Bair raised the two jibs and the spanker to catch more of the brisk wind on the aft starboard quarter. And under the slanting light of a waxing gibbous moon glittering on the water before them, away from Dirra they sailed and toward their unknown ends.

Late in the night a patrol of five men—a Fist of Rakka—came down to the docks and searched. They were looking for two strangers, two foreigners, two who might be spies. They were not Human, these two interlopers, or so the rumors said—a guileful influence at best; an enemy of god at worst. The priests of Rakka would question them, and they would answer indeed, for Rakka's priests were very effective in their methods of extracting answers from reluctant withholders and protesters. Hadn't they gotten the answers needed by merely holding a heated tong in the presence of the trembling cotton merchant, the merchant who had spent too long in corrupting foreign lands? For while drinking *kahwi* among his friends—one of whom was a Finger of a Fist—in an unguarded moment the merchant had mentioned selling his outlander boat to a pair of strangers, the ones, the spies, the infidels they now sought.

The boat was gone from its customary place when the Fist of Rakka arrived, and yet it might merely have been moved to another slip. After a long and fruitless search along the length of the docks, the Fist stood once again at the now-empty slip and stared through the moonlight downriver, seeing no sign of the foreigners in their foreign boat. If the infidels, the spies, were truly gone, perhaps the priests would send a dhow in pursuit. But for now the strangers had eluded their grasp. Grinding their teeth in suppressed rage, the Fist went away in anger, and woe betide any who stood in their way.

Down the Nahr Sharki they sailed, did Aravan and Bair, wind and current bearing them ever easterly. Now and again the river narrowed, the flow in these channels swift; then it would broaden again, at times greatly, and there the water shallowed and slowed, but the wind impelled them onward. Down a fertile river vale they went, past fields of cotton and grain and melons and other crops, past orchards of fruit and nuts and flocks of sheep lying under the stars, the land burgeoning with plenty, the winter season no hindrance in these latitudes.

Bair looked through the moonlight at the abundance. "Why would a land such as Khem, with all these riches at hand, why would such a land ever go to war? —Oh, I don't mean a war of defense, repelling some invader, but instead a war of aggression, carrying slaughter to a distant land."

" 'Tis Rakka—Gyphon—and His priests who drive them to do such," answered Aravan, "for He and they would rule all."

Aravan then looked at the moon-washed sky. "Here, Bair, take the tiller, for I would sleep."

"Take the—? But kelan, I know nothing of sailing."

Aravan looked at the guide pennants atop the masts. "Leave the sails set as they are and stay in midriver; the wind and current will bear us fair."

"But rivers meander, kelan, and should there come a great turn, the wind will blow from a different quarter."

"Aye, but not until morning will the river bend greatly, or so says my map."

Bair cocked a skeptical eyebrow. "Fair warning, Aravan: I might waken you ere the turn of the night should aught seem going awry, for a sailor I am not."

Aravan unrolled his bedding amidships, and as he lay down he said, "Fear not, Bair: as long as the air drives us swifter than the current, thou wilt be able to steer. Should the wind fall, though, then it's to the oars we must turn, for this craft will then be little more than a raft. As to thy sailing skills, on the morrow I will begin to teach thee, and ere we reach Adras in Bharaq thou wilt be a mariner fair."

On the second day of river travel they passed through a deep canyon, scarlet of stone and a league in length. A third of the way in and for a mile or more, in the shadowed high red rock to either side and carved in the crimson walls, great figures loomed, the gods or monarchs of lost ages, their faces weathered beyond recognition. Who or what they might have been could not now be told, for even the identifying cartouches were worn beyond redemption.

"Who might have carved these, and why?" asked Bair, looking up at the silent, towering giants.

Aravan shrugged. "As to the who: stone workers—masons, sculptors, and the like. As to why: mayhap it was decreed by priests, if these represent gods; but if they depict monarchs instead, then they were carved to give the sovereigns a manner of immortality, a permanent remembrance of who they were. But worship and immortality and remembrance of this sort fades, for even stone dies in the aeons, slowly slain by water and wind stealing away its substance grain after grain."

"Then these must have been here for a long while," said Bair, "for nought but vague features remain."

Aravan nodded. "Long, aye. Mayhap before even the Lian came."

Bair's eyes widened in wonder. "Before the Elves? But kelan, I thought the Lian were first to tread this world."

Aravan's brow furrowed and he turned up a hand. "That is not at all certain, Bair, for the Lian did find signs—sparse though they were—that others had been here before: *Kolaré an e Ramna*—the Hollow of the Vanished—is one such place."

"Ah, yes," said Bair. "The enclosed basin between Arden Vale and the Drearwood. Does anyone know who they were?"

Aravan shrugged. "Perhaps the Great Creator, assuming He exists at all."

Bair frowned. "You question the existence of the Great Creator?"

"Bair, one must always question his faith, seeking ever the truth." Aravan looked up at the looming stone figures. "Mayhap long past these represented gods, gods now unremembered, gods who never existed but who were yet believed in by people of faith."

Bair looked up as well. "Faith misplaced?"

Ere answering, Aravan had Bair let out a bit of rope on the main boom and then corrected the tiller, explaining why he had done so.

Bair nodded in comprehension and then gestured at the huge carvings and said, "Are you saying that these are gods who never were, and that this is faith misplaced?"

"Mayhap," replied Aravan, turning up a hand. "Some believe that that is the shortcoming of faith—the acceptance of something which cannot be shown to be true, but embraced nevertheless. Some say that is the blessing of faith as well—the strength to believe regardless of lack of evidence. These stone figures may represent nought but the longings of a folk seeking explanations for their existence."

"And the Great Creator is like these eroded carvings? Nothing more than a speculation to construe how we came to be?"

"Mayhap," replied Aravan.

Bair now stared at the river ahead, as if seeking answers, as if they might be lying just out of sight beyond the next bend. "How can that be, Aravan? I mean, what other explanation is there to all of creation than that of a Creator?"

Aravan shrugged. "Some believe that all is governed by intrinsic forces, forces we do not understand but natural forces nevertheless. Those who believe in this say that the whole of creation is not moved by gods, but instead sallies forth on its own." Aravan gestured at the river. "The water flows and things grow and birds fly and lofted rocks fall back to the ground and changes in the world take place, all able to do so without the intervention of gods. Life comes and goes and changes, all without gods seeming to do aught, even in the creation of new forms of life, or in the extinction of the old."

Bair frowned. "I do not understand. Do you mean that occurrences and situations govern much of what transpires in life rather than the gods? That the Great Creator is not needed to bring forth new types of life, but rather nature alone is enough?"

Aravan nodded. "Aye, Bair. Elvenkind has existed long enough to see things change, to see where nature and events alone cause the quenching of certain creatures, while other creatures which heretofore did not exist come into being. Heed, this I have seen for myself:

"There once existed white moths which flourished in the extents of vast fields of white stone on an island in the Bright Sea, some moths slightly darker than others, but all moths more or less white. These fields of stone lay along the route of migrating swallows, and though the moths were tasty morsels for the birds, 'the swallows seldom found enough to gorge themselves even though they passed through in the spring and fall, both times when moths were in abundance. And thus things stood for millennia. But amid great thunderous explosions, from the bed of the sea nearby there arose a firemountain which spread fine ash over all, turning the white stone of that isle into a vast extent of grey. The migrating swallows could then see the white moths against the grey ashcovered stone, and they began glutting themselves on this now-visible plenty. Yet a few of the slightly darker moths survived, and reproduced their kind, and here among this new crop of moths some were slightly darker than others. Year after year, more of the darker moths survived and produced even darker moths still, and, as the seasons passed, the swallows could no longer see them, grey against grey as they were. And now there exists in those grey fields of ash-covered stone myriad of grey moths. But of white moths, there are none. In this case it was nature and natural forces which gave rise to a new kind of moth, and some say that similar forces are at work causing the change in all, accident and happenstance playing no small part along with natural events."

"But that is just one isolated example, Aravan. Surely there needs to be others to explain the state of the world and all that lives on or in it."

"Oh, Bair, there are more."

"Such as?"

"I have been told by Lian who came to Mithgar long past that there was a time when ice covered much of this world, and in that time there came into existence many new animals, animals similar to but different from their predecessors, new animals of enormous size: the great bear, the hairy tuskers, the longtooth cat, mighty aurochs, others . . . huge animals all. It seems the smaller creatures simply couldn't survive as well as their larger kith along the icy reaches. Yet when the ice did melt, most of these large creatures were hunted out of existence by tribes of Mankind, just as the swallows hunted the white moths out of existence. But in this case Mankind was more savage than the swallows could ever be, for unlike the moths, the huge animals did not have time nor respite to adapt ere they were gone from this world. Who knows what they might have become had not man interfered? Not I, Bair. Not I.

"There is this as well, elar: I have seen embedded in stone the bones of giant creatures, Dragonlike but not Dragons. Some cataclysm long past implanted them in stone; how 'twas done I cannot say, but fixed in stone they are."

"Do you think they actually walked the world?"

"Mayhap, Bair, though the Priests of Rakka would say 'twas the Evil One—mayhap Adon Himself—who put them on this world to confuse Humankind."

"But Rakka *is* the Evil One, Aravan, and Adon the good. Yet they've just reversed it; how can they say such a thing?"

Aravan laughed. "They take it on faith."

Again Aravan had Bair adjust the angle of the sail, letting out a bit of the jib sheets as well, instructing him as to how the setting made the most of the wind. When it was done, Bair said, "You seem to be saying that faith is a bad thing, Aravan."

"Nay, elar. What I am saying is that faith in an untrue thing can lead one astray."

"Then how does a person know what is true and what is not? What to have faith in?"

Aravan turned up his hands and said, "In matters of faith, elar, the heart, not the head, must lead the way. Even so, Bair, ignore not what evidence there is to the contrary no matter where it may lead, even if thou must question thy faith, and even if it means thou mayest find thy heart was in error and thy faith was misplaced."

"But kelan," protested Bair, "to discover a faith is misplaced would seem a terrible thing. Doesn't the loss of faith leave a person adrift, just as we would be, were we to lose our ship's rudder?"

"Truth sometimes hurts, Bair, yet it is the truth nonetheless, and in the long run truth makes one stronger. And rather than drift aimlessly, one should set to the oars and get under way again . . . searching for truth, seeking a new rudder, for at times does the search for truth lead to a new faith—something unto which thy heart can cleave."

"You would have me question my faith in the search for truth?"

"Heed me, lad: to question thy faith is no misdeed, but to *not* question it is."

Bair sighed. "All right, kelan, yet I would ask this: if all things are the result of natural forces, then how do you explain the stars and the moon and the sun and the Planes themselves? Are they, too, brought about by intrinsic forces, forces we do not comprehend?"

"That I cannot say, Bair, yet someday we may know, assuming we ignore not any evidence which does come our way."

They sailed on in silence, each pondering the world and life and all of creation, and how all came to be, neither of the twain catching a glimmer of any answer therein.

And as they pondered, they passed beyond the reach of the mysterious, looming, crimson stone figures, massive giants carved by unknown hands for unknown reasons, which gave them no answer at all.

CHAPTER 26

Tales

March–April, 5E1009
[*Nine to Eight Months Past*]

Driven before winds and borne by the river current, Aravan and Bair reached Port Khalin in but four days, Bair bailing a time or two, for riding on the wind came the seasonal rains, though not heavy enough for the need to break out the three-part, canvas storm cover. They did not stop in Port Khalin, however, there at the mouth of the Red Bay, for black flags bearing sigils of white clenched hands flew high from the poles on the docks. And so onward they pressed, for of water and food they had plenty, but of patience to deal with the Fists of Rakka they had none. And so they sailed past the city and into the northern waters of the Sindhu Sea under the uncertain light of a nearly full moon now and then shining through rifts in the towering storm clouds sweeping blackly above.

The tempest washed over them nigh mid of night, the high winds driving the waves into the aft starboard quarter, the rain pelting down. They donned the weather gear which had come with the craft, Bair's oilskin coat inches too small, and secured the storm canvas from wale to wale and from cockpit to bow to keep out the rain and the swash of the sea. And driven before the gale the little ship ran, riding up and over the quartering waves running in and under the starboard stern and away from the larboard bow.

"Should we reef sail, Aravan?" called Bair above the moan of the wind, the lad using the term he had learned but yester.

"Nay, elar, no need to shorten sail, for we are running fair in this blow: fifteen knots I ween. Here, take the tiller, and I will trim sail to make even more."

As Bair took over steering the craft, Aravan uncleated each of the jib-sheets and loosened them but a bit, cleating each tight again, the jibs easing out a bit larboard. Then he let out rope on the boom to shift the mainsail larboard a touch. Finally, he angled the spanker a bit larboard as well.

"Ah then," he called to Bair, "mayhap we are making sixteen knots now."

For two days and then three did the storm blow, the rain seldom slackening, the aft-quartering wind hurling the two-masted bovo across the risen waves. And both Aravan and Bair bailed and bailed again, water from above pelting down and waves splashing across from below, the canvas cover keeping most of it out, though leak it did. Hence, they did not lie down in the hull to sleep, there where the water sloshed to and fro, but instead took turns sitting cross-legged below the canvas and resting in deep meditation. Yet resting and bailing were not Bair's only tasks, for he handled the craft as well, Aravan teaching him how to manage the tiller and sheets, and the way to set the sails in the blow.

And always did Aravan and Bair keep the main and jibs and spanker trimmed to make the most of the wind, the lines running through pulleys affixed to the masts and threading through guide-eyelets along the wales to come to the sheet cleats aft, the arrangement allowing the pilot to control all from the cockpit astern.

At mealtimes Bair would crawl forward under the dripping storm canvas to retrieve water and crue. And on more than one occasion he gritted, "I would give all I own for a good hot meal and tea. Even hot tea alone would seem as a gift from the gods."

On the second of these days during this storm-driven time—in spite of his earlier admonition for Bair to read the tale for himself—did Aravan tell Bair the full of the story of Elyn and Thork rather than relying on the simple summary he had told days before, for he deemed the lad should have that full knowledge as well. And tears stood in Bair's eyes when the tale was done, though the lad said they were but raindrops instead.

" 'Tis a sad tale, I know," said Aravan, "yet it is better that thou dost know it, for some knowledge is better than none, and more knowledge is better than a little."

"Tell that to Dodona," growled Bair, bailing, the rain drenching down.

Aravan smiled a brief smile and then said, "Mayhap, elar, within these tales I have of recent told thee—this one of the Kammerling, the other of the Green Stone of Xian—lie clues to something we might face in the future, yet what that might be, I cannot say."

Bair looked out across the storm-pitched sea and slowly shook his head. "Perhaps only Dodona knows."

And on through the downpour and waves they fled before the hard-driving, aft-quarter wind, Aravan guiding by dead reckoning. And just after dawn on the fourth of these days, the rain momentarily stopped though the gale did not, and above the crests of the rolling waves, off the starboard aft they could see dark bluffs towering up from the sea.

"Ah, me," said Aravan, "would that we were aboard the *Eroean*."

"Why so?" asked Bair, trying to wipe his drenched face dry with nought but his thoroughly wet fingers.

"Yon lies the grand isle of Malaga."

Bair frowned. "And . . . ?"

"Bair, were this ship truly the *Eroean*, we would be farther still—much farther—but, alas, we are not. Even so this craft has done well, for hurtling before this gale as we are, we have come nearly one thousand sea miles in but three days and some."

"Is that good? I mean, if a sea mile is the same as a land mile—"

"Nay, Bair, a sea mile is somewhat longer, some two hundred seventy strides more."

Bair frowned. "Regardless, a thousand sea miles in measure— or a bit more in land miles—it seems a far distance to travel in such a short time, but I know little of boats. So again I ask: is that good?"

"It is splendid! It means we have been running before this wind a middling of twelve or thirteen knots fair."

Even as Aravan spoke, again the rain came hammering down, and the bluffs were lost from view, and onward the little boat ran, hurled before the raw wind.

*   *   *

Another day the storm held, and another after that and then one more, and late in the afternoon on the seventh day, they rounded a shoulder of land off the larboard beam, a broad headland known as the Cape of Rhaman, the southernmost tip of the land of Quraq. And as they swung the craft north by northeast, the storm began to subside, and by the noontide of the eighth day of sailing the waters of the Sindhu Sea, clear skies shone above, though the following swells yet ran deep.

And Bair unlaced the three overlapping sections of the now-dry storm canvas, folding each up as he went, the lad glad to see the sun, saying that he would let Adon's light dry out the interior below. As he stowed the cover away in one of the side lockers, he paused and said, "Kelan, I just remembered something Dodona said directly before he vanished: 'Go and go now, else the coming storm will leave you in its wake.' That's what he said. Do you think he meant this storm?"

Aravan looked at Bair in surprise. "Mayhap, Bair. Mayhap. The gale we rode indeed does fit his words, for the storm drove us fair. Still, he could just as well be referring to the coming woe. Then again mayhap there is another storm we will fare into 'pon a future time."

"Argh," growled Bair, shoving the last of the covers into the locker, slamming the lid shut, and throwing the latches. "Oracular words: confusing riddles wrapped in obscure mysteries all tied up in impenetrable enigmas."

In midmorn of the following day, as Bair handled the tiller he said, "I have been thinking on our conversation of yesterweek, kelan, of the Creator and intrinsic forces, of nature and happenstance and accident and circumstance, and I would ask this: are not Adon and Elwydd, Garlon, Fyrra, Raes, Theonor and others, even Gyphon and Brell and Naxo and Ordo, are they not gods?"

"Mayhap, Bair."

"You mean there's even a question about them being gods?"

"I repeat: mayhap. Adon does not name Himself so, saying that even He is driven by the Fates."

"The Fates: are they real?"

"Incarnate? That I cannot say."

Bair frowned. "Perhaps the Fates are just another name for the Great Creator."

"Or another name for forces intrinsic, and happenstance, circumstance, and accident," replied Aravan.

Bair fell silent as wing on wing they sailed onward in the braw wind, now blowing from directly astern. But at last the lad said, "If Adon and Elwydd and all the others are not gods, Aravan, then why do so many worship them?"

"Mayhap they *are* gods, Bair, but then again mayhap they are but godlike beings."

"I fail to see the distinction, Aravan."

"The distinction, elar, is in how one thinks of them . . . and how they think of themselves."

Bair frowned, yet said no more, and on across the waves they fared on a northeasterly course, aiming for the port of Adras in the land of Bharaq.

Fourteen days it took altogether after rounding the Cape of Rhaman for them to reach the Bay of Adras, for their speed had diminished considerably from that of the storm-driven days, Aravan judging it to have been some six knots or so on this last leg overall. Still, in the middle of the day of the twenty-fifth of March—three days after celebrating the vernal equinox—they docked at Port Adras, twenty-two days ahead of the estimate Aravan had made back in Dodona's demesne: the camels had arrived at Dirra ahead of schedule, and the trip down the Nahr Sharki had gained another day, but most of the gain had come by gale-force winds blowing them swiftly along much of their way, and they had not needed to tack whatsoever on their journey across the sea. It was as if Fortune Herself had smiled down upon them, though Bair was more inclined to attribute the whole of it all to the foresight of the Oracle Dodona.

They spent the rest of that day and all of the next two arranging for care of the bovo, and acquiring horses and supplies for their journey unto Jangdi. Among their purchases were ropes, rock-nails, jams, snap-rings, climbing harnesses, ice axes, crampons, framepacks, and cold-weather clothing; they were after all going into the mountains, where such gear most likely would be needed.

And as they made their purchases, they asked for directions to the Temple of the Sky, but the merchants scoffed, saying that such was nought but legend and not to be believed.

"What will we do?" asked Bair upon leaving the last of the merchants. "I mean, even if Jangdi is a small mountain kingdom, still we could search forever."

"Fear not, Bair, there is yet one more place to visit—the shop of a friend. I met him some years back on one of my treks to find a yellow-eyed man."

And Aravan led Bair to the shop of a map merchant—an ancient named Dharwah. The old man was well pleased to see Aravan, as was Aravan to see Dharwah, the Alor looking past the wrinkles and age spots and palsied hands and shreds of white hair to find the young mortal man he once knew. Yet when asked, Dharwah knew not where the temple was, nor did anyone else in his shop—neither his aged wife nor his son, nor the now-grown sons of his son, though they all bowed reverently to Aravan, naming him *Velinimet* as they did so. Yet even though Dharwah knew not where the temple was, still he said, "I have heard of a headman in a village at the foot of Jangdi who is rumored to deal with the yellow-robed monks of that faraway fastness; if any would know of the Temple of the Sky, it is either the headman or the holy men with whom he does trade . . . if the rumor is true."

"And the name of this village and headman?" asked Aravan.

"The headman I do not know, but the village—" Dharwah shuffled through chart after chart, finally drawing one forth. "—ah, here it is." His finger touched a point on the map, and he leaned forward, the better to see. "The village is named Umran." He turned the vellum about for Aravan, saying, "Here, Velinimet, do you see?"

Aravan gazed at the map and smiled and tried to give Dharwah a gold piece, but the old man refused, saying that Aravan had more than paid for such by sharing some of his many charts garnered on sea voyages long past.

When Aravan and Bair left the map merchant's shop, Aravan carried the vellum showing the way north through Bharaq to the village of Umran there at the foot of Jangdi.

"They called you a name, kelan," said Bair. " 'Velinimet.' What does it mean?"

"Patron," replied Aravan. "It seems the charts I let Dharwah copy when he was a young man have served him well."

Bair glanced back at the map merchant's shop and said, "Then let us hope the map he gave us does serve us just as well."

In early morn of the following day, on the road to Jangdi, out from the city rode Aravan, two remounts and three lightly loaded packhorses trailing, with a Silver Wolf ranging to the fore. And the ward at the north city gate made no move whatsoever to stop the Elf and collect their customary toll; instead they scrambled into the gatehouse and slammed the door, breathlessly watching as the monstrous 'Wolf padded past, remaining in the safety of the gatehouse as the rider followed his savage escort and rode on through the portal and away.

North they coursed and north, faring across the land, slowly rising plains for the most part, a gentle realm of green. And there, too, did the spring winds blow and with them came the rains, and through downpours and blowing mist did they fare that day.

That evening in camp, as they huddled 'neath a hastily erected lean-to, Aravan said, "Bair, mayhap I should tell thee the tale in full of the final voyage of the *Eroean*, for I cannot say whether or no something therein may bear on our current venture. And 'tis better thou knowest the tale, even though having the knowledge may come to nought after all."

"Final voyage? When you took to the sea during the Winter War?"

"Nay, elar. I do not think of that as being her true final voyage. Instead I would tell thee of the voyage long before, there in the last days of the First Era."

"Oh my, kelan, tell me not if it brings you pain."

Aravan took a deep breath, and then let it out. "Though there are two others who know much of the story—two Pysks, Jinnarin and Farrix—none other than I know the full of the tale written in the *Eroean*'s log. Aye, heartache it may bring; even so, it is time I spoke of it to someone, and it may prove useful in the end."

Bair nodded but remained silent, the lad waiting for Aravan to begin.

"It all started on Rwn when a Pysk named Farrix saw plumes streaming down from the winter aurora to dive beyond the horizon, where nought but ocean lies. Leaving his mate Jinnarin behind, he set out to see what he could discover concerning this strange mystery. . . ."

Over the next three nights—two in camp, the third in a kindly crofter's byre—in a halting voice at times, Aravan spoke of Jinnarin and Alamar and a fearful dream, and of Aylis, his love, and of the crew of the *Eroean*, and the world-spanning search for Farrix, and of Durlok and a crystal cavern on an island in the Great Swirl, and of the destruction of Rwn and the vengeance wrought thereafter.

And throughout it all, Bair sat quietly and did not interrupt even a single time, quelling the questions myriad which rose to the tip of his tongue. For the lad knew that speaking of such was difficult at best for Aravan, and Bair would cause his kelan no additional grief.

The tale came to an end as they sat in the byre, the evening rain drumming on the roof above. And neither said a word when Aravan fell silent, his long story told at last. Finally, Aravan stood and opened a door and peered out at the blow. And in a husky voice, Aravan said, "Sleep now, Bair. I will wake thee at the turn of the night."

Bair stepped to Aravan and embraced him, and then took to his bed in the soft hay.

And the rain fell down and down, the sky weeping above.

As they readied for travel the next dawning, Bair glanced at Krystallopŷr, for the crystalline blade had been a tool of Durlok, and the black haft had been Durlok's staff, and Bair said, "Lor', Aravan, but it seems many things bear on this venture of ours, tokens of power not the least: Adon's Hammer, the Silver Sword, Krystallopŷr, mayhap my crystal, the Green Stone of Xian, and—"

"Hold, Bair," interrupted Aravan, as he left two silver pennies on the post by the door, there where the farmer would find them. "We know not whether aught other than your crystal and the Kammerling pertain to our mission, for Dodona spoke only of them and not these other things. Mayhap they are indeed connected with what we do; but then again mayhap not. Speculate, aye, but know that it is speculation, for connections heretofore unseen may emerge, yet do not assume that *all* things connect directly to a given matter at hand. Indirectly, aye; directly for some, mayhap; but directly for all things whatsoever? To this I do say nay."

While Bair laded the remaining goods on the second packhorse, he said, "Are you saying to wait, that all things reveal themselves in due time? Isn't that the road to disaster? Shouldn't we prepare for all possibilities?"

"All possibilities, nay, Bair, for that is an infeasible task. But to assess likelihoods, aye, given prudence as well as taking into account whatever facts there may be." Aravan cinched his saddle to one of the three riding mounts. "What I am saying, elar, is that life is much like a road to be travelled, with forks and branches lying ahead and leading to various ends; when travelling that road, the way before us is likely to become clearer the farther we travel, for as branches are encountered and information is gained and choices are made as to which fork to take, our next decision is likely more confined and the goal more easily seen. We should not delay overlong at a given fork, yet neither should we rush headlong down a path chosen, for we may pitch over a precipice; nor should we refuse to turn about and backtrack to a better place, given that the road behind yet lies open for us to reverse our course."

Bair snorted and lashed a final thong in place. "Adon, kelan, but you sound just like Dodona: forks and branches and choices, probabilities and possibilities. Just tell me the goal and point the way; I will find a means to get there."

Aravan grinned and shook his head. "Ah, the rashness of youth. 'Ware, elar, for that way leads to the opening of doors better left shut, or at least to be opened cautiously."

Bair sighed. "Such as tomb doors in the desert, eh? Djado doors, would you say?"

Aravan nodded somberly. "Djado doors indeed."

Forty or more miles a day did they fare northerly through the realm of Bharaq, Aravan changing mounts often so as to not overtire the steeds. Yet the Silver Wolf loped along in comfort, the daily journey but a jaunt to him. And the land steadily rose, slanting upward toward the high Mountains of Jangdi far in the distance ahead.

Now and again Hunter would bring down game, and they would have a hot meal in camp at night. At other times they stayed in byres and at inns, hostels along the way, farmers and innkeepers alike glad to put them up. Yet when they asked the way to the Temple of the Sky, there too they were told that such a place was but a legend, superstitious old wives' tales. And so they journeyed on, following Dharwah's map toward a village afar.

March passed and April came onto the land, yet the farther toward Jangdi they fared, the colder became the days and nights, and spring turned to winter again, though it affected neither kelan nor elar, for Aravan had the winter gear he had purchased in Port Adras, and it certainly did not trouble the 'Wolf, though the steeds needed extra rations of grain at dawn and dusk and blankets in camp overnight.

They came into a rolling hill country; "The foothills of the Jangdi Range," said Aravan.

"Foothills? But I see no mountains."

"They are foothills nevertheless," replied Aravan, "and the mountains are giants like no others, towering into the sky."

The following eve lying low on the horizon the peaks of the range could just be seen, though there were yet many days of journey lying ahead. Bair stood long on the crest of a hill looking at the snow-laden tiers. At last he came down to the campsite and said, "Seeing that fastness afar reminded me of a question: are there Renegade Drakes who refused the Pledge of the Dragonstone but who did not side with Modru, with Gyphon, during the Great War of the Ban?"

"Aye, Bair, some of the Renegades took no part in the war—Redclaw, Grimmtod, Raserei, to name three; mayhap there are others."

"Did they suffer the Ban?"

"Nay. And they yet have their fire, for they did not ally themselves with the forces arrayed against the High King and Adon."

"Then if they are Renegades, they are not bound by the Dragonstone vow; do they yet pillage, raid, sow destruction in their wake?"

"For the most part they do not; they seem to live by the pledge even though they refused the vow. Yet when the temptation is great, all three have been known to plunder."

"Such as . . . ?"

"Such as when Grimmtod destroyed the castle of Queen Gudlyn the Beauteous, there in the land of Jute, all to get to a treasured scepter said to be made of gems rare, perfect in their cutting, perfect in their breaking of light."

"Huah," said Bair. "Well then tell me this: for those Drakes who are bound by the pledge, what happens if they break the oath? What then?"

"By their vow they must return to Kelgor, to the Dragonworld, and come to Mithgar no more."

Bair frowned. "Why are Dragons even here on Mithgar instead of their own native world?"

Aravan laughed. "Ah, Bair, thou couldst ask the same of Elvenkind—"

"—or of the Hidden Ones?" interjected Bair.

"Nay, not the Hidden Ones, for when disaster struck their world they fled from there to here."

"Disaster? What disaster?"

Aravan shrugged. "That I cannot say. They seldom speak of it, and I do not question."

"Well, then, speak instead to the issue you raised, kelan: why indeed is Elvenkind here, and why the Drakes as well? Why do not both Elvenkind and Dragons remain on their own worlds, on their own native Planes?"

Aravan gestured about at the world at large. "Because, Bair, Mithgar is wild and tempestuous, full of adventure, whereas Adonar is quite calm by comparison, and *that* is why Elvenkind is upon Mithgar. But as to the Drakes, why they are here I know not. If I were to guess, then I would say it is because there are more Krakens in the Mithgarian seas than in the oceans of Kelgor."

"What in the world do Krakens have to do with anything, much less with Dragons?" asked Bair.

"Krakens are Dragonkind's mates," replied Aravan.

Bair's eyes widened in surprise. "Dragons mate with Krakens?"

"Aye. So say the Children of the Sea. There in the Great Maelstrom below Dragons' Roost do the couplings take place, Krakens rising to the top, Dragons plummeting down to be enfolded in a many-armed embrace and drawn under the cold waters of the Boreal Sea."

"Do they not drown? —The Dragons, I mean."

"Mayhap some do, the weakest of them, but for the most when the deed is done, the Drakes struggle to the surface and somehow manage to take to wing again.

"And ere thou dost ask, Bair, 'tis Sea Serpents who are the get of these matings, roaming the waters of the world for a time. But then they take to the abyssal depths and encase themselves in chrysalides. A deal later do they emerge—the males transformed into Drakes, the females into Krakens—and they go their separate ways until the times of the matings."

"But how do they—?"

"Bair, that is the extent of my knowledge, or rather, that of Lady Katlaw, as she was told by a Child of the Sea, and in turn told me."

"Lady Katlaw?"

"Aye. A healer on the Island of Faro there in the Twilight Waters on the verge of the Bright Sea."

"How did she come to learn of the Dragons and their mates?"

"Did I not speak of this when I told you of the final voyage of the *Eroean*?"

Bair shook his head, *No*.

"Well, then, in his youth, Alamar the Mage brought Lady Katlaw a Child of the Sea, one who had been swept onto the isle by a terribly fierce cyclone, the waters rolling up over the land and nearly drowning all. Sinthe was her name—the Child of the Sea—and she was hurt, and 'twas Alamar found her and took her to the lady's tower for healing. In the process of making her well, both Alamar and Lady Katlaw did learn the strange tongue of the Children—filled with clicks and chirps and whistles it is, much like the speech of dolphins, but riddled with words as well.

"Upon a time when I anchored at Lady Katlaw's isle, there in the Twilight Waters on the verge of the Bright Sea, then did I learn the tale of Drakes and Krakes and the strange matings between. It was many more years—two millennia, or so—ere I met Alamar the Mage."

"The father of Aylis," said Bair, his words not a question but a statement instead.

Aravan nodded but then fell silent and spoke no more that eve.

*　　*　　*

As they broke camp the following morn, Bair said, "I say, Aravan, if Dragons and Krakens can bear young on Mithgar, a place not their native world, does that not make all of their get impossible children, like me?"

Aravan grinned. "Mayhap, Bair."

Bair nodded and then said, "Think on this as well, kelan: you did tell me that Farrix and Jinnarin did have a child here on Mithgar, a lady Pysk named Aylissa. Yet they are not of this world. Is she, too, an impossible child?"

Now Aravan frowned in puzzlement. "I had never considered such, elar. As thou hast so cleverly pointed out, Drakes and Krakes and Pysks are not affected so, and mayhap there are more not of this world but who can bear young herein. As to the reason why, I can but speculate: mayhap Adon or Elwydd or another such being took pity on them and made them able to do so; then again, mayhap they are of the Middle Plane but of a different world; lastly, mayhap 'tis only Elves and Humans who are thus affected, neither Race able to conceive in the other's domain nor to create a child together . . . but for thee."

Aravan fell silent, staring at the ground, musing, and Bair said, "What of the Foul Folk, Aravan, can they bear young on Mithgar?"

Aravan looked up. "I think not, Bair; never has a Rûptish child been seen on Mithgar . . . not by Elves, not by Drimma, even though both have raided Spaunen strongholts: the Elves after the Felling of the Nine; the Drimma in their continuing war with the Rûpt."

"But they are here on Mithgar yet," protested Bair, "even though all the ways between have been sundered—all but the bloodways, that is. If my cousins, the Spawn, produce no young, then how can this be?"

"Elar!" snapped Aravan, "never call the Rûpt thy kindred, even though some blood of the Lower Plane flows in thy veins. 'Twas through a long-ago act not of thy making which placed it there. Aye, the blood thou dost have, yet the Rûpt have no part of thee; instead, thy true kindred are of Arden Vale and of Darda Erynian—the Great Greenhall—and even of Vadaria, but not a single soul of Neddra."

Bair said, "All right, kelan, I'll call them cousins no more."

Aravan looked deep into Bair's eyes, trying to see if his message had been truly accepted, but the lad looked back unflinchingly, and Aravan could not tell.

They packed more goods, and finally Bair said, "But still the question remains: if the Rûpt produce no young on Mithgar, then how can they yet be on this world?"

Tying up his bedroll, Aravan said, "It is told that Gyphon made the Rûpt, if not immortal, then very long lived, for as thou dost say, they are yet on Mithgar, though it has been millennia since the Great War of the Ban, when the Sundering of the Ways took place. Yet I do know thereafter upon Mithgar their numbers are dwindling, with the deaths of so many in sundry wars and skirmishes and with some taking the bloodway to their world. Only on Neddra can the Spaunen breed, or so I have been told by those who did travel to the Lower Plane ere the Sundering took place."

"Like the Elves," murmured Bair.

Aravan looked at Bair. "What?"

"The number of Elves on Mithgar dwindles, too, just as does the number of Rûpt," said Bair. "Death by war and misadventure make our numbers dwindle; too, some take the bloodway never to return, and we dwindle further still; and lastly, none of Elvenkind but me are ever born herein, and that only because my great-grandsire bore the blood of a Fiend." Bair paused and frowned and then said, "And if that is true, why then cannot there be an impossible child born from the mating of a Rûpt and a Fiend?"

Aravan slowly stirred snow into the campfire and finally said, "Heed me, elar: though others not of this world may bear young upon Mithgar, there is but one Impossible Child, and it is thee."

Bair sighed in resignation, but otherwise did not respond as he began lading goods on a packhorse.

On they fared among the foothills, snow falling now and again, the mountains to the fore ever rising, climbing up to the sky, and the road they followed narrowed and narrowed, with fewer and fewer villages along the way. They progressed for seven days without seeing a living soul or much in the way of movement, but for a pair of gliding motes in the far-off sky, flyers so distant that even to Elven eyes they were nought but specks soaring among the remote, airy peaks.

On the eighteenth of April in the early morn an icy mist swirled and parted and swirled again as they followed along the rising, snow-laden trail now passing along the flank of a small mount. On they went through the chill grey to round the shoulder of the hill and pass beyond. Down into a swale they fared and up again, the low-lying fog slowly churning with their passage. Yet eventually the mist parted a final time as rider and 'Wolf forged above the last of its tendrils along the ascending way, and when he came into the clear air, Aravan reined to a halt. Hunter came padding back down the narrow trail, and from a shimmering gloom Bair stepped forth.

"Why are you stopping, kelan?"

For an answer, Aravan pointed northward along the constricted snow-laden path, a path that wended mayhap another mile more ere coming to a small village sheltered at the foot of an enormous, overhanging massif of stone; there the trail went no farther, fetching up as it did against the colossal range.

Bair turned and gasped at the towering mountains, ascending up and up, their frigid, snow-covered crests lost above the lofty clouds. "Oh," he said, "oh my," and nothing more.

They had come at last to the Mountains of Jangdi on the day of the dark of the moon, to find the range entire nought but a vast barrier standing athwart the way.

CHAPTER 27

Hindrance

April, 5E1009

[Eight Months Past]

"Kutsen Yong frowned. "Mountains? Mountains?"

"Yes, mai lord," replied Ydral. "Mountains to the west standing athwart our way. Even so, there is a narrow path through—an old tradeway from long past."

"Then why are we stopped?"

"Mai lord, the scouts report the route is too narrow for aun rolling palace. Yet we can take aun golden tent with all aun comforts through and leave the palace behind, to be returned to Janjong."

"Leave my palace? Are you now a court jester, Ydral, or my advisor true?"

"I am aun most trusted advisor, mai lord, and this Jai do advise: to the north and south stand even greater barriers—fields of ice with yawning crevasses in the northern Barrens; the impassable Mountains of Jangdi to the south, with no roads whatsoever. The passage ahead, though narrow, is the most direct way, the route to take: three hundred miles and we are past the hindrance, mai lord, and all of the West will then lie helpless and trembling before aun terrible might."

"I will not abandon my palace."

Ydral's yellow eyes narrowed in cunning, for he would make this *fool* see reason. "Mai lord, there is ahn other way: turn about and return to Janjong and build a great navy and sail from the Jingarian Sea into the Sindhu, and thence southerly past the Cape of

Storms and into the Weston Ocean, and thence into the Avagon Sea to land aun vast army on the shores of Pellar to attack this so-called High King, the pretender who would usurp aun rightful rule. It would only take a year or two to accomplish such a great and glorious deed. The only alternative is to send aun rolling palace back to Janjong, while instead we take aun golden tent and comforts and use the narrow road to the west and arrive within a month. Jai know the road is a hindrance, mai lord, yet—"

With a dismissive wave of his hand, Kutsen Young said, "Then widen it."

Ydral's jaw dropped a fraction in astonishment swiftly quelled. "Widen the road, mai lord?"

Ire came into the eye of the Masula Yongsa Wang. "Only a fool would dare question me. Are you such a fool, Ydral?"

Ydral cast his yellow gaze downward, swallowing his sudden rage. "No, mai lord. Jai would never question tji, just as Jai would not have conceived such a solution."

Kutsen Yong leaned back against his silken pillows. "That, Ydral, is why *I* am the Mighty Dragon and you are not. I have shown you a third way to deal with such a triviality. When I am made a god by the Jìdu Shàngdi, the mountains themselves will part before me even as I approach. Until then, I will conquer the world in all the comforts I am due. Widen the road."

Clenching his fists, his nails drawing blood, hidden within the sleeves of his robe, Ydral bowed and backed away from the throne. "Indeed, mai lord, we will do such."

And thus it was that the vast army of the Masula Yongsa Wang turned away from slaughter and rape and pillage, and set to widening a narrow mountain road some three hundred miles in length to provide a way for Kutsen Yong in the comfort of his golden rolling palace to be drawn by forty red oxen into the trembling West.

And in the privacy of his own dark wagon, Ydral raged at this upstart fool of a Dragonboy for delaying Gyphon's return. He smashed alembics and hurled tomes, yet neither did aught to quell his fury. Nay, it would take the comfort of several young women to assuage his terrible wrath. Trembling in anticipation, he readied his very sharp knives and made certain the straps on the table were quite secure. And then he summoned his manservant and told him which ones of the herd to bring.

CHAPTER 28

Jangdi

April, 5E1009

[Eight Months Past]

Bair's gaze went up and up, up steep stone massifs and snow-laden slopes, past colossal granite crags and vast deep cuts and immense outcroppings, up monstrous pitches rising through lofty clouds and beyond, the icy pinnacles lost to sight past the billowing grey. And its <fire> spoke of durance and mass and strength and of reaching toward the sky. "Lor', Aravan," said Bair in awe, "is that Jangdi?"

"It is," replied Aravan.

Bair glanced at the village and then again at the towering slopes. "Well, then, now I know why they said the village lay at the *foot* of Jangdi."

Aravan sighed. "And somewhere within that vast range lies the Temple of the Sky."

"And we have to find it," groaned Bair. "We'll be climbing forever."

"Mayhap not, Bair. Let us go see the headman."

"Perhaps I'd better go as I am, rather than as Hunter, so as not to frighten any of the villagers."

Aravan nodded, undoing a saddle-tie and casting the thong to Bair. " 'Twould look more natural wert thou leading my steed, rather than walking in freely."

"I could ride bareback, you know," said Bair, "on one of the remounts."

"Aye, thou couldst, yet servants and children are more likely to talk freely to one they think their own than one who rides a horse."

"But even if there are servants or children, what if none of them speak Common? I mean, it's not likely any will know Sylva, Baeron, Twyll, Châkur, or the smattering of Kabla I have."

"Then improvise, lad. Improvise."

Sighing, Bair tethered the strap to a bridle ring and then whispered, "Come on, boy," and led the horse forward, Aravan sitting tall in the saddle, the string of remounts and packhorses following after.

As they approached the village and came in under the shelter of the great overhang of stone, a handful of wary men stepped forth, sheathed knives girted at their waists; behind them stood an assortment of old men and boys, some bearing cudgels, others rough staves like quarterstaffs. From barely cracked-open doorways and windows in the rough hovels behind, women and girls and grandams peered out, some with babes in their arms, others holding on tightly to children.

Light brown they were, the villagers, a saffron tinge to their skin. Their hair was black, but for the eldest of elders, and their dark eyes held a bit of a tilt, much like that of Bair's. The men were dressed in rough-spun garb, some with fleece vests, others with quilted jackets, all wearing boots made of what looked to be oxen hide, the covering hair reddish in color. The women, from what could be seen, also were dressed in coarse cloth, and they wore reddish, oxen-hide boots as well.

"Stop some paces away, Bair," said Aravan in Sylva, "and break out the bolt of red silk."

Chattering women flocked around Bair, fingering the fine red cloth, while the smiling headman in rapid Bharaqi speech invited Aravan into his hut, Aravan answering in kind. And just before stepping into the hovel, Aravan called back, "Break out the yellow silk as well, elar, and discover whatever you can about where the temple might be." And then Aravan was gone, leaving Bair towering midst a gaggle of women.

Bair handed the bolt of red to one of the women and then stepped to a packhorse and took down a second bundle, removing the waterproof cover. Yet when he turned to display the fine yellow cloth, the women gasped and backed away, some whispering *Purohit*.

"What is it?" asked Bair, speaking Common.

None answered.

He tried the other tongues he knew, even the Dwarven tongue Châkur, and still they did not answer, though he thought one of them—a grey-haired lady—looked in startlement at him when he spoke in Kabla.

Gazing straight at her, he held the bolt out wide in his left, his right hand out wide and upturned, miming puzzlement, and again he spoke Kabla, though his speech in that tongue was yet limited. "What? Why this"—he had no word for yellow or cloth—"this, um, robe, um, bad?"

The elderly woman he had singled out looked him in the eye. "Not bad . . . *mukad'das*."

Bair frowned, then asked, "What, um, mukad'das?"

For an answer, the woman pointed up at the stone overhead.

Bair looked up, seeing nought but the great sheltering overhang of rock, and then he looked back at the woman and shrugged, puzzlement on his features.

She raised her voice—"*Mukad'das! Mukad'das!*"—as if saying it louder would make him understand. Then she said something rapidly to the women about her, and another of the women—younger and a bit stocky—dropped to her knees in the light dusting of snow before Bair and raised her hands into the air and bowed thrice, and then stood and pointed at the cloth and said, "*Adhyatmik.*"

Bair frowned.

Bowing? To what? Kings? Rulers? What? And the yellow cloth? What does that have to do with—? Oh! The cloth is yellow and the priests are robed in yellow. Not bowing to a ruler, but bowing in worship instead. Adhyatmik, mukad'das, and purohit must mean worship or holy or priest or some such. But why did that first one point at the stone overhea—? No, not at the stone, but at the mountains! Where the priests are said to live.

Bair set the yellow silk back onto the pack frame and pulled out his dagger, the women gasping and backing away. But then the lad knelt in the street and swept aside the thin layer of snow. With the point of the dagger he scratched a representation of the

mountains in the frozen dirt, the younger woman now stepping
up to see what he had done. Bair then gestured all 'round at the
village, then scratched an X on his rough drawing, then pointed
at the X and then at the village and then back at the X again and
said, "Umran."

"Beshaq!" said the woman, gesturing about and repeating the
name of the village: "Umran."

He looked up at the woman and grinned, and then once more
pointed at the X and said, "Umran." Then he stabbed at a place
on the map and asked, "Purohit?" He pointed at another place.
"Adhyatmik?" He pointed at yet another place. "Mukad'das?"
Then he waved his dagger over all and turned up his hands. "Purohit? Adhyatmik? Mukad'das?"

The woman looked at his map and snorted in derision and knelt
beside him and held out her hand.

Hilt first, Bair gave over his dagger.

She brushed free a second spot in the road. Carefully she
scratched a depiction of mountains in the frozen dirt, taking great
pains to draw the slopes and crests and vales just so. . . .

A time later, Aravan emerged from the headman's hut. He found
Bair in one of the hovels, sitting at a table and drinking freshly
brewed *chai*—or so the Bharaqi named their tea. Several of the
younger women sat about the small chamber as well, and they
cast the lad dark-eyed glances and whispered to one another and
giggled.

"Well, elar, it cost us two of our horses, but I have vague directions to the Temple of the Sky," said Aravan.

Bair grinned and set down his mug. And he reached under his
jerkin and fetched out a square of yellow silk, with markings of
black thereupon. "Wherever it is, kelan, I have drawn us a map
which will help us get there."

Bair laughed uproariously at the astonished look on Aravan's
face, and the young women giggled as well.

"How didst thou—?"

Bair pointed at the woman who had overseen his sketching of
her map. "This is Juhi. She drew the map in the earth, and after
much hand signalling and speaking a few words of Kabla, I got
them to bring me a brush and pot of ink and I copied it onto the

cloth. But, kelan, they won't touch the yellow silk, and they kept pointing at the drawing and the mountains and making hand motions as if to ward off evil and calling the mountains *varjit*."

At Bair's words, the women cried out, *Varjit! Varjit!*

"Forbidden," said Aravan. "That is what it means. They do not venture therein, for the mountains are forbidden to them."

"Forbidden? But why?"

"The men would only say that something lives therein, and all who challenge the priests' edicts are never seen thereafter."

"What happens to them? —The ones who challenge, I mean."

Aravan shrugged. "They know not. Yet they do say the mountains are dangerous, and speak of creatures dire, though when I asked them to explain, they knew not what these creatures might be."

"Foul Folk? Something else?"

Again Aravan shrugged. "That I cannot say. Yet this I do know: therein are like to be rockfalls and abrupt storms in the summer, avalanches and icefalls and sudden blizzards in winter and spring and fall, frigid winds, crevasses, thin air, arduous terrain—"

Bair shook his head and held up a hand, stopping the flow of Aravan's words. "This sounds no different from other ranges."

Aravan nodded. "Aye, Bair, yet this range towers above all others, hence I suspect it is a difference in degree and not in kind."

"Harsher, you mean?"

"Aye, much. Yet not only would I think it to be more brutal, but these folk of Umran have been warned by the priests to stay clear, hence they do not venture there. The mountains are forbidden, at least the region to the north."

Bair frowned. "But, kelan, if they do not go into the mountains, then is my map reliable?"

Aravan turned to Juhi, and a lengthy conversation in Bharaqi ensued. Finally, Aravan said to Bair, "There is a small mount just south of the village, one we fared past along its flank on the way here. Juhi says that in spite of the warnings to not even look on the range, she has been up its height many times on clear days, seeking to see where the priests live, seeking to see the Temple of the Sky. Never has she espied it in all her trials, yet well does she know the general lay of the land, though not what lies on the far sides of each mountain unless a peak or a shoulder rises into view beyond. Hence I would say her drawing is fair to use as a guide."

"If no one has seen the temple, then how do the men know where it lies? Especially if they do not themselves look."

"Among the men was a white-haired, toothless elder who related an ancient legend as to where it is said the temple might be, a legend from times long past ere edicts forbidding travel therein came down from the priests."

"And these priests, what do they know of them?"

"Only that in the spring and autumn do they come and only on a moonless night. How they arrive, none knows, but of a sudden one of their like appears: small of stature, covered in yellow, hooded and secretive and ebon dark. He trades for tea and grain and tubers and salt and spices and other such and pays in coins of fine jade. The goods are placed in baskets lowered from the ledge above and hauled upward in the night."

"Then can we simply wait for them?"

"No, Bair, they have already come and gone this spring, and we dare not wait for autumn."

"Oh. I was hoping. Well then, there's nothing for it but that we go in and find the temple for ourselves." Bair turned the yellow-silk map about so that it faced Aravan. "Where do the men deem it is? The temple, I mean."

Aravan spoke again with Juhi, and she looked at the map and held a thumb and forefinger somewhat apart just above the silk, taking care to not touch it. Then she looked at Aravan and shrugged. Aravan said, "If her guess is correct, it's four or five leagues to the inch on the map." Aravan frowned at the drawing, then he put his finger down on the far side of a peak some six inches north and a bit west of the X marking Umran. "According to the old man, somewhere nigh here lies the *Aakash mei Mandir*—the Temple of the Sky—or so legend says."

Quiet gasps of indrawn breath whispered about the room as Aravan touched the yellow silk and spoke the name of the temple. *Varjit*, hissed some: *Forbidden*.

They spent all the next day with Juhi atop the mount she used to see into the range ahead, and though Bair looked with his special <sight>, he could find no sign of the temple in a range full of <fire>. Even so, they verified the accuracy of her map and made additions and emendations, and studied what looked from their remote vantage to be the best routes to the place beyond the shoulder of a far-off mountain, the place where the toothless old man had said the temple might lie. And they noted snowfields and icefalls and cirques and ridges and buttresses and headwalls and cols and other such along the way, at least as much as they could see. Too, they noted where the sparse tree line ended and scrub began, and where that ended as well—only stone and snow and ice in the heights beyond—for fuel would be critical in the melting of snow for water, as well as thawing out the food. As Aravan had said, "Remember DelfLord Balor's admonition, Bair: it is a great gamble, climbing at heights where there is nought to burn, for the climber can die of thirst with water frozen all about, or of coldness should the snow or ice be eaten for drink, or of starvation should the rations be solidly frozen."

The day after, in spite of sincere warnings of the villagers that something dire lived in the forbidden mountains, and in spite of the young women's entreaties to Bair, not a word of which did he understand, Aravan and Bair made ready to enter the Mountains of Jangdi; they would go the following morn. Aravan arranged with the headman for the keeping of the steeds, saying, "If autumn comes and the priests bring no word of our whereabouts, the horses are thine to do with as thou wilt." Too, he acquired two pair of snowshoes, one for himself, the other for Bair, for the route they had chosen ran through in notches and mountain vales, where the snow would be lying deep, at least as best they could judge. And Aravan reck'd the trip would take some nine or ten days altogether.

Bair looked at Aravan in puzzlement. "Ten miles a day, kelan? That's all?"

"Ten miles a day in the notches and vales and snows, and mayhap crevasse-laden fields of ice, Bair, but less than ten when we have to sharply climb."

Bair laded each of the frame-packs with two fortnights' stock of food—crue and jerky and a bit of tea—for though it was perhaps a trip of ten days into the mountains, if they found not the temple they would have to spend another ten days coming back out. He packed as well a supply of tinder to go with the flint and steel. He included a copper pot in which to melt snow for water, for part of the way they would find fuel from trees and scrub to burn; he added an oil burner to each pack . . . not for illumination, for Aravan had his Dwarven lantern for light, but instead to use as small stoves in the places above the tree line and scrub line, where there was no fuel to burn. From among the supplies they had brought north with them, they carefully selected what they would take and what they would not, striving to keep the burden to a minimum, while at the same time trying to assure they did not reject something vital.

"I say, kelan, why don't we let Hunter carry a pair of packs like saddlebags? —I mean, he can certainly bear more than both of us combined."

"But he cannot wear snowshoes, elar, and where we go the snow is bound to be deep in places."

"Ah. Oh, well . . ." Bair added two small mirrors to their packs, for signalling should the need arise.

That night they were feted by the villagers, and again warned of the peril, though none knew just exactly what that peril might be. At last Aravan pleaded that he and Bair had an early start in the morning, and when several of the women coyly invited each of them to sleep in comfortable goose-down beds, the Alor declined, saying the stable loft would be good enough. When Aravan translated this last to Bair, the lad looked at his kelan and sighed.

The next morning, their goods at hand, a distance from the village where the sheltering massif did not overhang, they stood and surveyed the vertical stone above. Nearby were gathered the villagers, watching in apprehensive silence as the two looked long and finally selected the route they would follow upward, a fairly easy climb for one trained by the Dwarves, as they both had been.

"I will take first lead," said Bair, cinching on his gloves and slipping into his climbing harness, already laden with jams and rock-nails and snap-rings, though much of the climbing gear was yet in the primary equipment bag.

Aravan looked at the lad and nodded.

Bair tied a figure-eight loop in his end of the climbing line and clipped it to his harness, then stepped to the face of the massif and studied the rock above, where a thin crevice split downward. He selected an appropriate rock-nail and reached as high as he could and hammered it in, the rock-nail pinging with a rising tone at each blow as it was solidly set. Slipping a snap-ring through the nail eyelet, he clipped the climbing line into the now-anchored ring. A second snap-ring he clipped to the first, and to this ring he affixed a stirrup cascade—a dangling set of connected foot loops, four hanging down to the left, four hanging down to the right. Finally, he glanced back at Aravan. "Ready?"

At his end of the climber's rope, Aravan looped a belaying hitch through a snap-ring fixed to his harness, and then used another snap-ring and a semigirth hitch about a sturdy tree as an anchor, affixing the end of the line to his harness as well. He then sat down with his back to the tree, the coil of climbing rope at his side, and cinched on his own gloves. He was now set to pay out line and to belay any fall Bair might have. He looked at Bair. "Ready. On belay."

His flanged mace dangling at his right hip, his long-knife strapped to his left thigh, Bair faced the wall once more and called out, "Climbing!" and using the stirrup cascade—left, right, left, right—he stepped up the four loops on each side, Aravan feeding out a bit of line. When Bair reached the top stirrups, he clipped a short anchor line to the second ring of the embedded rock-nail, and then selected another rock-nail and reached high and hammered it in, pings rising. He then fixed a brace of snap-rings through that rock-nail and called out "Slack!" When Aravan fed him a bit of line, he clipped the climbing rope through the top ring of the pair, and in the ring just under he fixed a second stirrup cascade. Unsnapping the short anchor line, "Climbing!" he called, and up he stepped into the second set of stirrups, testing the firmness of the rock-nail anchor, then putting the full of his weight on the support. He reached down and retrieved the first cascade and clipped it to his harness, then stepped on upward.

And thus did the ascent begin.

Up went Bair and up, hammering rock-nails or setting jams, clipping lines and cascades through rings, testing, unclipping and moving on upward, all with Aravan belaying. When the coil of rope had but four loops left, "Twenty feet!" called Aravan.

Standing on a ledge, Bair looked 'round for a suitable place to anchor a belay for Aravan to make his own ascent. The lad selected an upjutting horn of rock to do so, and by a leather-strap sling and snap-rings he moored himself to the projection and set up his own belaying gear. When he was ready, "Off belay!" he called down.

As Aravan got to his feet and freed his assemblage, Bair set a jam and two linked rings in a nearby crevice and unclipped a hank of line from his harness and fixed it to the top ring. "Rope!" he called below, casting the coil down while yet holding on to the free end. When he saw the line had not snagged, he cast the free end down as well.

Aravan affixed one of the packs to this second line, and Bair hauled it upward, anchoring it to the lower ring on the jam. Again he cast down the rope and hauled up the second pack; a third time he hauled up the unused gear.

When this was done, Bair called down, "Ready! On belay!" and Aravan—with Krystallopŷr harnessed across his back and a long-knife strapped to his right thigh—called back, "Climbing," and using his own stirrup cascades, up Aravan went, removing rock-nails and jams and rings and leather-strap slings as he ascended, clipping some to his harness, placing others in the equipment bag, and looping runners over his head and one shoulder. And above, Bair took up slack as he belayed, while Aravan climbed and retrieved gear. . . .

Aravan led on the next pitch, Bair on the one after.

And up the stone they went, alternating lead and follow, while villagers below craned their necks and watched and shook their heads in grim disbelief, yet the pair would not listen to reason, hence it was on their own foolish foreigner heads; they had been warned: it was forbidden.

When they topped the vertical massif, only Juhi was in a position to see as Aravan and Bair coiled ropes and bundled gear and shouldered their packs, then clipped a rope between them and, with the Elf leading and the tall lad trailing, onward they went, trekking northerly through a wide notch white with winterfall. And she stood on the crest of her small mount and watched until they crossed a far ridge of snow and disappeared downward beyond.

*   *   *

"Crevasse ahead," warned Bair, standing on an upjut as they paused for a drink of water. "A wide one. How deep I cannot say, but there seem to be snow bridges—at least that's what they look like from here."

"Where away?"

Bair pointed. "A furlong or so."

"Dost thou see thee a way past?"

Bair scanned the snowfield. "Not one at hand. I say we look at the bridges before going out of our way."

Aravan slipped his waterskin back under his coat. "I will continue to lead; I tread lighter than thee."

Onward they went, their cloaks and hoods pulled tightly 'round against the dry chill, and as they came to the crevasse, Aravan paused while Bair payed out more rope and then anchored it by driving the handle of his ice axe into the pack and taking a hitch about the helve. "Ready," called the lad.

Aravan stepped toward the gape, then shook his head. "This bridge sags." He eased a bit closer to the cleft. "It is quite deep, else we'd climb down and cross over and climb up again." He looked both left and right, then pointed. "Yon." He stepped back from the crevasse and when he was well away, Bair pulled the haft of his axe up and out from the snow and followed Aravan easterly.

Again Aravan rejected a snow bridge spanning the fissure, but the next one appeared to be firm enough, the arch deep and rounded on top.

As Bair anchored and payed out line, Aravan trod lightly across. Then he anchored as Bair crossed over, the icy walls plummeting downward into a shadowed bluish white a hundred feet or so before curving under and out of sight.

Onward they went, among sparse trees. The snowfield for the most part was hard-packed, yet split now and then with fissures: many of them were quite narrow, and the two simply leapt across; others they crossed using snow bridges; still others they clambered down and through and back up and out again; and some they altogether went 'round. Occasionally they came to wide reaches of loose snow, and in such places they used their snowshoes until they came to firm pack again.

Often they paused and drank, for the air was thin and the water helped stave off high-mountain sickness. And when evening fell, they camped down in one of the shallow crevices to be out of the wind.

As they took a meal of jerky and crue, and melted snow in the copper pot using winter-dried scrub gathered from a scant copse above as fuel, Bair said, "How far do you deem we came this day?"

"Nigh seven leagues, I ween," replied Aravan.

"Ha! I thought so. We've gone two days' travel in but one."

Aravan nodded. "Aye, but the way ahead is rougher. Didst thou see the icefall we must cross on the morrow, and the buttress down whence it fell?"

"Yes, but we'll make short work of that, I would think. And there's a chimney up the bluff."

By dusk of the following day they had gone but three more miles altogether.

Bluffs and crevasses barred the way, and fields of loose, drifted snow, and windswept barren stone ridges, and icefalls and ice-laden slopes. The two fared up and over all, using their gear when necessary, including crampons upon the icy ways. Alongside extensive lateral moraines they trod, and across fields of debris below avalanche chutes and other such reminders of winters now and past. And always did they keep one eye to the sky and the other eye out for shelter, for late-spring blizzards could strike at any moment. Yet all they saw in the sky were isolated drifting clouds and towering peaks and an occasional far-off flyer or two soaring among the remote peaks—falcon, crow, or something else, they could not say, for they were too distant to tell, beyond even Aravan's Elven sight to make out.

Deeper into the range they pressed and, except for an occasional cloud, the days were clear and the sun bright as spring came creeping unto these heights, and meltwater flowed in the late afternoons. But though the days were fair, the nights were frigid, and they camped in whatever refuge they could find, using crevices or digging out snow caves, once digging down into the snow 'round a solitary pine to make a tree-pit shelter.

Onward they went, past shoulders and through cols and along

gullies and up bluffs, the terrain ever rising, the nights ever more chill. And but for an occasional word and the crunch of their feet on hard-packed snow, the only sound they heard was the susurrus of the wind, though now and again even it paused to leave nought behind but an airy silence.

And still they had seen no sign of the Temple of the Sky.

In a buffeting wind on the dark afternoon of the ninth day of their journey, some eighty-five miles north and a bit west of the village of Umran and well above the tree line and scrub, gasping with effort in the rarefied air at that altitude, Bair finally clambered over the lip of a near-vertical buttress well-nigh five hundred feet high, twenty of which near the crest arched out in an overhang . . . then it was six more perpendicular feet to the top. As he gained the flat above, he collapsed to his hands and knees, sweat pouring down. On the edge of exhaustion and panting for breath in the sparse air, Bair levered himself to his knees and looked about, numb with the striving, his mind hazy at these heights. Past the broad ledge on which he knelt, a long slope led upward through a high-walled col, immense cornices of snow hanging above, looming out over the way. Only the darkening, cloud-laden sky showed beyond the crest of the pass, the wind driving the grey overcast northward above.

Brushing aside snow, Bair began seeking a suitable place to anchor a belay. He chose two narrow, deep cracks in the flat atop the ledge and set a jam in each, then affixed himself to them, and through a ring at his waist he set a belay hitch in the line leading to Aravan below.

"Off belay!" he called down. And in another crack he set a third jam and a pair of rings.

Then, "Rope!"

Grunting, he hauled up the packs and the spare equipment bag and affixed them to the third jam.

"Ready! On belay!" he called down and waited, his gaze on the ominous sky. He glanced back into the pass, and just then, silhouetted against the wind-driven clouds, one of the dark fliers slid across the far end of the slot and then was gone from view. Bair frowned, for in that brief moment it had not seemed to be a bird, but rather—

"Climbing!" came Aravan's call, and Bair dismissed his fanciful notion and turned his attention to belaying.

Up came Aravan and up, retrieving rock-nails, jams, rings, runners, and slings, Bair taking up slack and coiling rope as he anchored Aravan's climb. But the Elf moved slowly and rested often, for this high in the mountains the air was perilously thin.

Finally, Aravan clambered over the top and stood gasping as Bair, yet sitting, undid the belay hitch clipped to his own belt . . . and in that moment—

—one of the vast cornices of snow in the col ahead gave way, the great overhang crashing down, a vast wall of white tens of feet high hurtling toward Aravan and Bair.

"Avalanche!" shouted Aravan.

Bair whipped about to see the monstrous wave thundering toward him. Unclipping from the belay anchor and springing to his feet, "Trust the rope!" he shouted, and leapt over the precipice, Aravan jumping over as well, the gigantic crest of snow crashing through where they had been and hurtling outward into the thin air.

Both Bair and Aravan plummeted down the vertical face of the buttress—*zzz . . .*—the rope sliding through the last ring on the last jam wedged in the wall above as Aravan fell down and down, Bair falling below him, a wall of white plunging past and down as well. Then, some fifty feet below the overhang—

—*Thnn!*—

—the rope snapped taut—

—*Unh!*—grunted both Aravan and Bair, and, now out of control and spinning, the pair crashed into the rock of the buttress. As they rebounded, some ten feet below Aravan, Bair fell limp, knocked senseless by the stone.

And as tons upon tons of snow hurtled past, Aravan began rising and Bair dropping, for the lad weighed some twenty pounds more than his outbalanced kelan, and the rope slid ever faster and faster through the ring overhead, drawing Aravan back up toward the thundering avalanche above.

CHAPTER 29

Engels

April, 5E1009

[Eight Months Past]

Even as he swung about on the end of a tether sliding upward, on the second try Aravan managed to grasp the descending rope, the line running through his gloved hand and slowing to a halt in his grasp, stopping his rise and ending his elar's drop. Hauling up on the line, Aravan easily overcame the twenty-pound difference and down he went, unconscious Bair rising, the rope linking them sliding through the ring above.

And still tons upon tons of snow hurled over the lip above and plummeted past the two, to crash down onto the base of the buttress far below.

Like two spiders on a joined strand they were, and Aravan reached Bair just as the dazed youth was coming to.

"Bair, dost thou hear me?"

"Unh. Where—?" Bair struggled upright to see the avalanche of snow plunging past. He looked down at the four-hundred-fifty-foot drop below, and then to the face of the vertical rock some two or three arm lengths away, then up at the rope above. Finally he looked at Aravan and grinned. "Some fix, eh?"

Aravan grinned back. "Aye, elar, some fix indeed, yet one DelfLord Balor did train us for."

Bair nodded and winced and touched the back of his head and winced again.

The cascade of snow began to dwindle, the broad fall moving inward as the rush to oblivion began to slow. And as it diminished, Aravan unclipped a short length of line dangling from his harness and handed it to Bair.

Reaching up, Bair used this secondary line to tie a friction knot around the main rope above, a knot that would tighten when the secondary line was weighted, but grow lax when unweighted.

And as Bair tied the knot, Aravan said, "That was quick thinking, elar. 'Tis the second time my life was saved by 'trusting the rope.' "

"Second time?"

"Aye. Once during a Vulg attack did Gwylly save my life. 'Anchor!' he cried, as he set the jam, and below him I swung out and away, the Vulg crashing into the wall where I had just been."

"A clever folk, those Warrows, or at least Amicula Faeril is," said Bair, as from the knot he threaded the remainder of the short rope down and tied it through a ring at the waist of his harness, leaving some three feet of slack between harness and knot.

Aravan handed Bair a second short length of line, and Bair tied a second friction knot to the main rope below the first, and as close as he could to this second knot he affixed a pair of his stirrup cascades.

Even as he did so, the last of the avalanche dribbled past, a thin stream of snow blowing in the wind and cascading down atop the two. When it ended—"Ready?" asked Aravan.

"But what about you, kelan?"

"Ah, my lad, I get a free ride."

"Free ri—?"

Using Bair's weight and controlling his rise, Aravan began to ascend, the rope sliding through the ring above, Bair in counter descending. "Wait until I hail all is ready," called Aravan as he rose.

His jaw agape, Bair watched as his kelan ascended while he himself sank.

As he came to the last six feet at the top, Aravan halted his rise and set a jam into an upward v-crack, then using two snaprings and a runner, he managed to anchor the jam to the main line. Easing upward again, he came to the point where the twenty-pound difference in their weights was being held by the anchoring rig. With the line now belayed, both of Aravan's hands were free, and he quickly clipped a secondary line to the main one, clipped a short length of this second line into the final jam above and threw the remainder onto the lip overhead. Using a horizontal split in the face of the stone, he eased his heft off the main, letting the full of Bair's weight depend; the runner and rings and jam just below easily held. Aravan gathered his strength and skill and took several deep breaths of thin air and then unclipped his own harness from the main line and free-climbed the last few feet.

Snow lay upon the ledge, the tailings of the slide, and Aravan quickly cleared a wide space. He took up the secondary line and, brushing more snow aside, found Bair's original pair of jams and anchored the rope, taking out all the slack. Finally, he lay on the edge and peered over and called down, "Bair, there's a runner holding thy weight for the nonce, and should it break on thy ascent thou wilt fall but a foot ere jerking to a stop. Dost thou understand?"

"Aye!" called Bair.

In the rising wind, Aravan glanced at the ever-darkening sky and called, "Ready! On belay!"

"Climbing!" came the response from below.

Grasping the main line, Bair stood in the top stirrups, transferring the full of his weight onto the lower friction knot, the knot tightly gripping the main rope and supporting the stirrup cascade. He then slid the now-lax top friction knot upward three feet or so—the knot able to slide, for none of the lad's weight bore against it—until the line between it and his climbing harness drew taut. Then settling his weight back against this upper knot and the line to the waist of his harness, he caused the top friction knot to grip tight to the main line. With his weight off the stirrups, the lower knot relaxed, and he reached down and slid it up until it came to the upper knot. Once again he grasped the main line and stood in the top stirrups, and with his weight off the top friction knot he could slide it up again.

And thus in the scant air he came up the rope, like an inchworm climbing a thread, advancing up the rope toward the ledge overhead where Aravan lay and watched.

And as he climbed the sky darkened, and the buffeting wind grew stronger.

Halfway up Bair paused to rest, for he was gasping in the altitude, sweat pouring down his face. He leaned back in his climbing harness, his weight on the line between himself and the top friction knot holding him in place. A long loop of line dangled down twenty-five feet and then back up to his harness: it was the fifty feet of rope he had ascended so far. He affixed the top end of the loop to a ring on his harness, and coiled the remainder; now if his friction knots failed, he would not fall all the way back down to the bottom end of the line.

From above Aravan called down, "Hurry, elar, we need go onward, for the sky speaks of a storm, and we must find shelter ere it strikes."

Bair sighed and readied to inch upward again in the thin air, three feet at a time, weighting one knot, unweighting the other, and sliding the free one up the main line.

At last Bair reached the bottom side of the ledge above, the climbing rope dangling down in another long loop. He paused and managed to retrieve the runner and rings and jam Aravan had set, then, just as Aravan had done, he free-climbed the remaining six feet.

Gasping, he clambered over the lip just as flakes of wind-driven snow forerunning the oncoming storm hurtled past and up the col.

"Untie, Bair," called Aravan. "Make haste, for this ledge is no shelter, and the wind will be savage; we have to get through the pass and into cover beyond."

As Bair untied the friction knots from the climbing line, and the climbing line from his harness he said, "Can't we take shelter in the pass?"

Removing the anchoring jams and the one at the top of the climb, Aravan replied, "I think not, Bair. The col will act as a funnel and the wind therein will be quite brutal. Too, there is yet an overhang of snow above, and should it give way . . ."

"I understand," said Bair, untying the secondary anchoring line from the main climbing line as the wind-driven snow strengthened. "I hate to suggest this, but we could take shelter back at the base of this buttress."

Aravan began coiling the main line. "Nay, Bair. No time, for the storm is nigh upon us, and to be unsheltered on that wall in a blizzard would mean certain death. Besides, should we make it to the bottom and that second cornice give way, we'd be buried by unnumbered tons of snow."

"Then it's through the pass and hope we find shelter beyond," said Bair, tying off the coil on the secondary line.

Bair turned and looked about, and with a sinking heart asked, "Oh, kelan, where are our packs?"

For the first time Aravan looked across the ledge. "Where were they moored?"

Bair dug down through the tailings of the slide to find the anchoring jam and two snap-rings but nought else. "Over the edge with the avalanche, kelan, that's where they are; our equipment and food and fuel, all gone, buried, as you say, under unnumbered tons of snow."

Even as he said it, the wind howled as if in victory and engulfed them in hurtling snow.

Using the pry of his rock-nail hammer, Bair freed the jam and rings and clipped them to his harness. Then Aravan clipped a line to Bair, and together they headed upslope into the col, wind shrieking, snow racing past, darkness churning overhead, and on one wall of the pass above loomed a vast overhang of snow.

In a rage of white gone grey under the dark clouds above, and with the yawling wind hammering at their backs, into the deep pass they went, the snow knee-deep and heavy and hindering, since their snowshoes had gone over the rim with their packs and the surplus gear bag. In the rarefied air, their breathing was heavy and their progress strained, yet still they pressed on, unable to slow-step and conserve energy, for to do so in this blast would imperil their lives. And driven on the furious wings of the howling wind, blinding snow engulfed them, and had they not been roped together, one might have lost the other.

On through the pass they went, cataracts of snow cascading down from the wind-battered cornice above, until they came at last to the crest of the col. Yet in that moment the rope between Bair and Aravan went slack, though in the heavy snow Bair could not see why.

His lungs heaving with the effort of breathing thin air, his heart hammering with labor, the lad took up the line and followed it to find Aravan on his knees in the drifts, the Elf gasping.

"Kelan!" called Bair, the wind shredding his words and whipping them away.

"Kelan!" shouted Bair again.

There was no response from Aravan.

Bair had to put his mouth to Aravan's ear to be heard above the scream of the wind.

"Kelan!"

Aravan looked up at Bair, then shook his head and unclipped the line and weakly motioned for Bair to go ahead alone.

"No," shouted Bair. "You'll die up here. And if you don't go onward, then I won't either."

Aravan grimly struggled to his feet and, supported by Bair, took a single step and then collapsed. Bair, pressed beyond his own limits, fell as well.

Disentangling from Aravan, Bair, gasping, struggled to his knees. He coiled the line and clipped it to his climbing belt. Then, straining, he rolled Aravan onto his side and slipped Krystallopŷr from the Alor's back and transferred it to Aravan's chest, tying it to his harness. Then using two long runners and a sling, he fashioned a drag and clipped it to the shoulder straps of Aravan's climbing rig, and all the while the shrieking wind stole precious heat from the pair.

Panting, dizzy, black spots swimming before his eyes, Bair attempted to survey his work but found he had not the slightest idea of what he was looking at, much less whether or not it was suitable. Even so, with the last dregs of his will, a dark shimmering came over the lad . . . and Hunter stepped forth and threaded his muzzle through the sling, the loop sliding over his head to settle 'round neck and shoulder and chest.

And then the great Silver Wolf started down the slope of the far side of the col, dragging the Friend—the Elf—through the snow after. Even this grand creature was pressed to his limits, yet onward he went, seeking to get clear of the pass and the dangers therein, seeking shelter below. And the blinding snow hurtled past, the shrieking wind funnelling through the gap, the raging blast seeking to freeze these interlopers in their tracks.

Down went Hunter and down, dragging the Friend behind, finally to come to the mouth of the col, a plateau running beyond, a plateau where he could turn away from the pass, away from the path of any slide that might come roaring through. Yet he needed to find shelter, and soon, else the Friend he drew behind would perish. Hunter found a drifted-over, shallow ledge on the plateau, and dragged the Friend down into the lee. Then the 'Wolf dug into the drift, making a hollow. As he dug there came a rumble from the pass. Hunter looked up and through the whirling white, and he could just make out that the overhanging cornice on this end of the gap had crashed down, the mass not sliding but filling the pass with snow. Hunter continued to dig. Finally, he dragged the Friend into the recess and lay down beside him, curling about the Friend in an attempt to keep him warm.

And thus they lay, nine days away from where they had started, food and supplies and fuel carried off and buried by an avalanche, their route back blocked, and a shrieking blizzard cold beyond measure howling all about.

And the snow hammered past, some falling, some accumulating, and the drift began to grow once again, gradually burying the Elf and the 'Wolf.

Hunter awakened to silence.

The blizzard had blown itself out. The covering snow was illuminated from above; day had come.

The 'Wolf nuzzled the Friend. The Elf was breathing shallowly; he had not died, yet he did not waken either. Something was wrong.

But then Hunter heard the beat of wings.

Bair. The truename came unbidden unto Hunter's mind.

A dark shimmering came over the 'Wolf, and then 'twas Bair who lay listening. As always, Bair remembered everything that Hunter had experienced, yet unlike Hunter, Bair did not now hear the sound of wings.

Struggling upward through the drift, Bair finally won free. And blinking against the bright midmorning sunlight glaring off the crystalline snow, casting back his hood and wiping away sun-blinded tears Bair looked up to behold—

—*Adon, am I dead? Are these dark Engels I see?*—

—winged beings descending, great raven-black feathered pinions bearing them through the air. And armed with bows, down they came like crows gliding, spiraling down toward Bair.

CHAPTER 30

Interlude

May, 5E1009

[Seven Months Past]

At the touch of spurs, the warhorse reached full gallop within three running strides. Leaning forward in the saddle, the youth lowered his lance in the uncertain light as the target neared, and—*Thnk!*—the point of the weapon struck the wooden shield dead center, the target spinning 'round, the wooden morning star sweeping at the rider's head as the horse hurtled past, the lad bending low to avoid the counterblow.

"Oh, well done, my prince," called out Lady Eitel, as the youth wheeled his horse to enter the lists again, preparing to charge the target from the opposite end.

As he waited in the twilight for a squire to turn the silhouette to confront him—for at the end of its wild spin it had settled in the target groove facing the wrong way—Ryon raised his hand in acknowledgment of Eitel's praise. She simpered in return, then behind her fan she looked back and smirked at her ladies-in-waiting, knowing that any one of them would give her all to be in her position. For she, Eitel, Princess of Jute, planned to be the one to wed Ryon; then would those Fjordlanders pay, and dearly, for their retaliatory raids on her realm. And, as her mother, Gydwyn the Lovely, Queen of Jute, even though mad had wisely said, "What matter that you, Eitel, are ten years Ryon's senior? Nought whatsoever at all. To annihilate the enemies of old, *that* is the thing of importance, and you *will* have them crushed once you are the Queen of all Mithgar." Eitel the Exquisite was in perfect accord with her mother's plan. All that need be done was to catch this fool of a boy, and that, of course, would surely be accomplished when she got him into her well-used bed.

Yet even as Ryon readied for a last charge at the target ere the twilight was gone altogether, a page came running across the field to the side of the lad's horse, the prince bending down to listen. And but a moment later he handed off his lance to one of the squires and rode away from the field at a gallop, leaving Eitel to shift on her own, while the ladies-in-waiting behind her glanced at one another in the fading light, knowing smiles on their faces.

"My Lord Prince Ryon," called out the majordomo as Ryon strode into the candlelit chamber, "Lord Bruka of Blueholt and Lord Koll of Skyloft Holt."

Ryon, yet dressed in his armor, pulled off his gauntlets and cast them to the table. "My lords," he said, nodding at the Dwarven emissaries.

"Prince Ryon," growled Bruka, canting his head forward as did Koll, though the latter said nought.

Dressed in black-iron chain-mail shirts, with double-bitted axes slung across their backs, the two broad-shouldered Dwarves looked much alike, Koll being slightly the taller of the two, standing some four-foot-seven, while Bruka was an inch or so shorter. They wore plain helms upon their heads, black hair cascading down to the shoulders. Braided beards adorned their faces.

For their part, Bruka and Koll saw a brown-haired, brown-eyed, tall youth before them, standing some six foot in all. They looked at his sweat-stained face and his scarred armor and the calluses upon his hands, and they glanced at one another approvingly.

"Come," said Ryon, "let us sit and you can tell me why you are here."

As all took to chairs at the table, "We came to see your sire," said Bruka, "yet we are told he is gone to Challerain Keep."

Ryon nodded. "He and my dam are on their way to spend the summer there. In October they will return. Until then here at Caer Pendwyr I stand in the High King's stead."

Koll grunted as if somewhat surprised that a youth of sixteen was left in command.

Ryon smiled. "Can your tidings wait till October, or would you journey the five hundred and some odd leagues to Rian?"

Koll looked at Bruka and shrugged, and Bruka said, "We have already journeyed far to bring this news, though we know not what it portends."

"Say on, my lords," said Ryon.

"Skail is dead," replied Bruka.

"Dreja, too," said Koll, speaking for the first time.

"The Cold-drakes?"

"Aye," replied Bruka.

"When? How?" asked Ryon.

Both Dwarves turned up their hands, and Bruka said, "We discovered Skail's remains some months past, lying before his lair there in the mountains of Gelen, no wounds in evidence, a victim, we think, of the Ban."

Ryon cocked an eyebrow. "Victim of the Ban, you say. Why so?"

"His trove was intact."

"Ah, I see," said Ryon. "If he had been slain by a hero, such as Elgo—"

"Thief Elgo, you mean," growled Koll, Bruka nodding in agreement.

Ryon turned up a hand, "Let us just say that had the Dragon been slain by someone, the trove would have been taken. And since it was not . . ." Ryon paused but then said, "You claimed the trove for yourselves, I assume."

Bruka nodded. "The Dragonhide, too."

"Ah, yes," said Ryon. "—But tell me: why would Skail have stepped into the sun?"

Again both Dwarves shrugged, and Bruka said, "Who knows the minds of Dragons? Regardless, when we bore the news to the holt you name Skyloft, a party was sent to scout Dreja's nearby lair from afar, yet what we found was his remains lying before his cavern as well."

"No wounds in evidence?" asked Ryon.

"None," replied Koll. "We claimed the hide and trove, and gave a finder's fee to the Châkka of the Blueholt."

"Adon, but what a tale," said Ryon. "A dark mystery, too. Why would two Cold-drakes—sire and get, it is said—why would they have stepped into the sunlight?"

"We know not," said Koll, "but we have sent word to all Châkkaholts throughout Mithgar to send parties unto the lairs of any nearby Cold-drakes . . . or Cold-drakes afar for that matter."

Ryon's eyes widened in surprise. "Adon, do you believe that *all* Cold-drakes are dead?"

Again the Dwarves shrugged, and Bruka said, "As of yet, no Châkka have come bearing finder's fees, hence we do not know."

Ryon pursed his lips and then smiled. "Of all the places you and your kind have carried the message, I assume you have come here dead last."

Bruka smiled in return. "You are wily, Prince Ryon, and correct. All the Châkkaholts have been told."

Ryon laughed and shook his head. "Nicely done, my friends. Nicely done." And then he added, "Come, let us break bread together."

As the three stood, the majordomo said, "My lord prince, I would remind you that you are to have an intimate dinner with Princess Eitel."

Ryon's shoulders slumped, and he sighed, but then he brightened. "Then set two more places at the table, Aldor, for I would speak of things other than wicked Fjordlanders or of assuring the royal line." He turned to the Dwarves. "Let us talk of arms and armor and the forging of axes and swords." And with a jauntiness in his step, and sweat-stained and in sore need of a bath, Ryon led the emissaries to an intimate candlelit meal with a princess as mad as her mother.

On a swift packet sailing through the Straits of Kistan and engaged in a glancing battle with a crimson-sailed Kistanian dhow, a Realmsman ranged the decks of the fleet little ship, his bow in hand, the man winging deadly shafts at the Rovers and dodging deadly shafts in return. In a pouch under his jerkin was a coded journal, containing the astounding news that—in spite of their pledge to abstain from interfering without just cause in the affairs of others—Dragons had conquered the island realm of Ryodo, and a Jingarian queen now sat on the throne. Too, something dire was afoot in Jinga, yet what it might be, he did not know, his information sketchy at best, for he had not heard from his spies afoot in that land.

The Realmsman, a man of Aralan, prayed to Adon that the wind would pick up in the setting sun and the packet would leave this Rover behind, for he would have this news reach the High King, for though it dealt with matters afar, it might truly bear on the future of all Mithgar.

At Black Mountain in far Xian, in the darkness the great iron doors swung wide, doors forged long past by Velkki Gatemaster. Out rode Mages on horses—hundreds of Mages, hundreds of horses—a long journey ahead. They were bound for the Plains of Valon, for the Trine was coming.

Far below the ruins of Dragonslair, great hands split the now-cold magma stone, gemstone eyes seeing through solid rock as the Utruni made their way toward the great token of power lying 'neath. They would take this device in hand now, for the time of the prophecy drew closer, a prophecy spoken long past by the Utrun Lithon, now dead, a prophecy the Utruni alone did bear:

[*Uthr mnis klno dis . . .*]

> *In the time of the Trine,*
> *A Hammer to carry, be wary;*
> *The terrible Wage is Woe and Rage.*
> *In the time of the Trine,*
> *Where the Dragons are found, be bound.*
> *Find the One to smite for Right.*
> *In the time of the Trine,*
> *Unto the trapped King bear Kammerling,*
> *The Greatest Dragon to slay this day.*
> *In the time of the Trine,*
> *Champion of Fate, smite Greater Drake,*
> *In the time of the Trine, the Trine . . .*
> *In the time of the Trine.*

And now at last the Utruni clove through cold stone and unto the token of power: called the Kammerling by some, Adon's Hammer by others, and the Rage Hammer by others still. And Orth reached out and took up the great silveron weapon.

In a slow, heavy tongue, a tongue which sounded like rock sliding upon rock, Brelk said, "Now we must seek the Drakes."

"Nay," said ruby-eyed Chale, Orth's mate, "it is not yet the time of the Trine."

"But soon," said Orth, holding up the Kammerling and gazing at it, her great sapphirine eyes casting blue glints on its silvery surface, though by what light none could say.

"Then at the very least we should seek to see where they are," said Brelk, turning his viridian gaze through the stone of the world, seeking to see Drakes near and far, his sight passing over the corpse of nearby Frauth—get of Sleeth—lying at the mouth of its lair, for that Cold-drake was dead, slain by the Ban; deep in its cave lay a trove yet intact though Dwarves from Kachar drew nigh to claim it as well as the Dragonhide.

In the mountains far to the east, a great army widened a road. In all they had progressed nearly a hundred miles that month, Kutsen Yong's great oxen-drawn wagon not far behind the laboring Horde.

And in his golden palace awheel, not at all concerned over the arduous burden this was putting upon logistics and men, Kutsen Yong dallied with his new concubines, young virgins at his behest.

In his dark wagon elsewhere, Ydral seesawed between wrath and ecstasy, young virgins at his behest as well, their fate of another sort.

As to the Fire-drakes, they had been dismissed, but for Ebonskaith. After all, the Dragons could be summoned anytime at the whim of Kutsen Yong. And Ebonskaith, Mightiest of Dragons, sat in the mountains nearby and seethed, now and then roaring at the sky, and he plotted and schemed all to no end, for the Dragonstone held him in thrall.

In Arden Vale, Riatha sat on the west bank of the Virfla and polished the dark blade of Dúnamis, the sword having seen much use of late, and she wondered how her Bair fared: was he well? was he in a place of comfort? or was he instead in danger dire?

She did not know....

She did not know....

And sudden tears flooded her eyes.

CHAPTER 31

Phael

May, 5E1009

[Seven Months Past]

As the ebon-winged beings descended, bows nocked with arrows, Bair took his flanged mace in hand, though what he might do against assault from above, he did not know. Yet even as he gripped the helve of his weapon, he glanced down at his side where Aravan lay half-buried in snow, Krystallopŷr askew across his chest, the rigging Hunter had used to drag him with yet hooked to the Elf's climbing harness. And there was something strange about Aravan's <fire>, as if it were somehow changed or overlaid with <fire> not his own.

Bair knelt and placed a finger to Aravan's neck. His breath was shallow and his pulse was slow and weak.

Uncertain, Bair stood and took a protective stance in front of his kelan, then looked up at the dark-feathered beings spiralling down from above, their weapons in hand, missiles ready to fly.

Black they were, dark as night, like ebon men with great raven's wings, dark pinions flared wide as down through the air they came, seven altogether. And as they neared, Bair could see that what he had taken for clothing was instead overlapping black feathers as well, their sable bodies, including their faces, covered with dark plumage. And while six glided above, one alighted on the snow facing Bair, his wings spread outward and crooked, as would a hawk posture when threatened, ready for fight or flight. Smaller than a human, he was, perhaps standing nigh five feet tall, or so Bair did judge. His wings, however, fully extended would span tip to tip perhaps twelve or thirteen feet in all. To drive those great pinions, his chest was broad and deep, heavy with muscle. Something between that of a man and a bird, his face was wide of brow angling down to a narrow chin, and was covered with fine feathers, which grew in length as they progressed over the top of his elongated head, becoming a magnificent crest flaring wide at the back of the skull. And in his black-feathered face golden raptor eyes glared, savage and sharp and alert. His <fire> glowed brightly, and it was plain to see he and those above were a Folk, feathers, wings, and all.

"We come in friendship," said Bair in Common, lowering his mace to his side, "sent by Dodona."

At Bair's words, the being stepped backward a pace, but then replied in a language somewhat like the Bharaqi spoken in Umran, or so to Bair's ear it did sound, for the lad did understand one of the words: varjit: forbidden.

Aravan, you would pick this time to be unconscious.

Bair then spoke in his limited Kabla, struggling to find the right words, especially something denoting friendship, finally settling for, "We this place come. Dodona say come. We not bad." When it was plain he was not understood, Bair said in Sylva, "We come in friendship."

The winged being's eyes widened at the use of that tongue, and he relaxed slightly and said, "This land is forbidden to outsiders, and I see no falcon nearby."

Bair sighed in relief. *At last a language we have in common. And what's all this about a falcon?*

"Who *are* you?" asked Bair.

"I am Ala of the Phael."

Bair's eyes widened in surprise. "Of the Phael? Of the Hidden Ones?"

At Ala's nod, Bair hooked his mace back onto his belt loop and slipped the keeper thong in place. Then he held forth his hands, palms outward, showing they were empty and said, "I am Alor Bair of Arden Vale, and my companion is Alor Aravan of"—Bair frowned and then brightened—"of the Sea.

"We are sent on a mission by the Oracle Dodona to find the Temple of the Sky. But right now I would accept any shelter, for my kelan is in dire need." Bair stepped aside and gestured at Aravan.

The Phael looked at the Elf, his golden eyes widening. "A Lian?"

Bair nodded.

His bow at his side, the Phael strode forward, his wings now fully folded. "We were sent by the Guardian to find a Friend in need, though whether it is this Lian, I cannot say. To find his companion as well."

"We are surely in need, Friend and companion both," said Bair turning and kneeling beside Aravan.

"There is a test," said the Phael, reaching Aravan's side and kneeling as well.

"A test?"

"The Guardian said the companion would bear a falcon, and the Friend would have a blue stone."

"A falco—? Oh, yes." Bair fished about under his collar and drew forth the crystal, the falcon incised within. The Phael looked at the crystal and said, "A falcon, true, not as I expected, yet it will do." Then Bair winnowed the thong from under Aravan's collar, bringing the blue amulet forth. The Phael reached out and touched the stone. As he did so, Bair could see that the feathers on the backs of his hands and fingers were as tiny as minnow scales, and the palms and undersides of his fingers were bare, the skin black. Too, there was what looked to be dark down underneath the larger feathers covering the being's wrists and arms and body. The Phael nodded and looked at Bair. "He is a Friend, and thou art his companion, the ones we seek."

"I repeat," said Bair, "we need get him to shelter."

"It is not far," said the Phael, pointing northerly, "perhaps but two leagues by thy measure."

Bair looked. Five or six miles to the north, down a slope and across a basin and up another long slope, there atop a high, rough-sided mesa stood a large, squat, round stone building—its conical roof covered with snow, and ice hung down from the eaves—a building that Bair would have sworn had not been there but a moment ago.

"So close," murmured Bair. "We came so close."

"Yes," said the Phael, "closer than any trespassers before ye.

Even so, still ye must get there on thine own, or so the Guardian says."

"But I thought you were sent to help."

"Only to point the way."

Bair ground his teeth. "By Adon, who does this so-called Guardian think he is?"

"Why, he is the Guardian, the Keeper, the Shepherd, the Mystes, the Mentor," replied the Phael, as if it all were obvious. "None may question his ways."

"None question his wa—?" Bair glared at the temple and then at Ala, the Phael stepping backward from the enraged lad. Bair glanced down at Aravan and then back at the temple. "I'll show him which of us is a true Guardian." And he stripped off his cloak and laid it in the snow. Then he unfastened Aravan's cloak and drew it from the Elf and laid it atop his own. Unsnapping his improvised rigging from Aravan's harness, he redid the ropes to turn the two cloaks into a makeshift sledge of a sort. Then, struggling in the rarefied air, he wrestled Aravan onto the garments and fastened them 'round, then clipped the rigging back onto Aravan's climbing harness. Carefully he affixed Krystallopŷr in its sling lengthwise upon Aravan's chest. Surveying his handiwork, panting, he turned to Ala and said, "Time to go, birdman." A dark shimmering enveloped him and a Silver Wolf stepped forth; the Phael cried out in alarm and leapt into the air and away, dark wings churning. Hunter slipped the loop of the rig over his head, and sighting upon the rough-sided mesa, down the snowy slope he went with care, choosing his way through the snowfield, dragging unconscious Aravan behind.

Down he went and down, down the long white slant and into the basin, the Silver Wolf steering wide of crags and ice, Hunter keeping to where the snow was deep and soft through which to haul the hurt Friend, while high above flew the dark Phael, calls whistling among them, the 'Wolf paying the Phael little heed as he plowed on across the basin and up.

In the snow-covered scree at the foot of the mesa, Bair unclipped the climbing gear from Aravan's harness and added it to his own. He looked up the side of the rough stone looming above; fluted and cracked and ice-laden it was, with chimneys here and there. After long study, he selected a route. Clipping a wye-rigged line to the shoulders of Aravan's harness and then paying it out after, up the wall of the mesa he went, free-climbing the rugged stone, using his ice axe to clear a hand or foothold every now and again.

On a nearby prominence across a deep notch, Phael stood and watched.

Up he went and up, resting in the thin air often, occasionally setting jams or rock-nails and stirrup cascades to get past a difficult stretch. On he went and on, trailing rope behind, fastening a new hank to the old when needed.

And the sun slid across the day.

Finally, gasping, he reached the flat above, and there he rested awhile, the promised shelter at his back, though Bair stubbornly refused to turn and look at it other than to see it was made of grey-granite blocks.

Now to get his kelan up.

Bair looked 'round and cleared away snow and found a suitable spot to place three jams, snap-rings in each. He threaded a short length of rope through the rings and made a loop just long enough to reach over the side. Then he snapped several rings together in a large linked loop of their own, and over the side he clipped that circlet of rings to the anchored loop of rope. Finally, he fished the line tied to Aravan through the circlet, and then fixed the end to a ring at his own waist.

"Here we go, kelan," he said, and grasping the part of the line leading directly down to Aravan, he stepped back over the rim of the mesa. Using Aravan as a counterweight, down the rough face of the mesa he descended, the rope sliding through the linked snap-rings above, Bair controlling the twenty pound difference between his weight and Aravan's to descend slowly while Aravan rose upward in counter. "Another free ride, kelan," gritted Bair, and down he went, Aravan rising. One of the knots tying the long lines together came to the rings overhead and jammed, but Bair managed to work it through, the circlet large enough for him to do so, where a single ring would have stopped the knotted rope altogether. And down he went and down, to come to Aravan—still breathing, still unconscious, still something wrong with his <fire>. Bair clipped a line to Aravan's harness and cast the end free, the rope falling down the side of the mesa. Grasping this new line, Bair continued his descent, Aravan ascending. Finally, the lad reached the bottom, the Elf reaching the top. Bair then set a jam in a crevice and, using a runner and ring, he fixed the rope at his own waist to the anchoring jam and unclipped the line from his harness. Then, while Aravan dangled above, Bair rested a goodly long while.

At last Bair started upward once more, and after a prolonged, exhausting climb, in the late afternoon he reached the top of the mesa once more. Then straining to his uttermost limits, he managed to wrestle Aravan onto the plateau, collapsing by his kelan's side.

His legs wobbly, his lungs heaving, sweat pouring down, Bair struggled to his feet, and turning to face the grey-stone temple, he shouted, "All right, Guardian, you unfeeling bastard, we're here on our own!" And then he sank to his knees, his head hanging.

A door opened in the side of the temple, and a white-haired, white-robed man or Elf or being of some sort stepped out and trod toward exhausted Bair and unconscious Aravan. He came to a stop before the lad. "Welcome to the Temple of the Sky, Alor Bair."

Bair looked up, and his eyes widened in startlement, and he gasped in surprise, "Dodona!"

"No, boy, not Dodona, though we are of a kind. Even so, I knew you might come."

Even as Bair saw that the Guardian's <fire> was indeed like that of Dodona—like that of a silver <flame>—the lad gritted, "If you knew I was coming, why didn't you help?"

"Oh, I could have helped at any time, but I wanted to see just how worthy you were, to test your mettle here at the last."

"This was a test? Something to test me when my kelan could have died?"

"Oh, child, he would not have died. I merely made certain he didn't waken." The Guardian turned toward Aravan and whispered a word, and of a sudden Aravan's <fire> was as it should be. Aravan groaned, and his breathing deepened.

"Argh!" roared Bair. "You cast some sort of spell over him just to test me?"

"Indeed," replied the Guardian, his voice mild. "You were and are quite worthy, you know."

Completely nonplussed, Bair looked at the Guardian, not knowing whether to feel proud or angry, whether to thank him or strike out in rage; he settled for laughing aloud in frustration.

Aravan sat up and looked at Bair kneeling in the snow. "What is so funny, elar?" Even as he asked, Aravan's gaze swept over the rim of the mesa and out to the basin below. "And how did we get here?" Then, as raven-dark Phael came winging down, in amazement Aravan turned to watch them . . . and saw the old man. "Dodona?"

Bair laughed all the harder.

CHAPTER 32

Falcon

May–September, 5E1009

[Seven to Three Months Past]

Ten feet apart, at the vertices of an equal-sided triangle chalked upon the stone floor, the Guardian and Bair and Ala the Phael all sat facing inward. At the center itself sat Aravan, the Elf facing the old man.

"Again I warn you," said the Guardian, "what we are to do is most perilous. Are you certain you wish to proceed?"

Aravan looked down at the crystal pendant at his throat and then back at the Guardian. "Aye, else creation will fall."

"So says Dodona?"

"So says Dodona."

The Guardian sighed. "Then if you are determined, I suppose we must."

At this response, Bair felt his heart pounding, and he wanted to say, "Kelan, don't." Yet he knew what must be done, and he bit his lip and remained silent.

They had been in the Temple of the Sky for a sevenday, primarily recuperating from their ordeal. And in addition to Ala they had come to know several of the Phael—Volar, Fleogan, Soren, Dyfan, Avi, and Segl—the latter three, female, their crests somewhat smaller than those of the males. It was difficult for Aravan to tell them apart by sight alone, yet he had a good ear for their voices. As for Bair, he had little if any trouble identifying one from another, for the <fire> was somewhat different from Phael to Phael. These seven Phael were not the whole of the flight, Ala

saying there were many more, most on far patrol now that spring
had come to Jangdi, winterlike though it was.

The Guardian alone seemed to live in the temple, though Phael
had free access to the chambers. Still, the flyers seemed somewhat uncomfortable inside the grey-stone walls, and they did not
stay long within, preferring to live high in the peaks above.

Aravan and Bair had been given quarters of their own—monk's
cells, or the like, though when the temple might have had monks,
the Guardian did not say—each equipped with a cot and a chair
and a small writing table, as well as a chest at the foot of the
bed. Of course, with but a fraction of their gear, the rest having
been swept over the precipice by the avalanche, Bair and Aravan had little to store.

Dyfan and Soren and Segl had flown to the site of the fall to
search for the gear, yet they came back empty-handed.

As to their Dodona-given mission, the Guardian had known
why they had come, but he waited the full sevenday ere acting,
waiting for them to regain strength and to further acclimate to
the altitude, saying that they needed more redness of blood.

It was during this time of waiting that Bair studied the Guardian, and there came a day when he discovered that this old "man"
could take on any appearance he wished; on that day the lad had
emerged from his cell and strode into the central chamber, and
there the Guardian stood talking to several of the Phael, and Bair
could see nought but a silver <flame>. Then the <flame> *turned*
and stepped toward Bair and became an old man again, and he
smiled at the lad and said, "Some vision you have, my boy."
When Bair told Aravan what he had seen, his kelan merely nodded and said, "Faeril once told us that no matter his shape to the
eye, Dodona was at heart a silver spirit, and since the Guardian
is of a kind . . ." Aravan shrugged and turned up a hand, then
added, "Elar, many are the mysteries of this world. Thou hast
just discovered another."

And so they had rested a sevenday . . .

. . . but finally they sat in the central chamber of the temple—
the Guardian and Bair and Ala at the vertices of an equilateral
triangle, Aravan chalked within, a crystal on a platinum chain
about his neck, the pellucid stone resting alongside his own blue
amulet on its thong.

The Guardian turned to Ala. "Are you ready?"

At the Phael's nod, the old man looked at Bair. "Are you ready as well?"

Distress in his eyes, Bair sighed and said, "Ready."

The old man then turned to Aravan, but before he asked, Aravan said, "Ready."

"Then let us begin," said the Guardian.

All knowing the roles they were to play, they began, and but moments later . . .

. . . with Aravan in deep meditation—the Elf immersed in all he knew of falcons and of flight, for he had studied such in solitude long past in Darda Erynian and Darda Stor—and with Bair and Ala in a lighter state, and the old man in a seeming trance . . .

"Now, Shapeshifter, lend me your shapeshifting spirit," whispered the Guardian.

Not knowing whether he could even accomplish that which the elder had said was necessary, Bair tried to come to the state desired. He felt his entire being on the cusp of shifting, and tried to hold himself in that state, struggling to remain Bair, to not become Hunter. Yet he failed, and a large Silver Wolf now sat at the point where Bair once had been. And though he had seen it before, still Ala cried out in startlement at the sight of the huge silver beast.

"Bair," whispered the old man.

Once again the lad appeared, a frown on his face. "This is difficult, Guardian."

"Nevertheless, Shapeshifter, try again."

Again Bair tried, and again and again—sometimes shifting; sometimes not; yet also not achieving the proper state. But he continued until at last he held himself directly on the threshold of shifting, yet not a scintilla beyond or back.

And the Guardian said, "Flyer, lend me your soaring spirit."

Ala's wings extended, and in that moment Bair lost the edge, stepping back rather than transforming.

The old man sighed. "Let us begin again."

Aravan in the center did not move or in any manner show that he was aware of the failures occurring beyond the chalk lines.

Yet again Bair sought the verge, finding it once more.

And once again Ala extended his wings and dreamed of soaring.

"Aravan, lend me your Elven spirit to do with as I will," whispered the Guardian, yet by no manner did Aravan appear to heed, though the old man nodded in satisfaction.

And even though he was in a meditative state, Bair could see <fire> flowing from his own self to enwrap Aravan, and <fire> flowing from Ala to enwrap Aravan as well, <fire> it seems under the control of the Guardian.

"*Valké,*" whispered the Guardian, speaking the truename Aravan had chosen, the Twyll word for falcon.

Of a sudden there came a flash of platinum light, flaring throughout the chamber, and when it was gone before them in the chalked triangle sat a falcon, a male, a tiercel, raven-black as was Aravan's hair, a savage wild spirit glaring out from sapphire-blue eyes. About its neck dangled a crystal on a short, fitted, platinum chain, and a blue stone amulet on a shortened thong, as if the links and leather themselves had taken part in the transformation, shortening to fit the wearer.

Of Aravan there was no sign.

Bair and Ala were shocked from their state of meditation, and Bair gasped at the sight, and Ala whistled out in startlement, for although they both knew what they were trying to accomplish, still it was a wonder.

Wildness in its blue eyes, the falcon attempted flight, yet the chalk line intervened, and—*skree!*—the bird cried out in anger, enraged by a captivity it could not apprehend. And it tried flying upward, but as if unseen walls came up from the lines to a point some five or six feet above, the falcon fell back thwarted. Again it cried out in rage, and with its wings partly extended, the raptor awkwardly hopped and bounded 'round the triangle, seeking escape, finding none.

Looking on in dismay, the Phael's eyes flooded with tears, while Bair stared gape-jawed. Aravan had disappeared, but to Bair's gaze the crystal was now filled with <fire>—his kelan's <fire>—held within the shimmering lattice, a bright <burning> inside the figure of the falcon incised within.

"Oh, my," said Bair. "Oh, my."

The elder turned to Bair and Ala and snapped, "Come, come. We cannot let him stay in this shape."

Bair took a deep breath and, quelling his astonishment as much as he could, once more he managed to enter a state of light meditation, even though a wild black tiercel raged but an arm reach away.

Wiping away his tears, Ala nodded and fell into meditation as well.

"Now, Shapeshifter, lend me your spirit again."

Again Bair reached the cusp of transformation, not going beyond, not falling short.

"Flyer, withdraw your spirit," murmured the elder.

Slowly, Ala folded his wings.

"Aravan," whispered the Guardian, speaking the Elf's true name . . . yet no transformation occurred. Once more the old man turned to the Phael, "Withdraw."

"It is difficult to not think of soaring," said the Phael, breaking his meditation.

"Nevertheless . . ."

Again the Phael entered a meditative state, extending his wings and then folding them once more.

"Aravan," whispered the Guardian.

Again no transformation occurred, and the black falcon continued to seek a way out of the caging lines.

Now Bair broke his own meditative state. "We cannot leave him like this," said Bair. "We must find a way to transform him back, else he will be a falcon forever."

"You must calm him, Shapeshifter."

"But how?"

"That I cannot say, for I know him not well, yet calm him nevertheless."

Bair frowned in concentration, trying to think, trying to recall what might soothe a falcon's savage spirit, yet it was Ala who said, "I will calm him."

And with a series of murmuring chirps and callings the Phael spoke to the tiercel, and lo! the bird stopped hop-footing about the chalk-line cage, stopped *skree*ing in rage, and turned its savage blue gaze upon the winged being.

"Now, Shapeshifter," hissed the elder.

Bair slipped into a state of light meditation and mentally stepped the verge of transformation.

"Now, Flyer, withdraw."

And Ala once more extended his wings and dreamed of soaring and then of not soaring but of standing aground as a nonflyer instead, folding his wings as he did so.

"Aravan," whispered Mentor.

Again there came a flash of platinum light, and once more Aravan sat enclosed by the chalk lines; and the Alor looked about with a savage blue gaze which swiftly transformed to sane calm.

A month elapsed, and then another, and in the passage of time, day after day Aravan transformed into the shape of a falcon, the training not only to learn to shapeshift, but also to bond the tiercel to Hunter as well as to Bair, for as the Guardian had said, "It is to these two the falcon must be loyal, else all our efforts are for nought." And turn on turn, only the 'Wolf and the lad were permitted to feed the bird.

Here it was that Ala proved to be essential, for the Phael could calm the wild bird, and Ala was somehow able to persuade the falcon that neither Bair nor Hunter were a danger. And slowly the bird Valké came to trust the lad and the 'Wolf.

And gradually, the Guardian began to require less and less of Bair and Ala's <fire>, progressively diminishing their involvement until at last, though he had not been born to it, Aravan began to shift on his own, changing from Elf to falcon, and from falcon to Elf, without aid from aught but a clear crystal imprinted some twenty years past with the spirit of a falcon.

Still, Valké was but a savage creature, a savage creature where reason prevailed, though barely, for the falcon was driven by other urges, other needs from those of the Elf he once had been. And in a reversal of teacher and student—each feeling a bit strange as mentor became protégé and vice versa—it was now Bair who instructed Aravan, Bair who took the lead and Aravan who followed, Bair advising Aravan in the ways and perils of shapeshifting, reflecting what Bair himself had been taught, stressing the point time and again that the falcon Aravan became was a thing of the wilds—not some Elf in the shape of a falcon, but a falcon cunning beyond all others, a falcon who at times would have strange unfalconlike urges, urges and motives akin to those of Elvenkind, perhaps even akin to those of a particular Elf, an Elf named Aravan. Yet, the tiercel who once was Aravan only occasionally would think along those paths, and this but when Aravan held a strong concept in mind ere shifting. And just as was the case with Bair and Urus and other shapeshifters, the peril of shifting was ever at hand, for although Valké might again *become* Aravan, there was no guarantee he would, for Valké indeed was a falcon wild. And *that* was a danger that the tiercel and Aravan both lived with: Aravan might never again become Valké; Valké might never again become Aravan. The Elf Aravan was aware of this danger; the tiercel Valké was not.

Year's Longday came: Summerday. And not only did Bair and Aravan celebrate the solstice, but so did all the Phael, many of the dark-feathered beings arriving from their far-flung patrols in the days before. On Summerday itself, in the high noontide did the Phael take to wing, the flyers trilling and soaring in crisscrossing formations, dedicating their spirits to Theonor, whom the Guardian also served, or so said Volar when asked. "Adon's brother is Theonor, a god as dusky as we. He is the patron of all flying things, or so we do believe. And the Guardian is his agent on Mithgar."

Bair turned to Aravan. "Since the Guardian and Dodona are of a kind, then is Dodona an agent, too? And if so, whom does he serve?"

Aravan shrugged. "Thou wilt have to ask Dodona . . . or mayhap the Guardian knows, for it is beyond my ken."

When Bair did ask the Guardian about Dodona's patron, Elwydd was the answer.

July came, and with it a great rushing melt upon high, water cascading down the steep slopes, lakes forming in basins, the snowpack retreating upward, ice calving from glaciers, sheets breaking away from mountain faces to thunder down, stone appearing where winter had been. Too, grasses grew and there came a burst of flowers in the lower vales, and as if springing full-grown from the blossoms themselves, flies and bees and beetles and moths probed the pollen-laden depths. Birds came winging, gorging themselves on the surfeit of insects. Kimu came as well, up from the lower valleys into the highland meadows, the ante-lope-goats to graze upon the new-grown succulent grasses. . . .

. . . At last, in the heat of July, spring had come to the heights.

In July as well, after the Guardian impressed upon Aravan he must be well grounded ere changing from falcon to Elf—else he could fall to his death from a great height, or crash down from a small limb, or other such calamity—Valké was finally set free of the chalked triangle.

On that day in an outer chamber as the Guardian once again warned Aravan, in a flash of light the Elf was gone, and instead there stood the black falcon, crystal pendant and blue stone at its throat. Valké looked with wild sapphirine eyes at Bair, as if ex-pecting to be fed, but instead the lad proffered his leather-clad wrist and took him up and bore him outside. The falcon glared about, as if seeking prey. Taking a deep breath, Bair called out, "Fly, Valké!" and with an upward and outward motion of his arm, he released the bird.

Valké sprang forth, wings raging, and he flew out at a shal-low up-angle and over the rim of the mesa, soaring into the bright blue sky, Ala winging high above and calling as would a falcon cry. Then Bair glanced at the Guardian, and at the old man's nod, a darkness shimmered over the lad, and Hunter padded out to the far rim south and stood. After long moments, Hunter raised his muzzle to the sky and called, his howling wail long and mournful.

And lo! Valké answered, and sharply turned wing over wing and came plummeting toward the Draega, and in the last instance he flared his pinions wide to land at Hunter's side. And from a dark shimmering and a platinum flash of light, Bair and Aravan emerged, elar and kelan laughing and embracing one another. Ala, too, landed nearby and was embraced as well. And Aravan said, "Ah, elar, what a splendid thing it is to fly above the world so high."

And Bair grinned and replied, "Just as it is to freely run across the plains below."

The lessons continued, Bair clambering down from the tem-ple mesa to the valley below, where a 'Wolf then raced across the basin, a falcon flying aloft, Valké learning to scout the terrain ahead and guide Hunter from above, and Hunter learning to follow the bird's lead to passage or game or water, Ala aiding in the training, calling out Sylva biddings to the Draega and *skree*-ing behests to the bird.

By the third week of August, the training was complete; Hunter and Valké had each learned to work with the other, Valké finding game and routes and water, Hunter bringing down the larger quarry. Too, Aravan fitted Krystallopŷr's special sling to Bair, for the token of power defied transformation, just as did the crystal pendant and Aravan's blue stone of warding and Bair's stone ring. It was on this day, as Aravan was rebuckling the sling on the lad, Bair standing as the Elf fitted the harness to him, that the Guardian entered the chamber. He stood awhile, his gaze on the crystal-bladed spear, and then with a sigh and shaking his head he turned on his heel and left. Aravan watched him go, a puzzled look in the Elf's eye, and he took up the spear and studied it, wondering what the Guardian saw that seemed to concern him so. Yet it was but the weapon he had borne for millennia—a blade of crystal starsilver-mounted upon what once was a Wizard's staff, a gift fashioned on the western continent by a shy Hidden One named Drix. Many a time had this weapon saved a life as it took many lives in return. What was there about it that troubled the Guardian? Aravan did not know. Shrugging, he laid the weapon aside and turned once again to Bair, the lad standing patiently, leather loops dangling down.

After a while Aravan slipped Krystallopŷr into the spear-scabbard, checking for fit, making a few adjustments. At last he said, " 'Tis done."

Thumbs under straps and tugging, Bair tested the harness and then said, "Well, let us hope it doesn't break when I change, or be subsumed by my aura, as are packs and clothes and gear."

"If it breaks or is subsumed, then we will fashion one especially for Hunter," replied Aravan. "But for now, Bair, let us see."

A darkness enveloped the lad, and there stood Hunter, spear and harness in place. Aravan smiled and said, "Bair," and when the lad stood before him, he added, "As we suspected, elar, just as the leather thong on my blue stone seems to be part of that token of power, and the platinum chains on its own token, so too does the harness belong to the spear, shifting to fit the wearer at the time of <change>."

Slipping from the rig, Bair looked at the sling and spear as he laid it on the table. "Even so, the harness doesn't alter when simply handed from one wearer to another; only during shapeshifting does it— Oh, wait. I <see>. The rig is caught in my <fire> as well as the <fire> of the spear, such that when I transform, so does the rig conform, yet it remains part of the spear . . . just as the crystal and chain does for you, or the stone and its thong. It's all in the blending of <fire>, kelan, in the blending of <fire>."

Aravan sighed and shook his head, saying, "Would that I had thy <sight>, Bair. Would that I had thy <sight>." Aravan fell silent and took up the spear and again frowned at it in puzzlement, then looked in the direction the Guardian had gone.

It was at this time as well that one of the Phael scouts, Penna by name, reported to Ala that a great army slowly moved westerly through the Jangdi Spur, a wide scatter of mountains running northerly across the land from the Jangdi Range to deep within the icy barrens afar.

"Jingarian, they seem," said Penna, "though I did not approach."

Ala frowned and said, "Though it is none of our affair, these squabbles among the walkers, still Aravan and Bair may want to know. Come, let us tell them what thou hast seen."

And upon learning of the movement westerly, Aravan fell into pondering, but Bair asked, "What could they want?"

"I know not, elar," replied Aravan. "To the west lies Xian, the land of the Grey Mountains."

Bair turned up his hands. "Even so, again I ask, what could they want?"

Aravan shrugged. "Once long past it was said that dwellers in Xian came from Jinga. The folk therein have the same cast of features. Mayhap the Emperor of Jinga seeks to claim that realm and the people as his own."

"But I thought the Wizards of Black Mountain dwell in Xian."

"Aye, so it is believed, though that dark mountain has been closed to all since the time of Elyn and Thork. Even then those two could but access a handful of chambers, or so the legend says."

"Oh, I just thought of something, kelan," said Bair. "What if this army is the great woe from the East Dodona spoke of, the West all unknowing?"

Aravan frowned. "How great is this army, Penna?"

"Vast," she replied. "I could make a count."

Aravan looked at Ala, and, turning to Penna, Ala said, "I would have thee fly over this army and see what thou canst, verify whether they are Jingarian and what nation if not. Count their numbers. Keep a close eye upon them for should they turn south into our demesne, the Guardian will need to act." Then Ala looked at Aravan and Bair and asked, "Is there aught thou wouldst add?"

And Bair said, "No— Oh wait! Yes, there is." He looked at Penna. "If you see a yellow-eyed man, bring word immediately."

Fourteen more days they roamed the land, Hunter racing across the bowl, Valké flying above, Krystallopŷr ensconced in the spear-scabbard across Hunter's back, bird and 'Wolf working together as they had been trained.

It was as they were in pursuit of a kimu—the antelope-goat espied by the falcon and pursued by the 'Wolf, the little animal racing to the crags and up, where Hunter couldn't reach, Valké above crying in rage and repeatedly swooping down at the game, to little effect—that Ala and Penna came to land beside Hunter pacing back and forth below the kimu's refuge.

At the sight of the Phael, Bair emerged from amid a shimmering darkness to stand before the pair. "Call Valké," said Ala. "Penna has news of import. She has seen a man with yellow eyes, a yellow-eyed devil incarnate."

CHAPTER 33

Invasion

September–December, 5E1009

[Three and a Half Months to Days Past]

On the crest of a mountain in the Jangdi Spur sat the Fire-drake Ebonskaith, the great Dragon coldly seething—the summons would soon come, for the road was at last finished, and the march of conquest would begin anew. And as he sat on his pinnacle, once again he saw the black-winged Phael soaring nigh, and this time she overflew the column, staying in the low-hanging misty clouds to remain unseen by those below. Yet mist was no hindrance to Dragonsight, and so he watched her glide. And as she passed above the column and then took a perch upon a high crag to watch, Ebonskaith merely looked on and made no other move, for although he was held in thrall by the unworthy Human wielder of the Dragonstone, he had no duty whatsoever to tell him of the birdman above.

On an early September afternoon in Arden Vale, Riatha and Urus stood watch together atop the eastern bluff overlooking the gorge. To the north and south as well as across stood other sentries, the warders within sight of one another, now and again with cryptic hand gestures signalling up and down the long ravine that all was well; at night, too, did they signal, with coded birdcalls and other such, especially when there was neither moon nor stars; they would not again fall prey to a post falling unremarked.

It had been some eight months since the last assault by Foul Folk, yet none within the length of the vale relaxed their vigil.

And as Urus and Riatha swept their gazes along the depth of the dale and across the heights above, Faeril and Ancinda and Tillaron came climbing up the narrow, steep path, Faeril in the lead, the other two trailing and bearing a basket each.

"Your relief is here," said Faeril, topping the bluff and gesturing toward the two coming after. "But I thought we'd sit and have a meal before going back down."

As of a picnic they spread a cloth and laid the food thereupon—roast mutton and dark bread and apples in the main, though there was a handful of shelled nuts and a sweet candy or two. And Faeril fished out from one of the baskets five mugs and a bottle of dark Vanchan wine.

"Would that Aravan and Bair were here," she said, as she slipped the cork and poured the cups full. "Aravan always did like the Vanchan . . . said there was no better."

"In that he was right," said Tillaron, accepting his mug as he remained standing on watch while the others sat.

When all had been served, Faeril raised her cup and said, "Here's to Aravan and Bair, wherever they may be."

Riatha's face paled at this mention, yet she too raised her cup and drank to the salute.

Noting Riatha's disquiet, Ancinda Soletree leaned toward the Dara and said, "Take comfort in that Aravan is with thine arran, Riatha. Take comfort, too, in that Bair is well trained."

Riatha sighed. "Thy words are well-spoken, Ancinda, yet I cannot but be concerned. Surely Dodona did answer Aravan's question, else they would be back by now, for nigh a year has passed."

Faeril sat with her eyes downcast, and she said, "Let us hope you are right, Ancinda, in that they are well, else something terrible has befallen them along the way."

"Faeril!" snapped Ancinda sharply.

Faeril's face twisted into distress, and she said, her voice trembling, "Oh Adon, but we don't know. I mean, they could be anywhere, dealing with who knows what, and in deadly peril . . . or worse." The damman burst into tears.

Tillaron shook his head. "Peril, mayhap. Worse, nay, for no death rede has come."

Riatha blanched, and her lips drew thin.

Urus drew both Riatha and Faeril into his arms. "Let us hope Dalavar Wolfmage was right when he said Bair should walk with Aravan, for together they make a formidable team."

Riatha rested her head on Urus's breast. "Indeed, chier, yet would that we knew where they are and what has befallen and whether or no our ruse here at Arden is yet deceiving Black Magekind, or if they search elsewhere for our Impossible Child."

Across Xian marched Kutsen Yong's Golden Horde, the Masula Yongsa Wang's rolling palace trundling in its midst. And upon seeing the massed throng and the ebon-scaled Dragon above, villages and towns surrendered without a fight. Many a pagoda was consecrated to the Jìdu Shàngdi, Humans sacrificed in the ritual, Ydral enthralled in an ecstasy of carnage as he gorged on stolen <fire>. Yet as always, after the temple was sanctified in blood, Ydral raised one of the newly dead and asked about the Elf with the crystal spear. At times Ydral found his pursuer was far away, yet at other times the yellow-eyed man was puzzled by the answers he received, for there were days the dead could not seem to locate the Elf at all . . . either that or Ydral missed the answer amid the chorus of whispers and wails as the numberless wretched souls crowded forward to speak through the raised one, each striving to be heard, murmurs and hissings fading in and out, many voices talking at one and the same time through but a single mouth, some speaking of birds and Wolves and mountains, others telling of ships at sea and wars and lovers and myriad other things past, present, and future. Concerned over the failure to locate the Elf, yet wearied by the casting, Ydral, slaked in bloodletting, would take to his dark wagon to sleep the sleep of the sated. Tomorrow or the next, or within a week at most, there would be another conquest, another ceremony unto the Jìdu Shàngdi, another search for the Elf who pursued.

In September they came in among the Grey Mountains, which slowed them but a bit, for an old trade road wended through, and though in places it was narrow, and in other places bridges were long collapsed, a foregoing army of workers made certain that the oxen-drawn palace of Kutsen Yong would easily fare through.

In October they entered the realm of Aralan, and there they found an army standing across the way. Kutsen Yong was enraged, for uncowed by Horde and Dragon they seemed, ready to battle to the death, ready to face certain doom. And the emperor ordered his army alone to attack these fools who sought to defy him.

"But, mai lord," sissed Ydral, "why waste the lives of aun own men when many Dragons are at aun beck?"

"If it's death they crave," shouted Kutsen Yong, "I shall give it to them! Not a quick death by Dragonfire, but slowly and in agony, butchered by my Golden Horde."

The Golden Horde was loosed, swift steppe ponies thundering across the plains in a vast wave, the ground shivering under their hooves. And the mounted warriors launched arrows even as they galloped, some of which whistled shrilly, deliberately made so to terrify the enemy. And as they neared the ranks of the foe, many riders leveled lances, each point fashioned with a cruel hook and snare, while other of the horsemen drew heavy sabers, each cutting edge sharp and curved, the better to let blood as the rider flashed by. Behind came the foot soldiers running.

Masula Yongsa Wang! they cried as they smashed into and through the ranks of the defenders of Aralan, blood flying, men falling, death upon the land.

In spite of the Mage Warrior King's promise of a long and lingering death, the battle was swift and decisive, for the Aralanians were outnumbered ten, a hundred, a thousand to one. Even so they gave a better account of themselves than could be expected, and many of Kutsen Yong's men did not live to see the noonday sun.

Furious that any would think to oppose him, Kutsen Yong had every nearby town destroyed, old men and women and children slaughtered, babes dashed to death, crops burned, forests hewn, the land salted, and plague left lying in wait for any survivor who remained hidden. And not once did he use Ebonskaith or any other Dragons to do his bidding; given the opposition he had faced so far, Kutsen Yong had decided to save them for his encounter with the fool of a king who thought to stand above all.

In Pellar, Prince Ryon was called to the war room. When he arrived, his sire, High King Garon, beckoned the lad to a place at his right hand. At the table stood War Commander Rori, a tall, lean Vanadurin in his mid sixties, his yellow hair and beard shot through with silver. Bending over maps were Lords Stein, Revar, and Halen—three of Garon's most trusted military advisors—each in his mid forties. At Garon's left stood Fenerin, the Elven advisor's shoulder-length hair a deep chestnut. Also in the chamber were three Wizards, youngish-looking, one a female. And as well there was a mud-spattered Realmsman.

"Ryon, I want you to hear this," said Garon, and then he nodded at the Realmsman and said, "Speak, Rendell."

Rendell, a young man of twenty or so, turned to Ryon. "My lord prince, an invading Horde, vast beyond imagining, has come into Aralan from Xian. Not only are their numbers past counting, they have a Dragon, Ebonskaith, with them—"

"Ebonskaith!" blurted Ryon, looking from the Realmsman to his father and back.

"Aye, my lord. Ebonskaith, the Fire-drake," affirmed the Realmsman.

"But, Father, Ebonskaith is among the Dragons pledged; he is not one of the Renegades."

"Aye, son, yet hear the full tale out."

Ryon fell silent and looked to the Realmsman once more, but it was one of the youthful Wizards who spoke next. Small of stature and brown of hair and eyes and wearing a yellow robe, she clenched her fist and said, "We believe the Dragonstone is involved, for we cannot scry aught in Aralan, and only the Dragonstone has the power to deny us. Too, we believe this is connected to the time of the Trine, which is nearing, a time when a dreadful event of fire and blood will occur on the Plains of Valon."

The Mage fell silent and Garon said without preamble, "Ryon, I present Sage Arilla, and Mages Belgon and Alorn . . . of Black Mountain." The three Mages bowed—Belgon black-haired and dressed in a red robe; ginger-haired Alorn dressed in brown—and Ryon canted his head forward in return.

"But I thought Black Mountain to be closed," said Ryon.

Arilla smiled at the youth and said, "It was, Prince Ryon, but then it was not. Yet now it is abandoned and closed once more."

"This Dragonstone, what is it?" asked Ryon.

"We do not know," replied Arilla. "Though some claim that it has a hold over Dragonkind."

"It was once in Black Mountain, but then stolen," said Alorn.

"Damn Ordrune," spat Belgon.

"Ordrune?" asked Ryon.

"When the Dragonstone first came to us, it was he who administered to all Mages the oath of binding, but did not pledge himself," replied Belgon.

"It only occured to us long after we discovered the Dragonstone to be missing that just because someone administers an oath it does not mean he has taken it," said Alorn. "The rest of us were sworn; Ordrune was not. And Arin Flameseer finally discovered it was Ordrune who stole the Dragonstone from Black Mountain."

"When was this?" asked Ryon.

"Back nigh the end of the First Era," said Arilla.

Ryon's eyes flew wide. "Near the end of— But you are so young."

"We have <rested> since that time," said Alorn, as if that explained all.

Ryon shook his head. "Regardless, you now believe this Dragonstone is somewhere in Aralan?"

"Aye," said Arilla, "for after Arin and the others recovered the token, it was taken to Rwn. We thought it locked away forever . . . in vaults now sunk beneath the sea."

"Damn Durlok," said Alorn. "Damn *all* Black Mages."

"Enough of this talk of the Dragonstone," said Belgon. "Right now we are facing an imminent doom."

Lord Halen ran his fingers through black hair just greying at the temples. "This Trine you spoke of—"

"A coming alignment of the Planes," said Belgon, his voice pitched sharply, as if it were an event all should have known about.

Fenerin smiled and softly said, "Not all are privy to Wizardly knowledge, my lord Mage."

"Pah!" snapped Belgon, but said no more.

"And when is this Trine due?" asked Ryon.

"In March of next year," replied Arilla. "Some six months from now."

"Six months?" said Rori. "A short time to muster all needed to cast back this Horde from the East."

"Nevertheless, it can be done," said Ryon, looking at his sire.

Garon, short of stature and brown-haired and in his late fifties, nodded to Ryon and said, "In fact it must be done, else we are defeated ere we begin." Garon looked from advisors to commander to prince to Mages to Realmsman and took a deep breath. "Given that we muster the nations, I ask you, what then?"

War Commander Rori frowned and looked at Arilla. "Sage Arilla, you did say that an event of fire and blood was to take place on the Plains of Valon."

"I did," replied Arilla.

Rori put a finger to the map and said, "Then, my Lord King, I say we summon all forces to the Plains of Valon, here in the South Reich at the Argon Ferry, and draw the enemy there, for there they will have to win across the river in the face of your Host. And should they manage to cross over, then we can fall back to the high ground here in the cusp of the Red Hills and make another stand. And should it become a running battle, we can then fall back to the Gûnarring Gap or beyond, to a place that is strait where they will have difficulty in bringing their great numbers to bear."

Lord Stein, a burly man, shook his head and slammed his fist to the table. "Abandon Pendwyr? I say nay! Here we should be, for here too they cannot bring all their forces to bear on this narrow headland."

"But, my lord," said Lord Revar, "you would have us be trapped. I say instead we should hit them in the narrows of the Fian Dunes and—"

"Nay," objected Rori. "If their force is as vast as Rendell says, they will merely surround the dunes and crush us within their ring of iron."

Ryon looked at Rendell and then Rori. "If that is the case, War Commander, then perhaps our tactics should be strike and flee . . . as Galen did in the Winter War, when his meager one hundred faced ten thousand."

"Strike and flee?" sputtered Stein. "The King's Host? Never, I say! Instead—"

King Garon cleared his throat and gestured Stein to silence.

"My lords forget not what the Wizards have foreseen. Forget not as well the Dragon Ebonskaith, for he alone can conquer whatever Host we gather. And it is not as if we can use the same trick Prince Elgo used on Sleeth, for he was a Cold-drake and not one of fire." Garon turned to the Mages. "What of the Dragon, my lady and lords?"

Arilla looked at the Realmsman. "Was the Fire-drake involved in the battle you saw?"

Rendell shook his head. "Nay, my lady, he was not. Even so, he seemed to be with the invaders."

Now Arilla turned to the King. "My Lord King Garon, it may be that Ebonskaith yet keeps the pledge and will not be involved. Even so, even if he has broken his vow, then mayhap in a great conjoinment, we of Magekind can turn him aside."

"Conjoinment?" asked Ryon.

Belgon snorted, but Alorn said, "Many Mages link together and lend a wielder—a Sorcerer—their <fire>. His power is thus multiplied manyfold, and great deeds can be accomplished."

"And have ye a Sorcerer who can do such?" asked Fenerin.

Alorn nodded. "In this case, I am that Sorcerer."

"How many Mages can you link together in this grand conjoinment?" asked Ryon.

"Several hundred," replied Alorn.

Ryon's eyes widened in surprise. "How many of you are there?"

"The whole of Black Mountain," said Arilla. "Eleven hundred and twenty-three."

"And where are these Wizards?" asked Lord Stein.

Arilla smiled at War Commander Rori and then turned to Stein. "Across the river in Valon, all but a handful."

"Whom do you count as absent?" demanded Belgon.

"We three here," replied Arilla, "and Dalavar Wolfmage, wherever he might be."

Belgon snorted. "Dalavar? That shapechanger?"

"Think not to belittle Dalavar," said Fenerin. "He stood at High King Blaine's side at the Battle of Hèl's Crucible."

"Pah! Brave he may be, but a true Mage he is not," sneered Belgon.

Alorn turned toward Belgon. "I would not be so quick to judge. I hear he has some art of illusion as well as Seer's blood."

"Bah!" said Belgon. "With the Dragonstone involved, Seers are helpless. And Dragonsight sees through all illusions, and the foe has Ebonskaith. No, Alorn, Dalavar Wolfmage will have little effect on the outcome of this war."

As Alorn started to reply, King Garon held up a hand of staying. "We are not here to discuss the merits of Dalavar Wolfmage, my friends, but to devise a plan of action against the coming storm. And I have heard no strategy better than that which War Commander Rori has put forth, or the strike-and-flee tactics suggested by Ryon. If any have better ideas, let us hear them now."

In late November, Kutsen Yong summoned Ydral to the golden palace awheel.

"Yes, mai lord?"

Kutsen Yong gestured toward the kneeling courier before the throne. "My commanders send a message that they have occupied a small village up near the mountains in the north. I would have you go there and sanctify a temple to the Jìdu Shàngdi."

"But, mai lord, surely if the village is small, one of the lesser priests can—"

"Do you defy me, Ydral?"

"No, mai lord. It is just that—"

"Ydral, be still and heed: I want innumerable pagodas sanctified in the name of the Jìdu Shàngdi, many in each city and town, and one or more in every village, and, yes, one in each hamlet as well, temples in all the world, for all will come under my rightful sway. And when the Jealous God sees what I have done, then He shall raise me up to rule beside Him." At those words, Ydral blanched, his fingernails drawing blood from his palms, so hard did he clench his fists. Yet he remained silent, as Kutsen Yong added, "And who better to consecrate these temples than you, Ydral, my chief advisor."

"Who better indeed, mai lord," hissed the yellow-eyed man.

Kutsen Yong spoke to the kneeling courier. "You, messenger, shall lead my advisor and his personal guard unto this village of . . . of . . ." He snapped his fingers.

"Of Inge, my lord," said the courier, without raising his head. "The villagers name it Inge."

Ydral's eyes widened in surprise, yet he remained silent.

"Yes, Inge," said Kutsen Yong. "You seem to have heard of it, Ydral."

Ydral smiled. "Indeed, mai lord. Jai have passed by it a time or two in days of yore."

In Arden Vale a silver horn sounded, and a rider came galloping into the Elvenholt, her horse lathered. She flung herself from the mount and called out to a nearby Lian, "See to my horse," even as she dashed into the coron-hall, her black hair streaming behind, where she found Alor Inarion sitting in converse with Dara Riatha and Alor Urus.

Inarion stood as the visitor hurried forward. " 'Tis not often one of the Dylvana graces our hall."

Slender and small, standing no more than four-foot-six, the diminutive Dara sketched a bow, her blue eyes fixed on the Lian. "Alor Inarion, Warder of the Northern Regions of Rell?"

"Indeed. And thou art . . . ?"

"Dara Vail of Darda Erynian, and I am come to summon thee."

"To Darda Erynian?"

"Nay, my Alor. To Valon instead, and with all the force at thy command."

In the darkness of night before a cold Iron Tower on a moor in faraway Gron, three Warrows stood at the door of a tomb. Heavy was the stone and dark, all Dwarven made, perhaps. By the lantern they bore, the Warrows could see three names deeply carven in the rock, and under one of the names another phrase was added such that the whole of it said: DANNER BRAMBLETHORN, KING OF THE RILLROCK. Two of the Warrows were dressed in armor—a buccan in silver, a damman in gold. The third, a buccan, was dressed in plain leathers.

Together the three had managed to pry the door open enough to permit them to enter, yet, hesitating, they looked at one another, their jewellike eyes wide with apprehension.

"I like not this robbing of graves," said the Warrow accoutered in silver.

"Nevertheless we must do so," replied the damman in gold. "I mean, Aurion Redeye recalled the black, too." She shuddered in memory. "And I think none of us would defy him and chance another visitation. Besides, time is short, and the way to Valon is long, and the others will be waiting."

Gritting his teeth and gripping a dagger in his right hand, the buccan in leathers held his lantern high and edged into the blackness beyond, the others following after.

Realmsmen brought word to Caer Pendwyr: the Rovers of Kistan had sailed their ships to the southern ports on the Avagon Sea, and the armies of Hyree, Khem, Chabba, Thyra, and Sarain were gathering there.

Ebonskaith watched as the Phael flew high above, one now heading easterly away from the Golden Horde, the other winging toward a small village to the north, perhaps keeping watch on the yellow-eyed man. At times over the past weeks other Phael had come and gone, couriers perhaps. But now there were just two in the sky, and they flew on and on, until even vaunted Dragonsight could see them no more. And the mighty Fire-drake said nought of these birdmen in the skies.

In the village of Inge on the southern verge of the Grimwalls nigh the border between Khal and Aralan, there in the town square in a newly erected pavilion at an altar in the center stood a yellow-eyed man in pale lanternlight, a long, thin knife in a red-slathered hand, his arms slickened unto his elbows. And on the altar before him something crimson and glistening lay, with scarlet dripping down and pooling. Surrounded by soldiers clad in scale mail and bearing heavy, curved, unsheathed blades, were gathered the villagers: some stood weeping, looking away; others moaned in horror and stared at what had once been their mayor, unable to gaze elsewhere; yet others retched dryly, now bringing up nought but thin streams of bile, as they knelt in their own vomit. And the thing on the altar—a thing that had once been a man, a man tortured and flayed and finally eviscerated— a thing, though dead, spasmodically jerked a final time and then stilled; villagers cried out, those who were looking that way.

In front of the altar in blood and bile and feces and urine lay the discarded corpse of a maiden, stripped of skin and disemboweled, just as the mayor had been.

And though the sides of the pavilion were open to the chill, still the gagging tang and reek and fetor and stench strangled the very air.

And the blood-slathered man, his yellow eyes glistening, his entire being bloated with an energy not his own, gasping and panting, his mouth gaping wide in joy, looked down upon his achievement.

Yet trembling in ecstasy, the yellow-eyed man raised his face upward and spread his glistening arms wide and, in a voice like that of hissing vipers, in Common said, "With the blood of these worshipers of False Adon, on this most joyous mid-December night Jai do consecrate this new pavilion to the Jìdu Shàngdi, the god henceforth all will serve."

The yellow-eyed man gestured to one of the soldiers, who then called, "All hail the Jìdu Shàngdi, for He is the Jealous God!"

In hushed dread, a handful of villagers managed to choke out, *J-Jìdu S-Shàng* . . . their voices sinking to silence.

"Perhaps we need another . . . offering," said the yellow-eyed man, smiling, revealing pointed sharp teeth much the same as those of Rûcks or Demons, as he gestured at the red, slick thing on the altar.

Again the soldier called out: "All hail the Jìdu Shàngdi, for He is the Jealous God!"

And villagers shrilled in terror: *All hail the Jìdu Shàngdi, for He is the Jealous God!* Terrified voices chopped to silence, punctuated by stifled sobs.

With a dismissive gesture, the yellow-eyed man waved all away, and as they had thrashed them unto this place, so too did the soldiers begin flailing the long, supple switches among the villagers, driving them out and away and across the snow 'neath glittering stars in the frigid dark vault above, the low-hanging, half-silver moon in the west shedding no warmth at all.

When Ydral stood alone with his personal guard, he spread his arms wide above the corpse and gathered his will. Then, with his brow furrowed in concentration, he hissed, *"Ákouse mè!"* commanding the dead one to listen.

He dipped his long, grasping fingers into the blood and tasted it, savoring the coppery iron tang, then called out, *"Peísou moî!"* commanding the dead one to obey.

Ydral then let blood drip from his fingers into the dead man's punctured eyes and sissed, *"Idoû toîs opthalmoîs toîs nekroû!"* commanding the dead one to see what the dead can see, visions beyond time and space.

Ydral channelled the fierce energy he had stolen from this man and the girl below back into the corpse as he spoke the next decree: *"Idoû toùs polémious toùs emoùs toùs mè nûn diokóntous!"* commanding the dead one to look through space for the enemy who might now pursue.

As the stolen <fire> drained from him, he whispered: *"Heurè autoús!"* commanding the dead one to find the foe.

Now Ydral's teeth gritted as he spent more of that which he had taken, and he uttered the compelling words: *"Tòn páton tòn autôn heurè!"* commanding the dead one to discover the path of the enemy.

And then he decreed, *"Eipè moî hò horáei!"* commanding the dead one to reveal what it sees.

Now Ydral's entire being shook, as he came toward the last of the usurped <fire>, his voice canting, *"Anà kaì lékse!"* commanding the corpse to rise and speak.

And spending the remainder of the stolen <fire>, he spoke the final mandate, *"Egò gàr ho Ydrálos dè kèleuo sé!"* invoking his own name Ydral as he who commands the dead.

As of a legion of voices in distant agony, the chamber filled with unnumbered whispering groans, the corpse stirring. The guards shrank back in dread, moving to the edge of the pavilion as if they would flee, but fearing to do so. Ydral, his yellow eyes burning with a ghastly light, called out again, *"Anà kaì lékse; egò gàr ho Ydrálos dè kèleuo sé!"*

A wet, glistening hand reached up, as if trying to grasp the very air, blood seeping down exposed muscle. And slowly, agonizingly, the corpse rolled onto its left side, the flayed torso levering up, skin falling away as of a garment loosened. Broken-boned, raw fingers gripped the edge of the altar left and right, and the corpse steadied itself on its crimson-dripping arms. Again there came the massed groans of a multitude from a slack-jawed, lipless mouth, and, blood-wet neck muscles contracting and slackening and sliding, it turned its flayed head toward Ydral, punctured eyeballs in a skinless face staring at the one who summoned. Speaking as a single voice, a hideous choir of whispers filled the chamber. The guards mewled in terror at the empty sound, looking about for a place to flee, but daring not. And the voices spoke in a language the guards did not comprehend.

[*Varför ni . . .*] *Why . . . why . . . why . . . have you summoned me? . . . summoned me . . . summoned me . . . summoned me . . . summoned . . .* echoed the ghastly chorus of mutterers, whisperers, murmurers, different voices fading in and out, stronger, weaker, rising, falling, murmurs on top of murmurs, all asking . . . asking . . . asking. . . .

Ydral answered in the same tongue, the native tongue of these villagers, for those who delve into the forbidden art of *Psukhomanteía*—of Necromancy—need know many tongues, for they are at times . . . useful. "Seek not to evade *mehr*, dead one. Instead, do that which Jai asked! Where is the foe who has at times followed *mehr*? The Elf who bears the crystal-bladed spear."

Still the punctured eyes stared at Ydral, but his yellow-eyed gaze did not waver. At last, mid the sucking sounds of blood-wet, raw muscle, the corpse turned its head, searching, at last peering southeasterly and very slightly down. Myriad whispering voices hissed answers, simultaneous agonizing echoes murmuring, rustling, mumbling, as if numberless mutterers crowded forward, all speaking, each striving to be heard, murmurers fading in and out, many voices talking at the same time through the same slack, unmoving mouth, each whisperer describing a different event, a confusion of sissing babble.

. . . *Wizards gather . . . two follow . . . many march . . . black-winged flyer . . . King calls . . . Temple . . . Demon . . .*

Yet Ydral listened for the dominant whisper, not easily distinguished from the multitude, for as he had told one of his sons, one of several fruits of his loins—a son spawned upon Baroness Lèva Stoke at the specific request of her mother, Madam Koska Orso, who had summoned Ydral for just such a task, a son murdered not twenty years past by the same spear-bearing

Elf and four others—as he had told this son Bèla, *"Trust little the word of ahn dead soul, for unto the dead time has no meaning. They see the past and the present and the future all at once, all the same. Unless the Psukhómantis—the Necromancer—has the will and energy and endurance, the power to give focus, then the voices of the dead bring words of little use to the summoner, for they may bear ahn message meant for another entirely. Tji must listen carefully to find the truespeaker for tji. If tji can single out that voice, then words of value may come, as they did when Jai discovered that one who bears Elven blood will be mai doom. Concentrate, dominate, else what tji learn will lead to disaster."*

And so, heeding his own words, Ydral listened carefully, trying to choose from among the myriad of agonized whispers, trying to pick out the voice of the truespeaker who would answer his questions. And from the lax, gory maw of the dead one, mutterings filled the pavilion, murmurings, sissings, hissings.

Yet among the whispering voices, there was one stronger than the others, for the victim on the altar was newly slain, and Ydral reasoned that such a voice belonged to *this* corpse. *Spear borne by* . . . green weed . . . Jordians . . . Dwarves stand . . . three small ones . . . *Silver Wolf* . . . shackled to a wall . . . flay . . . *running under* . . . the bridge falls . . . *falcon in the night* . . . black armor retrieved . . . the ship . . . *they come* . . .

Ydral's eyes widened. "The spear is born by *ahn* Silver Wolf? Is Dalavar Wolfmage come?"

With unnumbered groans echoing through a jaw hanging slack, the corpse rotated its head about, muscle slithering wetly over muscle, cartilage creaking, bone grinding on bone. Oozing aqueous humor and blood, the ruptured eyes seemed to be staring through the winter night, seeking, seeing far beyond. And as the mutilated gaze passed over them, guards shrank hindward in terror, some backing against the pillars of the pavilion and making warding signs, others stepping just off the platform and into the snow, wanting to flee yet unable to face the consequences such action would bring.

Finally, amid the ghastly voices, the primary one spoke of the Wolfmage in Valon with six Silver Wolves, none bearing a spear.

Ydral frowned in puzzlement, for he knew of no Silver Wolves other than those with which Dalavar ran. Ydral turned to the corpse. "How near are the spear and the Draega?"

Countless sobbing moans issued forth from the gaping jaw, yet no answer came.

Now Ydral invoked the tongue of *Psukhomanteía*, of Necromancy, bidding the dead to answer as to the whereabouts of the spear: *"Tòn páton tòn autôn heurè!"*

Slowly the chorus of wails subsided. Finally, as if seeking, seeking, again the corpse rotated its head about, muscles sliding across muscles in blood, and looked southeasterly again. And as it did so, raw ligaments and sinews oozing scarlet drew tight and the gaping jaw closed, and a lipless smile spread over the face. In that moment there came a horn cry from the far perimeter guards, and then another bugle sounded and another, followed by several more. From somewhere there came a distant flare, quickly followed by a hubbub of cries in the hamlet.

Air sissed in through Ydral's clenched teeth and he looked out into the village, into the dimness beyond the lanternlight, and then he turned and bolted from the pavilion, his form changing even as he ran, and a dark Fell Beast on leathery wings fled northward through the winter night.

Behind on the altar the corpse wetly collapsed, blood and visceral fluids splatting wide.

The dead was dead again.

CHAPTER 34

Pursuit

September–December, 5E1009
[Three and a Half Months to Days Past]

Aravan paced back and forth in the snow, the kimu above on the crag quite forgotten. "A yellow-eyed devil incarnate?"

Penna flexed her wings and shuddered. "Aye. A flayer of women."

"Just like Stoke," gritted Aravan.

"Where?" blurted Bair. "Where is this yellow-eyed man?"

"North," replied Penna. "Midst a vast army heading westerly, now beyond the Jangdi Spur."

"How far?" asked Aravan.

"Five hundred leagues as I fly," said Penna. She glanced at Bair. "More aland."

The air went out from Bair's lungs. "Fifteen hundred miles through these mountains? And even longer by road? Oh, Aravan, he could be anywhere by the time I can get there."

"Would that I had my maps," growled Aravan. "We could choose the swiftest route for thee, Bair, and for Hunter."

"I can fashion thee a map," said Ala.

"Kelan, map or no," said Bair, "you should go on without me. As Valké you can get there swiftly; as Hunter I cannot. And Yrdal, if indeed it is Ydral, could be long gone ere then."

Aravan shook his head. "Remember Dodona's words, elar: 'A path will be chosen at the Temple in the Sky,' said he, and that thou must go at my side."

"But what if this isn't the true path?"

Aravan turned up his hands. "What choice otherwise has presented itself? Too, thou mayest be right, Bair: if a vast army marches on the West, it may be the great woe Dodona foretold as coming from the East."

Ala looked at Penna. "Didst thou number this army?"

"I could not count them," replied Penna. "I could but estimate: five hundred thousand or so; a quarter of them ahorse; the rest afoot; a great wagon train in their midst."

Bair eyes widened in shock. "A half a million soldiers?"

Penna nodded. "Yet that is not all, Alor Bair, Alor Aravan, for there is something worse—"

"Something worse?" blurted Bair. "What could be worse than a half a million soldiers marching on the West?"

"They have a Dragon with them," said Penna.

Bair gasped. "A Dragon?"

As Penna nodded, Aravan asked, "Dost thou know which one?"

"Ebonskaith, I ween."

Bair looked at Aravan. "The mightiest Dragon of all. But did you not say he is pledged, Aravan?" As Aravan nodded, Bair said. "Lor', if he's broken his vow. . . . A great Dragon, a vast army, and a yellow-eyed man: it cannot but be the woe from the East."

His blue eyes filled with ice, Aravan turned to Ala. "Go to the temple and make thy map. We will fly on thy heels."

Ala said, "Come with me, Penna, for I would have thee mark on the chart where last thou didst see these things."

As Penna and Ala took flight and headed for the temple, from a flash of platinum light and a shimmer of darkness, Valké and Hunter emerged and raced for the temple as well, the kimu behind yet trembling upon the crag.

"And this is the best way?" groaned Bair.

Ala turned to the lad. "There is no way swifter for one afoot as wilt thou and Hunter be."

Nearby stood the Guardian, watching Ala and Penna and Bair and Aravan, the old man saying little as the four of them pored over Ala's map.

"But nine or ten weeks?" said Bair. "Surely there is a better way." He looked across the table at Aravan. "Can we not go back to the sea and— No, wait. That will not do."

"Elar, there is nothing for it but that we take the route chosen," said Aravan. He turned to Ala. "Still, I would have you and yours keep an eye on the army and the Dragon and the yellow-eyed man, and bring word to us as to their whereabouts from time to time."

Ala turned to the old man. "Guardian?"

The elder stood in thought for long moments. Finally he said, "You ask permission of me to leave the Jangdi Range?"

Ala nodded.

"Although you need no sanction from me to go where you will, this I would advise: act as scouts and couriers as you have been asked, and be bearers of sustenance as well; aid in refining the route the lad and 'Wolf must take. I would caution you to do no more, elsewise you will surely change the natural course of events." The elder fell silent.

"We do so pledge, Guardian," said Ala. Then he turned to Penna. "Thou didst hear the Guardian, my love? I would have thee return to keep watch on this devil incarnate and his Dragon and half million men. I will send others winging to act as couriers and bringers of sustenance, to fly between and bring word to us, which will guide Aravan and Bair and Valké and Hunter to wherever this fiend and his Dragon and army have gone. Yet heed, as I so pledged to the Guardian, thus shall all the Phael do."

Penna nodded and prepared to go, taking up her bow and arrows. She stepped to Ala and they kissed, their arms and wings enwrapped about one another, and then she strode from the temple and took flight, winging away to the north.

Behind, Aravan and Bair leaned over the map again as the old man looked on, but his gaze was not upon them but upon Krystallopŷr instead, and a grave regard lurked deep in his eyes. After long moments the elder turned and took his leave without saying good-bye.

Days fled, weeks fled, as Bair and Hunter struggled through the great mountains, the Jangdi Range looming all 'round, Valké flying above, choosing the routes the Silver Wolf would take.

Yet there was no easy way, and often did Hunter give over to Bair to scale up or down a route the Draega could not manage. Each night in camp, Aravan and Bair would study Ala's map, the Phael often in camp alongside them, helping to choose the way.

The route Aravan and Bair followed was not one aimed directly at the army and the yellow-eyed man, but instead was the swiftest one northward which would get Hunter free of the range and onto the high plateau beyond; even so, September fled into the past, with Autumnday barely celebrated, for they rested instead, and did but toast the equinox with just a warm cup of tea. October came upon the range, and with it Bair turned sixteen; there, too, they celebrated only with a cup of tea. Winter snows began to blow high in the mountains and down in the vales. And still Bair and Hunter struggled through cols and up precipices and down vertical bluffs, Aravan aiding at every turn, especially at setting anchors at the tops of cliffs and feeding ropes down for Bair to climb, Valké flying up to the heights for Aravan to do so; or removing them whenever Bair had to rappel down the face of a bluff, Valké flying down afterward.

And Phael couriers came and went, reporting on the progress of the vast army and the Dragon, and the whereabouts of the yellow-eyed man, telling of the fiend's horrendous activities in pagodas and temples and pavilions along the way. Too, the couriers brought supplies to replenish the packs Aravan and Bair had fashioned at the temple to replace those they had lost.

November came and with it the true winter storms, slowing Hunter and Bair's progress even more. Yet on the fourteenth of November in late midmorn did Hunter come padding down through the deep snow in the Jangdi Foothills to step onto the high plains of Tishan, where Valké circled and cried above, the black falcon swooping over an old trade way leading into the Jangdi Spur.

Hunter stepped onto the beaten-down road and began loping west, following Valké.

At last they were on the track of the army . . .

. . . on the trail of a yellow-eyed fiend . . .

. . . and that of a Dragon as well.

*   *   *

In early December, as Hunter trotted at a ground-devouring pace across the western reaches of Xian and Valké flew above, Phael messengers came through the winter day, bearing word to Aravan and Bair that the army and Dragon continued westerly, while the yellow-eyed man rode north amid a great warding guard.

"They have gone their separate ways?" asked Bair.

Fleogan nodded, his crest ruffling in the chill air blowing down from the Grimwalls, the mountains lying low on the horizon in the north.

Aravan drew a sketch on a corner of Ala's map. "Where?"

Fleogan looked and pointed. "Here is the route."

Aravan frowned. "Perhaps they are headed to Inge."

"Inge?" asked Bair.

"A village here," replied Aravan, pointing at a place on the drawing.

"Soldiers are in that village," said Fleogan.

"From the great army?" asked Bair.

Fleogan nodded. "Three hundred or so."

Bair frowned. "Why would he leave his vast army behind merely to visit three hundred in a village of little import?"

Aravan looked at the sketch and then Fleogan and then at Bair. And Aravan's words fell cold. "He does not go to visit a garrison, but to consecrate a temple instead."

"Oh," said Bair, his lips drawing thin in distress.

The lad looked west and then north. "Which way, Aravan? Whom do we follow? The army and Dragon or the yellow-eyed man?"

Aravan stared at the snow-covered ground. After a moment he glanced up at Bair and said, "We go after the fiend."

Now Bair looked deep into Aravan's eyes. "This I must ask, kelan: is north the way to victory or the way to vengeance instead?"

Aravan took a deep breath and let it out, whiteness curling on the air. "Vengeance for Galarun's death is due, that I cannot deny; yet that is not why I say we should go north. Instead, the army and the Dragon are not foes we alone can defeat, but the yellow-eyed man we can. And if indeed he is the one who has the Silver Sword, what better token to bear into battle against the west-marching horde?"

"I pray to Adon you have chosen right," said Bair, "for west then north we go."

And in but mere moments a Silver Wolf loped across the flats of Xian, a black falcon flying above.

Following a trail of death and destruction, west they went into Aralan, and angled north up through the land, passing south of the Wolfwood, where Dalavar was said to dwell. Finally, they turned to the north toward the Grimwalls afar, the Skög lying to the east of them and the Khalian Mire to the west—the Skög an ancient forest said to be the eldest of all; the Khalian Mire a sucking swampland of bog and ooze and marsh and fen and morass and quag and sump, deadly to the wary and unwary alike. Neither place did Hunter and Valké, nor Bair and Aravan enter, for at nights they camped on the snow-laden prairie between. And there it was that Avi brought word that the yellow-eyed man had indeed gone into the hamlet of Inge, where a new pavilion was being erected even then.

With Valké overhead and leading, north and north loped Hunter through the day, the Silver Wolf and the raptor coming at last to the northern reach of the mire, and there they turned west for Inge, passing over the frozen rivers flowing down from the Grimwalls and through the foothills at hand to ever feed the swamp, the environs within steaming and warm in spite of the winter air, the <fire> within dark and ominous.

Night had long since fallen when they came within sight of Inge, and Hunter stopped in the shadows well short of the reach of the lanternlight seeping from the village. And as Bair stepped forth from shimmering dark, Valké swooped down and landed beside the lad, and there came a flash of platinum light.

"Oh lor', Aravan, the l—"

—a bugle sounded from the verge of the hamlet—

"—ight! We've been—"

—again there came a horn cry—

"—seen!"

Aravan clenched his fists in anger at Valké's unthinking act, and still another horn sounded. "The pavilion, Bair. Valké has seen the yellow-eyed man within. It is Galarun's killer."

Soldiers came running toward the two.

But Bair vanished, and Hunter, teeth bared and snarling, Krys-tallopŷr in its sling on his back, dashed away from Aravan, the 'Wolf racing toward the center of town, toward a pavilion where he knew a terrible enemy stood.

Behind, there came another flare of light, and a black falcon sprang upward into the air, the oncoming soldiers seeing it not, for they instead quailed back and down as a monstrous silver beast flashed past and away.

And as Hunter hurtled among the buildings and toward the lantern-lit pavilion, with Valké racing above, a bugle blew again, and then another, and arrows hissed out from the darkness and at the Silver Wolf, skidding short, arcing long, whispering by— hasty shots flying astray.

In the open-sided shelter, the terrible enemy turned and ran, and even as Hunter leapt past the line of warders and charged across the pavilion, hurtling over the bloody dead thing just then falling back onto the altar, the enemy ahead *changed*, became a hideous great creature flying up and away, Hunter's leap after falling but inches short.

Like a monster from the dawn of time, out from the pavilion and up it flew, leathery wings flapping, its fang-filled beak wide and shrieking, its eyes glaring yellow, clawed feet trailing after. Twenty feet across did it span, and fifteen feet was its length from the tip of its snout to the end of its lashing, whiplike tail.

Yet no matter the size of the creature, from above Valké stooped, pinions folded, the tips of his wings guiding, and down he flashed like a dark arrow, and talons raked across the Fell Beast's neck.

Skreigh! cried the monster as on upward it flew, the black fal-con below turning on a wing and flying skyward to come at the creature again.

A Draega ran beneath.

Into the Grimwalls flew the beast, up over a high, craggy bluff. And once more the falcon plummeted past, again raking the neck of the ungainly creature. While behind and thwarted by the rise, Hunter transformed into Bair, the lad cursing as he scram-bled up through the steeps, free-climbing by the light of the glit-tering stars above, and the low-hanging, half-silver moon in the west.

Beyond the bluff, again the falcon stooped on the Fell Beast, the tiercel *skree*ing as it dived, the leather-winged monster trying to dodge but failing, and once more talons slashed into flesh.

On the crests above, Fleogan and Penna and Ala stood and watched the chase, their hands gripping bows, their fingers straying to arrows only to fall back lax, the Phael wanting to aid, wanting to bring this creature down, yet making no move to do so, for the Guardian held their pledge. And in the vale below . . .

Greater, much greater than its small tormenter, the hideous monster could not escape the raking claws nor turn its huge body against the agile bird, and down the beast dived and down, and alighted in a dark cloud from which a black, Wolflike form, large as a pony, sprang forth running northerly. And as the dark creature hurtled across the snow-laden 'scape—*Skree!*—Valké cried in fury, for now he could not stoop on the running foe, for to do so would leave him upon the ground in the reach of the Vulg's lethal fangs. And so the falcon, wings raging, overtook from behind and raked at head and ears as it flew past and up and away.

And in the distance aft, although it was Bair who topped the bluff, it was Hunter who took up the chase, the Silver Wolf racing after the cries of an enraged tiercel.

And Hunter came upon the tracks of a Vulg, ancient foe of the Draega, and this Vulg ran in the direction of Valké's cries, and so did Hunter, for now he had a scent to follow.

On he raced and on, and of a sudden in the distance to the fore the cries of Valké ceased mid a flash of platinum light.

And moments later, Hunter came upon the Friend, the Elf sitting in the snow, starlight shedding down, moonlight aglance.

Of black Vulg or Fell Beast or yellow-eyed man there was no evident sign.

CHAPTER 35

Neddra

December, 5E1009

[*Days Past*]

Stepping forth from shimmering darkness came Bair. "Kelan, where is he?"

"Gone," gritted Aravan. "He vanished as Valké was flying up and away in a high turn. Where he went the falcon did not see, yet the snow tells the tale."

Bair looked at the muddle of tracks, pawprints of a Vulg mixed with those of a man or Fiend or whatever it was Ydral might be. And even as Bair read the signs, he felt a numb prickling in his chest— Nay! Not a numbness, but a tingling instead. "Kelan!" he blurted, reaching under his quilted coat and fishing for the chain 'round his neck. And holding out the stone ring, he said, "This is an in-between crossing. He has gone elsewhere."

"Did I not say the snow tells the tale?" said Aravan, an edge to his words. He slammed a fist into open palm. "The moment Valké saw him in the pavilion, did I know him: from the day Coron Eiron painted the portrait for me—a vision from Galarun's Death Rede—this monster's visage has been burned into my mind. He is Galarun's killer, the stealer of the Silver Sword, the sire of Stoke, Ydral. From that dreadful day long past in the Dalgor Fens until this very night, I had not set eyes on him." Aravan's voice grew bitter: "But now I have seen him, pursued him, attacked him, and yet he escaped my grasp." Aravan leapt to his feet and shouted in rage at the world, echoes slapping back from the Grimwalls 'round.

"But, kelan," said Bair, "if he has gone to a place where my blood will allow, I can follow him."

"Bair, I cannot send thee alone after that fiend, for it would be—"

"Am I not a Guardian?" protested Bair. "Too, if you let me take Krystallopŷr—" Of a sudden, Bair's words chopped short, and his eyes widened in revelation, for at Aravan's throat in the low-glancing light of the half-silver moon glinted the falcon crystal.

"Bair, again I say—" began Aravan, but Bair thrust out a hand to silence his kelan.

"Listen to me, Aravan, for surely what I say is right: tokens of power filled with <fire>, such as Krystallopŷr, can cross over when there is a bearer."

Aravan nodded, but remained silent.

"And surely when you become Valké, the falcon crystal is filled with <fire>, your <fire>, just as is a token of power . . . I have <seen> that it is so."

Now it was Aravan's eyes which widened in revelation as Bair continued: "And a creature not of the blood, but whose aura can be subsumed in the aura of another, another who *is* of the blood, that creature, such as a horse, or perhaps a falcon, that creature can cross the in-between borne in the aura—"

"—of the one who crosses!" exclaimed Aravan. "Oh, Bair, if thou art right . . ."

"One way to find out," said Bair.

Aravan glanced at the stars. "We are in the candlemarks of the mid of night, a time of crossing unto Neddra, or so I have been told. Let us hasten, Bair, for I would not miss this span, else we will need wait till the mid of night on the morrow, and Ydral will be long gone by then."

"Then bring on Valké," said Bair, taking his flanged mace in hand, "for I would not wait a day."

In a flash of platinum light, Aravan disappeared, Valké standing in his stead.

Bair held out his left arm, and with a stroke of wings the raptor sprang to Bair's wrist. With a sweep up and right, the lad transferred Valké to the pad on his right shoulder, the falcon muttering but stepping from the bottom of one limb to the top of another, talons sinking into leather, gripping, releasing, gripping again, as he turned 'round to face front.

When the bird was settled, with the stone ring held in his left, his mace in his right, Bair began, his voice rising and falling, neither singing nor speaking, but something in between. And he moved in an arcane pattern, a series of intricate steps and glides and pauses and turns, neither walking nor dancing, but something in between. And his mind became lost in the ritual, neither wholly conscious nor unconscious, but something in between. And he did these things in the marks of midnight, neither the morrow nor yester, but something in between. Snow lay on the land, a flowing solid yet not a liquid, but something in between. And he moved in a vale, neither plains nor mountains, but something in between. And Valké sat on his shoulder, in thought neither wholly a bird nor fully an Elf, but something in between. Krystallopŷr rode in its sling on Bair's back, and the falcon crystal rode about the raptor's neck, both filled with <fire> not their own. And in the deep marks of mid of night in the snow lying on the vale they moved, stepping in intricate steps, canting an intricate chant, Bair and Valké slowly fading, Bair's voice becoming soft... faint... silent.

And in the stillness left behind and on the high peaks above, Ala and Penna and Fleogan sighed and looked at one another and after long moments reluctantly took to wing, flying southeasterly through the night toward faraway Jangdi, for the ones they had guided for months and miles were now gone in-between.

Out from nothingness and into the night stepped Bair, the tiercel on his shoulder, the lad yet pacing and chanting. And when he could see the mountains rising about him, his movement stopped and his voice fell silent in the dark. Wrinkling his nose at a faint caustic scent on the air, he said, "Well, Valké, we are here, wherever here may be. If Aravan was right, then we've come unto Neddra."

Valké's sharp eyes glared about, and then he leapt forward, wings flared, gliding to the ground. And from a dazzle of light, Aravan stepped forth.

"Kelan, the glare," admonished Bair.

"Valké deemed it safe," said Aravan. "I kept the thought of

discovery in mind, and he remembered Inge." Then, "He is here," gritted Aravan, pointing to the snow. "Ydral."

In the dingy blanket was a muddle of tracks, booted feet becoming the prints of a Vulg running north.

"Shall we travel afoot," asked Bair, "or upon wing and paw?"

"By foot for the nonce," said Aravan, " 'Tis against Valké's nature to fly at night, or so I remember him thinking . . . complaining rather."

"Then here," said Bair, doffing his pack and beginning to unbuckle Krystallopŷr's harness, "you may need this soon, whether or no this is Neddra."

"Wait, elar," said Aravan. "Keep the harness. I will bear the spear in hand. Should Valké and Hunter be needed again, it will delay us less."

"All right," said Bair, reaching back and pulling the spear free and handing it to Aravan.

As Bair began rebuckling the harness, he looked about. "Do you deem this is indeed Neddra?"

"Aye," replied Aravan. "Look to the moon."

Bair glanced at the sky, searching. "What moon?"

Aravan pointed. "Yon through the gap to the west, just now setting. The darkness against the faint stars."

Following the direction of Aravan's outstretched arm, Bair at last saw what seemed an ebon disk sliding into the horizon, set where the moon should be. "A black moon?"

"Aye. 'Tis Gyphon's sneer at Elwydd."

"Some sneer," said Bair, fixing the last of the straps and shrugging the harness into place. Then shouldering his pack once more, he said, "Let's go, kelan," and together they set off at a jog-trot, following the tracks of the Vulg.

Out from the small vale they ran, to enter a grim, frozen 'scape of rock and twisted trees and sliding shale and scree, dingy snow and dull ice clinging, the land stark and barren. And the air had an ill-defined acrid smell, somewhat sulphurous, or so Bair did deem. "The air is faint foul," said he, as they trotted up and over a low, stony ridge.

"Now dost thou wonder if it is Neddra, elar?" asked Aravan. "E'en were the black moon turned bright and the air become sweet, still the desolation itself would speak of Gyphon's disregard. Some call this place Hèl, for 'tis bleak, blasted, and sterile."

"But Aravan, it must be fertile elsewhere. Even Rûcks and such have to eat."

"Mayhap, yet much of this world is this way, or so those who were here during the Great War of the Ban did say."

Bair glanced left and right. "Even so, still somewhere they must grow food. I do admit, though, kelan, there is less <fire> in this world than in Mithgar, at least in the place we now run."

On they trotted and on, following the lope of Vulg tracks; up and over icy outcrops of rock they went, stepping up slopes and down.

A league and a mile all told did they follow the twisting way, and finally as they topped a rise—"Hsst!" warned Aravan, stopping, crouching down, Krystallopŷr in hand, Bair crouching beside him.

On a high-rising hill in the basin below, flickering torchlight ringing its battlements, there stood a black fortress, dark and ominous, its ebon walls streaked with glazes of rime and long white runs of hoarfrost, Rûcks patrolling the icy walls.

And from where Bair and Aravan knelt in the snow, the Vulg tracks ran down the slope before them and toward the black bastion ahead.

CHAPTER 36

Muster

December, 5E1009
[Days Past]

With red flags flying, Vanadurin in the land of Jord raced across the realm, just as did their Vanadurin cousins in far-away Valon. Balefires were set atop the warcairns, for war was coming from the East, a war of blood and iron, a war where a Dragon rode the sky. And the Harlingar in the north now gathered at the High King's call, for, as they had done in the War of the Usurper some two millennia past, they would again ride to the side of the rightful High King in distant Valon, a place where their Harlingar kinsmen now dwelled.

In Aven, an emissary stood before the king in his palace in the city of Dendor. "My lord," said the delegate, "the High King would have you join forces with Garia to delay these invaders for as long as you can."

"What you ask, Realmsman, is that I come together with those who have no honor."

"Indeed, my lord, the High King knows he asks much of you. Still he needs you to buy time, for an army from the East is come."

"Not only do you ask that I join with the Garian thieves who defile my realm, but you also ask that we face a foe whose count of soldiers numbers in the hundreds of thousands, or so my scouts do say."

"Aye, my lord, the army now marching across Aralan is vast

indeed. Yet heed: each day Aven and Garia can delay the advance of this Eastern foe is a day gained for your women and children and the halt and old to flee into the West.

"And each day Aven and Garia can delay the advance is a day gained for the High King's muster to gather on the Plains of Valon.

"And each day Aven and Garia can delay the advance is a day gained in the setting of the High King's defenses to cut this Eastern army down to size.

"And so, my lord, the High King asks that the nation of Aven join with that of Garia in spite of the bad blood between and stand athwart the path and gain that one more day, a day at a time, for as many days as you can. And when you can no longer hold them, then the High King asks that in a running battle—delaying them as you go—you draw them down into Pellar and toward the Argon Ferry, for that is where the main muster will make its stand."

"But to join with the rabble of Garia?" King Dulon slammed his fist to the table in ire, and stood long in thought. Finally, he sighed and said, "Though Garia started this bloodletting between, and there is much they must pay for, still a common enemy raves through Aralan and toward our common border. It seems King Vlak and I have little choice but to throw in together.

"Realmsman, return to the High King and say this unto him: we shall join with Garia and hold the line for as long as we can—and for that I expect consideration when we settle with Garia in the end—even though I fear delaying this vast army from the East will mean a great loss unto Aven, mayhap e'en greater than that of King Agron marching into Gron long past."

In Riamon and Darda Erynian and in the Greatwood nigh, in Hoven, Tugal, Vancha, Basq, Gelen and Gothon, in Jute, Wellen, Thol, Dalara, in Rian and the Jillian Tors, in Harth and in the Wilderland, and all across the realms, word had gone out for the muster to gather on the Plains of Valon. And Elves and men and Baeron prepared—arms and armor, horses, wagons, food and medicines and other supplies—making ready for the long march and the deadly war to come.

So, too, did the Hidden Ones prepare, in the Weiunwood and

the Blackwood, though they would not leave their domains; yet should a foe come in among the forbidden places, woe betide that foe.

In Skyloft Holt and Kachar and Mineholt North, in the Quartzen Hills and Blackstone and mighty Kraggen-cor, and in the Holt of the Red Hills as well, Dwarves donned black-iron chain shirts and helms, and they took up axes and crossbows and warhammers and mounted their ponies and gathered their wagon trains and set out for the mustering point. Even the Châkka in Blueholt in Gelen set sail across the seas to come unto the war.

And in a small, quiet realm called the Boskydells behind a vast thornwall, there, too, went a Realmsman, bearing a coin of little worth, small and pewter and with a hole in the center depending from a leather thong, the coin a message hearking back to the Great War of the Ban, a summons to the Wee Ones living in the Seven Dells that the High King called as many as could come to his aid. Yet the Realmsman found that the Warrows of this thorn-guarded land already knew they were needed and were quite prepared to set out for Valon. It seems that a ghostly visitation had come to three of the Boskydellers—a damman and two buccen, each separately related by blood to three heroes of the Winter War—the apparition calling upon them to don royal armor loaned long past and join in the fight to come.

The Realmsman merely shook his head and rode on for Trellinath. After all, and in spite of the legends concerning them, these were a small Folk, quite insignificant; what matter that they joined in the battle, eh?

In Arden Vale, Inarion signalled to Elissan, and she raised a silver clarion unto her lips and blew a ringing call, and the column of Lian Guardians began their ride southward for Arden Falls and the hidden way beneath. From there they would go down into Lianion called Rell and leave the vale behind.

When word was brought by the Rûcken scout that Arden Vale was abandoned, the Black Mage Nunde cast forth his senses from his tower in the Grimwall Mountains, a tower just east of Jallor Pass, and he searched for the so-called Rider of the Planes. But the lad was not with the Elves faring south, nor was he in Arden

Vale. For a sevenday in all did Nunde search the world, seeking a particular <fire>, and still he found no sign of the one the damnable Elves had named Bair.

Good. Now I can call my watchers away from that accursed place of Arden Vale, the place where my apprentice Radok was slain. And since that crossbred mongrel of a boy has not left the vale—in what? ah yes, five years—he must have been slain in one of the raids I visited upon that gorge, else I would have scried him out. Hence, the prophecy of the Rider of the Planes is now ended . . . and the Trine is coming.

Nunde danced a small jig-step in glee.

CHAPTER 37

Fortress

December, 5E1009

[A Day and Three-Quarters to a Quarter-Day Past]

The sun dawned a dull red, shining through a yellow-brown haze, the air itself faintly sulphurous, as if somewhere nearby great furnaces belched poison into the sky. And from their aerie on the snow-laden slopes above, Bair and Aravan looked on as the black fortress below came to life, Rûcks and Hlôks and other such stirring.

Bair groaned and said, "They suffer not the Ban, kelan."

Aravan nodded. " 'Tis Neddra, one of the Untargarda, where the Ban rules not." Aravan glanced at the crimson sun. " 'Tis not Adon's light which shines down upon this world, elar, but Gyphon's bloody glow instead."

"Oh," said Bair. "I see." But then Bair frowned. "What are they guarding against, kelan?"

Aravan shrugged. "Mayhap this bastion was built to ward against invasion from Mithgar, or to launch invasions to there."

"But with the Ban," protested Bair, "none but their own can come from Mithgar, and no Foul Folk can cross to there. So why is it yet filled and warded?"

Aravan turned up a hand. "Given their nature, mayhap the Foul Folk war among themselves, and this dark stronghold may be but a pawn in that struggle."

Bair nodded, and a silence fell between them as they watched the fortress sitting atop the high-rising hill in the basin below.

Roughly square was the bastion, an outer wall running 'round, some twenty feet high and three hundred feet to a side and fifteen feet thick at the top, wider at the base, with bartizan after bartizan along its length full about, some fifty feet in between any given pair. A barbican sat atop the main gate in the south, a smaller barbican at the rear, with a road running up in a series of switchbacks to the main gate, and presumably a like road ran down from the postern gate afar. Between the bulwark ringing 'round and the main fortress itself, there lay an open space, a killing ground for any who had won their way up the hill and had breached the outer wall.

Centered within this outer wall, the black bastion itself stood: some sixty feet high it was and also built in a square, two hundred feet to a side with a great courtyard in the center, towers and turrets and a massive wall hemming the quadrangle in.

Scattered about the quadrangle stood a number of large, enclosed wagons with wooden walls and roofs, drivers' seats atop, coaches mayhap, though who or what they might transport neither Aravan nor Bair could say.

In the quadrangle as well was what looked to be a stable.

"Horses?" asked Bair.

Aravan shook his head. "Hèlsteeds, I ween."

"If they are Hèlsteeds," said Bair, "then I imagine there are Ghûlka within the bastion below."

Aravan nodded but said nought as they continued to watch, noting the patrols, seeking weaknesses and strengths.

Two outer and two inner towers sat in a small square and warded the passageway into the dark fortress, with great outer and inner gates and portcullises barring the way. At the northern wall of the main fortress, another four towers warded the rear entry as well.

With a tower at each corner of the main fortress and towers centered along each of its walls, defenders could bring great power to bear against any and all assailants who sought to claim the fort as their own.

"Where does Ydral stay?" asked Bair, taking a bite of crue. "And do you think this is his fort?"

"I know not the answer to either question, Bair, yet I was told by those who fought on the Lower Plane during the Great War that fortresses on Neddra have passageways beneath, and a chamber central to all."

"Ah," said Bair, "a central chamber. A place for the Silver Sword?"

"Mayhap," replied Aravan. "As soon as we know the routines of the fort and the best way to gain entry, then we shall see if indeed the Dawn Sword lies within."

"Then we are going inside," stated Bair, his mouth grim, his words not a question.

"Risky it is, Bair, yet to kill Ydral and regain the sword is worth all."

Bair looked down at the fortress. "How soon?"

"Mayhap three days or four, as soon as we can see which way is best."

Bair took a swig from his waterskin and as he corked it he paused, looking at the bag. "Then we're going to need more water, kelan." Bair looked about in disgust. "And even can we find scrub to burn, I don't fancy melting this tainted snow to get a drink."

Aravan smiled. "I have had worse, elar, much worse."

"Have you a plan?"

Aravan looked at Bair. "What wouldst thou do, elar, given what we see before us?"

The sixteen-year-old lad frowned and then said, "Until we have more knowledge of the fortress and the schedules and posts of the warders, we cannot venture within. Accordingly, I would have us move in the night from this side to a corner opposite, for mayhap we will see a weakness from a different vantage than the one here, for all I see at the moment is strength.

"Too, as we discovered in Jangdi, Valké has the vision to make out fine details from afar, better indeed than Elven sight. Hence, I would have him scout for us as well, but to do so we will need a way to shield the flash of light, especially if he is to take wing at night. Day would be better, though he should not get too near, not only because of arrows, but also to keep Ydral from knowing he has been followed here."

Bair looked at Aravan. "That's what I would do, kelan. Have you aught to add?"

Aravan smiled and clapped Bair on the shoulder. "Nought for the nonce, elar, for it seems thou hast grown a bit more cautious since a night in the desert apast. And as for the flash of light, mayhap my cloak will serve as a covering shield when I become Valké, and thy cloak when I transform back."

When Valké came gliding in low, using the mountain as cover, Bair doffed his cloak and waited. With a wing-driven backwash of air, the raptor alighted at hand, and then looked up suspiciously as Bair fetched him forward with a quiet chirp, the lad with a cloak in hand. Chattering in ire at being covered, Valké made his vexation known. "Aravan," whispered Bair, light leaking out from the flash within, the Elf now crouching beneath.

As Bair re-donned his cloak, Aravan said, "This did Valké see. The fortress can be climbed at any of the towers, for there the stonework is rugged, the joins somewhat gapped."

Bair frowned. "But the towers are where the warders congregate. What of the stonework between?"

Aravan shook his head. "Smooth and well mortared. If we free-climb, it's a tower or nought."

"What of the rime and hoarfrost? Won't it get in the way of free-climbing?"

"On the north wall, aye. But on the south sides of the towers, the feeble sunlight seems to have been enough to keep the stonework clear."

Bair looked at the fortress. "I can toss a grapnel atop the low, outer bulwark, but the wall of the main fort looks to be sixty feet high or so, and where I would have to stand to well throw the hook would add another ten."

"A long toss," mused Aravan. "Thou wilt have to muffle the tines."

"Would that Valké could fly up and you, kelan, set the grapple, but, alas, the flare of light would of certain be seen."

Aravan nodded glumly.

Bair took a deep breath and exhaled. "All right, then. We'll just have to find the weakest point and give it a try."

"Aye," said Aravan, then added, "By the by, two things: there is a switchback road running down the hill from the postern, just as we surmised, and, we'll not need to melt snow at all—Valké espied a running stream."

"A stream in Neddra? Probably poisoned," grumbled Bair.

*   *   *

On the second night, just after sunset and with a black moon riding overhead, they moved to another viewpoint, this one in the mountains above the northeast corner of the fortress, there where the stream flowed out from a narrow cleft in the mountain. The water itself was faintly bitter, but drinkable nonetheless.

Ensconced in icy, snow-laden crags, long did they watch, counting the warders, measuring the heartbeats it took for the patrols to make their rounds, noting that the outer wall was but lightly guarded, the inner wall more heavily so. Too, they noted that there seemed to be much greater activity on the walls than the night before, guards changing shifts every candlemark or so, with a gabble of voices drifting up, words lost on the air. It was as if some great activity were occurring or about to occur in the fortress itself.

As the bloodred sun broke the horizon, Aravan said, "Bair, rest. I shall stand first watch and take count of the daylight shift. I'll waken thee at the noontide."

"Rest I will," said Bair, "yet I think sleep will elude me."

The lad fell into slumber the moment he lay down.

As the sanguine sun crept across the yellow-brown sky, they rested and watched in turn: Aravan from sunrise to the noontide; Bair from the noontide till the ruddy dusk.

When Aravan awakened and returned from relieving himself, "What passes, elar?" he asked.

Bair said, "The ward on the outer wall is gone, and that on the inner changes shifts every candlemark or so. Too, there are fewer warders on the main fort than last night, and those who are on watch seem distracted, jittering about, watching within instead of without, as if anxiously waiting for the relief to come. What could be happening, I wonder?"

Aravan shrugged. "Who knows the mind of the Rûpt? Still, keep a close eye, for with distraction comes opportunity."

As dusk turned to night and the night itself eked on, they continued to watch, noting the movements below. And in the candlemarks beyond mid of night a wind kicked up from the east, driving dark clouds before it, gradually obscuring what few stars they could heretofore see.

"Mayhap a storm is riding on the wings of this wind," said Aravan, kneeling at one of the packs and fetching two biscuits of crue. "If so, 'tis a likely time to make our foray."

But Bair said, "Nay, kelan, now is the time, for although the corners and gates are yet warded, the two side towers between corners just went dark, yet I saw no warders march away."

Aravan turned and peered down at the fort. Torchlight burned in all the towers but the one centered on the west wall and the one centered on the east. "If empty, likely the warders went down through the tower," said Aravan.

"Well, *if* they are empty, can we get in before any take their place?" asked Bair.

"One way to find out," said Aravan, handing Bair a biscuit. "Eat this as we go."

"Should we not send Valké?"

" 'Tis night, and the cloak does not conceal all the flash of the change; the brightness may be seen. Too, by the time Valké scouts there and back, even if unguarded now, the towers may be warded again by the time we arrive. Nay, this may be our single opportunity. I say we go and go now."

"A time for boldness and dash, eh?" said Bair, as they shouldered their packs and began the descent down the steep way, snow cascading before them, the two keeping to what little cover was offered as they angled for the tower on the east.

With the gathering clouds obscuring the dim starlight and the setting ebon moon casting little or no illumination whatsoever, the night was verging on pitch-blackness, and were it not for the torchlight faintly gleaming from the corner towers and gateways, even Elven sight would have been thwarted. Yet this faintest of glow was enough for Aravan and Bair to quickly circle their way around to the base of the hill and upward, keeping centered on the east wall, farthest from the corners.

They came unnoticed to the outer wall.

Bair swung the padded grapnel a time or two, and then cast it, the trailing rope uncoiling after, and with a muffled *clnk!* it landed atop the barrier. Bair drew on the rope, the grapnel sliding across the banquette above and toward the parapet, where the tines caught. Testing the anchor, Bair nodded, but then turned to Aravan. "This I would say to you, kelan: our primary mission is to regain the Silver Sword; it is not to slay Ydral. If he happens to get killed along the way, so be it, but the sword comes first. And should we find the blade, then it's out and away and back to Mithgar, whether or no Ydral is slain."

Aravan looked at the lad intently, as if seeing someone new, and then with a sigh he reluctantly agreed.

Up the line they swarmed, Bair in the lead, Aravan coming after. When Bair reached the top, he cautiously looked left and right. The outer wall was unguarded. He clambered on over, Aravan right behind.

A ramp led down to the killing ground, and swiftly the two crossed through the darkness to the base of the central tower and 'round to the join on its southern exposure.

Up the rough stonework they scaled, passing by arrow slits in the tower wall, darkness and silence within. Up they clambered and up, now and again slowed by a patchy glaze of ice or frost. Finally, they neared the top, where Bair in the lead motioned Aravan to stillness, and they both clung to the stone without moving, for a wall patrol drew near. Guttural voices grew louder, along with the tramp of iron-shod boot. Torchlight shone brighter and brighter, and with his heart hammering in his chest, Bair pressed himself against the stone, as all 'round the darkness faded. Directly above on the wall came the light, and then passed onward, voices and light fading as the Rûpt tramped away.

Bair exhaled, noting for the first time that he had been holding his breath. When the patrol was but a distant murmur, upward he climbed, to slip over the parapet and onto the walkway above. Looking left and right as he slid Krystallopŷr from its harness, he turned about to motion Aravan up, to find his kelan standing behind, reaching for the spear and hissing, "Cast thy hood far over thy head and keep thy face down. We would not have them see just who and what we are."

Faces in hooded shadow, rightward they turned and stepped past a broad, tall, ironbound door; into the central east tower they silently glided, Aravan now in the lead, Krystallopŷr in hand, Bair following, his flanged mace gripped tightly. Along the interior side of the tower a wide trapdoor stood open, a great bar lying on the floor at hand to barricade the way should there be a need; a broad spiral stairway led down into the dimness, faint light seeping inward through quadrangle-facing arrow slits from the torchlit courtyard below. Down the stairwell went Aravan, Bair on his heels, and into another chamber, where again a trapdoor stood open, the spiral stairway continuing downward. To either side of the chamber, tall and wide ironbound doors stood open, revealing dark passageways within the fortress walls vanishing into darkness beyond.

"These doors, kelan, they are so huge, as well as the corridors beyond."

"Troll-ways," replied Aravan.

"Ogrus?"

"Aye."

On downward they went, passing through chamber after chamber, identical to the ones above. Four storeys in all did they descend, each fifteen feet high, ere they reached the level of the quadrangle, yet the stairwell continued down, twenty more feet or so, to fetch up against another great, ironbound door.

"It leads to the passageways below," whispered Aravan.

"To the sword, I hope, and perhaps Ydral," murmured Bair, his heart suddenly pounding again. Then, grimly, "Let's go."

Down the last of the steps they glided and to the shut portal. As Aravan reached for the ring on its ring-post, Bair whispered, "Recall, kelan, the last one of these I opened, something deadly came out," and he raised his mace in readiness.

Aravan paused, and then placed his ear to the massive door, listening.

Bair held his breath.

Finally, Aravan said, "A faint murmur of voices, no more."

Again he reached for the ring on its ring-post.

Again Bair raised his mace.

With a creaking of hinges, Aravan slowly opened the huge door, trying to minimize the sound. No creature, no monster stood waiting for them, but a babble of voices instead—squeals and laughter and shouts and a heavy panting and grunting of many throats.

A tall, broad passageway stood open before them, corridors

branching off left and right, faint light coming from somewhere ahead, and a musky scent rode on the air.

"To the center?" murmured Bair.

Without turning, Aravan nodded and stepped inward.

Through the doorway they crept, closing it behind, so as to leave it the way they had found it. Down the hall ahead they slipped, weapons ready, senses alert, Bair trying to identify where he might have heard such sounds before.

In the distance behind, the doorway banged open, the sound of running footsteps and voices echoing along the way. Bair turned to see torchlight bobbing down the hall toward him, and a surge of fear and rage and readiness for battle whelmed through him, but Aravan grabbed him by the arm and hauled him into the shadows of a cross-corridor. And they stood still, looking aside so that their eyes would not reflect light and give them away.

Past the byway ran the Rûpt, a Hlôk in the lead, Rûcks following, one bearing a torch. None whatsoever even glanced aside, but instead eagerly ran snuffling toward the sounds ahead, while behind, Bair found himself trembling—whether in relief or dread, he knew not—perspiration trickling down.

"Come," hissed Aravan, when the squad was well past. And on they went down the corridor toward a babble of sound growing louder.

"Kelan," whispered Bair, "there is a gathering ahead, doing what, I cannot say, but a gathering nevertheless. Is it wise to walk toward so many?"

Aravan paused and looked back. "This way leads toward the core. Wouldst thou have us turn aside?"

Bair turned up a hand in uncertainty.

Aravan then said, "Whatever is happening to the fore has their attention, I ween, and we need press forward until we find a way to Ydral's quarters and mayhap the Silver Sword, for you and I both deem the most likely place for them to lie is in the center of all."

On they pressed, faces enshadowed in their cloak hoods, nearer and nearer to the sounds ahead, voices calling out in Slûk, the grunting and panting and squeals and shouts louder and louder. And finally, just beyond a spiral stairwell to the right and leading downward, they came to an entrance into an upper tier of a brightly lit amphitheater, the noise nearly deafening. And down below . . . down below . . . in the center of all and writhing on the open floor were scores of Rûcks and Hlôks stripped bare and wildly coupling with others, groaning, gasping, shrieking, hooting. Here and there in the frenzy, Rûpt bashed kindred aside and took their places, while others furiously and eagerly swapped mates. To one side Spaunen cast their weapons down and stripped out of their armor and flung themselves into the fray.

"They're, they're—" blurted Bair without finishing his thought, his eyes wide in disbelief.

" 'Tis a breeding pit," said Aravan, "and filled with a Foul Folk I've not seen before: females."

"Females? I didn't know there were female Rûpt."

Aravan hissed, "What didst thou think, lad, that Foul Folk grew upon trees?"

"Well, I suppose I didn't think. I suppose I thought that somehow they, um, just *spawned*, or some such. But, Adon, they're no more than animals, and—" Bair's words chopped off and he pointed. "Aravan, look, we were right: Ghûlka."

In the roiling melee, three Ghûls strode across the amphitheater floor and dragged Rûcks and Hlôks away from lusting females and shoved them toward the walls, where reluctantly they donned armor and took up weapons and marched out and away even as others entered to frantically strip naked and hurl themselves upon the females vacated, who ardently reached up to pull them down atop.

"Overseers of the breeding," growled Aravan, stepping back and turning to the spiral stair running down the well on the right. "Come. Let us find Ydral."

"But won't this lead us down to the pit?" asked Bair, even as they descended.

"Mayhap," replied Aravan. "Yet mayhap as well there are more chambers below."

At the level of the pit floor they came to a landing. Leftward was a corridor like the one above, the furor of mating loud; the spiral stair, however, continued downward, and Aravan and Bair descended into the dimness below, sounds from the breeding pit echoing down after. At the bottom of the well they came into a rough-walled corridor curving to left and right.

"Which way?" whispered Bair.

"Yon," said Aravan, gesturing leftward, where faint light shown 'round the curve.

His heart hammering in his throat, Bair followed Aravan along the passage.

The light emanated from a torch ensconced along the leftward wall, and opposite was a shadowy corridor leading inward toward the center of the underground maze. A stench of death seeped outward from this dark passage.

"This way," hissed Aravan, stepping within.

Breathing through his mouth, Bair followed.

Along the corridor they went, deeper into darkness, their own shadows lost in the blackness ahead.

And then—

—Looming out before them—

—A huge figure—

"Kelan, look ou—!"

Something slammed into the back of Bair's head, hurling him forward, the lad smashing into Aravan and crashing to the floor, as down into darkness he spun.

CHAPTER 38

Flight

Winterday, 5E1009

[The Present]

*D*ragging. . . . Dragging. . . . Monstrous hands gripping, dragging. . . .

Stunned, Bair vaguely knew someone or something haled him
through the dark— No, not dark; light—

Roughly he was handled, his pack and weapons stripped from
him, and tight bracelets clasped about his—

Moments later, fully aware, Bair found he was shackled to a
wall in a lantern-lit, stone chamber. To the right, Aravan was also
fettered, manacles about his wrists, chains embedded in the stone,
the Elf awake and aware.

Before them stood a handful of Rûcks, crossbows in hand,
quarrels vaguely pointed their way. Beyond the Rûcks stood a pair
of hulking Trolls—twelve feet tall, at least—and Bair then knew
who and what had attacked them in the dark corridor, one from
the front, one from behind. Where the Ogrus had come from—
side corridors, niches, hidden doors—Bair did not know, only that
they had come. And even as he gazed about, with a sinking heart
the lad realized that he had slammed into his kelan, knocking Aravan down, and Aravan had not had a chance to bring Krystallopŷr into play. And now they were both—

Adon, we're in a death chamber.

—for Bair saw the flayed and disemboweled corpse of a Rûck
on a table to one side of the stone-walled room. As well there
was a table littered with various tools—knives, augurs, screw-dri-

ven clamps, fire irons, rasps, pliers, meat hammers, saws, picks, and other such—all instruments of torture. A cloying miasma of blood and feces, bile, urine, and the contents of split-open intestines permeated the chamber. One of the massive doors of the fortress stood shut directly across the room, and heavily curtained archways stood left and right, but what the drapery might conceal, Bair could not say.

This must be Ydral's evil sanctum, for who else would be so depraved?

Bair turned his head toward Aravan, and whispered in Sylva, *"Vio ron skyld."*

Aravan gave a slight shake of his head, and a tilt toward the Rûcks, all of whom swung the aim of their crossbows toward Bair.

"Tji say tji are at fault, boy?" came a sneering voice, and Ydral stood in the open archway to the left. He came stalking into the room, Rûcks and Trolls giving back before him as if in fear, some casting glances at the mutilated corpse on the table nigh.

"No, tji foolish child," sneered Ydral, looking up into Bair's face, then turning toward Aravan, "it is the fault of this *Dolh*, this Elf that brought tji here. How tji both crossed over into Neddra, Jai cannot say. But that tji did gives mehr great pleasure"—Ydral clenched a fist and glared at Aravan—"for now Jai can end once and for all this one's relentless pursuit."

With hatred burning deep in his yellow eyes, Ydral stepped before Aravan. "For more than five thousand years tji have sought mehr, ever since that cursed war when mai Lord Gyphon was cast down." Momentary bitterness flashed across Ydral's face, but then he triumphantly smiled. "But tji could not even draw nigh, could tji? Not only did tji not catch mehr, tji did not even know where Jai was." Ydral paused as if struck by a sudden thought. "Was that accursed Draega and black bird aun sending?"

Aravan said nought, his steely gaze on Ydral.

"Pah! It matters not, for Jai evaded them just as Jai evaded tji throughout the years." Ydral grinned a pointed-tooth smirk. "It was here, tji fool, here that Jai came, where tji could not follow, here to Neddra, here to mai mighty black fortress, here near the crossovers to Mithgar and others, mai fortress of the nexus.

"Here it was Gyphon Himself came to launch His invasion into Adonar.

"But that was then and this is now. Somehow tji did manage to find mehr here, and to do so tji had to defeat the Sundering. But how?" Again Ydral paused, frowning. "Bah! Jai cannot say for the moment, and yet tji and this boy are here in mai fortress now, and from Mithgar tji did come."

Ydral stared hard at Aravan, as if sight alone could ferret out the secret. Yet Aravan's sapphire-blue eyes gazed in grim silence into Ydral's eyes of yellow.

Ydral drew back from that unflinching, hard glare, then barked a laugh. "It matters not tji are silent at this moment, for Jai will extract that secret from tji. Oh, yes, Jai will, and it will give mehr much pleasure to have tji scream to mehr just how tji did it."

Ydral glanced at Bair and snorted. "Tji and this lackwit boy thought to invade this stongholt? Pah! Why do tji think Jai left the two side towers unguarded?" Ydral gestured at the nearby corpse. "Ha! Jai knew tji were coming all along, the boy and his pitiful weapons, tji and aun spear."

Ydral stepped to a table where lay the spear, along with a mace and two long-knives, as well as two backpacks amid a scatter of climbing gear.

As Ydral took up the spear, his eyes widened in shock, and he looked at what he held. And then he laughed and danced about and crowed in glee. And with two hands he held the spear overhead, his face lifted upward as well, and he shouted, "It matters not what that upstart fool does, for with this *Jai* shall rule Mithgar!" Ydral whirled about to face Aravan. "Jai have had mai doubts that Lord Gyphon would name mehr as His regent, perhaps instead choosing that pusillanimous Dragonboy. Yet now Jai have the means to assure He will choose mehr. And tji, mai unwitting pursuer, have delivered it into mai hands."

Trembling with excitement and gazing at the spear, of a sudden Ydral turned to the Rûpt and snarled at them in Slûk. And without a further word, Ydral stalked from the chamber, taking the spear with him, the Trolls following, and they went out the massive door and into a corridor beyond, leaving Aravan and Bair shackled to the wall, five Rûcks standing ward with crossbows aimed directly at the prisoners' hearts.

*   *   *

Time passed in silence, but for echoes drifting down from above. Bair's thoughts raced in futile conjecture, seeking a way out, finding none. After a while, "Kelan," murmured Bair, but with a raised finger and a slight shake of his head, Aravan signalled the lad to muteness.

Moments fled and moments more as down the spiral stairwell and along the corridor and through the massive open door there came the faint echoes of frenzied breeding.

And more time passed.

The Rûcks on ward began glancing at one another and muttering among themselves, talk which escalated to oaths and arguments, now and then breaking into shouts. Finally, they seemed to come to an agreement, and one approached Bair while the others leveled their crossbows at the lad; the Rûck tested Bair's shackles by jerking on the chains. Sneering, the Rûck moved to Aravan, the other four now turning their weapons upon the Elf. Again the Rûck yanked on the iron links and then paused, eyeing the crystal dangling from its platinum chain about Aravan's neck, the blue stone amulet lying alongside. He reached out toward the crystal, yet ere he touched it he jerked back his hand as if stung by something unseen. Lashing out, he backhanded Aravan across the face; the Rûcks behind cried out in alarm, Bair recognizing the name Ydral among their words of warning.

Snarling and backing away, the Rûck turned toward the others, and they moved off a few paces and squatted in a circle and one began casting—

Bair frowned. *What are they doing?*

—dice, or rather, knucklebones.

They're gaming, but for what? To see which one kills us? Who gets the crystal, who the amulet, and which one gets my ring? If so, why the words of warning? At least it seemed like a warning to me.

Of a sudden and with a shout, one of the Rûcks leapt to his feet and bolted out the door, stripping armor as he went.

And then Bair knew why they were casting lots.

The four behind continued rolling the bones.

And then another one scrambled up and away. . . .

And another after him. . . .

Until there was but one Rûck left.

Crossbow in hand, that Rûck stood by the door, peering into the dark hallway and listening to the sounds drifting down from above, paying no attention to the prisoners behi—

—platinum light flared throughout the chamber, and Valké—*skree!*—hurtled through the air, and even as the Rûck began to turn, again silvery light blazed, and Aravan slammed into the Rûck, grabbed him by the throat and crotch, and lifted him up to smash him down and break his back across one knee. The Rûck fell slack to the stone, dead before striking it. Snatching up the crossbow, Aravan turned to find Hunter struggling in his chains, the 'Wolf shackled to the wall.

"Bair," called Aravan, and from shimmering darkness Bair emerged.

"You got loose, kelan, but I—"

Swiftly, Aravan stepped to the table containing their packs and took up his long-knife, snatching up a key ring as well. He strode to Bair and as he unlocked the shackles he said, "Valké's wings slipped the fetters."

"But the irons, kelan, they were caught in your <fire>, and when you changed they should have— Oh, my, they did." Aravan's manacles dangled, the bands now too small to fit a person's wrists. Nevertheless, Valké's wings had come free, for the feathers had compressed to slide out from the encircling clasps, unlike Hunter's forelegs.

Aravan and Bair strapped on their long-knives and shouldered their packs and clipped on their climbing gear, and as Bair took up his flanged mace, Aravan said, "Let us look for the Silver Sword, for surely it is nearby. It is a thing Ydral would keep for the pleasure it gives him, remembering the slaughter in its taking. Can we find it, then we must run down Ydral ere he escapes again, for whatever he saw in Krystallopŷr bodes ill for the world and creation. I would have him dead ere that happens, and the spear back in my hands."

Moments later, weapons at the ready, they stepped through the curtained archway on the left, the one from which Ydral had first appeared.

"Adon," gasped Bair, slapping a hand across nose and mouth, for the reek of decay was overwhelming.

The lantern-lit chamber they entered was filled with flayed, eviscerated corpses lying on tables—Rûcks and Hlôks and even a great Troll—sparkling tools at hand: scalpels of all sizes, in the main, but forceps and pliers and augurs and saws and other such instruments as well. Too, there were glass jars and flasks containing harvested organs: eyes, hearts, tongues, livers, intestines, genitalia, and things Bair could not name.

Beakers and bottles filled with liquids and crystal salts and sulphur and powders lined shelves along one wall, alongside what looked to be a collection of skulls. And above a brazier with glowing charcoal a torso of a Rûck dangled from a hook, flesh blackened and split and dripping fat to sizzle on the coals below.

"What is he . . . ?" asked Bair, the biscuit of crue he had eaten while coming down the mountain surging up toward his throat.

Aravan shook his head. "Like sire, like son," murmured Aravan. Then—"Come. I ween the sword is not here."

They moved out from Ydral's blasphemous surgery and crossed the chamber to the archway beyond, Bair bracing himself for what they might find.

It was living quarters: a rumpled bed, chairs, a table, a desk, a chifforobe . . .

. . . which was all Bair managed to take in before he saw that the rumple in the bed was a corpse, a female corpse.

His biscuit of crue spewed outward, along with whatever else had been in his stomach.

"When thou canst," said Aravan, "search the chifforobe. I'll search the chest at the foot of the bed. And, Bair, 'ware poison needles and other such traps which might ward doors and drawers and lids."

Wiping his mouth on his sleeve, Bair stepped to the wardrobe. Using the hook of a flange on his mace, he pried the tall door open. Rooting about, he found nothing inside but clothes. One by one he pulled the drawers on the left side of the chifforobe all the way out from the cabinet and set them on the floor. There was nothing within any drawer but garments, and nothing behind, either.

Bair turned to see the contents of the bed-chest strewn about, the chest itself turned on its side. Aravan now examined the desk.

Bair pulled the chifforobe away from the wall and looked behind, finding nought.

Now Aravan moved to the bed. Lifting the mattress up, the female corpse sliding—"Bair!"—*thmp*, the corpse slipping to the floor.

Bair turned to see. Beyond the undercording—ropes crisscrossing back and forth from rail to rail to support the feather bed—on the floor lay a sword in a scabbard.

"Not a very original hiding place," said the lad.

"He did not mean to hide it," said Aravan, letting the mattress fall back and stooping down. "Rather he wanted it where he could easily reach it, touch it, hold it, stroke it, reliving the slaughter of the Dalgor Fens." Aravan stood, sword in hand.

"Is that it?" breathed Bair. "The Silver Sword?"

Aravan turned and drew the weapon from its sheath. The blade and guard were of brushed silver, the hilt wrapped with silver wire. Softly it glowed in the lamplight. "Many a time did I see this blade as Galarun bore it west. Aye, elar, this is the Dawn Sword, or so the Wizards named it." Aravan passed the weapon to Bair.

Bair frowned. "But, kelan, I thought the Dawn Sword held <power>, yet this holds no <fire> whatsoever . . . not even that of plain silver true. And the metal is soft—like silver pure—not a weapon with which to do battle at all."

Aravan held out his hand. As Bair gave the sword over to Aravan and Aravan slipped it into its sheath, the Elf said, "Here and now is not the time to debate the worth of this blade. Instead—"

A shrill cry split the air, and running footsteps fled away down the corridor beyond.

"Quick," said Aravan, turning Bair about and sliding the sword in its scabbard into the sling they had used to carry the spear. "We must flee. Someone has discovered the slain Rûck, and found us missing as well. Valké and Hunter may be needed to get us out from here, and Hunter must bear the blade, for Valké cannot."

Out from Ydral's quarters they fled, through the archway and across the chamber past the dead Rûck by the door and into the passage beyond.

Down this corridor and then leftward they ran, heading for the stair, and now they could hear a gong ringing somewhere, somewhere beyond the curved passage.

Up the stairwell they scrambled, even as they heard the running clatter of oncoming iron-shod boots.

"On up!" hissed Aravan, and they spiralled upward, passing by the archway leading to the breeding pit, those in the pit paying no heed to the tocsin.

Up they sped, and from below came the yells and the clack and rattle of pursuit hammering up the stairwell. A horn blatted out a cry, and an echoing answer responded from above.

With shouts and footsteps coming after, Aravan and Bair reached the landing where the stairwell ended; out into the corridor they darted, turning leftward away from the arena and toward the outer wall, toward the tower they had climbed for entry. Side by side they fled along the passage, only to see in the dimness ahead a squad of Rûpt, five in all, racing toward them.

Bair smashed down the Hlôk in the lead, his mace crashing through helm and bone and brain, black ichor flying wide as the Hlôk slammed sideways into the stone wall, his tulwar clanging free of his dead hand, even as Aravan's hard-driven long-knife slashed through the air to decapitate one of the Rûcks, the severed head bouncing down the hallway. *Waugh!* cried the Rûpt following, and they turned to flee. But Bair's mace smashed from behind and Aravan's long-knife pierced as well, and elar and kelan ran onward, leaving bloody slaughter lying aft.

They came to the portal at the inward side of the tower, and in they dashed, slamming the door to and dropping the bar across. Then up the spiral stair to the next floor and to the one beyond they ran, where they paused long enough to hurl the trapdoor shut and bar it as well.

Onward they fled up the curving stairway, throwing trapdoors to, barring some, leaving others merely shut. And horns blatted throughout the fortress.

Onto the walkway atop the wall they came, and in the quadrangle below, Rûcks and Hlôks ran thither and yon, and a Hèlsteed-mounted Ghûl waved a cruelly barbed spear and shouted orders in Slûk.

A bare glimmer of oncoming daybreak shone in the east, faint under the dark clouds roiling across the tainted sky, driven by a moaning wind. Aravan groaned and said, "We cannot cross over at dawn."

Bair glanced leftward, northward at the sky to see darkness coming. "Then we'll lose them in the mountains in the storm," said Bair, snapping open the tines of the grapnel.

Through the blow there came a shout, for warders atop the wall espied the two intruders and sounded the alarm. Forward leapt the Rûpt, charging toward Aravan and Bair, even as the lad set the hook and cast the rope over the side.

"You first, elar," hissed Aravan, stepping to the center of the walkway. Bair scrambled atop the parapet and looped the rope under one thigh and over the opposite shoulder, then he stepped backward from the rampart and began rappelling down the stone wall.

And up above, Rûcks and Hlôks raced toward Aravan, and at the last moment, a black-shafted arrow hissing through the space where he had been, the Elf turned and ran and leapt up to the battlement and sprang outward into free space, the Alor plummeting toward the snow-laden slope of the killing ground below. Past Bair he plunged, the lad crying out in horror.

But from a blaze of platinum light, Valké emerged, black wings hammering across the whirling wind, the bird calling out—*Skree!* —and twisting up and away.

Now black-shafted arrows sissed past Bair, even as a Hlôk above chopped a tulwar down across the rope, shearing it in two, and Bair fell the last twenty feet, slamming into the snow, tumbling down the killing-ground slope.

As a portcullis rumbled upward and gates swung wide at the main bartizan of the fortress, Bair floundered to his feet, entangled in the rope. In a trice the lad won free of the line, and from shimmering black a Silver Wolf emerged.

Toward the outer wall Hunter raced, zigzagging, arrows *thunk*ing into the ground fore and aft, left and right. Up one of the foot ramps to the banquette he ran and leapt across the parapet to the snowy ground beyond.

Leftward he turned, Valké *skree*ing above, Silver Wolf and Black Falcon fleeing, a silver sword in a sling across the Draega's back, for, though it had no <fire>, the blade had not transformed.

And out from the fortress galloped a Ghûl on a Hèlsteed, Vulgs racing alongside, Rûcks and Hlôks in their wake. To the gate in the outer wall they sped, the Ghûl shouting in rage, Vulgs snarling and milling about. Rûcks flung the portal open, and out from the wall burst the pursuit, turning leftward after the transgressors, Vulgs racing ahead of the main body.

Angling northward fled the Draega, a dark tiercel in the churning black sky above. And as they crossed the bowl of the basin, the gates from the rear bartizan swung wide and, bugles blaring, out boiled more Foul Folk.

Now the fugitives came to the slopes of the icy range, and onto the slopes and upward fled the Draega, under the falcon in the sky.

And behind came the baying pursuit.

On they ran and on, clambering up sharp slopes, veering among crags, now and again running alongside bluffs too steep to climb directly. And all the while the roiling skies above blackly threatened to break.

Still onward they ran and up, dark dawn becoming dark day. And as the slant became steeper, the pursuers neared the pursued.

Deep snow cascading in its wake, up the mountain steeps lunged the Silver Wolf, the yawling pack of Vulgs baying after. The howling Ghûl on a gasping Hèlsteed surged up the slant aft of the pack, and struggling alongside the corpse-foe and his scaled steed, the yowling band of Rûcks and Hlôks clambered up the cant as well. Now black-shafted arrows flew upward, some aimed at the Silver Wolf, others aimed at the dark falcon crying in rage in the churning skies above, both arrows and falcon buffeted by the shrieking winds aloft as the boiling wall of the oncoming storm drew nigh, and a forerunning blast drove snow swirling up from the ground.

Pursuers and pursued, up the steeps they strove, Hunter now and again glancing at Valké above, yet pausing not in his lunging run, while behind came the howling foe. Of a sudden the Hèlsteed squealed and pitched backward down the slant, the scaled creature smashing atop the Ghûl, bones cracking under the crushing weight of the beast. Yet snarling out commands, with spear in hand the corpse-foe rose to his feet and took up the chase afoot, though the Hèlsteed did not as it lay in the snow, its head and neck twisted awry, its cloven hooves drumming a tattoo of death.

Now Valké called out a *skree!* and veered to the right, but Hunter did not change his course to follow. Again the falcon called out, but the 'Wolf plunged on upward, toward the stormy heights above. Calling out once more, the raptor stooped, folding his wings and plummeting toward the Silver Wolf below. Just as Valké unfurled his pinions—*thuck!*—a crossbow bolt pierced him through, and with a wracking cry he tumbled down through the air to fall to the snowy slopes.

Even as the Rûcks shouted in glee, and in spite of the howling pursuit, Hunter veered rightward to come to the felled bird. And gently, in mouth and gently, the 'Wolf took up the wounded falcon, careful not to disturb the piercing quarrel, and then the argent animal plunged onward, up the steepening slopes, snow flying out behind.

And still the Vulgs came after, the huge black Wolflike creatures now gaining on the silver foe.

Up they ran and up, up through the screaming wind, while the black skies above seemed to darken yet further. At last Hunter topped the slant to come onto a circular flat, and ahead and curving 'round to the sides towered the hard face of a sheer stone bluff, trapping the small plateau in its looming embrace, trapping the 'Wolf and the falcon as well.

Hunter moved forward and gently laid Valké to the soft snow, then with a low growl whirled 'round and padded back to the precipitous lip of the dead-ended, stone-held flat.

Downslope, the yawling rout of Vulgs and Rûcks and Hlôks and the Ghûl lunged upward, fangs bared, blades drawn, arrows and quarrels nocked, cruel barbed spear in hand, murder in their viperous eyes. In the distance beyond and barely glimpsed through the blowing white stood the massive black fortress, its ebon walls streaked with glazes of rime and long white runs of hoarfrost.

With another low growl Hunter turned his back to the oncoming peril and stepped toward wounded Valké, and in that moment the howling blizzard swept over all, hurtling stinging snow shrieking across the whole of the mountainside.

At last the Vulgs topped the steep slant, Rûcks and Hlôks and the Ghûl right behind. And in the howling wind and hammering snow slamming into the stone-walled trap, they searched the full reach of the flat, yet they found no blood, no tracks in the snow blowing in the wind, no sign of the trespassers whatsoever; the fugitives they sought had completely vanished, as if they had never been.

Chanting and stepping and grasping his stone ring in his left hand, while cradling the quarrel-pierced black falcon in his right, Bair emerged from the in-between to find himself in a blizzard, wind howling all about, the snow flying so thickly he could see but a handful of steps ahead.

"Oh, kelan," he murmured, "I don't know where we are, but I've got to get you to—"

"—va—!"

—*What was that?*

The wind howled.

I thought I—

"—an!"

There it is aga—

"—rava—!"

A voice crying out. A female.

But what she might be calling, Bair knew not, for her words were whipped away in the wind.

"Over here!" he shouted in desperation, his arms now shielding the quarrel-pierced bird from the shrieking wind.

And then came another call: "Arava—!" The wind shredded her cry, yet the lad now knew the name she called and who it was she sought.

Yelling, "Here!" Bair stumbled in the general direction whence he judged she had cried. "Here!"

"—ravan! Ara—!" she cried, closer still. And then—"Aravan!"—her voice came clear, and Bair saw a snow-obscured someone in the blow ahead, and moving toward her he called out again, "Here!"

Rushing toward him came the figure, crying, "Oh, Aravan, Aravan, my love, is it really—?" Her words juddered to a halt as from her cloak hood she looked up at Bair, her gold-flecked green eyes flaring wide.

"Nay, my lady, I am not Aravan, but this dying falcon is."

CHAPTER 39

Vadaria

December, 5E1009

[The Present]

With the wind howling and hurtling snow before it, buffeted by the blow, the lady looked from Bair to the quarrel-pierced falcon in disbelief. "What? What did you say?"

Above the shriek of the air Bair raised his voice to be heard. "I said this is Aravan, or rather will be when he shifts back, but if we don't get him to a healer and soon—"

"Oh, Adon, Adon, now I know why Branwen and Dalor are both needed." She looked about as if seeking others.

"My lady?"

"Come, quickly. We must—"

"Daughter?" came a call in the blow, and a figure loomed out of the storm, his cloak flying about.

"Father, over here!"

The newcomer, a dark-haired, green-eyed, young ma— No, not a man, but an Elf? —No, neither man nor Elf, but something in between: his eyes with a bit of a tilt, his ears somewhat pointed—

Mage. He's a Mage.

Bair looked again at the lady, seeing like features.

She is of Magekind, too.

"Father, quick, where is Dalor?" the lady demanded, her voice tight with distress.

The Mage gestured vaguely into the blizzard. "He is up here

somewhere stumbling about in this bloody blizzard, Daughter, as you instructed. —And who is this boy with the bird?"

"Father, we've got to find Dalor now."

The Mage frowned, but ere he could say aught— "Father, now!"

In that moment—"Halloo!"—came a call whipped about in the moan.

"Dalor, this way!" cried the female, clutching Bair's sleeve and tugging him toward the call . . .

. . . and stumbling through the blizzard toward them, his cloak clutched about and holding tightly to the brow of his hood to keep it from blowing back, came a short, portly young Mage.

"Dalor, Dalor," cried the lady, "this falcon, you must heal him, and quickly."

"What?" exclaimed Dalor, aghast. "You want me to heal a bird? Nonsense. I know nothing of birdkind."

"But this is my beloved Aravan."

"The boy?" asked Dalor, looking up at Bair looming above him.

"No, Dalor. The falcon is Aravan."

"The falcon? But I thought Aravan an Elf."

"Yes," growled Bair. "Aravan is an Elf, and this bird is Aravan, though most of his <fire> is held in the crystal."

Snow lashing, the three Mages looked at the crystal. "The boy is right," snapped the lady's father. "The <fire> of an Elf *is* caught in the lattice of that pendant."

The lady turned to the healer. "Oh, Dalor, hurry, ere the falcon bleeds to death."

Dalor blew out his breath in irritation. "I can stop the bleeding, but to truly heal the bird, Branwen is the one you want. She knows more of wild things." Dalor turned to Bair. "Put it down, boy, and step back."

Bair gently laid the falcon to the drifting white, and as Dalor knelt beside it he looked up at Bair and the Mage. "You two, shield me from this wind. Healing a bird is bad enough, but in conditions like this . . ." He then looked at the lady. "Aylis, kneel opposite and buffer some of this swirl."

As Dalor bent over Valké, of a sudden Bair realized what the healer had called the lady Mage. *Aylis? Aylis? Aravan's Aylis?*

"But you're dead!" exclaimed the lad even as Aylis dropped to her knees across from Dalor to shield the falcon from the whirling blow.

"What?" snapped Aylis's father.

"I was told Aylis had died on Rwn."

The Mage shook a finger. "Then she's the most lively dead person you're likely to see, boy."

"If she is Aylis—Aravan's Aylis—and she called you 'Father,' then you must be Alamar," said Bair.

"That's right."

"B-but, Aravan said you were white-haired and crotchety. Besides, you are too young to be her sire."

"Look, boy, I have <rested> since Aravan last saw me."

"Sanguinem nullo modo!" muttered Dalor.

"Crotchety, eh?" said Alamar. "He called me that? Crotchety?"

Bair nodded, not taking his fretful gaze from Valké.

"I don't believe I'm crotchety," grumbled Alamar. "Instead it's that I do not gladly suffer fools. No, not crotchety. Not crotchety at all. Do you hear me, boy. Not crotchety."

Dalor looked up at Bair. "All right, lad. Take him up. We've got to get to the cabin and Branwen, where he can be properly healed. And be careful of the quarrel, else he'll begin to bleed again."

Bair leaned down and gently took up Valké and, shielding the falcon in his arms, through the howling wind and hammering snow toward the lip of the flat he went, Bair following Alamar, Aylis at Bair's side, Dalor coming after. And down a long slope they clambered, a slope like the one Hunter had lunged up while fleeing the Rûpt on Neddra.

"Where did you come from, boy?" asked Alamar, the two standing before the hearth in the small, one-room mountain cabin, the chimney moaning in the wind.

"Um, from Neddra," replied Bair, not taking his eyes from the three across the room hovering about the table on which Valké lay—Aylis, Dalor, and Branwen, she a tall, dark-haired lady, another Mage.

"From Neddra? Now *that's* a bit of news. The only crossing

we know of is the one to Mithgar on Rwn, though for some reason we can't seem to get over. Is the white grove destroyed?"

Now Bair looked at Alamar. "Sir, the entire island is no more. Rwn itself is destroyed and— Oh, wait! The only in-between crossing on Rwn led to— Tell me, sir, is this Vadaria?"

"Vadaria? Of course," replied Alamar. "But Rwn destroyed? No wonder we could never . . . —How?"

"How what?"

"Rwn, boy, Rwn: how was it destroyed?"

Bair blew out a breath. "Aravan said it was Durlok who did so."

"The Grand Wedding," groaned Alamar. "In conjoinment we tried to stop him, but failed in the end." He glanced at Aylis then back to Bair. "The wave?"

Bair nodded.

"Damn his eyes!" spat Alamar, slamming the butt of a fist into palm. "He will answer to me when I reach Mithgar. Perhaps through Neddra, now that we know there is a crossing from Vadaria to there, and of course there are crossings from Neddra to Mithgar."

Bair shook his head. "Durlok is dead. Aravan killed him; with the crystal of Krystallopŷr, he slew Durlok in the altar chamber on the island in the Great Swirl. And as for crossing between the Planes, I'm afraid you can't. You haven't the blood to do so."

"Durlok is dead? Slain by Aravan? Done in by his own crystal? Well and good. Well and good. Though I was hoping to do him in the eye myself." Alamar frowned and looked at Bair. "And what's all this about not having 'the blood to do so'?"

Bair took a deep breath and blew it out between pursed lips. "Sir, there is much history for you to catch up on, in particular the Great War of the Ban and the Sunder—"

Dalor stepped to Alamar. "We've got the quarrel out, and Animist Branwen has done all she can for the nonce, but if we can't change the falcon back to an Elf, I'm afraid he will die."

As a strong gust outside shrieked by, "I know how to shift him," said Bair, striding across the room, Alamar following, the lad adding, "All we need do is call out his name—Aravan—and Valké will transform back. Here, we'll just put him on one of the cots and—"

Even as Bair reached for the falcon, Branwen asked, "Does Valké need to be conscious for the change to occur?"

"Um, I think so," said Bair, frowning as he took up the limp bird. "Else how can he know to change?"

"Then I'm afraid we are done for," said the Animist, "for Valké is deeply in shock and unaware."

"Here, let me," said Alamar. "Go ahead, boy, put him on the cot."

As Bair laid Valké on one of the cots and Alamar sat on the edge and examined the crystal amulet, Dalor said, "What is your name, lad? I mean, we can't keep calling you 'boy.' "

"Bair."

"Bear? As in the woods?"

Bair shook his head. "B-a-i-r, the name my Baeron sire and Elven dam gave me."

"Baeron sire? Elven dam? Can that even be?"

"Well, my sire is not exactly a Baeron. You see—"

"What do you know of this crystal?" snapped Alamar. "And how did Aravan's <fire> get within? Was it a curse?"

"No, Mage Alamar," said Bair. "We went to Dodona and—"

"Dodona? The Oracle in the Karoo?"

"Yes. He said it was necessary that we go to Jangdi, for there Aravan could learn to use the crystal. We didn't know then what it would do, but you can see the result." Bair gestured at Valké. "It lets Aravan become a falcon, and the falcon become Aravan. Just as I can become—"

"What do you know of the <power> of its working?"

Bair turned up a hand. "All I know is that the Guardian at the Temple in the Sky—"

"A monk?" fumed Alamar. "This is terrible! Monks use <wild magic>. I may never be able to transform Aravan back."

Again a strong gust screamed past, rattling the roof, whirling down the chimney, swirling the fire. Above the howl Bair said, "The Guardian is not a monk."

Alamar raised an eyebrow. "Not a monk? Then we may have a chance. What kind of Mage is he?"

"I don't think he's a Mage at all," replied Bair. "Just what he is, I know not, though he and Dodona are of a kind."

Air hissed in through Alamar's clenched teeth. "The Guardian is of a kind with Dodona? How know you this?"

"Why, I saw it. As silver <flames> they both are to my <sight>. Too, he said so."

Alamar groaned. "This is even worse than monks' <wild magic>. This is of a <power> we do not even begin to comprehend. What kind of fools were you to let—"

Bair glared at the Mage. "Haven't you been listening? Dodona said it was necessary."

Aylis pressed out a soothing hand. "He is right, Father. If Dodona said it was needed, then it was needed."

Alamar sighed. "Indeed, daughter. If Dodona said so, then it had to be done. Still, I am concerned with how to shift this falcon back to Aravan, and <power> of this sort is—"

"Ah," said Branwen. "I have it. The key is in the crystal itself, in the falcon therein. . . ." The look on her face was one of intense concentration, and under her breath she hissed, *"Reddere Aravan!"*

A flash of platinum light blazed up in the cabin and then was gone, and where the falcon had been now lay Aravan on his side, crimson spreading outward from his breast, Aylis gasping in distress.

"Quick, Dalor, ere he bleeds to death," snapped Branwen, even then reaching to undo the pack and gear and strip his clothes from him, all of which came with the transformation. "Aylis, Alamar, give him room to work."

Murmuring, "Beloved, oh my beloved. Don't die. Please don't die," Aylis stepped back against Bair, her fists gripped tightly in tension, her knuckles white, distraught tears standing in her eyes, tears which she sporadically blinked away. And she stood barely breathing as Dalor concentrated and muttered strange words over the unconscious, white-faced Elf.

And the blizzard battered at the small cabin as if to tear it apart to get to whatever prey might be inside.

Finally, Dalor looked up at the others, his own face drained, gaunt. "I think he may live, though he is wounded most sorely."

At those words, Aylis turned and leaned against Bair and began to softly weep. And the lad took her in his arms and held her as she cried, and the wind moaned and shrieked in accompaniment.

*   *   *

Branwen stood at the table cutting at a slab of yellow cheese, Bair chopping apples at her side, and at the cot where Aravan lay, Aylis spooned droplets of gwynthyme tea into the Elf, Aravan reflexively swallowing.

"I would have gotten it, you know," said Alamar.

"Gotten what?" asked Dalor, resting on a cot before the fire, sipping gwynthyme tea, the air redolent with the minty odor, mingled with the aromas of stew and cheese and apples and bread.

Alamar gestured toward the bed. "I would have discovered the key to transforming Aravan back. It was quite simple, after all." Alamar frowned at the gold bracelet on his left wrist, a bracelet set with a dull red stone.

Dalor shook his head. "Alamar, it was <wild magic> I think, the same as is imbued in that bangle of yours. And you've been trying to determine how it does what it does for more millennia than I care to mention. No, I think Branwen was needed here, just as Aylis foresaw, not only to treat a wounded falcon, but to look into the crystal and release the in-held <fire> to transform the bird from falcon to Elf."

Alamar glanced at the bracelet, then with a dismissive sniff he looked away, saying, "I'd rather not speak of it, if you don't mind."

Dalor grinned and they quietly lounged for a while, the crackling of the fire and the chop of Bair's knife and the slice of Branwen's all overwhelmed by the moan of the blizzard outside. Finally, Dalor called out, "I say, Bair, when did you and the falcon come to Vadaria?"

"Why, just a moment or three ere Aylis and I found one another," replied Bair.

"What!" exclaimed Alamar, craning about to face the lad. "That cannot be. The only time one can cross the in-between to Vadaria is during the noontide. And the only time to leave is in the candlemarks of mid of night."

Bair shrugged. "Nevertheless, that's when we came: at dawn."

"Nonsense, boy."

"Father," said Aylis. "His name is Bair, not Boy."

"Mayhap there is somewhat else at work here," said Branwen.

"Aye," agreed Dalor. "If the boy, er, if Bair said he came at dawn, then I believe it is so. Tell me, lad, how did you know where the crossing lay?"

"Oh, I didn't know. Hunter found it. Sensed it because of the ring."

"Hunter?" asked Alamar. "Who is Hunter."

"Well—" began Bair, but Branwen said, "Ring? What ring?"

"Why, this one," said Bair, fishing the stone ring out from under his collar. "It was a birthing gift."

"Who is Hunter?" repeated Alamar.

"A birthing gift?" asked Branwen. "May I see it?"

Bair leaned down so that Branwen could get a close look.

"Answer me, boy, who is this Hunter?"

"His real name is Hunter, the Seeker and Searcher Who is One of Us but Not of Us, a name given to him by the—"

"Alamar, come look at this," said Branwen. "It glimmers of <wild magic>."

"Eh?" Alamar levered himself up out of the chair and stalked to Branwen and Bair. He took the stone ring in hand, in the firelight the jet inset casting a dark gleam to the eye.

As Branwen took up the kettle of stew and began spooning it into bowls, Alamar frowned at the ring, and then glanced at the bracelet on his own wrist, then peered at the ring again. "Oh, it's <wild magic> all right, just like my bracelet and that falcon crystal." He looked up at Bair. "Who gave you this?"

"My dam said none knew who brought the ring at my birthing, though she did mention that foxes barked in the vale that eve."

"Foxes? Ha! Pysks. They may not have crafted the ring, but I'll wager they delivered it. <Wild magic> indeed." He frowned at the ring again. "What does it do?"

"It sort of, um, tingles when I come nigh an in-between crossing," said Bair. "That's why Hunter knew a crossing was near, though Valké tried to guide Hunter by a different path, and—"

"Just who is this Hunter?" Alamar demanded.

"Why, he's—"

"Oh, my," called Aylis. "Dalor, Aravan turned on his side. Is he all right?"

Dalor rolled out of his cot and stepped to Aravan and laid hands upon the Elf.

"He's not about to waken, is he?" asked Branwen, pausing in her spooning of stew.

"No, no," assured Dalor. "I set a sleep upon him. He won't awaken until I lift it. The falcon took a terrible shock. He was pierced deeply, with attendant great damage to muscle and lung and tissue. All of that carried over to Aravan and he will need much rest and care to recover from that terrible quarrel strike." Dalor then looked at Aylis. "But as to this, it is a natural turning he does, and we'll have to keep watch that he doesn't reopen the wound. If and when he turns back, I will lay on hands again. In any event be ready to give him some more gwynthyme tea, for although the quarrel was not poisoned, still it was quite foul, and gwynthyme will burn out the taint.

"I will waken him on the morrow, but only long enough to take sustenance—a hearty broth, I believe—and to relieve himself, then it's back to sleep. A week or two, and then we shall see whether or no he can take a more natural course."

"Time to eat," said Branwen, setting the cauldron back onto the fire iron to keep the stew warm.

As they took the meal, Alamar said, "Boy, you spoke of a deal of history we needed to catch up on."

Bair looked up from his bowl and said, "Oh, Mage Alamar, it would be better if we wait for Aravan to awaken. I only know what I've read and been told, but my kelan, he lived it."

"Kelan?" Aylis glanced from Bair to Aravan. "I did not know Aravan had kindred on Mithgar."

"He's not my real kelan—my real uncle—Lady Aylis. But he always thought of my dam as a sinja—a sister—and so as a kelan he has been to me, though not by blood. Ha! Certainly not by blood."

"What's all this about blood, boy?" asked Alamar. "This is the second time you've spoken of it as if it were somehow . . . special. And you said I hadn't the blood to cross to Neddra, nor to cross from there to Mithgar."

Branwen eyed Bair closely. "Is there aught you need to tell us about crossing the in-between?"

Bair sighed. "It would be better if Aravan told you, but this is what I know. You see, during the Great War of the Ban—"

Alamar frowned. "War of the Ban?"

Bair nodded. "Yes, you see, when Gyphon and his minions invaded Adonar—"

"Invaded Adonar!" gasped Branwen. "Gyphon?"

Bair threw up his hands. "I'll never get to tell you of the Sundering if you don't—"

"Sundering!" exclaimed Alamar.

"Father!" snapped Aylis, glaring at Alamar, then turning her scowl upon Branwen and Dalor as well. "Bair is right. Let us hold our questions until the end."

Silence fell and all eyes turned to Bair.

"Well, it was in the Second Era of Mithgar"—Alamar raised a finger to interrupt, but Aylis slapped it down—"that Modru and his Hordes swept out from Gron in an attempt to throw down the High King, and . . ."

Aylis sighed. "So, without the blood, we cannot cross the in-between."

Bair nodded.

"Then how is it that you and Aravan were able to cross over?" snapped Alamar.

Bair took a deep breath. "That's another long story, Mage Alamar, but it must wait, for I am most weary; within the last day, Aravan and I invaded a black fortress, were stunned by Trolls and clinched in fetters, faced a dreadful foe, escaped, recovered the Silver Sword, fled the fortress ahead of howling pursuit, scrambled up mountains, where Valké was wounded, crossed the in-between in a blizzard, and came here. And I need sleep, for I am weary."

"But—" began Alamar, yet Aylis interrupted, saying, "No buts, Father. He needs rest."

Moments after lying down on a too-short cot, Bair was fast asleep.

The blizzard blew itself out sometime in the night, as Aylis spooned tiny sips of gwynthyme tea into Aravan.

Just after dawn the next day, Bair stepped outside the cabin and into the new-fallen snow. Alamar followed, calling out, "You never did answer my question, boy: just how did you and Aravan cross over?"

"I'll answer that when I get back, Mage Alamar. Hunter needs to bring down some game, for there is a broth to make and many mouths to feed."

"You never did answer that question of mine either: just who is this Hunter?"

"He is the Draega I become when I shift shape."

"A shapeshifter?" Alamar's eyes widened in surprise, and he glanced back at the cabin where Aravan yet lay. "You are a shapeshifter?"

Bair nodded. "A talent I inherited from my sire, though when he shifts he becomes a Bear."

"Hmm, they say that the Baeron have shapeshifters among them; your sire is one of these?"

"Aye."

"And he is the one you said is not exactly a Baeron?"

"Aye."

"Huah. But he a Bear and you a Draega? There is a tale here for the telling."

Bair shrugged. "Not much of one: you see, when Dalavar came to Arden Vale and—"

"Dalavar Wolfmage?" blurted Alamar. "From the Wolfwood near the Skög?"

"So they tell me."

"What was he doing in Arden Vale?"

Bair let out a sigh of exasperation. "Look, Mage Alamar, I've said it before, and I'll say it again: if you keep interrupting, I'll never be able to answer even one question, much less a barrage. Let us wait until this eve, and I'll tell the tale to all who wish to hear it. Besides, Dalor is to awaken Aravan today, and I want fresh meat for the broth, if not for today, then for tomorrow. And when Aravan recovers enough and is able, he will tell you all that has gone on in Mithgar in the—what?—seven thousand years since you've been absent?"

"Seven thousand two hundred twenty-eight years six months and a day, to be more precise," growled Alamar.

"All right. Seven thousand two hundred twenty-eight years

and a half dozen months and a day. But now I've got to hunt; we need meat for the broth and our table."

From a darkness Hunter sprang forth and loped down the slope for the valley below, leaving Alamar behind, the Mage shaking his head in wonder at the lingering trace <fire>, a small vanishing twist of <wild magic> swirling in the air.

Aravan opened his sapphire-blue eyes and looked straight into the gold-flecked green eyes of Aylis. And when he saw her, as of a barricade falling, a chill wall 'round his heart shattered and fell away, the warmth within blossoming to fill his entire being.

And he reached for her.

In spite of his wound he embraced her and whispered, "*Chieran. Avó, chieran.* My heart was dead but now it lives again. I will love thee forever."

And they gently held each other, and wept.

CHAPTER 40

Recountings

December, 5E1009–January, 5E1010

[The Present]

Hunter dropped the stag at the door of the cabin, and as Bair entered the one-room mountain hut, Aravan sat propped up in his cot, Aylis sitting at hand with a bowl of broth and a spoon. Branwen stood at the hearth pouring a cup of hot water over a shredded leaf of gwynthyme, making tea. Alamar and Dalor sat at the table engaged in some kind of game on a six-sided board scribed with black and white hexagons, red and green coin-shaped pieces scattered thereon, other, taller, carven shapes ranged 'round the edges ready to assault the center.

"I thought thee dead, chier," Aravan whispered.

"I thought me dead, too," replied Aylis, tears standing in her eyes, and she turned aside to wipe them away. Seeing the lad, she said, "Hello, Bair. Any luck?"

"Hunter brought down a stag," replied Bair. Then he looked at Aravan. "You're looking better, kelan."

"I feel rather wretched, elar," whispered Aravan, "but I ween 'tis better than being dead." A weak smile spread across his face even as Aylis's visage turned pale.

Bair also smiled, his eyes glistening. Then he said to Aylis, "Did I hear you say that you thought you dead? How so?"

Aylis took up another spoonful of broth and held it to Aravan's lips; Aravan reached for the spoon yet winced from the slight movement. He let his hand fall back to his side and allowed Aylis to feed him. After sipping the broth, he murmured, "Yes, chier, I too would know what happened."

Aylis sighed, her thoughts turning inward. "The crossing from Rwn to Vadaria is a— rather, was a particularly difficult one. When Durlok's spell succeeded, we broke the conjoinment and started the rite to make the passage. I bore father in my arms, for he foolishly had spent all but a flicker of his <fire> to—"

"To do my part in doing Durlok in the eye," said Alamar, looking up from the hexagonal, black-and-white board.

"Do him in the eye or no, it was foolish, Father."

"Bah!" said Alamar, returning to the game.

Aravan took another sip of broth from Aylis and then whispered, "Go on."

"There's not much else to tell, for even as that monstrous wave rose up to smash all, forerunning water even then rushing onto Rwn, that was when I crossed over, Father within a heartbeat of being dead, his <fire> so low that I could take him with me."

"It was a <flame> so feeble a candle were a thousand times brighter," said Dalor.

"Yes, yes," said Alamar, "tell me again how foolish I was." He moved a piece and smirked at Dalor. "Storm deflects eagle."

"Father, you would have died had not Dalor been at hand. He gave of his own <fire> to save you."

"Bah," said Alamar, "and bah again."

"Crotchety," said Bair.

"What's that, boy?" said Alamar, looking up from the board.

"I said, it seems you are yet the Wizard my kelan knew, in spite of your youthful look."

"Now see here, boy—"

"Tokko!" crowed Dalor. "Rock smashes throne."

"What?" Alamar swung his gaze back to the board, then looked accusingly at Bair.

"I've a stag to dress out," said Bair.

As the lad shut the door behind, he heard Aylis laughing gaily, Branwen chuckling, and Aravan coughing lightly.

Every day for the next two weeks, Dalor spent a bit of <fire> on Aravan, knitting tissue, repairing nicked bone, mending torn muscle, regenerating pierced nerves and the like. Too, every day, he awakened Aravan to take food and relieve himself, allowing the Elf longer and longer periods of wakefulness. At the end of the first week Aravan began feeding himself, and at the end of the second, he was taking solid food at the table.

It was during this second week that Year's Start Day did come: the first day of January in the One Thousand and Tenth Year of the Fifth Era of Mithgar. And though they were on Vadaria instead, where the count was altogether different; even so, the year did start there as well. And on that day did Dalor allow Aravan to begin telling the Mages the full story of what had passed since the destruction of Rwn: the death of Durlok in his crystal cavern; the Great War of the Ban; the loss of the Dawn Sword; the Battle of Hèl's Crucible; the slaying of Sleeth and the story of Elyn and Thork; the War of the Usurper; the Purging of Drearwood; the Winter War; the War of Kraggen-cor; the millennia spent in futile pursuit of Ydral and the successful pursuit of his son Baron Stoke; all those as well as many events in between, some of which Bair did not know, and all of which were news to the Mages.

And during the tellings, often did Aylis and Branwen gasp in distress at what had befallen Mithgar and the folk therein. Dalor took the news without comment, though occasionally did tears come in his eyes. As for Alamar, he cursed Modru and Andrak and Gnar and the Emir of Nizari and Stoke and Ydral as well as Durlok, even though most were long dead, Ydral the only one yet alive.

When Aravan spoke of the Sundering of the Planes, and of Rael's Rede of the Dawn Rider, and of Faeril's crystal-induced prophecy, then did Bair tell of his ancestry, and of the blood flowing in his veins. And then did the Mages look upon Bair with new eyes, for he was not just *any* lad, but one foreordained by Fate.

Shifting uncomfortably under their scrutiny, Bair said, "Look, Dawn Rider or no, I haven't done aught special."

"You've recovered the Silver Sword," said Branwen softly, glancing at the blade in its scabbard leaning against a wall. "You and Aravan."

"And you've gone between Planes," added Dalor.

"It's my blood which allows such," said Bair.

"Even so," said Alamar, "that does not explain how you came to Vadaria in the dawn instead of the noontide."

"Mayhap it's the ring," said Branwen. "Or rather the <wild magic> therein. Mayhap it lets the lad cross over in times otherwise disallowed." She looked at Bair.

Bair shrugged. "I've only crossed four times altogether: from Mithgar to Adonar and back, going on the dusk, returning on the dawn; then we crossed from Mithgar to Neddra, in the candlemarks of midnight; lastly we crossed from Neddra to Vadaria, and that was in the dawntime."

"All in times appointed, but for the last," said Branwen.

"During these crossings, what do you do with the ring?" asked Alamar.

"Why, I grip it. It seems the right thing to do."

"I think the ring is the key," said Branwen.

"So do I," agreed Dalor.

"I give up," said Alamar. "Ring or not, he crossed into Vadaria at a twixt time. As the boy said, it could be his blood—Demon, Spawn, Mage, Baeron, Elven—and whatever else might be."

"Whatever else might be, Father?" snapped Aylis. "Speak not ill of Bair's heritage."

Alamar threw up his hands.

In the third week, Dalor declared Aravan fit enough to begin sleeping on his own, the spells of slumber no longer needed, saying that within three weeks he would be reasonably well.

"Five weeks and no sooner since Valké was wounded?" groaned Bair.

"Lad," said Dalor, "ordinarily it would take months for even the healthiest to recover from such a wound; indeed, some would never recover, assuming they lived at all. Be grateful that I was nearby to aid your kelan in his time of need."

"Oh, I am grateful, Healer Dalor, it's just that the yellow-eyed man's trail grows ever cold."

"Yellow-eyed man?"

"Ydral," replied Bair. "And, I say, now that I think of it, just how did you and Lady Aylis and Mage Alamar all happen to be in the blizzard at that spot on the mountain in the first place."

Although Bair thought Alamar was adoze in front of the fire, the Mage snorted. "Boy," said Alamar, "did not Aravan tell you that Aylis is a Seer?"

"Umn, yes, that he did," answered Bair, then waited, but Alamar said no more.

"She saw it," said Dalor. "In a Seer's casting. Saw that Aravan and three others would be in that place at that time and one would be wounded. A Healer would be needed, or an Animist, or both, Aylis wasn't certain. And so she asked Branwen and me to come to the mountain with her."

"Three others?" said Bair. "But there was just me."

"What about Valké and Hunter?" asked Branwen. "If I've counted right, with you and Aravan that adds up to four."

It was in the middle of the third week of Aravan's recovery that Aylis came to her father and the others to ask that they take some time away from the cabin, so that she and Aravan could—

"I wondered when you would get around to that, Daughter," said Alamar, smiling.

"Father, we just want some privacy," declared Aylis, though her lightly freckled cheeks did redden.

Dalor raised a finger toward Aylis. "Mind you now, nothing rambunctious." And Aylis reddened even more.

"Well, I need to search for some pine nuts," said Branwen.

"And I need to, um, help you," said Dalor.

"Well, I could hunt, or rather Hunter could," said Bair, a puzzled look on his face. "But I don't see why we need—"

"Boy, are you as dense as a rock?" snapped Alamar. Then he leaned over and whispered, "Canoodling."

Bair frowned and looked at Aylis, gone completely red, and Aravan, who was shaking his head and grinning. A look of sudden enlightenment swept across Bair's face. "Oh. Right. Hunter will hunt."

And they scrambled for cloaks and boots and winter garments, and dutifully marched out the door, Alamar whistling an improvised ditty, Bair looking everywhere but at the two staying behind. . . .

. . . And when they were alone, Aylis and Aravan made sweet and gentle love.

*   *   *

The end of the fourth week came, with Aravan afoot. And, as he and Aylis took air outside, Aravan turned to Aylis and took her in his arms. As he held her tightly, he whispered, "Chier, we have no choice; Bair and I must go, else Mithgar and all creation may fall."

"I know," said Aylis, her tears bitter. "And if I could, I would go with you, but I cannot. Even so, you must come back to me."

In answer he held her even tighter.

When told that Aravan and Bair would be leaving, Dalor cautioned that another week or two were needed ere Aravan would be fit.

It was at that time Alamar took up the Silver Sword and said, "This is it, eh? Lost and found again. The token of power said to be Gyphon's bane."

Bair nodded. "I once told my kelan the mission Dodona set us on seems filled with tokens of power."

Alamar looked up from the sword and said, "How so?"

"Well, there's my ring and the falcon crystal and Aravan's amulet, of course. Then there's the Silver Sword . . . oh, and Krystallopŷr. And then there's the Kammerl—"

"Krystallopŷr," said Aylis. "This is the crystal Durlok used to destroy Rwn." She turned to Aravan. "This is the crystal made into the blade of the spear you told us of . . . the one you bear, which steals the <fire> from those it pierces?"

Aravan turned up his hands. "All I know is that when Truenamed it burns through the foe. As for stealing <fire>, that I cannot say."

"Oh, it has plenty of <fire> all right," said Bair. "An extraordinary amount. Fairly bursting with <fire>, in fact."

Alamar frowned at the lad. "How know you this?"

"I have <seen> it," said Bair.

"The <sight> a gift of his Mage blood," said Dalor, standing at the window, watching Branwen outside stripping pine nuts from cones. Then he turned to Aravan. "Perhaps the <fire> comes from the foes you have slain."

"In all the wars and skirmishes and encounters with evil, I have slain many," said Aravan.

Aylis sighed. "Bursting with <fire>."

Bair cocked an eyebrow. "I say, could that be why Ydral took it, trembling with excitement as he was, because of the <fire> it holds?"

Alamar thrust out a hand. "Trembling with excitement? Hold on, boy. As of yet, neither you nor Aravan has told me the full of what passed in that black fortress, and this sounds ominous. What did he say when he took the spear?"

Bair looked to Aravan, and the Elf said, "That with it he would rule the world. How this may come to pass, I cannot say, yet we fear something dreadful is drawing nigh, just as Dodona has said. Hence I deem it urgent we return to Mithgar—Bair and I—and find Ydral ere he can wreak whatever havoc he has in mind."

Alamar stared intently into Aravan's face. "Just what is the makeup of this spear you bear? Or rather did bear, before Ydral stole it."

"As I told thee, after the destruction of Rwn and the death of Durlok in the crystal cavern on the isle in the Great Swirl, we sailed to the western continent, and there the Truenamed spear was given to me by Tarquin, the Fox Rider you met, Alamar. It was forged by a Hidden One named Drix; what kind of Hidden One he may be, I cannot say, for he was too shy to appear, too shy to give me the spear himself."

"So far you have only told me that its blade was the crystal Durlok wielded, the one which slew him in the end. Poetic justice that. But what else went into its forging?"

Aravan turned up a hand. "The crystal itself is bonded by starsilver to a black helve; the helve itself is the staff that Durlok bore."

"Staff?" shouted Alamar, leaping to his feet and raging across the cabin. "Durlok's staff? Starsilver-bound to the crystal? Those bloody, bloody fools!"

"What is it, Father?" asked Aylis, apprehension on her face.

Alarmed, Branwen came running into the cabin, a pinecone in hand. "What—?"

"Fools!" spat Alamar once more, then groaned. "Those bloody, hedge-Wizard, <wild magic> fools. They didn't know what they were doing, and now the Trine draws near."

CHAPTER 41

Dendor

January, 5E1010

[*The Present*]

The general, his forehead pressed to the floor, did not look up at Kutsen Yong. "O Mighty Dragon, armed and armored they stand atop the walls, fire and rock, oil and arrow, spear and quarrel, bar and blade at the ready. They refuse to surrender."

"They defy me?" Kutsen Yong rose up in fury. "This affront shall not be borne, for I am the Masula Yongsa Wang."

"Aye, my lord," replied the general. "When you release the Dragons upon them, they will sorely regret their insolen—"

"Silence!" shouted Kutsen Yong.

Trembling, wondering what he had said that could possibly have upset his liege, the general clamped his lips tightly.

"You presume to advise me as to how to teach these Western fools a lesson?"

"No, my lor—"

"I said silence!"

As Kutsen Yong seethed in rage, the general began to sweat, for he knew of the capricious will of the Master of Dragons.

Kutsen Yong stepped down from his golden throne and stood above the commander. "This you shall do, *Chi'hwi'gwan*: with but fifty thousand men you will conquer the defiant city."

"Fifty thou—?"

Now Kutsen Yong knelt at the general's side. "And you shall lead them in every assault. If you do not do so willingly, then you shall do so on a pike."

"But, my lord, the Drago—"

Kutsen Yong leaned down and hissed, "You dare to question me?"

The general trembled and remained silent.

Kutsen Yong stood. "Go now, and do not come back until the city lies in ruins."

As the general crawled backward from the throne chamber of the rolling golden palace, Kutsen Yong regained his ornate chair of state.

And he sat and fumed.

Every city in the West had defied him. Every small town and hamlet had been abandoned, and everything of worth taken away: all valuables, all food, all men, all women, all children gone, nothing but scorched earth left in their wake. And now this city defied him as well.

Fools! Western fools! I will show them what it means to oppose me. Ydral will be in blood up to his elbows, should any survive my Golden Horde. And the plague rats will deal with any who manage to escape him.

"Ydral!" he called.

There was no answer.

"Ydral!" shouted Kutsen Yong again.

Still there was no answer.

"Attend me!" he commanded.

The Prime Mandarin rushed forward and cast himself face-down to the floor.

"Where is Ydral?" demanded Kutsen Yong.

"O Mighty Dragon, he is not back from consecrating the temple."

"Not back? But it was weeks past I sent him."

"My lord, just today his guard returned without him," replied the mandarin.

"What?"

"O Mighty One, they say he became a hideous winged thing and flew away, a silver beast in pursuit."

"A hideous winged thing?"

"Yes, O Masula Yongsa Wang, so they did say. Perhaps a thing such as that which is said to have been in the dark of the sky on the night of your birth."

"Send Ydral's guard captain to me," commanded Kutsen Yong, and as the mandarin scuttled back and away, Kutsen Yong reached out a hand and stroked the Dragonstone. . . .

On a distant tor, Ebonskaith shuddered.

Within a candlemark, his great leathery wings churning, Ebonskaith landed alongside the palace, the mighty Drake sending clouds of snow roiling into the air. Red oxen bellowed in fear, and Ebonskaith's long tongue licked out as if to catch a tasty scent on the air. Taking care to not look at the Dragonstone itself, Ebonskaith then turned his ophidian gaze upon the unworthy being who held him in thrall, the unfit creature even then clasping the stone holding captive the soul of the Dragon-King. A pace or two behind the 'Stone-wielder a man in armor stood, the scent of his fear strong on the air.

"I would have Dragons find Ydral and bring him to me," said the worthless ruler of all Dragonkind.

His voice sounding like great, rough bronze slabs dragging one upon the other, Ebonskaith asked, "Ydral?"

"The one who stood with me at the great summoning."

"Ah, the mongrel," replied Ebonskaith. "The yellow-eyed mongrel who rode away with his trifling guard."

Kutsen Yong smiled at this Dragon's naming of Ydral. "No matter what you call him, I would have him brought to me."

"I take it he is missing," said Ebonskaith.

Kutsen Yong gestured at the armored man, "Captain."

Perspiring, the captain said, "During the consecration of the pavilion, he changed into a flying creature and fled, a huge silver beast running after."

"Describe these things," said Ebonskaith.

"Leathery wings had the creature, though they did not match even a fifth of the span of yours," replied the captain. "Too, it had long neck and a fang-filled beak. More than that I did not see. As to the silver beast pursuing, like a Wolf it was, but much larger, perhaps the size of a pony."

"Ah," said Ebonskaith.

"You know this creature and beast?" asked Kutsen Yong.

"Perhaps," replied the Drake.

"Regardless," said Kutsen Yong, "I would have Dragons return Ydral to me here at my rolling palace. Not you, O Dragon of mine, but some of those under your dominion."

"It will take but one," said Ebonskaith.

"One?"

"Raudhrskal will go, for he has had dealings with Fell Beasts and knows their scent and manner."

"Fell Beasts?"

"Creatures like that which your yellow-eyed mongrel became," replied Ebonskaith. The Drake turned to the captain. "Where is this pavilion?"

"In a village called Inge, at the foot of the slopes of the mountains in the north, near a mighty swamp."

"I know the place. I will send Raudhrskal after."

Atop the walls of the city of Dendor, King Dulon stood with his men and watched as the black Dragon soared upward. "Arbalesters, stand ready," ordered the king, even though he knew not whether spears from the mighty engines could pierce Dragonhide.

Yet the Drake flew southeast and away.

With a sigh of relief, King Dulon ordered the arbalesters to stand down. Yet the king did not take his ease for, though the Dragon was gone, there remained a vast army ranged all about the city walls: a half million men, or so they had estimated, many times greater than the last army that had besieged Dendor—a Horde of Spawn during the Great War of the Ban. In that long-ago time with the help of Kachar the city had prevailed; but that was in the past, and here in the days to come his men could not possibly stand against the mighty force now beringing the walls, yet Dulon had pledged to the High King to hold out as long as he could.

Candlemarks passed, and candlemarks more, and then from the bartizan at the south gate there came a bugle cry, and even as Dulon and his men ran to answer the summons, he could see a contingent of the enemy rushing forward with scaling ladders to assault the walls.

"Loose the oil!" cried the king. "Ready the torches!" And bugles rang out the command.

Yet the main force of the foe stood fast, and nought but a

minor portion came—if fifty thousand strong can be said to be but a minor portion. On they came and on, shouting out strange battle cries, the fearsome force running no faster than the middle-aged man in the lead.

CHAPTER 42

Grotto

January, 5E1010

[The Present]

They are late.

Greylight looked up at Dalavar, the Mage pacing back and forth.

"They are late, Greylight," growled Dalavar, peering across the wide, grassy plains of Valon.

The Draega gained his feet and looked about, raising his nose in the air. Seeing nought, sensing nought, the great Silver Wolf shook himself, and then padded to the nearby thicket and cocked a leg; the remaining five Draega followed after and marked the thicket as well.

"Something is amiss," said Dalavar, when the pack gathered about him. "They should have been back by now."

The Mage fell into thought, and finally he said, "Perhaps we can go before them and prepare the way." He then spoke to Shimmer, using <words> arcane, and she canted her head to one side and listened attentively. And then she sped away northerly, as Dalavar watched her go. And then from a darkness, Shifter sprang forth and ran south, Greylight running at his side, Beam and Longshank loping after, Seeker and Trace running wide on the flanks.

And across the South Reach they sped.

A day they ran and then another, and in the setting of the sun they came to the fringes of a great encampment—warriors and horses, wagons and tents—but the 'Wolves did neither stop nor tarry. Across the wide grounds of the bivouac they loped, now passing among an enclave of gathered Wizards, eleven hundred or so. And when the Draega trotted past a particular pair, "Oh, my," said a female Mage, and the male at her side sneered, "Pah!" But the 'Wolves sped on.

At last in the deepening twilight they came to the banks of a great, wide river: it was the mighty Argon, and from the shadows of a small grove, Dalavar stepped forth. He led the Draega down to the ferry standing at the dock on the west bank, and there he arranged for a crossing.

The ferrymen were sore afraid when the great argent beasts came aboard, and in grim-lipped silence the men hauled for the opposite bank. And they were glad when the 'Wolves stepped ashore to vanish into the darkness beyond, one ferryman exclaiming, "He changed, he did, I saw it. The Mage became a great black beast, running with the others." And none of his ferry mates gainsaid even one of his words.

On they loped, faring southward and slightly west, stopping each night to rest in groves and swales. And in midafternoon of the third day beyond the ferry they came to the waters of Thell Cove. Along the shingle they ran, to come to the walls of a high bluff, great, frozen ripples in the stark stone, moss dangling down like concealing drapery cascading from above.

Padding now along a narrow ledge hidden beneath lapping water, deeps falling away to the right, they came to a ruffle in the stone, and here Shifter angled leftward to pass through a mossy curtain and into a hidden grotto beyond.

And there in the dim light of the sun shining blue through the pellucid water, riding at a stone mooring, a three-masted, silver-bottomed, blue-hulled Elvenship lay.

CHAPTER 43

Raudhrskal

January, 5E1010

[*The Present*]

In the cold mountain fastness of Garia, Ebonskaith settled onto a high icy peak, dark granite falling sheer below. Opposite, on a like peak sat the master of this domain—Raudhrskal—the rust-red Dragon furious that another Drake would invade his place of sovereignty, a fury further inflamed when Ebonskaith told why he had had the audacity to encroach on Raudhrskal's realm—

"He would what?" hissed Raudhrskal.

"Have you find the yellow-eyed mongrel Ydral," replied Ebonskaith.

Flames blasting from his throat, Raudhrskal roared in rage, the Skarpal Mountains ringing with long-lasting echoes of his furious wrath. And then he bellowed, "Am I his lapdog to go chasing after a thrown stick?"

"You cannot defy him, for he holds the 'Stone," said Ebonskaith, adding, "just as you cannot defy me."

Now the reddish-brown Drake turned his flat, scaly head toward raven-dark Ebonskaith, and yellow gaze locked upon yellow gaze. "At the time of the next mating, we shall see just who is the greater here," hissed Raudhrskal.

"If there is a next mating," said Ebonskaith, neither roaring nor breaking gaze.

It was Raudhrskal who looked away first.

"We must find a way to sunder the hold of the despicable god-made stone," said Ebonskaith.

Raudhrskal hissed agreement.

"Yet until we manage to do so," added the dark Drake, his tongue flicking out and back, "you are to follow the taste of the mongrel and deliver him to the rolling palace."

"You say the yellow-eyed mongrel is now a Fell Beast," said Raudhrskal, his words a statement and not a question. "I have had dealings with Fell Beasts ere now. They did not survive."

A small flame licked out from Ebonskaith's mouth. "Oh, the unworthy 'Stone-wielder did not ordain that the mongrel need survive."

CHAPTER 44

Leave-taking

January, 5E1010

[The Present]

Alamar slammed a fist down to the table. "Fools! Didn't they know the Trine was coming?"

"Father," said Aylis softly, "what has the Trine to do with aught?"

"Everything, Daughter, everything. You saw the runes in the crystal chamber. You heard what I said."

Aylis frowned, remembering that dreadful cavern and her father's words:

"Ha! None of these runes is now empowered, though they have been in the past."

"What do they do, Father?"

"Well, my best guess is that they let Durlok talk to Gyphon . . ."

"I remember," said Aylis. "You said the runes let Durlok speak with Gyphon. Yet I don't understand why that is so importan—"

"Runes?" asked Bair. "What runes?"

"The runes of <power> on the crystal floor," said Alamar.

Bair frowned, trying to catch an elusive thought. "Crystal floor?"

"Durlok's stronghold," snapped Alamar.

"Within the isle in the Great Swirl," said Aravan. Then he turned to Alamar. "What have the runes to do with Ydral taking my spear?"

"Don't you see?" Alamar looked at Aravan and then Aylis and then at Bair and Dalor and Branwen.

They stared back at him blankly.

"Tcha!" exclaimed Alamar in irritation. "The runes are empowered by the staff. Now Ydral will use it to do the same, and he will—"

Aylis shook her head. "But Father, how did he recognize it as Durlok's staff in the first place? And how would he know of its powers?"

Alamar threw up his hands. "How would I know, Daughter? You're the Seer, not I. Perhaps he once was Durlok's boon companion. Perhaps he and Durlok took a long voyage on Durlok's black galley, whiling away the time trading secrets. The important fact here is not *how* he knew of the staff, but rather *what* he'll do with it . . . and mark my word, he'll use it to free Gyphon."

Branwen drew in a sharp breath as Dalor glanced at Aravan and raised a hand in objection and said, "But Alamar, from what we've been told, after the War of the Ban, Gyphon was cast into the Great Abyss."

Branwen nodded in agreement and added, "He is trapped."

"Bah!" snorted Alamar. "The Trine is coming, and driven by Krystallopŷr—"

"Driven by what?" blurted Bair.

"Krystallopŷr, boy, Krystallopŷr. 'Fairly bursting with <fire>,' you said. The crystal itself is filled with <power>"—Alamar turned to Aravan—"from all those Rûcks and Hlôks and Trolls and Ghûls and other folk and creatures you killed with that blade. Sucked the <fire> right out of them, the crystal did. And since those hedge-Wizard fools didn't tell you how to safely discharge it, well, it's been storing up <power> for millennia, perhaps as much <power> as it held seven thousand years past when Durlok used it to destroy Rwn."

"But, Father," objected Aylis, "Ydral would need to know the truename of the staff to invoke the runes. And since he isn't a Seer—"

"Pah!" said Alamar. "Durlok himself would have protected the staff's truename from a Seer, just as he blocked you long past."

"Then how—?"

"You can't hide a truename from the dead, Daughter, and as we have heard, Ydral is a Necromancer."

"How do you know this?" asked Dalor.

"Why, the boy himself told us that Ydral was speaking to a corpse even as Hunter first sighted him," said Alamar, "and Aravan said that Stoke named his father Ydral a Necromancer."

"Like sire like son," murmured Aravan. "Ydral and Stoke both."

"Even so," said Branwen, "what has this to do with Gyphon?"

Impatiently, and in a condescending voice as if pitched to a slow student, Alamar said, "The Trine is coming, when the Planes will be in congruency—"

"That's what the Trine is?" said Bair, interrupting. "A congruency of the three Planes?"

"It's misnamed," said Dalor. "It is really the alignment of all the Planes, not just the principal three."

"Misnamed or not," said Branwen, "I would still like to know what this has to do with Gyphon."

Alamar glared at Bair. "If this young pup will just stop interrupting—"

"Father!" snapped Aylis. "Just tell us."

"Don't you see, Daughter? When the Planes are in alignment, the barriers between are lessened, and this includes the barrier to the Great Abyss. Ydral will go to the crystal cavern and invoke the staff and empower the runes and open the way, and given there is enough <fire> in the crystal, the barrier will fall and Gyphon will step across and be free."

"Oh, Adon," breathed Branwen. "If He is free upon Mithgar . . ."

"Then He will rule all of creation," said Dalor.

Bair slumped in a chair and groaned, "That's what Dodona meant."

"What's that, boy?" asked Alamar.

His face now drained of blood, Bair looked up at the Mage and said, "Dodona told Aravan and me that we were the last hope of the world and also perhaps its doom. 'Hope and doom both?' I asked. He merely nodded, but would explain no more. Little did we know that by carrying Krystallopŷr into the black fortress we were bringing the doom of the world with us."

"And all caused by those hedge-Wizard fools," gritted Alamar, "who starsilver-bound a crystal of <power> to Durlok's very own staff. Idiots!"

Aylis shook her head. "Father, blame not the Hidden Ones,

for when they fashioned the spear it was some seven thousand years ago, millennia past the previous Trine, long before the next. And it was long before the Great War of the Ban as well, hence they could not know that Gyphon would be banished to the Great Abyss. And as to the Trine itself, it held little interest to any but Wizardly scholars of the obscure and arcane, such as you yourself are, for then the ways between the Planes were open to any and all, and whether or no the barriers between were weakened, it mattered not. And so, the Hidden Ones could not have foreseen what the forging of the spear would bring."

"Pah, Daughter—" began Alamar—

—but Branwen said, "If it were so easy in foresight to see such, Mage Alamar, then why did you not see it yourself and warn against such in the future? No, Alamar, this time only in hindsight can you see with such clarity."

Alamar threw up his hands. "Hindsight, foresight, it matters not, if he's not stopped—"

"How can we stop him?" asked Bair.

"Retrieve the spear or destroy Ydral or destroy the runes ere he can summon the Great Evil," replied Alamar, "for if such is not done, then Ydral will use the staff to open the Trine-weakened way, and he will channel the power of the crystal through the starsilver binding and into the staff itself to lower the barrier and set Gyphon free."

Aravan, who had said little, now asked, "When comes this congruency, this Trine?"

"Just over two months from now," replied Alamar, "on Springday."

"When all things are in balance," murmured Aylis.

"And the barriers will be weakest at the exact moment of equipoise," said Alamar.

"At the meridian and lat of the isle of the crystal cavern, that will be eight candlemarks ere sunset," said Aravan, none questioning his words, for the gift of Elves is to know at all times where stands the sun and moon and stars. And then he stood and began gathering together his gear, saying, "Come, Bair, we must stop Ydral."

"But you aren't yet completely healed," protested Dalor, even as Bair scrambled to his feet and began repacking. "You've at least a sevenday or so before you can—"

"We have no choice," said Aravan, turning from Dalor the Healer to Aylis, her face gone deathly white, "for the time is short and our choices few and the distance to the Great Swirl is far, assuming we can return to Mithgar and quickly reach the *Eroean*."

"The *Eroean*?" asked Branwen.

"My ship," said Aravan. "None is swifter."

"But you'll need a crew," said Alamar. "Where will you round up one in time?"

"The only place where I might find the experienced mariners I need," said Aravan, "is upon Arbalin Isle. There I will go and take on a crew and thence unto Thell Cove where the *Eroean* lies."

Bair paused in his packing. "Alamar, is the island in the Great Swirl the only place where Ydral can summon Gyphon?"

Alamar frowned, then said, "It's the only place I know."

"There is one other," said Aravan, "a half a world away from the Swirl: Modru's Iron Tower in Gron."

Alamar snapped his fingers. "That's right. You told us. Modru: he nearly summoned Gyphon to the tower during the Winter War. But wait. Only in the crystal cavern will Durlok's staff be of use."

"Then we shall gamble that he will go there rather than to Claw Moor in Gron," said Aravan.

"My boy, it would be better if you'd wait a week," said Dalor, seeing no incongruity in calling Aravan a boy. "Then you would be completely healed."

As Aravan shook his head, Dalor added, "I know. I know. Time is short and the journey long."

"How far is it?" asked Bair.

Aravan paused. "From the Avagon to the Great Swirl, four thousand six hundred leagues—plus tacking—by the route we must sail."

Bair's eyes flew wide. "Four thou—!"

"And from where we will cross unto Mithgar, add another thousand or so just to reach Arbalin Isle and Thell Cove."

"Oh, my," said Branwen, "such a long way and so little time; 'tis sixty-four days till Springday. Can it e'en be done?"

"I know not, Lady Branwen," said Aravan, "yet we must try."

In spite of the tears standing in her eyes, Aylis said, "Isn't there some place to cross over that's closer to Arbalin than the mountains near Inge? And what about taking Dwarven fighters into your crew, as you did before? You will need such to face Ydral."

"There is no time to recruit such a warband," said Aravan, buckling the last strap of his pack.

"Besides," added Bair, "a warband might make things worse, for Dodona said that in the end Aravan and I must go together and alone." Bair frowned. "I say, kelan, does that mean we can't have any crew whatsoever?"

"No, elar. We must have a crew to reach the Great Swirl." Aravan looked at Aylis. "It's across the weed and into the isle that we must go alone, or so I deem."

Aylis began to weep softly, and Aravan took her in his embrace.

"But wait," said Branwen. "To get to Mithgar, won't you have to go back through Neddra?"

Bair nodded and clasped his ring. "I've detected no other way, and neither has Hunter in his hunting forays here on Vadaria. In this we have no other choice: it's back through Neddra or nought."

Aylis embraced Aravan all the more tightly at hearing Bair's words. "Oh, my love, it is so perilous," she whispered.

Aravan stroked her hair.

Dalon frowned. "If it's far to the Great Swirl, how will Ydral get there in time?"

"He'll fly," said Alamar with surety, "for did we not hear in addition to a Vulg he can shift into the form of a Fell Beast?"

"A flying creature most foul," said Branwen.

Alamar nodded and then added, "In fact, it is much shorter by the route he will take—flying directly over land and sea— than that which the *Eroean* must ply, for she must sail 'round a continent and a pole to get there. Moreover, by this time Ydral is probably already on the isle—or rather in it—preparing the way for Gyphon. Damn his Fell Beast form!"

"Wait," said Branwen. "Aravan can fly too, as Valké."

"Oh, Valké will fly," said Aravan, "but not to the Great Swirl; unlike for a Fell Beast, there is entirely too much ocean for a falcon to cross without resting, and there is no place for him to do so. Besides, Bair is right: Dodona said we must go together and alone in the end."

"But if not to the Swirl, when will Valké fly?" asked Branwen.

"When we reach Mithgar, Valké will fly ahead," said Aravan, "leaving Hunter to come at his pace. By the ti—"

"My boy, if you try to fly as Valké," interrupted Dalor, "I don't know what it will do to your recovery."

"Again I say, we have little choice," said Aravan. He turned to Bair. "By the time thou dost directly arrive at Thell Cove—"

"Directly? Directly to Thell Cove?" asked Bair. "But I thought I would be going to Arbalin Isle with you."

"Nay, elar. 'Tis Valké who flies to Arbalin, where I will gather a crew. At the slower pace of Hunter, thou wilt go directly to the cove, where the *Eroean* lies. The crew and I will meet thee there, and together we will ready the ship and set sail. Thereafter, we depend on Rualla, fickle Mistress of the Winds."

"All the more reason to hurry," said Bair, setting the sword in its sling. "I'm ready, kelan."

"But it is not the proper time to cross," said Alamar.

"It was not the proper time when we came," said Bair.

They stood on the plateau, stone walls rearing up on three sides to embrace the snow-laden flat.

Aylis, her face pale and grim, looked up into the blue eyes of the love she had lost then found again, only to lose him once more. In her embrace Aravan looked into the gold-flecked, green eyes he thought to never see again, and he brushed back a stray lock of her light brown hair shot through with auburn glints. "I shall return, chieran. I vow I shall return." And he took her face between his hands and kissed her one last time.

"I shall hold you to that promise, O my love," whispered Aylis. "Come back to me." She tightened her embrace one last time as if to store the feel of his arms, the feel of his form, the feel of his love, and then released him and stepped back.

Having said their good-byes to Alamar and Branwen and Dalor, who stood quietly by, Aravan and Bair trod through the snow and to the center of the small plateau, and in a flash of platinum light, Aravan was gone, Valké in his place.

Bair slapped the leather pad on the shoulder away from the upjutting hilt of the Silver Sword, and with a leap and a stir of wings Valké sprang to the perch, raptor talons clutching and releasing and clutching as the black falcon turned about to face forward.

Then with a final wave, gripping the ring in one hand and his flanged mace in the other, Bair began stepping and chanting, turning and pausing, stepping, pausing, gliding, canting, fading . . . and then he and Valké were gone.

And behind Aylis quietly wept in her father's embrace . . .

. . . while on a like plateau above a distant black fortress the lad and the falcon appeared.

CHAPTER 45

Prey

January, 5E1010

[The Present]

A lone with Valké on the small plateau, Bair glanced up at the wan red sun hanging low in the sulphur-tinged sky, the black moon high overhead. "Eight candlemarks or so till the darktide, Valké." He offered a wrist to the bird, transferring it to the ground. Then shielding it with his cloak from the eyes of any warders on the walls of the distant black fortress below, "Aravan," he whispered, and from a flash of light the Elf appeared.

"Should we wait for darkness, kelan?"

Aravan nodded. "Aye, elar, for the fortress stands between, the crossing to Mithgar some league and a mile straight beyond."

"Hmm," said Bair, peering at the bastion below. "I would gauge the fortress to be about the same distance away from here—a league and a mile, or so."

Aravan nodded and then frowned, as if trying to catch an elusive thought, but whatever it may have been slipped beyond his grasp. He took a deep breath and then said, "Come, let us rest while the sun is in this pungent, yellow-brown sky. We will start down in the shades of night."

And so they waited as the day slowly waned.

In the drear twilight Bair stood and walked to the edge of the precipice to see—

"Kelan," he hissed. "Come look."

Aravan rose to his feet and stepped to Bair's side.

Four miles outward and down, torchlight ringed the walls of the black fortress. But Bair pointed farther on, and some four miles past the dark stronghold, more torchlight glimmered in the valley beyond. "Is that where the crossing is?" asked Bair.

Aravan nodded grimly. "I deem it is so, elar."

"What do you think it means?"

"Valké will fly and see," said Aravan, even as he cast the hood of his cloak over his head.

"But Dalor said he did not know what it might do to you should Valké fly."

" 'Tis the swiftest way to discover whether or no this torchlight is at the crossing, and if so, what it may portend."

"But Dalor said—"

Aravan thrust out a hand of negation. "I will take care, elar." Aravan knelt in the snow. "Now make certain the light is shielded."

Reluctantly, Bair made small adjustments to the cloak all about Aravan to cover him completely, finally saying, "Ready, kelan."

Light flashed under even as the cloak vanished into Valké's aura, and—*skree!*—the black falcon took to wing.

Bair watched as the tiercel soared up and away in the darkening sky, the black moon now crossing the zenith. Yet in but moments, Valké turned on a wing and came gliding back down.

"This much did Valké see: Ghûlka and Hèlsteeds, Loka, Rucha, Trolls: they ward the in-between crossing. And another band roams the hills near the passage." Grimacing, Aravan rubbed his chest and shoulder on the side where the quarrel had pierced Valké through nearly four weeks past.

"Oh, kelan, are you all right?"

Aravan sighed. "I deem Dalor is right, for Valké cannot take wing for any long distance. Even so, this short flight did no lasting damage either unto him or me. Would that I could heal as swiftly as thy sire or thee, Bair, but I cannot, for he and thou art natural born unto thy shapeshifting, whereas I am not."

"I wouldn't know," said Bair, "for I've not been hurt badly . . . but for the Lamia sucking at my life at the Oasis of Falídii."

Aravan nodded. "And mayhap that would have killed another, Bair. Regardless, once thy sire did recover from a crushing that would have slain another, and if thou art aught like him, then thou wilt recover swiftly from injury. But as I said, I am not natural born to such."

"Well, if you are all right—"

"Elar, though hurting, I am well," assured Aravan, "and we must deal with what Valké saw."

"Are you certain that he saw Foul Folk? I mean, that's quite a distance away."

"He is a falcon, Bair," replied Aravan, as if that explained all.

Bair turned up his hands. "Well then, what will we do about those who block the in-between? And what of this band roving the hills?"

"As to that band, I think they seek us."

"Seek us?"

Aravan frowned. "Aye. I deem Ydral on his way back to Mithgar discovered our tracks, our scent, the trace we laid coming to the fortress when first we pursued him. Hence he knew we used that in-between to cross over from Mithgar to here, and he told a Rûpt jemadar or such. And when we fled from the fortress, the jemadar did set a ward to keep us from escaping back to Mithgar by that way."

"Well, if that's the case, why isn't *this* crossing warded?"

Aravan shrugged. "What wouldst thou surmise, elar?"

"Well, if I had to guess . . . mayhap they know not that this is an in-between as well. Mayhap they believe we merely vanished into the mountains above in the rage of the blizzard. And now they ward that southern crossing, expecting us to circle 'round to come to it once more." Bair cocked an eyebrow at Aravan.

" 'Tis as good a conjecture as any," said Aravan. "Even so, it leaves us with a dilemma: a band warding the way."

"Perhaps we draw them off," said Bair. "Provide a misdirection. Get them into another chase."

Aravan shook his head. "I am afoot, Bair, and as such cannot hope to outrun a Vulg, and Valké as yet cannot fly any distance."

"Perhaps Hunter alone could lure them away," said Bair.

"Mayhap. Yet 'tis thee who must make the crossing, for I alone cannot, and should they leave the in-between well warded or should the pursuit be close at hand, then we will most certainly fail."

"Adon, but you are right, Aravan, it is a thorny dilemm— Oh, wait. Ydral said the fortress was at a nexus, for Gyphon did invade Adonar from here. That means there is another crossing nearby, one leading to—"

"—to the High Plane," said Aravan, grinning, the elusive thought he had been chasing made crystalline clear by Bair. "And from Adonar we can cross into Mithgar."

"But where?" asked Bair, gesturing about. "Where is the crossing from here to there? And as to a crossing from Adonar to Mithgar, I have been to only one place on the High Plane which leads to the Mid, and I have no idea whatsoever where on Adonar that ring of oaks might lie."

"I know of several crossings from Adonar to Mithgar, and can we find the route Gyphon took to invade the High Plane, we can only hope that a crossing to Mithgar lies nearby."

"Not only that one lies nearby, kelan," said Bair, "but that wherever on Mithgar it leads, the way to the *Eroean* will not be even farther afield than the crossing in the Grimwalls nigh the village of Inge."

Aravan turned up his hands. "A chance we must take, for we have no better choice."

Bair nodded then said, "All right, then, where shall we look for a crossing?"

Aravan frowned in concentration, then looked down at the fortress and then at the warded crossing beyond, then left and right where valleys lay. "The cardinal points, I ween."

"The cardinal poin—? Ah," breathed Bair in enlightenment. "Can we hope that the black fortress, the nexus, lies in the center of all? Here we stand at what looks to be a league and a mile due north of the bastion. The warded crossing lies a league and a mile due south. If you have guessed aright, then a league and a mile due east or west should lie the crossing to Adonar."

"Or so I hope," said Aravan.

"What'll it be, kelan, east or west?"

Again Aravan looked left and then right. "The way to the eastern vale seems the easier of the twain."

"Then let us be gone from here," said Bair, taking up his pack.

*   *   *

Well into the night, the black moon sinking in the west, kelan and elar stood on a small, snow-laden hillock. "This is it," said Bair, gripping the stone ring, and looking back at the distant dark bastion. "But I think we are not on the cardinal point."

"Nay," agreed Aravan, "yet we are not far off."

"Well, hood yourself and huddle down, we've an in-between to cross."

In moments and with Valké riding on his shoulder, gripping his ring in his left hand and his flanged mace in his right, Bair began the ritual of crossing, his mind lost in the rite. Stepping, turning, pausing, gliding, chanting, singing, canting . . .

. . . and when he came to the end, the black moon had set.

Lor', I didn't cross over. What can it be? Think, Bair, think. I did the ritual correctly, that I know. I held the ring. Could it be that this isn't the time? That Alamar is right after all? That crossings must be made at certain marks of the day or night? But then, if that's true, how did we get to Vadaria when it was not an inbetween time?

Valké sprang down and then stood glaring at Bair. The lad whipped off his own cloak and held it out. Valké eyed the garment suspiciously, and with some reluctance hop-footed forward, and chirped in ire as Bair mantled him with cloth.

"I deem this leads not unto Adonar," said Aravan.

"But I have the blood of many—"

"Thou hast not the blood to take thee to the Dragonworld of Kelgor, nor the blood to step to Feyer, the world the Hidden Ones fled, Bair, and this crossing could lead to one of those. And I deem there are myriad other places where thy blood permits thee not."

"Well then, what'll we—? Oh. There is yet the cardinal point in the west."

Aravan glanced at the sky and said, "And not much time to find it."

Slowly, to keep from being detected, they worked their way about the basin to the north of the dark fortress, taking advantage of the crags and rocks and boulders lying at the foot of the mountain slope. At last they came to the easternmost opening into a westward-leading valley.

Yet ere they entered— *"Ssst!"* hissed Aravan, pointing south and away.

Coming into the basin from the south rode Ghûls on Hèlsteeds, Rûcks and Hlôks loping alongside, and black Vulgs ranging wide left and right.

"The searchers?" asked Bair.

"Mayhap," replied Aravan. "Let us be gone."

And into the broad westward vale they slipped.

As swiftly they moved downward and into the valley beyond, Bair said, "Kelan, in the reach ahead the <fire> grows stronger."

"A threat?"

"Nay, Aravan. It is in the land. Recall, when we first came into Neddra, I said that even the Foul Folk had to eat, and I deem this valley is one of those places used for the growing of crops, for in it lies a more fertile soil than that which we left behind, or so its <fire> would indicate."

"Let us hope it is an omen, then, for what might lie ahead."

On they pressed, Bair gripping the ring in his right hand as into the shadowy vale they went, fading dim stars ahead. Behind, in the east, the yellow-brown-tinted sky paled with the coming of a sulphurous dawn.

And onward into the valley they trekked, scrub and thorn reaching up through the dingy snow.

And now the rim of the red sun rose above the horizon aft, as sullen day broke aglance across the drab land.

Of a sudden: "Kelan! The ring, it tingles. A crossing is near."

"Then circle about and be drawn to it," said Aravan.

In the distance behind a bugle blew.

"And quickly," added Aravan, "for they may have found our tracks."

But Bair closed his eyes and clasped the ring, then began faring to the left.

Again a bugle blatted, and now came the howls of Vulgs.

Aravan drew his long-knife, though against a pack of the pony-sized Wolflike monsters it would be of little aid.

Bair paced toward a small hollow, a meager thicket of winter-barren trees therein.

Aravan looked back the way they had come. In the distance afar and silhouetted against the red sun, creatures topped the rise and paused, long shadows streaming down before them. Again a bugle blew, and then another, and howling in response they raced into the vale.

"Here, kelan," said Bair. "This is it."

Not saying a word, Aravan sheathed his blade, and then in a flash of light Valké took his place. With a short flight to Bair's left shoulder, the falcon settled into place.

Another bugle sounded, and atop the rise leading into the vale came Ghûls on Hèlsteeds, clots of snow flying up from hard-running cloven hooves.

Taking his mace in his right hand, and gripping the ring in his left, Bair began the ritual, while black Vulgs howled and sped toward the pair, the distance between fading swiftly.

And still Bair chanted, canted, paced, turned, paused, while bugles sounded and thundering Hèlsteeds and yawling Ghûls raced out of the bloodred sun, Rûcks and Hlôks running after.

Lost in the rite, Bair sang and glided, stopped and turned, paced and chanted, unaware now of his surroundings, though Valké on his shoulder glared at the oncoming doom, rage in the black raptor's eye.

Bugles blew and Ghûls howled and Hèlsteeds hammered through snow, Rûcks and Hlôks in their wake, and snarling Vulgs flashed to the brim of the hollow and leapt toward the prey, only to pass through empty space—

—for the lad and the falcon were gone.

CHAPTER 46

Adonar

January, 5E1010

[The Present]

"*W*augh!*" cried Eryndar, leaping to his feet, for someone or something began to manifest in the midst of the camp of the Elven hunters. " 'Ware!" cried the Elf, drawing his sword and pointing at the apparition beyond the fire. " 'Tis a *thing* crossing from Neddra!"

The other five Elves sprang up, swords drawn, ready to slay whatever this—this—

—"Wait!" called Talarin. " 'Tis a Baeron— No, 'tis a—"

But then whoever, whatever it was stepped fully into the clean, crisp air and new-fallen, crystal-white snow.

" 'Tis a large lad with a black bird on his shoulder, a falcon dark," said Gildor, lowering his blade but not sheathing it.

"Even so," said Eryndar, his own sword yet leveled at the youth, "he is come from Neddra."

The lad looked about, his eyes widening in wonder at the sight of a half dozen Elves ranged about a campfire and poised to attack or defend, the boy could not tell which. Horses tethered nearby stood alert, sensing tension. And even as he fastened his mace to his belt, the youth asked, "Is this Adonar?"

"It is," said Gildor. "Yet thou art not of Elvenkind, and all but the bloodways are sundered. Who art thou? And how can this be?"

"It's a long story," replied the lad. "Yet mayhap it will suffice for me to say that I am named Bair, the child of Urus, the Baeron, and Riatha, Guardian Lian!"

"Impossible!" cried Eryndar, his sword yet in hand. "This is a trick of Neddra, for none may be born of Elf and Man."

"No trick is this, Elven warrior, for some do name me the Impossible Child. Others call me the Rider of the Planes, while to some I am the Dawn Rider. For I am so named in Rael's Rede and in the Rede of Faeril the Warrow."

"Faeril I have not heard of, but the rede of Rael, we know it well, for she is my trothmate," said Talarin, "and the ythir of Gildor our arran." He gestured toward the golden-haired Elf at his side.

But Eryndar said, "Faugh! He is but a child, a youth, and as to him being the Dawn Rider, where is his horse? And so I say, how know we that this lad does tell the truth? This could be a trick of the Evil One, of Gyphon Himself."

"Nay," said Talarin, casting back his hood, revealing hair as golden as that of his son, "for Gyphon is trapped in the Abyss. Nevertheless, the question remains, how know we that this youth does not deceive?"

"Know by this!" cried Bair, and he reached over his right shoulder and drew the Silver Sword from its sheath and flashed it on high, where it glittered in the morning light of the diamond-bright winter sun.

A gasp went up from the Elves, and Eryndar cried, " 'Tis the Dawn Sword. I rode with Galarun and know it well." And then did Eryndar sheathe his own blade.

"Too, I have someone who will vouch for me," said the lad named Bair, holding a wrist out for the falcon.

But the black raptor flared its wings and sailed to the snow, and in a flash of platinum light, transformed into an Elf, a Lian they knew as Aravan, and again did all the Elves gasp in wonder.

"Eryndar, thou wert with me on the day Galarun fell," said Aravan. "Talarin, Gildor, we fought side by side at Hèl's Crucible."

"Aye," said Talarin, first to recover. "Yet how can this be that thou art a falcon and then a Lian?"

"As I did hear Bair say to Gildor, 'tis a tale long in the telling, and we have not the time, for once again Gyphon threatens all."

"Gyphon? But he is sealed in the Great Abyss," protested Arandar, running a hand through his black hair.

"Indeed," said Aravan, "yet a congruency of the Planes draws nigh, when the barrier between will be weakened, and the one who slew Galarun and stole the Silver Sword—a yellow-eyed Fiend known as Ydral—he has a token of power that will free the Great Evil." Aravan gestured at the lad, the boy sheathing the Dawn Sword, the Elves yet with blades in their hands following suit. "But Bair and I can stop him, can we get to Mithgar in time. We need hie to the nearest crossing."

"The nearest I know of I trod long past and is in Darda Falain, many days ride from here," said Talarin, Gildor and the others nodding in agreement. "It crosses into Darda Galion."

"Darda Galion?" said Aravan. "What good tidings!"

"But Aravan, that in-between to Mithgar has been sealed, lo, these many millennia."

"Aye, but for the bloodways. Yet heed, it is not sealed unto the Rider of the Planes and the falcon he bears, and our need is dire, for we have but sixty-three days to reach the center of the Great Swirl."

"Sixty-three days?" gasped Ellidar. "It cannot be done."

"We have a slim chance can we get to the *Eroean* in time," said Aravan.

"But Darda Falain is three hundred leagues hence," said Gildor, gesturing westward.

"Then these twain will need swift horses, remounts as well," said Talarin. He turned to Aravan and held out a hand toward the animals, a dozen steeds altogether. "Take every one of our mounts, riding and packhorses all, for we cannot aid ye elsewhere, for we cannot cross unto Mithgar to do battle at thy side. But list, as Gildor has said, ye are some three hundred leagues east of the in-between, and e'en with remounts—"

"We must try," said Aravan.

Talarin nodded and turned to the others. "Swift, now. Prepare the horses, and pack food for two, enough to last ten days, grain for the steeds as well." As the Elves fell to, Talarin said, "As for water, ye will find streams aplenty, and the ice is thin. Too, Alwynholt lies along the way, where ye may get fresh mounts."

Aravan looked about at the vale and asked, "Where are we?"

"In the reach of the Durynian Range, nigh Lyslyn Mere." Talarin pointed westerly down the valley.

"Ah, then, I know the mere," said Aravan, "and though I've not been to Darda Falain, I do know where it lies."

"Well and good," said Talarin.

"Yet the crossover in that Eldtree forest, I know not its place," said Aravan.

" 'Tis midmost, just east of Falainholt, no more than three hundred paces. Shouldst thou need a guide, then seek any in the holt."

Aravan glanced at the lad, standing quietly nearby. "We will have no trouble finding the crossing once we draw nigh. Yet we take all thy steeds and ye will be afoot; should we send some to aid ye?"

"Nay," replied Talarin. "We shall instead march to Eylinholt, a day or so south of here."

"Ready," called Eryndar, leading two saddled mounts nearby, the other steeds on long leads trailing behind, five tethered to each mount, each tailing animal bearing but a light load of food— oats for the horses, mian for the riders.

"No need for two saddled mounts," said the one named Bair. "I will go a different way."

"How so?" asked Eryndar.

"Thou shalt see," said Aravan, smiling, as Gildor without question tethered the animals together in one long string.

Now the lad turned to Talarin. "Dodona said unlooked-for aid would come along the way, and it has."

"Dodona the Oracle?" asked Talarin, his eyes widening in wonder.

"Aye. And we thank you for your help, for without it we would surely have failed, for Valké the falcon is yet recovering from a wound and cannot fly far, and the horses will serve our needs."

"Wound?" asked Talarin, turning to Aravan.

Aravan tapped himself high on the chest. "Rûchen crossbow quarrel. I would tell thee more, yet we have far to go and little time."

"Then go," said Talarin, "yet if we ever meet again, thou hast a tale of wonder to tell, and I would be among the first to hear it."

Aravan smiled. "Done and done, Alor Talarin."

Aravan then took the pack from his back and tied it to the saddle of the steed Eryndar had meant for the lad. Then striding forward, he mounted the lead horse. He looked at the boy and said, "Ready, Bair?"

And, lo! in a shimmer of darkness, the boy did vanish and in his place stood a Draega, and all the Elves did gasp in startlement.

"Behold! Like Dalavar Wolfmage is this Impossible Child," cried Ellidar.

Then Aravan called out, *"Cianin taegi!"* and heeled the flanks of his steed and galloped away, the Draega loping at his side, horses trailing after. Westerly they went, down the length of the vale, Aravan and an Impossible Child on an impossible mission to save all of creation from a deadly doom.

While behind, Talarin and Gildor, Ellidar and Eryndar and Arandar stood watching, and she who had spoken not until then, said, "May Adon guide their way." And so did they all echo the words of the Dara: the Dylvana Arin Flameseer.

West they went, and west, as the sun rose up behind them, down the vale and out from the Durynian Mountains and into the foothills beyond, pausing just long enough to water the steeds at crystal Lyslyn Mere and to feed them some grain and take on a meal of their own. And then they took up the journey again, Aravan changing mounts often and varying the gait to spare the steeds. Even so it was well into the nighttide ere they called a halt to the run, for the horses needed rest, as did Aravan and Bair.

Day after day they raced across the rolling, snow-laden wold, Aravan riding, a string of horses behind, a Silver Wolf ranging at his side. Each night they stopped to rest the mounts beneath winter-bright stars, the primary moon of Adonar silvery and gibbous and waxing, the daughter moon of that moon circling about the mother and reflecting her face, as it came from behind and passed across the silvery orb to disappear behind once more.

To the wonder of the dwellers therein, Aravan and Bair paused in Alwynholt to exchange spent horses for fresh. But ere the noontide of that fourth day had passed, they were on their way once more, leaving the thatch-roofed, stone-walled, warm-hearthed village behind.

For seven days altogether did they race across the snowy plains, and just ere sunset of the seventh day, they stopped at an ice-crusted, meandering stream, and as the horses took on water Aravan said to Bair, "Elar, we are but a half day or less from Darda Falain, and the steeds are not yet spent. I say we press on this night and arrive there ere dawn."

Bair looked up from replenishing his waterskin. "Hunter is not yet spent either, in fact is chafing at the pace: even with remounts the miles a day the horses cover is less than he can go. But, you, kelan, how fare you?"

"I am somewhat weary, but many leagues are yet left in me. 'Tis Valké I wonder at."

"Valké?"

Aravan nodded. "He needs must fly when we reach Mithgar, and when last he flew he was in pain." Aravan glanced at the low-hanging sun. "Even so, a few candlemarks hence seven days will have passed since then, and Dalor said 'twas a sevenday I must wait ere Valké tries his wings."

"On the morrow, then," said Bair, "just to be safe."

Aravan nodded. "When we cross into Mithgar." He called to the horses, and they raised their heads from the stream. And as he mounted up, from darkness Hunter came, and westerly they went once more, to run through the night for Darda Falain, full mother and daughter moons above lighting the way.

In among the Eldtrees they fared, pale gloaming all about though evening was long gone and the nearing dawn yet to come. Still the trees shed a dim glow, a testament that Elves lived among the giants, for the bond between the Eldwood Trees and the Elves did make the wood into twilight.

They moved toward the center of the forest, Hunter now in the lead, and in the trees above, *vani-lêrihha*—silverlarks—sleepily warbled, waking in the coming dawn. Inward they pressed and inward, then the great Silver Wolf turned sharply rightward to come to the brim of a wide pool in a small glade in the heart of the Eldtree wood. Mist curled up from the clear surface in the dawntime air, and still dusky twilight glowed from the Eldtrees all 'round.

And there did Hunter change.

"Did I not know better I would think I were in Darda Galion," said Aravan, dismounting. "This crossing is identical to the one I remember—nigh Wood's-heart it was—though I knew not whence it went."

"This is a crossing, all right," replied Bair. "So the ring says."

"Well, then, let us be on our way."

"What of the horses?" asked Bair.

"We shall take but one," said Aravan, pointing. "The others are trained to seek out an Elvenholt, and Falainholt lies yon." Bair turned about to see, and in the near distance the soft yellow glow of lanterns shone through the wood.

"And why would we take even one horse with us?" asked Bair.

"If Valké cannot yet fly, I will need to ride to the River Nith and across, and thence to the Great Escarpment. Then make my way down into Valon, where fresh horses are to be found."

"Ah, I see," said Bair. "But will this horse know the rite of crossing?"

"Bair, he will be caught in your aura, just as Valké is, and the steed will then know what to do."

They selected the freshest of the mounts—a grey—and with a slap or two sent the other animals trotting toward the light of Falainholt.

Then Bair mounted the remaining horse, and in a flash of light and a stir of wings, Valké sprang to his shoulder.

As an afterthought, Bair drew the Silver Sword, for if Dylvana were on the other side in Mithgar—for they did ward Darda Galion—he would have this token of good to allay any untoward concerns.

And then casting his mind into the familiar ritual, Bair began to chant, his voice rising and falling, neither singing nor speaking, but something in between; his mind became lost in the rite, neither wholly conscious nor unconscious, but something in between; and he visualized the steps, the glides, the turns, the pauses and passings. And the horse moved off, pacing in an arcane pattern, hooves flashing in a series of intricate steps, neither a dance nor a gait, but something in between. And into the mist rising from the mere they rode, neither air nor water but something in between. About the glade they pranced, in its smallness 'twas neither forest nor field but something in between. And dawn was in the sky, the light of the Eldtrees aiding, neither night nor day but something in between.

And even as Lian came from the Elvenholt, following the trace of the riderless horses back, they heard the chant, the cant, the pacing, and they rushed forward just in time to see a rider with a black falcon on his shoulder and something glittering in his hands, while above in the trees in a flurry of song and wings, silverlarks filled the air. And then the rider and falcon and horse faded, faded, and then vanished, gone in-between, the silverlarks gone as well.

And Lian turned to one another, wonder in their eyes, and in their midst a voice softly chanted:

> *"Bright Silverlarks and Silver Sword*
> *Borne hence upon the Dawn,*
> *Return to earth; Elves girt thyselves*
> *To struggle for the One.*
>
> *"Death's wind shall blow, and crushing Woe*
> *Will hammer down the Land.*
> *Not grief, not tears, not High Adon*
> *Shall stay Great Evil's hand."*

And then someone began weeping, for 'twas Rael's Rede, a prophecy come true: Mithgar was in deadly peril, and with it all of creation, and they could not help, for they could not cross the in-between.

And in a tiny glade by a crystalline mere in the dawntime upon Mithgar, a lad on a horse with a falcon on his shoulder and a Silver Sword in hand came riding out from the in-between and into Darda Galion and, somehow caught in his aura, thousands of silverlarks winged into the Eldtrees above, singing songs unheard on Mithgar for five millennia, their carols heralding a new day, for a new day indeed had come: it was the dawn of the twenty-fifth of January in the One Thousand and Tenth year of the Fifth Era of Mithgar.

The lad and the falcon were some three hundred leagues from Arbalin Isle in the south, and beyond lay a long ocean journey of four thousand six hundred leagues in all.

And as the Dawn Rider with falcon and sword came unto imperiled Mithgar, but fifty-five days and a daylight remained ere the doom of the Trine would fall.

CHAPTER 47

Mithgar

January, 5E1010

[*The Present*]

Even as Bair rode into the mists of the mere in the dawntime in Darda Galion, with silverlarks caroling as they flew into the twilight of the Eldtrees above, there came the cry of a silver horn ringing through the woodland—a call of assembly. Bair spurred forward, riding toward the cry. Within a furlong or two, he came into Wood's-heart, the Elvenholt central to the Larkenwald, thatch-roofed white cottages nestled within the forest. And central to the holt, Elves gathered—Dylvana Elves—astride horses and armed and armored, as if mustering for war. And as Bair emerged from the trees, the Elves cried out in wonder, for the Dawn Rider and the Silver Sword was come in among them, and silverlarks sang above.

A rider, a tall golden-haired Lian, surged forward to meet the lad, even as Valké sprang from Bair's shoulder and sailed to the ground. "*Hál!*" called the Lian. "*Vio Vanidar*, known as Silverleaf. And art thou the—?"

There came a flash of platinum light, the horses starting up and back, and as both Bair and Vanidar gained control of their steeds, Silverleaf cried out in amaze, for where Valké had been, now stood Aravan, and he grinned up at Vanidar and said, "Hello, old friend."

Silverleaf sprang down from his horse and embraced the Elf. And then he held Aravan at arm length and asked, "How can this be, my friend? Thou art not, or rather, wert not a shapeshifter when last I knew."

Aravan held out a hand to forestall more questions, and as Silverleaf released him, Aravan said, "As I told Alor Talarin—"

"Talarin! But he is gone unto the High Plane."

"Indeed, Vanidar, he is there. Nevertheless, as I told him but a sevenday past, 'tis a long tale in the telling, and we have not the time."

"Then, Aravan, thou wert there on the High Plane and now thou art here? Is the Sundering undone?"

"Nay, Vanidar, the bloodways yet rule. 'Tis only as a falcon can I cross and only when borne by this lad, Bair, child of—"

"—Bair!" exclaimed Silverleaf. "The child of Riatha and Urus?" He turned his attention to Bair. "When last I saw thee thou wert but a newborn and—" Of a sudden Silverleaf's eyes widened in enlightenment. "Ah, now I do see an answer to my question: thou hast the blood of two Planes."

Bair turned up a hand. "Four, actually, or mayhap five."

Silverleaf frowned. "Four Planes or five?"

Bair shrugged. "My ythir accounts for one Plane; the rest come from the line of my sire."

Silverleaf cocked an eyebrow and said, "Then answer me this, lad: is that sword I see in thy hand the blade said to be able to slay the High Vûlk Himself? And if so, then art thou the Dawn Rider come to aid in this time of woe?"

"Some do call me by that name," said Bair.

Silverleaf nodded. " 'Tis well and good, Dawn Rider, that thou hast come. Sorely do we need thine aid, for a vast army rages through Mithgar, coming from the East, leaving destruction, pestilence, famine, plague, and death in its wake, refugees fleeing before it. And the foe is aided by Dragons, and who can stand against such?"

"Dragons," said Aravan, sighing. "We heard 'twas but one: Ebonskaith."

"One or many," said Vanidar, "still the question remains: who can stand against such? And, aye, 'tis said Ebonskaith is in their midst, with rumors of more Drakes to come."

Aravan frowned. "More have broken the pledge?"

"Mayhap," said Silverleaf. "If true, it seems the terrible vision of Arin Flameseer is visited upon us at last."

Aravan took a deep breath and let it out. "What ill news thou dost bring unto mine ears, Vanidar, if this rumor be true."

"Ill news indeed, and so I ask, is this lad with the Silver Sword come to ride with us in answer to the High King's call?"

"That he is the Dawn Rider, 'tis true," said Aravan, glancing at Bair, "and it is the Silver Sword he bears. Yet we come not to ride with ye unto the High King's side, for we have another mission of e'en greater import."

A moan rose up from the Dylvana host at these words of denial. And Bair shook his head in disbelief and, casting his mind back to the tale Aravan had told him, said, "Slaughter did Arin Flameseer see, and blood and Dragonfire, a salting of the land, the hewing down of forests, plague and pestilence, famine and death following in war's wake, and midst it all a green stone, the Dragonstone; oh, kelan, this is the woe from the East Dodona foresaw. We must ride to join the allies, the Silver Sword in hand."

"Nay, Bair," replied Aravan, "for though the sword would be a mighty talisman to carry against the foe, still we must bear it with us unto the Great Swirl, for there it is meant to be, or so I do ween. Our mission is to stop Ydral ere the Trine does fall and he opens the way for Gyphon's return."

Bair groaned. "But we don't even know that Ydral has such in mind, or that he goes to the isle in the Great Swirl instead of another place, mayhap the Iron Tower in Gron."

"Elar, we must trust Alamar, for he has seen the crystal cavern, as have I, and the runes inscribed therein. Nay, though the High King's need is great, an e'en greater threat lies where we are bound."

Bair sighed and nodded in glum agreement and sheathed the Silver Sword in its scabbard in the sling upon his back, and all the host did sigh as well, for neither Dawn Rider nor Silver Sword would lead them into battle.

Aravan turned to Vanidar. "Go, my friend, and answer the muster, for we've another task."

"Would that thou wert with us," said Silverleaf as he mounted up, "for we are but a hundred blades, a hundred bows, and thou alone with thy spear be worth a thousand blades more."

"My spear," said Aravan, bitterness in his voice, "may prove the downfall of all."

Vanidar cocked his head, but Aravan thrust out a hand, saying, "Go, Vanidar, go. Answer the High King's call. Should we survive, I will tell thee then what has come to pass."

"And should we survive," replied Silverleaf, "I will do the same." With those words Vanidar sprang to his saddle and reined his horse about and signalled the bugler who blew a silver call. And leaving but a handful of Dylvana to ward the entire wood, the Elven band rode away to the north and east, trailing remounts and packhorses after; they were headed for the ferry at Olorin Isle, where they would cross the mighty Argon and then turn south, for horses could not fare down the Great Escarpment, needing to go 'round it instead.

"Dismount, Bair," said Aravan, "and give over the steed to the warders, and follow me to the map room in the coron-hall, I've a chart to show thee. . . ."

"This is the route Valké will take." Aravan traced a path southwestward from Wood's-heart to the port city on Arbalin Isle, lying off the coast of Jugo. " 'Tis some three hundred leagues altogether. But for thee, this is the way Hunter will go, three hundred leagues as well." Again Aravan traced a route, this time southeasterly and down the Great Escarpment, then nearly due south across the Plains of Valon to the Argon Ferry and south beyond, to come to the grotto where lay the *Eroean* in Thell Cove.

"But what if Valké can't fly, kelan?"

"He feels fit," said Aravan, tapping his chest, "as do I. Dalor said it would take a sevenday more to heal, and a sevenday now has passed. Valké is eager to take to the air."

Bair held out a hand of negation. "That is all well and good, kelan, but may not be the case, and so again I ask, what if Valké is not fit to fly?"

"Then as I said before, I will ride unto the escarpment and stride down into Valon below; 'tis a land of horsemen, a place where I would hope to find swift mounts to bear me onward.

Should that be the case, then thou wilt go at my side; elsewise, should Valké fly, then thou wilt hie for Thell Cove instead."

As Bair nodded, Aravan turned back to the chart. "Now heed me, elar, for there are risks along the way to the cove, the way Hunter must run." Aravan's finger stabbed to the map. "Here flows the River Nith, which Hunter must cross, the current swift and plunging over the lip of the Great Escarpment here at Vanil Falls. Beware Hunter trying to cross too close, else he will be swept over to plummet a thousand feet into the Cauldron below, and even a werecreature such as he may not survive such a fall. I suggest that he cross well upstream, say, at this place.

"Then here nigh the linn of Vanil Falls lies the way down the Great Escarpment," said Aravan, tracing the route. "The path is narrow, in places too strait for Hunter to pass. He will need to shift back unto thee to get beyond. Again, beware, for the drop is sheer, and shouldst thou fall . . ."

Aravan continued to describe the route, Bair nodding and fixing the chart and the crossings and warnings in his mind, hoping that Hunter would remember them as well.

They took a quick meal in the common mess, Dylvana softly telling them all of what they knew of the oncoming war. They spoke of the cities that had fallen, saying Dendor in Aven had held out the longest, even though it was but three days, or so the Realmsmen scouts in the hills south of the city had reported; there were rumors, however, that the so-called Golden Horde had sent but a paltry fraction of their might against the walls—a force overwhelming still—and that King Dulon and a significant number had managed to break through the ring of besiegers when the city itself fell, the walls torn down by a Drake, they say— Ebonskaith, mayhap. And just where Dulon and his men now were, none knew, though some said he was fighting a running battle southward. One of the Dylvana sighed and said, "Even so, even if true, 'tis but four thousand or so against four hundred thousand or more."

"Five hundred thousand," grunted Bair, past a mouthful of food.

The Dylvana gasped at this news. Bair shrugged. "Four hundred thousand, five hundred thousand, there is little to choose between. Dulon must feel like a gnat swatting at a Bear."

Aravan held up a hand. "Be not too quick to judge, for in the Winter War, Galen and one hundred fought against ten thousand to the woe of those he attacked. Dulon's odds are the same."

As to the rumors of more Drakes to come, news there was that Ryodo had fallen to dozens of Dragons a handful of years apast, and there were tales of Drakes raging across lands far to the east, aiding the Golden Horde.

Even though neither Bair nor Aravan had had any rest since the dawn of the day before, still they decided to press on. Outside in the compound, with Dylvana looking on and silverlarks singing above, Aravan said, "Art thou ready, elar?"

Settling the sword in its sling across his back as well as the pack he bore, Bair nodded and said, "Let us be gone."

In a flash of light, Aravan vanished and Valké took to wing, the handful of Dylvana gasping in astonishment. Up raged the black falcon and up, to circle twice and then arrow southwesterly, the raptor quickly lost to sight beyond the leaves of the twilit forest.

And when it was clear that Valké was well on his way, from a shimmer of darkness, Hunter sprang forth, the Silver Wolf running south, threading among the massive boles of the great Eld-trees, to be lost in the gloaming below.

Behind in Wood's-heart, the Dylvana looked at one another, their eyes wide in wonderment, and shaking their heads, they turned to the stables, for they had a forest to ward.

High above the Larkenwald did Valké fly, and by early midmorn he sailed beyond the Great Escarpment and into the air over the Plains of Valon. Below him, hares froze in their foraging as his shadow passed across, but Valké did not stoop, for the hunting of game was not his immediate concern. Instead the raptor had another goal in mind, one curiously unfalconlike, though he was yet a creature wild; even so, now and again it seemed he answered to the desires of an Elf named Aravan, a person he would never meet. And so, on he flew and on, above the snowy plains, ignoring birds and hares and voles and marmots and other such easy game.

Southwesterly he flew throughout the day over the white-laden land, now and then passing over hillocks the wind had scrubbed free of snow, revealing rich grasses yellow in winter, the wealth of Valon. Far to the west Valké could see a spur of mountains marching south out from the Grimwall: it was the Gûnarring. And though the falcon knew not its name, he did know that along that range the air would be good for soaring, for such was his knowledge of mountains and the winds flowing along the rises.

And across the plains now and again Valké could see armed and armored riders on horses, and leather-clad men marching across the snowy grasslands, wagons in their midst, all heading eastward as if in migration. Yet a migration this was not; they were instead heading for a great gathering; how he knew was a mystery to the falcon, but he pondered it not as onward he flew . . .

. . . and flew . . .

. . . while the low winter sun climbed up the sky and across and down again.

Finally, as twilight drew over the land, Valké passed above one of the wide trails the two-legs used, riding their horses, drawing their wagons, moving on their mysterious errands between places, going to and from their solitary bowers or collections of bowers to others, such as those places where they gathered in great flocks and lived in their wooden and stone and other such nests down on the flat ground itself.

And after passing across the trail, Valké espied a small woodland tucked up against low hills, and here he spiralled down to land on the snowy ground.

From a flash of light came Aravan.

As Aravan ate voraciously, he looked at the sky above. *I am just south of Pendwyr Road and west of the Red Hills. Valké has flown some one hundred and fifty-three leagues. Kala! No wonder I am hungry, but what a good distance he did fly. I should sight Arbalin by morrow eve.*

Completely spent, Aravan curled up in his sleeping bag among the trees on the slope and fell into exhausted slumber.

*   *   *

That night, entirely unaware of Aravan and he unaware of them, a company of Warrow archers rode past along Pendwyr Road, answering unto the High King's muster. Among the band rode three in armor—one in black, one in silver, and one in gold.

The Silver Sword in its sling, Hunter loped among the Eldtrees, the great 'Wolf heading southeasterly, following the course set for him by the Friend. By midmorning he came to a river, the current swift and running down from the mountains in the west, flowing easterly among the enormous Eldtrees. Hunter stood at the icy water's edge and lapped up a great long drink, and then he eyed the distant shore. He knew that somewhere downstream a thundering waterfall fell, for he could dimly perceive its roar, though distant it was. Too, the Friend had warned him that such lay on this river, and that he was to swim across and reach the far bank, where he was to follow along the flow. And so Hunter sprang into the rush, the water frigid for winter was on the land, and in powerful strokes of his legs underwater he struck for the opposite shore even as the stream bore him eastward. Many loping strides downstream he clambered out along the far bank and shook mightily, water spraying wide, and then began running again, vapor flowing out from his fur in long ghostly tendrils trailing behind.

As he ran toward the distant roar, the sun continued its climb up the sky, and just ere the noontide Hunter scented Elves, though faintly. And he paused to determine the direction, his nose leading him to a large slab of rock upjutting from the water and leaning against a steep fall of bank, forming a large, shadowed cavity 'tween slab and shore. From here came the Elven scent, and when Hunter looked into the hollow, he espied Elven boats moored and abob in the current.

No Friends here, only their scent, left in days long past.

Hunter went onward, the roar now quite loud, and he came to the lip of a mighty precipice over which the waters of the River Nith did flow. Down it plunged in a silvery stream, falling sheer into the depths below. Yet in the near distance another river coursed over the rim, this one much larger, and it was the primary source of the thunder, plummeting down the face of the Great Escarpment and into a massive roil of water far under.

Hunter cast about, finally seeing the pathway down, and along this slender way he did go. Yet soon he came to a place too narrow for him to pass, and from a shimmer of darkness came Bair.

Bair paused long enough to gaze about: he was on the narrow way down the face of the Great Escarpment, a thousand feet sheer to the land below; behind, the Nith hurtled out over the lip of the Great Escarpment, Vanil Falls cascading down into the westernmost reach of the vast churning pool known as the Cauldron. Some seven miles to the east, the Great River Argon plummeted over the lip and into the Cauldron as well; Bellon Falls it was named, its roar so loud as to make speech unheard; in the Cauldron did the waters of the tributary Nith join those of the Argon, the Argon to run on southerly to form the eastern border of the realm of Valon; in the distance beyond the mighty river lay the Greatwood, where Bair had trained with three princes some seven years past.

Bair was enthralled by the sight, yet within moments he was beyond the restriction, and Hunter once again followed the way down.

Several more times did Hunter come to narrows, and these did Bair step past, Hunter carrying on.

And as Hunter approached the foot of the path, out from a thicket bordering the roil of the Cauldron there stepped a Silver Wolf. And although it had been over sixteen years since Hunter had seen her last, still he knew her by her scent: it was Shimmer.

Together they raced across the snowy plains, running southward —Shimmer of Moonlight on the Water as the Gentle Breeze Brings Scents from Near and Far, and Hunter: the Seeker and Searcher Who Is One of Us but Not of Us. When they were far enough from the roar of Bellon Falls, Shimmer called for a halt. And by postures and whines and growls and quiet songs, she gave Hunter the message she bore. And in the same manner did Hunter tell her where he was bound, only to have her repeat what she had said before.

Once more they took up the run southerly as the sun crossed the rest of the sky to sink in the west.

That night, Shimmer sat ward over a sleeping lad, the boy gaining his first rest since dawn of the day before.

*   *   *

Once again Valké took to the sky, the morning fresh on the day, and southeasterly did he wing. And still on the plains below did armed and armored marchers and riders and wagons roll to the east, some faring on a track in the south, others on a track to the north, for the Red Hills stood across their way, and they were on headings that would bear them around the run of craggy tors. In the far distance Valké could see what seemed to be a river, and on it floated the waterborne bowers of the two-legged ground-walkers. Bound for another place altogether, Valké did not veer to examine these floating nests—some with their strange wings unfurled in the wind as they slowly moved upriver, others standing still, no wings evident whatsoever, just peculiar trees standing tall.

Southeasterly he flew and southeasterly, throughout the entire day, not stopping to hunt and eat or to take a drink, for odd, unfalconlike thoughts urged him to press onward, and press onward he did. And late in the day with the sun low in the west he came to a great nesting place of the walkers, their wooden bowers on land along the shore of the Avagon Sea, and there at a dock lay one of the great waterborne dwellings, its wings furled.

And Valké was drawn to this nest.

Down he stooped, plummeting, the tips of his wings guiding, men aboard pointing, and in the last moment Valké flared his dark pinions wide to settle on the deck near the bow.

And from a flare of light, Aravan appeared, sailors crying out in alarm.

Aravan looked about in wonder, for this was the *Eroean*, of that there was no doubt, and she was ready for sailing; mystery of mysteries, she was not in her grotto nor even in Port Arbalin; instead she was moored to a dock in Merchants Crossing here on the shores of Jugo.

As dawn broke on the land, Shimmer having delivered her message and having guarded the boy through the night, she and Hunter parted company, Shimmer running on her course, Hunter running on his. All day they loped on their diverging paths, and when darkness fell, they were twenty-five leagues apart.

When Bair took his meal that night, he was just south of the

Reach Road, the east–west artery running between the Gûnarring Gap and the city of Vanir—the capital of Valon.

Bair fell asleep as soon as he lay down, and he did not awaken as riders trailing remounts galloped past, couriers bearing news.

"Cap'n Aravan!" came a call.

Weary and voraciously hungry, Aravan turned to see—"Long Tom," replied the Elf.

Just emerging from belowdecks amidships, Long Tom turned and called out, "Brae, sound th' poipes, the cap'n o' th' ship be aboard."

Silence was his answer.

"Brae, y' gob, Oi said sound th' poipes, the cap'n be aboard."

Startled from his wonderment, the yeoman sounded the pipes, and Long Tom turned and came striding along the deck, the big man calling out to crewmen to shut their gapes ere they tripped over their own dangling jaws and to stop their gawking and whispering and get back to work. And then Long Tom came before Aravan and sketched a salute, saying, "Cap'n, 'e said you'd come."

"Who, Long Tom, who said I would come, and what is the *Eroean* doing here?"

"Why, 'im, that's 'oo, that Davalar Wolfmiage . . . it wos 'im what said you'd come."

"Dalavar," said Aravan, his word not a question. Then he gestured about. "Tom, there's a mystery here, and you can solve it for me. But I need food and drink. Is there a cook aboard?"

"Aye, Cap'n, 'n' a roight good'n', too. 'N' supper itself be cookin' in th' galley, e'en as we speak."

"Well then, I'll take a big meal in my quarters, while thou dost tell me all."

"Oi, Noddy!" called Long Tom, and a cabin boy came running, skinny and dark-haired and perhaps fourteen or so. "Fetch th' cap'n a meal, hot 'n' pipin'."

"Water, too, lad," said Aravan, "and plenty of it. Plenty of food as well. Enough to feed three or four."

"Who shall I have join you at supper?" asked Noddy.

"None, lad. 'Tis all for me."

Noddy's dark eyes widened in astonishment, but he turned and ran aft.

And Tom said, "Cap'n, I'll go t' th' lock-up stores 'n' fetch some ale, you look as if 'twere needed."

"Well and good, Tom, and meet me in my quarters, for I would hear how all did occur."

"All wot?" asked Long Tom, as he strode with the captain aft.

"This, Tom," replied Aravan, gesturing about. "How came the *Eroean* to be here in this port just when I would need her?"

While Aravan scooped food into his mouth as if he hadn't eaten for weeks, Long Tom told his tale:

" 'Twas Dalavar Wolfmiage wot brought th' *Eroean* t' Arbalin Port, sailin' th' ship wi'out no aid, 'n' a wonder wos that. Slipped in alone on nought but th' staysails 'n' began droppin' 'em as 'e entered th' mouth o' th' 'arbor, th' Elvenship glidin' t' th' pliace where 'e dropped anchor. We thought it wos you acome ag'in after six thousan' years, 'n' later one thousan', 'r thereabouts. But whin they sent th' loighter out, all wot debarked wos 'im 'n' foive Silver Wolves. Large as ponies they wos, but threatened not anyone.

"Dalavar recruited a crew, 'e did, lookin' hard at each man jack, as if seein' into th' very soul o' 'im wot wos bein' inspected—'r that's wot Oi thought, Oi did, 'n' it gave me th' shivers, roight enough, whin 'e wos lookin' at me. But there on th' docks, that's wot 'e did, lookin' hard at th' men, rejectin' some, acceptin' others, me among th' latter. But unloike the tales told by moi ever-so-many griate granther, them wot wos 'anded down t' me, th' Wolfmiage took no Dwarven fighters 'r any other kind o' warriors aboard, battlin' sailors excepted, sayin' that you 'n' another 'ad t' go alone at th' time o' th' Trine, 'n' wotever that may be 'e didn't say.

"Swore us t' secrecy, 'e did, 'n' took us aboard, 'n' then told us t' learn th' ship's riggin' 'n' quicklike, f'r you 'n' another'd be acomin' soon.

" 'N' 'e appointed me first mait, 'e did, me bein' a rigger 'n' a mait 'n' all, but Oi serve at y'r pleasure, Cap'n, 'n' if you'd loike another, Oi'll step daown, Oi will."

Aravan waved a hand of dismissal, managing to say through

a mouthful of food, "Dalavar made a good choice, I warrant, and I'll sail with thee as first mate until thou dost show me otherwise. Now go on with your tale, Tom."

Long Tom beamed, as he took up the story once more:

"Well, 'e told me t' sail 'er 'ere t' Merchants Crossin', 'e did, as soon as th' crew wos ready, 'n' so Oi did, 'n' so we did. 'N' 'e told me t' tie up at a dock whilst we waited f'r you 'n' t'other t' come.

"Oh, 'n' 'e left a message f'r me t' say t' you, 'n' it wos this: remember th' Dragonships, th' message wos, but whin Oi asked him wot it all meant, 'e said you'd know, 'e did, 'n' that wos that.

" 'Im 'n' 'is 'Wolves'r gone anow, 'n' that's a fact.

"As Oi said, 'e left me in charge, me bein' a mait 'n' rigger 'n' all, 'n' Oi showed th' crew th' ropes Oi did, 'n' we're ready t' sail, we are, anytoime at y'r command, Cap'n Aravan."

Aravan stopped chewing and took a long draught of water. "Then, Long Tom, prepare to cast off, for we must get to Thell Cove. I've someone to meet there."

As Long Tom stood and stepped to the door, he paused and said, "Er, Cap'n, beggin' y'r pardon, sir, but wot about th' other t' come, th' one 'e said t' wait for. Oh, don't take me wrong, Cap'n', me 'n' th' crew, we'll obey th' order, we will, but th' Wolfmiage, 'e said t' wait 'ere at Merchants Crossin', 'e did, f'r you 'n' one other t' come. 'N' t'other's not yet 'ere."

"That's who we go to meet," said Aravan. But as Long Tom nodded and turned to go, Aravan held up a hand. "Wait, Tom. Just what exactly did the Wolfmage say?"

"Th' Wolfmiage, 'e said t' wait 'ere at Merchants Crossin', 'e did, t' wait f'r som'n niamed 'Unter, 'n' t' wait 'n' not go sailin' off t' nowhere wi'out this 'ere 'Unter, 'n' that's wot 'e said, 'e did, tho' 'oo 'r' wot this 'Unter may be, Oi couldna say, Oi say."

Aravan frowned and stood and walked to a port and looked through the glass at the night sky beyond. Finally, he blew out a long breath and turned and said, "Then we wait, Long Tom. We wait."

Aravan stepped to the table and sat and resumed eating, motioning Long Tom to sit as well, Aravan pausing long enough to pour two mugs of ale, sliding one across to Tom.

And as Aravan ate, the Gelender took a long pull on his drink, then, as if screwing up his courage, he inhaled a deep breath and blew it out and finally said, "Oi, naow, 'n' wot's all this 'ere about you bein' a griate loopin' black bird, eh?"

Just ere sunset four days later, a Silver Wolf bearing a sword in a sling on its back came padding aboard, panting hard as if it had run long.

And Aravan called out to the crew, "Raise the gangway and cast off, lads, and stand ready at the sails and hauls; it's to the far seas we are bound, 'round the cape and 'round the pole and thence unto the Great Swirl. . . ."

And as men clambered up the ratlines, and others cast off the mooring lines and drew in the footway, in the breeze blowing 'cross the larboard bow Long Tom called out orders, Brae piping his commands, commands to raise those sails that would take them from the mooring and into the wide channel beyond. Slowly, majestically, the great ship eased away from the dock, gaining speed as more Elven silk was bent on. Westerly she turned, running with the wind, making for the open sea.

And as they left Merchants Crossing behind, there were but fifty days remaining ere the doom of the Trine would fall.

CHAPTER 48

Strife

January–February, 5E1010

[*The Present*]

On the southern marge of Aralan, in the foothills of the Bodorian Range, a contingent of Jordians waited in ambush, a wagon train nearing, moving slowly along the Landover Road.

"My lord," Bron said softly, "they come, and soon our lances will drink blood. Even so I would rather be riding at King Brandt's side on his way to the Plains of Valon."

Lord Holst glanced across at the young warrior mounted on a dun-colored steed. "I, too, regret that we are not with King Brandt. Nevertheless in this mission we do aid him greatly and aid the High King as well. How oft have you heard that an army does travel on its stomach? It can proceed no faster than its food supply. And since this so-named Golden Horde finds only scorched earth where it fares, if we stop the flow of supplies, we stop the army in its tracks."

Bron sighed. "Aye, Lord Holst. I know why we are here. Still, there be not much glory in the waylaying of wagons."

Holst shrugged and peered at the line coming west. "Stand ready," he ordered. "And quieten steeds."

The command was softly passed from warrior to warrior along the lengthy row, as still the train came on, outriders in the lead, other warders faring alongside the slow-moving wains.

Long moments lapsed and long moments more, and the lead riders rode on by, wagons trundling in their wake, and still the Jordians waited. But at last Holst signalled Bron, and the lad

raised his black-oxen horn to his lips and blew a mighty call—
Raw! Raw! Raw! Out from concealment thundered the Jordians,
horns blowing, lances lowered, steeds running full out.

On a crest afar Ebonskaith watched, and did nought to stop
the Jordians from overrunning the train. After all, the weakling
Human who now held him in thrall by that abomination of a
'Stone had said nought about protecting his vulnerable lines of
supply. And so the Dragon watched, as men slew men below.

Weary, midst a mixed band of Garian and Avenian warriors,
King Dulon sat in a small woodland on the banks of the Ironwater River. Two fortnights past, Dendor had fallen. Dulon and
four thousand had managed to break through the ring of besiegers, but two thousand more had been slain since then, including King Vlak of Garia. Nevertheless, the surviving Garians
had remained loyal to Dulon, and they continued to harass the
enemy, continued to strike and flee and draw them after, for that
was what the High King had asked of Dulon, and what he had
pledged to do. And now he sat in the mid of night and drank
cold water and ate cold crue and thought of warm fires and warm
food and Queen Beca, his oh-so-very-warm wife.

"My lord," hissed Pytr at his side, "someone comes."

Dulon looked up in the wan light of the waning, half-silver
moon to see a warrior approach. "Gurd," said Dulon. The man
knelt at the king's side, not in obeisance, but rather to speak in
soft tones.

"A force, my lord, two or three thousand I ween, nearing the
river upstream. Two miles hence."

"This side or that?"

"That."

"Invaders?"

"Nay, my lord, but just who they might be—"

In that moment a distant knelling came ringing along the ice
of the frozen Ironwater.

Dulon sighed. "They cross." He turned to Pytr. "Get the men
ready."

"Fight or flight?"

"I know not. Yet mounted I would have them."

Soon all the men were ahorse, the steeds standing quietly in the riverside woods there along the Sea Road, a tradeway from Dael in the north running south-southeast to the city of Rhondor on the Inner Sea, and then on to the Avagon beyond.

And they waited, weapons ready . . .

And waited . . .

In the moonlight they waited, every man's sight searching, seeking . . .

And still they waited.

And at last along the road came three broad-shouldered outriders, with a vanguard of a hundred or so a furlong or two behind, and two furlongs beyond them came the main body.

They were mounted on ponies.

Dulon let out a long breath of air and sheathed his sword, then rode out before the trio.

"Hail!"

"Kruk!" spat the one in the lead, and even as the rest of the men surged out from the trees and onto the road, he reached over his shoulder and drew a double-bitted axe from the sling on his back. The two behind leveled crossbows.

"Hold!" cried Dulon. "I am of Dendor in Aven, and these are my men."

From the oncoming vanguard there sounded a horn, and they and the host behind spurred ponies to a gallop, weapons in hand.

"Sheathe your blades!" called Dulon to his men. "These are *Dvärgvolk*! Allies!"

And as the men sheathed their weapons, so too did the trio relax their guard, for now they saw the blue-and-gold standard and had heard the name Dvärgvolk and so recognized the men for who they were. Even so, there was yet the vanguard and the main body galloping forward, coming to the aid of the outriders.

The scout in the lead turned and said something in Châkur—the harsh tongue of the Dwarves—and one of the two with the crossbows raised a horn to his lips and blew a resonant call.

"But I would not flee from these dogs," gritted Borak, DelfLord of Kachar.

"My lord," said Dulon, "although 'tis a boon you offer—your host to aid us in our running battles—the High King needs you at his side, for upon the Plains of Valon will this matter be settled, or so I am told. My task is to draw this so-called Golden Horde unto the banks of the Argon, whereas the duty of all others is to be at the warfield in Valon. Hence, I would beg you to ride on, just as the Jordians did, for the time is drawing nigh for the final conflict."

Borak growled and tugged at his black beard. He glanced across at Ravvi, his eldest son. Ravvi's black eyes flashed in the moonlight as he said, "I too would not run away from a battle, sire, yet King Dulon is right: we all of us are duty-bound, and our charge is to join with the High King's Host." Ravvi clenched a fist. "Yet heed! Once there, we and our kindred will join together, and then let these yellow dogs come to us for a taste of good Châkka steel."

Borak leapt to his feet and raised his axe on high and cried, *"Châkka shok! Châkka cor!"*

Châkka shok! Châkka cor! rang the response from all the Dwarven host.

Pytr flinched at the sound and glanced about, wondering if outriders from the Golden Horde had heard the mighty shout.

Noting the look, King Dulon sighed and shrugged.

Kutsen Yong stroked the Dragonstone and looked up at newly summoned Ebonskaith and demanded: "The cities are empty, the land barren, neither warrior nor maiden nor merchant nor peasant to be found. Where have they gone?"

Ebonskaith considered his answer. Finally, he said, "South and west they flee before your Golden Horde."

Kutsen Yong glared. "They flee before *me*, Dragon, not my Golden Horde, for I am the Masula Yongsa Wang."

Ebonskaith did not respond and merely sat by, the rage in his eyes unconcealed, much to Kutsen Yong's glee, and the unworthy wielder of the Dragonstone laughed aloud; then did Ebonskaith's wrath break free, and he roared flames into the sky. Men in the camp shrieked in terror and covered their ears; horses pulled loose from their tethers and bolted, screaming as would women cry.

"Enough!" shouted Kutsen Yong, his hands clapped over his ears.

The flame died.

"Do that not again unless so commanded by me," shouted Kutsen Yong.

For a moment naked fury stared out from Ebonskaith, but then he hooded his gaze.

"Ydral," said Kutsen Yong, "I would have him at my side. Where is he? And where is this Dragon you sent after him?"

Ebonskaith's tongue flicked at the corner of his mouth. "Raudhrskal has tasted the yellow-eyed mongrel's scent and even now follows the Fell Beast." And then Ebonskaith turned his head away and smiled, as much as a Dragon can.

Far to the south and east, across the Sindhu Sea did a Fell Beast wing above waters pale green. Clutched in its claws was a small shrieking man, brown skinned, as if from one of the isles of the Ten Thousand Isles of Mordain. It was the fifth victim the Fell Beast had captured so far and borne to its distant lair, for Ydral needed to gain more <power>; too, he had to eat.

Swiftly did the Fell Beast fly, for it sensed a thing afar, a thing in pursuit, a deadly thing the Fell Beast could not defeat. Above trapped hulks and to the center of the slow-turning morass did the Fell Beast fly, and midmost in this long, long swirl did the creature come to a steep-sided rocky isle. Down it swooped toward the upjutting mass, but it did not land thereupon; instead it soared just above the undulant water and 'round the perimeter of stone. And then through a large, jagged opening angling up from the sea the Fell Beast and its shrilling burden disappeared into the high-rising bluff.

At the place of the Argon Ferry, the river nearly two miles wide, Humans and Dwarves and Dylvana and Baeron and horses and ponies and wagons were massed along the eastern shore, waiting to ferry across to join with those who had come to the plains from the west. Fjordlander Dragonships and ships of the King's Fleet, longboats from Jute and crafts from Arbalin, rowboats and skiffs and dinghies and other such were pressed into service, along with the two craft of the Argon Ferry itself. On the far western shore where the warriors debarked, wagons were off-loaded, horses and ponies, too; and companies and squads and brigades formed up again and marched westerly and into the High King's camp.

Far to the north and east, three great beings set forth from the cold ruins of a recently extinguished firemountain. Through the very living stone of Mithgar the beings with gems for eyes did fare. They were headed southwesterly, toward the Plains of Valon, for the day of the Trine was near, and they bore with them a great token of power, a silveron hammer in hand.

Fighting running battles by day and resting in hidden camps at night, King Dulon and his men drew the Golden Horde south and west. Away from the Ironwater River did the king fare, and down through South Riamon, slowly pressing toward the southern bounds of the Greatwood. Along this marge, west they did turn, now riding among the Glave Hills, the mounds and hillocks and knolls with their valleys between giving shelter to his weary force—men and horses both.

Yet with each and every strike did the Golden Horde send more men after, and on this mid-February day, King Dulon and his mixed company—now less than a thousand in all—engaged the enemy again, fighting amid the hills, twining through notches and narrow vales, where the contingent of foes they now faced could not bring their full force to bear.

But then they came into a broad vale, and the enemy poured inward after.

"We have come to the last of our strength," said Dulon to Pytr, the lad yet at his side. "We have drawn them as far as we can, and here I fear it will end."

"Then, sire," replied Pytr, "though we be outnumbered three or four to one, let us give them a mortal battle and make each of our deaths cost dear."

The king nodded, and then said, "Sound the horn. A fitting end we shall have."

Pytr raised the horn to his lips and sounded a call.

The men formed up, grim looks filling their eyes, as into the face of Oblivion they stared.

Across the way the enemy formed up as well.

Again Pytr sounded a call, and lances were lowered and

couched by the Avenians who yet had them, and sabers were taken in hand. And at King Dulon's side, Gurd raised the blue-and-gold standard for the final battle.

And at a signal from the king, one last time did Pytr sound the horn—

—and lo! it was answered by a silver cry from the hills above.

And sleets of arrows came sheeting down into the ranks of the foe.

CHAPTER 49

Asea

January–February, 5E1010

[The Present]

"Cap'n, Cap'n!" Small Rob, cabin boy of the *Pelican*, ran pell-mell to the sterncastle and jerked open the door and flung himself down the short ladder and into the passageway beyond. "Cap'n!" he shouted again, even as he reached the captain's cabin and pounded on the door. "A ship o'erhales abaft."

Whitby, captain of the *Pelican*, jerked open the door. "What's that, boy? A ship astern?"

"Aye, Cap'n, and—"

"Do she bear crimson sails, lad?" demanded Whitby as he snatched up his coat and hurried down the passageway.

"No, Cap'n, just the opposite. Light blue, they are, like the sky."

"Light blue? Light blue? Now where have I— Oh, lor', can it be?" Whitby, a towheaded Gelender in his forties, captain of the *Pelican*, a merchanter out of Port Chamer in Gelen, took the three steps all in one leap. Swiftly he crossed to the aft ladder and clambered up to the sterncastle deck, the cabin boy right behind. At the taffrail and peering hindward stood nineteen-year-old Ensign Morrin, son of the company's founder, out to sea to gain some experience and "become a man." Orbie, the tall, gawky steersman, also gazed aft, though he kept a firm hand on the wheel. Down on the main deck, the day crew stood gaping hindward as well.

As the captain came alongside and looked at the o'erhaling

ship arear, the ensign said, "We didn't see it until but a moment ago; with her sails the color of the sky and her hull the color of the sea, it was as if she appeared from nowhere."

" 'At's right, Cap'n," chimed in Orbie. "We didn' see 'er till she was close on. Be she a raider?"

Whitby laughed and shook his head. "By gar, Orbie, no raider is she. Bell all the crew adeck. This they've got to see, for 'tis a legend come to life."

"Legend, Captain?" asked Ensign Morrin, as Orbie rang the bell.

"Aye, lest these eyes deceive, 'tis the *Eroean*, not seen in any waters since the Winter War."

"But, Captain, that's a thousand years apast."

"Aye," replied Whitby, "and before then she'd been gone from the waters a good six thousand years, but now she's back once more." And he stood and looked as onward came the *Eroean*, and the remainder of the crew scrambled adeck in answer to the bell. Mister Randall, first mate, came up the ladder to the stern-castle and, elbowing Small Rob to the side, he took a stance beside the captain.

And on came the *Eroean*.

Three-masted she was with a cloud of sails, three-masted and swift. Her bow was narrow and as sharp as a knife to cut through the waters, the shape smoothly flaring back to a wall-sided hull running for most of her length, the hull finally tapering up to a rounded aft. Two hundred and twelve feet she measured from stem to stern, her masts raked back at an angle. No sterncastle did she bear, nor fo'c's'le on her bow. Instead her shape was low and slender, for her beam measured but thirty-six feet at the widest, and she drew but thirty feet of water fully laded. Her mainmast rose one hundred forty-six feet above her deck, and her main yard was seventy-eight feet from tip to tip. As to the mizzen- and foremasts, they were but slightly shorter and their yards a bit less wide.

And running before the Northeast Trades, the ship came on and on, churning a white wake, all bit of sail she could fly standing in the wind—mains and studs, jibs and spanker, staysails, topsails, gallants and royals, skysails and moonrakers and starscrapers. South through the Weston Ocean she bore, bearing slightly west, on a parallel course to the *Pelican*, strong winds on her larboard beam aft.

"Lor', Cap'n, look at her run," said Small Rob. "Why, she must be makin' ten, twelve knots."

"More like fifteen, lad," replied Whitby.

"Fifteen!" blurted Rob. "And here I thought we were runnin' fair at six. But th' Elvenship, now, why, at fifteen she could sail the world in a week or so."

Whitby laughed. "Not quite, boy, not quite. And I ween she'll slow soon enough: the Doldrums lie ahead. Still she's the fastest thing afloat, or so the legends say."

"Hmph!" snorted Ensign Morrin. "'Tis a wonder why she doesn't just founder and sink."

"What do you mean?" asked Small Rob.

"Boy, you'll address me by my rank," demanded Morrin.

"I'm sorry, er, Ensign Morrin," apologized the lad. "Still, sir, I would ask: why would she founder and sink?"

"Just look at her," said the ensign, deigning to reply, "cleaving the waves as she does. Why, with that cutting prow, high seas alone should sink the vessel. It's foolish to have aught but a rounded bow: everyone knows that a good ship is designed to ride up and over the waves."

"Cod's head and mackerel tail," agreed the first mate, "so the ship builders say: the round cod's head smacks and batters into the waves, riding up over each crest, and the narrow stern leaves a clean wake with hardly any churn, all safe and sane."

"Indeed, Mister Randall," said Morrin. "And just look: the Elvenship is all wrong, her design foolish, mad—her prow sword-sharp and her stern club-blunt—built absolutely backwards!"

Randall nodded, adding, "And with that much sail, come a sudden gust, all her masts will splinter into flinders, or so I do say."

Captain Whitby smiled unto himself, and he said, "Why, then, it must be a pure wonder that the *Eroean* has managed to survive the sea thousands of years, flying all that silk and slicing right through each and every billow, water rolling over her decks."

"That's right, Captain," replied Randall, not at all recognizing the irony. "A wet ship, that one, and someday in heavy wind and wave she'll plow under never to return, if I do say so my-self."

But Orbie said, "I don't think she'll ever sink, in spite o' 'er mad design, for there be *magic* bound in 'er 'ull and *that* be what 'olds 'er up. As long as the magic endures, well, she'll ne'er founder, ne'er be sucked adown."

"Aye, Orbie, 'ee may be right," said Randall. "But mark my words, if she loses her magic, she'll sink down like a cold stone."

Morrin looked at the first mate and said, "And that's why, Mister Randall, no one will ever build another ship like her, for 'tis magic alone keeps her afloat."

Swiftly the Elvenship overhauled the *Pelican*, and as the *Eroean* passed and drew away, Small Rob's eyes flew wide and he cried out, "Lor', Cap'n, war that a *Wolf* astandin' just aft o' the bowsprit, or did my eyes deceive?"

Whitby, his own eyes wide in wonder, said, "It seemed a Wolf to me, lad, and a bigger one I ne'er seen."

Onward she sped, the Elvenship, her shoulder to the sea, her great cloud of sails run full out and filled from ties to sheets, the vigorous wind on her aft larboard and driving her on and on, her sleek hull soon lost over the horizon, her mast and sails following. And then she was gone, was gone, and even her wake disappeared, leaving the *Pelican* alone on the sea.

As they left the merchanter behind, Aravan came up through the main hatch from the lower deck, where the carpenters worked on a small Dragonship below, following the captain's plan. For back in Merchants Crossing, while waiting for Bair to appear, heeding the message Dalavar Wolfmage had left for Long Tom to deliver, Aravan had called the two ship's carpenters to the Captain's Salon. . . .

"I would have ye build me a Dragonship," said Aravan as he gestured toward the plans spread out on the table before him, and the pair, Master Gregori and Journeyman Willam, glanced at one another and stepped to the table to see. "Overlapping, clinker-built oaken strakes she will have," said Aravan, "and a tall pine mast. A Fjordlander ship, but smaller in all respects. Twenty feet from stem to stern I would have her, shallow-bottomed and four feet abeam, with but two feet from her narrow keelboard to the height of her top wale. . . ."

Aravan went over the plans, detail by detail, some of which made both carpenters mutter and shake their heads.

"She'll ne'er hold together, wi' planks that thin," said Willam, a man of Wellen, placing a finger on a measurement noted on the vellum.

Aravan said, "The strakes making up her hull must be planed spare."

"But Capitain," protested Gregori, the Arbalinian shaking his head, "they no be thick as boot leather." As Aravan laughed, Gregori stroked the lean jaw on his angular face and added, "A bit thicker than boot leather they be, but Capitain, why so thin?"

"For flexibility in the weed," replied Aravan. "With what little water she'll draw, and the narrow keelboard under, the give of her supple, shallow-bottomed hull along with the overlapping strakes will help her steer through that cursed grasp without the weed grabbing on."

"She wiggle like snake?"

Again Aravan laughed. "Aye, Gregori, she wiggle like snake."

Gregori turned to Willam and shrugged . . .

. . . and so the work had begun.

Aravan emerged from belowdecks and, glancing at the merchant ship falling away aft, he strode forward to the larboard-side short ladder and climbed to the low foredeck, where he stood alongside Hunter. The Silver Wolf glanced at the Friend, then faced front once more.

Above them flew the jibs—flying, outer, and inner—as well as the fore staysail, the silks filled and straining with the braw following wind. Behind them and arrayed up the foremain, main- and mizzenmasts, every bit of sail that could be rigged was filled to the full as well, including the stud sails extending outward to either side from the fore and mainmast yards up to the gallants.

Before them beyond the long bowsprit and as far as the eye could see stretched the dark indigo waters of the Weston Ocean, her wind-driven waves rolling above an unseen and vasty deep.

"Quite a sight, neh?" said Aravan, gesturing at the restless expanse.

A rumble sounded deep in Hunter's chest, yet what it meant, Aravan did not know.

They were some thirteen and a half days out of Merchants Crossing and running before the Northeast Trades, all the winds fair and favoring, for the full of the way across the Avagon and through the Straits of Kistan the seasonal Easterlies had driven them westward, and only now and again had they needed to trim, hauling the halyards a point or two to make the most of the following air.

Yet though nothing had slowed or delayed their journey, still as they had come to the Northern Kistanian Straits they had made ready for the worst—for here did the Rovers of Kistan lay in wait for the unprepared merchanters. And yet the *Eroean* had sailed through entirely unmolested—no attacks, no pursuit, no attempted intercepts—but that did not mean the Elvenship was alone in these waters, for many a red sail did they see, sails of the Rovers, pirates all, faring in their seagoing dhows. And though Aravan called the crew to stand by the ballistas, he did not turn to engage these oceanic brigands, for the *Eroean* had no time to spare. Nor did the brigands pay them any heed, for so too did it seem the Rovers of Kistan were on urgent missions as well, the ships of the crimson sails tacking against the easterly winds. And as the *Eroean* had fared westward past several of the lateen-sailed dhows, Aravan had said, "What ill do they fare east to commit?"

Bair had frowned in concentration. "Kelan, remember Dodona's words: 'The South prepares for war.' We saw armies— the Fists of Rakka—marching northward. Could it be that these Rovers plan on bearing the Fists across the Avagon and to the High King's shores?"

Aravan sighed. "Aye, elar, I deem thou hast the right of it."

"Isn't there something we can do?" asked Bair.

Aravan shook his head. "We can but hope the Realmsmen have borne word unto King Garon, for we cannot delay."

And so the *Eroean* had sailed onward, faring west, while crimson sails fared east.

Through the straits they had gone and into the ocean beyond, and they turned southwesterly, the shores of Hyree on the larboard beam.

But now they ran before the Northeast Trades in the open sea, Hyree no longer seen. And Aravan stood beside Hunter, both savoring the clean smell of salt on the air.

Of a sudden and from a dark shimmer Bair stepped forth, Hunter no longer adeck.

"He likes the clean smell of the sea, as do I," said Bair.

"Hunter?"

"Yes."

They stood in the prow a bit longer, nought but the sound of the hull *shssh*ing and the creaking of rope straining against wood and the occasional crack as silken sail flexed in the wind.

"Do we go by the shortest route?" asked Bair.

"Nay, elar," replied Aravan, "because of wind and currents, the shortest route is not always the quickest. Come with me."

Down from the foredeck and onto the main they strode, passing by sailors leaning on the toprail and watching the seas running aft, all the men turning to look with a bit of awe at the tall lad who was a 'Wolf and the Elf who was a falcon. As they came to the aft-cabin door, Aravan looked up at Long Tom on the low deck above. "Tom, I would have thy advice. Too, have Noddy come to the salon."

"Aye, Cap'n." Long Tom turned to the steersman. "Wooly, stay wi' th' wind, 'n' should it shift, well, send som'n' t' fetch me."

"Aye, Tom, I will at that," said Wooly, a stocky, dark-haired West Gelender.

"Noddy! Noddy!" bellowed Long Tom as he scrambled down the short aft deck ladder.

From amidships Noddy came running. "Aye, Mister Tom."

"Cap'n Aravan wants ye in th' saloon."

With Noddy bolting ahead, Long Tom followed the lad through the aft doorway and down the four-step ladder into the passageway beyond. As he passed one of the aft-cabin doors, Nikolai, the ship's second mate, suppressing a yawn while flinging on his shirt, came out from his cabin and followed, having been wakened by Aravan's knock, and summoned to the salon as well.

Along the passageway to the captain's lounge they went, passing by Noddy, who was then running back out.

In the salon, the mates found Aravan spreading out charts on the large central table, Bair standing at his side. As Aravan closed the map-table drawer and Long Tom and Nikolai stepped to the board, Bair frowned at the charts, then traced a line down the coast and 'round the Cape of Storms and across the Sindhu Sea to the Great Swirl. "This looks the shortest to me, kelan. But not knowing the wind and currents, what I have traced may not be the quickest."

Long Tom cleared his throat and said, "Aye, it does look shortest at that, yet looks 'r' deceiving, Mister Bair." Long Tom's finger followed a route of his own, saying, "This be th' shortest o' all."

Bair frowned. "But Tom, you've traced a great long arc down through the Polar Seas and back up to the Swirl."

Long Tom shrugged. "It be way o' th' w'rld, Mister Bair, it bein' 'round 'n' all loike a griate bludy ball—they say—'n' that be a fact, it is—they say—though why we don't fall off, well, that Oi couldna say, though Oi do suspicion it has somewhat t' do wi' them mysterious poles what some folk talk about. Regardless, this 'ere way be th' shortest, 'n' so Oi do say, Oi do."

Bair cocked an eyebrow skeptically, and, seeing the look, Long Tom said, "Lemme riddle you this, Mister Bair, for it's th' way it wos riddled t' me, 'n' by it Oi did learn th' ways o' th' w'rld 'n' th' poles 'n' all, Oi did. If th' w'rld be truly round—'n' I ain't sayin' it is, mind, but that be what they say—if you was atryin' t' get t' som' pliace fro' 'ere striaght through th' pole t' th' opposite side o' th' w'rld, 'n' if th' ice was instead open ocean, then 'ow would you go t' th' pliace you be tryin' t' reach?"

"Why, straight over the pole, Tom," answered Bair, glancing at Aravan, but his kelan merely smiled and waited.

Long Tom then stabbed a finger to a distant place. "W'll then look 'ee: th' Griate Island 'ere in th' Bright Sea be on the opposite side o' th' w'rld from where we be, 'n' if you go striaght over th' pole t' get t' it, then that'd be the shortest course, naow, roight?"

Bair slowly nodded, studying the map.

Long Tom grinned. "Then tell me, Mister Bair, just 'ow would you mark that route on this 'ere chart, it bein' a striaght run 'n' all?"

"Well, I suppose I would— Hmm. I would go straight down this way and then, er . . . Say! The run to the Great Isle would have to be straight, too. —Straight north from the pole. And the only way I can make it run due north is to jump over here and run straight back up if I could go straight through."

"Ha!" crowed Long Tom. "That be th' mystery o' th' pole, that jump, you see, 'cause th' closer t' th' poles you be, the shorter long distances are, 'n' that jump proves it, Oi say, or so Oi woz atold."

Bair, who had not heard a word Tom had said, yet puzzled over the map. "But since I can't run straight through, I would instead sail to the ice and follow it 'round and—"

"Not quite, Mister Bair," interrupted Tom. "Instead you'd run a long curve adown t' a point in between 'ere 'n' there 'n' another long curve back up t' reach your goal, 'cause—"

"Ah!" said Bair, suddenly enlightened. "Because the flat map we're looking at grows more distorted the farther south we go, the pole itself being the entire bottom edge instead of a point on a globe."

Long Tom scratched his head in puzzlement, frowning at the map. "W'll, that—"

"Oh! Wait! I see!" blurted Bair. "A straight line on a globe would look like a curve on a flat map, and so this arc you've drawn down into the Polar Sea and back up is indeed more direct."

As Aravan grinned at the lad, Long Tom said, "W'll, that be not th' way Oi learned it, but Oi suppose it'll do, Oi do. Regardless, this do be th' shortest way t' th' Griate Sw'rl, or so Oi say, Oi say."

Long Tom glanced at Aravan for confirmation, but Nikolai said, "Ah, but I no t'ink it be fastest." The second mate brushed a lock of black hair out of his eyes as he studied the chart, then, pointing to several notations, he said, "See current an' win's— here an' here an' here—all be agin' ship 'long coastal waters. Mus' be more better way, eh, Kapitan, some way faster, no?"

At that moment Noddy came back into the salon, the lad bearing a porcelain teapot and five earthenware mugs on a wooden tray, along with a small tin of honey and a short wooden spoon. "There be no milk, Cap'n. It be gone all blinky, cook says."

Aravan glanced at Long Tom, and the big man said, "Oi may be a Gelender, but Oi c'n drink it black, Oi can."

Noddy poured four mugs of steaming tea and looked at Aravan, and at a nod, poured one for himself. They passed the tin of honey about, Long Tom, Nikolai, and Noddy all taking generous dollops, Aravan and Bair forgoing any. And as they sipped, Nikolai said, "We do go faster way, Kapitan, no?"

Aravan smiled and set his mug aside. "Aye. A faster way, Nick, though a bit longer." He traced a course southwesterly. "Given favorable winds we will ride the Northeast Trades to the Midline Doldrums, where, if necessary, we will row and tow across, though at this time of year, the air may yet be with us. Past the midline, we continue southwesterly till we round the shoulder of Hyree." Aravan pointed to a turn in the land a hundred fifty miles to the east. "Then 'tis due south we run, the course taking us out of the north-bearing coastal current and into the open sea." Aravan looked up at Bair and then at Long Tom. "Were we to run the shortest course down the coast, not only would we be running against the current, we would be tacking against the wind. Yet out in the open ocean, we will then be running with the Southeast Trades blowing into our fore larboard quarter instead of dead against the course." Once again Aravan looked down at the map, his finger continuing to trace a run due south. "Down to the Calms of the Goat we fare and hope the wind does not die altogether. Once past the calms, the wind should be the Braw Westwards, blowing on our starboard beam." On the flat map Aravan now scribed a long arc, tracing the curve of a great circle route. "Once in the Braw Westwards we will sail thus, the wind shifting aft as we run, faring at last into the Westerlies in the waters of the Polar Sea, where the—"

"But kelan," interrupted Bair, "it's winter and the—"

" 'Tis winter in the north, Bair, but south of the midline the warm season now runs."

"Ach!" said Bair, smacking a palm to his forehead.

"Beggin' your pardon, Cap'n," said Long Tom, "but e'en in th' warm season, they say, they do, that sudden 'n' fiercelike winter storms can come ablowin' down in them Polar Seas, or so 'tis they say, and so 'tis Oi hear."

"Aye, Kapitan," chimed in Nikolai. "Long Tom, he be right, by damn. Sudden *beueri*—blizzard win's—break mast; blow ship down."

"All the better should the wind fiercely blow," said Aravan, "for in those lats they run with us, and I would have such hurl us along our way."

Bair looked into Aravan's eyes. "Did you not tell me that the *Eroean* was dismasted in a Polar Sea blow?"

Aravan nodded, and both Long Tom and Nikolai gasped and Noddy nearly dropped his mug. And Aravan said, " 'Twas in the opposite of the year, Bair—summer up north and the cold season south—when the winds hurtling 'round the pole are brutal, more fierce than that which now runs. Even so, should such a blow come upon us, this time I'll fly less silk . . . unless, that is, we have no choice but to run full out."

Aravan paused, and yet none said aught, and so he returned to the map. "Though 'tis the warm season in the South Polar Sea, even so it is chill, and the crew will have to dress warmly. Yet heed, as in all the waters of the world, the *Eroean* depends on the wind, and we can but hope the Westerlies will remain steady in those frigid waters as well. As the Gjeenians say, Rualla, Mistress of the Winds, is fickle, and She may turn Her back on us, even in that sea. Only in the storms of wintry summer do Her winds fully roar along the ice, and occasionally in the warm season as well; let us pray that such is the case now, for I would rather run reefed before a screaming howl than lug full silked in a calm."

Aravan looked about the table, seeking comment, finding none, and so he returned to the long arcing course. "Past this point of the polar ice will we run, and then onward and into the Braw Westwards again, and these we will ride unto the Great Swirl. There we will take the ship into the weed, fifty sea leagues or so. Then Bair and I will go on alone in the small Dragonship being built below."

Long Tom sighed. "You can't take some o' us wi' you?"

"Aye, Kapitan," added Nikolai, "I fight good with knife."

"Me too," said Noddy, his voice uncertain.

"No, Tom, Nick. And no, Noddy. All hands will be needed to back the *Eroean* out from the weed so she doesn't get caught like the others trapped in that mass. Ye'll bring her about and sail her to clear water, then south across the Braw Westwards and 'round to the far side, where ye'll run back and forth out of the grass along the eastern marge." Aravan glanced at Bair. "When we succeed—if we succeed—we will hie downwind to that reach and wait for the ship to find us."

And thus was the course laid out, the path the *Eroean* would follow, and they flew before the Northeast Trades the rest of that day and through the night, making just over fifteen knots, and all did pray that Fortune would keep Her smiling face turned their way. Yet as the noontide approached, the ship began slowing ... and slowing ... and slowing ... until all her silk hung lank.

With but thirty-five days ere the fall of the Trine, she had come to the Midline Doldrums, where not a breath of air did stir.

CHAPTER 50

Skirmishes

January–March, 5E1010

[*The Present*]

O ut from Wood's-heart rode Silverleaf and the Dylvana, one
hundred blades, one hundred bows, one hundred warriors in
all, answering the call of High King Garon. Out they rode and
away, remounts and packhorses following. Through the twilit
woodland they fared, great Eldtrees looming above, shedding a
gloaming down softly.

Throughout the day they rode, changing mounts often. Even
so they did not press the pace, for the journey ahead was long.
They splashed through Quadrill Ford in midafternoon, and then
the ford o'er the Rothro late in the day, where they made camp
for the eve.

Just ere noon of the following day they came to the ferry dock
on the west bank of the Argon, there nigh Olorin Isle, and they
were borne across ten horses at a time by the Baeron ferrymen,
Elves among the steeds. From the west bank to the isle they went,
and thence on a second ferry unto the eastern shore. It was well
into the night ere all had debarked.

The next day they rode northeasterly among trees at the south-
western tip of Darda Erynian, and that eve they came unto the
ruins of Caer Lindor, an island fortress betrayed and hurled down
long past during the Great War of the Ban.

They crossed the River Rissanin the next day to come into
Darda Stor, named the Greatwood by the Baeron; few of those

mighty men were now therein, having answered the High King's call.

Over the next days southeasterly they fared through the winter-barren forest, to come once again unto the rim of the Great Escarpment, only now they were to the east of the Argon instead of to the west. They continued on their southeasterly course as the days fled by, riding down a long slope as the escarpment slowly diminished, Silverleaf and the Dylvana aiming for the bank of the Argon below.

At last they reached the flats, the river to the right, Darda Stor to the left, and on they went and on, the February chill lying across the land, snow falling now and again.

It was mid-February, the seventeenth, when they rode in among the Glave Hills. And nigh the noontide they heard in the distance the skirl of steel on steel and the shouts of combat afar. And then the running of horses, the sounds of battle gone, the sounds of flight nearing.

With silent hand gestures, Silverleaf signalled the company, and up the wide slope of a broad rise they rode toward a long ridge above. Nigh the crest they dismounted and, tethering the steeds to gorse and furze and whin, they silently went on upward, bows in hand, arrows nocked. Widely spread, they crept to the crest to look down into a broad vale, and from below a horn sounded.

Arrayed against one another were two forces on horseback. To the left were some four thousand warriors astride rangy and winter-shagged steppe ponies. A flag flew in their midst: a sinuous, snakelike red Dragon on a golden field.

Again a horn sounded, and the outnumbered force to the right, nine hundred or so, lowered lances and drew sabers, and a blue-and-gold flag was raised at the fore of the riders there.

Silverleaf signed to the company to draw arrow upon the force to the left, and he gave another sign to Eloran. And even as the Dylvana raised a horn to his lips, the clarion below sounded a third time. In answer, Eloran blew the call to attack, and as one, the Dylvana company loosed a rain of death down on the Dragon-flagged brigade below.

First to fall was the Dragon-flag bearer, slain by a shaft from Silverleaf's silver-handled, white-bone bow. And but a heartbeat later, next to him fell the brigade commander, slain by Silver-leaf's arrow as well.

Ai! wailed those in the fore, even as Elven shafts slew. *Fubing! Syanging!*

Silverleaf knew not what they were crying, but "ambush" and "trap" seemed befitting, and the golden-tan warriors in the front turned their mounts about and struggled through the mass behind, horses squealing and kicking, as arrow-pierced riders fell to the ground.

"Trumps all!" cried Silverleaf, and Elves raised clarions to their lips, and a half a hundred silver horns called out, echoing from the hills, sounding as if thousands were coming, even as sleets of arrows hurtled into the ranks.

And below panic reigned as the Dragon-flagged warriors fled.

Within but moments the vale was empty of all but the men of Aven, and the bodies of the arrow-slain, a handful of steppe horses milling among the dead; and shortly thereafter King Dulon raised weary eyes to see one hundred Elves come riding over the ridge and down.

On the first day of March, at the end of a series of running battles, Silverleaf's eighty-three and Dulon's five hundred and nine came at last to the banks of the Argon, wounded in their midst. They had reached the site of the Argon Ferry there along Pendwyr Road. And Dragonships and other boats bore them and their steeds across, even as a contingent of the Golden Horde came into clear sight arear.

CHAPTER 51

Rualla

February–March, 5E1010

[*The Present*]

Stroke! ... Stroke! ... Across a mirrored surface slowly rolling with long, glassy swells, throughout the day and into the night the crews in the dinghies haled the Elvenship after, not a breath of air stirring but for the gasps of harsh-breathing men. Stripped to the waist they were, sweat rolling down, the rowing ceaseless save for the changes of crews.

Stroke! ...

Bair rowed as well, and his long powerful pulls were a marvel to all the men who saw. Yet with all of his strength, even he grew weary; and so did all the rowers change and change and change again as slowly the ship, towed on long hawsers, progressed through the dead air of the aptly named Midline Doldrums.

Throughout the night and all the next day did they row, and into the next night as well, the mirror of water broken by ever-widening ringlets from the dip and pull of oars, and the expanding vee-shapes made by slow-moving prows cutting the glaze of the sea.

Stroke! ... Stroke! ... Stroke! ...

In the light of a first-quarter moon sinking in the west, Bair stood on the foredeck of the *Eroean* and watched the silvery light glimmer and gleam on the spreading ripples and the slow heave of the undulant sea. Then he turned to his kelan and said, "Lor', Aravan, will the wind ever return?"

Aravan sighed. "Did I not say, elar, that we would be at the mercy of Rualla, Mistress of the Winds, and that She is a most fickle mistress? Well, so at Her mercy we are. And when She might favor us again, none I know can say."

Bair hammered the butt of a fist to the bowsprit block, and he growled, "Our need is great, and Rualla sleeps."

"Speak not ill of Her, Bair, for we would not have Her take umbrage."

"But time is vanishing, spiralling down like sand through a glass, and I feel so . . . so . . ."

"Thwarted? Indeed, elar, so do I. Yet there is nought to be done for it . . . other than that which we now do."

Stroke! . . . Stroke! . . .

. . . And the men rowed on . . .

. . . through the night and into the dawn, Bair taking another turn at the oars . . .

. . . and midmorning came, and with it a waft of air, and the silks gently belled in the breeze, the sails softly ruffling.

"Rualla lies somewhere to the fore," hissed Bair to his crewmates. "Let us follow this trace and hunt her down."

And with renewed vigor did all the men row—*Stroke! . . . Stroke! . . . Stroke! . . .*

Forward they haled the *Eroean*, and the hint of wind grew, until in late midmorn the sails filled, the wind blowing on the fore larboard quarter. Aravan recalled the rowing crews: the towing lines were cast off and hauled in; the dinghies were rowed alongside the *Eroean*, and swiftly the rowers clambered up the rope-and-board ladders, while the boats were lifted up on the davits.

When the crews were all aboard, Aravan called out, "Swing the yardarms, Mister Long Tom, and set a course due south. We've come to the Southeast Trades, and I would make the most of this air."

And as Long Tom piped the yardarms about, the silken sails filled one by one, and soon the ship was gaining speed, running south and into an ever-strengthening flow.

At the bow, Bair watched the prow cut through the water. And then he raised his face to the sky and whispered, "Thank you, Mistress Rualla. Your wind is most welcome, but could you make it a bit stronger, please, for the whole of all hangs in the balance."

At a speed of ten knots they fared the rest of that day as well as into midday of the next, but in early afternoon the wind on the forequarter fell off a bit, and, flying all the silk she could, eight knots was the best the *Eroean* could make.

She averaged this speed for a sixday, but as she neared the Lat of the Goat, her rate began to fall. And upon reaching the lat itself in the early afternoon, she ran into fitful winds, and the crew was hard-pressed to keep angling the yardarms and shifting the sails to make the most of the capricious breeze. Even so, the *Eroean* yet made headway, though slow it was; still it was a bit better than rowers in dinghies could do.

That afternoon and into the night and all the next day as well did fickle Rualla toy with them, stirring the wind this way then that, blustering and then failing, only to come from another quarter to swirl and dance about. But at last nigh sunset did She tire of this tease, or so it seemed, for suddenly She swung the air about to steadily flow out of the sinking sun and onto the starboard beam.

" 'Tis to the edge of the Braw Westwards we've come, Nick," said Aravan. "Pipe the sails about, for now it is we run southerly and southerly, down the long curve toward the South Polar Sea and through it to the ice and then back up and out and into the Braw Westwards once more to ride to the Great Swirl beyond."

And as the sun set and twilight came, Nikolai piped the crew, and soon the *Eroean* was running nearly due south at twelve knots, her sails filled with a splendid flow blowing abeam.

Down the long curve of the great circle she sped, the fine air carrying her on, and four days later the wind blew even more braw, the *Eroean* now slashing through the waves at fifteen knots.

Aravan ordered the extra lifelines rigged, for should the seas rise the decks would be awash with water, knifing through the waves as the *Eroean* did, the sea sweeping across and aft. And that was one of the secrets of the Elvenship's speed, for instead of sailing up one side and down the other she cut straight through all but the biggest of waves.

On she sped and on, her heading slowly turning as she followed the great circle, the steady Braw Westwards shifting from beam to the starboard quarter astern.

Rain came and went, storms sweeping like long, grey brooms across the whitecapped sea, but the *Eroean* did not slow. And the air grew steadily colder the farther south she ran. The crew began wearing their polar gear when adeck, and they kept it handy when below, for none knew when the weather might turn even more brutal above.

On the third of March in the late afternoon she came into the South Polar Sea, and now driven before the Westerlies, the ship cut through twenty-foot waves rolling o'er the deck. And then did Aravan call all hands below, all but Second Mate Nikolai, who stayed in the wheelhouse to guide the ship. And when the men were assembled, Aravan stood on an anchored table and called for quiet.

"I tell ye now that should any fall overboard into these frigid waters, the ship will not slow to save ye, for ere the *Eroean* can come about in these rugged seas, whoever has fallen in will by then be dead and swept away in the icy brine."

Some men murmured at these words, while others who had sailed these seas before nodded in confirmation. Aravan let the mutter run on for a moment, and then he held up his hands for quiet. A hush fell over the crew.

"Knowing this then, this I do command: when adeck, wear thy safety harnesses and safety lines, and clip onto the lifelines, and onto the ratlines as ye do climb, and to the sparlines aloft, and into the lookout rings above, for I would not have any lost unto this perilous, unforgiving sea." He looked down at Wooly and Fat Jim standing at the fore of the men. "And ye twain, should the weather and seas be such for ye to steer from the aft deck, clip onto the wheelblock eyelets as ye do steer, for I would not have ye fall o'er the taffrail and down. But as it is now, it's the wheelhouse for ye, where warmth and comfort await."

"But Captain," said Fat Jim, a squat, rotund, bald-headed Pellarian. "It's right hard to see from the wheelhouse, especially with spray on the glass."

"Well listen t' him anow, complainin' about seein'," said Wooly. "Heed t' me, boyo, 'tis in th' wheelhouse I'll stay, f'r I'd rather be blind than dead."

At this the crew hooted, and Aravan let the laughter run its course. And then he asked, "Be there questions?"

Men looked about at one another and shrugged. But Noddy held up a hand and said, "I would ask a question, if I may, sir."

At Aravan's nod, the cabin boy said, "Is the mission we are on so important that we have to sail across this dreadful sea?"

Aravan glanced at Bair and then back to Noddy. "Aye, lad, it is."

"Then sail it we will, sir," said Noddy, looking about.

And Long Tom said, "Aye, Cap'n, as th' lad 'as vowed, sail it we will, we will."

And so all the men did shout.

With the hard-blowing Westerlies driving the *Eroean*, the Elvenship flew through the waters at twenty knots or so, her knife-sharp prow cleaving waves, water sweeping adeck. Seldom did the men have to brave the hammering brine, for the howling wind blew ever west to east. Even so, the yardarms did need a bit of haling, something well under a point a day, for the craft was on a great circle course arcing through the wind. And the men were thankful for their polar gear and slickers and boots as they struggled across the deck, but most of all they were thankful for their safety harnesses clipped to the vital lifelines.

For two full days did she run swift and true through the frigid, wind-driven waters, but in late afternoon of the third day, just as the high-looming ice of the frozen polar continent was sighted off the starboard bow, the wind began to die, and at mid of night the ship was completely becalmed in a gelid, low-rolling sea.

Stroke! . . . Stroke! . . .

Once again did the men row and tow, though even after warming to the labor, still it seemed they were slowed by the chill seeping up from the depths of the frigid water below, and the deathly cold drift of air from the towering ice walls of the continent lying some five or so miles to the starboard; it was as if the frozen realm itself were offended by these warm-blooded interlopers who dared to encroach upon the surface of the frigid South Polar Sea.

Yet still the men rowed.

Stroke! ...

And as the ship crept along the towering, continental ice—"A *cold* <fire>," said Bair. "One which bespeaks of a grim determination to quench all heat, or so to my <sight> it does seem." Bair frowned and said, "Yet underneath all I catch glimmers of the memory of warmer days, as if this once were lush."

Aravan shrugged. "Mayhap so, elar, but for all the days of Elvenkind upon this world, it has ever been a frozen waste."

"Hmm ..." mused Bair. "Even so ... —I say, kelan, are we moving at all? I mean, it seems as if we've been rowing forever and not getting anywhere."

"We're moving, Bair, though slowly. See the wake?"

Bair glanced down at the sluggish ripples spreading outward. "Still, it's much slower than when we rowed through the Midline Doldrums."

" 'Tis the cold," said Aravan by way of explanation.

Stroke! ... *Stroke!* ...

Three nights and three days did the men row, and through the dark of the moon; and on that blackest of nights, just after passing the nadir, from the west the wind rose, the silks filling slowly.

"Recall the boats," ordered Aravan, "and when all are adeck, fly every bit of silk."

Swiftly the men and dinghies were taken aboard, and the yardarms were swung about, the sails bellying full, the ship gaining speed. But then looking back o'er the stern, Long Tom saw the stars vanishing along a rising line.

"Cap'n Aravan, look abaft," he called.

Aravan looked hindward, then said, "Batten down all, Tom, and hale in the studs. 'Tis a storm riding on the rising wind."

And within but a hand of candlemarks a shrieking blizzard o'erhauled the *Eroean*, wind howling, great waves driven before it, snow hurtling past, masts creaking and groaning under the strain, the staylines moaning as would a wind-driven harp wail in the screaming blast.

"Cap'n, we've got t' reef silk," said Long Tom. "Else th' masts'll splinter, they will. Oi say we sh'd fly only th' topsails, 'n' maybe a jib. We c'n keep headway wi' j'st them, 'cause th' tops 'r' high enough t' catch th' wind when we 'r' daown in a trough, but low enough f'r easy reefin, sh'd it come t' that."

"No, Tom. We have no choice but to leave the silks as they be. Three days we were becalmed, and our goal is far, and the time of the Trine draws near."

"But Kapitan," said Nikolai, "what of ice? We no can see. We hit ice, we go down."

Bair stood at the wheelhouse window. "I can watch for <cold-fire>, but at this speed whether or no we can veer in time, that I cannot say."

"We can only pray to Adon that he will keep our path clear," said Aravan.

Long Tom took a deep breath and said, "Then pray t' Adon Oi will, Oi will."

"Me, I pray to Garlon instead," said Nikolai, "for He be master of sea."

"Perhaps I'll pray to Dark Theonor," said Fat Jim at the wheel. "They say He is Lord of the Sky."

"If I were to pray to anyone," said Bair, peering out at the raging sea, "it would be to Rualla, Mistress of the Wind, fickle though She may be."

And on through the black of night hurtled the *Eroean* amid thundering, one-hundred-foot waves, her masts straining, her stays wailing, her decks completely awash. Once before had she been driven such, and she had but barely survived, her mizzen and mainmast shattered to splinters, only her foremast intact. And now she ran in a like blizzard, her mission just as dire . . .

. . . for she was some four thousand miles from her goal, and there were but eleven full days and a daylight left ere the doom of the Trine would fall.

CHAPTER 52

Argon

March, 5E1010

[*The Present*]

As the last of the craft bore Silverleaf and Dulon and their horses o'er the width of the Argon River, the vanguard of the Golden Horde rode to the banks and looked across at the mighty force High King Garon had gathered to face them. And the men of Moko and Jinga pondered, for it was the greatest host they had seen since the invasion of Ryodo. Even so, the Golden Horde was led by the Masula Yongsa Wang—the Mage Warrior King. And did he not have Dragons at his behest? And yet the men of the vanguard looked at one another, none daring to speak what was on his mind, for Kutsen Yong—the Mighty Dragon— had been most capricious of late. Did he not withhold the Dragon and send but fifty thousand against the well-defended walls of Dendor? By whim, some said. To punish, said others. Dare not to anger him, said all. And now they stood and gazed across at the far shore, estimating the count of men, yet seeing among those distant forces what appeared to be children bearing bows.

Leagues away and deep in the living stone of Mithgar, three huge beings—twelve, thirteen, and sixteen feet tall—came southward, splitting the stone before them, sealing it up after, the one in the center bearing a puissant token of power. With great gemstone eyes—ruby and sapphire and emerald—they sighted upward through the very rock itself, by what light, none could say, yet peer upward now and again they did. And far off in the sky a mighty Dragon winged, and it was this Drake they followed, for he was the only one on the move. Most other Dragons—including the dead Cold-drakes, the ones who had not been stripped of their skins—lay nigh their lairs or within.

King Garon stood at the fore of his war commanders and advisors, and their advisors as well, Prince Ryon at his side, all looking across the Argon River as a vast army came along Pendwyr Road, a huge golden wagon rolling in its midst, a dark Drake high above.

Garon sighed. "I was hoping it would not be true, yet a Dragon rides on the winds of war."

" 'Tis Ebonskaith," said Inarion, Warder of the Northern Regions of Rell, peering upward at the Drake.

"In Jordkeep we tell the tale of Ebonskaith's battle with Black Kalgalath long past, much of it witnessed by townsmen of Halfen, there on the Boreal Sea," said King Brandt. "It is told that Black Kalgalath finally won, but barely. And now with Kalgalath no more, surely Ebonskaith reigns as the greatest Dragon of all."

"A Dragon we might have to face," said Garon. He turned to Mage Arilla. "Do you know how to defeat the Drake?"

"Debate now rages among my kind," replied the Sage. "Yet whether we can influence him through subtle means or whether we must take direct action—"

"Subtle means? Direct action?" asked the wee damman in golden armor.

"Indeed, Lady Buckthorn," replied Arilla. "Can we simply maze his mind, we may win that way—through guile. Some, though, Belgon among them, say that lightning or cold will win the day, while others advise fire—for Drakes fight Drakes with tooth and claw and fire, or with acid and poison gas if they be Cold-drakes instead."

"But is there any other way to battle the Drake?" asked the damman. "Something we who wield not the astral <fire> can use instead? A weapon or mayhap a lure?"

Arilla glanced about and, seeing no Dwarves standing nigh, in a quiet voice said, "The Dwarves of Blackstone advised we use heavy shafts tipped with the deadliest of poison and hurled by ballistas, saying that the *smüt* of the Hidden Ones—the Fox

Riders, in particular—should do the deed. When asked, they said they attempted to try it once, yet the Drake was upon them ere they were ready to cast the bolt. We then asked where they got the Pysk poison; they would only say it was left over from a successful campaign against a band of Trolls at the end of the First Era. They would answer no more, for it seems their pride was pricked by this failure of arms against the Drake. Too, that we would even question them about this loss stung their Dwarven pride, and they stormed off in high dudgeon."

"Just like a Dwarf," said Inarion. "Even so, their plan may have merit."

"Well, although we have ballistas here," said Garon, "we have no Fox Rider poison."

Ryon looked at his father. "Then, as Lady Buckthorn has suggested, can we not offer the Drake something which will win him to our cause? Neither cunning nor guile nor force nor poison, but something Dragons desire?"

Garon frowned and looked to his advisor, Fenerin. The Elf smiled at Ryon. "Art thou thinking of the prize Arin Flameseer and her band offered Raudhrskal long past?"

"Something of the sort," replied Ryon.

Fenerin turned up a hand. "Ah, Prince Ryon, we have no Krakens here, and I cannot think of aught else that would turn a Drake's head."

"Except mayhap the lost Dragonstone," said Arilla.

"Again, Sage Arilla, you name a thing we do not have," said Garon, as he gazed across the river at the massing foe. "Even so, if you can find a way to deal with the Dragon, then we hold an advantage. Even though we are outnumbered, still I believe the River Argon is a formidable ally, and we will win, slaying them even as they try to cross against the Fjordlander ships and those of the Jutes as well as those of my fleet." Garon looked at the bow of Lady Buckthorn. "And many will fall to the slings and arrows of the Warrows, as well as our other missileers, and we will kill them with our swords and axes and spears and maces and morning stars and other fell weaponry as they try to step ashore; for on the river and when debarking then they will be most vulnerable." Garon paused and sighed and looked at Arilla.

"On the other hand, if you of Mage-kind cannot stop the Drake, then I am afraid we are fordone."

A hard glint came into Ryon's eye. "But we will fight regardless, eh, Sire?"

Garon nodded. "Aye, Son, that we will, for by fighting we purchase time for the young and old, for the halt and the lame, and for our loved ones to mayhap find safety in the west."

Elsewhere among the host, Vanidar Silverleaf sat with Riatha and Urus and Faeril and spoke to them of the remarkable day when a rider had come through the dawn with a falcon on his shoulder and the Silver Sword in hand. And the trio wept to know that Bair and Aravan on that day had been safe. And they wept for they did not know whether the two were safe still, for this much Silverleaf had gleaned from what the two had said: they were on a perilous mission, one involving Ydral, an isle in the Great Swirl, a rune-marked crystal cavern, and preventing Gyphon's return ere the time of the Trine did fall.

South of the ferry and along the west banks of the Argon, a Dylvana scout stood on a knoll peering downriver. Of a sudden she started, and crouched down so as not to be seen. Along the opposite shore, a horseman towing a remount galloped north. Robed in black he was and turbaned. As the rider passed beyond, the Dylvana stood and watched him race away. A frown on her face, she turned and peered back the way the dark-robed man had come, and what she saw caused her to gasp in surprise. She stood long moments and long moments more, counting, estimating, and then, spinning on her heel, she ran down the back slope of the knoll and leapt astride her own steed and spurred forth, remount trailing, as north and away she fled.

Kutsen Yong had his rolling golden palace moved to the fore, and he summoned Ebonskaith to his side. "I would have you give me advice, Dragon: just how would you propose that I cross this great river?"

Seething with pent rage, Ebonskaith sat and glared at Kutsen Yong.

"Speak up," said Kutsen Yong, stroking the Dragonstone.

Thus forced to respond in spite of his wrath, Ebonskaith hissed, "There is a great woodland to the north, where you may send men to hew timber and make many floats with which to launch an attack."

"That is one way, Dragon. Name another."

Ebonskaith gazed at the opposite shore. "Across the way lie many boats. This night you can send companies of swimmers across to fetch them to be used as ferries."

"That is a second way," said Kutsen Yong. "Name another."

Ebonskaith gazed up and down the river, and his eyes widened slightly as he looked south. "Then I advise you wait."

"Wait?" Kutsen Yong reached for the Dragonstone. "Why should I wait? I believe instead I will summon your brethren and put an end to this usurper who would take my rightful place."

In answer, Ebonskaith pointed across the river and slightly south, where a slight Elven rider towing a remount galloped toward the High King's camp.

"What has that lackey to do with me?" demanded Kutsen Yong.

Now Ebonskaith pointed south once again, this time on the near side of the river, where a black-robed rider came racing toward Kutsen Yong's own minions. He was stopped at the perimeter by the warding ring.

"And what has this fool to do with me?" hissed Kutsen Yong.

A third time Ebonskaith pointed, and this time he directed Kutsen Yong's gaze down the flow of the river itself, where hundreds of crimson sails came gliding into view, and on the opposite shore afar a mighty force of dark-robed warriors and horsemen came marching north to the heavy beat of drums, black flags flying in their midst, sigils of white fists scribed thereon.

And within the living stone of Mithgar, three Utruni—one bearing a silveron hammer—continued faring toward the Plains of Valon as a date with Destiny drew nigh.

CHAPTER 53

Perilous Waters

March, 5E1010

[The Present]

The shrieking wind howled easterly, hurling snow and ice and the *Eroean* before its brutal blast. Great greybeards loomed over the ocean, dwarfing the tall Elvenship; up she would ride toward each towering crest, her sharp prow to cut through, her hull to slam down—*Whoom!*—upon the far side to plummet into the chasm below, then up she would ride again, sailing on slopes and crests and slants, for not even the *Eroean* could cut straight through the bulk of these mighty waves. And blinding snow and spray hurtled past, coating halyards and staylines and masts and yardarms and sails with ice, fouling pulleys and weighing down silks and glazing ropes and sheathing the decks. Her masts creaked and groaned, and her halyards moaned like a great stringed instrument sawn by the howling wind, as 'round the bottom of the world hurtled the Elvenship driven by the blizzard dire.

In the wheelhouse only Bair had any sort of vision into the blow, the lad with his <sight> watching for a glimpse of <coldfire> to the fore as the ship hurtled over each crest—*Whoom!*—and drove for the one beyond.

"Keep a sharp eye, elar, for 'tis the season of calves," said Aravan.

"By damn, Kapitan," called Nikolai above the yawl of the storm, "e'en if cub see ice on line, I no t'ink we maybe steer one side before we smash up."

Aravan nodded grimly. "We've no choice, Nick. We must run full out."

Whoom!

Long Tom shook his head. "Cap'n, Oi do say ag'in, Oi do: wha' wi' this wind 'n' all silk aflyin', well, we're likely t' lose th' masts 'n' sails 'n' all, 'n' that be moi opinion, it is, 'n' so it is." Then he added, "As th' lad said, 'n' you did agree, 'twas just such a storm in th' Polar Seas when she were dismasted afore."

"Indeed, Tom, it was. Yet when we repaired her, I had the stays strengthened, running doubles where singles ran before. Nay, Tom, she'll hold up in this wind, though we may lose some silk."

At these words Long Tom grinned and said, "Well then, Oi say, if it's j'st a bit o' silk we lose, well then, that'll be all roight, it will."

Whoom!

And onward plunged the *Eroean*, her rigging shrieking, her masts groaning, her timbers moaning, the hull booming down into the frigid brine beyond each curling crest, while monstrous waves rose up and smashed down and the storm-driven wind thundered past, and the fact that it was the warm season south mattered not at all to the dark and cold South Polar Sea.

Three days the *Eroean* ran before the brutal blow, her overall speed some twenty-two knots, and now her course took her out from the peril of the continental ice as she gradually swung points to the north and away. And in the thundering wind, sailors clipped to the safety lines slipped and slid across the icy deck to hale on the halyards and change the set of the sails as they followed a direct line on the globe on the way to the Sindhu Sea. Even though dressed to withstand the blast, still the men spent as little time out in the savage blow as completing the task allowed. Oft the pulley blocks would be jammed with ice, and a fresh crew would scurry up the frozen ratlines to the yardarms to break loose the pulley sheaves above as another crew scuttled forth to free the sheaves below and change the set of the sails. Then back down would come the high crew, and across the sheathed deck all would scrabble through the hatches and into the warm shelter 'neath. And though battered by the wind and snow and ice and losing their footing to fall, none was lost to the polar brine, for all did clip up to the lines.

And the masts groaned and ropes thrummed under the shrieking burden as great greybeards and the Elvenship hurtled through the days and nights and across the frigid sea.

But in the wee candlemarks of the fourth day of the storm the blizzard blew itself out, leaving the seas heaving in relief, great waves yet rolling, a strong wind yet flowing, clouds streaming overhead. Slowly the seas settled as east-northeast the ship ran, and in midmorn, just as the sun broke through, Aravan announced to all that they had again come into the Braw Westwards. And at fourteen knots they sailed into the southern bounds of the deep blue Sindhu Sea.

Four days later in midafternoon—"Weed ho!" cried the foremast lookout.

Bair on the foredeck peered into the distance ahead, and yet he could not see what the lookout had descried, though the <fire> to the fore was an abysmal bilious green.

Aravan came to the bow, Noddy trotting at his side, Nikolai coming after.

Long they stood and looked, Noddy up on the stemblock and holding to a foremast stay.

Northeastward they sailed and northeastward, and of a sudden Noddy gasped. "Lumme, Cap'n, but there she be."

Ahead lay a pale green sea, the waters slowly turning deasil. They had come to the Great Swirl at last, and within the heart of that vast, churning, clutching morass lay an isle some six hundred and sixty miles away, a crystal cavern down within . . .

. . . and but four days remained ere would come the cusp of the equinox, when the doom of the Trine would fall.

CHAPTER 54

Blood and Fire

March, 5E1010

[*The Present*]

"O Mighty Dragon, he seeks Ydral."

"Ydral?"

"Yes, my lord."

Kutsen Yong turned away from the captain and frowned up at Ebonskaith.

"Why ask me?" hissed Ebonskaith, turning his face toward the black-robed, turbaned man beringed by guards and standing a short distance away. "He is the one seeking."

"Bring him forward," commanded Kutsen Yong. "I would hear what he would say."

King Garon peered southward. "The Fists of Rakka, Lady Vail?"

"Yes, my Lord," replied the Dylvana, "and a great fleet."

"And their numbers?"

"I did not stop to count, yet their numbers are fully as great as ours."

"And the ships?"

"Mayhap two thousand in all," said Vail. "Mayhap more."

Garon blenched and looked at his own ships moored on the western shore: barely four hundred, counting those of the Fjord-landers and Jutes.

*   *   *

Trembling with fear at the nearness of the Dragon whose rage seemed but barely contained, the turbaned man, a white fist emblazoned on his black robe, salaamed to Kutsen Yong, who demanded, "Why have you come?"

The Southerling rose up, his eyes widening at the Dragon mark upon the face of the man on the throne. "Are you the one named Ydral?"

Ebonskaith burst into laughter, and the Southerling flinched down and away.

"Fool!" spat Kutsen Yong. "Do I look as if I would be Ydral? He is my lackey, my lapdog."

"Even so, I have been ordered to speak with Ydral, leader of this vast horde, and if not to him then to the second-in-command: the Mage Warrior King."

Once again Ebonskaith burst into laughter, and once again the man flinched down.

Kutsen Yong leapt to his feet in fury. "Did you not hear what I said? Ydral is my lapdog. I am the Masula Yongsa Wang, and only I command the Golden Horde."

The brown-skinned man was taken aback, and he bowed once more. "Forgive me, my lord, I knew not you were he, the one I was sent to find, could I not find Ydral, he who is soon to become the regent of Rakka."

Kutsen Yong frowned. "Regent? Regent? And just who is this Rakka?"

"Why, my lord, He is the god whose rightful rule was usurped by the one named Adon."

"Dolt!" hissed Kutsen Yong. "You speak of the Jìdu Shàngdi. And *I* am to be His regent, and then His equal, not that fool Ydral." Quivering in anger, Kutsen Yong said, "Deliver your message to me, else you shall answer to my Dragon."

The turbaned man fell to his knees. "O mighty lord, spare me, for this is what I was sent to say . . ."

"They've stopped," said Tillaron, peering southward at the great army standing in rows and files and waiting, even though the heavy drums continued to beat.

The High King had divided his forces, the bulk of whom now

faced the throng to the south, for they were on this side of the river, while the Golden Horde was not.

"Why?" asked Ancinda, frowning. "Why have they stopped?"

"And what's in those panelled wagons, do you think?" asked Faeril. "Completely covered as they are. There are so many."

"I know not the answer to that, wee one," replied Tillaron. "But as to them just standing there, it's as if they are waiting for some event."

Urus looked at the sky, the sun now standing at the zenith of its mid-March arc, a half-moon rising in the east. "Perhaps they are reconsidering," he growled.

"I think not," said Riatha. "Ever has the South been foe of the North—Hyree, Kistan, Chabba, Sarain, Khem, Thyra, and even some tribes of the Karoo. Nay, Urus, they've come to war upon the High King, and war upon him they will."

"Then why are they waiting?" asked Faeril. "I mean, look at them, and look at those across the river. Together they outnumber us at least three to one . . . to say nought of the Drake in their midst."

Tillaron frowned and looked back at the High King's camp. "Mayhap they wait because they know that instead of a Dragon we have Mages in our own midst—eleven hundred or thereabout, or so I have been told."

"They are beyond our range," said Arilla. "The Golden Horde stands some two miles away across the width of the Argon, and the Southerlings stand off the same."

Ryon frowned. "What of this great conjoinment? The one you spoke of weeks past. Does it not increase the range?"

"Aye, my prince," said Alorn. "Still, should we use our <fire> to attack or defend against the Golden Horde and the massed Fists of Rakka, then what shall we use to fend the Drake?"

"Pah!" snorted Belgon. "There are among us some who have the skill to strike with elemental force. The rest of Magekind is here to lend their <fire> to those of us who can."

"What of illusions or other such tricks of guile?" asked Commander Rori.

"The Drake sees through such," said Arilla. "Even so, when they attack—if they attack—as soon as they are within range, we can deal with the common soldiers, though precious <fire> needed to fend the Drake will be spent in battle instead."

"And Ebonskaith?" asked King Garon. "What of him?"

Arilla sighed and glanced at Belgon. "We have decided to try a lightning strike, should it come to that. When it appears they are ready to move, Alorn will form the grand conjoinment, and half the Mages will join in, and then acting through Alorn, Belgon will cast the bolt itself."

"I thought you were to try to confuse the Drake," said Ryon.

Belgon shook his head. "With lightning the results are evident, whereas none knows whether or no the mind of a Dragon can be mazed."

Now it was Alorn who shook his head. "Nevertheless we should try. Can we simply befuddle him then he will—"

"Bah!" snorted Belgon. "Why spend <fire> on an unknown when—"

Arilla held up her hands and stepped between the two. "Fight not again a fight which has already been fought. The council in their wisdom has decided, and I say let be!"

Alorn turned away from Belgon's sneer as King Garon glanced at Arilla and sighed.

Down went the sun and down, sinking into the west, the waxing half-moon chasing it across the sky, and still the Southerlings held fast, neither attacking nor retreating. At last the eventide came, and night followed, the moon shining down from above, and just as the High King's Host began to relax, then did the ships of Kistan raise sail, the crimson seeming black at night, and with the wind abeam they began to move upstream. Too, from the ranks of the standing foe there sounded the clatter of hasps and latches, and shortly thereafter the heavy drums hammered louder and louder; the Fists were on the move.

"My Lord King," called Commander Rori, "I do not understand: they come to fight at night!"

"Stand ready!" commanded King Garon, mounted upon a dun steed.

Near at hand spread out in a long row stood a company of Warrow archers. "My Lord," called the damman in golden armor, "the moonlight and starlight is all to the good, and we and the

Elves can see quite well, as can the Dwarves, but the bulk of this host is Human, and those archers will need to see a bit better else they'll not be as effective as they might otherwise be."

"Fear not, Lady Buckthorn," replied the King. "When the Mages decide they are close enough, then shall we—"

Up from the ranks of the Southerlings shot streaks of light, flares to bloom and hover above the High King's Host, illuminating all, and sleets of arrows came winging out of the darkness to pierce men and horses alike, animals screaming, men yelling as down they were felled.

But in that moment the flares above were extinguished, and like flares bloomed over the foe. Swiftly did Warrows and Elves and men loose arrows, and yet even as they flew, darkness fell, the flares quenched, though the shrieks of wounded and slain Southerlings came echoing on the air.

Up streaked more flares from either side, yet none whatsoever did bloom into light.

But then a vast wall of fire came rushing forward from the foe and toward the King's Host, and all did quail, but even before it arrived it vanished, as if snuffed out by forces arcane.

They have Black Mages among them, came the whispered word.

"That's why they waited until night," gritted Ancinda.

"Till night?" asked Faeril, her bandoliers full, extra knives ringed 'round her belt, a throwing dagger in each hand.

"Black Mages suffer the Ban," said Ancinda.

Faeril nodded in understanding, but then her eyes widened in revelation. "The wagons! The panelled wagons! That's where the Black Mages were. Sealed up out of the sunli—"

Prepare to battle in darkness, came the order. And though Elves could see well by starlight alone, and Warrows and Dwarves by the moonlight above, it was the men put at great disadvantage, for how could they tell their own? *"For Adon!"* cried Commander Rori, and it became the cry of the Host, and as the two forces rushed together—arrows flying, swords slashing, spears piercing, maces bashing, morning stars crushing—*For Rakka!* came the answer from the foe.

And the Elves were deadly with their superior sight, and they hewed and chopped and hacked and pierced, and yet where one man fell another ten would take his place.

Ducking and dodging, the Warrows found it difficult to loose their arrows, yet when they did, the shafts were fatal.

And shouting *Châkka shok! Châkka cor!* and singing dirges dire, Dwarves of Kachar and Mineholt North and Kraggen-cor and the Red Hills and Blackstone, and from other mineholts afar, hewed with axes and smashed with hammers and morning stars. Even so, many were the men and few were the Dwarves by comparison, and Châkka fell slain upon the field.

As for the men of the Host, the Vanadurin of Valon and Jord were afoot, their horses as likely to kill friend as to slay the foe. So, too, afoot were the men of Wellen and Jugo and Pellar and Hoven and Vancha and the other nations who had answered the High King's call. And so the steeds were gathered as the battle had begun, and haled to the corrals, where they were penned along with the ponies of the Dwarves and Warrows. And though they were away from the strife, the smell of blood was on the air, and where the ponies and untrained steeds trembled in distress, the warhorses screamed in rage.

And as to the men afoot, with saber and spear and long-knife and sword and mace and hammer and morning star did they hew and crush those who called out *Rakka!* in response to *Adon!* And yet the enemy gave as good as it got, and for every foe that fell, so did a friend.

Among the men raged the Baeron, the great warriors hewing and bashing, while within their ranks and roaring in rage, huge Bears slashed with claws.

As for Wizardkind, though they could attack individual warriors—and here and there men burst into flame or fell senseless or ran screaming from phantoms only they could see—the Mages for the most part were nullified by the commingling of the forces in melee, for then the Wizards could not use their powers to attack on a broad scale. And the foe numbered in the hundreds of thousands, and the High King's spellcasters on the field numbered just over four hundred in all, for concealed behind mazing walls of illusion—conjury to protect them from all but the Dragon and those Dark Wizards who could pierce illusion as well—six

hundred Mages stood off in grand conjoinment, waiting and waiting for Ebonskaith, and yet the Dragon did not come.

And in many places on the battlefield, fire bloomed, lightning
flew, and frigid vapors hissed, and bursts of darkness struggled
with bursts of light, as Mages and Black Mages duelled one another, one side ageing even as it fought, the other not, for they
drew <fire> from the warriors engaged in the vast battle, fear
and woe and agony and dying all about.

And out on the Great River Argon, beyond the range of the
Mages afield, ship met ship, some ramming with great underwater beaks, others casting grapnels and boarding the foe to battle hand to hand; and crews manning ballistas cast flaming balls
made of a blend of pitch and sulphur and naphtha upon one another's craft, infernos raging aboard the vessels of friend and foe
alike, and shrieking men leapt overboard ablaze. Fiercely did the
battle rage, and though they gave good account of themselves
and took many a foe ship with them, outnumbered as they were
five or six to one, down went the Dragonships and the King's
vessels into the gentle, slow current, the river quenching the fire.

And none were there to stop the Golden Horde from boarding the ships of the victorious Kistanian fleet, to be ferried across
the wide Argon.

Out on the plains of Valon afar stood Dalavar Wolfmage and
six Draega. And as he watched the battle, Dalavar's fists were
clenched, his knuckles white, his vision blurred, for tears stood
in his eyes. Yet he made no move to join the Allies, for to do
so might jeopardize that which might come. "That is the trouble
with prescient vision," he said to Greylight. "I know too much
to go to their aid, for the chances are slim as they are, and I
would not have us diminish them one whit."

On land the battle sawed back and forth, the High King's
forces slowly gaining the upper hand, but then—

"My Lord King," cried Commander Rori, "the Golden Horde,
they come."

His sword covered in blood, King Garon, yet mounted,
wheeled his horse about, and watched as—silhouetted against
ships aflame—a vast throng smashed into the allies flank.

Garon called to his bugler ahorse, and in moments a silver
cry rang through the air, repeated by black-oxen horns of the

468 / DENNIS L. McKIERNAN

Vanadurin and the argent clarions of the Elves. And within the
melee, a portion of the King's forces swung about to face this
new threat, the Host now outnumbered three to one and fighting
on two fronts.

Still the battle raged, but at last Garon called out again to his
bugler, who rode to the King's side, "Sound the withdrawal. We
must fall back unto the Red Hills for—"

Thuck!

A crossbow bolt slammed full blown into the High King's
chest. And in bewilderment he looked at the shaft and then to
his bugler and said, "Sound the withdrawal, Ryon," and then fell
from his horse dead.

CHAPTER 55

Morass

March, 5E1010

[The Present]

As into the fringes of the weed they sailed, Bair peered over the side at the *Eroean*'s prow cleaving the pale green water. Down within the brine running aft he could see long branching tendrils of grass-green wrack.

"Noddy," said Aravan, "a weighted line forward to plumb."

As Noddy rushed away, Nikolai looked at Aravan in puzzlement. "But Kapitan, water here be deep."

"Indeed, Nick," replied Aravan. "But we will use the line to collect weed and judge how thick it is."

"Ah!" said Nikolai, grinning. "Clever Kapitan." Then he looked to the fore and asked, "How far in we sail, eh?"

"When last I was here," said Aravan, "we penetrated some hundred forty sea miles ere the weed imperiled the ship, yet conditions may have changed 'tween then and now, and we may run short or long of that mark."

"When you last here, Kapitan?"

"At the end of the First Era," replied Aravan.

Nikolai's eyes flew wide in astonishment. "At the end of . . . —By damn, that be, what, seven, eight t'ousan' year?"

Aravan nodded but did not otherwise reply.

Noddy came up the short ladder to the foredeck, a weighted plumb line in his grasp. "Here be, Cap'n."

Nikolai took the burdened line from Noddy, saying, "I cast bob; let run deep; see what she bring up." The second mate gave the plumb a vertical length of slack, then stepped to the side rail and whirled the bob 'round a time or two and cast it hard to the fore and out a bit starboard, the cord uncoiling smoothly, the lead weight flying far to land with a small splash.

As Nikolai fed line out, Bair, who had said little, turned to Aravan. "Kelan, this place . . . its <fire> is quite dreadful, and it speaks of clutching, seizing, holding all within its malignant grasp."

Even as Noddy gasped at these words, Aravan said, " 'Tis an evil quag, elar, trapping ships unfortunate enough to sail within its deadly domain."

"Trapped ships, Cap'n?" said Noddy.

"Aye, lad," said Aravan. "The closer we come to the center, the thicker is the weed, until it is nought but a grasping snare, seizing ships and never releasing them, ships unwittingly caught—storm-blown, ill-captained, or ill-fated, it matters not—all have been lost."

"Lumme," breathed Noddy, scanning the horizon ahead, "a sea of lost ships lies somewhere in there?"

"Aye, Noddy, and I would not have the *Eroean* suffer the same fate."

Nikolai drew up the sounding line, tendrils clinging here and there. "Not many weed, Kapitan. *Eroean* run through this forever."

Aravan sighed. "It will change, Nick. Indeed it will change."

Throughout the remainder of that day and into the night did the Elvenship sail, the weed growing thicker by the mile, the ship slowing with the drag. Even so, Aravan kept all silk flying in the gentle wind, for time was short and somewhere ahead the *Eroean* would come to a halt. And the last leg would be sailed in the small Dragonship lying belowdecks, the craft finished, supplies laded—water and food, along with gear they might need.

Nigh mid of night, Aravan and Bair stood surveying the craft, her well-caulked, clinker-built hull painted a dark blue above the waterline, and silveron below, for Aravan had used some of the precious starsilver paint to coat her bottom and narrow, flat keelboard. Her silken sail and mast were hued sky-blue. An echo in color she was of the *Eroean*.

"Ah, but she is a fine craft," said Bair, turning to Master Gregori and Journeyman Willam.

The two carpenters bobbed their heads, and Gregori said, "A good ship—*Buona la nave*—she is."

"Knowin' how the Dragonships of th' Fjordlanders run," said Willam, "this one ought to fly spanking 'cross th' water." He gestured toward a single flat-bottom craft stowed to one side. "Not like this scow here."

Aravan smiled, for that "scow" was but one of the small crafts he and his Dwarven warband and Jinnarin and Alamar and Aylis and a handful of others had sailed through these waters to the isle long past. "They served their need," said Aravan.

"Oh, Cap'n, I didn't mean to slur it," said Willam. "It's just that, um—"

Aravan held up a staying hand. "I know, Willam: this craft should fare much swifter."

"That's right. Exactly. Beat that one and any like her all hollow she will."

"Has she a name, kelan?" asked Bair.

"Nay, but wouldst thou like to choose one?"

Bair pondered a moment. "I would call her *Little Drake*, but Drakes are all male, and this ship's a she, and I certainly don't wish to name her *Little Kraken*." He turned to the carpenters. "What have you been calling her?"

Startled, they looked at one another and flushed.

"Well?" said Bair.

"*Femina solutus*," mumbled Gregori.

As Bair frowned, Aravan broke out in laughter, and Willam blurted, "It's because th' way she's built, Cap'n, flexible and all, just like you wanted."

Bair turned to Aravan. "What does it mean?"

Yet chuckling, Aravan said, "Loose lady, Bair. It means loose lady."

Bair shrugged. "Well, it seems a perfectly good name to me. The *Loose Lady* she'll be."

"Quite fitting," said Aravan, yet grinning.

Willam looked at Gregori, and they both blew out a sigh of relief, for it was clear the lad didn't know the connotation of the name, and Captain Aravan thought it amusing.

"Well, lads, fetch some crew and raise her topside," said Aravan, "for we will need her ere long."

Dawn came and onward they sailed, moving steadily toward the center of the Great Swirl, the *Eroean* covering one hundred forty sea miles in all within this pale green sea, the same as one hundred sixty miles aland. And all the while the weed gradually thickened until the amount gathered by the plumb line at last became substantial. Aravan once again stood on the foredeck, and in early morn he finally called out, "Heave to and maintain!" and Long Tom brought her about directly into the wind, the silks flapping lank, the bosom of the sea slowly rising and falling as of a sleeping creature softly breathing, the weed acting to smooth the waves into long, gentle swells.

"We're dead 'n th' water, Cap'n," called Long Tom, as slowly the ship drifted, the current driving the Great Swirl carrying her in the weed deasil.

"Stand by for to lower *Loose Lady*," called Nikolai, the little Dragonship now rigged to the davits.

In his cabin, Bair strapped on the harness to carry the sword, and as he took up the weapon in its scabbard, he withdrew the blade and <looked> at it again. Unlike everything else in the world, everything else Bair had <seen>, this one thing held no <fire>, no <aura> whatsoever. Shaking his head in puzzlement, the lad slid the blade back into its sheath and slipped all into the harness. He hooked his flanged mace to his belt and looked around the cabin one last time. Then he took a deep breath and stepped outside, heading for the main deck above.

Aravan stood waiting at the small craft, his long-knife strapped to his thigh. And he gestured Bair aboard and clambered in after. "Lower away," he called.

As the crew payed out the davit lines, Long Tom leaned over the railing. "Oi'll bring 'er abaout, j'st as you said, Cap'n, 'n' sail 'er t' clean water. Then run th' Braw West'ards south 'n' around th' Griat Sw'rl t' t'other soide 'n' run 'er back 'n' forth waitin', Oi will, 'n' so will we all, Cap'n. 'N' so will we all."

With a sketched salute Aravan acknowledged Long Tom's words, and then the *Loose Lady* settled into the weed and water. As kelan and elar cast loose the davit lines, the crew above shouted three cheers, and then broke into a gabble of well wishes, though none of them knew just where the two fared nor why, only that it was vital. After all, hadn't they sailed through the blizzard from Hèl itself just to reach this place?

Using oars, Bair and Aravan rowed out from the wind-shadow of the *Eroean*, and then raised the sky-blue silk. Aravan set the lines on the spar and at the bottom corners of the square sail to angle the silk into the Braw Westward wind, and into the Great Swirl they fared, the morning sun bright upon undulant waters.

Behind, in a flurry of activity, the crew rushed to the halyards, and under Long Tom's command, the *Eroean* fell away on the wind, her speed gradually increasing the farther south she fared.

And within but a handful of candlemarks, Aravan and Bair and the *Loose Lady* were alone on the pale green sea.

Northeasterly they sailed, northeasterly, the angle gradually changing as the slow-turning morass of clutching weed churned 'round a distant point unseen.

The day slowly passed, the sun riding up from the horizon and overhead, then sliding down the western sky. There was little to do but sit and talk, or to stand and stretch, and only now and again did they have to clear the weed from the angled-back steerboard, for with her shallow draft and flattened keelboard and the overlapping strakes of her flexible hull, the *Loose Lady* ran quite clean through the weed-laden brine. They took meals and water and, modesty notwithstanding, they relieved themselves over the side, just as they had done when sailing from the city of Dirra in Khem down the river to the Red Bay, and then across the northern Sindhu Sea to Port Adras in Bharaq.

Gradually the weed thickened, and Bair leaned over the top wale and peered down.

"I say, kelan, there are small fish swimming among the leaves."

"Aye, Bair, and it shelters tiny crabs and shrimp and mollusks and other creatures, too."

Bair fished up a strand of the leafy tendrils; the frond was long and lank, thin-stemmed and branched, with narrow pale green leaves curled at the very tips to form tiny snags, snags which hooked on to other strands to form an entangled mass floating just under the surface. Diminutive berries grew on tender stems along the branches, and as he watched, a tiny snail slowly enveloped one.

As Bair examined the plant, Aravan said, "This weed, 'tis only green here in the Great Swirl. In the other waters of the world, 'tis reddish brown and not thick."

"Reddish brown?"

"Aye."

"Why green here alone, and red in the rest of the world?" asked Bair.

Aravan shrugged. "I know not, elar, yet when last I was here my crew said it was the curse of this place."

Bair sighed and cast the weed back. "Given how its <fire> appears, I would not gainsay them at all."

They both fell silent, pondering, and deeper into the morass they fared . . .

. . . and thicker grew the weed.

It was just after dusk in the light of the waxing gibbous moon when they saw the first trapped ship far to the starboard. What kind and where from they could not say, for it rode low in the water. Even so, they could see the hull had rotted, great gaping holes in its side.

" 'Tis held up by the weed," said Aravan, even as Bair started to ask. "The tales say that ships will be held so forever, yet I think, ship by ship, the bottoms will rot completely away, the ballast stones to plummet into the depths below along with any dense cargo, and finally the hull and decks will succumb to the brine, and then they will be gone."

"Mayhap, kelan, that is what feeds the weeds: the rot of wood, the rust of iron, the unravelling of the fiber of ropes, along with whatever is in the cargo that decays and crumbles and withers into scale and powder and pulp and slush and ooze."

With added regard Aravan looked at the lad. "Mayhap thou art right, elar."

Ere dawn they passed another craft trapped in the weed. Aravan steered wide of it, for his amulet signalled peril. Bair looked with his <sight> upon the dismasted, half-sunken hulk, its timbers shattered, a sickly green growth of slime and weed blotching the hull and covering the structures adeck. "There is a terrible black <glow> emanating from the wreck, as if something hideous dwells therein."

"Somewhat like the Lamia?"

Bair shuddered. "Yes, kelan. Somewhat like that."

"Then keep a sharp eye out, lad, though what we may do against such, I cannot say, for Krystallopŷr is gone."

Bair frowned and reached over a shoulder to touch the hilt of the Silver Sword in the sling upon his back. "Mayhap this?"

Aravan shrugged.

And on they sailed in the predawn marks, another hulk on the horizon, this one burning with green witchfire. And still the clutch of the Great Swirl slowly churned, bearing them and the hulks to the larboard.

Resting and sailing by turns, through night and day did they fare, the *Loose Lady* passing among derelicts, some afar, others near, some glowing with a <darkness> to Bair's <sight> and causing Aravan's amulet to grow chill, still others burning with witchfire, as if in mortal torment.

And all the ships they passed were worn beyond endurance; grey and lifeless they were, and a pervasive air of decay hung over all. Many were strange in design—reed boats; massive, half-sunken arks; ships fitted with banks of oars—all of them fallen into ruin, masts and spars hanging awry, some ships scarred by fire. And in one place they could not say what kind of craft had even been there, for only a long, wet mound of wood pulp rode upon the weeds.

"A graveyard of ships," said Bair.

"Aye," replied Aravan. . . .

. . . And on they sailed and on.

On the morning of the third day, Aravan awakened Bair and softly said, " 'Tis Springday, Bair, the day of the Trine."

Bair took a deep breath, and he looked to the fore, and then did his heart sink.

The island was nowhere to be seen.

But sometime after the noontide, an isle came into view, rearing up out of the sea, its looming walls stone and sheer. "Ah," sighed Bair. "Is that it, kelan?"

"Aye, elar, the center of the morass."

"Then we should be there soon."

Yet the ship slowed and slowed, for there the weed was even thicker—and ever thickening as well—as if to prevent any from reaching that goal. And the *Loose Lady* slowed to a crawl.

They broke out the oars and rowed, giving the sail what aid they could, and slowly they drew closer to their goal, even as the sun arced down in the west.

Of a sudden, in late afternoon, the little Dragonship broke into clear water, the submerged growth behind like a great green wall falling sheer into abyssal depths below. The island itself lay some two miles ahead across the open water.

As they shipped the oars, "Where is the entrance to the cavern?" asked Bair, sweat rolling down his face.

" 'Round the isle, on the southern side," replied Aravan, adjusting the set of the sail.

"How far?"

"At the angle we'll take, mayhap four miles or so."

Bair helped swing the yardarm about, the wind blowing abeam. "How big is the isle?"

"Some four miles east to west, three miles athwart."

"And how much time is left ere the cusp of the Trine when all things are in balance?"

"Four candlemarks."

Bair sucked air in between clenched teeth. "Will we make it, kelan? Will we get there in time?"

Aravan took a stance at the steerboard and grimly replied, "Only if Rualla is kind."

And across the open expanse they sailed, the water made ebon by depth, the *Loose Lady*'s silk full to the brim with the light breeze blowing o'er the starboard beam.

And candlemarks burned away, the sun riding down the sky, and they skimmed 'round the shoulder of the isle—high and sheer and stone—and then angled due east, Aravan adjusting the set of the sail as Bair handled the steerboard.

"Two miles to go, Bair, and two candlemarks left," said Aravan.

Bair looked at the filled silk and said, "But the wind is now behind us, kelan. Shouldn't we be there and into the crystal cavern ere the cusp of the Trine does fall?"

"Mayhap so; mayhap not; I cannot say," said Aravan, as he took over the tiller.

And on they sailed toward a date with destiny, or so Bair did hope . . . as well as dread. Another mile they fared, the light wind yet abaft.

"Step forward, Bair," said Aravan, "and stand ready to guide me in. The entrance to the cavern should be in sight. 'Tis a great cleft in the stone."

"But I thought you told me it was hidden by illusion," said Bair as he stepped toward the bow.

"It was, yet when Durlok was slain, his spells came to an end, the illusion among them. But e'en were it yet so, mayhap thy <sight> could detect such and see beyond."

"Perhaps," said Bair, ducking under the sail. And of a sudden he gasped and pointed.

Aravan squatted down to see past the silk, and then he, too, drew in his breath . . .

. . . for above a dark, jagged cleft rising up out of the water and cleaving into the sheer wall of the isle, as if guarding the entrance, a rust-red Dragon lay.

And nearly the full of the sun now rode along the midline, a candlemark away from the exact time and place when the cusp of the Trine was due.

CHAPTER 56

Retreat

March, 5E1010

[The Present]

By the time the Allies escaped, nearly three hundred thousand friend and foe lay dead and dying upon the battlefield. Though most of the casualties were Human, all had suffered loss—Elves, Warrows, Dwarves, Baeron, Southerlings, Easterners, men of the King: hacked, stabbed, pierced, bludgeoned, and crushed upon the slaughterground, with skulls smashed, bones broken, limbs severed, intestines spilled, muscle and sinew and tissue cloven, blood running and pooling and coagulating, and the cloying odor of feces and urine and bile rising upon the air. And mingled with the caws of dark gorcrows settling down for a feast, moans and weeping and cries for help and cries for release and cries for loved ones keened across the dawn, yet few if any were answered. And down among the fallen lay a slain High King, a raven plucking at his dead eyes.

As for the sound of war and combat, there was none, for when the Allies had finally managed to disengage—the rear guard battling valiantly against staggering odds—there was no immediate pursuit, for the Southerlings had suffered great losses, as had the Golden Horde, and these two foes paused, counting the dreadful toll, while waiting until the remainder of the Eastern force could be ferried across the Argon.

West went the Allies, falling back toward the Red Hills, and they left behind a burning encampment—tents, wagons, supplies, whatever they had not enough time in the fury of battle and the haste of withdrawal to gather up and take with them. And as fire blazed and smoke rose into the sky, west they went, dead and dying left behind, war or surrender lying ahead.

At the fore rode Ryon, High King now, the set of his mouth grim.

Three days they slowly fared along Pendwyr Road, to come at last to where the Red Hills on the left verged on the route they followed.

As they approached the tors and crags—"Here we will make our stand," said the seventeen-year-old High King.

"My Lord," replied Lord Stein, "I know this is what we planned, but the numbers of the enemy are much greater than we deemed, with those blasted Southerlings coming when they did. Should we not fall back to Gûnarring Gap or even farther to someplace even more strait, where the enemy cannot bring the full of his force to bear?"

Ryon pondered a moment then replied, "My father said that by standing in battle whenever and wherever we could, we would give our loved ones more time to perhaps find refuge in the west. As tempting as your strategy is, Lord Stein, we will save it for later."

Riding a pony nearby, Dalek, DelfLord of the Red Hills, growled, "My Lord King, though I cannot long sustain such a great army as is here, we can always take refuge in my holt."

"I thank you for the offer," said Ryon, "yet that would leave us trapped as badgers in a hole, and would free much of the foe to pillage, plunder, and rape. Nay, this is where we will make another stand, for here they cannot come at our flanks."

From her pony Lady Buckthorn said, "But then, my lord, should we lose again, how will we draw them onward? I mean, backed up against the Red Hills, won't we be trapped?"

"Nay, my lady," replied Fenerin, the Elf smiling down at her. "The place where we go was chosen with care. There is a back way out."

"What if the foe finds the back way?" asked the damman Warrow. "Will he not block our escape or come at us from behind?"

"Mayhap," replied the Lian, "yet it is a long way 'round, and he would need split his forces, weakening his hand. Either that, or we should be gone ere then."

The damman was not through with her questions, and so she and Fenerin spoke on other matters, as the King led the remainder his forces—one hundred and fifty thousand strong—into a small vale.

And there in the glen did he array his ranks, there where his flanks were not exposed. And across the road lay the southern bounds of the Plains of Valon.

Amid the squawking and squabbling crows and ravens, men scuttled across the field of battle, looting the slain, stripping both friend and foe alike. Often fights would erupt over some choice piece, and from such now and again a new corpse would join those already on the field.

Kutsen Yong stood on the verge of the slaughter. "How many?"

The mandarin before him trembled in fright. "Almost one hundred thousand," he repeated, his voice but a whisper.

"What?" roared Kutsen Yong. "This so-called High King slew one hundred thousand warriors of *my* Golden Horde?"

"And a like number of the Fists of Rakka," said Ebonskaith, his eyes hooded in satisfaction. "Some two hundred thousand dead, yours added to theirs."

"Bah! What care *I* for these Southerlings? It is the High King's affront to *me* that needs avenging." Kutsen Yong turned to the mandarin. "And how many of them did we slay?"

"All told, a like number," replied the mandarin.

"Good then. Two hundred thousand of the enemy dead."

The mandarin wailed and fell to his knees. "Forgive me, O Mighty Dragon, I meant a number like unto the dead of your splendid Golden Horde—some one hundred thousand of the foe were slain in all, fighting us and those of the South."

"Two to one," said Ebonskaith, this time the satisfaction creeping into his clangorous voice. "For each one of them slain, two they did kill, fully half of them yours."

"They will pay for this insult to me," vowed Kutsen Yong, stroking the Dragonstone. "Oh, yes, they will pay." He motioned to his commanders. "Come, let us go in pursuit of them."

Up from their knees rose the warlords of his Golden Horde, and swiftly came the cries of horns sounding throughout the weary army. Groaning, they gained their feet and mounted their horses. And horns sounded among the surviving Fists of Rakka as well, and they, too, readied for the long forced march.

Kutsen Yong looked about. "Where is my golden palace?"

"O Mighty Dragon, there is no craft large enough to bear your golden palace across," said the mandarin.

Kutsen Yong's face twisted in wrath, and he turned to Ebonskaith and pointed to the mandarin. "Fly him up high and out over the plains and then drop him. I would have him ponder my great disappointment as he falls down through the sky."

In midafternoon of the third day, an outrider from the vanguard came galloping back toward the cortege of the Masula Yongsa Wang. Hurling himself from his horse, the messenger flung belly down before Kutsen Yong. "O Mighty Dragon, we have found the enemy in an enclosed vale of these hills; the so-called High King is trapped."

"Now he shall see who is greater," snarled Kutsen Yong as he reached for the Dragonstone.

Dawn of the next morning found the two forces facing one another: the King's Legions—one hundred and fifty thousand warriors in all—in the vale looking out; the Golden Horde and the Fists of Rakka—their combined numbers nearly four times greater—looking in.

But then from the morning horizon all 'round there came the heavy beat of vast leathery pinions, as hundreds upon hundreds of Dragons winged through the sky, all to settle on the crags and tors of the Red Hills above the High King's Host and bellow their rage in unbridled fury.

And as horses reared and screamed in terror and the Allies blenched in dread, and as the Golden Horde and Fists of Rakka gasped in fear, from his golden tent upon the Plains of Valon came the victorious laughter of Kutsen Yong. . . .

. . . And far under the Plains and down in the living rock, three huge beings with gemstone eyes made their way toward the place where the Dragons did gather, just as the prophecy they followed foretold.

For this was the day of the Trine, and here in this place the cusp would come in the early marks of midmorning.

CHAPTER 57

Trine

Springday, 5E1010

[*The Present*]

Trembling with apprehension, Court Astrologer Tyan bowed low, and without raising up said, "I but serve, O Mighty Dragon; what is it you wish of me?"

Kutsen Yong looked up from the woman he was with, and then with a negligent wave dismissed her. As she clutched her clothes to her bosom and quietly and hastily withdrew through the rear of the tent, Kutsen Yong stepped to the fore and gestured toward the Host. "On this day will die the upstart who would claim to rule the world. Name for me a most propitious time for this to be done."

Breathing a sigh of relief and yet keeping his eyes downcast, Astrologer Tyan said, "O mighty Masula Yongsa Wang, in this place on this day the heavens will be in perfect balance when the sun has risen a quarter of the morning sky upward. I have seen it to be a most auspicious time for the Dragons to be loosed."

"Dragons? Fool! I do not intend to loose the Dragons. They are merely here to show my might."

"You intend to send men instead?"

"Yes. Men. I would have this upstart know I alone am his doom."

"Many will die, O Mighty Dragon, men of the Golden Horde. Men of the Fists of Rakka as well."

Kutsen Yong smiled. "Death matters not to a god."

*   *   *

Her ears assaulted now and again by a Dragon bellowing out in rage, Sage Arilla turned to Alorn, her look grim. "We were not certain we could handle even one Drake, much less the hundreds now gathered."

"You are right, Arilla," replied the Sorcerer, glancing at Belgon, then staring back up at the Dragons gathered high on the tors and crags all 'round. "Even with a grand conjoinment, our chances of success with but a single Drake were dubious at best."

As Belgon snorted, Alorn added, "It would seem Arin Flameseer's wild-magic vision is visited upon us at last."

"Bah!" said Belgon. "Granted, she did recover the Dragonstone, yet as to her so-called vision, hers was the imaginings of a—" Belgon's words jerked to a halt as a stir rippled throughout Magekind. Wizards yielded back, as of a sea parting, for Dalavar Wolfmage came among them, three Draega along each flank ranging fore and aft. Without speaking to any, Dalavar passed beyond the gathering and went onward toward the root of the vale to face the Dragons above, the Wolfmage seeming small and meek compared to the mighty Drakes on high.

He stood a moment in concentration, 'Wolves ringing 'round, and then emerging from Dalavar came an image of himself, a phantasma rising up through the air and flying toward the Drakes.

And Belgon snarled, "What does that fool think he's doing? We must stop him!"

"Nay, Belgon, let be," replied Arilla, "for he cannot possibly make things worse than they already are. And knowing Dalavar, he may actually improve them."

Belgon snorted in derision. "Bah! I say we stop him now."

"Too late," murmured Alorn, "for he now parleys with the Drakes."

But even as Alorn spoke, Belgon strode off toward Dalavar, the Wolfmage encircled by Draega.

And Dalavar's phantasma flew up to hover before Redclaw, the Renegade Drake the greatest of Dragons, save for Ebonskaith.

And as of great, rough bronze slabs dragging one upon the other, Redclaw spoke: "You seek to fool me, spellcaster? 'Tis but an illusion you throw."

And lo! in the same clangor of bronze on bronze, Dalavar replied to the Dragon in the tongue of the Drakes, which none among the Host could understand, save for a handful of Seers. Dalavar's words in the Dragontongue set the Drakes to wonder, and they looked not at the illusion, but at the one who cast it, and these are the things revealed of Dalavar by the Dragonsight: one who was neither a Mage nor a Demon nor a Rûpt, but a mix of all three, a breedling, a spellcaster, a shapeshifter, now surrounded by six true Draega of Adonar, and this in itself was quite meaningful, for Draega did not easily give their loyalty to anyone.

"Nay, Lord Redclaw," replied the phantasma, "I know I cannot fool your eyes, nor those of any Drake, yet I did this only to gain the attention of you and your kind. Heed, for this I would say." The hovering figure gestured downward. "Those arrayed below are not your enemy, but allies instead, for they but serve Adon."

"Bah!" hissed Redclaw. "What care we of Adon Plane-Sunderer? He argued that none should meddle in the affairs of others, as if He believed it true, yet see what He did to prove Himself false: He sundered all ways but for those of the blood. And by doing so he has meddled in the affairs of Dragons, for should we return to Kelgor—a world of beauteous wonder, a land of glorious thundering mountains spewing flame, their flanks running with flowing molten stone, a land of raging storms and lightning wild, of fire fountains and steaming cauldrons, of roaring maelstroms and tempest-tossed seas and other such furious marvels—should we return, then we are barred from ever coming back to this place of many mates, and we know not whether they would follow by the undersea crossing at the place of coupling. Yet heed: not only did He belie His own words by sundering the ways, He reft Drakes of Fire, those who aided Modru in that which you call the Great War—Great War, pah!—and imposed a Ban upon them here upon this world, relegating them forever unto the darkness. And it is Adon Meddler, Adon Falsetongue who has done this to us. So why should we *not* think of those who side with Him as being among our enemies? Why should we consider them as allies instead?"

Dalavar answered. "Much of what you say is true, Mighty

Redclaw; even so, your true enemy stands yon." The phantasma gestured toward the Fists of Rakka and the Golden Horde.

"Why say you that?" hissed Redclaw.

And Dalavar's Dragonlike words did clang out, "I say so, for they serve Gyphon."

Now did all the Drakes roar in rage, and the air was filled with their thunder, and the Host as well as the Fists and the Horde quailed under this assault, especially the Southerlings and those from the East, for all Dragon eyes were focused upon them in nigh-unquellable wrath.

Among the Golden Horde, Kutsen Yong turned to see the cause of the roar, his gaze searching for the reason, and then did he espy the small figure hovering before the Drakes. Kutsen Yong turned to Ebonskaith. "What is that in the air—a flying man?"

" 'Tis but an illusion of Magekind," hissed Ebonskaith, compelled by the 'Stone to reply.

Kutsen Yong stroked the talisman. "What is it he is attempting to do?"

"To persuade the Drakes to come to their side."

Kutsen Yong laughed. "The fool! It is *I* who hold the Dragonstone."

And then it was Ebonskaith who bellowed in fury, his shout of rage joining that of his brethren.

Long did the uproar last, but finally, when the clamor died, Redclaw spat, "Gyphon! It is He who crafted the god-wrought stone which holds us in thrall; it is He who trapped the soul of the one therein. Those who serve Him are our enemies indeed. Break us free of this unendurable subjugation and we will gladly let the Legions of the High King be."

Now the image of Dalavar began to fade, and as it did so it said, "Nay, it is not within my power to set you free, yet there is a remote possibility that your circumstance may change. If so, remember my words and heed."

And then the illusion was gone, leaving pondering Drakes behind.

And down below, Belgon at last reached the Wolfmage and,

glaring, said, "Seek not to meddle, Dalavar Hedge-Wizard, else the wrath of the Order will fall upon you."

Greylight's hackles rose, as did those of all of the Draega. Dalavar spoke, something between a word and a growl, and the pack did settle. Not deigning to reply to Belgon, Dalavar smiled at the great Silver Wolves and said, "Come, my friends, our work here is done. Now all is left to the Fates. Let us go speak to the Warrows, for I would know how they came to be here." And with that he strode away, leaving Belgon sputtering behind.

As midmorn approached, the opposing forces stood arrayed and facing one another, one hundred fifty thousand on one side, nearly six hundred thousand combined on the other.

And on his throne at the fore of his vast array sat Kutsen Yong, Ebonskaith at his side. And the sun crept up and up, toward the time of balance, Kutsen Yong now and again glancing at his royal astrologer, the man watching a shadow on a dial set upon the ground and holding up a staying hand and saying, "Not yet, O Mighty Dragon, but soon."

Kutsen Yong scowled at the enemy, then turned to Ebonskaith. "Tell me, where sits this so-called High King?"

Ebonskaith glanced across at the Allies. "Just where he should be. Centermost among his Host." That Ryon was now High King, Ebonskaith did know, for with his Dragonsight he had seen King Garon fall in the battle four nights past. And Ryon did sit at the head of the High King's Host.

Kutsen Yong shaded his eyes. "Where?"

"There by the scarlet and gold. The one on the black steed."

"That *boy* is the High King? The one who would rule over *me*? He is but a child!" declared Kutsen Yong.

"Indeed," said Ebonskaith.

But standing by his horse, the Warlord Chuang looked up at Kutsen Yong and bowed. "O Mighty Dragon, you were but eleven when you became Emperor of All."

In fury, Kutsen Yong shouted, "Fool! You compare that boy to *me*?"

The warlord flung himself prostrate to the ground before the Masula Yongsa Wang. "Forgive me, O Mighty Dragon. None compare to you."

Mollified, and as if to stop the Drake from slaying the groveling fool, Kutsen Yong held up a staying hand to Ebonskaith, who had not moved at all.

Kutsen Yong glared down at the warlord. "Resume your place, for soon we will assault the fool child king."

Jemadar Khazuul, leader of the Fists of Rakka, said, "O Mighty Dragon, would it not be better to wait until nightfall? For then our Dark Mages will stir."

"Bah! I need no Southerling Mages to come to my aid, for I have Dragons at my beck, though I use them not at all."

"But, my lord, the casualties . . ."

Kutsen Yong shrugged. "What matter another hundred thousand dead, or three hundred thousand for that matter? They gladly lay down their lives for me, for *I* am the Masula Yongsa Wang, who will soon be a god."

Opposite stood the High King's Host—Humans, Elves, Baeron, Dwarves, and a company of Warrows. Among the Wee Folk, three were accoutered in chain shirts—a damman in gold and two buccen, one in silver, the other in black. And though they bore bows nocked with arrows, sheathed at their waists were long-knives, swords to ones of their stature: in a green scabbard at the damman's belt was an Atalar Blade, silver with golden runes; at the silver-armored buccan's side and ensconced in its leather scabbard rested the Elven long-knife Bane, its blade and blade-jewel down in the sheath unseen; and in the black-armored buccan's plain scabbard was a long-knife seemingly nought but plain steel. Resolutely stood these three, with leather-clad Warrows spread to either side, Prince Ryon not far away. And these Wee Folk, steadfast and grim, and their company of deadly archers, had slain foe beyond number; even so, the foe that remained was yet beyond number still. The damman in golden armor glanced up at the hills behind, then looked at the teeming enemy before them and gritted, "I believe a Dragon now blocks the back way out. If so, we are truly trapped."

"It matters little, I think," said the buccan in black beside her, eyeing the Fire-drakes above.

Nearby, a Kingsman also looked up and said, "It seems they've quieted down. I wonder why they bellowed before."

"Didn't you see?" said another. "Was a Wizard what flew up to them and set them to roaring so."

"Yar, I saw, but what could he have said?"

The other shrugged. "Mayhap the Wizards can do something about the Dragons and all."

"Like what?" asked another.

"I dunno. Use magic or some such."

A Lian Alor mounted nearby overheard the talk, and he glanced at the Dara beside him, casting his mind back to the Great War of the Ban, remembering . . .

Phais's eyes widened. "Ye can fend Dragons?"

A grim look came over Imongar's face. "Mayhap in a great conjoinment of Mages, can we find a sorcerer to be the focus and wielder of the bonded <fire>, though the casting needed is like to slay all thus merged."

Loric reached across and took Phais's hand, and she looked at him, sadness in her brown eyes. And Loric looked up at the Dragons and began humming a Death Song, and Phais began singing the words, and soon all Lian and Dylvana joined in, their voices soaring high, for it seemed that Death was soon to come for them at last.

As the Elves sang, seventeen-year-old King Ryon sat ahorse at the fore of his host, his colors at hand—a golden griffin rampant upon a scarlet field. But Ryon wasn't the only seventeen-year-old Royal in the ranks that day, for arrayed to either side were his comrades from the past: to the right Prince Äldan sat astride a bay at the fore of the Vanadurin from Valon; on the left and mounted on a buckskin sat Prince Diego at his father's side, the two at the head of the lancers from Vancha. Only sixteen-year-old Bair was missing from the four who had trained together in the green galleries of the Greatwood but seven years past. And though Ryon had inquired, none he had asked knew whatsoever of Alor Bair's whereabouts.

Far and away in the Sindhu Sea alongside the sheer stone of an isle midst the slow turn of the Great Swirl, the *Loose Lady* sailed on the wind toward the dark, jagged opening in the looming rock ahead. Above the gap a rust-red Dragon raised its head and watched as the craft approached.

"What shall we do, kelan?" hissed Bair.

"We have no choice; we must go on."

"If it comes to it, perhaps we can dive overboard and swim underwater and in."

"Mayhap, Bair, yet if the Drake is opposed, then no matter what we try, I deem we have but a slim chance of succeeding."

"Know you which Drake he is, kelan?"

"Given his mien, 'tis Raudhrskal, or so did Arin Flameseer describe him long past—rust-red in scale she said he was, though mayhap crimson in deed."

"Why is he here, of all places?"

"I know not, elar, yet speak with respect, for Drakes are quick to anger."

And on they sailed, approaching the Dragon, and, as they neared, a curl of flame licked at the corner of the Drake's mouth. And when they were a furlong or so from the entrance, he fixed them with a yellow ophidian eye and in a clangor of words the rust-red Dragon boomed, "Elf and breedling, falcon and 'Wolf, you are not what you seem."

"Aye, Lord Dragon, we are not," called Aravan, continuing to sail on.

"Have you come to hinder or aid the yellow-eyed mongrel within?"

And as Aravan angled the sails and turned the craft to the larboard on a straight run for the gap, he said, "Lord Raudhrskal, we have come to hinder."

Raudhrskal puffed up in vanity at the mention of his name, for it meant he was known among the Elves. But then looked down at the two. "He is inside, performing some rite. He has slain one Human, then raised the corpse. Now he prepares to slay another."

"Then we must go forward," said Aravan. "Bair, stand by to row."

The rust-red Drake raised his right forelimb and looked at his saberlike claws and flexed them. Then with a negligent gesture he said, "Run him out, if you will, for I would a Fell Beast slay."

Under the Plains of Valon and down in the living stone, three Utruni, one bearing a silveron hammer, made their way toward where the Dragons were gathered. And yet they were uncertain as to whom to give over this mighty token of power, or where that champion might be.

"Only the Dragons show up plain," grumbled Brelk, gazing upward even as he sealed the stone after.

At the fore, Chale clove rock, making the passage they followed. He looked at an angle through the earth at the height of the sun. "We need to hurry. See Ar's light. The cusp of the Trine is nearly upon us."

"We can deliver the Rage Hammer, but where and to whom?" asked Brelk.

Orth said, "To the Champion of Fate we must go, but who that might be is not known, yet 'tis here the prophecy commands we bring it, and so he must be somewhere nigh."

Searching with gemstone eyes, only ephemeral forms did they see, for the nature of their sight was to peer through solid stone, and Humans and Elves and other such seemed no more substantial than vapor. Yet Orth's gaze widened and she drew in a breath. "I think there must be two armies standing off against one another, for there is much steel above. The force in the hills bears arms and armor like unto that of the High King. The one on the plains carry weapons of the South and East."

"I agree," said Chale, squinting. "And the army in the hills seems hemmed in. Could it be that the High King is trapped? If so, the prophecy says 'Unto the Trapped King bear the—' "

But Orth barked, "No! Not the High King. Look!"

And where she pointed a Dragon sat at the fore of the force from the East. Beside the Drake on a vaporous platform sat an ephemeral being. But neither of these two did capture their gaze, for gemstone eyes upon a gemstone stared, and the soul trapped therein.

Of a sudden, Orth gasped and said, "Now do I understand the true meaning of Lithon's prophecy. Chale, to that Drake by the 'Stone we go."

Obeying without question, Chale turned and began making his way toward the great form of the Drake at the fore of the ranks of the High King's foe.

And as they went, Orth began intoning the rede:

[*Uthr mnis klno dis . . .*]

> "In the time of the Trine,
>> A Hammer to carry, be wary;
>> The terrible Wage is Woe and Rage.
> In the time of the Trine,
>> Where the Dragons are found, be bound.
>> Find the One to smite for Right.
> In the time of the Trine,
>> Unto the trapped King bear Kammerling,
>> The Greatest Dragon to slay this day.
> In the time of the Trine,
>> Champion of Fate, smite Greater Drake,
> In the time of the Trine, the Trine . . .
> In the time of the Trine."

And swiftly did the Utruni cleave through the stone, for the time of the Trine drew nigh.

Quickly Aravan and Bair dropped sail and took up the oars, and in through the large, jagged opening—wide at the base and narrowing to a point high above—they rowed the *Loose Lady*. Into a long, strait passage they went, coarse stones sharply jutting out along the angled sidewalls, fragments of quartz glittering here and there. Daylight shone in under the surface of the water, making it luminous, and no bottom could be seen below.

On inward they rowed, the channel some eighty feet wide down at the water's edge. The angled ceiling of the passage rose and dipped, coming down as low as fifty feet in places. In they went and in, their shadows preceding them down the strait, daylight receding behind, the hollow sound of surge echoing from the gloom ahead, rhythmic, like some great creature breathing. Of a sudden the channel came to a vast cavern, a broad lagoon within: some hundred and fifty feet across it was, with perhaps twice the breadth, the ends left and right cloaked in dimness.

And *lo!* the walls all about sparkled like diamonds.

"More quartz," breathed Bair, "like the falcon crystal, only trapped in the walls instead."

"Aye," replied Aravan, "the crystal cavern ahead is made entirely of—"

A distant scream came echoing on the air.

While crystalline walls danced in the light reflected from the undulant waves, the cavern sighing with the surge, leftward they angled, across the understone lagoon, rowing for all they were worth, racing toward a landing gripped in the shadows on the far side of the grotto, there where stood a long stone quay.

As they passed above the heaving waters, all below was clutched in a blackness so impenetrable that a thousand hideous creatures could dwell therein unseen. And yet they paid it no heed as onward they sped.

At last Aravan and Bair reached the quay, and Aravan leapt to the stone dock, a mooring line in hand. Bair clambered to the landing after, where he drew the Silver Sword from the sling on his back. Securing the craft, Aravan said, "I have been here twice before, and well do I know the way. Stay at my side."

When Aravan stood, Bair handed over the blade, saying, "Kelan, I deem this is yours to wield, should there be a need."

Aravan looked at the lad, then nodded and took the weapon in hand, then gestured toward a single corridor leading away from the dock, a rough-hewn tunnel some fifteen feet wide and half again as high.

Even as they entered, there came again a scream echoing down the passage, and toward this cry of agony they ran, a dark shimmering enveloping Bair out of which Hunter sprang. And Elf and Draega ran toward the sound, Aravan silently, Hunter's claws clicking faintly on the quartz-laden floor. Into the dimness they sped, the walls about them layered with crystal, Aravan's stone amulet growing more chill with every step. Leftward curved the passage, past a junction where a small tunnel split off to the left. With Hunter pacing alongside, Aravan ignored this side branch and ran beyond, down the main passageway curving back to the right.

Onward they ran and onward, passing by another passage splitting off to the right, the floor of the main corridor now sloping upward and continuing to curve gently to the right. Again they came to a branch splitting off to the left, but on past it they went, and from the fore they heard dark words chanted, and a bright glow shone down the way. Still the main corridor continued to slope up and curve to the right, the respiration of the cavern lagoon fading as they went. And as they pressed ahead, Aravan's amulet continued to gather cold unto itself, silently warning of peril.

Some four hundred fifty feet onward, again they came to a junction, one corridor bearing left and the other straight ahead. But Aravan did not hesitate, and he took the left passageway, the one from which came the aureate glow.

On they ran, passing a large area on the left filled with crates and bales and barrels, covered with lichen and scale, supplies from a long-lost age.

Another hundred fifty feet they went, the light ahead growing brighter, and once again they passed a cache of goods stowed in a hollow on the left, the crates and barrels faring no better than those before.

Now they came toward an opening into a chamber from which the golden light glowed. Aravan stopped a few paces away, Hunter halting as well, and quietly the Elf breathed into the Silver Wolf's ear, " 'Ware, for 'tis the crystal chamber."

Now they eased forward, and a side of the chamber came into view. The ceiling and wall were made up completely of footwide, yard-long, six-sided shafts of crystal—blunt-pointed steles closely packed and jutting out at random angles into the room. The uneven floor was crystal as well, as if there once had been huge crystals jutting up here, too, but ones that had been broken away and the surface crudely adzed. And the chamber glittered with an aureate light emanating from an as-yet-unseen central point. And runes came into view, their forms hacked in the floor, the shapes somehow jarring to the senses, almost as if they were writhing obscenely even though they were fixed in hard quartz.

Taking a deep breath, Aravan stepped to the doorway, Hunter at his side. The floor jagged down into a huge, circular chamber, fully two hundred feet across and lined with great crystals sparkling in the golden light. The rough-cut floor formed a large, shallow hollow, and down in the center, where a massive crystal block served as an altar—blood pooling on its surface, two slain Humans lying at the base—there stood Ydral, his arms raised high, Krystallopŷr in his right hand, golden radiance streaming outward. And on the altar in the shimmering light, a beautiful manlike figure stood, his feet firmly planted in the blood. And behind the figure yawned a rift in the air, and it pulled at the eyes and yet what the eyes saw the mind could not comprehend, for beyond the rift was neither light nor dark, but a *nothingness* instead.

Of a sudden the flow of <fire> from Krystallopŷr ceased, and the rift in the air vanished, yet the golden glow remained, now emanating from the being on the altar Himself.

Running silently, Aravan rushed through the doorway and across the malignant runes, Hunter leaping ahead.

Yet in that moment Ydral looked up to see the attack, and he gasped and drew back. But the one with His feet in the blood, He turned and looked, and with a negligent wave of His hand, Aravan and Hunter slowed and slowed and then did not move at all, and the Silver Sword fell from Aravan's lax hand and struck the floor with a soft *ching*.

Here in this place and across the world and throughout the worlds beyond, suns rode square on midlines, and now had come the Trine.

In the air above the island Raudhrskal fled away, for not even a Dragon can vie with a god, and Raudhrskal knew in the cavern below a god had surely come.

Kutsen Yong looked over at the astrologer. "It is time," said the man at the dial. "All things are in balance."

But even as Kutsen Yong prepared to give the order, the ground before Ebonskaith began to bulge.

Though they strained to break free, neither Aravan nor Hunter could move, for Gyphon held them fast in His gaze, and they felt the weight of His power.

"Fools!" hissed Gyphon, Rakka, the Jìdu Shàngdi, the Great Evil, the god of a thousand more names. "Did you think to stop me? You cannot, for even now *My* revenge draws nigh, and Mithgar and the Middle Plane will be Mine, and thus all of creation. And none whatsoever can stop My rightful destiny."

Gyphon raised a hand toward Aravan and Hunter and said, "You were fools ever to seek to slay Me."

And a blackness began to form about His fingers. But then He smiled and lowered His arm, the blackness fading. Turning to Ydral, He said, "As a minor reward, My Regent, you may kill the Elf and his cur."

Ydral trembled with a shiver of ecstasy, and then his form began to change. . . .

Beside the throne with a *crack!* the earth split open, and up came three great Stone Giants—twelve, thirteen, and sixteen feet tall—Chale first, his ruby eyes glinting in the morning sunlight.

Yahhh . . . ! shrilled warriors nearby, and they reeled back from these monstrous beings, the astrologer howling and casting himself facedown and covering his eyes.

Ebonskaith's gaze widened in surprise, for these three had come upon him unaware, his Dragonsense overladed with so many warriors at hand. And they had the Kammerling with them! He took a deep breath, preparing to flame. Yet wait! The hammer was not empowered.

Kutsen Yong screamed, scrambling away from his throne, trying to flee, tumbling down the steps, the Dragonstone lost to his grasp and rolling away. *"Taeji Akma! Taeji Akma!"* he shrilled, the voice of Old Tal whispering in his mind: these were red-eyed Earth Demons, come to drag him down to the center of the world to live forever in agony in the endless fires. Shrieking, on hands and knees he scuttled for the Dragonstone.

And now Orth held out the Kammerling and stepped toward Ebonskaith, offering the silveron hammer to the dark Drake.

Yet Kutsen Yong snatched up the Dragonstone, and mid his screams he shrieked a command to Ebonskaith—*"Destroy!"*

At that same moment, Chale turned his ruby eyes onto Kutsen Yong, and the Mighty Dragon, the Masula Yongsa Wang, dropped the 'Stone once more and shrilled in fear of the red-eyed akma, and he scrambled back and away.

Even as Orth held out the silveron hammer, Ebonskaith reached forth with his saberlike claws and took it in his grasp. And *lo!* the Kammerling flared into life, coruscating light erupting forth, for it was empowered by a fury beyond bearing; a Rage Hammer it truly was. And Ebonskaith now looked directly at the Drag-onstone, and he raised up the blazing hammer, but hesitated, say-ing, "Forgive me, my lord, for what I am about to do." And even as he said it, the light of the hammer began to wane.

"Destroy!" shrieked the Kutsen Yong again, reeling back from Chale's red-eyed gaze.

And at the detested sound of Kutsen Yong's voice, Ebonskaith screamed in fury, and once more the Rage Hammer blazed to life, and with all the power of his unbearable wrath the great black Drake smashed the hammer down onto the god-wrought stone, and it shattered into a thousand shards. And as it burst apart, a vast aethyric wave rolled throughout all of Mithgar, and at that mo-ment—

In Darda Galion the silverlarks burst into glorious song, while—

In a crystal cavern on a remote isle mid the Great Swirl, Gyphon screamed in agony and staggered, clutching His head, while—

Up from the shards rose a great golden Dragon, gleaming in the morning sun, scales here and there glimmering of brass and copper, bronze and brown, obsidian and silver, emerald and ruby and topaz and sapphire, all the colors of Drakes. Up and up he towered, each and every Drake moaning under the golden one's benevolent gaze. And still he grew to become gigantic, his form fading as up he loomed, and then he shredded into tatters, into wisps, as of smoke in the wind, to vanish altogether. And when the golden Drake was gone, Ebonskaith, weeping uncontrollably, dropped the hammer, its flare extinguished. It lay on the ground glimmering until Orth reached down and took it up.

As Gyphon staggered under the aethyric blow, the bondage upon Aravan and Hunter was loosed, but even then a huge, black Vulg leapt for Aravan's throat, only to be intercepted in midair by a Silver Wolf. And Draega and Vulg, ancient and eternal foes, met one another in fury, blood flying wide as silver met black.

Shaking off the enthrallment Aravan stooped down and took up the Silver Sword and tried to step toward Gyphon, but could

not, for the golden glow surrounding the Jìdu Shàngdi held Aravan back, even as—

Snarling, Hunter clamped his teeth on the black Vulg's throat,
and Hunter shook the beast as if he were no more than a rat,
while—

The aethyric wave past, grimacing, Gyphon lowered His hands
and shook His head, recovering—

Unable to penetrate the protection surrounding Gyphon, as Aravan had done countless times on countless practice fields with
swords and ricks of hay, he hurled the Silver Sword . . . and it
flashed through the shimmer of light to slam blade-first to the
hilt in Gyphon's abdomen and impale Him through and through.

Gyphon's eyes flew open in horror, and His mouth stretched
wide as if in agony, but no sound came out, yet it was a scream
nevertheless, a scream which pierced all of Mithgar, all of the
world, indeed all of creation: in Darda Galion the songs of the
silverlarks chopped to silence; in Darda Erynian and elsewhere,
Hidden Ones looked at one another in startlement, as did the
Elves on Adonar; in the Grimwalls and on Neddra, Rûcks, Hlôks,
Trolls, Ghûls—Foul Folk everywhere—fell down grovelling in
pain, their hands clamped over their ears, trying to stop a scream
they could not; on Vadaria as well as on the Plains of Valon,
Mages gasped—even the Black Mages in their closed and latched
coffinlike boxes in the panelled wagons among the Fists of
Rakka—and in a remote fastness high in the mountains in a snow-
bound cabin on Vadaria, four Mages—Branwen, Dalor, Alamar,
and Aylis—looked at one another in dread.

"What is that?" asked Alamar, frowning in distress.

And Aylis whispered, "The death of a god, I deem, yet which
one, I cannot say."

And thus it was that gods, Demons, Dragons, Mages, Hidden
Ones, Utruni, Elves, Warrows, Baeron, Dwarves, Humans . . . sentient life everywhere heard the silent and agonized scream, including a rust-red Dragon fleeing across the Sindhu Sea.

And in the crystal cavern, Gyphon, impaled on a sword He
could not touch, burst into light and furious flame, and Aravan
staggered back, shielding his eyes even as the rift into *nothingness* opened behind the Jìdu Shàngdi to engulf the god and the

fire and the light, and Gyphon fell screaming in terror and agony and death back into the endless depths of the Great Abyss.

Yet weeping uncontrollably, Ebonskaith snatched up Kutsen Yong in his saberlike claws, the Masula Yongsa Wang shrilling in dread, and the greatest Dragon of all held Kutsen Yong on high for all Dragons to see. And he bellowed out in the Dragontongue, "The soul of the Father of all Dragons is free of the abomination, free of the god-wrought thing. Dragonkind is no longer in thrall to the power of the Dragonstone. Now, my brethren, turn on the Golden Horde and on the Southerlings, and with flame and claw, destroy them whole."

Even as the Drakes, roaring in rage and grief and relief, launched into flight from the crags and tors and hurtled toward the great and terrified army out on the Plains of Valon, still weeping, Ebonskaith drew down shrilling Kutsen Yong and hissed, "You unworthy fool, you did not tell me *what* to destroy, and so I destroyed that which I most hated as well as that which I most loved."

And then without further word, Ebonskaith rent Kutsen Yong asunder—blood, guts, bone, tissue, vital fluids flying wide.

And in the crystal cavern, by a faint glow emanating from Krystallopŷr, Aravan turned to find Bair standing over a Vulg with its throat torn out, the lad bleeding from gashes on his arms and legs and face.

"Elar, the Vulg poison—"

"Fear not, kelan. Silver Wolves are immune to such. The poison was gone from Hunter's veins even as he changed back."

Bair looked about. "Gyphon . . . ?"

"Impaled on the Dawn Sword and slain"—Aravan gestured at the gaping rift—"and fallen back into the Great Abyss."

Bair's eyes widened in shock that a god had been slain, and that it was his kelan who had done such.

But then Aravan looked at the Vulg. "Ydral?"

"He's dead, kelan, truly dead, for he was slain by me, by Hunter, and werebeasts slaying werebeasts makes them truly dead."

And with these words, something long clutching Aravan's soul vanished. And as tears came into his eyes, Aravan said, "Galarun, thou art avenged."

But even as he said it, a drift of air began flowing inward, and there came a tinkle as crystal shattered along the wall. And Bair looked at the yawning rift with his <sight> and winced and tore his gaze away, saying, "The Great Abyss, it is yet open. I see <fire> flowing into the gape from the runes and the crystal all 'round. Kelan, we must flee this place."

Bair snatched up Krystallopŷr to use its faint light as a lantern.

" 'Ware, elar, for it is yet Truenamed," warned Aravan.

Bair nodded and said, "Let's go," even as the wind grew stronger.

And he and Aravan fled the chamber, now thrumming with energies unseen to all but those with <sight>. Down the corridor they ran, into the breeze, and to the waiting craft. As Aravan untied the mooring line, "Krystallopýr," whispered Bair, the faint light in the blade vanishing, and he slipped the spear into the sling on his back, which once held the spear and then the Silver Sword and now held the spear again.

Casting loose they rowed swiftly across the ebon lagoon and then out the strait channel and into the daylight beyond, the sun yet two fists above the horizon, seven candlemarks from setting.

Of Raudhrskal there was no sign.

On the Plains of Valon mid the thunder of wings and the roar of fire and the shrieks of fleeing men and horses, a vast slaughter took place as Dragons, their rage loosed at last, with flame and claw slew the whole of the Golden Horde and the mighty Fists of Rakka, as well as burning the fleet and the men of the Rovers of Kistan. And Dragons rent open the panelled wagons of the Black Mages, and even as Dark Wizards shrilled in horror and withered from the Ban, Dragonfire burned their dust as well.

And the Mages and Elves and Warrows and Baeron and Dwarves and men of the High King's Host looked on in abhorrence, some unable to turn away, others weeping in dismay. And as the killings went on and on, Sage Arilla turned to Alorn and said, "This is what the Seers foresaw, this slaughter on the Plains of Valon."

*   *   *

As Aravan and Bair exited the cavern and came into open water, even then the air began flowing more sharply into the gap behind, and the isle itself began to shudder.

"Raise sail," called Aravan, and up went the blue silk, and they set out tacking easterly, against the inflowing breeze.

Stronger grew the wind and stronger. And Bair glanced back toward the isle. "Kelan, look!"

Aravan turned to see the isle collapsing in on itself, the *nothing* at its heart—the Great Abyss—swallowing the island whole.

And now the wind began to howl, shrieking toward the gape, and the water and weed flowed inward, too, dragging the *Loose Lady* back toward the suck.

Above the scream of the ever-rising wind, Bair shouted, "Kelan, neither Hunter nor I can escape this doom, yet you must change to a falcon and flee, else you, too, will be slain."

"Nay, Bair. I'll not abandon thee."

"But you must!" shouted Bair.

Aravan shook his head. "E'en were I of a mind, nothing whatsoever, not even Valké, can fly against this gale."

And in the howling wind, as the *Loose Lady* hurtled toward the gape, Aravan began singing a Death Song. Yet Bair's eyes widened and he shouted, "Nay, Aravan, you are wrong, for there *is* that which can fly against the wind." Bair pointed outward and upward, and winging toward them came sweeping a massive shape—it was Raudhrskal the Dragon come back, and he swooped down and snatched them up from the *Loose Lady* and bore them into the sky.

Up he flew and up, battling against the wind, and down below the sea churned, and the surface of the water *tilted*, forming a huge, twisting funnel, as of a monstrous maelstrom spinning 'round, sucking hulks, ships, seaweed, and the *Loose Lady*, all down into the Great Abyss. And even hundreds of miles away, out on the edge of the Great Swirl, the *Eroean* battled valiantly not to be caught in the suck, but slowly it, too, was being drawn centerward by the inblowing wind howling down the slant of the sea. And over the width of the world, the waters of oceans began flowing away from their basins and toward the Sindhu Sea.

Flying above, Aravan watched as air and water and weed and

hulks disappeared downward. And he despaired and cried out, "All the world will be sucked into that great maw."

But Raudhrskal, using his Dragonsight, said, "Elf and breedling, you have with you creations of Gyphon which might save the world, do you know their truenames."

Aravan frowned and began to protest, "We have nought—" but then he gasped, "Krystallopŷr! —But how?"

Now Raudhrskal said, "That which opened the Great Abyss mayhap has the power to close it."

"We are no Mages to cast spells," shouted Aravan.

"Truename the tokens which unlocked the way and destroy them, and the passage will be closed again," said Raudhrskal. "Or so I do believe."

"But we know not the truename of the staff," cried Aravan.

Struggling, for Raudhrskal's claws interfered, Bair drew the spear from its sling, then looked with his <sight> at the dark helve, but even then he was not certain. "Kelan," he called, "the staff may yet be enabled, for Ydral did not disempower it, did not speak its truename. If so . . ."

"But how do we destroy tokens of power?" asked Aravan.

"Crystal and staff, I know not," replied Bair. But then he looked again with his <sight> at the helve and blade and at the gap below. And his eyes widened in revelation. "Kelan, they are of opposite <fire>. Mayhap they have the power to destroy one another."

"Dost thou mean to cast Krystallopŷr into the Great Abyss?"

"Aye," shouted Bair, "with staff and blade empowered."

But Raudhrskal said, "Heed, if I fly close enough for you to do so, even I may not be able to win free."

"What is there to lose?" called Bair above the howl. "For if the world itself vanishes into that gape, we will all die regardless."

Thus it was decided, and as air shrieked inward and as weed and water and hulks slid down that monstrous gullet, and as the *Eroean* yet miles away slowly spun toward certain death, down swooped Raudhrskal, the rust-red Dragon aiming toward the center of the maw.

"Krystallopŷr," whispered Bair, and the crystal blade sprang to life.

Down hurtled Raudhrskal and down, and just above the whirling gape he tried to level off, his mighty pinions raging in the howl, and yet even he was being drawn inward.

"Now!" shouted the Drake. *"Now!"*

And Bair cast the crystal and dark staff, bound together by starsilver, toward the vast *nothing* below. Down it spun and down to disappear within—

WHOOM!

A vast thunderclap blew water and air and weed and hulks and a Dragon up and away.

And a great wave rushed outward in an ever-widening ring, diminishing as it expanded, but even so it nearly capsized the *Eroean* some four hundred miles away.

But the *nothingness* was gone, the Great Abyss closed, the waters of the sea yet turning. Gone, too, was much of the Great Swirl, hulks along with it, as well as the splendid *Loose Lady*. Of the rocky island that once stood in that place, there was no sign. The crystal cavern had vanished, along with Gyphon and Ydral, one slain by a Silver Sword, the other by a werebeast dire.

Wave after wave washed over the sea, as if some enormous rock had been dropped into the water, each wave less than the very first one which had nearly swamped the *Eroean*. Long Tom had managed to gain control of the ship, and he swung her about so that she met each subsequent crest bow first, riding up and over the billows and down the far sides. Evening fell, and the waves diminished to long, low swells, and though he did not expect Aravan and Bair and the *Loose Lady* for several days, still Tom had the ship's lanterns lit and brought adeck to serve as beacons, for although a silvery gibbous moon rode low in the eastern skies, still he wanted to make certain that the cap'n and lad could find the *Eroean*, assuming they had survived *whatever* catastrophe had occurred there in the Great Swirl.

And he slowly tacked westerly, Nikolai with a bob and line calling out that the water was clear of weed. But then a lookout cried, "Oh lor', the moon!" Tom turned and looked aft and up, but the great shape that had slid across the silvery orb was by then gone. And yet there came a great whooshing sound, as if from monstrous wings, and then swooping toward them low across the sea came an enormous dark shape. Amid the shouts of sailors and a wild scrambling of men—some fleeing belowdecks, others trying to bring ballistas to bear, yet others dropping to their knees to pray—Raudhrskal, booming laughter, deposited Aravan and Bair on the afterdeck of the *Eroean*, and then flew up and away.

CHAPTER 58

Homecoming

March–June, 5E1010

[*The Present*]

With the wind on the starboard stern quarter, and the *Eroean* running south-southeast, Aravan, Bair, Long Tom, and Nikolai stood about the map table in the Captain's Salon, Aravan marking a course on a chart. Once again Noddy served tea, his face yet filled with the wonder of Aravan and Bair having been borne through the air by a Dragon.

"You true mean run ship through the Silver Straits?" asked Nikolai, looking at the route marked.

"I do," replied Aravan, "for 'tis the quickest way, and we need to hie back to aid the High King."

"Aid for why?" asked Nikolai.

"There's a great army from the East marching into the West, Nikolai, and they have a Dragon in their ranks."

"Lor', another Dragon?" gasped Noddy.

"Aye, Noddy: Ebonskaith. Not only that, but the Rovers of Kistan are on the move as well, as are the Fists of Rakka in the South, and I deem they prepare to invade the High King's realm as well. War has come unto the West, and we need return as swiftly as we can."

"But, Kapitan," said Nikolai, "how we fight Dragon?"

"I know not what we can do against a Drake, but I do know that we can harass the Rovers," replied Aravan, "if we are not too late already."

Long Tom clenched a fist. "Ah, naow sinkin' them bloody roiaders, that Oi understand, Oi do."

Noddy frowned. "From what I've heard of the Silver Straits, it's a bad crossing. And the weather is getting even colder down there. I mean, we came through a terrible blizzard j'st t' get here, Cap'n, so why not go back the way we came? —Only this time stay out of the Polar Sea. I mean, lookin' at the map, it seems shorter the way we came than goin' through the Silver Straits."

Aravan canted his head in assent. "Shorter in distance, Noddy, but longer in time. By running for the strait we run with the wind, whereas by heading for the Cape of Storms we run into the teeth of the prevailings. Hence what looks to be shorter turns out to be longer with the tacking."

"Rualla," murmured Bair.

"Rualla indeed," replied Aravan.

And so, even though the South Polar Sea sank deeper into coldness as spring did rise toward summer, the *Eroean* ran on a great circle route, aiming to course through those dire waters, heading for a perilous strait and the Weston Ocean beyond.

Day after day, southeasterly they sailed, the wind blowing braw and fitful by turns, their course slowly angling toward due east. Out of the Sindhu they ran and across a short stretch of the Bright Sea, faring south of the Great Island and into the South Polar Sea. And each day the sun rose later and set earlier, for summer drew nigh—the cold season south—in the depths of which there would be days of no sun whatsoever here in these southern climes. And into these stormy waters they fared, and all did pray that this time no blizzard would find them, especially in the pinch of the narrows. Yet the closer they came to the polar continent, the more brutal became the weather, and through snow and sleet the *Eroean* ran, the hard-blowing, shrieking wind sometimes to the fore, sometimes aft, and sometimes howling abeam. And every day was shorter and darker than before, yet forward they fared 'neath ever-ominous skies.

But life belowdecks went on as usual in the pitch and roll of the ship, men playing at dice and cards or singing chanteys to the quaver of Fat Jim's squeezebox.

Life went on as usual for Aravan and Bair as well, and when

they weren't on the small, sheltered bridge guiding the ship through dark waters, or past ice, or measuring their progress, or performing other shipboard duties, they would often sit in deep discourse, such as the evening during a meal in the Captain's Salon when Bair said, "I have been thinking on our conversation of a year or so past, kelan, when we were on our way to Bharaq."

Aravan raised an eyebrow. "We spoke of many things on that journey, elar."

"Hearken back to our discussion on the nature of gods and the Great Creator, of intrinsic forces, of the natural world and happenstance and accident and circumstance."

Aravan nodded and took a sip of tea.

Bair took up a chunk of bread and dipped it into broth and popped it dripping into his mouth. He chewed a bit and then swallowed, Aravan waiting for him to speak. And Bair said, "Then at that time did I ask you this: are not Adon and Elwydd, Garlon, Fyrra, Raes, Theonor, and others, even Gyphon and Brell and Naxo and Ordo, are they not gods?

"And you replied 'mayhap,' and went on to say that Adon does not name Himself so, saying that even He is driven by the Fates."

The ship rode up and over a wave, and Bair captured his cup of tea as it slid across the table. Then he looked at his kelan and said, "Perhaps those we name gods, Aravan, are nought but beings of great <power>; that a so-called god can be slain seems to say it is true."

Aravan turned up a hand. "Mayhap 'tis so, elar, yet heed: none knows just who made the Silver Sword, at least none I've spoken to. Whether Wizard or god or mayhap Dwynfor—the greatest of the Elven swordsmiths—or someone else altogether, I cannot say. Yet if it *were* a god who forged the blade—Adon, Garlon, Theonor, or anyone else thou didst name—then it seems to me that a god could indeed fashion a god-wrought weapon to slay another god."

Bair slapped the table in frustration. "Then, kelan, you *are* saying that these so-named gods might truly be such."

Aravan shrugged. "Or not."

As Bair groaned in exasperation, again the *Eroean* rode up over a wave to boom down upon the far side.

Aravan frowned. "The seas are getting rougher. I think we need quickly finish our meal and hie to the wheelhouse."

And so, leaving the question unresolved as to whether those godlike beings whom Bair had named were true gods indeed or merely entities of great <power>—a question whose factual answer neither one of them knew—Bair and Aravan hastily finished eating and then went to the sheltered bridge.

Still did Rualla run wayward, blowing this way and that, and at times the Westerlies shifted completely about to become Easterlies instead, blowing directly against the ship, and here the *Eroean* would tack into the wind on long and arduous beats. But always she made progress, and on the day she sailed through the Silver Straits, the sky was blue and the aft wind brisk, and nought untoward occurred. It had taken the *Eroean* some thirty-one days to come to the Silver Straits, thirty-one days for the crew to fear that which loomed ahead—the most dangerous waters in the world, but for the Great Maelstrom—and yet when they had come to the straits, she lay as calm as an Elven mere.

Onward they pressed and onward, Rualla as fickle as ever, and three days later she sailed into the far southern waters of the Weston Ocean.

Even so, on the journey so far she had fared at an average speed of but a bare six knots, and Aravan grew more testy with each passing day.

Fickle Rualla indeed.

Up through the Weston Ocean the *Eroean* went, angled across the full width of the sea, and the crew rowed through the Calms of the Goat, and then again across the Midline Doldrums. Finally, into the Straits of Kistan did she go, and now did the crew man all the ballistas. Yet they espied no crimson sails of any Rover ship, and so onward they sailed, tacking against the Easterlies, and still they found no Rovers.

On the tenth of June—some eighty-one days after setting sail from the Great Swirl—they glided into the harbor at Port Arbalin to find a city under construction; from what they could see it had been burnt to the ground.

No lighter came out to meet them, and so Aravan and Bair

and Fat Jim, Brae, and Long Tom—the big man with a pensive look on his face—set out in a dinghy and came to the docks, those that had been rebuilt. And there they did discover that the war was over, the Golden Horde and the Fists of Rakka and the Rovers of Kistan had been done in by lo! a great host of Dragons, perhaps every Dragon in Mithgar.

"Slaughtered to the last man and horse and ox . . . all wagons burned, all ships, too, and some say a great, rolling golden palace was burnt as well," said the harbormaster. "Served 'em right for what they did to Port Arbalin: torching the buildings and killing those they found. —Most of us ran away."

"Wot about Larissa?" asked Tom, a strain in his voice.

"Larissa?"

"One o' th' escorts down t' th' Red Slipper," replied Tom.

"Oh. The ladies. They was all out of there the moment all of them crimson sails came into view. But after the raiders and such left, the 'Slipper itself was the first place rebuilt, and the ladies are all back now."

Long Tom whipped off his cap and looked at Aravan. "Cap'n, if it be your pleasure, Oi'd loik t' go see 'er naow, Oi would, 'n' make certain she's all roight."

"Go, Tom," replied Aravan.

As the big Gelender rushed away, the harbormaster said, "A funny thing, though, some days after the raiders sailed on, the water in the sea, it dropped a foot or so . . . on the same day the Dragons kilt all the foe. Like somethin' somewhere drank a big gulp to make it sink like that, and it ain't come back, neither."

"The Abyss," muttered Bair, glancing at Aravan.

"What?" asked the harbormaster.

"I think it fell into an abyss," said Bair. "If so, it's gone forever."

As the harbormaster shook his head in 'wilderment, Aravan turned to Fat Jim and Brae. "Row back to the *Eroean* and have Nikolai rotate the crew on shore leave over the next two days, you two among the first. Any who wish will find me at the Red Slipper, and tell the full crew I will pay for all."

"Aye, aye, Cap'n," replied Fat Jim smartly, a great smile on his face.

As the men took to the dinghy, Aravan and Bair started for

the 'Slipper. "We'll stay for two days and celebrate with the crew, for they did most splendidly. But on the third day we'll set forth for Ardenholt. It's time thou didst let thy loved ones know that thou art yet alive."

Bair nodded. "I suppose they are wondering; after all, it's been—what?—oh my, a year and eight months since I left."

Aravan grinned. "Dost thou not mean since thou didst run away?"

Bair flushed, but said, "I was a Guardian of age."

Aravan held up a hand as if to make peace. "Indeed, as thou didst make plain to me more than once."

Silence fell between them as they strolled on, heading toward the Red Slipper. But then Bair asked, "What of the *Eroean*? I mean, are we just going to leave her behind?"

"For the nonce, aye, yet with Tom and Nikolai and this crew she will be in good hands."

And unto the 'Slipper they came.

Over the next two days did they celebrate with the crew, resting, drinking, eating, revelling, gambling, fighting, and whatever else came to mind. And on the morning of the second day a wagon arrived bearing a tun of dark, heady brew from the Holt of Vorn, and Aravan purchased the lot to lade out to the *Eroean*'s crew, two hundred fifty-two gallons in all.

As Aravan raised his tankard to Bair's he said, " 'Ware, elar, for Vornholt ale is quite potent, and I caution thee to go easy."

"Easy, kelan? I'll have you know I can hold my own with any. —Hoy, Long Tom, come and join us."

As Aravan shook his head at the folly of youth, Tom came to the table, a tiny redheaded woman on his arm. "Cap'n, Mister Bair, Oi'd loik y' t' meet Larissa. She's agreed t' be m' woife."

"Hai!" exclaimed Bair, raising his tankard. "This calls for a toast, wouldn't you say?"

The celebration lasted long into the night.

The next morning, pale and trembling, Bair stumbled down to the common room, his clothes awry, one boot in hand, the other on the wrong foot. He lurched to the table where Aravan sat at breakfast. "Kelan, kelan, I think I made love to a dark-eyed woman last night, but I can remember nought. I mean, when I awakened she was in my bed, or I was in hers, I really don't know which. What'll I do?"

Aravan burst into laughter.

And in that moment Bair looked at the rashers of bacon lying on Aravan's trencher alongside four runny eggs and, gagging, he slapped a hand over his mouth and raced for the door. But ere he reached it he looked about in desperation, and finding not what he sought, he threw up in his own boot.

And so they stayed an extra day, giving Bair time to recover. And whenever a certain dark-eyed young lady smiled at him, he reddened.

And he drank no more ale from the Holt of Vorn.

That day as well Aravan spoke to Long Tom. "We sail for Merchants Crossing on the morrow, and there will I leave thee in charge of the *Eroean*, Tom, for I will be gone for a time."

"How long, Cap'n?"

"Mayhap a month or two."

"Then, Cap'n, will it be all roight if Oi bring her back t' port here? Oi mean, som' o' th' crew, well, they'd loik t' help rebuild th' town, 'n' we c'd take shifts aship 'n' ashore, 'n' that'd keep th' *Eroean* shipshape 'n' all, it would."

"Well and good, Tom, as long as she's kept in good state, ready to sail. Hear this, though: when I return we may simply weigh anchor to take her to her own hidden docking and moor her until she's needed again."

At these words, Long Tom's face fell. "Oh, my. Oi wos hopin' . . ." Tom sighed, then said, "Y'r pardon, Cap'n, she's your ship 'n' all, 'n' well, we'll do wote'er 'tis you command, we will."

"I'm sorry, Tom, but just as thou dost cherish Larissa, so do I cherish someone as well."

Bair, who had been sitting with his head in his hands, looked up. "Fear not, kelan, I will of certain take you back to her."

The next dawning found the *Eroean* setting out for Merchants Crossing, her crew well feasted and well satisfied, though some yet seemed under the weather, a condition with which Bair now could well identify, though he himself seemed recovered in full.

Ere the noontide the Elvenship dropped anchor at that port, the city itself nought but ruin, for the Rovers and Fists had visited there as well. And saying farewell to the crew, Aravan and Bair set out in a dinghy, Nikolai and Noddy rowing, all hands adeck and cheering.

As kelan and elar debarked from the dinghy, Nikolai said, "By damn, Kapitan, you come back we sail 'round world, eh?"

"Oh, but that'd be wonderful," said Noddy, his eyes agleam.

"Mayhap," replied Aravan, "can we find a way."

At these words, Bair touched the stone ring on its platinum chain at his throat and sighed.

And then they said good-bye and set out for Arden Vale, pausing only long enough to stop at the place of the crofter who had boarded Aravan's horses, only to find burn and char.

"I came to tell him to keep the steeds," said Aravan, surveying the wrack, "for thou and I, elar, have no need of such."

"Blast the Southerlings for such ruination," said Bair.

Aravan nodded and said, "Given what we heard of the war's end, they paid for all in blood and fire." Then he took a deep breath and said, "Come, Bair. Arden Vale awaits."

And from a flash of platinum light and a shimmer of darkness Valké and Hunter sprang, the falcon flying above and to the north, the 'Wolf racing below.

It was as they were crossing a corner of the West Reach of Valon and heading for Gûnarring Gap that seven Silver Wolves came loping alongside Hunter, and he paused and greeted each one, they greeting him, and they did know one another's scent.

That night in camp and the next two as well, Dalavar sat with Aravan and Bair, six Draega lounging nearby, and the Wolfmage told them of the war—as much of it as he knew—some from his own knowledge, other gleaned from a colloquy with the great Dragon Ebonskaith after the war, and yet more learned from conversation with Faeril.

It was this last he spoke of first: telling of the Rûpt invading Arden Vale—and then did Bair leap to his feet, ready to rush home that instant. Yet Dalavar and Aravan and Shimmer managed to calm him down. For it was over and done, the Spaunen slain, the threat gone, the rebuilding begun. Yet when Dalavar named the Elves who had perished, silent tears flowed down three faces, and no more was said that eve.

The next night, though, Dalavar spoke of the Dragonstone and Kutsen Yong and the march of the Golden Horde, of the fall of Dendor and King Dulon's running battle and his rescue by Silverleaf's band, of the Utruni and the Rage Hammer and Ebonskaith's destruction of the 'Stone and the loosing of the Dragons upon the Golden Horde and Fists of Rakka along with their Dark Mages. And when he told them of his conversation with Redclaw, Bair took on a peculiar look, as if pondering some question of great import, yet the lad said nought.

In turn did Aravan and Bair tell Dalavar of their own ventures, though it seemed that Dalavar did know some—or perhaps much—of what they had done.

Dalavar spoke little of his own involvement in events: not of the prescience he had inherited from his mother and used to good effect, even though he could sense nought of the Dragonstone, but followed the Kammerling instead. Nor did he speak of his casting of illusion, nor of his part in the first battle of Arden Vale, nor his single-handed sailing of the *Eroean* from its grotto to Arbalin Bay, nor of his selecting a crew, one ready to sail when Valké and Hunter arrived.

Yet Aravan and Bair clearly knew how key Dalavar had been, from the time he had come to Arden Vale to greet the birth of Bair, to the very last day at the end of the war when he reminded the Dragons just who the true enemy was. Key indeed had been Dalavar, and even now Bair did wonder if Hunter and the pack coming together nigh Gûnarring Gap was by chance or design, and if by design was there something of great import within Dalavar's words, but he cast that thought from his mind as Dalavar spoke on.

Over three days did Greylight, Shimmer, Beam, Seeker, Trace, Longshank, and the one known as Shifter run with Hunter northward, Valké flying above. And each night of those days did Dalavar take up the tale, as did Aravan and Bair on nights two and three. And kelan and elar came to know of the prime events of the war, while Dalavar learned how very close Mithgar and

all of creation had come to being shackled under the rule of
Gyphon, and how very close the world had come to being sucked
into the Great Abyss.

The following day Shifter and the rest of the pack left them,
the seven Draega veering for Quadran Pass, while Hunter and
Valké continued north, and only forlorn howls and the *skree* of
a falcon marked their parting.

As lavender twilight stole over Arden Vale a Silver Wolf loped
through the dusk and past the Lian pickets, the warders signalling
one another that Hunter was home again. And they heard a tiercel cry and looked up in the darkening sky, stars beginning to
shine, and lo! 'twas a black falcon flying above as if pacing the
'Wolf in the oncoming night. On they went toward Ardenholt,
leaving wondering warders aft, for a falcon and 'Wolf to be running together was an unheard-of thing.

Now Hunter came in among the cottages, and there he did
pause, Valké to wing-over and spiral to earth to land beside the
waiting 'Wolf. And out from a shimmer of darkness and a flash
of platinum light Bair and Aravan emerged. And they looked
about, their gazes seeing burnt cottages, gutted by fire, stone walls
standing but roofs gone, the thatch nought but traces of ash lying
on char within.

"Oh, kelan," said Bair in distress, "Dalavar was right: the war
came here, too."

Grim-faced, Aravan nodded. "Aye, elar, it did. Yet such is the
way of it: none is safe from conflict. Even so, the spirit of this
vale is strong, and this too shall pass—even now is fading."

"Fading?"

"Aye. Dost thou not hear the music?"

Bair listened. Faint on the air came the sound of song.

Together they followed the melody toward the center of Ardenholt. As they came to the heart of the thorp they could see a
new-built coron-hall, its windows ablaze with the fulgent light of
lanterns. And from here did harp and flute and timbrel play and
Elven voices sing, for it was Summerday, Year's Long Day, one
of the four turns of seasons celebrated by the Elves with banquet and song and tale and ode, this year special, for it was one
which held two Summerdays to keep the mark of the seasons

true. And Bair and Aravan stepped through the twilight and up to the veranda and into the bright hall. And as they entered a hush fell over all, and then Riatha rushed forward, weeping with joy, for her arran had returned, and she hugged him fiercely. Faeril, too, came running, Urus right behind, and they did embrace the lad and Aravan, all receiving hugs in return, Bair sweeping Faeril up to do so. And the air was filled with questions: where had they been? what had they done? did they know of the High King's muster? of his death? . . . and more.

Finally, Inarion summoned them all to the dais, and an extra two places were set at the head table, and food and drink were served to the pair, and Inarion forbade any questions be asked until these two were replete.

Aravan and Bair set to with a vengeance, for it had been long since they had had Elvenfare. And while they ate and drank, again song and music filled the hall. But at last appetites were sated, and when Aravan and Bair both declined another serving, then did Inarion call for silence. When it fell he bade the two to relate all that had happened to them since that October night when they each had left the vale ". . . for we but know fragments: those related by Silverleaf when the Dawn Rider came with the Silver Sword into Darda Galion, bringing silverlarks in his wake."

Inarion gestured to the pair, and Aravan leaned over to the sixteen-year-old and murmured, "I would have thee tell our tale, elar, for I deem thy sire and ythir and amicula, as well as mayhap dark-haired Elissan, would hear the story from thine own lips."

And Faeril, her jewellike eyes asparkle, said, "Oh, yes, Bair, please do tell."

Slowly Bair stood—a tall, gangly youth, but a lad soon to come into his full height, though not yet into the full of his heft. In the silence he looked about at Elven faces eager to hear what had befallen the two, and tears came into his eyes to be back with those he loved, even as his mind returned to the night Hunter left the vale to find Aravan, and all that had followed thereafter: Bair recalling dressing like K'affeyah nomads and the voyage across the Argon Sea; the camelback journey through the Karoo and the djado oasis and the near-fatal encounter with the Lamia; the Kandrawood and Dodona; the journey through Khem and sailing to Bharaq; Jangdi and the avalanche and the Phael and the Guardian; the falcon crystal and the training of Aravan and Valké; the pursuit of Ydral into Neddra and the black fortress, and capture and escape with the Silver Sword; the crossing to Vadaria with Valké pierced through; the finding of Aylis and Alamar and Branwen and Dalor, and the healing of bird and Elf, and the reunion of lovers; the crossing to Adonar to emerge among Elves, and the Elves giving over their horses, as if they, too, had been waiting to aid; the coming back to Mithgar on the dawn, silverlarks in the air; the desperate voyage of the *Eroean* to the Great Swirl, and that of the *Loose Lady* across the clinging morass; the crystal cavern and Ydral and Gyphon and Raudhrskal and the Great Abyss.

All of those things did flash through his mind in the instant he took to survey the hall. He blinked away his tears and took a deep breath and glanced at his beaming ythir and sire and amicula and then at Aravan, and finally he turned back to the assembly and said, "There are two things I would say before I begin the tale, and they are this: Galarun is avenged, and Gyphon is dead. . . ."

Startled gasps filled the hall, followed by an uproar of questions. Bair let it run on for a bit, but finally raised his hands for quiet. And when it fell, he said, "Although our venture has its roots reaching long into the past—back to when the gods did debate over free choice and control; back to when a Dragonstone was made; back to the forging by unknown hands of a Silver Sword and a hammer; back to when the sword was stolen and a vow was made; back to when my amicula in a crystal thought to be a falcon; and back to many other things, up to and including my birth—for me it all began with a promise I made as a child, and then again on an October night when a Guardian I became. . . ."

AFTERMATH
AND
ECHOES

CHAPTER 59

Aftermath

June, 5E1010–March, 6E1

[The Present]

Four days after returning to Arden Vale, Bair awakened in the night with the realization that Dalavar Wolfmage indeed had spoken of an occurrence of even greater import than the mere events of the war. And Bair sat on the edge of his cot and pondered what to do. Finally, he rose and dressed and stepped from his chamber. He moved toward the writing table to prepare a note, but the aroma of freshly brewed tea was on the air, and from the shadows Riatha said, "Wouldst thou have a cup with me?"

Bair nodded and sat, and she poured. As the lad took up his cup, Riatha said, "Thou art dressed as if to hie on a journey, and I deem I have seen in thine eyes a lingering from the war."

"Ythir, the mission I took up with Aravan is not yet fulfilled. There is still that which must be done as perhaps as important— or even more so—than that which we have done so far."

Riatha raised an eyebrow, and Bair plunged on. "I need to speak with Adon Himself."

Now Riatha's eyes flew wide. "Speak with—?"

"Adon, Ythir. Adon."

Riatha took a deep breath and then slowly exhaled, and she calmly asked, "About . . . ?"

"About Durlok's staff and Krystallopŷr and the Dragonstone. About prophecies and auguries and redes. About a stone ring and an amulet of warding and a falcon crystal. About tokens of power fashioned long past with destinies set to come to fruition in these days. About a debate long ago concerning free choice versus control. And about what Redclaw said to Dalavar concerning Adon, the Drake naming Him Adon Plane-Sunderer, Adon Meddler, Adon Falsetongue. For all those things I have named and more do I need to speak to Him."

Riatha turned up both hands. "But why?"

"To take Him to task."

Riatha leapt to her feet. "What?"

"To take Him to task," repeated Bair. "Oh, don't you see, Ythir? Redclaw was right, but only partly so." Bair threw out a hand to forestall Riatha's objections. "Hear me out, Ythir: no matter Adon's intentions, the full of the tale is, we have all—all Elves, Hidden Ones, Warrows, Baeron, Dwarves, Humans, Dragons, Mages, Utruni, even the Foul Folk—we have all been used as mere pieces in a vast tokko game played by those we name gods. And it's time it stopped."

"But Bair, surely thou canst not believe—"

"But I do, Ythir. I do. Look, if Adon and Gyphon had settled this between them long past—by combat to the death, if necessary—then we wouldn't have been mere pawns in that long-played game."

Now Riatha did frown and sit again, her look thoughtful. She sipped her tea and then said, "What thou dost say is in part true, but let me ask thee this: if it had come to combat to the death, and if Adon had lost, then what would the world be like under the heel of Gyphon?"

Bair's eyes widened, for clearly he hadn't thought of such. And from a doorway to the side, Urus said, "Mayhap, lad, mayhap all the things you name, the things which you and Aravan and we and many others did, in this time and in the past, mayhap that *was* Adon's and Gyphon's combat to the death, and only by Adon using us could Gyphon be defeated."

As Riatha poured a third cup of tea and set it before Urus, Bair sat in deep thought. But at last he said, "Nevertheless, Da, I need to speak to Adon still, for I am the only one who can do so and return."

"But what is it that you would say to Him?" asked Urus.

"Just this: things have been done which now need undoing, the Sundering of the Planes for one."

Riatha gasped, and then said, "Oh, Bair, if the ways between the Planes were opened, then we could, we could all once again . . ." Her eyes filled with tears.

Urus reached out and took her hand and stroked it, and then said to Bair, "I deem she would have you do so."

Bair nodded and then said, "I will ask Aravan to go with me, for as I say, this is but a continuation of the same mission we took on times past, he much longer than I."

Bair and Aravan were gone from Mithgar for nearly three months, elar and kelan travelling to the Ring of Oaks in the Weiunwood to cross the in-between. And when they returned, a host of Elves came, too—Daor and Reín among them, Riatha's dam and sire—for the ways between the Planes had been made whole again. . . .

"What?" Riatha looked at Bair in puzzlement.

"I said, Ythir, that the ways to and from Neddra have been made whole as well, and the Ban has been rescinded."

"But why?"

"Oh, don't you see, Ythir, any interference subverts free choice, free will, not only for us but for all."

"His argument was quite eloquent," said Aravan, "and in the end he not only persuaded Adon, he persuaded all who attended: Lian, Dylvana, and the gods."

Riatha turned to Urus. "But to free the Foul Folk to work their will . . . ?"

"Mayhap without Gyphon and His agents driving them," said Urus, "they will be less inclined to do their ill."

"For that, Bair has a plan," said Aravan, grinning. "One with which I am in hearty accord."

"What?" asked Faeril. "What is it?"

Bair ran his fingers through his long, silvery hair. "Just this, Amicula Faeril. . . ."

It was a warm Springday on Vadaria, when in a small cote in a grassy glade in a silver-birch grove, Aylis heard a tapping at her open door. She set aside the mortar and pestle and turned about with but barely enough time to say, "Oh, my love, my love," ere Aravan took her in his arms and silenced her with a kiss.

EPILOGUE

Echoes

Times Following

[*...And Beyond*]

And so the Ban was annuled and the ways between *all* the Planes were restored, including the way to Neddra, where the Foul Folk dwell, and to Kelgor the Dragonworld.

Whether or no Adon on His own would have rescinded the Ban and opened the ways between the Planes, none can say. Yet Bair did go, and Adon did act, and though scholars argue on many things, on those two things they do agree.

Hence even Gyphon's creatures were set at liberty to roam whence they would in spite of their penchant for malevolence, though they continued to prefer the night for doing dark deeds.

Yet the Rûpt were in part thwarted, for when Bair and Aravan went to Neddra and across to Vadaria, and found Aylis and Alamar and the others and told them the good news, they also told them Bair's plan. And led by Alamar, then did Magekind conquer the black fortress, holding it as a bulwark against Spaunen using the nexus to invade other Planes. And a fortress full of Mages is a formidable bulwark indeed.

They located many of the other ways to Mithgar and the other worlds, including the crossing in Gron. And here, too, Magekind set up wards against the Rûpt, barriers and fearsome illusions triggered by Foul Folk trying to leave Neddra.

Concerning the meeting between Bair and Adon, we have only descriptions of such and no written record. There were, however, two Elven tapestries woven concerning discussions of free will versus control, but again we have only descriptions of such: one tapestry depicted the debate between Gyphon and Adon, wherein the gods first argued the issue; it shows what can only be described as "beings of light" of various hues—shafts of light tinted gold, silver, bronze, and all the jewel tones imaginable—gathered in a vale, two beings in the center, one silvery white and one shimmering like oil on water, representing Adon and Gyphon, respectively; this tapestry is a reweaving of the one which was destroyed—along with priceless scrolls and tomes—by fire when the Ardenholt coron-hall burned down during the Rûpt's first raid on Arden Vale; this tapestry is based on a description by Dara Phais, for she was there at the time of the debate. The second tapestry is much like the first, yet it shows a tall, sixteen-year-old lad in glade center, a lad speaking to the gathered gods—who are again depicted as beings of light—and to members of Elvenkind. As to the true faces and forms of the gods, who can say? Bair with his <sight> did describe them as being much like Dodona and the Guardian, though much <brighter>. Where are these tapestries now? Again, who can say? for they vanished along with the Fey at the time of The Separation.

As to the scrolls and tomes burned during the Ardenholt Raid, Elves toiled for many years scribing anew much of what had been lost, and it is said that Bair journeyed to the Boskydells, to The Root, and then to The Cliffs to obtain a replacement copy of the *Ravenbook* for the Ardenholt archives. Even so, all could not be replaced, and many things which were written are lost forever.

Scholars also agree that Kutsen Yong was of certain the one Dodona had spoken of when he said ". . . by a man born of a corpse," for Teiji, his mother, was dead when her belly was cut open and Kutsen Yong was delivered into the world.

They agree as well as to the reason why great Dragons— Cold-drakes all—were found slain across the face of Mithgar, their troves intact, for when the Dragons were first summoned by Kutsen Yong wielding the Dragonstone, *all* Dragons were compelled to comply, Fire-drakes and Cold-drakes alike, but at that time the Ban was in effect, and all Cold-drakes suffered the Ban, hence, even though they fought against the unbreakable call, still they had to answer, some dying at their lair entrances, others falling dead while flying toward Janjong—wherever they were on their journey, when they came into daylight, they were slain. This is verified by the fact that when their hides were taken for treasure, the muscle and tissue and bones within withered unto dust. However it is said that in remote fastnesses Ban-slain Drakes still lie, their treasures waiting to be found.

Scholars single out the most fortuitous event of the war as being Orth's realization of the true meaning of the Prophecy of the Kammerling, in particular the lines:

> *Where the Dragons are found, be bound.*
> *Find the One to smite for Right.*

In this pair of lines—in particular the words "Find the One to smite for Right"—Orth realized that "the One" referred to the first line of the couplet, and therefore "Find the One" meant to find the "One Dragon" who would smite for Right.

In the case of the next couplet—

> *Unto the trapped King bear Kammerling,*
> *The Greatest Dragon to slay this day.*

—the "trapped King" referred to the soul of the Father of all Dragons trapped in the Dragonstone. And since the next rhyme—

> *Champion of Fate, smite Greater Drake.*

—referred to a "Greater Drake," in this case the Father of all Dragons, then the "Greatest Dragon" (as opposed to the Greater Drake) had to be Ebonskaith . . . which meant that Ebonskaith was the "Champion of Fate." Hence, Ebonskaith was to wield the Kammerling and smite the Greater Drake, the Father of all Dragons, which meant smiting the Dragonstone and shattering it to free the soul.

Hence, Orth managed to correctly interpret the rede which had erroneously been assumed all along to mean that the Kammerling—the Rage Hammer, Adon's Hammer—was meant to slay the greatest Dragon, when instead it was meant to free that soul from the Dragonstone, the 'Stone itself a token of power forged by Gyphon.

Speaking of tokens of power, as to why so many came together in these end days, scholars, as did Bair, attribute it to the machinations and stratagems of both Gyphon and Adon, for each token had a destiny foreordained, and the fulfillment of each came to pass, as is described herein.

And scholars have concluded that Gyphon's downfall came about not only because of heroes wielding great tokens of power, but also because of His vile crossbreeding of Demons with Foul Folk producing Fiends; for it was from the blood of a Fiend mixing with one he raped, and she in turn giving birth to twins, and one of those in turn birthing Urus, he in turn siring Bair. All in all a fitting justice they deemed.

Scholars also concluded that when the Elves of Arden Vale left to answer the High King's call to muster on the Plains of Valon, should any Black Mages have <searched> for Bair or for Aravan—and there is some cause to believe that Nunde would have done so—those two were at that time either on Neddra or Vadaria, and so any such <search> would not have detected either one.

Some scholars speculate that Arin Flameseer, with her <wild magic>, foresaw in fire the coming of Bair and Aravan from Neddra to Adonar, and that horses would be needed; thus she arranged for the Elven hunting party to be there at the critical time. But that is speculation only, and not as yet confirmed.

Scholars also speculate that the inherited Mage blood in Urus was by then too attenuated for him to have <sight>, but the infusion of Riatha's Elven blood is what gave Bair his <sight>, for scholars argue that Mages themselves seem to be part Elves.

Finally, they agree the waters of the world had been somewhat lowered by that which fell into the Great Abyss, and coastlines were slightly changed, though not as much as that which would come later, when shallow seas would become land, deep seas would become shallower, and coastlines would run beyond their present bounds, the continents themselves altering in shape, land appearing where there had only been sea bottom before, such as the lands south and north of the Avagon coming closer together along their new shorelines. No map along the margins of the seas would remain unchanged. But that would come much later than the events herein.

As to particular folk in this tale, these are worth noting:

Coron Eiron and many others returned to Darda Galion, and once again Wood's-heart became a place of joy.

Aravan and Aylis were reunited to go among the Planes where they would. But as to the adventures they had, those must await another time for the telling, for they have no part in this recounting.

Faeril continued to live in Arden Vale in the cottage that she and Gwylly had shared. Her life, though not as long as other Warrows', was gentle and filled with love. And always did Bair come to her and tell her of his ventures—where he had been, what he had seen, what joys and perils he had faced. She lived some eighty-eight years in all, but then in the eve of a splendid Autumnday she passed on, some saying that on that soft moonlit night Gwylly had come for her. . . . She was greatly mourned.

High King Ryon survived the rampage on the Plains of Valon, and when it was over and he came back unto Caer Pendwyr, where he found Eitel the Exquisite waiting. And he sent her packing back to Jute. Instead he married the Lady Dresha, a princess of Valon, and together they ruled Mithgar for many a day. Too, did he declare that Year's End Day of 5E1010 was the last day of the Fifth Era, and that Year's Start Day would be the first day of the Sixth.

Bair himself did wonder just where one of the in-between crossings at the nexus went, the one to the east of the black fortress, the one he and Valké could not step through, and with the restoration of the ways, eventually he and Urus and Riatha did cross over there. And what they found was horror.

Concerning the three chain-armored Warrows—one in black, one in silver, and one in gold—who stood with Ryon upon the Plains of Valon, the story as to how they came to war is strange indeed, both the tale concerning the obtaining of the black armor—for it was far from the Boskydells and in the land of Gron—as well as the tale when they went to return the black chain, only to find Modru's iron mask missing from above the Iron Tower's gate, and what happened afterward with the Myrkenstone knife and all . . . but again, neither of these is part of this tale.

Thus passed several millennia, but the world itself had changed, for the nature of Humanity was such that over the centuries the Wee Folk and Elves and the Hidden Ones and others were pressed back and back by Mankind's encroachment and his destructive ways. And so all the folk we today would name Fey began crossing the in-between to escape Humanity. With their numbers dwindling, the Fey finally held council and decided to go elsewhere, though not all agreed. Hence perhaps not all the folk of lore and legend are yet gone from this world; perhaps some Hidden Ones still live deep in the old-growth forests that yet remain . . . or soar in the lofty skies above the remote high peaks of distant continents . . . who can say? All that is truly known is a great Separation occurred, making Mankind the poorer for it.

Still, the ways between the Planes are yet whole, and if one but knows the steps and the chant, the glide, pause, turn, and pace, the cant, melody, threnody, and the rise and fall of voice, and the location of an in-between, then crossing from here and there is quite simple. But even if you know none of these, now and again the Trine weakens the boundaries, and if you happen to be at an in-between place at an in-between time, at twilight or dawn or midnight or noon, and if conditions are right—a fog, a mist, or other such—and if the place is close-matched from Plane to Plane, then visions of other lands, other realms may appear, new worlds in otherwhere places afar; and you may see Fey, some so fair of face and form they will steal your breath away, and perhaps your heart as well, and some so fearsome that you will shriek in terror and flee back the way you came.

As to those who crossed over, it is unknown whether Aylis and Aravan were among these, for the oceans of the Earth are vast, and perhaps somewhere the graceful Elvenship cuts the waters of one of our own seven seas. On the other hand perhaps the *Eroean* remains hidden in some grotto in a secret cove on this world. But mayhap Aravan sailed it unto another world altogether. After all, it is said that there are mysterious places upon the seas where ships are said to vanish, and mayhap Aylis and Aravan are sailing the *Eroean* on the indigo waters of a deep blue sea on a world on the far side of elsewhere.

Regardless, it was thus The Separation did occur, and as far as we know, Mankind was left alone in the world, the Hidden Ones, Warrows, Elves, Dwarves, Dragons, and all other creatures and peoples of legend going beyond, leaving the world of Mankind much dimmer.

Mayhap some day, if Mankind ever learns how to nurture this world rather than to rape it, mayhap the day will come when the Fey Folk will return.

. . . One can only hope . . .

. . . One can only hope . . .

. . . For I would hear a silverlark sing.

'Tis deeds, not blood, which

determine the worth of a being

Afterword

For those who might wonder, *Silver Wolf, Black Falcon* is the sequel to *all* the other Mithgarian tales. Although each of these tales stands on its own, altogether they are part of the overall story arc mentioned in the Foreword, a story sweeping throughout millennia of time, characters and events and deeds in one tale profoundly affecting those in others, all to plummet down through time to bear fruit—both bitter and sweet—in this tale of the Impossible Child. Taking each of these tales in historical order and singling out a minimal number of key events, we have: *The Dragonstone*, wherein the 'Stone itself and its terrible prophecy is revealed; *Voyage of the Fox Rider*, in which the crystal cavern is found, Krystallopŷr is forged, and although the 'Stone is not mentioned it is swallowed by the sea; the *Hèl's Crucible* duology, wherein the ways between the Planes are sundered, the Silver Sword is stolen by a "man" with yellow eyes, Aravan takes up the quest to find the blade and avenge Galarun, the Ban is imposed, and Gyphon is cast into the Great Abyss; *Dragondoom*, in which the stolen Kammerling is found by two unexpected allies and is plunged into the heart of Dragonslair; the story collection *Tales of Mithgar*, wherein there are tales involving Ydral's son Baron Stoke, Beau Darby, Modru, Dalavar Wolfmage, and others; the *Iron Tower* trilogy, in which Modru nearly frees Gyphon from the Great Abyss; *The Silver Call* duology, wherein the Dwarves invade Kraggen-cor, the place where Bair spent time training with Aravan, without which it is doubtful they would have survived; *The Eye of the Hunter*, in which we first meet Faeril, Aravan first hears the name of Ydral, Urus weds Riatha, and Bair is born at the end of that book (a birth reprised at the beginning of this book).

Of course, in addition to those few noted above, there are many other events and people and deeds contained within these tales, entirely too many to list herein, but which echo down through the ages to directly impinge on the trials and lives and actions of others; like dominoes falling, the causes and effects in one age lead to causes and effects in others, deeds and events rattling down through time producing deeds and events of their own, perhaps to never end. It is left up to the readers of the full arc to discover the many more connections contained therein . . . such as High King Aurion Redeye telling three Warrows that he would recall three suits of armor at need, or the significance of a small pewter coin being used to rally the Boskydells, and other such.

As Beau Darby would say, "It's all connected, you know."

—Dennis L. McKiernan
January 1999

About the Author

Born April 4, 1932, I have spent a great deal of my life looking through twilights and dawns seeking—what? Ah yes, I remember—seeking signs of wonder, searching for pixies and fairies and other such, looking in tree hollows and under snow-laden bushes and behind waterfalls and across wooded, moonlit dells. I did not outgrow that curiosity, that search for the edge of Faery, when I outgrew childhood—not when I was in the U.S. Air Force during the Korean War, nor in college, nor in graduate school, nor in the thirty-one years I spent in Research and Development at Bell Telephone Laboratories as an engineer and manager on ballistic missile defense systems and then telephone systems and in think-tank activities. In fact I am still at it, still searching for glimmers and glimpses of wonder in the twilights and the dawns. I am abetted in this curious behavior by Martha Lee, my help-mate, lover, and, as of this writing, my wife of forty-three years.

Dennis L. McKiernan
HÈL'S CRUCIBLE Duology:

In Dennis L. McKiernan's world of Mithgar, other stories are often spoken of, but none as renowned as the War of the Ban. Here, in one of his finest achievements, he brings that epic to life in all its magic and excitement.

Praise for the HÈL'S CRUCIBLE Duology:

"Provocative...appeals to lovers of classic fantasy—the audience for David Eddings and Terry Brooks." —*Booklist*

"Once McKiernan's got you, he never lets you go." —Jennifer Roberson

"Some of the finest imaginative action...there are no lulls in McKiernan's story." —*Columbus Dispatch*

Book One of the Hèl's Crucible Duology
❑ **Into the Forge** 0-451-45700-5 / $6.99

Book Two of the Hèl's Crucible Duology
❑ **Into the Fire** 0-451-45732-3 / $6.99